RESISTANCE

RESISTANCE

G. D. BRENNAN III

Tortoise Books
Chicago, IL

FIRST EDITION, JUNE, 2012

Copyright © 2012 by Gerald D. Brennan III

All rights reserved under International and Pan-American Copyright Convention
Published in the United States by Tortoise Books
www.tortoisebooks.com

ISBN-10: 0-6156-2596-7
ISBN-13: 978-0615625966
Alkaline paper

This book is a work of fiction. All characters, scenes and situations are either products of the author's imagination or are used fictitiously. Any resemblance to actual events or locales or persons, living or dead, is coincidental.

Cover photograph provided through arrangement with the German Bundesarchiv. Photo credit: Bundesarchiv Bild 183-N0220-507 / Photographer : Unknown

All interior photographs are from ČTK (Czech Press Agency) and are used with permission.

Tortoise Books Logo Copyright ©2012 by Tortoise Books. Original artwork by Rachele O'Hare.

Recollections of General František Moravec

"I believe that all souls are created equal and that each soul belongs to itself, is a law unto itself, independent."
— Tomáš Masaryk, Father of Czechoslovakia, as quoted by Karel Čapek in *Talks with T. G. Masaryk*

INTRODUCTION
Washington, D.C.
February 1964

"My life has been full; I've seen a lot. I've begun to forget the details and exact chronological order, but even my forgetting has a method to it: everything over and done with I simply toss out of my head so as to leave it free and tidy; it's like clearing off a desk. Yet to be frank, I can't say everything, and not only out of consideration for others: I doubt one ever has words adequate to one's innermost feelings. A good reader will find me between the lines of my books."

— Tomáš Masaryk, as quoted by Karel Čapek in *Talks with T. G. Masaryk*

HOW can one honestly summarize one's own life?

I suppose it is easy for some, but mine's been more complicated than most. As a young man, I fought in the First World War; while middle-aged, I played a key role in the Second, and now that I am old, I have found a bit part in the Cold War, which may yet become the Third. Having been exiled in each of those wars, and having spent several years of active and implacable resistance to two of the greatest tyrannies of the 20th century—Nazi Germany and Soviet Russia—my family and friends are now prodding me to write down some recollections.

This is no small task for a man my age, though. Many events are so far removed from my mind that, when I recount what little I remember, I can't quite believe I am still the same person. Decades pass, and as we evolve into different versions of ourselves, even the most significant memories fade unless we turn them into stories; those few people who have been there alongside us do not always recall the same events we do, and only the artifacts and documents from the past can reconcile the discrepancies.

Indeed, my current life contains few of those reminders. Certainly it is more boring, and so I will describe it first, briefly, so I can get it out of the way and move on to the epic dramas of my youth.

I commute to work via public bus, in a routine so banal that I can scarcely sort out my recent memories by year, let alone by week or day. Small things give me my only pleasures—if I can sit and read the newspaper during my ride, the day is off to a good start. On busier mornings, I stand and hold the crossbar with the unread *Washington Post* under my arm and stare out at the dingy neighborhoods, block after block of disheveled brick houses with big front porches.[1] I still haven't given up the professional habits of my earlier life, so I scrutinize the other commuters—mostly businessmen wearing winter trench coats over blue or gray or black suits—as the bus lurches about and lumbers to the curb to pick up still more businessmen in suits. I am sixty-nine years old, but rare is the day when anyone gives me their seat. In my youth I wouldn't have minded, but now, with the aches and pains of a slowly breaking

---

[1] Once you get past the whitewashed monuments, Washington's an ugly city, full of decrepit neighborhoods, destitute Negroes and pompous politicians. At any rate, it hardly compares to my home, Prague, which I still honestly believe to be the most beautiful city in the world.

body, it irks me. A petty complaint, perhaps, but that's all most people have in America.

My job, too, is boring and banal, at least by my standards. For security reasons I cannot say much about it, other than that I work in the Pentagon, as a civilian employee of the United States government. I sit at a beige metal desk festooned with a paper desk calendar, a black phone, a typewriter, and several reference volumes and factbooks about Eastern Europe. Behind it, I have a variety of outdated and relatively uninformative newspapers from Prague and East Berlin and Warsaw and Moscow. From time to time I check out classified publications, type up classified reports, and send them off, always mindful that, should any action come as a result of my work, the results will most likely remain classified. I don't mind the secrecy—indeed, I'm quite comfortable with it—but I do miss the certainty that my efforts have consequences. Too often, I stare in despair at the impossibly slow sweep of the clock's black hands, waiting for time's release. I would retire, but without at least the daily changes of scenery, I fear I would feel even more useless.

When night comes, I nod off under the bus's harsh lights until it drops me off two blocks from home.

I live in a modest house in outer D.C., with a modest Plymouth Valiant out front that I only drive to pick up groceries. My children moved out long ago to raise children of their own, so most nights, the house is as quiet as a tomb. Usually my wife has cooked dinner. Sometimes she will surprise me with a recipe from home—roast duck or dumplings or goulash—but more often it's meatloaf or pot roast or hamburgers. Afterwards I read and smoke in my recliner, while she watches television from the sofa and empties my ashtray as I fill it. Perhaps this is why I've finally gotten around to writing these memoirs—life has become so sedate that the only potential source of excitement is in memory.

I'm not sure if I want to write about all of my life, or even about all of its eventful highlights. For my successes have been bloody and controversial, and when I talk about them, the words taste as bitter as wormwood. But I do at least have a lot to say about my failures[2]. So I will set down a recollection of my nation's slow death in the years

---

[2] For my fellow Czechs and I, there is sometimes a grim pride and comfort in failure. It is not pleasant, but it is at least familiar. Sometimes it is all we have.

leading up to the Second World War, and contrast it with the happy optimism of my country's birth—and only then, perhaps, will I set down something about my so-called successes.

As in most stories told from memory, I will probably embellish it here and there. I will leave out the boring parts for the sake of economy, and leave out other parts for other reasons. I have told most of it before, to friends and family, and like all good stories, it changes slightly with every retelling.

But it is still basically true.

CHAPTER 1
Podmokly-Prague
March, 1935

"As in looking at a person, in looking at a nation I am mainly concerned with soul and spirit…Morality and humanism must be the goals of every individual and every nation. No nation has a right to its own special set of ethics."

—Tomáš Masaryk, "Czechs and Slavs: The Time of Kollár and Jungmann"

THE Second World War started—for me, anyway—in March of 1935, in the dingy train station waiting-room of a tiny town near our frontier with Germany.

Others concentrate on other dates; the Americans, those loveably optimistic Johnny-come-latelys, go on and on about 7 December 1941 and the bombing of Pearl Harbor. (A dramatic event and a dramatic date, a day of fire and infamy, but late.) The Soviets, those hateably pessimistic drunks, spout off *ad nauseum* about 22 June of that same year, when an endless black wave of Nazi tanks and troops started rolling eastward with such speed and force that it only stopped six months later at the gates of Moscow. (Never mind that the rest of Europe had already been fighting for two years.) The British and French came into it on 3 September 1939, and the Poles had been invaded two days prior, so Germany and her first three armed antagonists all at least have a year and month on which to agree. (Never mind that the Japanese and Chinese had been fighting since 1931.)

And never mind the history lesson: this is about my war.

The town, Podmokly, isn't in any history books. And even I couldn't give you an exact date—the really life-changing events often sneak up on you unheralded, on days when you forgot to double-check the calendar before you headed out the door. (How many millions of Americans saved their newspapers the day after Pearl Harbor, with their six-inch headlines screaming WAR? And how few of them saved the papers that had actually landed on their doorsteps that fateful morning, the ones with a half-dozen small bland headlines, unremarkable except for that soon-to-be-famous date on the top?) I believe Freud said there's no such thing as premonition: we just remember events differently once we know what they caused.

As I mentioned, my war started in a train station waiting room. It was thoroughly unimpressive, like most truly historic places—we have to screw brass plaques to their walls or erect pedestals so we don't lose track of them. I remember battered timetables tacked to walls whose corners were darkened by shadows and grime. The grubby floor would have needed massive quantities of ammonia to be even halfway presentable, and even then, the cracked ancient tile, in all probability older than my country, would have still been an eyesore. Dark wooden benches, their edges worn smooth by years of travelers, filled the center of the room.

On one of them, I sat reading a newspaper, looking like a bored commuter—or so I hoped.

The man I was waiting for, a Mr. Radek, arrived just before 5:00, accompanied by two of our policemen in ill-fitting uniforms and two healthy, ruddy, handcuffed Germans. I'd been reading and waiting for fifteen minutes, but when they arrived, I kept reading and waiting. I knew who they were but didn't want them to know I was there, not just yet. (In my line of work, I'd learned it was best to structure one's life so as to take in as much information as possible while giving away no more than necessary.)

Radek removed his hat, then shook the raindrops from his trench coat like a peacock smoothing out its feathers. Our policemen nervously eyed their charges, Herr Müller and Herr Faber. Those two alone appeared unperturbed; lacking anything better to do, one of them wandered over to read the train schedules.

"Planning on coming back, Herr Faber?" the shorter policeman asked in hesitant German.

"Herr Müller and Herr Faber have been convicted of espionage and are only being released in exchange for our Captain Kirinovic." Radek spoke their language impeccably, his tone haughty, distant, icily correct. "Under the terms of their release, they are forbidden from returning to Czechoslovakia. Should they return, they will be arrested and imprisoned for the duration of their sentences, which are ten and twelve years, respectively."

"No, I don't plan on coming back." Faber spoke, smirking. He doubtless knew Czech and probably also could function in Slovak, but he didn't deign to attempt either language.[3] "No offense to Herr Müller, but I'd much rather share a bed with my wife than a jail cell with him."

"Me?" Müller snorted, then turned to the policemen to plead his case. "Officers, let it be known that I suffered most in that cell. The conditions were intolerable!"

---

[3] My country's two languages share about 85 percent of their vocabulary and rules; Slovak is admittedly the cleaner of the two, a pure mountain language, while Czech has been polluted by German through centuries of coexistence in Bohemia and Moravia.

Radek made an irritated face. "We treat our captives well. It is…"

"Oh, it wasn't anything your people did," Müller interrupted. "No, it was my own stinking countryman. Have you ever known a man whose flatulence could actually wake you up in the middle of the night? And not from the sound—from the smell!"

The taller policeman chuckled and nodded appreciatively.

Müller continued: "Last month—and, mind you, I hadn't even seen a woman in months—I was dreaming of this beautiful big-titted blonde I knew in Köln. And, miracle of miracles, I'm just about to have her when…*pppfffffhhhth*—I'm being asphyxiated!"

"That's what you get for taking the bottom bunk," Faber grinned.

Müller waved a dismissive hand at his countryman. "Another night's sleep ruined. Make no mistake, officers, I suffered most. Herr Faber may be glad to see his wife, but she won't be glad to see him."

The policemen chuckled while Faber prepared his counterargument.

"I didn't say I'd be glad. I only said it'd be better than prison. *Marginally* better. I'm trading the handcuffs for the ball and chain. And even the prison cooking was better than hers."

Radek cleared his throat and glared at the Germans. "As I was saying, we treat our captives well. It is the mark of a civilized country."

Faber smirked again. "Cuff our hands in front, then. So we can sit, instead of staring at train schedules like bored commuters."

Müller chuckled; this time, our policemen didn't join in.

Again Radek glared. "Our courtesy has its limits. You'll…" He paused, interrupted by a train whistle that sliced through the background static of rainfall. "There's the train. You'll get them off soon enough."

After that, silence reigned, leavened by rain and the approaching train, which soon chugged to a stop. Through water-smeared windows at the end of the station—the only ones that had even been half-washed, it seemed—I saw three blurred forms dart out and dash under the awning, dragging one disheveled laggard.

The first man entered alone and surveyed the room as if conquering it: the diplomat, I presumed. Behind him came two burly men in sleek trench coats—Gestapo, possibly?—their shoulders darkened by their swift passage through the rain. Between them stood—I use the word loosely—a handcuffed third man, a slovenly, stubbly, nearly-unrecognizable mess in an ill-fitting and unbuttoned trench coat. Captain Kirinovic.

How he'd changed! Though he'd been my subordinate for two years prior to his disappearance—his abduction, I still believe, at the hands of the Germans—I'd have passed him by if I'd seen him on the street, perhaps assuming he was a beggar or a drunk. After eleven months in their hands, he was a shattered husk—but the Germans we were returning were healthy and well-fed.

That infuriated me.

I turned a page, leaned forward, breathed heavily, and raised my newspaper higher with clenched fists; now it was no longer my shield from their eyes, but their barrier from my rage.

"Mr. Radek, I presume?" I heard but did not see the German diplomat speak—in his own tongue, of course.

"Herr Bruckner, yes? Let's get this over with, shall we?"

Their feet shuffled about in an awkward, un-choreographed first dance.

Bruckner spoke again: "For the grave crime of espionage against the German Reich, Captain Kirinovic has been sentenced to twenty-five years in prison. The sentence is hereby remanded, and he is hereby released into the custody of the Czechoslovakian government, in exchange for the release of Herr Faber and Herr Müller. Should he return to Germany under any circumstances, he will be re-arrested and re-imprisoned for the duration of his sentence, plus any additional time imposed for subsequent acts of espionage."

"S-so g-good to be h-home," someone who sounded like Kirinovic mumbled.

"Likewise, Herr Müller and Herr Faber have been arrested, convicted of espionage, and sentenced to twelve and ten years, respectively. They are hereby released for transport back to Germany and in exchange for Captain Kirinovic. If they return, they will be re-imprisoned for the duration of their sentences, which are ten and twelve years, respectively. Now, I have several documents from the Justice Ministry that must be signed…"

Again everyone shuffled about; keys jangled, and handcuffs opened.

"He sounds like a broken phonograph," Müller or Faber mumbled.

"S-S-So g-good to be ho-home," Kirinovic observed.

"Him, too," Faber or Müller mumbled.

Curious, and calmer now, I lowered the newspaper and peered over the ragged top edge. A janitor had silently materialized and was actually mopping the floor. Faber was rubbing his wrists, wrinkling his nose at the scent of ammonia and the sight of the lowly anonymous Czech; Müller was stretching and grinning. Both called to mind chubby teenage bullies, joking about farts and tits.

"Goodbye, gentlemen," Müller said brightly. "I'm looking forward to never seeing you again!"

The Germans departed. My countrymen watched them go; rainy silence returned.

"Are we waiting for someone else, sir?" one of our policemen asked at last.

"Yes," Radek said, sounding rather displeased. "I was told a man named Moravec was going to meet us here. I don't know what he looks like, though. I don't know anything about him, actually."

I folded the newspaper and stood up.

"Mr. Radek? I'm Mr. Moravec. I'll be driving Kirinovic back to Prague."

Relieved to be relieved of his burden, Radek shook my hand. "Ahhh, yes! Here's your man."

"So g-good to be h-home." Kirinovic mumbled.

"Good to have you back, Kirinovic."

His eyes seemed distant, unfocused. I extended my hand to shake his, but he just stood there, staring beyond me.

Hesitantly I spoke again. "We will debrief you tomorrow, but for now, I'll drive you…" His eyes didn't quite follow mine. "…back to Prague, where your wife and children are…" My voice trailed off.

I moved my hand up and down directly in front of his eyes and they flickered ever so slightly, like a candle, then stilled, and became expressionless brown beads.

"So good to b-be home." Kirinovic said.

*   *   *

We drove back in a nondescript black Skoda Popular I'd checked out of the motor pool. (I say "we," but Kirinovic remained immobile—incapable, apparently, of even watching the scenery.) Not that there was much to see—we drove through an endless succession of villages made drab by the dreary weather, and away from numerous gloomy hills that grew flatter before melting at last into the earth. Rain pelted the windshield intermittently, then faded to drizzle, then ended; the angry clouds went their separate ways, but in no particular hurry. Above them, the sky darkened.

Back in Prague, I spotted a turnoff leading into Letná Park. On a whim, I wheeled in and parked under the looming oaks, with our hood pointed over the high bluffs.

I killed the engine.

"So...g-good to be home." Kirinovic said.

"We are home," I said, wearily, flatly. "See?"

Indeed, from our vantage point we could see all of Prague[4]—massive black bridges stretching across the Vltava, Hradčany looming off to our right, and gaslights lining the ancient tangled streets below, painting the cloud bottoms in cold pale yellow.

Again I spoke, perhaps showing my frustration. "See? This is Prague. We are home. Can you remember anything? Anything at all?"

Somehow something stuck in his head: a slender connection was made, and stayed. His face flickered ever so slightly, and for the first time he turned slowly and looked almost directly at me. After hours of nothing, this act of normalcy felt eerie.

"They g-gave me scopolamine. So much s-scopolamine. I didn't tell them anything."[5]

---

[4] Indeed, years later, the Communists would choose this same spot to erect a massive statue of Stalin, visible from all of Prague—a statue that wasn't complete until Stalin was dead and out of favor. The sculptor took his own life a week before it was completed, and the statue eventually had to be dynamited, because it was too great an embarrassment. According to legend, Stalin's head rolled down the bluffs and fell into the Vltava, where it remains to this day.

[5] Scopolamine was truth serum—crude, but occasionally effective, like many things the Germans did. Given a high enough dosage, though, there was no truth left to tell.

Was it real? Was he now lucid? Dare I hope? I wanted to shake him but feared disturbing these tenuous connections. "How much? How long ago?"

"So much scopolamine. S-so good to be h-home."

*   *   *

I kept my promise and drove him to his house, but I took my time, dilly-dallying uncharacteristically, like a husband who's lost his paycheck at the roulette wheel. (I'd known all along it was going to be a subdued homecoming; there are no speeches or parades, no pomp or circumstance, in our line of work.) Kirinovic's wife greeted me cheerily at the front door of their apartment. Nervous and tongue-tied in a manner I'd never experienced even with the sternest of my superiors, I explained the situation. My heart grew heavier, pulled ever lower by her mood as it fell from excited to quiet to downcast. Still, she bravely promised to do what she could.

A week later, I was poring over reports when the switchboard operator patched through a call. On the line, I heard Mrs. Kirinicova[6] sobbing audibly in anger and frustration while the children cried loudly in the background. Despite several pressing matters, I left work early that day. That week, we committed Kirinovic to an asylum for the insane, where he was to remain indefinitely at government expense.

In two years he was dead, and our country was well on its way to sharing his fate.

---

[6] In Czech, nouns normally change their case depending on a variety of arcane rules. Proper nouns get a different ending to indicate possession; for example, Masaryk Station becomes Masarykovo Nádraží, because the station "belongs to" Masaryk. In a similar fashion, female surnames are usually changed to indicate that they "belong to" their husband or father; for instance, my wife is Mrs. Moravcová, and Kirinovic's was Mrs. Kirinicova.

CHAPTER 2
Prague
September, 1913

"When I was a schoolmaster and taught philosophy, the boys used to come to me, and ask about this and that; they could not understand when I used to say—I don't know. They were astonished at the kind of philosopher I was who had not an answer for everything."

—Tomáš Masaryk, as quoted by Karel Čapek in *On Thought and Life*

"**WHY** are you here?" Professor Masaryk asked us on our first day of class.

This was the beginning, for me—not the beginning of my war, but the beginning of my adult life, the planting of a seed, of sorts. This was long ago, back in the dying days of the old Austro-Hungarian Empire—before I was a spy or a soldier, before the Great War and our country's rebirth. We were in good old Charles University, in a dark medieval[7] stone classroom with our backs to the open windows and the happy crowded streets of old Prague.

In 1913, Masaryk was not only a professor but a prominent national figure of some repute; he wore glasses, a severe goatee, and an air of casual but complete self-assurance. I was a teenager, quite unsure I even wanted to be here.

"You, son." Masaryk pointed directly at me. "Why are you here?"

"Well, sir." I shifted upright, composing myself and an answer. "My parents have high expectations of me. But I didn't have any definite ideas about how to meet them. So I suppose this is the path of least resistance."

My classmates, many of whom no doubt felt the same way, chuckled. So, too, did Masaryk.

"A good answer," he said. "Honest. Is it easy, then, to study? Easier than, say, working on a farm or learning a trade? Do you find it easier?" Masaryk pointed at another student, a ruddy-faced farm lad who looked like the mud from the fields was still drying on his boots.

"I've always had a talent for memorization, sir."

"Well it won't do you any good here," Masaryk said. "Memorization's fine for the smaller things, learning your multiplication factors and what-not. But I want to help you learn how to think, which is something altogether more difficult. This book here…" He lifted a leather-bound copy of Plato's *Republic* and thudded it down on his podium. "…you can memorize passages from it and recite until you're blue in the face. And you and I will both be bored. Moreover, I'll feel like I've failed, unless you can apply it to the problems of modern society. All of Western Civilization is a footnote to Plato. He was my first political teacher, and his interests are still our interests. You…"

---

[7] When I say medieval, I literally mean it; my *alma mater* was founded in 1348.

Here he pointed to another student, a burly older-looking youth. "Name something you're interested in."

"Wireless telegraphs," the youth said with a challenging smile.

"All right." Masaryk said without skipping a beat. "What do you think Plato would have said about wireless telegraphs?"

"'What's a telegraph?'" another youth said, pretending to be a perplexed Plato, and the class exploded in laughter.

Masaryk, too, had the good sense to laugh, to roll with the punches and wait a few seconds for the room to quiet. "But Plato did speak about such things. Not about telegraphs directly, of course, but about communications. The spread of information. The way leaders can choose to appeal to reason and intellect, or to the baser human motives: fear and anger, lies and half-truths and demagoguery. So many people don't understand this, even now—the trappings of life may change, we may have newspapers and telegraphs and railroads and steel ships and even aeroplanes now, but human nature is essentially unchanged over the millennia. Unchanged! The classics, and the Bible, they discuss things we're still dealing with! Suicide. War. Prostitution."

Here the class snickered and giggled. Masaryk waited, then spoke just loudly enough to calm the troubled waters.

"All right. I know that's a word you didn't expect to hear in class. A dirty word, a scandalous word, some would say. They tried to get me removed once for teaching about prostitution. Not for advocating it, mind you! Just for having my students discuss its causes and consequences. They said I was 'corrupting the youth.' Fortunately there was no question of me drinking hemlock…" He turned his attention back to the fresh-from-the-farm youngster. "Memorization. I'm glad you said that. What would be the point of all this memorization?"

"Kn-knowledge, sir?"

"Knowledge. Knowledge is important! Everyone must have knowledge. Farmers must know how to plant their crops. Storekeepers must know how to run their stores. Students of history must know that Napoleon fought the battle of Austerlitz on such and such a date, and the result was such and such. But knowledge is fragmentary. My knowledge may not match your knowledge. Sometimes there's agreement, and sometimes there's discord. Take science, for instance. One man will publish a scientific theory, and everyone will agree with it, and it

26

becomes accepted knowledge. We think it is true. And then another fellow will come along, and he'll say, 'That first fellow, his theory wasn't exactly right.' And then *his* theory is accepted knowledge. And even when everyone accepts the accepted knowledge, one man will emphasize one part of it, and the next man will focus on something else. Do you see what I'm saying?" he asked the young former farmer.

"Y-you don't like knowledge, sir?"

"On the contrary! The more we use knowledge to broaden our picture of the world, the better we are in a position to know God, the creator and mover of all. But knowledge can be unreliable. And it can never be complete. It is a living, unfinished work. So what can we rely on?"

We looked uncertainly at one another. What kind of teacher was this, who thought knowledge was unreliable?

"You." Masaryk pointed to a bookish, bespectacled youth.

"Faith, sir?"

"Faith. Faith in what? Belief in anything can be called faith. Science, law, mathematics…"

"Religious faith, sir?"

"Religious faith. Faith is more valuable than knowledge. But faith can lead us astray as well. Unfortunately religion is so often unkind, inhuman, harsh; take the cruelties that the Jews of the Old Testament committed in the name of what, according to them, was the true God! Similarly the Mohammedans. Personally, I'm a Christian, and I believe in faith as Jesus practiced it. A living faith that manifests itself in deeds more than words, a faith that spreads like a flame. But Christianity, too, can lead people astray if it isn't practiced with love and humility. So many Christians had the Gospel of love but spread their faith with fire and sword! They devised the Inquisition, and they taught people to hate those who held other beliefs. So any faith can cause turmoil and calamity! Faith can be unreliable, too! We can't agree on whose faith, and whose interpretation of that faith, is right! So what can we rely on?"

"Science and philosophy, sir." I said.

"Science and philosophy. Why those two things?

"Science for the visible world, sir, and philosophy for the invisible."

"Interesting," he said appreciatively. For a hubristic moment or two I actually thought I'd led him to something new. Then he looked down skeptically. "But aren't those the same as knowledge? Why rely on them, if they are unreliable?"

"They are better than religious faith, sir. Faith seeks to control and direct people, but science and philosophy don't."

Here Masaryk pondered. "But isn't the teaching of scientific knowledge also the directing of souls? Haven't we also got scientific churches, sects, and heretics? A scientist or a philosopher communicates his thoughts and findings in just the same way that priests and preachers set forth their doctrine. If scientists and philosophers could do so, they would command. They claim grace and infallibility as certainly as the Catholic Church. Look at the French Revolution and you'll see what havoc can come from those things alone, without religion. Think of it, the scientists and philosophers also are only men, and for man it is not always a matter of truth, but also of glory, prestige, and bread, that unholy trinity of temptations that Jesus faced and Dostoyevsky wrote so eloquently about. So, again, their knowledge can be unreliable."

"Still, sir, their knowledge can lead us towards the truth."

"The truth." He smiled. "This is something substantial. Knowledge is fragmented and sometimes contradictory, but truth is unified. Truth is whole, even if knowledge is not. And knowledge is only useful if it gets us closer to the truth. To reason, the Word, what the Greeks called the *logos*. To God. Wouldn't you agree?"

"Do you equate truth and God, sir?" I asked.

"Do I equate truth and God? Yes. Yes I do."

"What if we don't believe in God, sir?"

"An excellent question. What if we don't believe in God? The fate of modern man suggests it is very traumatic not to. The increase in suicides in Europe over the past several decades seems correlated with the increase in secularism. Dostoyevsky basically said that the atheist will end up either a murderer or a suicide. Now, he may have overstated his case, but I do agree that there's a certain…loneliness to atheism. If you don't believe in anything larger than yourself, it is easy to end up adrift. Void of purpose. Alcoholic, which is perhaps just a slow and cowardly suicide. Isolated."

"How is that anyone else's business, sir?"

"Like the Stoics said, what's good for the bee is good for the hive, and vice versa. Personally I think that the individual and society both suffer from the individual's atheism. Without a belief in the immortal soul, and in our common brotherhood under one divine Father, it's difficult to truly love one's neighbor as oneself. And without that sentiment, we can't build a society that truly looks to the well-being of all of its citizens. Even individual lives become unbearable, if people only look to their own ends. Now…" (Here he smiled.) "…I believe in freedom of thought and conscience. I believe in religion without compulsion. So I'm not going to grade you poorly if you disagree with me. If you can truly think, and defend your thought process rationally, that's fine with me. But we can all at least agree on the importance of the truth, yes?"

Here we all nodded and murmured assent.

"Who, then, has the truth?"

"Y-you do, sir?" the farm fresh youth said, tentatively. The class chuckled.

"Top marks for this lad!" Masaryk exclaimed. "You are done for the term." Again the class tittered. "Ahh, wouldn't that be easy, if I had the truth! No, the truth in its entirety is far too big for any of us to grasp. What is truth? We can say things that are true, or tell stories that are true, but they are mere pieces of the truth, little rays of light compared to the brightness and fullness of the sun. The perfect truth, the pure form of something, is an ideal that we can aspire to but never quite reach—and yet we cannot abandon it! When we discuss Plato and his metaphor of the cave, we'll see more of this—some people live their entire lives in a cave, seeing images and shadows of true things, but never seeing the truth in all its fullness. But we, as educated men, have an obligation to seek out the truth and carry it to all who have not yet seen it! And in this task we can look to the example of our national leaders. And by that I mean not Austrians or Hungarians but Czechs and Slovaks."

Here the classroom got very quiet.

"Yes, I said Czechs and Slovaks. I believe…" Here he looked right and left, as if agents of the Hapsburg throne might be spying on us at that very moment. "I believe the Czechs and Slovaks share a common heritage and a common future. I believe that someday, we will have our own nation, free from the tyranny and absolutism of the Austrian monarchy. You men know of Jan Hus, yes?" There were nods and murmurs. "Hus, of course, was one of our earliest national heroes, a man who typified our spirit and history by his principled resistance to the Catholic Church and his determination to see the truth prevail. He paid for his beliefs, he was burned at the stake, but he fought the good fight. His goal was to find a way to follow Our Savior without cowering in fear and whispering to intermediaries and getting tangled up in robes and pompous ceremony. In the end he inspired many to resist tyranny and absolutism and Caesaro-papism. Anyway, here is his prayer. And yes, even though it is a prayer…" (Here he nodded at me.) "…I think it's something we can all agree to: 'Seek truth, listen to the truth, learn the truth, love the truth, speak the truth, keep the truth, defend the truth with your very life!'"[8]

---

[8] Like most effective politicians, Masaryk repeated himself frequently and returned to the same themes often in the course of intellectual discussions. Indeed, I re-read many of his works to jog my memory on these events, so I'm not sure which of these thoughts I heard firsthand and which I read later. For further exploration of his themes and thinking, read his books, particularly *Suicide and the Meaning of Civilization, Modern Man and Religion, The Spirit of Russia, The Meaning of Czech History,* and *The Making of a State* (Original Czech title: *The World Revolution*).

CHAPTER 3
Prague
March, 1929

"Do not ascribe to the soul what you find on the body—or perhaps only on the overcoat."

—Tomáš Masaryk, "Czechs and Slavs: The Time of Kollár and Jungmann"

IN 1929, after I had served for over a decade as an officer in the Austro-Hungarian and then the Czechoslovakian Army, my superiors asked me to become a spy. And I told them no.

* * *

"No?" General Syrový asked, incredulous, as I stood at parade rest in front of his desk. Syrový, like myself, had been an officer in the Czechoslovakian Legion in Russia during the Great War. He was Chief of the General Staff, perhaps the most decorated officer in the army, and certainly unaccustomed to young majors disagreeing with him. "You're telling us no?"

"I'm respectfully asking you to reconsider the assignment, sir."

"Relax, Moravec," General Krejčí stood at Syrový's side. "I'd like to know your reasons for this."

I relaxed, just a little. "I think it would be best for both the army and myself, sir."

In an army as small as ours was, you ended up knowing virtually all the officers, by reputation if not personally. Syrový was all starch and polish; Krejčí much more flesh and blood. I'd acquired a reputation for independent thinking and unconventionality, but perhaps I was taking it too far.

"General Krejčí here seems to think otherwise, Moravec." Syrový spoke gruffly and leaned forward in his chair, as if a brusque demeanor alone would make me change my mind. He cut an imposing figure: bristly white hair, row after tight little row of ribbons, desk and bookcases nearly immaculate, room smelling of ammonia.

"Honestly, sir, I don't quite see it. I'm a soldier, not a spy." I wondered if I was making a career-ending mistake, but there was no point in second-guessing.

General Krejčí stroked his chin, unperturbed. It seemed he wanted me in this assignment far more than I did. Now he stood and gestured to a wooden armchair. "Sit down, Moravec."

Obediently, I sat.

Krejčí paced. Overall his demeanor was far mellower than his superior; he had a build more typical of a middle-aged man, and his hair was thinning, imperfect.

"You like being a soldier, yes?" Krejčí gazed off into the distance, through the medieval-looking iron window frame at the stone buildings outside. "You like the public acclaim, the sunny parades, the glory of it all? Marching triumphantly through downtown Prague while the public cheers the successful conclusion of the war?"

"I don't think any of us who have seen the Western Front believes this is a glorious profession, sir," I replied.

Krejčí smiled. "Must be the women, then. Women love a man in uniform, yes, Moravec?"

"I'm happily married, sir." I smiled a little. He knew that, too. "I'm only interested in doing a good job. The rest of it is just…" I made a dismissive motion.

"What seems to be the problem, then, Moravec?" Syrový asked, clearly impatient.

"Well, soldiering…it's an honorable profession at least, sir. And I consider myself an honorable man."

"And spying's dishonorable?" Krejčí asked.

Perhaps I shrugged my shoulders. At any rate, I didn't disagree.

So Krejčí continued. "The army's all about appearances, I know. White-glove inspections, parades, and so on, and so forth. 'If it looks good, it might be good, but if it looks bad, it is bad,' my first commanding officer used to say. So that's it, yes? You think it looks bad. You think of cloaks and daggers, secrecy and lies. Dark things done in dirty places. Men betraying other men, then running away to the tavern to drink away their demons."

"That sounds like the dime-store novel version of it, sir." I said. "I'll admit, I don't know much about spying. But I do highly value the truth, sir. I suspect spying requires a lot of dishonesty, and, again, I like to think I'm an honest man."

Krejčí's eyes twinkled. "You like to think you are, or you are?"

"Sir, I…"

My protest was pre-empted. "Either way, I think you're perfect for the job," Krejčí said. "Anyhow, being a spy's more about discretion than dishonesty. Mailing letters with a post office box for a return address, instead of an office or a home. Wearing a coat and tie instead of a uniform. Letting two foreigners converse next to you on the train without revealing that you understand every word because you speak perfect German. In general, it's about revealing as little information as possible and getting as much as possible in return, which is not the same as dishonesty. If we wanted dishonest men, you wouldn't be here."

"Surely there are other honest men in the army, sir," I said in final protest.

"You've been spoken highly of by everyone who's come in contact with you, from President Masaryk on down. You speak several languages fluently enough to pass as a native—German, Russian, Serbian, English, French. And you're an independent thinker. Unconventional. We like that, too," Krejčí said.

"General Krejčí likes it," Syrový said, frustrated. "We've already cut your orders, anyway. You're assigned to the Intelligence Section of the First Army here in Prague. Under General Bily."

Bily was a martinet, a disciplinarian. Strict, severe, and worse than Syrový, everyone said. Still, what could I say? "Yes, sir."

"Report to Bily on Thursday," Syrový said. "He'll tell you more about your new duties."

*   *   *

"I can tell you nothing about your new duties," General Bily told me on Thursday. "I don't even know the names of the officers on my own intelligence staff."

I said nothing. I didn't know what to make of this. Here was a smaller but brighter office than Syrový's, and a smaller desk. And a neater, more disciplined man, which I'd not have thought possible— he wore an impossibly precise pencil-thin moustache, and he sat ramrod straight, as rigid as a new cadet in military school, with nary an indication of ordinary human discomfort. Behind him on the bookcase, his books were all stacked in height order, biggest on the left to smallest on the right, all perfectly vertical. All horizontal surfaces were thoroughly dust-free; there was nothing on the wooden desk but a pen and a desk calendar, on which he'd written brief reminders in lettering as precise as a draftsman. His wooden floor had been waxed to a high gloss, and everything metal or brass or otherwise remotely able to be polished had been polished; I was surprised he hadn't figured out a way to shine the walls.

"But I can tell you this." Bily looked through me with narrow, incisive eyes, and leaned forward ever so slightly. "We'll be at war with Germany someday. Everybody up on the General Staff is worried about the Austrians, those incompetent idiots; everybody's been concentrating on spying on them. Trying to figure out if the Hapsburgs will return to power, reporting in the meantime on their activities in exile—which archduke is screwing whom, in what hotel, and so on, and so forth. I don't know whether I'm reading intelligence reports or scandal sheets some days; I'm surprised they're not giving us rundowns on favorite positions and proclivities. But the Austrians don't matter. Even if the Hapsburgs return, and their empire totters back to life like some…reanimated corpse in a mad scientist's lab, the Austrians will never again be a great power."

"No, sir."

"And meanwhile, Germany's dead set on it. They've been very secretive, but we know they are re-arming. When we go to war with them—not if, but when, mind you—the First Army will bear the brunt of the fighting. And we know nothing about the Germans we will face. We don't know how many troops are facing us, we don't know their standard doctrine and tactics—in short, we know nothing about the German Army. My intelligence staff has told me nothing. I hope you can tell me something. Report to the First Army Intelligence Office on Monday."

"Yes, sir."

"And stop wearing your uniform."

"Sir?" I asked, perplexed.

"I don't know much about spies, but I know the whole point of being a spy is that you're not supposed to advertise who you work for."

*   *   *

Over the weekend, I read up on the theory and practice of espionage, from some battered old hardcovers I'd checked out of the First Army's dusty library. There were only three such books, all from the Great War—one by a German, another by an Austrian,[9] and a third by a Frenchman—and ranging in quality from useless to marginally useful. So on Monday, I still knew very little about what I had to do.

---

[9] Recently, curiosity got the better of me, and I tracked a copy of this book down in a dusty old bookstore near Georgetown. It was *Memoirs of a Spy: Adventures along the Eastern Front,* by Nicholas Snowden—a pen name for a Hungarian spy named Miklos Sultez who had coincidentally served in Galicia in the First World War, not far from where I'd begun my military career.

The intelligence office was near the other First Army offices in Dejvice—a high part of Prague with wide sunny streets. Trees were budding and birds chirping; it was an impossibly cheerful spring morning, so perfect it was almost a caricature. Despite my misgivings, the weather made it hard to feel truly apprehensive about anything. Before heading through the large wooden doors, though, I double-checked the address, then my watch: 7:53. (I'd learned that, when all else fails, show up early and stay late, especially when you're in charge.)

Upstairs were worn hardwood floors, ancient off-white walls, and a main room with a wall of rickety unwashed windows which somehow let in enough sunlight to highlight the dust in the air. In the main room were four desks, with four uniformed officers hunched over four typewriters, pecking slowly at the keys. Their backs faced a frosted glass door for the office of the director. The floorboards groaned at the disruption to their routine as I waded hesitantly through the room; all four officers looked up, wary but silent. I knocked on the door.

A fellow major answered; he was about my age, with darker hair, and a pudgy face; already he was going bald, and he had about him a distinctly unmilitary air, despite the uniform he wore. In fact, he reminded me of a farmer, or perhaps a farm animal. (Did I have any special premonitions about him? Or was I just caught up in the general excitement and significance of the morning? At any rate, this man, who unfortunately shared my last name, was a man I'd hear about often.)

Our first and only conversation went something like this:

He stuck out his hand, smiled, said: "Major Moravec."

"Yes, pleased to meet you." I shook his hand firmly. (Another good rule of thumb—show up early, stay late, and have a firm handshake.)

"And you are..." he said, drawing the last word out to make the sentence a question.

"Here to relieve you. Surely General Bily mentioned you were being reassigned?"

"He sent a brief message saying someone would be relieving me today. If it's you, where's the uniform?"

"General Bily told me not to wear one. He said in this line of work I shouldn't advertise who I worked for."

"What a marvelous answer!" He smiled, pleased. "Sharp logic, impeccably precise! The kind that can cut like a sword through all the bureaucracy and red tape! Still, General Bily didn't even tell me your name. You are…"

"Major Moravec," I said, perplexed. "General Bily didn't say who I'd be relieving. He claims to not even know the names of the men on his intelligence staff. Your name is…"

"Major Moravec," he said, perplexed.

Behind us, one of the officers, a white-haired captain of about fifty, came up with a report in hand.

"Major Moravec?" he inquired.

I turned around. So did the man I was replacing, whose name, apparently, was the same as mine.

"Major Moravec?" I asked, extending my hand again.

He got it. "Major Moravec!" he said brightly. He shook my hand and turned to the old captain, whose face now wore the confusion that had just left ours. "Captain Šnejd, you have something to discuss?"

"Yes, sir. About the payment of agents, I…"

"Major Moravec will handle it. The new Major Moravec!"

"The new Major Moravec?" Šnejd said, still baffled.

I extended my hand, somewhat gleeful at the improbable idiocy of it all. "The new Major Moravec!"

Šnejd still stood there, uncomprehending.

"Later," the old Major Moravec explained. "He'll handle it later."

"Of course, sir." Šnejd beat a hasty retreat.

Meanwhile, the old Major Moravec beckoned me in and closed the door.

"I'm Emanuel Moravec," he explained. "And you are?"

"František," I replied. "You were in the Legion?"

"Yes. I fought at Zborov. And then in the Great Anabasis.[10] And you?"

---

[10] The bulk of our nascent army found itself trapped in Russia at the conclusion of the Great War and during the Russian Civil War. In typically absurd Czech fashion, they extricated themselves by going the long way around, across Siberia and through Vladivostok on the Soviet Union's Pacific coast, arriving back in Prague in 1920. This was the Great Anabasis. (Or the Czechoslovakian Anabasis, if you're not Czechoslovakian.)

"I made it out just in time to avoid that, fortunately. After Zborov we went north through Arkhangelsk, then to France, then Italy. I came back to Prague with Masaryk."

"Lucky you!" he exclaimed.

"How does it feel to be leaving?" I asked, settling in to the chair that faced his desk.

"Sad," he said. "This was a great job. How does it feel to be arriving?"

"Confusing. I'm still not quite sure what this job entails. My superiors didn't give me much guidance."

"Nor did mine. That's what made it great. I had such freedom, such latitude and discretion." Moravec gazed wistfully out the frosted glass door at the shadowy shapes of his quartet of subordinates; I'd never seen anyone develop nostalgia so quickly.

"Ahh, yes. I've had postings where my superiors were standing over my shoulders with a magnifying glass, watching everything I did. It's nice to have a little breathing room and make some decisions for yourself!"

"Well, you'll have plenty of breathing room here!" Moravec chuckled. "If you're sick of all the stifling rules and regulations and routines, the endless exercises and tiresome tasks you faced in your previous army assignments, this job will be a breath of fresh air. Only the uniforms reminded me I was still in the military, and if you don't have to wear those, even, this should be paradise! And as for making decisions…as soon as I get out of your hair here, you'll…be able to make all the decisions you want. Actually, I should probably just…collect my things…" Abruptly he stood, opened his desk drawers, and started rooting through them.

"If you have any guidance, I'd very much appreciate it," I said hopefully.

"Oh, it's like any job," he said. Having satisfied himself that there was nothing in the desk worth taking, he closed the drawers, then walked over to the coat rack.

"How so?"

"You'll spend the first couple weeks wondering how you got the job, and the rest of the time wondering how everyone else got theirs!" He put on his uniform jacket and buttoned it, then grabbed the doorknob.

"Major Moravec!" I stood abruptly. An anxious tone crept into my voice; I lowered my volume so my new subordinates wouldn't hear it. "I hate to admit this, but I have no clue what I'm supposed to do once you walk out the door. What do I need to know?"

"Are you good at managing money, Major Moravec?"

"I'm…" Managing money? "Yes, I suppose so."

"That's all you need to know. Money management. In fact…that is one thing I do need to show you…" Hastily, he walked back behind the desk, moved his chair—my chair—to the side of the room, then pulled up the small rug that sat beneath it and felt along the floorboards with his fingers. Pushing down on the end of one particular board caused a rectangular section to tilt up; he plucked it up and placed it atop his desk.

Down in the hole in the floor sat the door to a small safe.

Moravec spun the dial several times and it opened obligingly. Stacks of bills, several times more cash than I'd ever seen at one time, lay bundled within—hundreds of thousands of crowns, apparently.

"What's this for?"

"Recruitment and payment of agents."

"Incredible."

"What, did you think they come to us because we're good people? Because they just want to do the right thing? Because they believe our country is better and nobler and more virtuous than theirs? Ha! What agents we recruit, we buy. These are the operational funds we're provided to do so."

"Well, yes, I had some sense of that from what I've read, but…it's a lot of money!"

Moravec's eyes gleamed brightly. Grunting, he squatted to better reach the cash. "Yes. It's a lot of money. Here. Let's count. They'll want a receipt showing I signed it over."

For the next few minutes, he hauled bundles of bills out of the safe and placed them in even rows atop the section of flooring that was sitting atop his desk. It seemed enough to start a casino.

"Three hundred thirty-one thousand crowns, yes?" Moravec said, after we'd counted it all.

"Three hundred thirty-one thousand crowns," I agreed.

"You'll find you have considerable discretion in how to spend these monies!" (As he made out the receipt, I noticed his watch. It was expensive, ornate; it would have cost two months' worth of salary, for the average major. His pen, likewise, was much nicer than I'd have expected.) "Šnejd can show you reports from the various agents. There are some reports in my desk drawers, as well. The combination to the safe is here…" (He wrote it down—I can still remember it! 34R-26L-13R.) "…but I strongly recommend memorizing it. And here…" Again he bent down to fish around inside the safe, and pulled out a ledger book. "This ledger book is where you record payments to the various agents."

He dropped the book on his desk—my desk—next to the cash. Curious, I opened it and leafed through. There were entries for various agents, each of whom was identified by a letter and number rather than a name: X-14, Y-34, V-19.

"Thank you," I said, before looking up to find he was already halfway out the door.

"Goodbye, Major Moravec!" he exclaimed with a nod of the head.

Out in the main room, Šnejd had been hovering; spying his opportunity, he fluttered on in, his ill-fitting uniform blouse—incredible!—not entirely tucked in on one side. (I don't know which vexed me more: that he wore his uniform so poorly, or that he wore it at all. Apparently General Bily's simple logical maxim had never occurred to anyone here.) He looked older than anyone else; perhaps he knew what was going on, at least. Like General Krejčí had said, armies tend to view slovenly appearance as a visible indicator of deeper dysfunction, but perhaps this was one of those cases where you couldn't judge a book by its cover.

"Good morning, Major Moravec!" Šnejd snapped a sloppy salute.

He held the salute, so at last I stood and returned it, feeling strange doing so in civilian clothes. "Good morning, captain. Does everyone in this office wear a uniform?"

Šnejd's face, the only bright spot on him when he came in, now dimmed. Dim-witted, perhaps? "Of course, sir. We're…proud soldiers. We must look the part."

"I see." I sat, looked at my open desk drawer, saw four paper folders, and pulled out the one for Šnejd. Inside was a single sheet of paper. There was nothing in the other three folders.

Brightness returned to Šnejd's face as he spotted a new chance to shine. "I recruited that agent, sir!"

"Really?" Well, this at least was something. In the land of the blind, the one-eyed man is king. "How did you find him?"

"He found me, sir!"

"Really."

Suddenly having so much money lying about made me nervous. Was Šnejd the type to pocket a bundle if I got distracted? Probably not—such initiative might be beyond his imagination. Still, I started returning the bundles to the open safe.

"Yes, sir. He sent me a letter saying he is a sergeant in the German *Wehrmacht* and he wanted to sell me some information. So I arranged a meeting, over a weekend when he had some leave, and he told me enough to put that report together."

"Really. How much does one pay for information like that?"

"I paid him one hundred crowns, sir. Minus expenses for lodging and food."

"One hundred crowns."[11] Putting away another bundle of cash, I paused and deliberately stared at it; it held fifty thousand crowns.

Šnejd seemed not to notice. "I haven't had any contact with him since that, sir."

"What a surprise."

Sarcasm slipped past Šnejd unobserved—like so many other things, apparently. Undaunted, he continued. "I try not to keep contacts too long, though. You can never be too careful in this business! For instance, I once had to carry some valuable information from Vienna back to Prague. I was on a standard passenger train, and everything was going smoothly. Then, much to my alarm, I spotted an Austrian policeman."

"How did you know he was a policeman?"

"He...he was in uniform, sir..."

"So what did you do?"

---

[11] One hundred crowns was at that time worth about six American dollars.

"I threw the package out the window, sir! Better to lose the information than to risk discovery!"

Now it was my turn to be confused. "When did you go back to retrieve it?"

"I...I didn't, sir," Šnejd said, surprised I was derailing his story. "I changed trains as soon as I could, to make sure I wasn't being followed, and made my way on to Prague."

I imagined the whole scene—Šnejd bumbling and fearful, fumbling the package out the open window. Perhaps no one even noticed him until he did that, and at that point, they probably just took him for an imbecile. Incredible. A walking masterpiece of satire and absurdity; his escapades sounded like episodes from *The Good Soldier Švejk*.[12] Part II, Chapter 1: Švejk's Misadventures in the Train. A line from elsewhere in the book popped into my head, a line one of Švejk's superiors barked at him: To call you a half-wit would be a compliment.

Still, there was no sense getting upset. Obviously there was nothing I could do with this man. "Well, it's a good thing you weren't caught."

"You can never be too careful in this business, sir! You always, always, have to watch your surroundings and stay alert at all times."

Behind him, the door was still open; I noticed the other three officers peering closer, listening intently and trying to hold in laughter. I strangled a smile. "Yes, I can see I've got a lot to learn, Captain Šve…"

"Šnejd, sir! At your service!" Again he saluted, spun to leave; the others straightened so he wouldn't see them laughing.

Putting the cash away, I noticed the open ledger book. "One more thing, Šnejd!"

He spun on his heels. "Yes, sir?"

"Could you bring me any reports you might have for…" I looked down to double-check. "…Agents X-14, Y-34 and V-19?"

---

[12] Jaroslav Hašek's *The Good Soldier Švejk* is one of the classics of Czechoslovakian literature, and one of the first widely-read war satires; its titular character battled the Austro-Hungarian bureaucracy with feigned innocence and veiled insolence, avoiding real effort all the while, and endearing himself to Czechoslovakian readers. (Such performance had been par for the course in the Great War; I'd been a pretty apathetic soldier myself in those days, as will be described later. But this was different; we were no longer draftee cannon fodder in another nation's army. We were volunteers in our own.)

"Who, sir?"

"According to this ledger book, they are three of our most important agents. Responsible for the majority of funds we've disbursed."

"I beg to differ, sir. I've never heard of them."

"Would you have heard of them?"

"Oh, yes, sir! Major Moravec put me in charge of all the agents!"

I leaned back and sighed. I could see I had a lot of work to do.

CHAPTER 4
Galicia
July-December, 1915

"In the end we must discriminate between right and violence, truth and falsity, reality and fiction, in those cases also where previously men resorted to arms. I think that the last great war proved clearly enough the needlessness, harmfulness, and stupidity of warfare."
—Tomáš Masaryk, as quoted by Karel Čapek in *On Thought and Life*

SUMMER of 1915 found me, quite unexpectedly, an officer in the Austro-Hungarian Army, a.k.a. the K.U.K.[13]

With scarcely a warning, what everyone soon simply called the Great War had burst upon the continent like a summer thunderstorm that previous year. It swept up and scattered Europeans of my generation by the millions, taking them away from hearth and home and depositing them into a new world of machine guns and barbed wire and trenches. By the time everyone had settled into their new hellish routines, I was on the Eastern Front, riding a horse alongside a ragged column of soldiers marching along a dusty road, on my way to fight for a country I didn't believe in.

In the morning, we'd all been upbeat, at least. Soldiers on march are at their best mid-morning; there is a spring in their step and the confidence that comes from having a rifle in hand. At such times, even for a reluctant army like ours, everything is glorious and multi-hued, green countryside and cyan sky and yellow sun and gray uniforms.

But now it was late in the day. The sinking sun had washed out the bright colors; dust now clung to sweat-sticky skin and coated the pike-gray uniforms and field packs. Most of the men had drained their tin canteens, and their legs and feet were weary. Many had slung their Mannlicher rifles[14] over their shoulders; nearly all looked up at us, their horse-mounted officers, with a resentful glare. Meanwhile we trotted up and down the column (four platoons in line, trailed by a horse-drawn field kitchen and an ambulance-wagon) and shifted our saddle-sore bodies uncomfortably. Truth be told, I'd have switched places with any one of them right then, if only for a different discomfort. But we are all assigned our own individual burdens, and seldom can we so much as swap them.

All day the road had been clogged with our motley army: sluggish infantrymen, cavalry hussars and dragoons in ridiculous uniforms, sleepy pack animals, overburdened trucks coughing and wheezing and breaking their wooden-spoked wheels in the deep ruts. There were refugees coming the other way, too, Gentiles and Jews, some shuffling downcast, others placing worried hands on tottering carts on which they'd seemingly loaded all their worldly possessions. So it had

---

[13] Kaiserlich Und Königlich—German for "Imperial and Royal."

[14] The brand of choice for the K.U.K. and, more recently, Lee Harvey Oswald.

been a halting march, with lots of fits and starts.[15] Now the road ahead was clear, and up ahead we could hear a rumble, like distant thunder but more menacing: artillery.

On the long road ahead I spotted a lone man on a piebald horse, wreathed in a cloud of dust. A messenger, perhaps? He galloped until he was nearly upon us, then slowed his horse to a trot and sidled up to me. Now I saw he was a fellow lieutenant, perhaps a staff officer.

"Good afternoon, lieutenant." He handed me a sealed envelope. "This is for your commanding officer."

"Orders from the front?"

"They want you to billet back here for the night. Everything's a disaster up there. The 41st regiment somehow ended up fighting the 17th regiment for the past seven hours. Anyway, there's a small inn a few minutes up the road—you might want to pull in there."

"Seven hours?"

"Bukovinians and Slovenians—no one in either unit even spoke the same language. And it seems the factories have been having problems making our field uniforms a standard shade of gray."[16]

"Correct me if I'm wrong, but…we are advancing, right? How is that possible?"

He smirked "They say the Germans are doing well up north."

"Still."

"Yes, I don't think we're helping them out much. The Germans say going to war alongside us is like fighting while shackled to a corpse. But the good news is, compared to the Tsar's troops, we're crack professionals!" He grinned, then turned his horse around and spurred it into a gallop again.

I wheeled my own horse around, trotted back to Captain Sagner, and handed him the envelope. He read it in silence, perplexed, then

---

[15] Not that we were in a hurry—our company was a march company, a designation invented by the K.U.K. indicating that we existed solely to be plugged into the front line as a replacement for an exhausted unit. In short, we were officially cannon fodder.

[16] Throughout the K.U.K., field coats and pants ranged in original color from blue-gray to powder blue to dark gray to light gray-green, and faded to various additional shades depending, one presumed, on the shadiness of the war profiteers who had manufactured them.

upset. An old army quip popped into my head: commanding in the K.U.K. while at war was a war itself. The captain scanned the sides of the road; there were rows of poplar trees on either side, and empty fields beyond.

"The messenger said there was an inn up ahead, sir."

"Go scout it out," he said.

Eagerly, I coaxed my horse around and spurred it on down the road, free at last, if only for the moment. Sooner than I expected, I came upon a large grassy clearing where sat the inn, an ancient building with an open porch, carved dark wooden columns, and a stately air of country dignity. I found the proprietress and explained our needs; she said we could billet there for the evening.

Before long, the front of our column appeared, and I shepherded the men off the road.

In front of the inn, they shucked their field packs off their weary shoulders, then stacked their rifles in circles, like the skeletons of teepees I'd seen in picture books of the American West. Once we barked orders to fall out, everyone turned their attention to their individual cares—some wandered off to fill canteens, while others brushed the dust from their uniforms, then sat to remove their boots and gingerly inspect their reddened and blistered feet.

My batman was near, a burly bearded fellow with eager hungry eyes, Corporal—Baloun, I think his name was. I dismounted and handed him my horse's reins, and Baloun led him to the water-trough at the front of the inn. I'd downed a couple canteens' worth of water by the time he came back.

"Humbly ask, sir. When will we be eating?"

"Soon, corporal. See? They're setting up the field kitchen now." Indeed we could see the cook hovering around the field kitchen, filling the copper cauldrons with potatoes and cabbage, then setting the fires underneath.

"Thank you, sir," Baloun said, and disappeared.

I directed the men to pitch their shelter halves, then scouted out the rooms in the inn for my fellow officers and I to spend the night.

Before long, the cook had finished, and the men were shaking off their lethargy and queuing up for their supper. Few orders were given, or needed—no news travels faster among soldiers than the word that there's food for the eating. Once they'd been herded into some semblance of a line, they shuffled past the large cauldrons while the cook awkwardly ladled food into their eager mess kits. Bland food, nothing special; bad food and not quite enough of it, like the old joke goes. But nobody expected better from the Austro-Hungarian Army. At any rate, they were hungry enough that nobody complained too much.

After the men were set to eating, Captain Sagner disappeared inside.

He returned after a couple minutes with two brandy snifters in hand, one of which he discretely gave to me. "Officers' mess is going to be inside, Moravec." he told me in quieter tones. "The proprietress is cooking up a goose for us. They've got a decent selection of wine and brandy, too."

I nodded. Franz Joseph's army had been born aristocratic and would die that way.

"Should be quite the feast," he said.

"Thank you, sir." I retrieved rolling papers and tobacco from my front pocket, then sat on a bench on the porch to prepare a cigarette. Captain Sagner sat beside me, and Lieutenant Lukáš soon joined us. We drank and smoked leisurely.

Out on the road, a cart trundled slowly into view, wobbling haltingly underneath a towering mass of haphazard housewares. Beside it, a florid little peasant with a bushy moustache hovered, brandishing a riding crop—a refugee, apparently a fellow subject of the Emperor, already safe behind the lines but looking to go further from the fighting. The animals' mouths foamed; there was panic in their eyes as they strained at their harnesses; still he whipped them mercilessly. At last the lead horse plunged to its knees and toppled to its side, tangling its harness and panting heavily.

The peasant tried to coax the dying horse to its feet. Some of our men looked up from their mess kits curiously.

Now a line of ambulance trucks pulled up behind, heading also from the front. They had no way to pass the cart on the narrow road; on our side, there was a ditch, and a line of poplars hemmed them in on the other side. So the lead ambulance let loose with a plaintive bleat of the horn, and the farmer kept trying to get his horse up, and the ambulance honked again impatiently.

Captain Sagner huffed. He set down his brandy, stood, smoothed the front of his uniform, and walked over to the road. Over the ditch he went with a dignified little leap. He said not a word to either the peasant or the ambulance driver; he merely drew his revolver and emptied it into the dying horse—eight reports from the M98, sharp and loud over the distant artillery noise. Now all the men were watching. Captain Sagner holstered his weapon and returned.

The peasant now tried in vain to drag his horse off the road. Again the ambulance driver honked, and now he yelled out the window at our unmoving soldiers.

Several soldiers reluctantly stood up and ambled over. One cut the tangled harness with his bayonet. He and the others then grabbed the dead horse's legs; squatting and grunting and heaving, they dragged the carcass off the dusty road and rolled it into the ditch. Corporal Baloun sat there and watched, curious but detached. When none of them were looking, he reached over with his fork, speared a potato from another man's mess tin, and wolfed it down. Then he stole another potato from a second man. Then he took a third potato and put it in a fourth man's tin, but not before taking a single bite.

On the road, the peasant returned to whipping his horses, but with three animals instead of four, the cart moved so slowly that it might as well have been stopped. Again the ambulance driver honked.

One of the sergeants leapt to his feet. Before the men who'd dragged the horse could sit back down, he ushered them back over to the cart. Grumbling, they clambered up on the wheels and sides and started rooting through the peasant's possessions, looking at first with care and discernment, then getting increasingly agitated as they realized there was nothing of value, and finally throwing things off willy-nilly until the cart was about a quarter lighter.

Frustrated and angry, they returned to their cooling food. The men whose potatoes had disappeared looked suspiciously around for the culprit, and settled on the one with the extra potato.

Up on the road, the peasant was looking through the assorted mound of housewares next to the cart—rugs, clocks, stools, drawers—trying to see if there was something in there he still wanted. And the ambulance driver let loose a very long, very loud and very impatient blast from the horn.

Reluctantly the peasant returned to his horses and started goading them along yet again. Once he had passed his discarded junk, he edged his still-slow wagon towards the ditch so the ambulances could pass.

Unfortunately, the first driver didn't wait for him to move; he gunned the engine to try to pass on the right, but there wasn't quite enough space, and his front wheel struck something. There was a loud snapping noise, and the ambulance bucked to a halt. Frustrated, the driver leaped out of the cab and darted around the front to survey the damage.

Meanwhile, the peasant and his cart trundled on.

"Jesus," Captain Sagner said. Again he set down his brandy and left the porch. He rounded up a new handful of soldiers and led them over to the broken ambulance. There he desperately tried to give form and purpose to the shapeless mass of men, but his efforts seemed pointless; some of the men wandered over to the pile of junk and started aimlessly poking through it.

I wanted to help, for the sake of the men in the ambulances, if nothing else. But it looked as if my presence would not make an iota of difference. As usual in this army, our efforts lacked purpose, not people. So I plucked my tobacco and rolling papers from my pocket and assembled two more cigarettes.

"When I was a child in Čáslav, we were let out of school early once," I said to Lieutenant Lukáš, perhaps feeling the need to explain my apathy. "They shepherded us over to the railway station to greet the Emperor when his train passed through town. We were all standing there in neat little rows, singing, 'Glory, glory,' when his train pulled in. And of course, being the condescending Austrian he was, all he could blurt out in our language was, 'I'm so glad to see you, my dear Czech children.' Anyway, his train pulled off practically before he could finish the sentence, and the wind blew the locomotive smoke in such a way that we were covered in soot, coughing. And I thought: 'This old fool thinks he's our father?' Since then, I've never much cared for Austria-Hungary."

"Me, neither," Lukáš admitted.

"When the war started, I really thought I'd find a way out of this mess. Something medical, perhaps. I really tried hard, though. I gave them every excuse but old age."

"Me, too," Lukáš said.

"I wanted to continue in my studies. Perhaps become a philosophy professor. It's odd. If we'd been born a few years later, we would have missed all this. But because we were born in 1895, we're here for the duration. It is a most regrettable situation. It is against my nature to not do my best. But how can I give my best to this?" I shrugged haplessly, indicating this army, and this war.

"Do you think it'll be over soon?" Lukáš asked.

"We're fighting the Russians, so who knows who will manage to lose first? Either way, I hope it'll be over quickly. Home by Christmas, perhaps. Back to the classroom for the spring term. I was studying under Masaryk; perhaps I'll be able to continue under him."

"Tomáš Masaryk? I've heard he left Prague."

"Really?"

"Yes, back in December." Even though no one was within earshot, Lukáš lowered his voice. "The rumor is he headed abroad to organize some sort of…resistance to Austria-Hungary's rule."

"Interesting." I remembered our days in the classroom, and his talk of a Czech and Slovak nation. Perhaps it was now more than talk.

We smoked and sat. Out on the road, the ambulances were at last rolling. Among our ranks there was a brief confrontation between the soldiers with the missing potatoes and Corporal Baloun. However, Baloun defused the situation by leading a delegation over to the peasant's dead horse. Under his leadership, the men hacked the carcass apart with bayonets. Again the cook stoked the field kitchen's fires, and its little chimney puffed merrily away as he started cooking up a horse-meat goulash in his copper cauldrons.

Presently the proprietress came out and ushered my fellow officers and I inside, and we dined in fine style by candlelight on dark wooden tables.

Night fell. We returned to our pleasant little porch for after-dinner cigarettes. The men had pitched their tents and built a roaring fire. I snuck back inside and scraped some potatoes and roast goose into my mess kit; I found Baloun outside in the fire-lit night and gave it to him for a late night snack. Then I hovered about and basked in the warmth as the men ate and sang and told stories and tried to ignore the distant battle rumble.

*   *   *

For the next several months, our army advanced, no thanks to me.

Given my later career and rank, it may seem surprising that I was such an indifferent and lackluster soldier back then, but that army, on that front, had that effect on many of us.[17] Here we were, my men and I, fighting in only the loosest sense of the word, more often marching forever along roads made muddy by autumn rains, unsure if we were advancing or retreating, or why. I know we re-captured Przemyśl, which the Russians had taken after a long siege, but my memories of that time consist not so much of events but strange scenes: horses torn asunder by high explosives and left to rot in the summer heat; a single naked foot and lower leg hanging from the branches of a tree; enough abandoned field guns and rifles to equip several armies, if only there were soldiers who cared enough to hold on to them.[18]

Certainly I saw nothing that would strengthen my affection for Austria-Hungary, and as the days dragged on, my apathy only increased. The K.U.K. showered us with medals at the slightest provocation, hoping to stave off such feelings. But they came anyway.[19]

Perhaps the only good thing about the Eastern Front was that it wasn't the Western Front. Those of you who have absorbed the popular

---

[17] A few years ago I read an excellent book by an American Negro author which described an event in the American South called a battle royal wherein two Negro boxers would be blindfolded and placed in a ring, more for comedy than sport, so they could flail aimlessly at one another while spectators watched and laughed. Picture such a conflict, then imagine it magnified a million-fold and waged not with boxing gloves in a ring but with rifles, horses and artillery pieces across hundreds of kilometers of open country. Picture this, and you can imagine the Eastern Front in the Great War.

[18] The art world would later say that surrealism was born in the trenches; it certainly seemed an appropriate response to the strangeness of that war.

[19] Because of these experiences, when *The Good Soldier Švejk* came out after the war, I could relate to the titular character. Only I was in charge of a platoon of fellow Švejks, which made everything seem all the more pointless.

imagery of the war probably assume it was all trenches and machine guns and cratered muddy wastelands, but our front lines were at least more fluid in the latter half of 1915. When things finally bogged down that fall, our army took some time to even figure out that we needed to build trenches.[20]

So great was the mutual apathy, though, that we and the Russians built our emplacements up to three kilometers apart, and kept the fighting to a minimum. In some places there were entire populated villages, peasants and cattle and dogs and ducks, living their lives as usual between our two lazy armies.

---

[20] The Russians, who had fought the Japanese in 1904 and 1905, at least knew that much.

CHAPTER 5
Prague
March, 1929-April 1934

"We shall always be a tiny minority in the world, but when a small nation achieves something with its limited means, what it achieves has immense, exceptional value, like the widow's mite. We are not inferior to any nation in the world, and in some respects we are superior…The problem of small nations is that we must do more than others and do it better. And if anyone sets upon us with force, we must hold our ground. Holding your ground is everything."

—Tomáš Masaryk, as quoted by Karel Čapek in *Talks with T. G. Masaryk*

ON a rainy Friday in 1929, soon after I became a spy, Kirinovic (who was then one of the junior captains on my staff) came knocking on my door—in civilian clothes, I was glad to see.

I'd been holed up in my office; it was one of those dreary rainy mornings when you bury yourself in work because everything else— even looking out at the other soggy downcast pedestrians still slogging to work—seems miserable.

"Good morning, sir. I've prepared a new report on…" Kirinovic started to talk, then stopped when he realized I wasn't looking directly at him.

"Hmm." I peered over his shoulder. In true Czech fashion, I hadn't directly ordered the men to stop wearing uniforms, but I'd brought it up in such fashion that all of them but one had figured it out. Indeed, two of my subordinates were sitting bolt upright at their desks, diligently hammering away on their typewriters in their pristine civilian suits. Meanwhile, Šnejd, still in uniform, was packing his personal effects into a cardboard box.

Following my gaze, Kirinovic glanced over his shoulder. "So Captain Šnejd is leaving us, sir."

"Yes. What have you got for me?"

"I…" Now Kirinovic was looking back again, with what might have been a sympathetic gaze. Šnejd was shaking hands and saying his goodbyes; he waved at Kirinovic, who gave an acknowledging nod before turning back to me. "I am a little sad to see him go, sir. He was a character. Almost like a mascot for the office."

"Are you saying we should have kept him on for sentiment's sake?"

"No, sir. I just…this is very new to all of us, sir."

"It's new to me, too, Kirinovic."

"My wife's just had a baby, sir, and I'm hoping I can…"

"Can you give an honest effort to the job that's being asked of you? Regardless of what else is going on in your personal life?"

"Yes, sir," he said, at last sounding almost confident.

"Very well then, that's all I ask." He seemed a nice enough man—too nice, perhaps. At any rate, this was not the time for niceties. "I'm getting the sense that a lot of things weren't recorded here. We are a branch of government, Kirinovic. We have been entrusted with public money. So we have to keep track of what we do. Our meetings with agents, our expenditures, we have to be accountable. And I have the sense that the old Major Moravec wasn't accountable."

"I'll be honest, I didn't always know what was going on around the office, sir. But there was a lot that was not written down."

"Perhaps that was by design," I said. "At any rate, I need to know what's going on. And if all you know is that you don't know what's going on, let me know."

"Very well, sir." Kirinovic nodded and made as if to turn and leave.

I spoke again, impatiently. "The report, Captain?"

"Oh! Yes." Kirinovic looked down at the manila folder in his hand and made a sound as if surprised to find it there. Sheepishly he handed it to me. "I've been preparing a report on a new rifle the German Army's fielding, sir."

*   *   *

"The K98k Mauser is a 7.92 mm shoulder-fired bolt-action rifle," General Bily read aloud from my report as I stood in front of his desk. Only this time, he seemed ever so slightly less rigid; he actually leaned back in his chair a little. "It has a maximum range of 700 meters, or 1000 meters if a scope is mounted."

Here perhaps I puffed my chest out a little, still proud and military at heart despite my civilian attire.

Bily looked up at me and pursed his lips; he closed the manila folder but kept talking, almost as if he'd read the report already. "It is intended to replace the older Model 98s used during the Great War. It will..." Here at last, he paused. Turning around, he plucked a magazine from an impossibly neat stack atop his bookshelf, leafed through the pages, and resumed. "...it will be available throughout the German Army by mid-November, thanks to an expedited production schedule."

"Sir, how did..."

With the barest hint of what could have almost been a smile, he lifted the periodical so I could see the cover. "*Wehrmacht* magazine. It only costs twenty crowns a year. You should subscribe."

To that I could only mumble a crestfallen "Yes, sir."

He tossed the magazine on the desk, nodding at me to pick it up. "Tell me things I can't find out myself, Major Moravec—information that isn't publicly available. Recruit agents. Buy documents."

"Yes, sir."

"I see you're wearing civilian clothes now. That's good. You still look too military, though."

"Too military, sir?" There had been some strange things about my current assignment and my work thus far, but to get that criticism, from that man, seemed the height of absurdity.

"Perhaps it is your posture. Your bearing. You'll have to do something about that."

"Yes, sir." Now they wanted me to unlearn the fundamentals. I slumped, crestfallen.

"That works," he said. "Don't get down on yourself, Major. This is still peacetime. Armies are allowed to make mistakes in peacetime. And mistakes are inevitable. Only the man who does nothing makes no mistakes."

*   *   *

In most jobs, you'd get in trouble for reading the newspaper at work. But after that, I insisted on it.

Most mornings, the outer office looked like a study in laziness, with Kirinovic and the others relaxing in their chairs, leisurely leafing through the broadsheets over steaming cups of tea while the sun streamed in the eastern windows. There was, of course, focus and purpose to the perusals; our small section was soon reading and typing out summaries of every major publication and every military periodical in Germany. To find secrets, I decided, you first had to find out what was publicly known and use that as your jumping-off point.

Erasing everyone's military bearing, loosening spines stiffened by years of parading and drill, took some ingenuity. Our final method was artfully simple—I suggested to the men that they should use personal items usually forbidden for able-bodied soldiers: umbrellas, knapsacks, canes, walking sticks. Walking sticks in particular worked wonders to create the unmilitary appearance we were looking for; they cultivated an artful and gentlemanly asymmetric slouch which seemed the very opposite of purposeful military perfection. So after some concentrated efforts, we figured out how to look like spies—which, sad to say, usually just meant looking like normal people.

But we hadn't yet recruited any agents.

* * *

Some time in July, Strankmuller, a new divisional officer subordinate to our section, dropped in to my office. Appearance-wise, he was short and baby-faced: a little pudgy for an officer, but that perhaps made for a better spy.

It was one of those sweltering days when you open the windows but the hot and lazy air refuses to go anywhere; there were beads of perspiration dotting Strankmuller's face, but he gave no indication of distraction as he stood there outside my door.

"Come on in, captain," I said; he obligingly followed, and I shut the door.

"Sir." Strankmuller spoke calmly but purposefully.

"What do you have for me?"

"An anonymous letter, sir." He handed it over. "The sender mailed it to our division headquarters. He says he's a junior officer in the *Wehrmacht* and that he's willing to provide us with his unit's mobilization plans. He provided instructions for us to contact him if we're interested."

"Well, that might be worth some money," I said. "Let's arrange a meeting with this man. Ask him for documents. Give him…we'll say ten thousand crowns."

"Ten thousand crowns, sir?" Strankmuller seemed aghast.

"If people come to us, I'm going to give them a reason to keep coming back. Wait in the outer office and I'll bring it out to you."

He closed the door behind him.

I made out an entry in the ledger book, opened the safe, and rooted around for the money. Double-counting the crisp bills, it occurred to me that this Strankmuller could easily take half of the money to the bar or the bank or the baccarat table, pay the agent with the other half, and no one would have any clue—his agent would still get a fair amount of money, and I would still get a credible report. Obviously I didn't want to plant the idea in his head by mentioning my thoughts, or even joking about them…

I realized I'd lost count of the money. Enough overanalysis, I told myself—if I don't trust my subordinates, I should get rid of them.

I slammed the safe shut and shoved the cash in a plain envelope. Then I walked out to Strankmuller and discreetly pressed the envelope into his sweaty palm.

"Bring back something good," was all I said.

* * *

"What do you have for me?" I asked when he returned a week and a half later.

"Well, sir, I arranged a little tryst at a bed and breakfast near the frontier."

"You spent the evening with him?" I gave a sly smile. "Captain Strankmuller, that's really above and beyond the call of duty."

Strankmuller suppressed his own smile. "No, sir. I had to get home before the wife started asking questions, so I just left the money on the bed and left. But I think I got my money's worth, sir."

Strankmuller opened his briefcase and produced an intriguing series of documents stamped with an impressive and authentic looking divisional seal.

"Good work, Strankmuller."

"Thank you, sir," he said, and left.

Leaning back in my chair, I perused the papers. They did look good. And yet, something seemed off. The documents seemed…calculated, somehow. Not like real internal documents with all of their abbreviations, undecipherable acronyms and bureaucratic inside jokes, but like papers designed to be read by someone who didn't know anything about the organization they described.

It was time to go home, but I found myself sitting there, staring at the typewritten papers and the ink-stamped seal.

* * *

That night I got back to our apartment to find my daughter asleep in the crib, a duck roasting in the oven, and my wife peeling potatoes. On the dining room table, she'd placed candles, the good dishes, the nice linen: a fancy dinner. Our anniversary. I'd obviously not given it as much thought as she had.

Sneaking up from behind, I caressed her as she worked next to the stove and kissed her on the side of the back of the neck, by the wispy fringes of her beautiful brown hair. "Good evening, beautiful."

"How was work, František?" she asked.

"Oh, not bad."

"Not bad?"

"Exciting, actually."

"How so?"

"Oh, you know. New ideas, new undertakings."

"How come you never wear your uniform any more?"

"What are you making there? Potatoes and…"

"Duck. And vegetables." Looking over her shoulder, she smiled a little. "You could see that."

"I was too busy concentrating on your loveliness."

"Good answer." She whirled about, put her hands in mine. A little smile fluttered across her face. "Funny you should say 'concentrating.' You seem very…distant lately. Lost in thought."

"What was that?" I asked, feigning obliviousness.

"Very funny. You seem…evasive, too. You don't talk about your work. And I haven't seen you in uniform for months. Sometimes I wonder if they've kicked you out of the army and you haven't had the nerve to tell me!"

Pulling her to me, I kissed her. "Yes, my beautiful. I'm still in the army."

For a few precious seconds, nothing existed outside of us. I pressed close to her as she leaned against the counter. We breathed heavily.

"I've got to finish dinner, handsome." She gave me a final peck, then turned away.

"Here, let me help with the potatoes."

I grabbed a knife and a wooden cutting board and got to work. The potatoes had an interesting texture; I bisected them and carved out the eyes, noticing their firmness and consistency. I experimented a little with the knife: it cut the potato into crisp, firm shapes.

"František?" she asked.

"Yes?"

"Stop playing with your food."

* * *

As soon as I sat down the next morning, I rang up the local telephone exchange, had them connect me with Strankmuller's divisional headquarters, and summoned him to the office.

By late morning, he was standing in front of my desk, perplexed and a little nervous. Wordlessly, I crumpled the documents he'd brought in—all those documents with their fancy inked divisional seals—into a massive paper ball, and threw them in the wastebasket.

Now I opened my desk drawer and produced a steak knife.

Strankmuller looked at me as if I'd gone mad.

From the drawer, I pulled out a raw potato, which I then cut in half.

"Oh, none for me, sir." He smiled thinly. "I had a big breakfast."

"Very funny. They're fake."

Strankmuller swallowed hard. "Fake, sir?"

Atop my desk, I whittled away at one of the potato halves until I'd created a flat surface. Then I inscribed a simple pattern on it, opened my inked pad, dipped the potato in it, and stamped it on my desk calendar.

"The divisional seal?"

"It was the most impressive thing about the documents. Which got me thinking, why have such an impressive seal on such unimportant documents? So I did a little experimenting last night. I think they're forgeries."

"Why, sir? If someone wanted to feed us bad information, there are easier ways."

"We paid him, didn't we? That's why."

Strankmuller looked miserable. "I'm terribly sorry, sir."

"It's OK, Strankmuller. I told you to."

"Still, sir."

"At any rate, we'll vet our sources better next time. We'll start by asking them questions we already know the answer to, to establish their bona fides."

"I just..." Strankmuller exhaled, frustrated. "I hate making mistakes like that, sir."

"Don't worry about it. Only the man who does nothing makes no mistakes," I said. The words felt foolishly optimistic, and I felt embarrassed just saying them.

* * *

"...and those field exercises are scheduled to end at the end of the month, sir," I told General Bily at the conclusion of a meeting a couple months later. My eyes dared to dart up to the clock. I sighed: yet another brief briefing.

"Very well," he said, then looked up, inquisitive. "Something's on your mind, major?"

"Can I be honest, sir?"

"Have you not been?" he asked, with what might have been a smile.

"I've been optimistic, sir. It's not exactly dishonest, but I'm not sure it's exactly the truth, either."

"You're leading an intelligence section. Leaders have to be optimistic about what they've accomplished and what they're capable of. Otherwise their subordinates won't follow them, and their superiors will either fire them or start scrutinizing their every move."

"Still, sir. It seems like we're making too many mistakes and not getting enough information. And I know you've said that's understandable, but it is frustrating."

"Frustrations highlight the path to future success, as long as you don't keep trying the same thing over and over. You've been making progress. I can tell. I've been reading the reports. They've been getting better, little by little. You're keeping track of all these informants, yes?"

"Yes, sir. Some of them have been providing...very reliable information actually, sir. But they're all low-level sources."

"Well, God willing, they'll move up in the ranks and keep providing information. As I've said before, I don't know much about intelligence, and in the past I hardly ever dealt with my intelligence staff. But I've learned in life that if you hold on to the geese that lay the golden eggs, you usually come out well in the end. So I have a sense you're on the right track."

"Thank you, sir."

"As I said before, we're at peace now, so we can afford to make slow progress and a few mistakes. I don't expect the war to come soon." Now he looked down, eyes heavy. "It will come, though."

"That doesn't sound very optimistic, sir."

This time General Bily really did crack a little smile. "Leaders have to be realistic, too. Otherwise, their subordinates—and their superiors—will think they're full of horseshit."

I suppressed a chuckle.

"It's all right to laugh at my jokes, Moravec."

"Is that an order, sir?"

"Is that an order?" He shook his head. And—miracle of miracles!—he actually leaned back and chuckled. "I know I have a reputation as a disciplinarian. A martinet. A prick. I'll be honest, I cultivate it. I'm sure you've figured out already as an officer that you can start out strict and ease up a little, once people have proven themselves, but you can't start out easy and only lay down the law when your subordinates let you down. People lose all respect for you when you do that. But you…you've proven yourself reliable. So far. So I'm hereby giving you permission…" Here he looked me in the eye with a twinkle and another smile. "…permission, mind you, to laugh at my jokes. If they're funny."

"Yes, sir," I said, smiling.

"Don't laugh at all my jokes, I hate yes-men and ass-kissers."

"No, sir, I'd never be one of those."

"Of course, not."

"Never, sir."

"All right. Back to business." Just like that, the mask came back up, and the human playfulness vanished. He wasn't exactly frosty now—just devoid of temperature. Now he glanced over the report I'd briefed him on. "This here. This is a good report." Opening his desk drawer, he plucked out a rubber stamp, and stamped the report, firmly but neatly: FOR THE MINISTER OF DEFENSE.[21] "I've been sending the good reports up. You may not have a lot of agents and sources yet, but you've done very well with what you have."

"Thank you, sir."

---

[21] Among the unfortunate legacies our country inherited from Austria-Hungary was a predilection for bureaucracy, and an over-reliance on rubber stamps.

"Honestly, I've never wanted to get my hands dirty by working too closely with my intelligence staff. Throwing cash around, operating in very ill-defined scenarios without a lot of rules—even though there are good reasons for all of it, it almost seems like you're gangsters rather than soldiers. In the past I felt it wisest to keep my distance. But you're starting to get results. And I've never gotten results from my intelligence staff before. So I'm pleased. For now. Keep it up."

"Yes, sir," I said, pleased.

*   *   *

In the coming years, I established rules and guidelines for my officers. Procedures that had been informal and haphazard became systematic; we picked up some tools of the trade and sharpened others. My men became freelance journalists and photographers, because those jobs offered a good cover for their activities. We recruited more agents, and put together catalogs of information. We checked new information against the old, to verify it and fill in the blanks and, by interpolation, get still more information.

All the while, we wrote reports and sent them skyward, like rockets of bureaucracy. Our creations were most like signal rockets—we were going for altitude and reliability, rather than sheer explosive effect. Still, the reports made it higher and higher. Soon they were landing on President Masaryk's desk.

And as the reports became more important, I became more important. I became a lieutenant colonel, then a colonel. I found myself packing up my desk at the smaller office and unpacking it at the much larger office of the army's General Staff, reporting directly to General Krejčí rather than General Bily. I had a bigger staff now. Lieutenant Colonel Tichý. Strankmuller, now a major. A young and energetic captain named Fryč. And Kirinovic.

In Germany, the Nazis were on the rise, too. When I started in intelligence; they'd been brown-shirted street brawlers, and now they were running the country. And in April of 1934, a scant month after I'd moved up to the General Staff, they kidnapped Kirinovic.

CHAPTER 6
Galicia-Siberia
January, 1916

"…I observed that our men were loath to report to duty; they behaved as though being sent to the slaughterhouse…"
—Tomáš Masaryk, as quoted by Karel Čapek in *Talks with T. G. Masaryk*

DESPITE the relative lack of danger or effort in our part of the Eastern Front, and the infrequency of actual fighting, I grew increasingly disillusioned. So on a moonlit night in January of 1916, I assembled my men in one of the dugouts.

In this dim subterranean room, we were out of the cold, and out of sight of any enemies—or friends—that might have ventured into our section of the trenches. In the cramped dirt room my platoon looked up at me, their faces lit by flickering candlelight.

"Good evening, men," I said, and the scattered quiet voices ceased their chattering. "As you know, none of us joined this war eagerly. Many of us thought it would at least end soon. But it's looking like that won't be the case. And lately, I've been wondering why I'm fighting on behalf of Austria-Hungary, a country whose leaders share neither our language nor our values. What's more, I find myself wondering why I'm fighting our fellow Slavs in the Russian Army."[22]

From the crowd of fire-lit faces came an unruly but enthusiastic chorus of yesses and here, heres.

Energized by their enthusiasm, I continued, a little louder. "At any rate, I've found myself in an army I don't like, fighting for a cause I don't believe in. What's worse, I'm asking you men to follow my orders and possibly risk death for a country I can't even contemplate dying for. And I can't in good conscience ask you to do that any more."

Now there was applause and still more chatter, and a single anonymous question: "What do you plan on doing, sir?"

"I'm going to walk out of the trench!" Again I found my voice rising, filling the cold room with the fiery certainty and idealism of youth and inexperience. In all my war experiences up to that point, I could not remember having nearly as much enthusiasm. I found myself thinking of Masaryk, of old lessons about Plato, and prisoners in the cave, and the fire of truth. "I'm going to keep walking until I see a Russian, and I'm going to surrender to him!"

"What do you think they'll do, sir?"

---

[22] Pan-Slavism ended up being a major factor in the dissolution of the Austro-Hungarian Empire and a major impetus for many of my countrymen to leave it, as will be apparent throughout the narrative.

"I...I imagine they'll welcome us. I've heard of others going over, other Czechs and Slovaks. Whole units, even! They'll be glad to see us, I'm sure."

Everyone else had heard those stories, too—rumors were rife in our army. Now I heard "Can I go too, sir?" and "To the devil with the Archduke!" and "Why didn't you say anything earlier, sir?"

"Shh!" I said, motioning for calm and quiet. This was not what I had expected. Perhaps I smiled. "Very well. If any of you wants to go with me, please raise your hands."

Every hand shot up.

"If news of this gets out, they'll imprison us." I looked both ways, as if the Archduke's minions were waiting in the shadows to arrest us. "So we might as well leave tonight."

All around, there was excited murmuring. I walked to the mouth of the dugout, peered out, and spied the nearest ladder. The men stacked their rifles haphazardly against the dugout wall—no need for them now. Someone blew out the candles, and orange warmth gave way to cold blackness. The far trench wall gleamed pale bluish-white, icy and bright. I walked out into the cold night, clambered awkwardly up the rickety wooden ladder, and stood alone on the parapet of the trench. The men looked expectantly up at me; they huddled together in the pale moonlight, with plumes of frosty breath dissipating above them.

The snow had fallen several days ago, but there was still not a single footprint in front of our trenches, nor a crater. No, all I saw was a vast expanse of snow, as large and pristine as I have ever seen, moonlit and bright and stretching off forever. The sky was midnight blue and speckled with an impossible number of stars; to the north, but still in front of our lines, I could see a distant house with a lonely orange window and a single plume of silvery smoke rising from it.

I waited to make sure all of my men made it out of the trench. (Elsewhere our lines were quiet; either no one noticed our departure, or no one cared.) Then I turned around and started walking, and my men followed single-file, a silent centipede crawling out of our dying army.

We walked forever. Our faces and feet numbed; our boots grew heavy with snow.

After an hour, I was nearly frozen, but at last I spotted a slender trench slashing across the whiteness. Did the Russians care we were coming? I raised my hands in the air and motioned for my men to do the same. Still, there were no shots, no shouts, and no signs of life as we shuffled towards them.

When we were just a few meters away, a lone sentry nervously sprung out of the trench and raised his rifle in the air over his head in anxious supplication.

"I surrender! I surrender!" he exclaimed excitedly in atrocious German.

"Shh!" I said, gesturing for him to calm down.

It took several minutes of gestures and pidgin Russian to make him realize that we were the ones surrendering.

*   *   *

That was my first exile, and the one which caused the most second-guessing.

After some deliberation and confusion, the Russians at last grouped us together with other erstwhile Austro-Hungarian soldiers and shipped us in drafty boxcars across the blank white wastelands.

After several days of nearly blind and seemingly mindless travel, our train pulled to a halt in a frozen forest somewhere in Siberia.

Our rusty boxcar doors creaked open; we saw soldiers in the Tsar's pompous, ridiculous uniforms standing alongside the train, lazily cradling their rifles. With gestures and shouted commands in bad German and worse Czech, they told us we needed to disembark.

Unhurriedly, we tumbled out of the dark train and into the impossibly bright day, blinked against the glare, and slowly started walking. Beneath massive snow-covered pines we trudged, huddled together in bunches, with the Russians spaced along the sides of our lumpy column. It was perhaps midday; the sky was a cold pale blue, and the sun, indifferent to our plight, provided no heat—only light. None of the guards—for it was clear by now that they were guards and we were prisoners—treated us poorly, per se; rather, our Slavic brethren treated us like a mild nuisance, but one preferable to front-line duties.

I found myself walking next to Corporal Baloun.

"Humbly report, sir. I'm incredibly hungry."

"I am too, Corporal."

"Humbly report, sir. I'm hungry enough to cook and eat one of my comrades."

"I'm sure they'll feed us when we get to wherever we're going, Corporal."

After trudging for several cold weary hours, we rounded a bend and saw a wooden gate yawning before us.

We marched through it, and into a vast clearing of thick tree stumps. There were long log huts and, at the edges of the clearing, towers manned by sleepy soldiers. A weak barbed-wire fence, perhaps an incidental afterthought, ringed the clearing; it looked too inconsequential to hold back anyone but a complete imbecile. Still, it was clear that we had arrived at a prisoner-of-war camp.

By this point, I was strongly wondering if I'd made the right decision. Still, despite the lax supervision, I gave no thought to escape. After all, where would I escape to? Prague? There was no question of that. If the distance alone hadn't made it impossible, I knew that I'd be arrested and imprisoned as a traitor if I returned. And besides, I'd led my men here. For better or for worse, it was now home.

CHAPTER 7
Prague
April 1934 – April 1936

"Money is the sinews of all war."
—Tomáš Masaryk, *The Making of a State*

WHEN I told General Krejčí about Kirinovic's disappearance, we were walking across the Charles Bridge, under the watchful gaze of the looming dark statues lining both sides. On the Vltava, ducks paddled about in the cool spring sun. Besides them, and the occasional passerby dropping breadcrumbs for their benefit, there was no one to observe us, let alone overhear us. Not a bad spring morning: a little brisk, which accounted for the lack of pedestrians, but both of us were glad to get out of the office.

"How do you know he was kidnapped?" Krejčí asked.

"He's been missing for a week with no explanation, sir."

"Perhaps he went to Germany to meet with an agent. They could have arrested him there, legitimately."

I stopped walking.

Krejčí, too, stopped, turned, and paid closer attention.

"I make my men keep diaries on everything they do, sir. On every contact they make. I arrange airtight cover identities—usually as freelance journalists or photographers. There's no way for the Germans to know who they're working for. Everything they do, everyone they meet, could have another explanation, a safe, innocuous explanation, to protect them from giving the real one. But even so, I don't let them meet agents in Germany without getting my approval and writing down where they are going, and why, and when they'll be back. And Kirinovic isn't my best officer, but he is my best diary keeper."

"Could it have been desertion? Suicide?"

"He's happily married, sir. A wife, a child, a second child due this week."

"A lot of responsibility. Some men would run away from that."

"Not Kirinovic, sir. He was ecstatic about this second child. And he was well prepared; he was a thrifty man. He was living comfortably within his means. He had no debts. No dark secrets."

"You sound certain."

"I make it a point to know my men, sir. I track their financial status, their family situation, their personal habits. The Austrian spies who served in the Great War, their superiors kept track of all of their vices, even how many cigarettes they smoked.[23] And I try to do the same, because I've had men with problems. Alcoholics. Gamblers.

---

[23] Another tidbit I'd gleaned from the Snowden book.

Womanizers. I get rid of men like that, sir. They're unreliable. Kirinovic wasn't one of those men."

We started walking again. Perhaps I expected that my self-righteous speech would put General Krejčí on edge; instead, he looked pleased.

"You like this work, don't you, Moravec? When I first interviewed you…what was that? Four years ago?"

"I think it was five, sir."

"Anyway, I knew you were the right man for the job. I knew, even though you didn't."

"As you know, I accepted this assignment very reluctantly, sir. And with many reservations. But I'll admit, it has gotten under my skin, sir." I gazed out at the Vltava, the beautiful low buildings lining the banks, the hills and bluffs off in the distance, now painted with the first fragile brushstrokes of spring color. "And it's not just another duty assignment. It takes a heavy toll. You have to neglect so much else. Everything else, really. Your social life, hobbies, friends, even family."

"That's a lot to neglect. Even for the oldest profession."

"Second oldest, sir. According to Exodus. Joshua sent spies into Jericho when the Jews were trying to enter the Promised Land, right before they blew the city walls down. They stayed at the home of Rahab, a prostitute. So that's older."[24]

"Prostitution and espionage? I'm surprised to hear you link the two, Moravec. When we first talked, so many years ago, you seemed more concerned with honor and dignity and other…soldierly virtues."

Again I stopped, turned, and stared at my superior. "I've kept my virtue, sir. You wanted honesty? Well, I've been honest." General Krejčí had a particular talent for getting under my skin. Others, like General Bily, applied external pressure—demands, deadlines—but with Krejčí, everything was an inside job.

"So you don't find it as…distasteful as you'd imagined?"

"I'll admit, there are some distasteful aspects to the work, sir. But the rewards are also great, if you keep in mind your sense of purpose and your love of country." Jesus, was I really being this holier-than-thou? To this man? I chuckled. Time to break the ice a little. "Besides, sir, if anything, I feel more like a prostitute's customer than a prostitute.

---

[24] Joshua, Chapter 2.

Only instead of paying someone for their body, I'm paying them for their mind. Their conscience."

"Their soul?" Krejčí's eyes twinkled; clearly he was enjoying this.

"I'd rather not think of it that way, sir," I said defensively. "The people we recruit are doing the right thing. They're just doing it for the wrong reason. That's what balances out the ugly aspects of this job, for me at least. At the end of the day I know that, although we often have to pay for information, although we sometimes have to take advantage of human weaknesses, our country is on the side of right and…"

Again I'd stopped walking. Now Krejčí was laughing. "I'm not judging you, Moravec! I got you into this, and you're getting excellent results, so I'm not about to complain about your methods! You're making me look good!"

"Thank you, sir."

We stood there; I watched the river lazily disappear under the bridge.

"It does make me wonder, though," Krejčí said at last. "Surely there must be a lot of Germans with those problems you mentioned. Alcoholics. Gamblers. Womanizers."

"The sources who come to us, who need money and are willing to sell their secrets for it, usually it is because they have those problems, sir. That's why I don't tolerate such men on my own staff."

"Well, I'm sure there are more where they came from. And in higher places. You've been letting these people come to you. I wonder if there are ways to find them."

"Find them, sir?"

"Just a thought."

In silence we hiked back up the sidewalks toward Hradčany, hemmed in now by the rows of buildings that loomed over the narrow stone streets.

"Thank you again for the report," Krejčí said at last when it was time to part ways. "And let me know what you find out about Kirinovic."

"Yes, sir."

*   *   *

Back at the office, my staff had completed their daily newspaper summaries. Strankmuller had been conversing with Fryč, but when he saw me, he followed me into my office and closed the door behind him.

"We know what happened to Kirinovic, sir." He dropped a copy of the *Völkischer Beobachter*[25] on my desk; the headline read:

CZECHOSLOVAKIAN SPY ARRESTED ON GERMAN SOIL!
DASTARDLY FOREIGN AGENT IN GESTAPO HANDS!

*   *   *

Kirinovic's case was potentially a major issue in our dealings with Nazi Germany.

When the Germans announced they were putting him on trial, we retained the services of a prominent—and expensive—Berlin lawyer. Meanwhile the Nazi regime ramrodded his case through what they still called a court system. There were no real concessions to the rule of law: the court proceedings were closed, the evidence undisclosed. They sentenced him to twenty-five years of hard labor. And that was that— what could have been a serious matter of contention, wasn't. Our government was in no position to challenge their decision on what seemed to them a relatively minor matter, and it became almost an afterthought, lost in the avalanche.

Meanwhile, they'd been flooding our country with agents and spies. Our court system generally gave lighter sentences, so when it came time to negotiate Kirinovic's release, we had to trade away two spies we'd caught in flagrant acts of espionage.

Five years before, General Bily had said war was on the way; I'd believed so, too, but I'd thought about it in general, distant terms—until we received our agent back shattered, drugged and drooling, after having treated their men with care and civility. That infuriated me. And that let me know that, yes, it had started.

This was war, and there was no point in expecting reasonable behavior from them. If we were to have any chance of surviving, we had to spare no effort in building and maintaining our networks. It was no small order—we were trying to get secrets out of a country where

---

[25] A notorious anti-Semitic rag, nonetheless very useful as a gauge of Nazi Party moods and priorities.

everyone already spoke in whispers, fearful of the secret police and that extra-legal legal system. But this was war. How could we set limits for ourselves when our very survival was at stake?

* * *

As part of our war, we started a bank.

The bank was a small, legitimate bank in a frontier town. Most of the tellers didn't even know they were working for Czechoslovakian military intelligence. Likewise, many customers came in and out transacting, seeing and doing all the same things they would see and do at a normal bank, and never knowing they were dealing with us. These people were small-fry, and we had our nets set for bigger fish.

Once we got a license to operate in Germany, we plastered newspaper ads all over the Third Reich. People say money talks, and ours was screaming:

> IN DEBT?
> NEED MONEY FAST?
> GET QUICK PAYDAY LOANS OF UP TO 1000 REICHSMARKS!
> FAST, EASY CASH!
> WE PROMISE COMPLETE DISCRETION!

General Krejčí was right, it turned out. There were many Germans in dire straits—alcoholics, gamblers and womanizers. And many of them didn't want their superiors knowing of their debts, so they were more than willing to go to a foreign bank to buy time to sort everything out.

And when they came in gasping for money, tangled in their nets of debt, we had a simple way of figuring out whom to keep, whom to use for other purposes, and whom to throw back. Our method was so unobtrusive, in fact, that none of them knew anything out of the ordinary was going on.

We made them fill out their loan applications.

One by one, they'd come in, fill out the form, and sit down with the loan officer. The officer would review all the standard information: name, address, and most importantly, occupation.

For most applicants, it was nothing significant: professor, machine-tool operator, draftsman, shopkeeper, mechanic. But every so often, the answer would interest us—if someone said they were a major in the *Luftwaffe*, for instance. At this point, the loan officer would lean forward a little in his chair and say, "Thank you! I promise we'll give your application our full, undivided attention."

Captain Fryč would swing through the bank every second Friday, and the loan officer would review the potential lendees with him. "We have someone you might be interested in. A major in the *Luftwaffe*," the loan officer would say, before handing Fryč the application sheet with the man's contact information.

Only then would our case officers get in touch with this *Luftwaffe* major. Even then, they wouldn't tell the target who they were, or how they'd come across him. They'd just mention that, if he was willing to, say, take microfilm photographs of any important papers, documents or plans that might be floating around the office, he would have money in his mailbox at the end of the month.

So after a few short weeks, that *Luftwaffe* major would be staying late at work on Friday afternoon, taking documents into the janitor's closet, locking the door, and taking pictures on a microfilm camera helpfully provided, of course, by us. On the way out, he would drop the film canister under, say, a park bench near the Brandenburg Gate.

And then those other loan applicants would come in handy. Someone else—a draftsman, perhaps—would pick up the film canister, get on the #29 tram, and attach the film to the bottom of the first seat with a simple piece of gum, and mark the tram car with a piece of chalk when he got off.

That night, the mechanic would search the silent empty trams parked in the dark marshalling yard and find the film canister. The next day, he'd take it to, say, a shopkeeper at an antique store, and tell him, "This was found on the #29 tram." The shopkeeper would smile, nod and put the film canister next to his register.

In a day or two someone would drop into the store and ask if anything had turned up in the lost and found. The shopkeeper would hand over the film canister. The customer would then get on a train for the Czechoslovakian border.

So it turned out that even a police state like Hitler's could be penetrated. And the best thing about it was that all these people were just links on a chain, taking information from Point A to Point B without really knowing what they were doing or who they were doing it for. If these couriers were arrested, all they could say, even if tortured, was, "Every week, I picked up a canister under the first park bench near the southwest park entrance. And I dropped it off under a seat on the #29 tram." Unless they caught our agent in the act, the Gestapo would still not know who our spy was, or who we were. And even if the Gestapo staked out the places the courier had mentioned, they'd still come up with nothing, for by then we would have sent an emergency signal to the other members of the network—something simple, like a chalk mark on a particular lamp post, for instance—and they would have gone to ground.

So it worked well. Within a few years, the mighty Third Reich was riddled with spies. That *Luftwaffe* major would take his photographs, and in a couple of days I would have on my desk, say, the entire aircraft production schedule for the *Luftwaffe* over the course of the next two years. (And he would in turn get enough money to cover his prodigious losses at the baccarat tables.)

In that particular case, we passed the information on to the British and French so they could plan their own aircraft production schedules. The French were skeptical, but the British at least took us seriously and ramped up their aircraft production as a result. (This was at a time, mind you, when the Germans were prohibited from rearming by the Treaty of Versailles. They had not yet publicly admitted that they even had an air force.) Those who have studied the Second World War know, of course, that Britain's air rearmament allowed them to prevail during the Battle of Britain; few know that we had helped get it started.

CHAPTER 8
Siberia-Dobrudja-Odessa
January-September, 1916

"But in war there is much besides the fighting of heroes. By the side of it there has hitherto been a whole system of abominations—lying, greed, baseness, vindictiveness, cruelty…"

—Tomáš Masaryk, *The Making of a State*

SURVIVAL soon became our top priority in the camps.

Things were, of course, completely different than I'd expected, but as so often happens in wartime, what had been unimaginable soon became routine. Daytimes, they would feed us—potatoes, gruel, or the occasional piece of unidentifiable meat. This was far worse than what we'd left behind; this was horrible food, and barely enough to lessen the hunger pangs for a few minutes. (Even Corporal Baloun grew slender.) Between "meals" we would pick the lice from our meager bedding, or heat crude pokers over fires and listen for the satisfying pop and sizzle as we ironed those abominable creatures from our clothes. The men staged races with the cockroaches they'd trapped; they'd drop the creatures in the center of a circle and see which one reached the outside first. No one had any money, but they placed bets anyway using I.O.U.s, tallying up wagers and amassing winnings and debts that would probably never be settled up. Meanwhile, I played chess with other officers, using crude boards assembled from scraps of paper and slivers of wood. With the help of the friendlier guards I studied Russian, and under the tutelage of some of our former countrymen (Bosnian Serbs who, like us, would have preferred fighting our army to serving in it), I learned Serbian. It was tempting to fritter away my days like the others, but even in captivity there are ways to spend your days productively, provided you look hard enough.

Still, at night I would stare up into the blackness of the unlit hut and wonder how long this would last.

Whatever pretense of military discipline we'd had soon evaporated; the men didn't want to hear it, and the other officers and I didn't want to enforce it, beyond the barest rudiments of cleanliness and human decency. Outside the log huts, spring thaws turned what had been a forest floor into a muddy morass; it was all we could do to keep the rough wooden hut floors somewhat clean.[26] Hygiene was made all the more important by the difficulty in maintaining it; sickness was endemic, and rumors of typhus at similar camps trickled in from the guards.

*   *   *

---

[26] We didn't want mud on the floors, but it worked well on the walls; we'd daub it between the logs in an effort to lessen the drafts.

One night as I lay half-awake in my rickety wooden bunk, Corporal Baloun spoke.

"Sir?" His voice was tentative and distant in the empty darkness. "Are you awake, sir?"

"Yes, corporal," I mumbled wearily.

"Humbly ask, sir. How long are we going to be here?"

"I don't know, corporal."

"I am wondering if we made the right decision in leaving our army, sir."

"It will work out, corporal," I said, not wanting to admit my own thoughts along those lines.

He tried to continue the conversation, but I rolled over and feigned sleep until it became real.

* * *

Two days later, a Russian general arrived and summoned us to the center of camp.

At last the days were getting consistently warmer; sprigs of green were pushing their way up near the rotting stumps of the trees from which they'd hewn our huts. The general found one such stump; he clambered up on it and tottered unsteadily, ridiculous in his Russian uniform with its epaulets and unnecessarily big hat.

My fellow prisoners clustered around, a motley assemblage clad in various non-uniform combinations of uniform parts.

"Greetings!" the general exclaimed in halting Serbian. "We are recruiting our brother Slavs from Bosnia and Hercegovina to fight alongside us in a new Serbian Legion! Your fellow Serbian, General Jivković, will be leading a division alongside us, and we are looking for volunteers to serve underneath him! So I would like to invite anyone willing to serve in this unit to please come forwards!"

All around, men started chatting excitedly. On a whim, I started pushing my way forward. I'd taken only a few stunted steps when I felt an insistent hand on my shoulder.

"Humbly ask, sir, where are you going?" Baloun whispered.

"To volunteer. They're recruiting a Serbian Legion."

"You're not Serbian, sir."

"I've learned the language. Perhaps I can put it to good use."

"You're going to leave the camps, sir? Go back to the front lines?" He sounded perplexed; he had never seen me eager for a fight. For that matter, neither had I.

"Why not?" I chuckled and shook my head. "It'll be a change of pace. At any rate, the food'll be better."

       * * *

It turned out I was wrong about the food.

When I remember my time fighting alongside the Russians, one image sticks out: a soldier shooting dogs.

After being armed and equipped, a tedious and uncertain process which called to mind the worst dysfunctions of the Austro-Hungarian Army, we had been sent to the Dobrudja.[27] There was no more Corporal Baloun, nor very many Czechs or Slovaks; the Serbians and I fought alongside Roumanians and Russians, and we were fighting Bulgarians. But on those haphazard front lines, everything was chaos on levels that were previously unimaginable. All of the normal functions of an army—combat, movement and resupply—were further complicated by barriers of language and apathy, the latter fueled by the increasing sense that no one in the Russian Army (with the possible exception of General Brusilov) knew what the hell they were doing. We rarely had trenches, even—the front wasn't stable enough and the ground wasn't dry enough to build them.

One day in late August, after we'd gone at least twenty-four hours without either a meal or a message about when a meal would arrive, I ordered one of my soldiers to shoot some of the dogs that were always prowling in front of our lines.

So amidst the chaos, confusion, and complexity of service in yet another collapsing army being supplied by yet another collapsing country, the food chain alone became simple, because it was now a cycle: living dogs ate dead soldiers, and living soldiers ate dead dogs.

       * * *

Here and there we shot Bulgarians, too.

In the first week of September, we were advancing, and we shot them, and then the Rumanian and Russian units on our flanks collapsed, and the Bulgarians shot us.

---

[27] A marshy area between the Danube and the Black Sea.

It may seem strange, given my initial apathy about all things military, that I started taking soldiering seriously. But at the time, it seemed the most rational choice—if Austria-Hungary somehow survived the war, we'd be unable to return home. (There is this notion that people do not change their character, but I know from personal experience that this isn't quite true. People do change, but in a slow, almost glacial evolution. Rarely are there 180 degree reversals, or even right-angle turns—usually we change course a few degrees at a time. Sometimes these changes cancel each other out, and sometimes they compound. It was in such manner that I eventually went from indifferent young soldier to enthusiastic middle-aged spy.)

I digress.

During one of those battles in the latter half of 1916, I was leading my men across a cornfield when a retreating Bulgarian suddenly turned back towards us, raised his rifle, and fired.

I tumbled to the ground in pain, clutching my ankle.

From where I sat, surrounded by a forest of verdant stalks that were just tall enough to block my view of the battle, there was no way for me to influence the outcome. So I listened to the shouts and shots as the fighting ebbed and flowed, and I sat there in the soft dark earth and dressed my wound, and I turned my head dreamily as the occasional bullet whisked through the corn, invisibly clipping ears and stalks, tearing off green leaves and sending them fluttering leisurely down to the black earth.

Before long, the fighting tapered off; each shot grew farther and farther apart, like popcorn cooked on the stove when it's almost done. One of my sergeants found me, hoisted my arm over his shoulders, and hobbled with me back to headquarters.

*   *   *

The Serbian Legion sent me back to Odessa by jouncing ambulance and coughing train.

On the way back, staring up at canvas truck covers or at the bottoms of other stretchers hovering inches above my face, I contemplated my fate. Other men might have prayed. But how could one believe in God in the midst of such insanity? For those few days I was angry; I knew I should not have expected anything involving the

Russians to go smoothly. My only consolation was that, amidst so much ineptitude, Bulgarian marksmanship was also abysmal.

Russian doctors were incompetent, too. So I refused anesthetic when they operated on me, so they wouldn't take my foot off while I was unconscious. Almost fifty years later, I can still see the faint scars on my palms where my hands clenched the sides of the steel operating table.

In the end, I kept the foot. But I started wondering if the war was lost.

CHAPTER 9
Moscow
July 1936

"The fact that we are surrounded on all sides by a big German neighbor, impels a thoughtful Czech to cautious and definitely wise politics."

—Tomáš Masaryk, as quoted by Karel Čapek in *On Thought and Life*

WITH Germany re-arming, it was clear that our small country needed some big friends. President Masaryk had tended to look towards the West for allies, seeing in those democracies the liberalism he wanted for us, but President Beneš, who had taken over from Masaryk the previous year, gazed eastward.[28] So after concluding a treaty of alliance with the French, we signed one with the Soviets.

One clause of our treaty with the latter called for intelligence sharing between our spies and theirs. And so, in July of 1936, several of my men and I boarded a passenger train in Prague, wearing shabby civilian clothes and carrying ordinary suitcases full of material to share with them over the course of a two-week stay in Moscow.

In order to further conceal our journey, we had chosen a roundabout route, traveling down through Rumania to cross the Soviet frontier not terribly far from where I'd fought alongside the Serbs. There we disembarked, rumpled from travel, lugging our suitcases out the narrow train doors and down the cement train sidings.

"Greetings, gentlemen!" I looked up to see a Soviet major in a brown uniform. He grinned, which didn't improve his appearance; those teeth he'd somehow kept were also brown. "I am Major Gletkin. Welcome to the Soviet Union."

Gletkin ushered us down the train station sidings, past boxcars and tankers being loaded and unloaded.[29] Through the grimy windows of the drab station house, we saw lethargic citizens huddled on benches, eating crackers and making tea; some had blankets strewn about them, as if they'd been there for days.

Following our gaze, Gletkin spoke again. "I regret that there will not be time to tour our glorious station here, but the Moscow train is waiting." With a forceful urgency inadequately papered over by

---

[28] It was hard even then to see the wisdom in this point of view, and, of course, subsequent events have proven its folly. Our Czechoslovakian Legion had, after all, fought the Red Army during the early years of the Russian Revolution. And for years after that, the Soviets had been pariahs, a backwards nation on the edge of Europe that always seemed to be either threatening to export their chaotic revolution or turning inwards to grapple with their own demons. They hadn't even been a member of the League of Nations until 1934.

[29] The Soviets used wide-gauge train tracks, which—either by accident or by design—helped maintain their isolation from Europe. Because of it, everything that crossed the border had to be transferred to new trains—ourselves included.

politeness, he shepherded us down to several shiny forest-green train cars. The hindmost was open, and a porter gestured for us to ascend the rear stairs. As we hefted our suitcases and jostled singly through the narrow door, Gletkin remained outside. When all of us had boarded, he looked around to make doubly sure there were no stragglers. Only then did he step aboard.

We stowed our luggage and surveyed our car. Apparently it was a dining car; there were lace-covered tables with fruit baskets overflowing with apples, oranges, bananas, pears and grapes; platters of rye bread and caviar and sausage and salmon; champagne and vodka chilling in icy buckets.

"An impressive spread, yes, gentlemen?" Gletkin asked.

"Yes, thank you," I replied. "This is wonderful. I am truly impressed."

"It is the least we could do," Gletkin said. "Our country has one sixth of the world's land mass and a tenth of its population. With such bounty for our citizens, how can we not be generous to our guests?"

Our train chugged out of the station, picked up speed and swayed back and forth on the uneven rails.

I steadied myself, then picked up a porcelain plate and started picking at the bread and sausage. Looking out at the countryside, I saw fields lying fallow and noticed tractors rusting in the shadows of unpainted wooden barns. "I spent some time here during the Great War. I was well acquainted with Russian hospitality."

"Our people have always been known for their generosity." Gletkin must have missed the tone of irony in my cordial words. "And with such a benevolent leader as Comrade Stalin, how could it be otherwise?"

"Of course." I was about to expound when the train hit a particularly rough patch of rail; the contents of my plate spilled to the floor.

"I apologize for the unsteady ride," Gletkin said as he helped me clean. "Foreign saboteurs have wreaked havoc on our railways."

"Of course."

"We will do everything we can to make the trip as smooth as possible, I promise."

"I spent a lot of time in Odessa. A beautiful city! I was hoping we might be able to walk around a bit once we get there," I said as I deposited the soiled food in the wastebasket.

"Ahh, yes. Regrettably, the schedule does not permit much sightseeing along the way," Gletkin replied as if genuinely sorry. "Unfortunately we will not be able to leave the train until we get to Moscow."

For the benefit of my men, most of whom didn't speak Russian, I translated this exchange.

"Unfortunate, indeed," Strankmuller smirked.

* * *

"This does seem a strange journey, sir," Fryč said as the smoky locomotive pulled us across the endless monotony of the Russian steppe.

We were alone in our compartment. The last we'd seen of Gletkin, he was drinking with Strankmuller and the others down in the last car, but still I leaned closer and spoke softer.

"It is odd, isn't it. Traveling in a sealed train, like Lenin."

"Even beyond that, sir. Our mere collaboration is…strange. You've read the same reports I have, sir. Behind the facades, the five-year plans, the dams and factories and glorious industrial facts, they're suffering. Famines, forced collectivization. I'm not sure they're any better than the Germans."

"We aren't surrounded by Russians. We're surrounded by Germans."

"Still, sir. It seems a rather cold calculation. To align ourselves with an ideology so foreign to our ideals, just to further our national interest…"

"Our civilian leaders are in charge of our foreign policy," I said. "Beneš believes we must align with the Soviets. I can't honestly say I'm excited, but we all must do as we're told. And I will say this: What are we supposed to base decisions on, other than the national interest?" I asked. "Given the fact that it isn't in our power to set this world right, I'm all for national interest. I'm more concerned about whether this will be a useful collaboration."

* * *

We disembarked in Moscow, sweaty and smelly and tired and disheveled and hung over. A Red Army delegation greeted us, their brown uniforms dripping with ridiculous ribbons and medals. This made for an awkward first meeting, a muddle of salutes and handshakes.

At last General Uritsky, the handsome and polite officer leading the delegation, ushered us into a line of waiting black limousines. As we drove through the Moscow streets on our way to the Hotel Metropole, there was no concealing the glumness of the people; they stood in great lines in their shabby clothing, slowly shuffling in their endless queues, waiting for who knew how long to get who knew what.

The Metropole was a beautiful building, a polished stone holdover from earlier days of opulence. Our line of cars parked on a side street, and we got out. I looked around, excitedly, remembering a story President Masaryk had once told me.

"What is it, sir?" Strankmuller asked.

"President Masaryk..." (It was impossible to think of him otherwise, even though he was now out of office.) "Masaryk was here during the Great War. He had come to Moscow to round up support for our cause. And the Bolsheviks were fighting cadets loyal to Kerensky's government. He was out on the street when suddenly he heard rifle fire, and he turned and saw a skirmish had broken out. There were bullets whistling past his ears, and he saw this man ahead of him duck into a doorway. So Masaryk decided to follow him, just to get safely out of the firing line—it must have been that doorway there!" I pointed excitedly. "It was the side door to the Metropole, and there was a man inside who was holding the door closed."

"Why, sir?"

"He said he couldn't let Masaryk in unless he was a guest of the hotel. And there was fighting very near behind him. And he asks again, 'Are you a guest of the hotel, sir?' and Masaryk just said, 'Damn it, man! Quit playing games and let me in!'"

"And..." Strankmuller didn't understand.

"He didn't want to lie. Even to save his own skin, he did not want to lie, because he so valued the truth. He told me the story because it had been an absurd situation, but what I took from it was that he didn't lie. That's how he always tried to conduct policy, on a basis of honesty and truth."

Gletkin shepherded us into the lobby, and we stopped for a smoke before they showed us to our rooms.

"Is that how we conduct our business, sir?" Strankmuller asked. "Always with an eye on the truth?" He flashed a small impish smile and looked down at our rumpled civilian suits.

I took a heavy drag from my cigarette. "We do what we can, Strankmuller."

*   *   *

For several days, we discussed intelligence with the Soviets. Or rather, we talked, and they listened.

Most of our working sessions took place in stifling wood-paneled conference rooms under glowering oil portraits of Heroes of the Revolution; here and there, one could see nails sticking out of walls, or vaguely light rectangular patches where it seemed other portraits of former heroes might have been removed. My men stifled yawns and fought off sleep while their fellow officers presented information on Nazi Germany's rearmament. The Soviets remained alert and scribbled attentively as we talked.

Long days passed, followed by longer parties; the Soviets worked hard and played harder. Here and there we were trucked off to view other impressive sites, dams and canals and factories under construction, all purportedly world-class and state-of-the-art, vast edifices of steel and concrete and ego. But at no time did we have the opportunity to go where we pleased, or visit anyone who didn't know we were coming.

*   *   *

Near the end of our stay, we were at yet another reception, an afternoon party in the lobby of their intelligence headquarters.

"A toast to our Slavic brothers," Tichý proclaimed, hoisting a shotglass of vodka amid a circle of upraised arms, Soviets and Czechs.

They had a sense of what Tichý had said, but I still repeated the words in Russian. Our Soviet counterparts nodded, faces flushed and eyes heavy-lidded. They were in the middle stages of inebriation, where tongues were loosed but not limbs, and one could still walk without ricocheting off walls and other inanimate objects. All of them drank. One muttered under his breath.

"What was that?" I asked.

Obligingly, the sloppy man repeated himself. "Our reactionary Slavic brothers."

"Reactionary?" I asked.

"I mean no offense. You are good enough fellows, it seems. If war does come against the Germans, we might stand a chance, with your brains and our brawn. But you are still reactionaries."

"So what? We're reactionaries, you're revolutionaries. What does it matter?" I asked, possibly a little tipsy myself.

"Now is a time of consolidation, here in our bastion of glorious socialism," Gletkin said. "But in time the revolution will spread. And you will find yourselves on the wrong side of history. This talk of Slavic brotherhood is nice. Blood is thicker than water…"

"What about vodka?" someone exclaimed.

"And vodka is thicker than blood!" Gletkin smiled. "But class is stronger, still."

I nodded, not in agreement but in appreciation.

"Come now, why this disagreement?" General Uritsky asked grandly.

"There is no disagreement here. Only education," Gletkin said. "These men are our kin. Blood brothers, or cousins, at least. Only they are on the wrong side of history. I am not telling them to confront them, but to help them!"

"I know plenty about history," I said. "It does not move according to some political ebb and flow. It is not as simple as charts and diagrams, patterns and progressions, thesis and antithesis and synthesis.[30] It goes where it will, and you cannot hammer it into any ideological mold. It is stronger than any mold. It will break your ideology."

"It will break yours," Gletkin smirked. "Someday the revolution will come to your country. And you will have to come down on the right side of things, or leave."

"Gentlemen, there's no need for all this," Uritsky interjected. "We have had a wonderful and productive visit, and we have learned a

---

[30] Many Marxists fit history into such childish patterns. By their reckoning, most history happens because some thought or idea or movement comes about—a thesis—which is then met by a countervailing force, or antithesis, whereupon the two will fuse together in a synthesis. For a further look at the foundations of Marxist historical thought, read Hegel's *Science of Logic* and Marx's *A Contribution to the Critique of Political Economy*.

lot. Our Slavic brothers," he said, nodding at Tichý, "...have done some wonderful work. I am jealous, I'll admit. I do wonder, how have you managed to construct such an apparatus?"

"How have you not?" I asked.

"We have spies and sources," Uritsky said.

"How effective are they?" I asked. "You and I both know that, despite being a smaller nation with fewer resources, we have much more information than you do on the Germans."

"You share a common frontier with them," Uritsky said.

"So do the Poles, but I don't see you inviting them to conferences. Let me ask you this. Your spies and agents, do you recruit them on the basis of ideology?"

"No," General Uritsky said, but he looked away involuntarily: a lie.

"I think you do. And that is your undoing. Those in Germany who share your views are nobodies; they're prisoners or underground types unable to express their views. I doubt very much that you will be able to recruit anyone with real and useful information on that basis. You cannot catch fish with hooks and no bait!"

"We do not need to catch any fish," General Uritsky said. "They jump into our boat!"

"What are your hooks and bait?" Gletkin asked. "Capitalist greed?"

All around, the Soviets chuckled—red-faced Reds smiling smugly.

"Say what you will about capitalist greed, it has built us a great network," I replied.

"It will be your undoing," Gletkin said. "Sooner or later you will run into people who can't be bought, because they believe in something bigger. And using such techniques will leave you vulnerable to deceit and backstabbing in turn. If people let themselves be bought by you, they will let themselves be bought by someone else for a higher price. Greed cannot be trusted."

"Can ideology?"

"Always. Since our ideology allows us to provide our people with everything according to their needs, they will not turn their back on us. You, on the other hand, have no ideology. Your democracy is a tool for factory owners and class oppressors."

"We have an ideology," I said. "We believe in truth."

"That's ridiculous," Gletkin said. "Everyone believes in the truth. That's like saying you believe in the sun."

"Do you believe in truth?" I asked. "You've taken us far and wide, shown us all manner of projects and constructions, recited all manner of numbers and statistics, and yet not once have you allowed us to see anything for ourselves. You present us with these great bountiful spreads, but do your people eat this well? You say you believe in truth, but I think you fear it."

"That's preposterous. Any tour guide behaves as we do. We have taken you to the things that are worth seeing," Gletkin said. "As for the truth, the truth is what is useful."

"That's ridiculous," I said. "Truth is what's real."

"Is it? These things your capitalist society promises, they are glittering lies. These great things that Comrade Stalin has led us to, they are the truth. Our Communist might speeding past the West while it remains mired in depression and economic collapse, that is the truth. It is you who fear it."

"Truth is everywhere," I said. "The totality of everything, the way it really is, without false optimism: that is the truth. If you look at some things and not at others, that is not the truth."

"And yet you do not look at the things we have placed in front of your eyes!" Gletkin said, and again his comrades laughed.

"Well, let's drink to the truth. At least we can agree on that, even if we argue its definition," I said. A white-clad waiter had brought forth another round of drinks, and I hoisted mine—wine. "Pravda vitězí."[31]

"Pravda vitězí." Gletkin drank, and smirked.

Of the wine I took but a sip. The conversation lost its seriousness, and I lost interest.

Now I had no desire to drink further, and I wandered off. Soon I found myself alone in a side hallway, the conversation and laughter echoing distantly from around the corner. Here on the wooden walls were fourteen portraits: ENEMIES OF THE REVOLUTION, the wall proclaimed in bold gold Cyrillic. I recognized Kerensky, Kolchak, and

---

[31] Our national motto: Truth Shall Prevail.

Kornilov, then realized that the last portrait had been turned over so as not to be seen. Curious, I looked around and made sure I was alone, then turned it around.

It was a picture of the father of our country, Tomáš Masaryk.

* * *

After we were driven back to the Metropole, I told Major Gletkin I was turning in for the evening, and ascended the elevator to my floor. Once there, I simply walked down the hallway to the stairwell, descended to the first floor, and poked around until I found a back exit. (The secret to poking around is to not look like you are poking around; you have to simply walk from one place to another, eyes straight ahead, without tentativeness or uncertainty or surprise at anything you see.) None of the hotel employees gave me a second glance as I made my escape.

Out on the evening streets, I was confronted with what I had until then only glimpsed obliquely. Ordinary citizens walked to and fro slump-shouldered, seemingly defeated by the simple realities of their daily lives; their gaunt faces, hungry and unhealthy, eyed me suspiciously. On the street corners they waited in herds to cross the street; there were no traffic signals, only angry policemen with whistles. It seemed no one had any desire to jaywalk, even.

"Greetings, comrade," I said in Russian to a man who made eye contact with me; his eyes bulged, and he walked right past me.

With the next several people I saw, I did exactly the same thing, and I got the same results. It was surprising, the lack of public freedom, the evident fear inherent in so simple a task as running errands. I placed my hands in my pockets and felt my house keys. Without thinking, I found myself rubbing them like a talisman; certainly it would be all the nicer to use them next time, after this strange interlude.

Then I saw a cluster of citizens standing around and chattering, their excitement in stark contrast to everything and everyone else I had seen on the streets. They jostled and angled to see something in a store window. The building in front of which they stood looked no different from many of the others I'd seen; it was another grimy brick building with cloudy windows. But I caught snippets of chatter as I strained to see what they were seeing:

"This is incredible! Comrade Stalin has done a great thing for us!"

"This is truly a wonderful day!"

"I haven't seen such a thing in ten years!"

Among the swaying heads I now caught a glimpse of the object that had caused such amazement: a single bushel basket of tomatoes.

* * *

Back at the Metropole, I could not get back in through the rear doors, so I took a chance on the lobby. There in a leather chair sat Major Gletkin, smoking. Next to him in the ashtray was a pile of ash and stubbed-out cigarette butts.

"Where are you coming from?" he demanded sharply.

"I went for a walk outside," I said simply.

At this his face went pale as a ghost. He inhaled, deeply shaken. At last he spoke: "You were trying to recruit spies."

"I wanted to meet some of your glorious citizenry. I wanted to ask them about the wonders of their socialist paradise. Don't you trust their devotion to your ideology?"

"Our citizens will not be your spies. They cannot be bought, or caught like fish," he said at last, loudly.

His nervous eyes darted past me, looking for—what? A superior? A fellow spy watching him watching me? He leaned closer, and for the first time, he spoke as if we were equals: "Tell no one of your excursion. For your sake, and mine."

* * *

The trip to the Soviet Union gave me little hope for meaningful collaboration with them, and I told my superiors as much, including President Beneš. But it also truly convinced me at last that our intelligence operations were on the right path.

CHAPTER 10

Odessa
April 1917

"It was strange. I was like a wound-up machine. I could think of nothing but our campaign against Austria; I saw nothing else, felt nothing else, I was hypnotized by it. The only thing I cared about was the war—what the day-to-day situation was, how things were going at the front—and whom to speak to next, how to reach people and arouse their interest."

—Tomáš Masaryk, as quoted by Karel Čapek in *Talks with T. G. Masaryk*

DURING the Great War, wounds like my ankle injury could be epic campaigns in and of themselves. They'd bleed profusely, then heal partially; if you were unlucky, they'd grow puffy and hot with infection, the nearby skin red and tight as a drum, and you'd again be a candidate for an amputation you'd avoided the first time around; if you were lucky, they'd heal over the course of several months.

So in the spring of 1917, while Russia's chaos was accelerating, I was recuperating, spending my evenings and most of my days in hospital wards populated by other wounded soldiers of varying nationalities and states of disrepair, some hobbling on wooden crutches, others confined to beds, others ambulatory but wrapped in bandages or slings, still others missing arms or legs, or disfigured. When I stopped to think about it, I knew I was lucky, but I usually didn't stop to think about it. (Hospitals are, by their nature, depressing places; no amount of white paint can conceal that simple fact. Open windows can never quite dispel the miasma, and what fresh air they bring is counteracted by the desire to be outside and healthy.)

To get some mental escape and hone my Russian, I sought refuge in their literature, taking advantage of a motley collection of battered books that some kind soul had deposited ages ago on a forgotten bookshelf in an abandoned corner of the ward. During my convalescence I read *Crime and Punishment* and *The Brothers Karamazov* and *Anna Karenina*; I even plowed through *War and Peace* in two weeks of furious reading. And every now and then, I'd get some literal escape to replace the literary—when there were no strikes or demonstrations, the pretty young Ukrainian nurses would wheel the wheelchair-bound around town, down the tree-lined streets, past Odessa's schizophrenic architecture (onion-domed churches and baroque opera houses side by side) and through its bucolic parks.

On one such excursion I spotted a familiar figure bounding up the Richelieu Steps, a distinguished gentleman wearing a black suit and a white goatee—old, but so energetic he seemed electrified.

"Professor Masaryk!" His familiar face, after so many months of lonely exile and recuperation, made me exuberant.

Lost either in thought or determined action, he didn't notice me.

Over my shoulder, I called out to the nurse: "Irina, push me over there." Obediently she wheeled me across the street to the top of the steps to head him off.

"Professor Masaryk!" I exclaimed again.

At last he looked up, curious, then walked over with a bright gleam in his eye. Enthusiastically he pumped my hand; in all my subsequent life, I cannot recall a handshake that brought me so much delight.

"Ahhh, yes…Moravec, isn't it?"

"Yes, sir." They say the great politicians get that way because they're good at remembering you—such simple gestures, at the right moment, can win undying loyalty.

"How are you? You've…been wounded, I take it?" In his voice I heard nothing but genuine and humble concern.

"Not too badly, sir. They didn't hack off my foot, and I seem to be recovering, so I'll probably be straightened out before all this is over…" I gestured up and around, indicating the omnipresent war.

"This is…" He gestured to my nurse.

"Sorry. Irina, my nurse." Over my shoulder I spoke to her in Russian: "Irina, this is Professor Masaryk."

"A pleasure, sir," she said.

To my nurse he spoke in flawless Russian: "Is he being a patient patient?" or words to that effect.

I looked over my shoulder to gauge her response. Wordlessly she wheeled my wheelchair around and made as if to push me down the endless stone staircase.

"That bad, huh?" Masaryk asked.

"I'm joking, sir. He's no worse than most. It is a frustrating situation for all of them. To be living like old men in what should be their prime years."

"See, Moravec? Not only beautiful, but wise." Now he switched to German, so she wouldn't overhear. "You're a young single man, you should treat a woman like this with the reverence she deserves. Who knows? Like it says in the Bible—the people who look the lowliest often end up becoming the most important of all!"

"Sorry, sir."

"Oh, Lord knows I'm not judging you! It took me a while to realize the truth of it myself. How are you, though?"

"Oh, you know. Same old, same old," I said.

He narrowed his eyes and looked at me suspiciously, and we laughed.

"No, it has been the most...bizarre odyssey, sir." I gave a brief rundown of the strange turns that had brought me here, from my time in the K.U.K. to my adventures alongside the Russians.

"Ahh, yes," he said appreciatively. "Tolstoy said Russia was going to be Europe's salvation. That doesn't look likely in this war."

"Tolstoy," I echoed. "I just finished *War and Peace* myself, sir. At last."

Here, unaccountably, he chuckled.

"What's so funny, sir?"

"Oh, when I used talk to my friends at the coffee houses in Prague, our conversations so often just turned into comparisons of books we'd read. And not meaningful discussions, either—just 'I've read this' and 'I've read that' and 'You should read this' and 'You should read that.' And so on and so forth in this...endless cycle of intellectual narcissism. And I can't complain, because I'm as guilty of it as anyone! But I guess it is the same old, same old after all."

"Surely we can have a meaningful discussion, sir!"

"If your nurse doesn't mind." Here he switched back to Russian. "Irina, I hope you don't mind us talking at length!"

Irina laughed. "It's a nice day, sir. And I like getting out of the hospital as much as the men do!" Still, we started moving, seemingly by collective unspoken assent.

"I like how Tolstoy viewed history," Masaryk said. "It's more the product of millions of little decisions by lowly peasants and soldiers, than of the so-called big decisions by the so-called great men. After all, what does it mean, history? Is it the story of politicians? Of military figures? Of battles? The fate of a people is also written in its culture's products—if you read Goethe's *Faust* or Dostoyevsky's *The Brothers Karamazov*, you'll learn as much about the Germans and the Russians as you will through their history. And even when looking at that history, the mighty leaders often are constrained by factors outside their control, while the lowly peasants and soldiers actually have the freedom to make decisions. We always want history to make sense, but inevitably it is complicated and chaotic. Which is why we're here."

"Why are you here, sir?"

He switched back to German. "I've been on a sort of…" Here he looked over at the nurse, trying to make sure she understood nothing. "…secret mission. During the course of the war I've gone from Rome to Geneva to Paris to London. And now I'm here."

"And what is your purpose here, sir?"

Now he looked about as if there still might be spies shadowing us. "Resistance to Austria-Hungary's rule. Not at home, of course, armed rebellion or things of that sort, for that would be impossible. But a revolution from abroad that will lead to our independence."

It seemed impossible—I'd heard rumors about it, of course, but seeing him in the flesh, my mild-mannered professor, and hearing it from his own mouth, tales of intrigue and espionage…"That's…quite a vision, sir."

"It's been my life. It's consumed me for the past…two and a half years now. I daresay I haven't had two good nights' sleep in a row since 1914. The only relaxation I get comes from a few hours' sleep a night, a few minutes of recreational reading a day…" He raised his hand to show me the book he was carrying—something by Zola. "…and some brisk walking, which is why I was down by the waterfront. The vast bulk of the day is political work."

"So, from philosophy teacher to politician…"

"It's not such a great change of pace. You know how much of philosophy deals with politics. Or rather, if you don't know, I should have failed you! Aristotle, Plato, Augustine, Aquinas. I always liked Plato's notion of the philosopher-king."

"Is that what you're trying to become, sir?"

Here he chuckled dismissively. "Hardly. No, in the West, my task was just…propaganda. Conducting newspaper interviews, talking with leaders of our colonies in France and here, writing to the ones in America, trying to get everyone united around our program. Meanwhile my cohorts, Doctor Beneš and others, have been smuggling news and information into Prague via codes and ciphers, so that the people will have something to counter the Austrian propaganda."

"Sounds like a lot of dueling propaganda, sir."

"Yes, except that they dispense false propaganda, whereas I believe ours must be honest. In politics, in propaganda, exaggeration is ultimately harmful and lies are worse. As it says in the Bible, the truth will set you free."

"The truth, sir?"

"Yes, I know. What a novel concept in politics! But I've learned in my public life, if you pursue truth first, popularity will come, whereas if you pursue popularity, it will come and go, and you'll be left with nothing.[32] But as Jesus said, "Seek first the kingdom of heaven, and these other things will be given to you in turn.""

Here I looked up at him skeptically, as if there actually might be stars in his eyes.

"Ahh, yes. I forgot—I'm dealing with my favorite rational agnostic. Well, church and state must be separate, of course—I think that's America's greatest contribution to the world of ideas. But we needn't run away from religion's influence. In fact, I think the attitude of 'Love thy neighbor as thyself' is the only possible basis for a true democracy, because in actual fact there is no equality among the stars or men—only as immortal souls are we really equivalent."

"Perhaps, sir." I smiled thinly.

"At any rate…the truth. That is still my goal. To let the Allied governments know the truth, that we are unsatisfied under Austria-Hungary and that we are willing to fight for our freedom. I've talked to the French and the British, and now that the Americans are in it I will have to talk to them, too. I'm not sure they want to redraw the map, but we have to let them know that Austria-Hungary's dismemberment will be good for Europe. We have to give the Allies a coherent political program, a purpose, so that all this death and slaughter, this suicidal mania that has convulsed Europe, will at least accomplish something—a better peace for all, a peace based on self-determination, for all nations."

---

[32] Early in his public life, Masaryk had been swept up in the public debate concerning historical manuscripts which were purported to be epic retellings of early Czech history. Masaryk had argued convincingly, and correctly, that the manuscripts were fake—flying in the face of popular nationalistic sentiment, which had latched on to the manuscripts as evidence of the glorious past which most Czechs wanted for their nation. Later on, he had also taken an unpopular course by speaking out on behalf of a vagrant Jew, Leopold Hilsner, who had been falsely accused of a ritual murder.

"That sounds like quite a program, sir."

"Ahh, yes. But people eventually stop taking you seriously if it's only talk. So here I am taking action—trying to live an active life like Prince Andrey, I suppose. Which brings us back to Tolstoy, that crazy old bat."

"You talk like you knew him, sir."

"Actually..." The expression on his face somehow combined impishness and sheepishness. "Actually, I so enjoyed his work that we corresponded at some length. And I visited him three times, here in Russia, when I was a professor. He was an old man, of course. It is always a disappointment to see legends in the flesh, Moravec! I wouldn't say to avoid it—just be aware that you may be underwhelmed. Anyway, I found I didn't agree with him on many things. He mentioned me in passing in one of his books,[33] in fact, because of a disagreement we'd had. Jesus' dictum to 'Offer no resistance to evil,' he took that very literally, whereas I thought it important to draw the line between defense and aggression. Why not resist evil if it's attacking you? Rather than letting it overcome you, why not resist? If one has to die, why not the person who started the problem?"

"Why not, indeed, sir?" Here at last the old man was making some sense.

"But Tolstoy was right about the freedom of the lowly and the constraints placed on the leaders. As your case shows, and mine. I have to take action and organize a force and send it into the field. I don't have many options open if I want to be heard—I just have the option of doing this poorly or well. But fortunately for me, many other Czechs and Slovaks made the same decision you did. There are enough people in the camps that we should be able to organize a Czecho-slovakian Legion much like the Serbian Legion you were in. I think we can organize a force of fifty thousand men. If we can do that, and become recognized by the other Allies as co-belligerents, we will be in a much better position.

---

[33] Masaryk's modesty made this seem like nothing important, but in truth, it was. In *The Kingdom of God is Within You*, the foundation stone of 20th century pacifism, Tolstoy mentions corresponding with an unnamed Czech professor, whose attitudes and aims seem to indicate that he was none other than our own T. G. Masaryk.

If we can participate, truly participate in the war, we will have a say in the peace."

All this time we had been walking away from the harborfront, down sleepy tree-covered side streets and shadow-dappled sidewalks, past sleepy apartment buildings with drawn drapes. Now we found ourselves in front of some official-looking building, and Masaryk gestured as if he were about to go inside.

"It was good catching up with you, Moravec. Keep your ears open. We will be recruiting soldiers for our legion, and you will have the chance to fight again. For now…" Again he nodded towards the building. "For now I must attend to some business."

"Yes, sir." We shook hands, and he darted inside.

As Irina wheeled the wheelchair around, I wondered: was the old man mad? Fifty thousand men—it seemed absurd! And looking back at the building, I wondered what purpose he could possibly have inside. Russia was in such turmoil that I found it hard to believe he could find any person worth talking to, any functionary with the authority and the ability to help him out on his quixotic quest. It seemed every day brought news of new chaos; already the Tsar had abdicated and Kerensky had taken power, and there had been massive strikes and peace demonstrations in many cities. And Lenin in his sealed train had returned from exile, ready for revolution.

Still I shook my head in appreciation when I realized what had happened. I'd assumed that Irina had been pushing me back to the hospital via a roundabout route, but all along, he'd been leading us his way without me realizing it.

CHAPTER 11

Prague-Kraslice-Chomutov-Prague
April-July 1937

"The issue of capital punishment has always weighed heavily on me. I have lost many nights pondering over whether to sign a death warrant, and the days when I have done so I mark with a black cross on my calendar…"

—Tomáš Masaryk, as quoted by Karel Čapek in *Talks with T. G. Masaryk*

OUR conference with the Soviets had convinced me we were where we needed to be. And so we kept to it, fishers of men with nets of money.

And then a big one just jumped in the boat.

One day in 1937, I came back from lunch to find a large stack of mail on my desk. Usually I whipped through it, reading every letter immediately, then throwing everything that didn't absolutely need to be kept in the bag to be burned. But today one letter-sized packet gave me pause. It was addressed to "The Chief of the Czechoslovakian Intelligence Service, General Staff, Prague" and stamped PERSONAL AND CONFIDENTIAL. I tore it open and scanned the first few lines of the cover letter:

Sir:

I offer my services as an agent. First off, I shall state the areas where I can provide information:
  1. The build-up of the German Army, with regards to:
     a) Infantry
     b) Panzers…

Immediately, I closed my office door and rang Fryč on the intercom.

"Sir?" Static crackled at the edges of his voice.

"I'm going to need some time alone, Fryč, which means no appointments and no visitors for the next hour. If the president comes by, make sure it's urgent before you let him in."

"Yes, sir."

Settling in to my desk chair, I fished in my vest pocket for my cigarettes, lit one, and studied the document intently.

The letter methodically listed virtually every secret we could have possibly asked for, in typical German thoroughness, as comprehensively as a department store catalog. There were no itemized prices, though. Its author wanted 100,000 Reichsmarks for the whole thing. Given the scope of the information, that wasn't a problem; he also wanted to arrange a meeting in Germany, which was.

After an hour of smoke and study, I rang the intercom again.

"Fryč, I need you in here."

117

"Yes, sir."

"Bring Colonel Tichý and Major Strankmuller with you."

When all three men were in front of my desk. I showed them the document.

"I received this in the mail today. I want each of you to read it separately. Then come back and give me your opinion, one at a time."

They left. I waited. They read the document in rank order, then appeared before me one at a time in the same sequence.

"It's a trap, sir. Under no condition should we respond," Tichý said.

"Thank you, Colonel. I'll take that into account," I said, and dismissed him.

"If we respond, sir, they'll abduct our agent. Just like Kirinovic," Strankmuller told me.

"Thank you, Major. I'll keep that in mind," I said, and nodded for him to leave and send Fryč in.

"This can only end in disaster, sir. The possibilities of it not being real are ninety-nine to one," Fryč opined.

"Thank you, Captain. I'll take that into account," I said.

"And the one? I don't trust it, sir."

But I trusted the one. Or rather, I didn't want to throw it out.

So we made alternate arrangements.

* * *

After a month-long series of negotiations and counter-proposals flying back and forth between P.O. boxes in Czechoslovakia and P.O. boxes in Germany, the four of us found ourselves standing in the shadows of the public square in the small Sudeten town of Kraslice on a black Tuesday night, waiting for our mysterious German, whom we'd labeled internally as A-54.

We didn't know what A-54 looked like; we only knew he wasn't here yet. The only person in sight was a drunk who had stumbled out of one of the nearby pubs and now staggered towards our silent quartet.

We stood our ground as he approached.

"Enshuldigen sie, bitte," he said to none of us in particular.

"Damn it, speak Czech, man! This isn't Germany," Tichý exploded.

Lifting his heavy head, the drunk looked at all of us in turn. He laughed condescendingly before staggering off.

"It might as well be," Strankmuller said. "Most of them speak German, read German and want to be German. If you're looking for countrymen who will treat us like countrymen, sir, this is the wrong place."

"We had to meet here," I said. "I rejected a meeting in Germany and one in Austria; if we kept playing hard to get, we probably wouldn't have heard from him again."

We waited, silent. Unspoken was our fear that the Germans were trying to stage an abduction, as they'd done with Kirinovic. In Germany or Austria it would have been child's play; here, in a region riddled with German sympathizers and a part of town not 100 meters from the frontier, it would not have been much more difficult.

Still, we'd done what we could to protect ourselves. In the darkened alleyways, hidden from sight and the flickering gaslights, we'd placed a dozen armed policemen. If the Germans tried anything, we'd at least give them a fight.

"A-54's to meet us at 11:00, sir?" Fryč asked.

"A-54's meeting us at 11:00," Tichý said. "He'll walk from the border to the far end of the square, head this way, then set his watch from the clock on the steeple."

"The clock on the steeple is stopped, sir." Strankmuller interjected.

"He'll pretend to set his watch, and you'll go out to meet him, Strankmuller. And then, the car. At any sign of trouble, our police are ready to step in," Tichý said. "Right, sir?"

"I know we're taking a risk meeting here." I added, to show I wasn't a hopeless optimist. "Everyone knows this isn't a lot better than meeting him in Germany. But big rewards only come from big risks."

So we were ready for trouble. But we weren't ready for what happened at 11:00: nothing.

11:15 passed, then 11:30. None of us had even suggested that nothing would happen. Perhaps they'd been planning an abduction after all; perhaps they'd spotted our precautions and called it off.

"Half an hour late," I said, looking at my watch as if it would suddenly change its mind. "There's no point in waiting any longer."

"Well, sir, at least it wasn't an abduction," Strankmuller said breezily.

Often I let him get away with remarks that would have sounded insubordinate coming from someone else's mouth. But tonight I glared at him.

"I'm sorry, sir, I just…" Strankmuller tripped over his tongue, he was backtracking so quickly.

"Round up the police and tell them what's going on," I ordered coldly. "We're headed back to Prague."

And then it happened.

"Sir," Strankmuller pointed.

Someone was wandering into the middle of the square, carrying two suitcases and several rolls of papers. As we watched, he pretended to set his watch.

Strankmuller had volunteered to make first contact, so I slapped on the back. "Go to him."

Purposeful and bold, Strankmuller walked up to the man. They exchanged greetings, and Strankmuller turned to signal us that everything was on the level. Tichý, Fryč and I got in the black Skoda. Fryč cranked the starter, and the car coughed to life. He put the car in gear, eased up on the clutch, and pulled up next to the square so Strankmuller and the stranger could get in.

"Good evening, gentleman," our mystery man said through the passenger window. He wore a bristly haircut and wire-rimmed glasses; he was most likely military, and probably Prussian; his bearing was easygoing, but attentive. "You can call me Karl. And you are?" he asked me.

"The senior man here," I told him.

"Fair enough," Karl—in lieu of a real name, I still thought of him as A-54—said.

"We're going to take you somewhere to talk," I told him.

"You want to abduct me?" A-54 smiled thinly as he clambered awkwardly in the front, handing us his briefcases and papers. "Very well, but I must be back at work tomorrow with my samples."

"Very well," I said, and we drove off.

For twenty minutes, Fryč drove down winding country roads. Outside the twin ovals of our headlights, one could scarcely see; their penumbra brushed over trees and fences without even giving any sense of the farmhouses and hills that surely lay beyond.

"Take a right here, Fryč," I said when I saw a signpost for Chomutov.

"Fryč," A-54 said. "Captain, perhaps?"

"A good guess," Fryč said.

"Militaries are all the same. Nobody has lieutenants on their General Staff. And the low-ranking man always drives. Which doesn't make that much sense to me, but then again I rather enjoy driving."

"Clever and observant," I observed.

"It comes in handy in our line of work," A-54 said.

"It certainly does." So he was a spy, too.

Presently we drove through Chomutov; here at last were lighted windows, sprinkled like salt on the dark rooftop silhouettes. On the far end of town was a two-story stone house with a man standing in the drive out front, backlit by the open door.

"Here we are," I said.

Fryč nosed our Skoda into the drive and killed the engine.

Our car doors opened. I collected A-54's maps and briefcases. Across the back seat, Strankmuller and I exchanged disbelieving glances, amazed that he'd simply walked across the border with this much sensitive material. It was almost too much to comprehend. When I stood up, arms full, I caught A-54 eyeing me.

"My men are going to take a look at these, if you don't mind," I said by way of explanation.

"Be my guest, sir," he said, and we walked inside.

In the narrow first-floor hallway, I handed everything to Strankmuller, mumbled instructions in his ear, and watched him dart upstairs. A-54 turned and watched him go. I gestured in front of him towards the living room, where two chairs and a coffee table awaited.

A-54 sat.

"Care for a drink?" I asked. "Coffee with brandy, perhaps?"

"That sounds wonderful, sir."

Now I whispered instructions to Fryč, who nodded and walked into the kitchen to prepare the drinks. A-54's back was towards him, but I could see Fryč pouring a hefty shot of brandy in one coffee cup, and barely a splash in the other. He held them aloft for my approval; I nodded, and he brought them out and set them on coasters in front of us.

"Well, now." I settled in at last. "I take it you mailed us the letter?"

"Yes, after much deliberation."

"What is it you want?"

"I'd like to earn as much money as possible." (He smiled.) "And I'd also like to stay alive to enjoy it."

"That's it?"

"There are...other motives, too..."

"Other motives?"

"My fiancée is a Lutzian Serb, for instance, not a German. So there is some difficulty for me because of that. Still, I'd be lying if I told you these other motives were of greater importance."

Behind A-54, Strankmuller stepped around the corner at the bottom of the stairs and waved: a quick signal that everything was working fine upstairs. (Earlier in the day, we'd installed a brand new German-made AEG K1 Magnetophon[34] up there, then drilled a hole through the ceiling and run a wire down the corner of the room and across the hardwood floor under the rug. The wire led to a microphone concealed in a floral arrangement on the table.)

"As you were saying..."

"As I was saying, sir..." A-54 continued. "I'd like to stay alive to enjoy it. So I'll give you what I can, and I won't take any assignments from you. I have my limits, and I've been in our profession long enough to know that when men in my position exceed their limits, it usually ends very badly." A-54 sipped his coffeed brandy and made a face, surprised but also pleased at its strength; then he raised his eyebrows, and his drink in salutation.

I returned the gesture, then sipped my brandied coffee. "Well, now that we're sitting down to drinks, perhaps you will give us your name and position?"

---

[34] The technology to record and play back sound on magnetic tape was very much in its infancy in the 1930s; the Magnetophon was the only device of its kind available anywhere in the continent, if not the world. We'd procured ours covertly from our enemies using front companies, after laborious effort, and at prodigious expense.

"I'd prefer not to...Colonel Moravec." He settled back in his chair, complacent. "The material I've provided, and the material I will provide, will speak for itself. If you don't want to pay me the whole fee right away, if you want to establish my bona fides first, that's understandable, but I..."

Behind him, Strankmuller was trying to catch my attention. They'd been photographing and inspecting the documents; I'd told him to run downstairs immediately if they uncovered any forgeries.

"Excuse me," I told A-54, then stood and walked over to talk to my subordinate.

"Sir, I don't believe this—it's too good to be true," Strankmuller said in a stage whisper. "He has a copy of the German Frontier Defense Plan, even!"

I thought of Major Gletkin—I wished he could see this! What we had shown the Soviets the previous year was all well and good, but this was another level of accomplishment entirely.

A-54 turned to see what Strankmuller was holding. "Ahh, yes. The *Grenschluss*," he said, loudly enough that we both turned around. For the first time all evening, A-54 smiled. Like a conjuror, he produced a neatly folded sheaf of papers, which he'd obviously been holding back for dramatic effect. "And while we're talking defense plans, I have another one to show you. Yours."

My heart sank. If authentic, it meant there was a spy in our midst. And it looked authentic. Which meant A-54 was, too.

"You can send this upstairs for your men to look at, Colonel. They should be able to confirm its authenticity without too much difficulty."

"Thank you." I handed the papers to Strankmuller; he disappeared. Heavily, I sat—wishing, perhaps, that Fryč had mixed my drink stronger.

"As I was saying, sir, I'm sure you'll want to establish my bona fides first," A-54 said. (Despite all the elaborate choreography, the sheer effort I'd put into stage-managing this, it was unclear now which one of us was running the show.) "And I know you want everything to be in order before parting with so much cash. So I can continue to send you information, and together we can decide when I've given you 100,000 Reichsmarks' worth. Your assistant has no doubt already figured out that there are some invaluable documents in here. Information, for instance, about the links between my countrymen and your supposed countrymen, the agitators in the Sudetenland."

Here I leaned back. "That is...a topic of interest to us." He could tell I was truly eager; we'd long suspected the Germans were meddling in our internal politics, but we'd never had concrete proof.

"Colonel, I will be able to provide much more. All this is but a sample. But again, I will do so on my terms. Which means none of the standard spycraft. No contact men, no dead drops, no radio transmitters."

"How do you want to maintain contact, then?"

"I will cross the border and send you letters from your own territory," he said. "We will establish post-office boxes here in Czechoslovakia that I can check regularly."

"We?"

"You and I, Colonel. Again, I don't want to tell you my name or position, but I will tell you that my rank is high enough, and my party number low enough, that I can cross the border at will."

"That's fine with us," I replied.

For the next few hours, we talked and drank our brandied coffees. I grew edgy, and A-54 got tipsy, and all the while my men photographed upstairs. A-54's proposed arrangements were fine with me; sources like him got to write their own rules.

And they got to set their own fees; as morning drew near, we returned A-54's samples to him, and we also gave him the full 100,000 Reichsmarks in cash—to establish our bona fides. For the benefit of our accounting staff, we made A-54 sign a receipt for the money; I filled it out with a caffeine-jittery hand, and our newest spy signed "Karl" in a sloppy drunken scrawl.

Then we drove him back to Kraslice; he dozed intermittently in the front seat, head resting against the window or lolling about.

Dawn was breaking as we pulled into town—an ugly unpleasant dawn, the only kind you get when you've been up the whole evening. Fryč parked the car and nudged our passenger awake. A-54 rubbed his stubbly face, got out, and stretched. We watched as he trod tiredly across the dead empty town square, carrying his suitcases full of secrets and cash. Catch and release.

* * *

We now had some more fishing to do.

When I went to General Krejčí and told him there was a spy in our midst who'd given the Germans our defense plans, he turned white as a sheet. Then he was ill for three days straight.

But A-54 had given us some clues during our lengthy discussion. Not much: a postmark from an envelope. A date on which, and a location from which, our frontier defense plan had been mailed to the Germans. Slender evidence—but sometimes that was enough.

After a few days of frantic research and unpleasant interviews out at various divisional headquarters, we had a suspect, one Captain Kalman.

Counterespionage work doesn't win you many friends; Kalman's commanding general was furious at us for our suspicions, and Kalman was alternately indignant and defiant, but we took him back to Prague anyway, and placed him in custody for questioning.

* * *

"How long are you going to keep me here, sir?" Kalman asked on the sixth day.

"As long as I have to," I told him, and leaned my forearms on the small table that practically filled our cramped little room. (As settings go, it didn't get much simpler—brick walls painted white, a single hanging incandescent light bulb, a battered table, two old but sturdy wooden chairs, and the two of us.) I knitted my eyebrows, feigning confusion at his feigned confusion. "Why are you acting so confused? You claim you weren't in the town in question on the date in question, but you still haven't asked why we're questioning you. Which tells me you already know what this is all about."

"Very well. Why are you questioning me, sir?"

"I'd rather not tell you," I said, smirking at my own absurdity.

"Sir, with all due respect, this is very…perplexing." He leaned towards me; his words pled fealty, but his body said defiance.

"You're a suspect in a criminal investigation. You can't expect us to tell you everything."

"I do expect to find out what I'm charged with, sir. I have that right; this isn't the Soviet Union."

"I know for a fact it's far nicer than the Soviet Union."

"Still, sir. At some point you have to either let me know what I'm accused of, or release me."

Perhaps it was my imagination, but I thought I saw a glimmer in his eye, and the corner of a smile—the self-satisfied look of the murderer who's getting away with it not because the police don't know he did it, but because they have no evidence.

Bile rose in my throat. "It is...outrageous that you ask for the protection of the state after betraying it to a state that does not provide such niceties. But still we'll give you that protection in time. You'll get justice, even if you haven't earned it."

"Justice." Kalman snorted. "This isn't justice, sir. And if you say it is, I don't trust you."

"You have no reason not to."

At this, Kalman leaned back in his chair, smirked a little, and lit a cigarette. Again came that look of awareness. "Have you ever read Plato, sir?"

"I studied him under Masaryk, before the Great War."

"Masaryk," he repeated, as if unimpressed by both our first president's name and the fact that I'd known him before he was the president.

"He said all of Western Civilization was a footnote to Plato."

"Well, sir, he was right about that, at least," Kalman conceded, friendlier now. "I taught myself Greek, to read Plato in the original."

"So we've both read Plato. What of it?" I asked. "Is this going to be a...roundtable of intellectual narcissism?"

"One quote of his pops to mind here, sir. 'Mankind censure injustice fearing that they may be the victims of it, and not because they shrink from committing it.'"[35]

"You know nothing of my motives, Kalman."

"You can say what you want about your motives, sir, but your actions are what they are." Kalman leaned forward, put his forearms on the table. Did he expect sympathy? "Please understand how...traumatic this is for me, sir. In my entire career, I've never had so much as a note of reprimand. With that in mind, don't you think this is rather absurd, sir?"

---

[35] *The Republic*, Book I.

"I'm well aware of your service record, Kalman. I've read your file extensively, and your commanding general spoke very highly of you. That doesn't mean you're innocent."

"But I don't think you understand what it's like to fall victim to such a monstrous mistake, sir. You may know on an intellectual level, but knowledge and understanding are different things. Ordinarily you wake from a bad dream and there is this moment of extreme relief. But this is the exact opposite of that, sir. It is like waking into a nightmare every morning. Even if I'm released tomorrow, my reputation, my career…"

"We're talking about your life here, Kalman," I interjected angrily. "That's what's at stake. Just so you know."

"Perhaps, sir." Kalman actually smiled; his demeanor changed abruptly from defensive to optimistic. "Or who knows? Perhaps your career. I think if I were you, I'd hate to stake my reputation on a false slander of an innocent man."

"Perhaps you need more time in your cell to think, Kalman."

Frustrated, I stood so violently my chair would have tipped over had the wall not been so close behind. Then I stormed out.

Out in the hallway, I bumped into Strankmuller as he was leaving the bathroom.

"Still nothing," I said. The ancient walls were thick as a fortress, but still I spoke as quietly as if Kalman were next to us.

"How long are we going to keep him, sir?" Strankmuller asked.

"I don't know. We have to either charge him or release him. And he knows it. What's more, I'm being told the same by General Krejčí. And without a confession, there's just no evidence. Or at least none we can use against him if we put him on trial."

"Nothing? Nothing at all, sir?"

"If this goes to trial in the criminal courts, it's bound to attract heavy newspaper coverage. And I'm sure the Germans read our newspapers as avidly as we read theirs, if not more so. So we can't very well say in open court, in front of the whole public, how we got our information."

"No, sir, I guess we can't. 'Your honor, we know this man's a spy because we have this very high-ranking spy of our own, and…"

Strankmuller chuckled bitterly and shook his head. "But you're sure it's him, sir?"

"I'm sure it's him. I don't understand why he'd do it; he seems a stable man. He's happily engaged and financially secure, he's not a big drinker." Again I thought back to the previous summer and my conversation with Gletkin. Was this what he'd meant by backstabbing? "Every superior's given him high marks. But his story just doesn't add up. I'm sure it's him."

"And he's told you nothing, sir?"

"Not only has he told me nothing, he's acting just the way you'd expect a man to act after being wrongly accused: shocked, hurt, and righteously indignant, in all the right proportions. But it all seems like a façade. Behind it, there's this air of arrogance, like he's enjoying this, somehow. Like we both know he did it and we both know I can't prove it."

"Perhaps he's proud of that, sir."

"Proud?"

"Perhaps."

Proud. I thought about that as I walked back. Outside the room where I'd been questioning Kalman, a sergeant was standing guard, waiting to take him back to his cell.

"Sergeant," I said.

"Yes, sir?"

"You can take the prisoner back to his cell now."

"Yes, sir."

"One other thing, sergeant." I leaned forward and lowered my voice. "I want you to put him in handcuffs, and leave them on overnight, and leave the lights on in his cell. In fact, keep someone in there, watching him."

"This is...very irregular, sir."

"If anyone asks, tell them it's a protective measure. I have reason to believe the prisoner is despondent about his imprisonment and humiliated by the accusations. He may attempt suicide."

"Suicide, sir?"

"You can never be too careful, sergeant."

"Yes, sir."

I peered in the small window in the door to the interrogation room. Kalman's back was to us; he was leisurely smoking a cigarette, as if he didn't have a care in the world.

Proud.

*　　*　　*

That night, while walking home from work, I spotted a crowded little bookstore I'd been meaning to visit for a while, a snug little place half-buried in a garden-level storefront, peering out at the feet of passing pedestrians. On a whim, I descended the stairs and popped in. I spent ten minutes searching endless disorganized shelves for a copy of *The Republic*, then lost track of time while paging through the various dialogues, and got home to find that dinner was already on the table. My wife was evidently frustrated; I tried to placate her with warm pleasantries, but found myself silent during dinner, absently picking at my dried-out duck until it got cold—or rather, colder.

After dinner, I sat reading by lamplight well into the night, long after my wife had changed into her nightgown and gone to bed.

*　　*　　*

The next morning, Kalman was disheveled, edgy and tired.

"How did you sleep, Kalman?"

"Sir, this is an affront to basic decency. What is it you want, sir? To humiliate me? To make me want to take my own life? Is that it? To spare you the difficulty of a trial? To get me to take my hemlock in my cell, for the good of the public?"

"So you're Socrates now, Kalman? A rather vain comparison, don't you think?"

"Even if that's your game, sir, I don't believe in suicide."

"Of course not. You're Catholic, correct?"

"Correct, sir. Besides, as Plato said, 'Man is a prisoner who has no right to open the door of his prison and run away...A man should wait, and not take his own life until God summons him.'"[36]

"Plato also said that, 'Truth should be highly valued; if a lie is useless to the gods, and useful only as a medicine to men, then the use of such medicines should be restricted to physicians; private individuals have no business with them.'"[37]

---

[36] *Phaedo*.
[37] *The Republic*, Book III.

"So you're allowed to lie, sir? As a spy, you're a physician, looking out for the good of the body politic?"

Here he'd caught me off-guard. Taken aback, I smiled. "To be honest with you, I hadn't thought of it that way."

"To be honest with you." Kalman shook his head. "Does that mean you haven't been honest?"

"I've been honest, Kalman. And truth shall prevail. I've always believed that."

"Ahh, yes. Truth shall prevail. And I suppose all you want is just to help it along, to come here and bring it to me in my cave."

Here I just gave him a skeptical look.

"Still, it's a good motto your professor picked for our nation. I wish it were always true. But as Plato also said, 'No one is more hated than he who speaks the truth.'"[38]

"Will you be hated if you speak the truth, Kalman?"

Kalman paused. Perhaps he smirked.

I continued. "If you really believe in what you've done, why not speak the truth about it? Doesn't the Bible say, the truth will set you free?"

Now Kalman chuckled, snorted, shook his head. Despite knowing better, he spoke. "Do you really think the truth will set me free, sir?"

At last.

*   *   *

After lunch, we left Kalman cooling in his cell, handcuffed again. I peered in to see him awkwardly fumbling with his cigarettes, his handcuffed hands straining to get one out and lit; he burned his fingers on the matches but never asked the guards for help.

Meanwhile, my men set up the Magnetophon next door to the interrogation room. They drilled a hole and snaked a wire in through the ceiling, then placed a microphone atop some steam pipes, where he hopefully wouldn't notice it. When we at last brought him back to the little room with its table and two chairs, it was wired for sound.

"What now, sir?" Kalman asked.

"Confession?" I suggested.

---

[38] Kalman attributed this to Plato, but I have not been able to find a source for the quote.

Behind Kalman, I saw Strankmuller's face in the window in the door; he nodded and signaled that all was fine next door.

"Confession and absolution, sir? That works with the church, not the state. Confession and execution is what you're offering."

"We'll see what we can do, Kalman. If you help us, we might be lenient. If you don't, we won't."

"A clever promise, sir. Very one-sided."

"I can afford to be," I said. "Are you afraid of death, Kalman?"

"I'm not, sir. 'Either death is a state of nothingness and utter unconsciousness, or there is a change and migration of the soul from this world to another…Now if death be of such a nature, I say to die is to gain; for eternity is then but a single night.'"[39]

"Plato also said there are other things men should fear more than death. Slavery. Dishonor."

I glared at Kalman and leaned forward; he shifted uncomfortably.

"How much did the Germans pay you?"

Here he grew indignant. "Really? Do you think I would..."

I pounded the table. "How much?!?"

Kalman hesitated, then spoke: "I didn't accept any money, sir."

*   *   *

"I then assembled the materials over the course of the next several months," Kalman's voice said, crackly on the magnetic tape but loud enough for the entire courtroom to hear. Everyone—judge, prosecution, defense counsel, visitors in the gallery—listened with rapt attention to the final portion of the questioning. "When I was on leave, I took the train to Cheb, two hours away from home, so as not to call attention to myself if the materials were intercepted after I sent them off. And there I simply put everything in an envelope addressed to the German General Staff and sent it off in the mail."

"Again, I ask: why?" My own voice, the voice of the past me, sounded strange to me.

"I've told you already, sir. You may think my reason petty, but I have nothing to add to it."

---

[39] *The Apology.*

That concluded the questioning, and the tape. The prosecutor, a beefy, red-faced man, let it run out. After the *click*, he sat there so everyone could contemplate this in silence. At last he stood.

"Your honor, I have nothing else to present."

"That's all, counsel?" So new was the technology of recording on magnetic tape that the judge had never experienced anything remotely like this—a prosecutor's entire case consisting of one tape recording and no witnesses.

"That's all, sir." The prosecutor gave a little shrug as if to ask: Do I need more?

After a short recess, Kalman's lawyer, a wiry little man with wire-rimmed glasses, stood to make his arguments.

"Your honor, this case is without precedent in the history of Czechoslovakian criminal justice. We are being asked to determine a man's fate based on nothing more than a strip of magnetic tape. A recording of a conversation during which the defendant was obviously under great duress. I don't see how this can be…"

"Enough!" Kalman exclaimed abruptly, surprising everyone, most of all his attorney. "I said what I said! I'm not going to lie and pretend otherwise."

* * *

A month later I stood alone in a stone courtyard.

It was a bright late summer day, perfect in appearance if not feel: the skies were as blue as I'd ever seen, and there was not a breath of wind. I'd put on my uniform for the first time in what seemed like forever; it didn't fit as well as it should have, and I tugged uncomfortably at the jacket. The sunlight, too, was unpleasant and feverishly warm.

Atop the gallows, the hangman, the chaplain and two guards stood waiting. As I watched, another squad's worth of guards came out of the building and stood four to a side at the bottom of the wooden stairs. The noose was already tied; the rope hung unmoving, as if made of lead.

Another man, a lieutenant, came out of the building and walked up to me. We exchanged salutes—something I hadn't done in a while.

"They'll be bringing him out in about a minute, sir."

I nodded, and the lieutenant walked back to the doorway to wait, content to leave me alone. On the wooden platform, the priest and the hangman were conversing. What do two such men talk about at such moments? Probably nothing of substance.

What brought me there? Duty, I told myself, although if I hadn't come, no one would have commented on my absence. Duty was a short, sturdy, handsome word. But perhaps I had darker reasons. As Kalman pointed out, I could say what I wanted about my motives, but my actions were what they were.

Then they were there in the doorway: a captain, four more guards, and Kalman, who stopped once he stepped outside. He bent forward, and the captain listened respectfully, then nodded his assent. One of the guards produced a set of keys and unlocked Kalman's handcuffs; the latter rubbed his wrists and gave a proud nod in my direction, then walked the last few steps without hurry or delay, as carefree as if he were taking a promenade in the park.

He ascended the stairs.

On the platform, he conversed briefly with the others, but I couldn't make out the words. What do two such men talk about at such moments? Probably everything. Then Kalman leaned forward and the priest raised his hand in blessing. Absolution? Perhaps the priest knew more than I did, now.

Now the hangman took the rope and placed it around Kalman's head, then turned the noose so the knot lay on his shoulder.

"Have you any last words?"

"Yes. Long live my country." These words were spoken for all to hear. Again Kalman looked directly at me, and gave—no, not a smile. Perhaps it was a self-satisfied smirk, or maybe just a look of acknowledgement.

And now, the black hood. The world saw his face no more.

The hangman stood back and gave the signal for the trapdoor.

Abruptly—so abruptly it took my breath away even though I'd been waiting for it—Kalman dropped. He jerked, swayed, and stopped. His neck—his body's neck, now—was bent sideways at an unnatural, impossible angle. He had become a corpse.

I breathed heavily but did not look away.

CHAPTER 12

Odessa-Kharkov-Arkhangelsk
April-October 1917

"Freedom, sir, is just as hard as duty. We feel that to will hurts. To will is labour; to decide tires, it is the creation of something new. During the War I envied the soldiers, that they were ordered about, that they could only obey, and need not decide. I had to decide, to command even all the time, not only to think, but to will terribly."
—Tomáš Masaryk, as quoted by Karel Čapek in *On Thought and Life*

SOME short weeks after my talk with Masaryk, a fellow Czech came to the hospital to recruit for the Czecho-slovakian Legion.

I signed up immediately.

I was starting to see that Masaryk was that rarest of human beings—a man whose plans actually came to fruition, whose goals were so compelling that other men started working on them too, and in such numbers that it seemed the world itself was doing his will.

The strength of his willpower became clearer once I left the hospital and joined our legion as it took shape in that chaotic revolutionary year of 1917. In the countryside where we marched and trained, we saw bewildered peasants with fields but no crops, and apathetic soldiers with uniforms but no rifles; at army offices, we met bureaucrats and clerks who said *nyet* to every request because it was the only answer that gave them confidence. But somehow amidst that confusion, our troops actually grew more organized, became whole units, and procured weapons. (In the latter case we often just took the weapons and ammunition from Russian army depots; the soldiers there usually didn't know who their superiors were, much less whether their superiors wanted them to stop us.)

And as all of this happened, Masaryk was there, spending nights with us in tents or billets, cheering us up with his sheer doggedness, drawing strength in turn from our enthusiasm. It seemed he was everywhere and everything; he was a commander, an advocate, a quartermaster-general making arrangements for further equipment and finding funds for transport, and over and above all, a catalyst for all of our actions and reactions.

* * *

Once our unit was formed, we took to the field to help in the Kerensky government's 1917 summer offensive. We fought near Zborov and acquitted ourselves well—much better than the Russians whose country we were, in theory, defending. Their army was plagued with apathy and desertion; when this offensive bogged down, many of them simply left the front lines, "voting with their feet," as Lenin later described it.

Masaryk knew the Czecho-slovakian Legion had to fight where it would be of use, and so we left the front, too. Everything didn't go according to plan for all of us in the Legion.[40] But amidst the sheer madness enveloping the country—the petty blackmails and briberies, the trains that waited in the station while their engineers begged for coal or cold hard cash—my unit embarked in Kharkov and transited the collapsing country, all the way up to Arkhangelsk. There we embarked on a ship, a coal-fired four-stack rustbucket that looked like it would sink from our weight as we walked up the gangplank.

After we set sail, my fellow soldiers and I had to chose between rotting in the fetid, airless compartments belowdecks or suffering the wet misery of the rain and sea spray topside. Meanwhile our decrepit liner churned across the surging gray Arctic Ocean, then down through the North Sea towards England.

---

[40] Indeed, much of our Legion did not make it out of Russia that year. As mentioned in a previous footnote, those troops ended up as belligerents not in the Great War, but fighting alongside the Whites in Russia's civil war.

CHAPTER 13

Prague-Kraslice
April 1937 – September 1938

"…I have long ago resigned from the fold of fetishistic wordmongers and nationalistic fanatics."
—Tomáš Masaryk, "Czechs and Slavs: The Time of Kollár and Jungmann"

WE had caught the spy in our midst and removed a grave threat to the nation. But still there was more to be done.

So I found myself in uniform again, on my way to brief President Beneš, who had succeeded the ailing Masaryk not long before. Next to me and a half-step behind, Fryč, also uniformed, carried an armful of maps and charts.

We walked confidently the vast sunny stone courtyard atop Hradčany—how could one be less than confident on such a morning? Our uniforms were trim and sharp, though mine had required an expeditious visit to the local tailor. Our shoes shone like obsidian, and the cobblestones themselves practically gleamed in the low morning sunlight, which also glinted off rooftops and silhouetted a thousand church spires in the city below.

Past saluting gate guards we strode, then inside the looming castle and down long shiny hallways; our heels clicked authoritatively on the marble floors.

At last we found ourselves outside Beneš' office, where his secretary, Táborský, looked up at us over the wire rims of his glasses. "You have an appointment, Colonel…"

"Moravec," I said. "A briefing."

Slowly, deliberately, Táborský looked over his appointments book until he found the line item for us. "Ahh, yes. Go on ahead and start setting up."

Inside, the president and his official photographer were poring over a series of glossy black-and-white photographs taken at a recent state dinner to which I'd respectfully declined an invitation. Despite his experience as a diplomat, Beneš still seemed new in this job; he was a short and severe man who, unlike Masaryk during his presidency, still looked as if he'd have been more comfortable at the head of a classroom than at the head of a country.

"Ahh, yes. Colonel…Moravec, right?" he said, looking up from the pictures spread out on his desk.

"Yes, sir."

Beneš glanced at his watch. "I'll be done with my photographer momentarily, Colonel. You and your assistant can start setting up."

"Thank you, sir."

Fryč and I got to work, setting up a map of the country on an easel and pulling out typewritten briefing materials. There really wasn't much to do; I'd only brought Fryč along so I'd have an extra set of arms and not look like a bumbling idiot.

Meanwhile, Beneš perused the photos, visibly unhappy.

"This one's good. And this one." From dozens of shots, he selected two. "And throw out the rest."

"Throw them out, sir?" the photographer asked, as if hard of hearing.

"They look bad. I look like a dwarf. See? In the future, please take your pictures from more favorable angles."

"Yes, sir."

"That will be all."

Pursing his lips, the photographer policed up his photos, carefully keeping separate the ones President Beneš wanted preserved. He made as if to walk out with all of them, but Beneš nodded towards the trash can. Reluctantly, the photographer tore the rejects in half and tossed them out. Then he followed Fryč out through the large wooden doors.

Alone at last with Beneš, I gave him a typewritten briefing summary and grabbed the wooden pointer from the map easel as he settled in behind his desk. Behind him, the windows looked out on that same panoramic view one saw from the courtyard, only here one saw it without obstruction; I tore my eyes from it reluctantly when I saw Beneš was ready.

"Shall I begin, sir?"

Beneš nodded.

"Very well, sir. I'm here to brief you on German strengths. And our weaknesses." With the pointer, I traced the crescent of our border with Germany. "As you well know, sir, the German government has been making a lot of noise about our ethnic German population in the Sudetenland."

Beneš harrumphed and gave me a look as if I'd told him that the sky was, in fact, blue. "As if I didn't already hear enough from Herr Hitler about our 'suffering minority.'"

"And as you also know, sir, our defenses against Germany are of necessity concentrated in the Sudetenland."

"Please tell me something I don't know yet, Colonel," he said brusquely.

"What you don't know yet, sir, is that we've recently recruited a highly placed German agent, whom we refer to internally as A-54."

"What does the A stand for?"

"Agens." Agent, in English.

"Of course."

"Sir, A-54 has recently and decisively confirmed for us something we've long suspected. The Germans in the Sudetenland, Henlein[41] and Frank[42] and our other supposed countrymen who are agitating for more 'rights' and more 'freedoms', are doing so under direct orders from Nazi Germany. Hitler's plan is to stir things up, to get them to ask for union with Germany, and to make the matter subject to international arbitration."

"These are political issues, Colonel. Tell me about our military issues."

"This is a military issue, too, sir! Hitler's goal is to annex the Sudetenland. If that happens, we will be defenseless."

"*If* that happens," Beneš said. "Personally I'm not worried about it, Colonel. As *you* no doubt know, we have mutual defense treaties with both France and the Soviet Union. They will stand by us if Hitler gets greedy."

I, for one, had my doubts about the Soviets. After seeing the decrepitude of their country, I didn't trust that they'd be able to offer real help. And Fryč's arguments had perhaps influenced me; I wasn't sure I wanted them on our side. But what choice did we have?

"Yes, sir," I said. "There is that possibility."

"What can you tell me about the German military?"

"Very well, sir. Militarily, the situation is worse than we expected. We've been piecing things together for some time, but A-54 has given us our first complete look at the puzzle. The German Army currently has twenty-one infantry and three panzer divisions. By year end, sir, they will have thirty-eight infantry and five panzer divisions.

---

[41] Konrad Henlein, leader of the Sudeten German Party (SdP).
[42] Karl Hermann Frank, at the time the deputy leader of the SdP, later State Secretary of what the Nazis referred to as "The Protectorate of Bohemia and Moravia."

The *Luftwaffe* is already larger than the British Royal Air Force, and by the end of 1937, sir, it will be larger than the British and French air forces combined."

"Do the British and French know this?"

"A better question is: do they believe it, sir? You cannot persuade people who choose not to listen. We've already given them information on the buildup of the *Luftwaffe*. The French refused to pay heed, sir. And the British haven't yet done enough. At any rate, sir, the Germans are formulating a new kind of warfare using their air and ground forces together. And all indications are that they are going to use it first on us."

"That's an interesting supposition, Colonel."

"With all due respect, sir, it is no supposition."

"This information from your Agent A-54. Could it be part of some scare campaign designed to provoke us into an aggressive over-reaction?"

"No, sir! We've seen plenty of other evidence of their efforts." I leaned on his desk. "Do you know how many German spies we've arrested, sir?" Impatient, I didn't wait for an answer. "Last year, sir, we arrested 2,900 German spies and *agent provocateurs*. That was in 1936 *alone*, sir. And that's information we know on our own, sir, independently of A-54. Coupled with his information, sir, it's clear that Nazi Germany is preparing for military action against us."

Impassioned, I forced myself to stand back, pause and let him think this over.

Beneš leaned back in his chair, unimpressed, or at least, underwhelmed. "I do agree with you, Colonel…in principle. These are areas of concern. And the Sudetenland question is of course vital to our defense. But Hitler doesn't have the political strength outside Germany to force the issue. Our Allies, taken together, French and Soviet and British, are still stronger than Nazi Germany. If Hitler wages war, it will be a European war, in which he will stand alone against great odds. If he's smart, he will avoid such an undertaking, and we'll be fine. And if he tries to provoke a fight, he will lose in short order, and we'll be fine."

I didn't say anything. Perhaps it was for fear of saying the wrong thing, and losing the chance to change his mind later.

It seemed like he took my silence as an opportunity for more lecturing. "Have you ever read Plato, Colonel?"

Not this again. I took a deep breath before responding: "Extensively, sir."

"You don't like Plato, Colonel?"

"I liked what he said about sophistry, sir. Being clever in your use of words and arguments to obscure the true meaning of things."

"Ahh, yes. It's a tactic most politicians use, even those that won't admit to it."

Here I nodded appreciatively.

Again Beneš spoke. "Plato also once said, 'The people have always some champion whom they set over them and nurse into greatness. This and no other is the root from which a tyrant springs; when he first appears he is a protector.'[43] That is what Hitler is now to the Germans—a protector who has reversed the humiliations the British and French so unwisely inflicted after the Great War. But if he provokes a confrontation and loses, he'll no longer be a protector, and the German people will no longer suffer his tyranny. That's why regimes like Hitler's—founded on force and aimed at the lowest instincts of their people—always fall in the wake of their first reverse. It is a sociological law."

A sociological law—perhaps I tried not to grimace. I've always distrusted such statements; history shows that no school of thought can describe (or more importantly, predict) human behavior, except in the broadest and most general terms. But President Beneš had been a student and later a teacher of sociology, and it obviously still informed his vision of the world. They say that, when the only tool you have is a hammer, everything starts to look like a nail.

"Do you not agree, Moravec?" Beneš leaned back in his chair, complacent.

"The only pattern I see in history, sir, is that people and nations are always trying to repeat their greatest triumphs, and avoid their biggest failures. Hitler probably thinks of himself as another Bismarck, a man who will be able to make war against his enemies one by one while everyone else stands by."

---

[43] *The Republic,* Book VIII.

"That's why I've signed treaties with the French and the Soviets. This time, the Germans won't be able to fight all of Europe piecemeal."

"Yes, sir," I said. What else could I say?

"It was a worthwhile briefing, Moravec. Thank you."

"Yes, sir. I'll keep you posted as things develop."

*   *   *

Over the next several months, as 1937 ended and 1938 began, things developed. That is to say, they got worse.

Every Monday morning, Captain Fryč would pass through Wilson Station with the brass key to a small post-office box. Every few weeks, he'd find a blank postcard in there with a postmark from Kraslice.

When we got that postcard, we knew A-54 wanted to meet. We would send a postcard of our own with a seemingly innocuous message. A few days later, we would drive to Kraslice, pick him up, and drive to the safe house in Chomutov.

Over coffee—plain, regular coffee—one fall afternoon, he laid out documents detailing something the Nazis were calling Plan Green. This called for their government, aided and abetted by Konrad Henlein and Karl Hermann Frank and our other so-called countrymen in the SdP, to incite riot and sabotage in the Sudetenland, then use the disorder as a pretext to invade our country, restore the peace, and annex the Sudetenland. Plan Green had been drafted by Reinhard Heydrich, a rising star in the Nazi security apparatus. It was breathtaking in its sophistry: Sudeten saboteurs became martyrs; Czechoslovakian police became oppressors; German invaders became liberators. These were monstrous lies—I quaked with rage as I read them.

*   *   *

Amidst the somber warnings of looming conflict came news that, though expected, was no less upsetting. President Masaryk had passed away, aged eighty-seven.

While his body lay in state in Hradčany, the people paid their respects in numbers that would have been remarkable in a country ten times our size. Over those few days, some 600,000 people ascended the steep cobblestone streets in reverent silence, waited in line for hours, and filed through the stately castle to say their final farewells to our country's father.

Then on 21 September came the last goodbye. Syrový and Krejčí led four other generals as pallbearers; they bore the casket to a howitzer carriage in a stone courtyard. The scene was nearly colorless; gray buildings and black clothing on the mourners made the khaki uniforms on the generals seem washed out by association. Only our flag, the tricolor red, white and blue draped over his casket, seemed vivid.

President Beneš and others made speeches—all short and unmemorable next to the immensity of the man who had left us. The heads of various heads of state and diplomats nodded in sympathy, although not all had come out of sympathy. (Few occasions can summon forth crocodile tears like a state funeral; among the attendees was Karl Hermann Frank.)

At any rate, Masaryk's bier was joined by a soldier from every language group in our country—one soldier each who was by ancestry Czech, Slovak, German, Hungarian, Ruthenian and Polish.[44] The horse-drawn gun-carriage and its escort pulled slowly out of the Mathias Gate to the larger outside courtyard where the funeral procession had been forming up.

After the dead president came the live one, and Beneš was in turn followed by soldiers and members of the Czech Legion, men I had fought alongside in the Great War, all marching in glorious solemnity under perfect blue September skies. (Incredibly enough, given subsequent events, the soldier heading the honor guard was none other than Emanuel Moravec; our careers had followed parallel arcs, and he, too, was by then a colonel.) I, too, could have participated; instead I stood amidst the onlookers, silent and anonymous in my civilian clothes. The procession headed down the hill and over the Charles Bridge, and through vast silent crowds in black—a million strong, they said[45]—on its way to Wilson Station.

* * *

In those dark months of simmering confrontation, my men still read the German newspapers every morning, taking comfort in the regularity of routine. I was reading our own Czech dailies, knowing

---

[44] It was fitting for this man. After all, Masaryk's first and foremost field of study had been philology, not philosophy—literally, love of language and love of the word came before love of wisdom.

[45] An equivalent crowd in America would number 20 million.

many things that never made it into the paper, but wanting, as a citizen and student of history, to have the public record of those events on hand. And I remember so many of those grim headlines from the next depressing year:

PRESIDENT BENEŠ ORDERS 176,000 TROOPS TO SUDETENLAND

and

SUDETEN GERMANS COMPLAIN OF TROOP PRESENCE

and

ENGLISH TEAM ARRIVES TO INVESTIGATE SUDETEN GERMAN GRIEVANCES

* * *

At around that time—perhaps eight or nine months after Masaryk's funeral—I found myself in a tavern with a British diplomat, a fact-finder and grievance-investigator on Lord Runciman's[46] staff. We'd originally set out to get lunch, but he'd wanted to have a few drinks, and now it was a lot closer to dinner. Not that I was complaining.

"I could use another one, if you don't mind," my red-faced companion said.

"I never mind, sir."

Our waiter was buzzing about near the bar; I signaled him and he made a beeline for our table.

"A..." The Briton started to order but didn't get far. "How do you say 'beer' in Czech again?"

"Pivo," I said.

"Pivo, proshim!" the diplomat ordered with a sloppy flourish of the hand, then again turned back to me. "They didn't teach ush the really important Czech words!"

"And you, sir?" the waiter asked me. "Another vodka?

---

[46] The leader of the English delegation sent by Prime Minister Neville Chamberlain to seek a solution to the Sudeten crisis.

"Prosím," I said, and the waiter gave a knowing nod. Like all good waiters, he vanished as quickly as he'd appeared, then reappeared with our drinks before I had time to wonder where he'd gone.

"A good waiter," I commented, for no particular reason.

"An adequate waiter. Waiters should anticipate demandsh, not…react to them. But at leasht the beer is good! What's this brand of beer called, Mr.…."

"Mr. Havel," I said.

"What's your first name?"

"Ladislav."

"Can I call you Ladislav?"

"If you prefer!"

"You're buying the drinks! I'll call you whatever you want!"

"Thank you, sir."

"Sir! Call me Bertie, Ladislav!"

"Sorry, Bertie."

"Oh, hell. *You* can call *me* whatever *you* want. Shince you're buying the drinks…"

"Compliments of the Foreign Ministry!" I said, raising my drink in salute.

"Either way, you're taking care of things. Sho you call me whatever you want, as long as you don't call me a taxi!"

"Very good, sir!"

"Bertie!"

"Bertie."

"I must say, you hold your liquor well, Ladislav."

"It comes in handy in our line of work."

"Yes it does."

"The beer is called Staropramen, by the way. You know, we have more brands of beer than any nation except Belgium."

"Well, I wish I could shtay and sample them all! But we probbly won't be around mush longer."

The pub wasn't terribly crowded—at least, not enough to excuse Bertie's apparent level of intoxication. Not that I minded. There were a few tables up front, but no one was close enough to eavesdrop without us noticing—or without me noticing, rather. Bertie looked like he didn't much care who heard him. Still I leaned a little closer.

149

"So Lord Runciman's found all the facts he's going to find, then?"

"I...you seem like a good guy, Ladislav, so I'll tell you thish. I don't know how many facts Lord Runciman was looking to find. Either that, or he found 'em all before he left England, and he jusht wanted to *look* like he was looking. There's always that differensh between perception and reality. 'shpecially in diplomacy."

"Ahh, yes, there is."

"You really do hold your liquor well! My hat's off to you, Ladislav!"

"Your hat's off already, Bertie!"

"My metaphorical hat! My invisible diplomatic hat, not my real hat."

"There is such a difference between the perceived and the real, though, Bertie."

"Yesh."

"The newspapers perceive things as if there is this two-sided story, where both sides are reasonable, and as long as both sides have a dialogue, everything will be all right."

"Everything will be all right!" Bertie exclaimed, loudly enough that a few of the patrons turned our way. Perhaps I'd overdone it with the Staropramen plan.

Still I continued, quieter: "We're not so sure about that. Others in our government have information proving—proving, mind you—that Hitler is manipulating this crisis to make it look like the Sudeten Germans are the victims of the trouble, and not the perpetrators."

Perhaps I was wasting my breath. Bertie's head hung heavily; I couldn't tell if he heard me, or if he was going to remember what I'd told him.

At last he shook his head violently. "It doeshn't matter what you prove or how you prove it. I probably sh-shouldn't tell you thish, and I'm only telling you because you sh-eem like a g-good guy. Anyway, even if Lord Runciman finds more facts, Pa-Prime Minister Chamberlain..." Bertie leaned towards me and placed a sloppy, heavy hand on my forearm, a just-between-you-and-me buddy buddy hand. "...Chamberlain won' go to war on your behalf."

*   *   *

"He won't go to war on our behalf, sir," I told President Beneš at our next meeting.

Behind him, the city was basking in glorious sunshine. A mosaic of sunlit tiled roofs stretched off into the distance outside our open windows. Perhaps out there, people were actually enjoying their summer.

"Then we'll have to give Henlein more concessions," Beneš said. "If we remove all irritants to the peace…"

"Beg pardon, sir. How are we irritating the peace?"

"The troops we put there at the start of the present crisis…176,000 troops…if we pull them back now that things have settled down a bit…if we prove ourselves completely reasonable and show 1,000 percent goodwill in the Sudetenland, this crisis will fizzle out eventually. The Germans will have to be reasonable, too, or they will be isolated. It is a sociological law."

* * *

On a perfect mid-September evening in 1938, Strankmuller, Fryč and I piled into a Skoda convertible and drove to Kraslice for a meeting with A-54. Though the heat had abated, the crisis had worsened.

In Kraslice, we found ourselves surrounded by a scene more chaotic than any I'd seen; had I not known better, I'd have thought we'd crossed the border by mistake. Hordes of angry townsfolk crowded the nighttime streets—shouting, surging, screaming crowds. Bedsheet swastikas and crude passionate German slogans floated above the teeming masses upon unseen hands, illuminated by fiery torches.

Here and there, we saw guns.

We saw them in eager hands or crude holsters or sticking out of pockets; it was not a pleasant sight.

"This 'urgent meeting' better be just that," Strankmuller said under his breath, leaning over so his words wouldn't travel outside the open convertible. The disbelief we all shared went unspoken: were things really this bad now? Inside our own country?

Fryč kept a light foot on the accelerator; our car crept slowly and carefully through the riotous crowd. The Skoda Superb felt tiny and insignificant amidst the fierce mob; we sensed that the slightest provocation—a careless turn of the steering wheel, a rough nudge with the bumper—would turn their fury against us. We were of course in civilian clothes, but next to me on the seat was a briefcase with government documents and our military IDs. I moved it down between my shins and the seatback; if this crowd, in this mood, found out we were Czechoslovakian officers, there was no telling what they'd do.

In the passenger seat, A-54 at last spoke up. "We're heading back to Chomutov, correct, sir?"

"Of course," I said.

* * *

Not so many kilometers away, Hitler was reaching the climax of a speech in front of an immeasurably larger and more orderly torch-wielding crowd, at the culmination of the annual rallies in Nuremburg. His voice—that mesmerizing, eloquent, impassioned, deceitful voice—was being beamed via radio across his country, across Europe, and to just about every home and apartment in the Sudetenland.

"…I am speaking of Czechoslovakia," Hitler said, and the crowd roared.

"This state is a democracy, that is to say it claims to be founded on democratic principles, since the overwhelming majority of its inhabitants were compelled one day to accept and adapt to a country which was manufactured by the Western powers at Versailles. But this 'genuine democracy' immediately began to oppress, to ill-treat, and to deprive of their vital rights the majority of their inhabitants."

* * *

As we inched through the clots of protestors clogging the streets, I noticed a crowd of angry youths surrounding and shoving an elderly Jewish man whose wide eyes betrayed obvious fear for his life. The man tried to remain calm but to no avail; once he raised an arm to ward off the blows, someone grabbed it and pulled it out of the way. Another angry fist smashed into his nose, and he fell to the ground and disappeared under the backs of the frenzied horde. Was this our country? Was this Czechoslovakia? Even had we been in uniform, our foursome would have been powerless to stop this; as it was, I was thankful for our anonymity, and embarrassed by our impotence.

By the time we cleared the crazed crowd, Kraslice had unmistakably degenerated into full-bore riot: we'd seen beatings, smashed storefront windows, random fires. As we at last turned onto the road to Chomutov, Fryč gunned the motor, understandably eager to put some distance between us and the ugliness.

*   *   *

"Amongst the nationalities that are suffering oppression in this state there are three and a half million Germans." As a speaker, Hitler had a strange inertia. It took him a few minutes to get warmed up, but once he got going, his passion and intensity carried him forward implacably—and carried others along with him. "These Germans—they too are God's creatures! The Almighty did not create them so that they could be given over to a hated alien power. And he did not create the seven million Czechs that they should watch over—much less that they should outrage and torture—these three and a half millions!"

*   *   *

Cresting a hill near a small hamlet in the countryside, we saw—no, impossible!—a roadblock, lit by flickering torch-fires. Several cars were pulled across the road so as to block all passage. A dozen men with guns stood guard.

Fryč slowed, hesitant. "Should I turn around, sir?" he yelled over the rushing air of the open convertible top.

"Go where? Back to Kraslice?"

"Just stay on the road," A-54 said.

Strankmuller gave him, and me, a perplexed look. I could read his thoughts because I was thinking them, too: since when is A-54 giving the orders?

Fryč coasted to a smooth halt and killed the headlights. An armed posse wearing crude swastika armbands surrounded us.

The leader walked up. "Can I see some identification, gentlemen?" he asked—in German, of course.

Our only identification was the briefcase with our military papers. No sooner did I glance at it than the leader of the posse noticed it, too. "What's in the briefcase, gentlemen?" he asked, then reached in and grabbed it.

One of his accomplices was carrying a knife in a sheath; he pried the briefcase open. By the firelight, the two men read the papers; a satisfied, sinister smile spread across the accomplice's face.

"Now if you gentlemen will excuse me for a moment," A-54 said, and got out of the car. Strankmuller and I traded uncertain glances. My house keys slipped out of my pocket on the seat; I grabbed them, hoping I'd have the chance to use them again.

Leaning over, Strankmuller whispered in my ear: "What was that you said a while back about an abduction, sir?"

* * *

"The conditions in this state, as is generally known, are intolerable," Hitler continued. "In the name of the right of self determination imposed on them by a certain American President, Mr. Wilson, over three and a half million Germans are being deprived of their right of self determination. They are being systematically ruined and subject to a slow process of extermination."

* * *

Several steps away from the car, A-54 and the Sudeten leader conferred, too quietly for us to hear. Strankmuller gave me a dirty look. I looked away at A-54, who was showing some identification of his own to the posse leader. The man nodded, visibly impressed, then flashed A-54 a "Heil Hitler" salute, which A-54 returned.

A-54 got back in the car.

The leader handed me my briefcase. His minions got behind the wheels of their own cars, cranked the engines, and moved them off the road so we could pass.

Fryč didn't need to be told twice, or even once; he put the car in gear and drove away as quickly as he could without looking eager. Once out of sight of the roadblock, I looked back in its direction, then leaned forward to confer with A-54.

"I was starting to think we'd be shot in our own country by our own supposed countrymen." I yelled over the wind of the slipstream. "What did you tell them?"

"I told them the truth, of course," A-54 said.

"The truth?"

"'The truth shall prevail.' That's your national motto, right? Yes, I told them the truth—that I'm a high-ranking officer and a long-standing Nazi Party member, and that you men are Czechoslovakian spies who are working with me."

Strankmuller chuckled. "It is the truth, sir."

"It is the truth," I conceded with a relieved half-smile.

* * *

"The misery of the Sudeten Germans is indescribable," Hitler continued. "As human beings they are oppressed and treated in an intolerable fashion. When three and a half million members of the German race, a people which numbers nearly eighty million, may not sing a song they like simply because it does not please the Czechs, or when they are beaten until the blood flows solely because they wear stockings which offend the Czechs—this may cause the worthy representatives of the British and French no concern. But this *does* concern us, and if these tortured creatures can find no justice and no help on their own, they will get it from us! The depriving of their rights must come to an end!"

* * *

"I do have a favor to ask of you," A-54 said, raising his voice and craning his head, straining to be heard.

"Yes?"

"I have been tasked with establishing radio transmitter sites in your country for our agents to send reports back to Germany. I was wondering if you and your men might be able to help with this, sir."

"Help with this?" Strankmuller echoed.

"Towards what end?" I asked.

"I'll give you my word that you'll know the location of every transmitter we have on your soil. You will be able to monitor the agents in charge of them and feed them disinformation if necessary. And I will complete my task more quickly than my superiors are anticipating, thereby earning myself a pat on the back and increased trust and responsibilities, which I will then use to get more information for you. It's to everyone's advantage, sir."

"Perhaps," I replied.

* * *

Hitler's speech built to its feverish climax. "What the Germans demand is the right of self-determination that every other people possesses, the right of self-determination that President Wilson promised to Europe but that was denied to the German people at Versailles. The German people want this right! They do not want mere phrases! I am in no way willing that here in the heart of Germany a second Palestine should be permitted to arise. The poor Arabs are defenseless and perhaps deserted. The Germans in Czechoslovakia are neither defenseless nor deserted, and the world should take notice of that fact. Germans, National Socialists, you have the right now once again to carry high the German head! All of us have the duty to never again bow the head beneath an alien will! Let that be our vow! So help us God!"

* * *

That night, the Sudetenland melted in a fury of riot and fire.

Dawn broke on scattered columns of smoke and blazing newspaper headlines. We'd spent the night holed up in our safe house, going over newly-obtained details of Germany's war plans; that morning, we avoided Kraslice and sent A-54 home via train instead, then drove back to Prague ourselves, while behind us the Sudetenland still seethed. Several gun battles broke out; at least one Czechoslovakian policeman was shot dead, possibly by the same armed German thugs we'd seen in Kraslice.

Only a few short months before, President Beneš had withdrawn the troops he'd sent in to the Sudetenland when we'd gotten wind of Plan Green. To restore order, he had to send them back in yet again.

Which, of course, Hitler regarded as intolerable—a cause for war.

* * *

Again I briefed the President in his office, with that gorgeous panorama that I now barely noticed. This time, General Krejčí was standing by my side.

"Politically, the situation is grave," President Beneš told us. He leaned forward in his chair and folded his hands worriedly on his desk. "Prime Minister Chamberlain is flying to Germany to meet personally with the Führer. The fate of the country may well depend on what Chamberlain does at this meeting."

"I already told you, sir, what Chamberlain will do."

"I still think the British and the French will fight if Hitler pushes his luck. With that in mind, what is the military situation?"

Krejčí cleared his throat. "Sir, if we have to fight the Germans alone, it would not be good. Perhaps we could hold out for three weeks. But if the British and French and Soviets fight alongside us…Moravec, tell him what you told me."

"Sir, according to our A-54, if the Germans sent enough troops against us to decisively defeat us, they would have to leave their Western

Front virtually unguarded. The French could lead with their marching bands and go all the way to Berlin."

*   *   *

But of course nothing of the sort happened.

At Munich, Chamberlain and Daladier,[47] in consultation with the Germans and the Italians, decided the fate of our country. They did not feel the need to confer with us. Meanwhile the Soviets remained on the sidelines, under no obligation to act so long as the French sat on their hands.

Chamberlain flew back from Munich and stepped out onto the tarmac at Heston Aerodrome to a riotous reception from the gleeful public. Newsreel cameras recorded the scene for posterity. Umbrella in hand, he stepped up to the radio microphones and read aloud from a sheet of paper.

"We, the German Führer and Chancellor, and the British Prime Minister, have had a further meeting today and agreed that the question of Anglo-German relations is of the first importance to Europe. We regard the agreement signed last night as symbolic of the desire of our two peoples never to go to war with one another again. We are resolved that the method of consultation shall be the method to deal with any other questions that may concern our two countries, and we are determined to continue our efforts to remove possible sources of difference and thus to assure the peace of Europe."

Chamberlain leaned back, satisfied, and let those words sink in to ears still ringing from the cataclysm that had ended a generation before. Surrounded by the credulous crowd, blissfully unaware that he was in the process of becoming one of the iconic images of 20th century folly, he triumphantly raised the paper he'd been reading, and spoke again: "My good friends, this is the second time that there has come back from Germany to Downing Street peace with honor. I believe it is peace in our time!"

*   *   *

"I believe it is a betrayal," Krejčí said that afternoon.

I believed his assessment.

In a cavernous room at the Defense Ministry we sat, surrounded by junior officers milling about, tending to maps, charts, and paperwork:

---

[47] The French Prime Minister.

all purposeful chaos. Munich and Chamberlain had thrown everything off, though; no one knew anything. If we went along with this straitjacket of a peace settlement, would our country end up dismembered? If we fought, alone, would the British and French come to our aid? Or stand idly by and watch Hitler crush us? Would the Soviets come to our aid, alone? Did we want them to? According to the terms of our treaty, the Soviets were only obliged to help us if the French did, so it all came down to that. Personally I'd have preferred to fight, regardless of the outcome, but then again my war had already started.

"What kind of diplomacy is this?" Krejčí continued. "The West, they drew our borders. And now they tell us, 'Either you can sacrifice your border regions peacefully, and leave yourselves indefensible for the good of Europe, or you can fight and go it alone, regardless of whether we or other countries are obliged to come to your aid.' What do they expect us to do? What would they do in our shoes?"

"Surely we'll fight, sir."

"In the Bible, it says to offer no resistance to evil, to turn the other cheek. But this isn't being slapped, this is being strangled. They say everyone will fight when they're being strangled. At that point, it's hardly a conscious decision; when the blood is cut off from your brain and your survival is at stake, you'll fight, automatically. So surely we'll fight."

I nodded. Krejčí stood and paced and looked for something to do.

In lieu of further pointless griping, we went back to work; he had status reports to hear and orders to give, and I had information to assemble and briefings to prepare. Still I kept an eye on the secure phone from Hradčany.

Half an hour later, it rang.

General Krejčí picked it up, and the room slowed down to listen.

"I…I understand, sir. It will be done." Krejčí put the phone down and spoke, to the hushed room and to no one in particular. "President Beneš has just decided…" His voice, which had made it so far without showing the strain, at last broke. He rubbed his hand in his face, then regrouped. "…decided to capitulate."

*   *   *

That week's newsreel footage—helpfully provided to the world by Nazi Germany—showed happy clapping civilians lining the town square in Kraslice while jackbooted Germans marched past under sunny fall weather, wearing shiny new equipment. Everything looked as neat and orderly as a parade—which, for all intents and purposes, it was.

Conveniently, no one was on hand to film the unhappy refugees streaming back to that part of Czechoslovakia which remained, theoretically, free. Democratic-minded German speakers, Czechs and Jews threw clothing and bedding and haphazard bundles of pots and pans into overburdened automobiles or atop wood-wheeled wagons; they rode out of town, or trudged slump-shouldered while their former neighbors hurled jeers, insults and rocks. And no one hosted peace conferences to call attention to their plight, or made speeches to demand their rights.

* * *

In that lofty office in Hradčany only four short days later, President Beneš sat with his back to the window and read the final draft of a short, simple letter.

I wasn't there, but I've heard enough about the scene that I envision it now perhaps more clearly than if I had seen it.

Outside, the gray cityscape was tinged with fall's colors: ochre and amber in the nearby hillsides, and down along the Vltava. (It's strange how the warmest colors appear when it's about to get cold.) Perhaps Beneš stared out and saw the beautiful view as if for the first time; sometimes moments of high drama can make us oversensitive, and moments of loss can make us appreciate what we're losing; we take fresh note of everything and see everything as if for the first time; all that we are saying goodbye to looks fresh and clear and new. But then again, President Beneš was always a hard worker, a man of almost superhuman focus, so perhaps he took no note even on this extraordinary morning.

I am told he read the letter aloud.

"It is with a heavy heart that I offer my resignation as President of Czechoslovakia. May God save us from this German menace."

He sighed, and signed.

At first he tried to remain in the country as a private citizen, but the Germans made it known through diplomatic channels that this was unacceptable, so some weeks later, he made arrangements to leave.

Perhaps when he was ascending the stairs to the airplane that was to fly him to exile in London, the reality of what was happening finally sank in. I am told he cried as he took his seat and looked out the window at the country he'd helped found, the country he'd led, the country he now fled in disgrace.

*   *   *

In the British Parliament, a lowly MP from Epping stood amid the stone and velvet and old wood. In a clear and firm voice, he spoke about Prime Minister Chamberlain's recent diplomatic "efforts."

"We have sustained a total and unmitigated defeat," Winston Churchill said. "And do not suppose that this is the end. It is only the beginning."

CHAPTER 14

The Italian Front-Padua-The Dolomites-Prague
October-December 1918

"It is evident that relations between nations are not only a question of political power, not only of the sword, the spirit also conquers the world…"

—Tomáš Masaryk, as quoted by Karel Čapek in *On Thought and Life*

BY the autumn of 1918, my men and I were in action for the final time.

We'd endured a bewildering year: marches and countermarches, fittings for new equipment, days at crude rifle ranges, travels by train and ferry and foot from England to France, then weeks staring across the shell-churned muddy wastes of No-Man's-Land on the Western Front. Then came relief from the line, followed by more travels too numerous to remember, let alone discuss in detail. At the end of it all, we found ourselves in northeastern Italy.

Those of you who have read Hemingway's *Farewell to Arms* know that the Germans and the Austrians had dealt the Italians a stinging defeat at Caporetto that previous year. The inept Italians had been knocked back all the way to the Piave River, and now, with help from the British, the French, and our newborn army, they were trying to reclaim their lost territory.[48]

The final offensive here began in October; we headed north to the Alps on the heels of the disintegrating Austro-Hungarian Army. It was strange—surreal even—to shoot at men wearing uniforms that we ourselves had worn not so long ago.

It was also odd to think of that conversation with Masaryk in Odessa just over a year before—and to realize that he had so completely realized his goals. For my countrymen and I were now fighting alongside the Allies, fighting not only for an end to the war and our exile, but also for a spot at the peace table and a voice in the postwar settlement. Masaryk had wanted to field an army. He had aimed at that goal when it had seemed an impossible dream, and now it was as real as the rifles in our hands.

*　　*　　*

But Masaryk in that fevered year was not content to sit back and contemplate the army he had wrought.

After our meeting in Odessa, he had circumnavigated the globe: east across Siberia, over to Japan, and across the Pacific. Once in America, he re-established old political and social connections with important people, wealthy people, people who knew people who knew President Wilson. With their help, he held functions and fundraisers in

---

48 I say newborn army, but for all intents and purposes, we were part of the Italian Army. We wore Italian uniforms, carried Italian rifles, and served under the command of General Piccione.

the glittering parlors and marbled halls of America's moneyed class, where he attracted still more supporters, adherents, and funds. And he gave speeches, too, including one outside Chicago's Blackstone Hotel which drew a hundred thousand spectators.

At any rate, by the end of Masaryk's time in the United States, the war was at last drawing to a close. And the American government, which had done so much to bring that about, now supported Masaryk's goal of self-determination and recognized us as co-belligerents.[49] So in October of 1918, while still in the United States, Masaryk declared Czechoslovakia's independence. But he made sure to do so in a way that showcased his flair for the symbolic and the dramatic, a way that seemed guaranteed to secure the sympathies of the American public, and their leaders—he arranged for the ceremony to be held at Independence Hall in Philadelphia.

* * *

Meanwhile in Europe, Austria-Hungary had continued its disintegration. Our citizens at last rose in peaceful revolt on 28 October, ending centuries of Hapsburg rule and making real the independence that Masaryk had declared just over a week before in America. According to the news reports and the accounts I later heard from friends and family, there were gatherings in the streets of Prague and triumphant celebrations throughout the country; statues were toppled, and crowds cheered.

* * *

When I next saw Masaryk, in December of 1918, he was no longer a professor, but a president.

The war had been over for a month. Our National Council[50] in Paris had proclaimed him the head of state and telegraphed the news to him across the Atlantic. He embarked on an ocean-liner and returned to Europe in triumph, homeward bound. He had left England in secrecy; he

---

49 When the United States first entered the war, President Wilson had had no particular desire to dismember Austria-Hungary, but thanks in no small part to Masaryk's efforts and intellectual leadership, in 1918 he began speaking about self-determination. This point I must re-emphasize, because it bears so heavily on the birth and death of our nation—self-determination may have been President Wilson's eventual end goal for Europe, but it had been Masaryk's idea first.

50 A cohort of fellow exiles who had worked with Masaryk throughout the war.

returned amidst a flurry of publicity, greeted and treated to a parade by the Coldstream Guards. Then he'd traveled to Paris, where he met with Prime Minister Briand not as a supplicant and private citizen (as had been the case at their previous meeting) but as a fellow head of state. And now he had arrived in Italy, where my company had been tasked with escorting him on the penultimate stage of his homecoming.

It was a chilly gray day; the clouds were so low we might as well have been indoors. We assembled in the piazza in Padua and stood at attention beneath the ancient stone buildings. There was not enough room for a proper parade, so our leaders walked past us to review the troops—first General Piccione, and then Masaryk walking side by side with Victor Emmanuel, the King of Italy.

Mercifully, they kept the ceremonies short. There were no speeches or grand gestures—everybody seemed to be in a hurry to get out of the cold, so the review was more perfunctory than proud. Then Masaryk and the King headed into the train station, surrounded by note-scribbling journalists and camera-clicking photographers.

When the assemblage had disappeared, an Italian major walked over to the head of our formation.

"You men can go home now," he said.

We retrieved our packs and shuffled off towards the train to load our rifles and our gear for the final trip.

*   *   *

Our train left the pan-flat coastal plain and chugged its way north on a route that was to take us across Austria, our much-diminished former overlord. Past countless mountain villages we rolled, villages full of little white houses and buildings with snow-dusted orange roofs, each town slightly smaller than the last, or so it seemed as we steamed up, up, up the deepening folds of snowy earth and into the gray and jagged Dolomites.

Recent events had proceeded at such a fantastic pace that I'd hardly had time to think, let alone think of reading, but now I had a chance to relax, and I found myself perusing a copy of Clausewitz's *On War*. I'd made some progress when I heard a familiar voice.

"Moravec."

I looked up to see Masaryk himself standing in the aisle of the train car, and I leapt to my feet to shake his hand, lurching awkwardly as the train rocked and swayed.

"Sir!"

"I thought I recognized you back in Padua. Sorry I couldn't stop and chat!"

"No worries, sir," I said, trying not to grin. One of the privates had recently vacated the aisle seat across from me, and I gestured for Professor Masaryk—President Masaryk—to sit. "Please, sir. Have a seat if you're so inclined."

"Thank you." He settled in, and we leaned into the aisle from each side, trying to talk to each other while both facing forward.

"How are you holding up, sir?"

"It's been so long; I'm eager to be home. These four years feel like forty." He stroked his white goatee pensively, looking tired in a way I'd never seen. "I have to keep reminding myself I'm not a private citizen anymore, though! It is quite an honor that the National Council's bestowed on me, but I find myself…hemmed in, by all the pomp and ceremony, by all the duties and restrictions. Tolstoy was right about leaders having no freedom!"

Absent-mindedly, I fidgeted with my book.

"What are you reading there?"

"Clausewitz, sir."

"A little late to be learning about war, isn't it?" he asked.

"I think I'm just trying to make sense of it all, sir. He's got some interesting notions…"

"Such as?"

"Well, sir, I'm reading now about the 'fascinating trinity' of factors that influence events on the battlefield. He speaks of violence, hatred and enmity as being one portion of the trinity; also of chance and probability and the randomness of creativity; and also he mentions the effect of reason and policy."

"I'm sure you prefer reason and rationality to the others," Masaryk said.

"Rationality—yes, it's interesting. In fact, the trinity might better be expressed that way, sir, as the rational, the non-rational, and the irrational."

"How so?"

"Well, there are rational factors—logical decisions by a country's political leadership, and well-planned military actions, and things of that sort—that influence events. But there are also irrational decisions, ones based on the passion and emotion of a people rather than thought or analysis by their leaders. War fever, or the stubbornness that made the French commit so many men at Verdun, for instance."

"And the non-rational?"

"Chance. Happenstance. Those roll-of-the dice occurrences that sometimes determine the course of events. The kingdom that was lost for want of a horseshoe nail."

"Does all this studying mean you're going to stay in the army?"

"Perhaps, sir. I never fancied myself a soldier but..."

"Well, I've not met many men who've known what they were going to do with themselves so early in life, myself included. But give it some thought. We owe our independence to men like you, and only with your help will we be able to keep it."

"Begging your pardon, sir. We owe it to you."

"Bah. Without an army in the field, without soldiers doing the bidding of the National Council, no one would have paid me any heed. You men did a tremendous job. I don't mind telling you—I hate war, but I love soldiers. I hope we don't have to go to war again any time soon, but if we do…"

Suddenly I became aware of a couple of civilians in rumpled suits making their way towards us; one pointed at Masaryk. Both held writing tablets, and one carried a camera around his neck; it seemed I'd seen them hovering about the fringes of his entourage in Padua.

"Sir." I gave a nod in their direction. "I think those men are reporters."

"Let them come over," he said. "We would not be making this trip without the public support we've been able to drum up in France, in England, and especially in America. As I was saying…" Now the reporters were upon us, and I wondered whether he was addressing me or them. He cleared his throat. "As I was going to say, we will need about fifty years of peace to consolidate the country we've built."

"To consolidate, sir?" one of the reporters asked.

167

"We're a small country surrounded by big countries; perhaps nine million Czechs and Slovaks, with the Czech half of our country surrounded on three sides by seventy million Germans in Germany, in Austria, and within our own borders. And we yet have only the rudiments of a government and a civil service. If we want to survive, we'll have to build a strong army…" (Here he gave a nod to me.) "…and other strong institutions."

"You must be excited, though, sir, that your efforts have come to fruition."

"Honestly, I'm most concerned with what to do next. The peace conference will of course be a major undertaking. We have earned a place there, and we have to make the most of it."

"Will you be attending, sir?"

"Doctor Beneš will be attending. There is too much work for me in Prague."

"What do you expect will be discussed there, sir?"

"Boundaries, final terms of the peace, the map of Europe—these things are as yet unsettled. Assuming the Allies draw up our frontiers according to the traditional boundaries of Bohemia, Moravia and Slovakia, there will be perhaps three million German speakers within our boundaries. Three million, as compared to nine million Czechs and Slovaks. We convinced President Wilson of the importance of self-determination as the basis for lasting peace in Europe—if this is truly to be a war to end all wars, we need to establish democratic nations in place of the old absolutist empires. But drawing boundaries on a map is never so simple. How is one to divide people? By language? By religion? By sentiment? By ideology? Because you will get different maps when you rely on those different things. Take language—there are French in Belgium, France and Switzerland; there are Germans in Germany, Austria and Switzerland. So we have languages with more than one nation, and we have successful nations—not monstrous absolutist failures like Austria-Hungary, but successful nations—with more than one language. The Swiss, for instance—they would not say they were French, Italian, or German, especially after this cataclysm—they would say they were Swiss."

168

A reporter spoke up. "Is that what we want for our country then, sir? Some sort of power-sharing, with different peoples living within the boundaries?"

"I don't know how we can avoid it. Again, drawing maps gets messy. It is particularly odd for us—having fought to get rid of Austria-Hungary's rule, it's odd that we'd want different ethnicities in our country. But if we want defensible frontiers, I don't know how we can avoid it. And if we do unto others the way we would have them do unto us, if we look at how Austria-Hungary treated us and do the opposite, if we hold fast to our national character, everything will work out. So, the Swiss can be a model for us. And the Americans, too. They have no ethnic tradition…"

Another reporter edged in: "You like the Americans, don't you, President Masaryk?"

"I'm married to one, I have to like them![51]"

"So the country has a Czecho-slovakian father and an American mother!"

We all chuckled at that one. But Masaryk plugged on. "Bah. Palacky was the father of our country. The national awakeners—I'm just following in their footsteps. But we can and should emulate the Americans. They were born of revolution from an autocratic power, so their people naturally supported our cause."

"Were there times you thought you'd fail, sir?"

"I'll admit, I had some difficult moments. In London I was periodically shadowed by an Austrian spy, a man posing as some sort of journalist or photographer." He cast a beaming smile at the assembled newsmen. "But Doctor Beneš sent word about him, and we were able to confront him. Then when I went to Russia, I had to travel under a false passport and a false name, unfortunately."

"Unfortunately?" one journalist asked.

---

[51] Masaryk had married Charlotte Garrigue of Brooklyn in 1877; she'd lived in Europe with him ever since, and had remained in Prague during his odyssey. Incidentally, his wife normally would have become Mrs. Masaryková, but he was somewhat forward-thinking in such matters and didn't have her change her name so as to indicate possession, as is the norm in our country. What's more, he even took her surname as his middle name, and had her retain her maiden name as her middle name, so they are known in the history books as Tomáš Garrigue Masaryk and Charlotte Garrigue Masaryk.

"I value the truth, above all things. But unfortunately there is no revolution or war without deceit and lies. As I said, Austria-Hungary has sent spies after me, and I don't doubt that they would have detained me, shipped me home, and hanged me, if they'd had the opportunity. So before I went to Russia I removed all English and French labels from my clothing, and some contacts at Scotland Yard provided me with a fake passport and a fake name, so that if I was apprehended no one would know who I was."

This was all incredibly amusing, and perplexing—my old professor, sneaking about like some sort of secret agent! I hadn't remembered him talking about this, so I threw a question his way: "What was your fake name, sir?"

"Thomas Marsden," he chuckled. "I asked for the same first name and the same initials, so I'd turn my head if I was supposed to, and so if I accidentally signed the wrong name it would still look the same! Of course, when I got here, I found that the cleaners back in London had written MASARYK in indelible ink on my shirt collars, in big block letters! But I'm on my way home, and I've done what I set out to do, and I didn't have to lie too much, so it worked out."

I'd been watching him, mesmerized, but now I realized that the reporters had been joined by a considerable entourage of dignitaries and soldiers, a collage of faces watching him hold forth.

Here someone interrupted: "You spoke of a national character. Does that hold true for everyone in the country, sir? Czechs, Slovaks, Germans, Hungarians?"

Masaryk took their edginess in stride. He leaned back on the train bench, settling in. "The Czechs and the Slovaks are one people, I believe. Linguistically and culturally, the similarities far outnumber the differences. As a philologist, that has given me much of my impetus in my public life. As for the Germans, I heard a story once that illustrates the difference between the Czech and the German character. It is about killing...of cats." Here he paused, and stilled the motley assemblage with his silence. "In the Sudetenland, there was a landowner who bought a farm with two tenant farmers, one Czech, one German. And this landowner did not like the cats on the farm. Now, the cats were necessary—they kept the mice under control so they wouldn't eat all the grain. But the landowner was inexperienced, and he didn't know this. So he told the two farmers how much he hated the cats, and how he didn't want to see them on his land. So the Czech farmer consulted his wife, and he asked if she thought the landowner wanted him to get rid of the cats. And the wife said, 'Certainly. That must be what the man wants.' So the Czech farmer reluctantly began killing the cats, without directly talking to the landowner about it. Meanwhile, the German just asked the landowner: 'Do you want me to kill all the cats?' And the landowner said, 'Yes. Kill the cats.' And so the German did as he was told. After that, the mice ran riot. They started eating all the grain. And the landowner knew that, if this continued, he would be ruined."

"Was the landowner Czech?" one of the reporters asked.

Masaryk chuckled. "Yes, he was Czech. So he did not reverse himself outright, but he started talking in front of both tenants about how he missed the cats, now that they were gone, and how they did have some good qualities, after all. So the Czech farmer wasn't sure what to do. He told his wife what had happened, and said, 'Do you think he wants cats again?' and the wife said, 'Yes, that's most likely what he wants.' So quietly, little by little, and again without consulting the landowner, he bought some cats and started letting them loose. Meanwhile, the German tenant went directly to the landowner, and he said, 'Are you instructing me to get more cats?' And the landowner said, 'Yes. Get more cats.'"

"So the Czechs and Germans will not mix, then?"

"I wouldn't say that. They each have their tendencies, but one is not better than the other. This German directness can be more useful than Czech fuzzy-headedness! Perhaps we can use the strengths of both cultures to benefit our nation. Again, look at the Swiss. Or better yet, the Americans. They're a democracy that has absorbed a great many ethnicities and peoples, because they have something stronger—a national idea of pragmatic self-improvement. And we, too, have an ideal—the search for truth, the unending resistance to earthly authority and royal absolutism. And the truth shall prevail."

Now any antagonism in the questioning was gone, replaced by a scattered but heartfelt chorus of "Here, heres" before the assemblage started dispersing. Amidst the chaos, an assistant came up from behind and tapped the president on the shoulder.

"Sir," he asked. "Sir, I have been instructed by Dr. Beneš to get your input on the parade."

"The parade?"

"Apparently, sir, there is to be a homecoming for you when we return to Prague. I am to telegraph them from Bujedovice so that everything will be in place. Of course, your escort of soldiers is here, but the carriage, the…"

"Carriage?" Masaryk said. "Have you been listening at all? I don't intend to ride around in some…gilded carriage, like some…royal pain in the ass!" Everyone laughed, including the hapless assistant. "No, we need something a little more democratic, a little less ostentatious. Something like a pleasant, plain, open-topped motor car."

"Sir, this is December. Are you sure we can't…"

"So much the better. If my soldiers have to be out there in the weather, I'll be out there in the weather. I can bundle up. Let me see what you've planned."

Masaryk stood and followed the aide out of the train car. I leaned back, closed my copy of Clausewitz, and stared out the window; close by, rocks and terrain flashed past, and far off, in the cold distance, one could see jagged stony mountains.

* * *

At the station—what would later be known as Wilson Station—we clambered single-file out of the train cars and assembled on the concrete in the shadow of the railway awning, the old painted-iron latticework of the open-air train terminal. From outside we could already hear the noisy chatter of rising voices.

We waited. Despite the telephoned and telegraphed arrangements, all was still chaotic and uncertain—such events are always madness behind the scenes, in direct proportion to the order and discipline being presented to the public. But at last all was set. There was a cannon-shot to herald our arrival, then speeches by President—President!—Masaryk and Dr. Beneš. We marched out into familiar old Prague with its stone buildings and winding tangled streets that I hadn't seen for over three years, down a route that was to take us over the Charles Bridge and up Hradčany.

Had I not seen it with my own eyes, I would not have believed the reception, the tumultuous, joyous, teeming mass of people that braved the cold and lined the streets to greet their new president. Our country was so young it didn't even have a flag yet, so our citizens just clapped and waved and cheered.

My men and I still wore our Italian Army uniforms, the same we'd had since arriving in Italy so many months ago, but no one in the crowd knew our army didn't even have its own uniforms yet. We marched in two lines on either side of the street, rifles on our shoulders with bayonets gleaming at the end; between us rode the president, beaming at the grateful citizens from the back of his motor car.

CHAPTER 15

Prague
February-March 1939

"In a small nation there is special danger that prudence degenerate into duplicity and unmanly lassitude. External slavery induces internal slavery, and dishonorable means are adopted by feeble individuals believing that they are serving their country. This happened in our country."

—Tomáš Masaryk, "Czechs and Slavs: The Time of Kollár and Jungmann"

SO much unpleasantness happened in the dark cold months after Munich that it would be tedious to recount it all here.

The winter of our discontent—if ever there was cause to dispute Shakespeare's genius, those five words alone could win the debate on his behalf, and in summing up late 1938 and early 1939, I can do no better than to steal from the Bard. Our country's death was not two discrete events, but rather a creeping necrosis. After Beneš left, our new government decided it needed to be obsequious to the one across the border. The *Wehrmacht* had grown seven-fold in the past four years, while our army had been bisected in the hopes of placating them. So our army was half demobilized and half demoralized; Krejčí was forced out; Syrový was dusted off and returned to his old post as Chief of Staff. Jews were being hounded from public office, and officers were being evaluated on their Aryan characteristics. Those spies we'd seized in our undeclared war of espionage were being released from prison, under orders from senile old Emil Hácha[52] and his army of puppet cronies.

And I'd been ordered to stop spying on Nazi Germany.

Yet in the beginning of 1939, I found myself at the same tavern where I'd met with Bertie those long months before. The same waiter was taking my order—some routines can come in handy—and my lunch companion was British. Again.

"Vodka on ice," I told the waiter, and again he gave a knowing nod and turned to my companion. We were taking a late lunch; the place was empty enough that no one could sit close by and eavesdrop. My companion had his back to the door, and we were in the back, so no one could see us through the big plate glass windows with STAROPRAMEN painted on them in bold green and gold.

"I'm fine with ice water," the other man said with a sly smile. "A clear head comes in handy in my line of work."

"Our line of work, Major Gibson."

"So you've heard about my promotion. I'm impressed, as always, Colonel."

---

[52] Hácha had been one of the country's best lawyers and had served as President of Czechoslovakia's Supreme Administrative Court before becoming President in the wake of Beneš' resignation; by this time, however, his best days were behind him.

"In our line of work, we have to keep tabs on both our friends and our enemies. Especially lately, when our friends have been less than reliable."

"Well, you've proven quite good at keeping tabs on friends and enemies alike."

"Are we meeting so you can flatter me, Major?"

"You agreed to this meeting, Colonel. I proposed it, but you set it up. So let's not pretend you don't want to be here."

The waiter brought our waters and took our orders. Gibson waited for him to clear out before resuming the conversation.

"I am not doing this to flatter you. My organization is very impressed with your organization's accomplishments. The Germans themselves, the *Abwehr* in particular, rate you as the best intelligence outfit in Europe. Ahead of ours, even."

"I know, Major." Here I couldn't suppress a slight smile. "I read their mail, too. There's no greater source of satisfaction than to be held in high esteem by your enemies."

"They feel that way for good reason," Major Gibson continued. "The information on German re-armament, particularly aircraft construction, has been most helpful; the Royal Air Force thanks you, as do the rest of our armed forces. It's obvious you have sources no one else has, whose intelligence is more thorough, more accurate and more prescient than everyone else's. So we'd like to find ways to co-operate with you in the future. Or rather, to keep co-operating, because you've already been most excellent at sharing information."

"You didn't co-operate when it mattered."

"Our Government didn't co-operate. In time, we'll have a new one. I wish our Prime Minister had listened to you, but that's in the past now. At any rate, we'll all be fighting the Germans eventually. And you want to be a part of that just as much as I do."

I sipped my water, felt its icy chill on my teeth. "Get to the point, Major."

* * *

"We're going to transplant our entire intelligence service from Czechoslovakia to England."

I'd herded the men into my office, or at least the most important ones: Tichý, Strankmuller and Fryč. Now I leaned back in my chair so they could absorb this.

The room was too small for anonymity, but still there were murmurs of perplexed displeasure. As usual, Strankmuller spoke first: "England, sir?"

"Where else? France? The Soviet Union? At any rate, we have to go somewhere. We've all seen the reports. We know Hitler won't be satisfied with the Sudetenland. So we have to leave."

Again, I heard murmurs. I didn't reproach them. I'd have done the same in their shoes.

"All of us, sir?" Strankmuller again.

"We'll leave some people here underground. I know for a fact that the Germans have detailed knowledge of our personnel, so it will have to be junior officers who aren't known yet, and retired men. But we'll move most everything else. The bank accounts for our agents must be transferred to safe locations in Zurich, Stockholm, and London. Codes, ciphers and codebooks will likewise have to be moved. As an added precaution, we will issue new code names to all of our agents. And we, too, will go."

* * *

"We'll go, then," I told Major Gibson.

"It's for the best," he said. "Your country's in crisis; the natural instinct is to stay and fight. Or even just to be here for the hard times. But with your responsibilities, the work you've done and the work you'll still be needed for, this is what you need to do."

I nodded. "Ever since Munich, it's been difficult to get anything accomplished here. People kiss up to power—it's the way of the world. And Munich showed where the power is at in Europe. Men I once considered more patriotic than myself are now putting circus contortionists to shame as they bend over backwards to kiss German ass."

"I'm sure it's frustrating."

"On one level, I empathize." I felt the need to at least defend my countrymen, not because they were right, but because they were my countrymen. "It seems like the only decisions are hard decisions these days. President Beneš decided not to fight alone, and I would have made a different decision, but I could see where he was coming from. Still..."

"Do you view him as the legitimate president, still, even though he's in exile?"

"More legitimate than Emil Hácha?" I snorted and shook my head.

"I suppose that's a yes," Major Gibson said, then gave a wry sly smile. "Shouldn't you be more respectful of your new president, Colonel?"

"A man who listens to every German whisper? Who tries to meet every demand before it's even demanded? I can't decide..." Here I paused. Was this treason or honesty? "...I can't decide whether he's just too senile to say no, or..." My sentence trailed off into mute frustration.

"The only decisions are hard decisions," Major Gibson echoed.

"I am concerned about getting out of the country unobserved. Hácha's opened the prisons. He's released every German spy we've arrested in the past six years. And since we're not even imprisoning German agents any more, no one knows how many more they're sending across the border."

"I took the liberty of making some preliminary plans," Major Gibson said.

"You assumed I'd say yes?"

"I knew you wouldn't go to the Soviet Union or France, and you couldn't stay here. We will charter an aircraft for you and your men. You can pick the date for us to fly you out."

"If they get the sense we're going to England, the Nazis will make arrangements to apprehend us. And if our files fall into their hands..."

"I'd recommend moving those things first, discreetly—the confidential files, bank accounts, and so on, and so forth. Then destroy what you can't move, and then move yourself and your people last. With a chartered plane, we should have enough seats for you, your wife and children, and a handful of your officers."

Leaning back in my chair, I breathed heavily, thinking.

"We can talk more about this in a few days," Major Gibson said. "I know this is a lot to throw at you at once. If you want to sleep on it, that's fine."

"I…" This. This was a lot to contemplate. The only decisions are hard decisions. "I can't take my wife and children."

"Why not?"

"Can my men take their wives and children?"

"Obviously that's a serious concern." For the first time in the conversation, Major Gibson was taken aback. "We'll have to get them out at some point. But, to get so many people to the airport at once, women, children, and get them on to two or three planes…"

"So they can't."

"We'll probably have to make other arrangements for them. Smuggle them out afterwards."

"Then we'll have to make the same arrangements for my family." The sentence just came out, without premeditation.

"Are you sure, Colonel?"

"If I bring my wife, my men will notice I'm doing something they can't do. I fought in the Austro-Hungarian Army; I know what happens when leaders do things their men can't do. They'll know I put my family in three seats that could have gone to three of my men. They'll know I left three of their peers back here and in greater danger, to say nothing of *their* families."

"That's your decision?" Major Gibson asked.

"That's my decision. As a fellow officer, I'm sure you can understand."

"Still, your family…"

"Believe me, Major, I don't want to leave them behind. I'd send them out ahead of me, if we could do so without alerting the Nazis. And I hope my wife never finds out I had to make this decision. But that's what it boils down to. I can't bring three family members without my men knowing." I smiled guiltily. "But I can bring three more men without my wife knowing."

"Spoken like a true professional, Colonel."

*   *   *

"So on the morning I give the signal," I told my men, "those of us who are leaving will go about our normal morning routine. We'll kiss our wives goodbye like we're going off to work, but instead we'll head off to the airport, where a chartered plane will be waiting to fly us all to London."

Now they were really agitated; my office was abuzz.

"I'm not looking forward to doing it, either," I said, to quell the disturbance.

Fryč stepped forward and spoke: "What will become of them, sir?"

"I don't know yet. We'll make other arrangements. For my family, too, we'll have to make other arrangements. But this isn't happening tomorrow; we have some time to figure all this out."

"How much time, sir?" Strankmuller asked.

*   *   *

"How much time?" I asked A-54.

"Eleven days," he said.

Chomutov was gone, as dangerous for me as Berlin would have been; we were waiting for coffee to percolate in the kitchen of a new safe house in Prague, not fifteen minutes from my office. He'd sent the blank postcard to my home, not my office, which said a lot about his general skittishness about our office gossip finding its way back to his superiors; we'd met at a fall-back location we'd set up before Munich. Still, he'd walked in proudly, on his own, while I'd snuck in through the back door, alone. I didn't want my superiors to know I was still meeting with agents from Nazi Germany, and I didn't want to be seen by the German spies who were possibly already tailing me. Did I really trust A-54 more than my countrymen? It was starting to seem so.

"Give me details."

His battered leather briefcase lay behind him on the kitchen counter; from it, he produced a typewritten document stamped DAS AMTSGEHEIMNIS on top. "On the morning of 15 March, 1939, the unoccupied portions of Bohemia and Moravia will be occupied by four German Army Corps and incorporated into the German Reich. Slovakia will be set up as an independent state. Bound, of course, by military and economic treaties to act in accordance with the Reich."

"A puppet state." Next to me the Silex percolator was still slowly brewing; I fidgeted, inspecting it.

"These moves will be presented to the world as peaceful acts designed to restore order. We're not expecting any resistance."

Almost without thinking, I gave him a dirty look. Even those precious few friendly Germans could be so…smug.

At last the percolator stopped percolating; I poured myself a cup. "Coffee?" I asked.

"Sure."

"Cream and sugar?"

"I'll prepare it myself, thanks," he said with a slim smile.

"Are we still hung up on that?"

"I almost *got* hung up on that!" he exclaimed. "I had a devil of a time explaining that hangover. Not that I didn't enjoy the meeting, mind you."

"I wish I had time for a few today, to take my mind off the insanity." I sipped my coffee. "This will probably just get me agitated."

"Last year, even six months ago during the height of the Munich crisis, your country could have put up a stiff fight. This year we both know that won't be possible," he said, sounding a little more sympathetic, at least. "You might find this interesting, too."

Again he conjured up a document as if from thin air and handed it to me. I skipped the memo information and read the body:

> In accordance with our operations to ensure the safety of the German Reich, all members of Czechoslovakian Military Intelligence are to be rounded up and interrogated with great severity, in order to learn the identity of all source agents within the German Reich. Highest priority is given to apprehending the following officers:
> 1) Colonel František Moravec.
> 2) There was no point reading aloud any more. Nearly all of my men were on the list. Remembering Kirinovic, I shuddered.

"What are your intentions, Colonel? Interrogation with great severity—I'm told it's rather unpleasant."

"We're making arrangements to avoid it," I said, perhaps somewhat testily. "The details of which I would prefer to keep to myself."

"Very well, Colonel. I didn't mean to pry. And the details anyway are not of my concern. I only ask that you destroy or remove any

183

files or documents related to me before my countrymen can capture them. I'd like to avoid it, too."

This chastened me; in my frustration, I'd forgotten how much he was risking on my behalf. "You have my word we won't let that happen. And thank you for all you've done for us. Your assistance has been invaluable."

"Thank you, Colonel. This needn't be goodbye. I'd like to keep working for you."

Had I heard him correctly? I wasn't sure, and wasn't sure I believed him. From what I'd seen, most relationships ended like this, with promises of continued contact and lies, to each other and to ourselves: I'll see you in six months, I'll write every week. Perhaps his motives were better than I gave him credit for, purer than personal enrichment and survival. Still, it seemed too good to be true.

"You'd like to keep working for us?"

"Certainly," he said, as if he'd had no thought of not doing so. "Why not?"

"Very well." Producing a piece of paper and a pen, I jotted down two addresses from memory. I wasn't going to hold my breath waiting for a blank postcard, but at any rate I would give him a method to keep in touch. "Here are two P.O. boxes. One in the Netherlands, and the other in Switzerland. Contact us in a month and we will make new arrangements."

"Thank you, Colonel." He shook my hand, firmly. "We'll be in touch. This is not goodbye, but *auf wiedersehen*."[53]

*   *   *

"Is this goodbye, then, General?" I asked General Bily at his apartment. Morning light, filtered through puffy low clouds, coated the kitchen in a soft glow: a day without shadows.

"Let's not get sentimental," he said. Gently he filled my teacup, then his, then sat. Unwilling to serve himself first: a hallmark of any great officer. "I can't imagine it will be a long war."

"I wish I was staying here with you, sir."

"Let's not get foolish, either," he said. "An old man like myself should get along fine. I can get away with a lot; nobody pays you much attention past a certain age. Say, sixty-five. You can spend your time

---

[53] The literal translation is: Until we meet again.

outdoors sitting on park benches, feeding the pigeons and acting confused, and no one gives you a second look. Whereas I'm sure they'll be looking for you."

"You'll have to lose the military bearing, general."

Here he smirked. "I'll have to get used to not being called 'general.'"

"Once a general, always a general, right, general?"

"Something like that. I'll be fine, though. And I know you've got a lot of worries these days, but you're doing the right thing by going. There's this myth that officers need to be wherever it's most dangerous. Stupidity, I say. It's the type of thing Syrový would say."

"He…" Here I lost my temper, then found it after a brief search. "He hasn't listened to a single report I've given him, sir. I'm absolutely flabbergasted."

"Are you surprised? The man doesn't have a brain in his head," Bily said. "The Germans will probably have to march into his office before he'll believe you. Amazing how far a clean uniform and a couple rows of medals will get you in this army, no?"

Theoretically, I should have stood up for my superior. Instead, I smiled.

"Anyway, officers need to be where they can do their job most efficiently. For junior leaders it is usually the front, but for senior officers it often isn't. You're going where your duties take you."

"I appreciate that, sir." I sipped my tea. "Major Gibson told me the same thing, but it means more coming from you."

Perhaps I said it without real emotion; perhaps his words were no real comfort against the enormity of what we had to do. At any rate, Bily wasn't convinced. "You still sound like you don't believe it."

"*You're* staying here, sir…"

"I'm going where my duties take me. I don't expect you'd be able to run an intelligence network from here in Prague." He sipped his tea, looked at me. "And you can't expect me to run a resistance from London."

*　　*　　*

For the next several days, Captain Fryč made an endless succession of trips down long hallways and steep staircases to a brick alley behind the General Staff Building, carrying armloads of dense cardboard boxes and canvas sacks. There in the perpetual shadows, he'd load everything into the trunk of a car whose driver (Major Gibson, disguised) would then drive via a circuitous route to the British Embassy. From there, we were shipping everything to London via diplomatic pouch. Already our country was crawling with spies, and these days I didn't trust our mail any more than I trusted the Germans.[54]

Meanwhile, we contacted our agents in Germany and made provisions to maintain contact after the move. If we were going to co-operate with the British, I needed to make sure we still had enough of a network to make it worth their while.

* * *

In keeping with the general absurdity of our national character, the powers-that-be kept having our regularly scheduled meetings, and I found myself attending one late on the afternoon of 14 March, sitting at a conference table at a windowless room in the Defense Ministry.

Never, no matter how full my bladder, how tired my brain, or how imminent my holidays, have I been so impatient to leave a meeting; I found myself shifting uncomfortably in my chair and checking my watch every thirty seconds or so. I can't even remember much of what was said; the enormity of what was going to happen filled my mind so completely that little else could enter. Would the Germans really be here tomorrow? That forewarned future seemed impossible to fathom, especially when set against the readily observable normalcy of our routine meeting.

"One more thing," General Syrový said when it was almost over. "Colonel Moravec seems to think we'll be invaded tomorrow by the Germans. As to why they would do this, when we've done everything possible to not only meet their requests, but anticipate them, I have no idea." He pursed his lips and made a skeptical face. "But just in case something like that does happen, I'm transmitting orders to all divisional headquarters tonight. There is to be no resistance. All units will be confined to barracks. German commanders will be received with the proper military courtesies. No armaments are to be destroyed, and no documents are to be burned. All files are to be left intact."

---

[54] With as many spies as they had in our country at that point, it would have been child's play for them to, say, bribe someone at the post office to get a look at all of our mail; I know I'd have done it, if I'd had their resources.

Syrový stared right at me when he said this. Had he gone senile in his old age, like Hácha? Anticipating requests from the Germans—did he think we were waiters instead of soldiers? And as for our files, did he not realize how many files we had? They were filled with names and detailed information on informants and spies—not just A-54 but perhaps thirty major and one hundred minor ones, Germans who had betrayed their country for reasons good and bad, but who might be burned in every sense of the word if their files weren't.

For the first time in my military career—or at least, since those dysfunctional early days in the Austro-Hungarian Army—I rolled my eyes at a superior officer.

Still, I had my orders.

*　　*　　*

In the basement of the General Staff building sat a furnace that was used to burn important documents. Ordinarily such tasks could be entrusted to junior personnel, or even personal secretaries, but these days I wasn't taking any chances on Syrový or anyone else countermanding my orders.

So as I pulled open the cage on the decrepit freight elevator, I knew that the man I'd delegated would be hard at work. And sure enough, there he was: Strankmuller.

Next to him was a mountain of empty cardboard boxes, illuminated by the fiery furnace. At his feet, two or three were still full.

"Major Strankmuller, I just came from a meeting with the other officers of the General Staff," I said wearily. "Apparently we're not supposed to be burning documents."

Strankmuller paid me no heed but silently bent over, picked up the last few boxes, pulled out the manila folders within, and threw them into the furnace's gaping maw. Then he turned towards me and acted surprised to see me. "I'm sorry, sir. Did you say something?"

"I've been told that we're not supposed to be burning documents."

"Sir, I can honestly report to you that we are not burning documents. Any more."

"Very good, Major." From my pocket I pulled a handwritten list. "The plane to London's sitting on the tarmac at Ruzyně Field. There are eleven seats. Here are the people I want in them."

I handed him the list, and he gave it a quick glance.

"Don't burn it," I said. "Round them up, and I'll talk to them in two hours. We fly tonight."

"Everyone on the list has to go, sir?"

"They can stay if they want," I said. "But the Germans have a list of their own with a lot of the same names. And they're liable to come looking for anyone who stays here." I turned to leave, thinking again of Kirinovic and interrogation with great severity.

"Where are you going, sir?"

"Home, to get a toothbrush, a razor and a change of clothes."

"What are you telling your wife, sir?"

* * *

"Sweetheart."

Tentatively, I stepped through our front door at our apartment. For the last time? My brain told me I wouldn't be back here, couldn't be back here, before the Germans came rolling into town tomorrow, but still it seemed unreal. These surreal thoughts again didn't match my surroundings—hearth and home, the familiar and real and routine.

My driver was waiting downstairs with the engine running. My house keys remained in hand—I knew I wasn't going to be here long. From the kitchen, my wife walked in, perplexed.

"You're home early, František."

"I'm going on an overnight trip to Moravia. I need you to pack an overnight bag for me while I talk to the girls."

"All right." Her brows knitted. Did she know something was up? Perhaps.

"Use the thin briefcase. I'll need my razor, my shaving soap and shaving brush, my toothbrush, three pairs of underwear, three pairs of socks, two pairs of pants, and three shirts."

"Three shirts?"

"I may have to stay a few extra days. There's money in the nightstand. Please, hurry! I do have to leave soon."

From over by the dining room, my girls came running. My heart broke.

"Daddy!" Hanyi said.

"Daddy," Tatiana echoed.

"You're home early, daddy! Can we play checkers before dinner?"

"Yes, play checkers with us, daddy! We haven't played in a long time!"

"I can't, girls. I have to go away for a few days for work."

"When you come back, can we play?" Hanyi asked.

"When I get back, we can play."

"We can play this weekend?"

"When I get back, we can play." I hated this. Someday, you'll understand, girls.

"You promise?"

"I promise." It was a much worse interrogation than I'd expected from them. "Right now, I have to tell you something very important, though. Tomorrow you don't have to go to school!"

"No school tomorrow?" Hanyi asked.

"I thought you wanted us to go to school always," Tatiana said, confused. (Children have a knack for recording your important statements and only playing them back when they are inconvenient for you to explain.) "So we can grow up big and smart."

"Just not tomorrow," I said. "There are going to be some bad men around, and I don't want you to get hurt."

"Will the bad men have guns?"

"Some of them." What kind of man was I? What kind of soldier? Knowing what was happening, knowing what my family might be faced with if—no, when—the Germans came looking for me? Knowing so much more than my family knew, and yet not only telling them nothing, but fleeing like a thief in the night? It felt cowardly; I was a soldier. Who was I supposed to defend, if not my family? This was…

No. It was best this way. Staying would accomplish nothing. And this way, when the Germans come, my wife and children can honestly say they know nothing.

Mercifully, my wife returned from the bedroom right then, with my briefcase in one hand and a wad of crowns in the other. "What's going on, František? Where did this money come from? This is three months' salary."

"Keep the girls home from school tomorrow, OK?" The suitcase was packed; I leaned over, took it, and kissed her goodbye. For three months? Six? A year? Forever? "Thank you! I love you!" Again, I kissed her goodbye, but I lingered longer this time.

"You're not staying for dinner?"

"No. I really must go. I love you. I'm sorry." Again I kissed her, lingered, then tore myself away.

* * *

Alone at the office, I opened my safe and another suitcase, this one empty. I filled it with cash, bundle after bundle, in neat even rows. Reichsmarks and Dutch gulden were all we had left in there; we had no more need for Czech crowns.

* * *

Ruzyně Field.

Our headlights sliced through the small parking lot, across the sides of cars and lampposts, as the driver pulled in.

Now the sun had gone down and the March air had started to chill; the stars hung distant and cold, and to the north a band of them had vanished behind what looked like a massive ragged swath of dark clouds. According to the calendar, spring was nearly upon us, but it felt like the dead of winter.

"You know what you're to do tomorrow, right?" I asked the driver, a baby-faced corporal in civilian clothes who had only been with us for the past few months.

"Yes, sir. I'm to go to your apartment and tell your wife that I took you to the airport, that you flew to safety, and that you'll communicate with her as soon as is safe and practical."

"Correct."

Now everything at last felt real, now that we were stepping out of the car and our placid routines. My suitcases—one with cash, one with clothes—were in the trunk; the driver opened it and grabbed them, and I took them. We looked across the lot—Strankmuller, Tichý and a junior officer named Palecek stood waiting by one of the black Skodas from the motor pool.

"I can take it from here," I told the driver. "It's probably better if you don't go inside. I'm assuming they're watching."

The driver nodded mutely.

"Don't report for duty tomorrow, but don't...don't do anything foolish, either. Just the errand I gave you. We'll strike back when the time is right." Again the driver nodded. He was a good soldier: smart, attentive, taciturn. I knew, somehow, that this was the last time I'd see him. "This will all make sense tomorrow," I said by way of final explanation.

"Thank you, sir." We shook hands. "Safe travels, wherever it is you're going."

As he drove off, I lugged my suitcases over to where my men shivered and smoked.

"Palecek had to drive, sir" Tichý said. "What should we do with it?" He nodded at their car.

Our whole organization was evaporating and dispersing tonight; we were of course going to London, and the men who had to stay behind were heading underground, to clean apartments.[55] All in all, we were disappearing without leaving much residue, but this car was an exception. On a whim, I unlocked it, rolled the passenger window down all the way, grabbed the keys from Palecek and left them in plain view on the front seat—an anonymous gift to an anonymous citizen, courtesy of the Czechoslovakian government, which would be dead by sunrise, at the ripe old age of twenty.

"Let's get inside," I said. "We don't know who's watching."

Inside, almost inconspicuous amidst the smattering of other travelers in the small new terminal, stood the others: Bartik, Tauer, Fort, Frank, Sláma, Fryč and Cigna. They stubbed out cigarettes in ashtrays and hoisted their leather suitcases and cloth overnight bags; no one seemed in a mood for chit-chat.

I led the way to the customs desk. There was no way to bypass it without drawing attention. The new agent on duty leaned back in his chair, uniformed, authoritative, snide. 24 hours from now, he was going to be unemployed.

"Do you men have your exit visas?"

"Not yet."

"Are you leaving the country for business or pleasure?"

---

[55] Clean in the espionage sense, as well as the normal meaning; we'd set them up in the past week, paying cash, and there were no written records of them anywhere at our offices—and thus no way for anyone whom I didn't trust to even know where they were.

"Business," I said. "We sell machine parts; we're meeting some customers in London."

"What are you carrying?" he asked, with a nod at my briefcase full of cash.

I raised my suitcase but didn't open it. "Machine parts."

"Please show them to me, sir," the agent said again.

At that point I was wondering if I should present some identification and browbeat the man into submission—obviously not something I wanted to do, given that we were trying to leave without creating a ruckus.

Fortunately, a senior agent I knew walked up and gave a nod. "It's OK, Vaclav. I know them."

Vaclav disappeared, and our friend—Tomáš?—took my passport and stamped it.

"Sir," he told me, leaning forward and cupping his hand over his mouth like an amateur agent. "Sir, some of these men have been hanging around the terminal for hours."

"My men? I know."

"No, sir. Others." His eyes flickered up towards a lone man, standing with his back to the wall and keeping steady eyes on the room.

"Thank you."

"Perhaps you and your men should wait out in the hangar, sir."

As I watched, the lone man walked to a telephone booth, fished in his pocket for change, and pulled open the folding wood-and-glass door. A German agent, no doubt. Was he keeping tabs on everyone leaving the country in the final hours? Waiting to summon help to stop us from leaving?

"Perhaps."

The man in the phone booth dropped in his money and dialed, but looked over his shoulder at us as he did so. I didn't want to find out who he was calling. Should I have planned this departure differently? I wondered, then stopped myself. There was no time for, and no point to, second guessing. Automatically, I checked my watch—as long as we took off soon, everything should be fine.

Again I led the way, my arms hanging heavily as they held their suitcases; my men followed like ducks as we walked behind the customs desk and out a small service door into the chill night winds we'd only just left behind.

We walked across the cold open expanse of tarmac towards a corrugated metal hangar. Inside, our tri-motored Fokker gleamed under the electric bulbs.

The pilot walked over, wiping grease from his hands. "Are you the charter flight to London, sir?"

"Yes, that's us."

"I think we'll have to wait until morning, sir. There's a major snowstorm on the way. The wind's been picking up; I had a devil of a time getting her on the ground. It's not safe to fly in this weather."

"It's not safe for us to stay on the ground, either."

"Let me do a quick preflight check and we'll see for sure. But my gut says we're going to be stuck here." Back he went to the aircraft, tugging on flaps and ailerons, kicking tires, looking everything over in no particular hurry.

Through the gap in the hangar doors, I could see the first flakes of snow blowing horizontally. The wind was picking up. What did that mean, in the grand scheme of things—that fate, or God, was trying to keep us here? Or just make our departure interesting? Despite my wonderings, I could not believe that. The weather did not know we were leaving. My men were clumped about, chit-chatting at last and blowing on their hands to stay warm; the pilot's back was turned; my mind turned to a more practical question.

Reichsmarks or gulden?

I opened my briefcase, pulled out a bundle of Dutch currency, and counted out a decent wad—hopefully more than enough to change his mind, but not quite enough to make him think we were fools.

I walked over, tapped the pilot on the back, and pressed the money into his hands. "Perhaps this will help your decision."

He looked down, mentally counted it, and grinned. "Well, sir, I like your thinking. Hopefully I'll be alive to spend it!"

He unlatched the rickety aluminum hangar door and pushed it open.

We clambered into the back of the cold dark airplane, stowed our bags behind cargo straps in the back, sat down, and shivered in the seats, silent, staring down the aisle towards the cockpit door, or out the windows, or off into blank space.

A few minutes later the pilot had clambered up front, and the propellers started turning. The engine drone filled the cabin as we taxied out of the hangar.

Still the snow was picking up, whipping across the runway in delicate wisps. Not only was the weather bad, but our flight path took us across Nazi Germany, so if we were forced down by the storm, I didn't honestly know if I wanted to survive the crash. Then again: night flying in bad weather meant they couldn't send Messerschmitts up after us. Was this good or bad? I didn't know. It didn't matter. It was what it was. We were doing what we had to do. Everything else was out of our hands now.

So I tried to relax.

Impossible.

What good were my efforts, my whole career, the sacrifices made and demanded, if it was all ending like this? If my country was now to be subjugated? When would I be back? How soon would I be able to get my wife out? My daughters? How would they find out I'd left? What would they think of me? These thoughts sank from my head into my heart, where they became an impossible black weight. Something fell out of my pocket and onto the seat; when I shifted to see what it was, it dropped to the metal floor with a sad sharp clatter: my house keys. I picked them up and held them tightly as I pressed my forehead against the cold cabin window.

For the second time in my life, I was going into exile.

The engine drone picked up; we accelerated unevenly down the runway. And suddenly came lurching flight; low above the runway, the plane buffeted and bucked as the pilot fought the heavy gusts. Still we drew away from familiar ground and watched buildings and terrain recede beneath us. Far sooner than usual, the lights of the city flickered and disappeared as we ascended into the clouds. My eyes welled with tears; I knew it would be years, if ever, before I returned home.

THE BIRTH OF A NATION; THE DEATH OF A STATESMAN

(Clockwise from top left) T.G. Masaryk reads on 26 October 1918 at Independence Hall; T.G. Masaryk returns to Prague on 21 December 1918; E. Beneš at T.G. Masaryk's funeral, 30 September 1937.

THE SUBJUGATION OF A NATION

Hitler looking out over occupied Prague, 15 March 1939; German troops parade with Hradčany in the background.

A TYRANT RISES

R. Heydrich (Right) and K.H. Frank in front of Hradčany.

AN EXILED ARMY PREPARES TO STRIKE BACK

(Top) E. Beneš talks to members of the exiled Czechoslovakian Army; (Bottom, L-R) J. Gabčík, head of Operation Anthropoid; J. Kubiš of Operation Anthropoid.

Assorted Documents Related to
OPERATION ANTHROPOID

From the Archives of the Czechoslovakian Defence
Ministry, Praha

Collected and Assembled by J. PERNES

Translated and Arranged by MAJOR T. HALKA
CAPTAIN M. LEDNEK
And CAPTAIN S. CERMAK

Prepared for BRIGADIER GENERAL FRANTISEK MORAVEC

FROM: MAJOR T. HALKA
TO: BRIGADIER GENERAL F. MORAVEC
RE: COLLECTION OF DOCUMENTS RELATED TO OPERATION ANTHROPOID
DATE: 29 NOVEMBER 1947

Sir:

Attached, you will find all of the documents we have been able to assemble and translate regarding Operation ANTHROPOID. Our efforts are ongoing, and we are still sifting though materials related to the event's aftermath. However, given your verbal instructions, and the country's current political situation, I thought it wisest to present you with what we've assembled so far, and let you do with it as you will.

For clarity's sake, we have numbered the entire collection of documents consistently, and we have included a header section with each document indicating the dates and locations of the events described. Where possible, we have also made note of when and how each document was acquired. We have, however, assembled the documents, sections of documents, and journal entries in rough chronological order, rather than presenting everything serially. Should you present these documents to interested English-speaking parties, they will have a clear picture of these events, and your role therein.

It should be noted that there are questions regarding the historical accuracy of some documents, particularly the purported diary entries of K. H. Frank. Given Frank's wartime duties and general temperament, it strains belief to think that he took time out of his schedule to report on the events described herein on or about the days that they happened. However, the original diary was found among his personal effects following the liberation of Praha, and seems to be written in his handwriting. There is some speculation that he perhaps prepared it in the waning months of the war—well after the events in question, but in advance of the war crimes trials he surely knew he would face—as a way of sanitizing his involvement in various atrocities. (Another theory is that he kept a diary during the war but rewrote it later, for the same reasons.) We are nonetheless including several portions

here because it does, at least, provide a glimpse—
however inaccurate and inauthentic—of German
motivations, actions and attitudes during several
important junctures. The author is obviously not around
for further questioning on his role, so we must rely on
what sources we have.

A note on translations: We discussed how best to handle
those documents which were originally written in
German. The consensus was that we should use Czech
place names, and English translations of German words.
I trust you will find this a satisfactory solution.

                                    Respectfully Yours,

                                    MAJOR TOMAS HALKA

```
DOCUMENT:    #47
DESCRIPTION: NARRATIVE OF J. KUBIŠ
PLACE:       CLOSE TO NEHVIZDY, OCCUPIED CZECHOSLOVAKIA
DATE:        29 DECEMBER 1941
```

Clouds cloaked the dark continent below our Halifax bomber, blotting out sight of our occupied homeland as we headed home. It was the end of our exile. The beginning of our mission.

I craned my head to peer through the small round window. It was above the wing, so even in perfect conditions one couldn't see much. But this was a moonless wartime night. All Europe was in blackout darkness. And under the weather. Over the North Sea the skies had at least been clear. I'd been able to see stars above us and a distant dim horizon beyond the dark wing. An infinite number of stars above and an infinite darkness below. Formless and flat and inky black. And now, nothing.

Giving up, I sat still. Looked at nothing in particular. Everything inside was lit red. All other colours washed out. The aluminium cabin walls, green zinc chromate spars and ribs and aircraft skin. Tan parachute straps and harnesses and the metal buckles and the green parachute coveralls. Under them, we wore regular clothes specially designed to look normal. No labels to betray their English origins, and no fabric beyond the meagre wartime norm. It had been strange getting dressed at last for this. Civilian suits, then parachutes. Like an eventful night on the town.

After we took off, there had been a long boring lull. For hours we'd been sitting in the cramped rest bay. Above the bomb bay and behind the cockpit, four to a side. Every man rubbing shoulders, and knocking knees if he slouched. Every man alone, with only his relentless thoughts and the engine drone in his head. War is mostly waiting.

"Kubiš." By name, someone was calling me. Valčik. With so few Czechoslovak soldiers in England, many of us knew each other. But with the other groups we were now supposed to play stupid. Even now we did not know their missions. So I kept my mouth shut.

Undaunted, he called me again. "Kubiš." Across from me, Gabčík shot him a nasty look.

I looked over. "Yes?"

"Can you see it?" Meaning home.

"No." I looked back to my front. Eyes on Josef's midsection, unfocused. Much of your time as a soldier is spent staring straight ahead, showing no emotion, like an automaton. This was the first spot of conversation we'd had in an hour and a half.

Three hours ago, the navigator's voice had come crackling over the intercom to announce that we'd crossed the coast. Then the tail gunner caught a glimpse of a German night fighter, and we heard the aircrew chattering over the intercom. We hadn't been talking very much. Not even Josef, which was rare. But the tail gunner's notice shut us up completely. As if our silence would make a difference.

But we'd gotten away. And I was not bored any more. I cannot speak for the others but I felt that strange mix of excitement and apprehension one feels at the jumping-off point of all such undertakings.

For the past few minutes, there had been a change in the propeller sound. Descent. An uncomfortable change in the pressure on the eardrums. Presumably we were almost home.

"Are you sure you know where are we?" Captain Sustr asked over the intercom.

"We've got a top-rate navigator." Flight-Licutenant Hockey's voice said. "Unfortunately it gets difficult without ground references, but we do pretty well with dead reckoning."

"How are we close to the first drop zone, then?"

"How close? About twenty minutes," Lieutenant Hockey said. "We should probably-"

Abruptly the plane lurched and there was a noise like a single rifle shot. Suddenly the engines strained for more power.

A chorus of anxious anonymous comments ensued. "Jesus and Mary" and "Bloody hell" and the like.

"I think I lost the trailing aerial," Hockey said. "The cloud bottoms are lower than I thought. I might have snagged a tree on the descent."

Snagged a tree? Jesus and Mary. Josef and I traded anxious glances. Far away, an antiaircraft piece boomed. Firing blindly, no doubt, but rattling me a little on the inside.

I breathed deeply. No one had promised us an easy mission. MUSIL had mentioned the odds again and again. He hadn't called it a suicide mission, but he also hadn't said it wasn't. Even if we succeeded, which was certain by no means. So we'd known what we were getting into. They'd even issued us L-pills. One dozen each. Eleven too many, Josef had joked. Still it was jarring, actually being here. Living things that you had only just been thinking about, or training for.

"I was going to say, we should probably get the first team ready," Hockey said on the intercom.

Captain Sustr emerged from the bomb-aimer's alcove and gestured at Josef and I. Our comrades shifted, and we waded through their knees and then climbed down behind the bomb bay to the tail. Weeks before, the SOE technicians had cut a circular hole in the floor down there and installed a round parachute hatch. While Sustr got everything else ready, Josef and I re-checked our straps and harnesses. Made sure the risers were above our shoulders so they would not rip our arms off during the jump. Then we clipped our static lines to the cable above and waited.

At five minutes, Sustr unlatched the hatch. We abruptly felt the frigid cyclone of December air eddying up inside. When the chill hit my face I felt even more anxious. No, I felt excited. No, I felt alive. As alive as possible for a person to be. Heart pounding strong and veins full of adrenalin. Everything in the red-coloured cabin looking as sharp as if the lines had been etched with a diamond.

Then came the signal. The green light and the buzzer.

Josef sat down. His legs dangled in the windy black hatch hole. Then Sustr tapped his back and he pushed himself forward and disappeared. Whisked away into the slipstream. Only his static line remained. A strand from a spiderweb.

Sustr manhandled our equipment over to the hole. Down it went with a whoosh. Out into the void.

I sat on the edge of the hatch finally. Like a swimmer getting ready for a cold pool. This would be violent, though, a river not a pool. To be honest I was scared but I think this is normal in such situations. Everything now was happening fast and in a few seconds, to turn back, it would be too late. I had not been having serious thoughts of this, but soon it would be not possible. Air pushed against my calves and then I felt the tap on the back and I pushed myself forward and fell into the violent darkness.

I fell through the cyclone of rushing air. Felt the violent shaking and twisting of my body, then the jerk of the static line pulling out my parachute. Heard the whoosh of the bomber's tail passing far above me in the night. Then the whoomp as my parachute caught air.

Then came darkness. Stillness. Suspended I hung in the sky.

Reaching above me, I could tell my risers had twisted. A minor problem. I grabbed them above my neck and pumped my legs as I would on a bicycle. I felt my body slowly spin, and I looked up as I untwisted. Back at RAF Wilmslow I'd realized there was no sight on earth more beautiful than a full parachute canopy above you. Now I could barely make out its outline, but it felt like everything was fine. It felt like it was snowing. I could not tell if it was windy. When you are borne on the wind you cannot feel the wind…

Down I slammed. Snow and dirt and parachute risers everywhere. I twisted my body like they'd taught me so I'd land on fleshy parts and not smack knees or elbows or head. And I realized I hadn't released my knapsack, or my parachute. It was filling back up with wind, and I had to grab my canopy release and stand up. And then in a big lumpy mess I had to wrap the parachute. Only then did I stop and stand still.

I was home. After two years of exile.

In the middle of a great snowy field I stood alone. Around me was an indistinct milky darkness. In the distance I could barely see a ragged spiky dark band of trees. The cloudy night sky was featureless. Already the Halifax's propeller drone had faded.

This was all wrong. Where was Josef?

At the limit of my vision I just barely saw a squirming dark lump. Awkwardly hugging my bulky parachute, I ran over. Josef was writhing in pain and trying to release his canopy. I dropped my parachute and bent down to help him.

"What happened?"

"My foot. I did something to my foot. Fuck!"

It was so dark that I couldn't make out his face or features. He was a writhing black cursing shape.

"Can you walk?" I asked of him.

"I'll try." He rolled over and struggled to his feet. But I could tell he wasn't standing right. And when he tried to take a few steps I heard a yelp of pain and he toppled into my arms. Grunting, I helped him back down.

"Fuck. Perfect jumps in England, and now that it's for real…" Gabčík said. Then I think he smiled. "I guess I should just be glad there isn't a welcoming committee."

"We are in a field," I said.

"Yes. Very good, my friend. We are in a field."

"MUSIL said it would be a wooded area. Hilly."

"Maybe they missed the drop zone," Josef said. Then he winced as he tried to move his foot.

"Maybe they navigated wrong." If so, where were we? I made myself to ignore the anxiety. The sudden taste of bile rose in my throat.

He sighed. Not in despair, just in thought. "I'll bury the chutes. You do a reconnaissance."

With that I grabbed the electric torch from my knapsack and set out. Reluctant to leave Josef alone but there were no other options. A chill wind cut through my cheap suit and coveralls as I stumbled over the frozen furrows. Already the snow was several centimetres deep.

Not since I was a little boy had I felt so alone.

We had parachuted into German-occupied Czechoslovakia. We were exiled soldiers. Spies now, really, since we weren't in uniform. Eligible for summary execution if captured. Under orders to carry out our mission completely on our own, with no help from our countrymen. So we had to get our bearings and cache our weapons and bivouac before dawn. And Josef couldn't walk.

Snow caked my shoes. My face was numb. I wedged my hands down in my coverall pockets and clenched my arms tight against my sides. Still my body shook with cold as I walked.

In the darkness a large shape took shape. A wooden farmer's shed. With my bare numb cold hands I groped the coarse plank walls. Then I found a door and a latch. It gave way and I stumbled inside. Tumbled over something in the darkness. Fumbled for my electric torch. There it was safe to use, but out in the field it might have attracted attention. And on that night in particular, any attention was unwanted.

When I pressed the brass button, the torch blazed forth. After the darkness of the snowy field and the dimness of the red-lit bomber it was blindingly bright. With its beam I swept the floor and the walls. Saw farm equipment. Rusty hoes and shovels and a tiller and a plough and, hiding under a dusty canvas tarpaulin, the shape of a cart such as one might use to load hay. And I felt safer. Felt again like a little boy, surrounded by the familiar things of my childhood. To warm up my hands I blew on them. But I didn't want to dilly dally while Josef was still out in the cold. So I turned the torch off and headed out.

Now there were yellow spots in my night vision. I blinked hard and struggled to follow my footsteps.

In my absence Josef had hollowed out a spot between two furrows. He'd placed the parachutes in there and covered them with snow. Now he sat huddled and shivering. Blowing on his hands. It was plain to see where the parachutes were but if it snowed more it would cover them up, God willing.

"Let's go," Josef said.

I hoisted him up and put his arm around my shoulders. We stumbled heavily across the frozen field.

Inside the shed he took off his left shoe and sock. I held the torch so he could see the foot. His big toe was tilted downward at a strange angle. There was a ridge between the toe and foot where there should have been nothing. It was like a bunion on top of the joint. A dislocation.

With his right hand, Josef pulled on the toe, while pressing on the joint with the left. He gritted his teeth. Pulled harder. There came an audible pop like a knuckle cracking, but much louder. Josef took a deep breath.

"Are you all right?" I asked.

"That hurt a bit," he admitted.

"A bit?"

"Get the equipment. We'll eat."

Again I went into the snowy dark. Criss-crossed the hard cold field until I found our equipment. It had been packed in a padded bundle and I had to drag the whole thing back to the shed, heaving and panting all the way.

Once I'd wrestled it through the door, we rustled through it. Pulled out chocolate bars and tins of bully beef. I unwrapped my chocolate.

"Don't eat that!" Josef exclaimed, just before I took a bite.

"Don't eat it?"

"Eat your bully beef first. Then you can have dessert."

"Yes, father," I said, then took a big bite of the chocolate. Still I smiled, glad for the humour.

We ate ravenously after that. Trying to regain our energy.

"We'll hide the equipment here," Josef said. "Then I think we can find a better spot for us before morning."

"A better spot?"

"This thing…" he nodded at his toe. "I might need to lay up for a few days. I don't want to be in the same place as the equipment, in case anyone finds us."

We finished our chocolate bars and bully beef. Sorted out our knapsacks and kept the easily explainable. Sleeping bags, clothing, food, and electric torches. Everything else we hid under the canvas-covered cart. We put on wool hats and gloves and bundled ourselves tighter against the cold. Josef stole a rake to use as a walking stick, and I helped him put a splint on his toe. Then I slipped one of the Colt automatics into my pocket and we headed out.

Already the sky was lighter. Already the snow was tapering off. Through the field we trudged again. Away from the light patch on the horizon.

MUSIL had good reasons for launching the mission when he did. Summer nights were too short for the Halifaxes to make it from England to Czechoslovakia and back under cover of darkness. But winter, too, had its disadvantages.

Early in the morning, or so we were later told, a local man left his house to poke around. He had heard the large plane flying low in the night, a very unusual sound. The first unexplainable thing he found was a line of footprints trekking across the fallow winter field. These he followed backwards, to see where we'd been, rather than forwards, to find out who we were and where we'd gone. So first he came to the shed. Further into his field, the tracks split up. Became confusing. But after a few minutes he found a single set of footprints leading back to the smudge in the snow where I'd fallen to earth. And it was clear the footprints had originated there. Had come from nowhere. From thin air.

Meanwhile we walked wearily. Or rather, I walked and Josef hobbled. From his face I could tell how terribly his foot must have hurt. But since we'd left the shed he had not said a word. Instead he just gritted his teeth and clenched the rake. It wasn't a terribly sturdy tool, though, and after half an hour the head broke off. Which wasn't surprising, I suppose. When you use things for the wrong purpose, a purpose beyond them, they wear out quickly. A spoon will last forever if it stays in the kitchen. But if you use it to dig up rocks in the field it will bend in no time.

Still Josef made the most of my mobility and his slowness. Here and there he sent me across the fields to scout ahead and report back. The first few times, nothing looked promising. All I saw were empty fields and occupied farmhouses. Windows lit by oil lamps. Doors on which we could not knock. So we kept going. And the winter sun took its time waking. And when it did it refused to peek out from the cloudy cover.

The third time Josef sent me ahead, I happened across a limestone quarry. It was in a strand of bare birch split by an access road covered in virgin snow. Through the dead white trees I saw a vast blank pit with a strand of pines on the far side. Everything was as still as a crypt.

This was a harsh morning. A grey day without shadows. No time of day is as cruel as morning after a night with no sleep. Sunlight itself feels like blasphemy. Like a dull razor hacking off two days worth of stubble without the benefit of shaving soap. My weary mind could not tell if this was the best place for us, or if I just did not want to find anything better. All I knew was that everything else was wrong. MUSIL had mentioned hilly countryside with few inhabitants. Dangerous for parachuting but good for hiding. This was the exact opposite. Safe parachute country, but farmhouses everywhere.

Retracing my steps, I found Josef still hobbling. Gritting his teeth with no thought of quitting.

The home stretch took impossibly long. Or so it felt at Josef's speed. When we arrived I made as if to walk on the access road, but he put out a hand to stop me.

"We don't know how long it has been abandoned. If someone sees fresh footprints, they might get curious."

So we picked our way through the trees, and circled the vast pit. Why are big, open spaces so compelling? Far down at the bottom we could see a rusty lorry and two creaky cranes. Neither had stirred under their fresh snow blankets. If we fell in, it would be a long time before anyone found us. Would they ever figure out who we were or where we'd come from? Would the war be over by then?

At the edge of the pit, a ramp ran down to a ledge that circled the rim. There, set in the quarry wall, I saw what looked like a wooden door.

Again I walked ahead of Josef. My feet were numb and my shoes were soaked through with melted snow. But I didn't care. At the end of such a trek the discomfort ceases to be discomfort and instead becomes a point of pride. When I got to the wooden door and wall I saw they covered a man-made cave carved out of the limestone.

By the light of the open doorway I inspected the cave. Truly there wasn't much to it. Rough limestone walls. Dusty work tables and stacks of tools covered in cobwebs. Rusty wheelbarrows. A lone light bulb, powerless. The wooden structure built to cover the cave entrance was just solid enough to keep out a most of the light, but barely any of the cold.

Finally Josef caught up with me. "Nice place you have found."

"What do you think?"

"Those farmhouses are looking better and better," he said as he hobbled in. "Get a nice meal and warm up with the farmer's daughter."

"With all these shovels, we can dig our own graves."

"You're in a dark mood. Even for you." Josef grinned. "Not until it's all over, my friend. For now, we'll take this. We can lie up for a few days and then make our way to Plzen. Find that address MUSIL gave us. The safe house."

"If it is a safe house."

"What else would it be? He said it was a safe house."

"He also said we'd be dropped in good weather. And in wooded country. Not farmland with no place to hide."

"Well, we're here," Josef said, sounding blissfully untroubled. "It doesn't matter how things were supposed to happen. We have to deal with what did happen." He set his crude walking stick down and stripped off his knapsack. Started unrolling his sleeping bag and making himself at home. Then went back, rooted through his knapsack and pulled out a map. "Think of it this way. We've found an out-of-the-way place. Lucky us."

Someone knocked on the door.

Jesus! My heart raced. My hand turned off the electric torch. Slipped into my coat pocket and around the pistol. The stranger called out "Good Day" in perfect Czech, which was good for him because he didn't wait for an answer before bursting through the door.

Alarmed, he stood silhouetted in the doorway. A worried middle-aged man with a moustache. We stared at him while he looked back at us. He knew something had happened which was not supposed to happen.

"Can I help you, sir?" Josef asked coldly.

"Yes, I just…I came over to do some skating on the pond over there."

"Where are your skates?" Josef asked.

The stranger had no skates and no answer. Finally he said: "I was…I was wondering what you gentlemen were doing here. This quarry's been abandoned since the war started."

Josef sprung to his feet. His foot. He tried to look casual but winced in pain. "Ahh! Such a shame, too!

Hopefully we can start it back up. We're surveyors, you see."

"Where's your surveying gear?"

"At the office. Just down the road in Plzen."

"Plzen?" Despite his own confusion, the stranger looked at Josef like he was a drooling idiot. "What happened to your foot?"

"I hurt it surveying."

Our visitor could tell the excuses were lamer than Josef. Then his eyes darted over to the pocket where my hand was obviously holding a pistol, and he knew he was no longer in control of the situation. "Yes, of c-course," he stammered. "I'm just…I'm a farmer, and I was trying to figure out…well, I want to ask this question without getting shot, but…"

"Shot?" Josef asked.

"Yes, your friend has his hand in his pocket, and I could be wrong, but it looks like he's…holding a pistol."

"A pistol?" Gabčík pretended to be stupid. And I made him appear so by picking that same moment to calmly draw the pistol. Gabčík followed the stranger's wild eyes to the gun in my hand, now an open secret, and looked at me like I was the one who had lost my mind.

To Josef I shrugged. To the stranger I spoke: "How did you find us?"

"I'm sorry, I just…I woke up last night and I heard airplane motors very low, and this morning I found footprints in the field and…" As he spoke, he grew more agitated. Raised his hands like we were in an American gangster film and this was a hold-up. Which I suppose it was, but for information instead of money. "…and parachutes, and guns and explosives in the shed, and tins of bully beef from England!"

"Where are we, then?"

"N-N-Nehvizdy!"

Josef and I gave each other a confused look. Nehvizdy?

"About thirty kilometres east of Praha!"

"Jesus and Mary. We're not even close to Plzen," I said to Josef, and he gave me another look like I was crazy for talking in front of the stranger. "He already knows. Besides…" I gestured with the pistol.

"I'm a patriot! I'm in SOKOL! I know people in the resistance who can help you!"

"We're not supposed to make contact with the resistance," Josef said wearily.

"Why not?"

"How do we know you're telling the truth? You could be a collaborator, for all we know."

"Look, I'm sorry I followed your tracks here. I should have minded my own business. But I swear, whatever you're here for, I can help you out!"

Now I edged closer to Josef. Said in a stage whisper: "Maybe we should hear him out."

"What? One minute you're pulling a gun on him, and now you want to trust him?"

"Just…" the stranger hopefully interjected.

"Quiet," I barked, then motioned with the gun. "Lay down on the ground. And…put your hands over your ears."

"Please," Josef added.

Obediently the stranger lay down. Unfortunately he had been holding the door open, so lying down meant letting go of the door. It clattered shut, leaving us in near darkness.

Afraid he was going to make a move, I fumbled for my electric torch. Turned it on and shone it on the prone stranger.

"What do you want to do?" Josef asked.

"I don't know. We are sort of in a bind here."

"MUSIL made it clear. We're not supposed to make contact with the resistance."

"He didn't say anything about them making contact with us," I pointed out. "Besides, the plan is already shot to hell. With your foot, and us so far from our safe houses. This is going to take longer than anyone planned…"

Reluctantly Josef nodded. Then he nodded again at my automatic. "You might want to put that away then, if we're going to make friends with this man."

"Good idea," I said, and put the pistol back in my coat pocket. "You can get up now," I told the stranger.

Josef helped him to his feet. He dusted off his clothes.

"We're terribly sorry about the inconvenience, sir," Josef said. "We do appreciate any help you can give us. My friend is tired and stressed out."

I shot Josef a dirty look.

"Well, you are!" Josef exclaimed. "It's fine! I am, too!"

"These are stressful times for all of us," the stranger said.

"Are you really willing to help us after all this foolishness?" Josef asked with a wry smile.

The stranger chuckled. Shook his head and rubbed his face. "Yes. Sure, why not?"

"Wonderful," Josef said.

"Let me go home and get you some food." He pushed open the wooden door, and I turned off my torch.

"Is there a police station in this town?" Josef asked.

"Yes," the stranger said. "Only two men, though."

"Czechs or Germans?"

"Two Czechs. Why?"

"Go into town. See if anyone else knows we are here. Don't ask questions. Just observe and listen. Especially see if there is any unusual activity at the police station. I am very sorry about all this. It is a very difficult position we are in here."

"It's all right," the stranger said. "These are difficult times." He gave a nod and a little smile and raised his hand in awkward salutation before leaving. The rickety wooden door closed with a clatter and again we were in the dark.

Exhausted, we slept the sleep of the dead in the cold dark cave.

After the stranger had left, we'd gone out and cut pine boughs to lay the sleeping bags on, for added warmth. Both of us wondered if the stranger was for real. But we were too tired to go anywhere else.

Hours later, I awoke to a knock on the door. In the darkness I didn't remember who I was or where I was or how I had gotten there.

Fumbling, I found the torch and pressed the button. The bulb flickered and died. Josef and I scrambled about and bumped into one another. It occurred to me that I hadn't even asked the stranger for his name.

Again came the insistent knock.

I pulled the door open and the stranger stood alone. He held aloft an oil lantern and carried a small knapsack. Behind him, all was black night, but the lantern cast a friendly orange glow.

"I thought this might come in handy," he said. He carried it in and set it on the work table. It bathed the cold stone cave in warm living light.

"Thank you, my friend," Josef said.

"I've also brought you some food." He opened his knapsack. Pulled out a loaf of bread, some hunks of cheese, a half bottle of brandy, and some Christmas cake wrapped in waxed paper.

"What's happening in town?" Josef asked.

"Nothing. I looked through the window of the station. One of the policemen was sleeping. The other was playing solitaire."

"You said we're in Nehvizdy?" Josef asked.

"Yes."

"We need to get to Praha."

"That will not be a problem. The train goes right there. And a friend of mine can give you the name and address of a man in Praha who is in the resistance."

"I don't want any talk of our presence here," Josef said.

"We have learned how to keep our mouths shut these past few years," the stranger said.

The oil lamp cast giant black shadows of us on the rough rock walls. They danced in the flickering orange light.

"What did you hear of home, back in London?" the stranger asked.

"I heard a lot of things. I didn't know what to believe," Josef said. "President Beneš speaks often of the resistance. On the radio he says the national flame is bright and can never be extinguished. But others told us not to get in touch with the resistance. They said it was compromised. Riddled with spies and agent provocateurs."

"The Germans have been very active," the stranger said. "There were protests and demonstrations early on. But under Heydrich, not so much. There were many arrests and executions when he took over. Those who have survived have done so only by cunning and suspicion and endless guile. I think there are several intact cells. But don't be surprised if the people you meet are as wary of you as you were of me."

"Will they help us?"

"Yes, I think so."

"We need the utmost secrecy," Josef said. "You cannot tell anyone we're here."

"I will keep your location secret," the stranger said. "But I will need to get in touch with my friends so they can arrange to get you and your equipment to Praha. Just to be curious, why didn't you hide your parachutes better?"

"I did the best I could," Josef said. "I said a prayer it would keep snowing and cover them. I was disappointed."

"Maybe it was for the best. It led me here," the stranger said. "Who knows what God wants for us?"

"We are grateful for the help," Josef said.

"Yes. I am glad for the chance to give it," the stranger replied. He introduced himself as Antonin. (I do not think it was his name, which is why I'm including it here.) Then he asked who we were.

"Zdeněk Vyskočil," Josef said, then nodded at me. "And this is Ota Strnad."

After Antonin left, Josef put out the lamp. We spent the rest of the evening in darkness.

```
DOCUMENT:            #4259.10.10.1941
SUMMARY:             ASSESSMENT OF SS SUPREME GROUP LEADER
                     REINHARD HEYDRICH, REALM-PROTECTOR OF
                     BOHEMIA AND MORAVIA
PREPARED FOR:        MUSIL
PREPARED ON:         10.10.1941
```

Reinhard Heydrich, whom the Germans have recently appointed as Realm-Protector of Bohemia and Moravia, has long been a rising star in Germany's security apparatus. Some have suggested that his recent posting to Praha represents a sort of internal exile, or fall from grace, but it is perhaps more likely the result of his own internal manoeuvrings. It is believed that Heydrich wants the autonomy this posting affords him, because any successes in this role will reflect on him alone, and will make him a candidate for positions of greater responsibility.

Physically, Heydrich is blonde, with blue eyes; he's athletic, but strangely big-hipped. Still, among the upper echelon of the SS he perhaps most closely embodies the Aryan ideal, which may account for the special place he apparently has in Hitler's heart.

In rank, Heydrich is currently an SS Supreme Group Leader, basically a paramilitary police general in charge of the RSHA. This organization, whose name may be translated as Realm Home Security Office, is a shadowy umbrella organization within the SS, tasked with supervising the Secret State Police (Gestapo), the Criminal Police (Kripo), Security Service (SD), and virtually every other police function in the Third Realm. So in essence, Heydrich controls the apparatus which sucks the enemies of the Realm off the streets of Berlin and Hamburg and Munich and spits them out in dark gaol cells and shallow unmarked graves. In this role, he controls a vast network of informants and spies. Over the years he has accumulated an extensive collection of files on various real and perceived enemies of the Realm. Amongst these rows of filing cabinets, with their manila folders full of documents and photographs, he also reportedly has extensive and detailed files on a number of his peers and superiors—basically everyone in the upper echelons of power in Germany. These files, of course, remain under lock and key; access to them is tightly controlled. Reportedly they are only available with Heydrich's personal permission, and under his direct supervision.

Upon being posted to Praha, Heydrich launched a wave of arrests and executions; presumably he sought both to impress upon our people his seriousness, and to show his own superiors that there were urgent tasks which had not been carried out by the previous administrators.

Given his continued role as head of the RHSA, he would still be well justified in spending most of his time in Berlin. (Indeed, his duties take him back often, and continue to earn him favour among his superiors. Some are already speculating that he will eventually succeed Hitler.) Still, since his appointment, he has spent the bulk of his time in Praha. In Berlin he may be a crown prince, but in Praha he is king.

```
DOCUMENT:              #4260.10.10.1941
DESCRIPTION:           ASSESSMENT OF SS GROUP LEADER KARL
                       HERMANN FRANK, STATE SECRETARY OF
                       BOHEMIA AND MORAVIA
PREPARED FOR:          MUSIL
PREPARED ON:           10.10.1941
```

Karl Hermann Frank is currently the State Secretary of Bohemia and Moravia, responsible for many administrative functions, and for liaison with members of the Czech puppet government, but subordinate to Heydrich.

As mentioned in previous memoranda, Frank hails from the Sudetenland, where he was a seller of political books and pamphlets and, later, deputy head of Konrad Heinlein's Sudeten German party. Like Hitler, he has the rabidity of the non-German German speaker who longs to be more German than the Germans.

Physically, Frank is an ugly man with a severe face somehow compelling in its ugliness. He has one glass eye, the result of a childhood accident.

Reportedly, Frank had originally sought Heydrich's job. In September, prompted by the evident success of President Beneš' newspaper boycott, he flew to Berlin. According to our sources, he suggested to Hitler that events in the Protectorate were getting out of hand. By his reckoning, the Czechs were more willing to listen to Czechs in London than Germans in Praha. (The head German in Praha at that time of course was Neurath, an old-fashioned diplomat who's reportedly loyal to Hitler, but not necessarily a National Socialist.)

It didn't happen that way. Hitler agreed on his overall assessments, but he didn't promote Frank. (Perhaps there is something people find lacking in this lackey, for he seems to have a talent for becoming the second-most-important person in any structure.) At any rate, Hitler reportedly listened instead to Heydrich, who had swooped in with a plan of his own. And Frank was made second-in-command, with the official title of State Secretary.

DOCUMENT: #4260.10.10.1941
DESCRIPTION: ASSESSMENT OF EMANUEL MORAVEC, FORMER
                    COLONEL IN THE CZECHOSLOVAKIAN ARMY,
                    CURRENT COLLABORATOR AND MEMBER OF
                    GERMANY'S OCCUPATION GOVERNMENT
PREPARED FOR: MUSIL
PREPARED ON: 10.10.1941

Emanuel Moravec is one of the most puzzling, and perhaps embarrassing, cases of collaboration with the German occupation. He has played a leading role in Germany's propaganda efforts, particularly in his frequent radio broadcasts on behalf of the German occupiers, and he seems destined for a greater role in their administration.

Physically, Moravec is somewhat squat and flabby, and his demeanour is somewhat uncouth.

Nonetheless, Moravec had an extremely successful career in the Czechoslovakian Army, owing, perhaps, to his extreme intelligence and his facility with words. As a young officer, he fought at Zborov, then served with the Czechoslovakian Legion during the Great Anabasis. He briefly served as an intelligence officer while a major and was relatively unproductive there. (There were allegations of financial impropriety, against which he defended himself quite ably. At any rate, nothing was ever proven.) When he returned to the line units, however, he made a name for himself with his innovative and unorthodox solutions to field problems. By the time of Masaryk's funeral, he was so esteemed within the army that he was chosen to lead the honour guard.

During the late 1930s, Moravec also began writing newspaper columns on defence matters. He was a loud and prominent voice against German actions before and during Munich, and prominently called for the nation to resist Germany alone if necessary to avoid the shame of the Munich settlement.

After Munich, however, his attitudes underwent a sudden and perplexing about-face. He apparently began working for the Germans, making pro-German news and opinion radio broadcasts, and earning their trust. Following the events of March 1939, he took a prominent place among the propaganda organs of the German government. Unlike some officials, who have maintained their patriotism in such roles and have discreetly funnelled information to us, Emanuel Moravec has been, by all accounts, a willing and enthusiastic collaborator.

It has been speculated that his financial and personal situation led to this change; he has two ex-wives and various child support obligations, and he is currently in a relationship with a woman who was once his maid, a relationship which reportedly began when he was 44 and she was 16.

```
DOCUMENT:     #47
DESCRIPTION: NARRATIVE OF J. KUBIŠ
PLACE:        PRAHA, OCCUPIED CZECHOSLOVAKIA
DATE:         5 JANUARY 1942
```

Soon the unpleasant dark cave was behind us. Josef and I sat side by side in bright white daylight, watching the countryside roll by as our train chugged towards Praha. Past snowy fields. Furrows of cold soil. The straight rows played tricks on the eyes. Made it look like a stick-man from a flip-book cartoon was running beside us.

"Do you think they'll come through for us?" Josef asked.

"They've come through so far," I said. Antonin had provided us with food. Train tickets. Contacts in Praha who would help us. In the train compartment we were alone, but still we spoke cryptically. Low tones, and no proper nouns. Truth with the specifics washed out.

"I still don't like it," Josef said. "Especially the business with the packages."

We had left our equipment back in Nehvizdy. Everything we needed for the mission: the Sten guns, the grenades. Antonin's friends had said it would be best if we went ahead on our own and they smuggled the weapons into Praha later in the boot of someone's car. Josef had hidden a single automatic in the suitcase he'd borrowed. Enough to get us in trouble, but not enough to do what we'd been sent here for. Besides that, all we had were our forged identity papers and our wits. And the L-pills.

"What choice did we have?" I asked. "They're on our side. Would you rather have them against us?"

"I didn't say this wasn't our best option. I just said I didn't like it. We're relying on people we're supposed to avoid. When we get to Praha, when we get our...equipment back, I want to rely on them as little as possible. MUSIL had his reasons for telling us what he told us."

Our train rumbled. Rocked gently. Outside the land rose and fell like swells on the sea. After France fell I had seen the sea for the first time. On our trail of tears. After a life land-locked in Central Europe it looked incredibly vast. All of the land I'd seen had been tamed. Forests swept aside, roads inlaid everywhere, fences erected, land ploughed under. But the sea seemed proof positive of man's eternal weakness. So much of the earth's surface that we could skate across and skim from but never conquer.

"Would you have done anything to him?" Josef asked.

"Him?"

"Antonin."

"We had to talk tough, to take care of the situation. I don't know what else I might have done if pressed." I really didn't. Years as a soldier, followed by our time in France, have taught me that you don't know what you're capable of until you do it or don't do it. And that goes for good things and bad.

"I'll be honest, I was glad I wasn't in your shoes," Josef said. "I'm glad all I had were words. If it had been a policeman or something like that, someone…working for them, that would have been one thing. But a situation like this…threatening people we are sworn to protect…I just wish I knew whether to trust these people."

"We have no choice, now," I pointed out.

By the time we rolled into Praha, the grey skies had dimmed. Winter's early darkness always made me glum. Dumb, numb, I stared out the window. Buildings crammed together. Huddled for warmth, roofs blanketed white.

Finally the train slowed and the tracks branched out. We stood and filed into the hallway. Outside, signalmen threw the big mechanical train yard switches. Beyond them, the station loomed. A yawning awning, swallowing us up.

Finally we stopped. Stood and waited in silence. Then at last there was movement up ahead. We shuffled ahead, then stepped from the narrow vestibule down onto the cold cement apron. Stood between passenger trains whose black locomotives belched coal smoke at an awning of old cold iron. Dark and depressing.

In silence we moved among the crowd. I walked. Josef limped. Announcements crackled. German, then Czech. Posters in both languages, warnings and advertisements, but no familiar names in either one. Up ahead people were bunching up. Another delay. I sighed, then gasped when I saw the reason.

There stood a line of policemen. Uniformed Czechs, our countrymen, with a plainclothes German agent backing them up.

They'd made a line across the gap between our train and the next one over. Two black locomotives hemmed us in. Facing them were two more. Ugly things with large white Vs painted on their snouts.

Josef had the pistol in his suitcase.

I willed myself to take a deep breath. No place to run, true, but maybe no reason to, either. Josef and I traded glances and soldiered ahead.

I stepped up to a pink-cheeked youngster probably five years younger than myself. He looked embarrassed and apologetic. Still he frisked us down, made us open our knapsacks. What was the appropriate emotion? Blankness? Mild irritation? Sympathy for the tedium of the work?

He asked Josef to open his suitcase.

If Josef hesitated, I didn't see it. He flipped over the suitcase and pressed the spring-loaded buttons. Opened up the suitcase. Nothing visible but clothes. He'd packed the pistol well.

The guard gave a quick glance and a nod. And he let us go. Patted Josef on the back, content we were just ordinary people.

I helped Josef as he hobbled through the station doors. We stood inside a large half-domed booking hall. A semicircle of large ticket windows surrounded one side, facing giant stone pillars out front. There is a strange hush in such places. A conspiracy of silent anonymity. One man walked close by us. Made something close to eye contact.

"Excuse me, sir. This is Wilson Station, right?" I asked.

Alarmed eyes responded. Perplexed. Or was that my perception? Anyhow he kept walking.

"Let's just go," Josef said.

Outside, a broad boulevard. A smattering of taxis with their breath hanging behind them in the cold air. Commuters almost faceless under hats and scarves, shuffling slump-shouldered into the station. Defeated by the workweek. I spotted two with the yellow Star-of-David sewn on their jacket shoulder.

We crossed the street to a desolate park sloping down from the station. Barren trees clutched at the twilight sky. Wide stone slabs lay prostrate on the snowy lawn. Remnants of a shattered monument. And above, a proud German sign in bold black-and-white: "Here stood the Wilson Memorial, which was removed upon the order of the Realm-Protector, SS Supreme Group Leader Heydrich."

North we walked. Around the park we trudged. Found a street sign on a building. Richard Wagner Street. A German name. Depressing.

"We've got the directions from Antonin," Josef said. "We'll find it."

He led the way. The street sloped down and we could see a bleak white and grey panorama of buildings. Neither of us were from Praha, which was one of the criteria MUSIL had used in choosing us. Better out-of-towners memorising maps than locals getting trapped by forgotten connections and random encounters, he'd figured. That would be all it would take to blow the mission. First someone sees you, someone you knew. Then they mention it to a mutual friend, who says he'd thought you had gone abroad with the exile army. And before long, innocent whispers find their way back to guilty ears. Stressful. I only felt peaceful when I forgot to think. When I looked at the physical world and saw only what was. Snow dusting all horizontal surfaces. Brick window ledges. Tram wires like spider webs. During inspections we'd had to dust all horizontal surfaces. Bookshelves. The cross-members on metal bed frames. The tops of light fixtures. The Germans had dusted the streets and thrown mounds of snow on the sidewalks, and now it was getting dirty. White mounds turning black. Or did our countrymen still keep the streets clean? The same people manning the ploughs as back in March of 1939, when our country fell and the Germans marched in unopposed by anything more formidable than a snowstorm?

I stepped off a kerb and almost got flattened by a German lorry.

"Jesus and Mary," Josef said.

"I keep forgetting we're driving on the right now," I replied.

"German ingenuity for you," Josef said.

At the foot of the hill we turned right. Headed back across Richard Wagner and then up a long sloping street. Doggedly, Josef hobbled. Staying at his pace was tedious.

Onward and upward. Behind us, the low sun shone straight up the streets, gleaming off the snow and ice. Our trek could not compare with what we'd gone through in training, but it was still tiring. (Today's problems are the only real problems.) The street slope was not steep, but it was relentlessly consistent. Meanwhile trams glided by with white-painted Vs on their windows. People stood in hordes awaiting them. We passed a storefront where another group stood slackly. Sorting through their pockets for ration books and money. Some appeared to grumble but most looked blank. Accepting everything, all the new routines.

"Strange," I said. It felt not like home, but like another new foreign country. One that happened to share our language. A dark parallel land.

"Strange how?" Josef asked.

"This doesn't seem strange to you?" I asked, nodding at the lines of frustrated consumers.

Josef stopped. Adjusted the crutch beneath his arm. "We had these things back…" Back in England. "We've seen all this before. Rationing and shortages. We just haven't seen them here. The war is the war everywhere. There is only one thing truly different. Do you notice it?"

"There's no bomb damage."

"Two things, then. There are also men our age in civilian clothes."

"Don't you feel the anxiety?" I asked.

Josef smiled. "If there is any, it's something we're feeling, because of our situation. We're the ones who can't trust anyone."

I wondered. I was hungry. We hadn't taken our bully beef with us, because of the labels.

"I'm hoping they'll be able to feed us when we get there."

"I'm hoping there is a there," Josef said. Stopped. Fiddled in his pocket for a piece of paper. HAJASKÝ, it said, and gave an address in Žižkov. "Maybe they wanted to get rid of us without a fuss. Maybe they gave us an address and train tickets and took our packages so there wouldn't be any messiness."

"You have a low opinion of our countrymen," I said.

"I have a high opinion of most of our countrymen. But I do consider every possibility. Obviously not everyone is interested in doing the right thing at this instant. Not that I blame them, entirely. Why should they be asked to fight the Germans with nothing, when we had a chance to fight with a whole army?"

"Should we think the same way?"

"Of course not. We have to inspire these people. Awaken the nation yet again. The people we ran into, I think they want to help us. But there always is that chance…" He shrugged.

Onward and upward we continued. Now I felt alone in the stone city. Here the street was lined with dead winter trees. In the flats above us, women were pulling down heavy blackout curtains. The swath of sky between the dark building silhouettes was itself almost dark.

Finally we found ourselves on the street. A short little stub of street book-ended by flats on one end and a busy intersection on the other. In the twilight Josef re-read the address. Looked at his watch. Looked at the address. Took a deep breath and looked over at a dark multi-storey multi-flat building wedged between two similar buildings. Made a sign of the cross and made for the buzzer.

Someone emerged just before he rang. I grabbed the door before it closed and we snuck inside. Acted like we lived there. There was a long entrance hallway and an open staircase leading down to the courtyard and up to our fate.

We climbed to the third floor. Found the flat.

We knocked on the door.

A minute passed. Slowly.

And then the door opened. A man stuck his head around the door. A middle-aged man. Wire-rimmed glasses. Severe suspicion. He looked us up and down. "Yes?"

"We have a letter from Antonin," Josef said. "He said he spoke to you on the telephone."

The door opened wider.

We walked inside. HAJASKÝ stopped us in the foyer.

"You said you have a letter?" he asked.

Josef nodded.

"Can I see it?"

Obliging, Josef pulled the letter from his breast pocket.

Silently our host read the letter. He then showed us around. Not that there was much to see. A living room scarcely large enough for its contents: a worn-out blue cloth loveseat, a dark wooden radio, a sad little lamp fighting a desperate rearguard action against the advancing night. Through those front windows, one could only see cobblestones and brick. Barely a sliver of the near-dark sky. Then HAJASKÝ pulled down the dark-blue blackout shade and that, too, disappeared. We might as well have been in a basement. We passed a front bedroom nearly filled by the bed inside. And a window that didn't deserve the name because it faced a brick wall less than a metre away. HAJASKÝ gestured, and we threw our knapsacks in, then followed him back to the kitchen. Dark wood cabinets. Cracking green tile floor. A small breakfast table. An ancient gas stove.

"I must say, it is an honour to have you here, Zdeněk." HAJASKÝ said. He was warmer but still wary. "I'm sorry you had to walk all the way up from the station. Žižkov is quite hilly."

"No worries. We've faced worse," Josef smiled.

"I won't ask your purpose here, but I trust it is something worthwhile. Something we'll all be proud to be a part of."

"It is, sir," Gabčík said. "Where did you say your water closet was?"

"There." HAJASKÝ nodded at a slender door at the back of the kitchen. There was a little bite sawn out of it.

"Your water closet's attached to the kitchen?" Josef asked.

HAJASKÝ shrugged. Josef hobbled past him and pushed open the door. I saw the reason for the notch. The toilet bowl had been placed so close to the door that, without the bite, you wouldn't have been able to open or close it.

"They put in a new toilet a couple years ago," HAJASKÝ explained finally. "But it was bigger than the old one."

Through the half-moon in the door, I saw Josef's left foot, now swollen and black and blue. Gingerly he was adjusting the crude cloth bandages they'd given him in Nehvizdy. It looked painful.

Above the table hung a crucifix and a small framed portrait. Presumably his wife and son.

"Your son lives here?" I asked.

"He's gone." HAJASKÝ explained. In prison? Exile? Down the street visiting a friend?

"And your wife?"

"Gone." To the butcher's? To England? Dead? Compared to him, I was a blabbermouth. Maybe that was a good thing. Maybe that was all that remained of the resistance. The tight-lipped ones.

We sat in awkward silence. Finally Josef emerged.

"So you ran across Antonin?" HAJASKÝ asked.

"Yes. We were…we were fortunate." Josef hobbled over. Plopped down on the remaining chair.

"Good." HAJASKÝ said. He spoke again, voice heavy and earnest. "I am truly glad that you came. I will help out in any way I can. There are far too few like you. I must admit, though. You gave me a fright. They say the Secret Police usually come early in the morning. When most people are sleeping and it's likely to catch them at home. Still, unexpected knocks on the door always make the heart flutter these days."

"We're sorry, sir,' Josef said.

"It is all right. It is good that you're here. The trip went well?"

"The train ride went surprisingly well," Josef said. "Or maybe I shouldn't have been surprised. These are Germans that took over, after all. It was somewhat of a disappointment here, though, to see the street names."

"They've changed many of the names," HAJASKÝ said.

"Yes," Josef said. "Yes, they did mention that back…"

"Back in London?" HAJASKÝ asked.

"They mentioned it to us," Josef said. "We had some maps that were smuggled out, but they were not entirely recent." Now he grinned awkwardly. "Between that and the lorries driving on the right, I'm amazed we were so lucky as to get here in one piece. We could have just as easily been…mangled by a lorry, or…picked up and shot in some dank basement somewhere…"

"Shot is lucky if they pick you up," HAJASKÝ said wearily.

"Shot is lucky?" Josef asked.

"Yes, for all involved. If they shoot you outright it is a beautiful thing. Like a kiss from Hitler himself. That means they don't get what's in here." HAJASKÝ tapped his temple with an index finger. Then took out rolling papers and tobacco and started assembling a cigarette. Seeing Josef's hungry eyes, he offered it to him. In short order, the three of us were beneath a heavy blue-grey cloud.

"What else can you tell us?" Josef asked.

"What do you know?"

Josef shrugged. "We've heard a lot of things."

"Well, they rounded up a lot of people. Both when they first took over, then that fall, after the first National Day. Then it got even worse when Heydrich came. I feel lucky just being free. Now, some of our friends, we know how they met their end. That is to say, we know that they met their end, at the gallows or the firing squad or the guillotine in Pankrác. But some of them, they just disappeared. Were they tortured? Are they collaborating? Both? We don't know. And when it comes to the Secret Police, and their ways of extracting information, you don't want to know. There is a room at Peček Palace, where people sit when they've been brought in for questioning. A holding area, with nothing in it but rows of benches and four blank white walls. They call it 'The Cinema.'"

"The Cinema?" Josef asked.

"Yes, not only because of the seating, but because when you're in there, you watch the motion pictures in your head of what they're about to do to you. No speaking, no moving around. Just you alone with your thoughts and four blank walls. Some men, the weak ones, they break just from that."

"But there are other things in store?" Josef asked.

"Of course," HAJASKÝ said. "Better not to have the mental images beforehand, I assure you. These aren't exactly surgical procedures, and they don't always work very well. But if you die before you even get to the operating table, everyone can sleep a little easier."

"So you've got a better reason for these than we do, even," Josef said lightly, with a nod at his cigarette.

But now HAJASKÝ was distant. Thinking. Eyes looking far past us. He took a deep drag from his cigarette.

Finally he spoke: "It is a guilty feeling. Feeling glad when something like that happens to a contact, or a friend. But you do sleep easier, knowing you won't be woken early by a knock on the door."

Josef nodded. Now we were all lost in thought. A few silent drags, and Josef spoke again. "I take it we're sleeping here tonight, then?"

"Yes, but I have to send you somewhere else tomorrow."

"Do you need me to go?" Josef asked. Nodded at his foot.

"Your friend can go by himself, I suppose," HAJASKÝ said. Colder than he had been. "I want to help you. And I will, as much as I can. But if I know my friends, they'll want to get to know you before you spend too much time getting to know us."

"We are who we say we are," Josef said.

"They'll want to make sure. On the surface, it looks like everything is as it seems, but we want to know what's up here, too." Again HAJASKÝ tapped his temple. "Our methods are of course far more reasonable. But still we have to verify these things."

Morning.

Sunlight blasted like a howitzer through the windows of the packed rush-hour tram. Josef's pistol hung heavily in the knapsack. I stood, hand clutching the strap, body knocking against my countrymen as the car rumbled down steel rails inlaid in the cobblestones. So many people it was hard to breathe. (How do people live in cities in peace, let alone war? Or take trams everywhere? They always say you're packed like sardines, but sardines don't stand, they lay flat. Relaxed. Better packing that way. Less dead space. Gravity's on your side. But obviously it wouldn't work on the tram. You'd crush the people on the bottom. And getting on and off would be a chore, so it would defeat the purpose. Could shelves work? Sleep a few more minutes during the commute. Shelves. Like an ambulance or a catacomb. Yes, I was thinking about catacombs back then!)

Next to me an old man exhaled. Breath like rotten fish. Still I didn't say a word. The day before at Wilson Station, or whatever they were calling it, that man had known I hadn't been around for a while. Better to keep quiet. Easy not to say the wrong thing when you don't say anything. Anything you said could prove you'd been away. Asking about the white Vs painted on the tram windows, and on the noses of the locomotives, and on the cobblestones in Old Town Square. Was it still Old Town Square? I didn't know. The Germans had given so many things new names. But I had a new name, too. Had to remember: Ota Strnad. Had to turn my head if anyone said "Ota." So we also gave things new names because it suited our purposes. But our purposes were better. (It is purpose that matters, not actions. Right? But actions speak louder than words.
Still, things are what they are. With or without names. We make names so things make sense and tell stories so events make sense, but things are what they are, with or without names and stories. But when the present is gone, what do we have of it but words? And maybe some objects, too. But the useless ones, the artefacts, are unexplainable without words. And what do we know of the future without words? Plans and drawings, these are like words. Representations of things, but not things. Ideas. Like our mission before it started. An idea.)

Golden sun slanted through the tram windows. Highlighting faces. Fibres on coats. Streaks on the window and paintbrush marks in the large white V. Turning everything orange and yellow. Yellow stars on overcoats: I had seen plenty of them on the street. The sun made everyone squint and turn away. Causing more bumping and grumbling. Civilians complain about many small things. Who has been tested by flame will not be faded by the sun. I knew I must be strong. As a soldier, I must be. Not to look down on them, but for their sake. To save them.

Shifting uncomfortably against the crush of bodies, I fished in my scratchy wool trousers for a crinkled piece of paper. Pulled it out, amidst grumbles from the fish-breath man. Now it slipped from my fingers. Panic! I dove for it. More complaints. What choice did I have? The last thing I needed was for that to get stuck on someone's foot. Disappear out the door. Awkwardly I worked my arm up to read the paper. Still more grumbles. If they knew who I was and what I was doing, would they still be grumbling? I wondered. But I said nothing in response. (Silence is anonymity. Silence is golden. But silence is consent, too. And all we had done so far was to grumble.)

I unfolded the paper. Another address. Above it, a code name: JINDRA.

JINDRA's address was another multi-flat like HAJASKÝ's. A corner building next to a tram line in Smichov, south of the Hrad and across the river from Old Town. Yellow brick walls, large windows. A buzzer next to the main entrance, but as I stepped up to it, an elderly woman with her arms full of packages emerged, and as at HAJASKÝ's I slipped in unannounced.

The main hallway was dark. Chilly. Silent as death. Past the first burned-out light bulb I saw a staircase. Despite the quiet I bounded upstairs. Hesitated there and dug the sheet from my pocket. Lit a match and saw something scurry down the hallway, darker than the darkness. A mouse. Living in corners and shadows. Chased by cats and traps. Well, traps don't chase anything, but still. In the barn we used to feed the cats and set the traps but now I could sympathize with the mice. Enough thinking. I had to trust these people. That's what I had told Josef and that's what I wanted to do. Still I could feel my knapsack heavy with dark possibilities. The pistol I had not wanted to leave behind. Should I put it in my overcoat? Yes.

I took a deep breath and knocked on the door.

Several dead seconds passed.

Finally the door swung open, and a man not much older than me eyed me warily from the bright flat.

"JINDRA?" I asked hopefully.

"Who are you?"

"HAJASKÝ said you'd be expecting me."

"I'm not JINDRA." He eyed the paper I still held in my right hand. Looked at me with disgust now. Snatched the paper before I could say anything. "Get in here."

The flat was a corner unit, large and well-lit. Colder, dustier and messier than HAJASKÝ's. Everything was faded. A washed out sofa and rug. Hardwood floors, well-worn. The windows offered good views up and down the street in two directions.

By them, an ugly bald man kept watch. His face was made worse by the nervous way he sucked on his cigarette. Wordlessly, the younger man handed over the paper I'd carried.

"What the hell is this?" JINDRA asked.

"His," the other man said, pointing at me.

"You wrote the fucking address down? Jesus and Mary." For a few more incredulous seconds he stared at the paper in his left hand, then awkwardly used the same hand to take another heavy drag from the fag end in his mouth. Angrily he stubbed it out in the ashtray on the coffee table. His right hand had never left his pocket. It gripped something. A pistol? "Are you trying to infiltrate our network or just destroy it?"

"What the hell are you talking about?" Now I was getting agitated.

"Why did you write this address down?"

"I didn't think it would be a problem."

"You didn't think at all, apparently," JINDRA spat back. "Think, man!" Temples throbbing. He placed a hand on his rage-red face and tapped the side of his head with his forefinger. "Use your fucking head! Memorize these things!" Now he pointed at the sofa. Barked. "Sit."

I sat. Still he stood. Paced. Breathed deeply. Spoke venomously. "If they get you, and you have a piece of paper with an address on it, they get someone else. Maybe they get me."

"This is your place?" I asked.

"It's none of your business whose place it is," the other man said.

"No, it isn't," JINDRA echoed. Again he looked anxiously out the window. Again I noticed the automatic in his pocket.

"Maybe he isn't one of us," the other man said, about me.

"Why wouldn't I be?"

"London's given no mention of you," JINDRA said. "They've said nothing about any special missions."

"Maybe they didn't want you to know," I said simply.

"There's no reason they shouldn't have."

I lit a cigarette. Smiled. "If they get you, and you know about the special mission, maybe they get me."

"We don't know who you are."

"Who else would I be, other than who I've said I am?"

"A German. An agent provocateur. You know, HAJASKÝ sent his wife and child away when he got word that you were coming."

"His wife and child?"

"In case you weren't who you said you were."

"Your friends found our parachutes. Our weapons."

"The Germans have done some very elaborate special missions of their own," JINDRA said. "And as I said, we've heard nothing from London. So I took some precautions for this meeting. We're being watched, through the window, by our own people. I haven't survived this long by taking chances," he said. Kept his hand on the pistol in his pocket but tapped it against his hip just to make sure I knew that it was, in fact, a pistol. "Just so you know where I'm coming from."

Calmly I withdrew my pistol from my overcoat and set it on my lap, my hand still on the grip. Smiled, said: "Just so you know where I'm coming from."

JINDRA nodded. "Who are you, anyway?"

"You can call me Ota Strnad."

"You want our help and you won't tell us your real name?"

"What's yours?" I asked.

"None of your business," the other man said.

"I will tell you this," JINDRA added. "I am involved with the highest councils of what remains of the resistance here. For this level of involvement, I have paid a price. I live a life in which there can be no peace. I live as a man who has officially ceased living, who knows only rootlessness and anxiety. In the past year and a half, I haven't slept more than a week in the same bed. And the only reason I've survived so long is because I've taken precautions about whom I contact. So I need to at least know why you're here."

"I will only tell you this," I said. "We are soldiers. And we were dropped in on a special mission ordered by President Beneš himself."

"What kind of mission?"

"I can't tell you."

Again JINDRA's face started to redden. "You parachute in on behalf of a president who folded to the Germans after Munich…"

"After being sold out by the French and the British!"

"…who folded to the Germans after Munich, left his country with his tail between his legs, and who exhorts us to further struggle using radio broadcasts sent from the safety of London. Then you find yourselves in a bind and ask us to take chances on your behalf when we don't even know you…"

"Does your organization take any chances at all?" Again I was getting upset. "Or is it here just to keep itself alive?"

"Our organization is doing what it needs to do to survive! You think you can drop in, ask for help, and then question how we do things? We can't be of any use to any one, if we end up in German prisons. The early heroes of the resistance, General Bily and the others, they didn't take such precautions. They met openly in cafes and taverns. And guess where they are now? Dead or in prison."

"Well, we're here to do something worthwhile. That's all I can tell you."

"That's all." JINDRA said. Not a question. An angry accusation.

"How do we know we can trust you?" I asked.

JINDRA smirked but did not otherwise reply.

"We weren't supposed to contact you. This wasn't part of our plan. They provided us everything we needed. Supplies, clothes. Identity cards, the best the British could provide…"

"Let's see them."

Wriggling, I fished out my identity card and handed it to him. He examined it in the harsh sunlight and smirked.

"This is one of the worst forgeries I've ever seen."

"Really?"

Now he took out his own card and placed it side-by-side with mine. His anger gave way to frustration. And sympathy, perhaps? "See? These ink colours are all wrong. The papers are completely different weights, and yours isn't perforated on the top edge."

"Jaroslav?" I asked, reading his card.

"I have many names," he said. "And many IDs, all genuine. We know people who know people who work for the Germans. They can get us identity card blanks, authentic blanks. So we can make authentic documents. Ours aren't really forgeries, because they are literally the real thing. As for yours, well, the Secret Police aren't known for their brilliance, but a twelve-year-old would know this was a fake. You're lucky you weren't stopped."

"We're lucky," the other man said. Emphasized the 'we.'

I thought back to our conversation with HAJASKÝ. "I'm sorry," I said.

"Well, the good news is, I believe you now. If you were an agent provocateur, the Germans would have given you better cards than this," JINDRA said. "I know all this may seem excessive. But under this occupation, you barely trust your own family. You trust your friends even less. And strangers, not at all."

"Is that why you don't trust London?" I asked.

"We listen to them. As for trusting them…" Now JINDRA turned to the other man. "You have a little Churchill in your radio, right?"

The other man nodded.

"A little Churchill?" I asked.

"It's illegal to listen to radio broadcasts from outside the Realm. Very heavily punished. All radio sets produced in the Realm have been made so they can't receive shortwave broadcasts. But we have devices in the radios so we can hear them anyway." JINDRA walked over and turned the dial on the radio. Through static you could hear the voice of a far-off announcer. "…for listening to the BBC Czech service. Your voice of truth…" JINDRA clicked the radio off. "We can listen to them a lot easier than they can listen to us. I don't even know if we have any working transmitters these days."

"No?"

"The Secret Police have been tracking them down. When it comes to radio signals, it is far more dangerous to give than to receive."

"Can you turn it on again?" I asked. Just hearing a voice from England felt miraculous.

JINDRA obliged. Static again, and President Beneš' voice now. "…again, the Czech people will not submit to the German occupiers. Even now, there are acts of sabotage and resistance. But more is needed. Every little bit helps. Workers, call in sick. Work slowly. Resist by any means possible. Much can be accomplished by playing dumb. Feigning ignorance, like the Good Soldier Švejk. But more is needed…"

"What have you been doing, then, in this resistance?"

"Well, they asked us to boycott the German-run press, and we did. And there was the V-for-Victory campaign."

"I've seen Vs around," I said.

"Yes. Under cover of blackout, people would sneak out and write Vs in chalk. In the street, on buildings. A small thing, but it at least let people know there was an active resistance. And of course, there was an extra meaning for us. Pravda Vítězí. And I do believe that the truth shall prevail. But sometimes I think Beneš cares more for prevailing than for the truth. Because the truth is it isn't possible for us to do as he demands. The French, the Belgians, the Dutch, they're close to England. They have coastlines. They can infiltrate people more readily. But we're at the heart of an occupied continent. And so what are we supposed to do? Rise up and be cut down? Anyway, the Germans keep us from doing much, and they have even co-opted the V. They couldn't stop it, so they just started painting their own everywhere. So where does that leave us?"

"We will be doing something worthwhile. Trust us."

"It's Beneš I don't trust," JINDRA said. "Masaryk, during the first war, was at least realistic in his expectations. But Beneš…"

"Can I trust you?" I asked.

"I will get you new identity cards, you and your friend," JINDRA said. "You'll have to lie low for a spell, but we'll get you better cards so you don't have to worry about getting stopped, and medical excusal forms, so the Germans don't wonder why you're not at a

factory. But for now you'll have to head back to
HAJASKÝ's and lie low. Come to think of it, you might
be better off without this," he said, holding up my
identity card. "If they stopped you and you didn't have
it, they'd detain you, but they might just think you
were some dumb nobody. But if they saw this, they'd
know something was up."

"Well, toss it, then," I said.

"Better yet…" JINDRA grabbed my matches and lit my
card. Then his.

I gave him a perplexed look.

"That one had outlived its usefulness. Having you see
it just gave me one more reason to get rid of it. As I
said, I have many names."

Our cards shrivelled to grey ash. The flames drew near
JINDRA's fingers and he set them down in the ashtray.
Somehow the cards retained their shape even as the
paper shrank. You could still see the writing. JINDRA
broke them up, mixed the ashes with the remains of the
week's cigarettes. Dusted off his fingers and then
picked up the paper on which I'd written the address.
Set that alight, too. "Keep it all in your head next
time," he said. "That way you can at least lie."

Cold darkness fell upon the stone city.

Our tram rumbled to a stop. Passengers grumbled. Humbled commuters, slump-shouldered. Incapable of anything more substantial than the evening commute. No one looked you in the eye any more. All stared off into space. At the mind's empty horizons. When someone boarded, there was a mute shifting of reluctant bodies. No more interaction or effort than necessary.

In the morning there had at least been a vitality and energy. Caused, perhaps, by the cheer of sunlight and the hope of a new day. Not possibility, but the illusion of possibility. But now the winter sun had made its early exit, putting even the illusion to rest. It was as if no one had hope for tomorrow beyond today's status quo. No gain but no loss, either. No new announcements or headaches from the Germans.

The tram started again. Heading north. My eyes wandered. Up at the lights. Over at the blue-uniformed conductor waiting by the clamshell doors to collect tickets. Sideways at the posters. Memfis cigarettes, Bat'a shoes, and the "Winter Help" clothing drive to aid German soldiers saving Europe from Bolshevism on the snowy Russian steppe. Slogans, German on top, Czech on bottom.

I envied the blank faces. While I pitied them, I envied them. My automatic hung heavily in my knapsack. A secret I couldn't share. As long as they kept their heads down, they could come and go and enjoy the simple things, at least. Whereas I had to lay low at HAJASKÝ's like a criminal. Cowering like a coward. Was this what we'd trained for? To come here and put people at risk with our mere presence? I wondered if we'd have been better off back in England.

```
DOCUMENT:    #27
DESCRIPTION: PERSONAL DIARY OF K.H. FRANK
PLACE:       HRADČANY, PRAHA, OCCUPIED CZECHOSLOVAKIA
DATE:        12 JANUARY 1942
```

It is time, I feel, to set down some observations on the past few months.

My life has been quite frustrating lately, but it is a strange frustration, the kind that you can hardly explain to others because your problems sound to them like good fortune.

When I was a nobody, a bored and lonely young man sitting behind the counter at that dusty old bookshop in Karlovy Vary, I would daydream of big things, grandiose things. I had been a soldier of no great distinction, and then had gone to law school and dropped out; still I imagined some great change in fortune, some sequence of events by which the world would become aware of my talent and importance. I imagined a successful career in politics; I imagined speaking to great crowds and stirring them to great things; I imagined myself leading a country.

Eventually I realized, as all young men must, that I needed to either abandon my daydreams, or take action to make them a reality; hence those years of toil in the Sudeten German Party. And it did seem at last that those things were coming to pass!

How great was my frustration, then, when the Leader chose Heydrich last September and placed me second under him! I have written about it at some length already in these pages; still I can't entirely make my peace with it. And this, I think, is why even my wife cannot comprehend my frustration: to her, and everyone else, I am a man of some importance, but to me, the distance between where I am and where I want to be is so miniscule compared to the distance I've already gone that I can't believe I cannot cover it.

And these feelings initially played out in our working relationship, unfortunately; it seemed almost a natural cycle, with hot resentments rising from me, and cool condescension coming down in turn from the frosty Realm-Protector.

Still, for all my initial frustrations, all my hopes and desires that have not yet come to pass, I have to concede that Heydrich and I have started to develop a worthwhile and stimulating working relationship.

We had a meeting this afternoon in the Castle. Heydrich has, I must admit, an exquisite office, of which I am somewhat jealous. It was the same one used by President Beneš and, before him, Tomáš Masaryk; more recently, Hitler was photographed looking out its windows on the one and only night he stayed here. (I was there that night, behind the cameraman, quite unaware that he was taking what would prove to be one of the iconic images of our Leader; no matter how close one is to the camera, one never quite sees what the camera sees! But this is, after all, the capital of the last country the Leader conquered without firing a shot, and I think there was something special in his eyes for the camera to capture that day, a distillation of the depth of vision that has brought our nation such triumphs over these past few years.) Heydrich's desk, too, was most likely used by the only two presidents of this abominable nation; it's a beautiful piece of work, so I suspect it's been around since the Hapsburgs. Heydrich, though, keeps it entirely empty, except for a blotter and a set of pens. No calendar, no notes, no sentimental knick-knacks, no evidence of his identity or intentions, except what's locked away inside. But not devoid of personality, because to reveal so little reveals much—a man of admirable discipline and self-control, our Realm-Protector, a man who never lets his sentiment get the better of him: a man, I must admit, that I now find myself aspiring to emulate!

Geschke was there during that meeting, giving some report or other about illegal behaviour among the Czechs. [Translator's Note: Hans Geschke, an experienced National Socialist Party lawyer, was head of the Secret State Police in Praha at the time.] "There has not been much activity, my Lord," I remember him saying at its conclusion. "Most of the what we've seen has been from black marketers."

I recall that Heydrich smirked. (He smirks more than he smiles, it seems!)

"Shouldn't we do something more about them, my Lord?" I asked.

"There is not much more to do, other than publicizing the arrests, and emphasizing that those who are not breaking the law have nothing to worry about. These things are best handled by Moravec's people."

"The Minister of Public Enlightenment, my Lord?" Geschke smiled.

"They always come up with the right words for these situations. They can put out their usual spiel, and the Czechs will keep turning each other in. As usual. If we take too active a role now…" Heydrich shrugged and left the sentence unfinished, except in our minds.

I recall looking out at the city spread out behind him. Today it was a bleak winter expanse of whites and greys, monochrome roofs and spires and hills under low clouds.

"They are a nation of denouncers and whores," Geschke said. "If we locked up everyone who gave us information, we wouldn't have enough gaols to hold them all."

"Emanuel Moravec is the biggest whore of all," I added. "I'm surprised you rely on him, my Lord."

"I rely on him to be himself," Heydrich said. (I've gotten so used to his postures that I can close my eyes and see him lacing his slender fingers together on the edge of the desk and leaning back, self-satisfied.) "Intelligence coupled with ambition and devoid of scruples is the best combination to have in an individual. Reminds me of…" He shrugged, indicating himself, perhaps.

"Moravec has no principles, my Lord," I reminded him. "After Munich he was begging their army to fight us, alone if necessary, whatever the cost to their nation. And now, to have him turn to our side?"

"He had the intelligence to abandon his principles when they became useless," Heydrich replied. "And what better job for a turncoat than turning words around? Our words sound so much more credible to Czech ears when coming from a Czech mouth. At any rate, this is the best way to deal with these things. Everything is calm here. The Slavs are slaves, we all know this. If we treat them as anything else…" Here at last Heydrich turned and looked out the window at the snow-choked city.

We waited to make sure he had finished. Finally I spoke. "Is that all, my Lord?"

"Unfortunately not," Heydrich turned back from the window. "Back in October, when we were gathering the fruits of our previous work, we arrested a Czech spy named Mašin who was sending transmissions and reports back to their so-called government in London. The arrest itself was unremarkable. But the information he was sending was shocking…a comprehensive catalogue of secrets, detailing decisions made at the highest levels of our government. If he had picked the locks on my desk drawers and raided the contents, he could not have come up with more information. In fact, very few people would have even had access to all that knowledge. Myself. Or you," he said, pointing at me. (I must admit—that made me nervous!) "Or you," he said to Geschke.

Geschke squirmed. "My Lord?"

"Or Paul Thummel, the head of Military Intelligence. Now I know it wasn't myself or you, Frank. And I'm pretty sure the head of the Secret Police contingent here wouldn't do such a thing."

"Pretty sure, my Lord?" Geschke dared a small smile.

"Geschke, haven't we already questioned Thummel?" I asked.

"We have, my Lord. Abendschon headed the investigation. Thummel denied everything." Geschke turned to Heydrich and continued. "In fact, if I remember correctly, my Lord, you ordered his release."

"I did," Heydrich said. "And do you know why?"

None of us spoke.

"Because by the time he'd been in gaol for a week, I'd received personal phone calls from Bormann, from Canaris, and from Himmler, all demanding his immediate release." Heydrich paused to let us contemplate this. (He rarely admits to being outmanoeuvred, largely because he is rarely outmanoeuvred. He fancies himself a skilled fencer but is even better at bureaucratic combat, the endless thrusts and parries exchanged via telephone and teletype among the higher echelons of power in the Third Realm. I must admit again, I have much to learn from this man!) "Bormann and Canaris I can handle. But when your own boss starts demanding something…" (We all know how rare it is for Himmler to countermand his most trusted subordinate. Himmler's brain is called Heydrich, everyone says, though of course no one says it louder than a whisper. [Translator's Note: The phrase works better in German: Himmler's Hirn Heist Heydrich.] Some even skip the specifics and say "HHHH" with a knowing nod.) "This man's been in the party longer than I have," Heydrich added ruefully. "The friendships he's made, he isn't the type of person one can just…"

"So we didn't get any information from Thummel, my Lord?" I asked.

"No. He knew he didn't have to talk," Heydrich said. "He knew he wasn't going to be interrogated with any great severity. But I know the truth. So I want you to put men on him, Geschke. I want to know all there is to know. The next time we pull him in, I want no one to question his guilt."

"Foul, my Lord," I said, relaxing at last. "It rankles me, working alongside a traitor like that."

"It may be the best possible thing for us," Heydrich said.

"How, my Lord?" Geschke asked.

"The whole Military Intelligence apparatus is soft. Weak. Unwilling to do the hard things our national destiny demands. Here in the Protectorate, we in the SS have free rein, as we should, but elsewhere in Europe…" He pursed his lips, and made an unpleasant face. "At any rate, if we can prove to the Leader that Thummel is unreliable, perhaps we can make him realize their whole organization is unreliable. And then perhaps we will have these same responsibilities elsewhere. If we do, we can make the whole continent as peaceful as the Protectorate. And then perhaps the Americans and the British will stop trying to…" He shrugged hopefully. "The Americans did what they needed to do to pacify their continent, and people complained at the time, but now? Nothing. And, granted, we are dealing with established and somewhat civilized cultures, rather than savages with painted faces, but still, in fifty or eighty years, perhaps..." He turned again to look out the window; I sensed the meeting was over at last.

"You are a man of vision, my Lord," I said at last. "We will make these things happen. By the way, when are you flying to Berlin?"

"Next week," Heydrich said.

(He has mentioned the trip in passing a few times, and I gather it is rather important—something about the Jews. I must confess—for as much as I'm learning from the man, I am hoping his other duties become time-consuming enough to draw him back to Berlin. Sometimes I think it would be nice to have a freer hand here, but Heydrich—Heydrich, of all people!—is holding me back. He seems overly concerned about keeping the Czechs happy, for some reason!)

```
DOCUMENT:          #7280.10.7.1947
DESCRIPTION:       EXCERPT FROM POSTWAR SUMMARY OF KNOWN
                   ACTIVITIES OF R. HEYDRICH
PREPARED FOR:      MUSIL
PREPARED ON:       10.7.1947
```

Heydrich was driven to Ruzyn ĕ Field on Tuesday, January 20th.

He had to fly to Berlin for an important meeting, but it was one of those occasions where he was flying, as opposed to being flown. His driver later recollected that he loaded two suitcases and a valise into a Fieseler Storch, a bug-looking light utility plane. Then Heydrich strapped himself into the pilot's seat, taxied onto the bleak frozen runway, and took to the sky.

He reportedly landed in Berlin a few hours later, where a luxurious grey Mercedes awaited. He was driven to a stately grey mansion next to a frozen lake in the Berlin suburb of Wannsee.

A set of minutes from this meeting recently came into the possession of Robert Kempner (who was recently one of the prosecutors at the International Military Tribunal in Nuremburg). Based on these, and on clandestine interviews with other participants, it has been possible to assemble a relatively detailed account of that meeting.

The attendees consisted of thirteen of Germany's leading bureaucrats; they sat at a long wooden conference table and discussed the fate of Europe's Jews.

"I want to emphasize that these are issues which have already been decided at the highest levels," Heydrich said, early in the meeting. "All that remains is the execution. There are, at best guess, eleven million of them in Europe, of which perhaps only half a million lie in areas outside our control. We have no excuse not to deal with this issue. Since emigration is not an option…" He shrugged. "There have already been great efforts made. But so far, everything has been very ad hoc. Especially the disposals. For our troops, doing this work face to face has been…" (One attendee recalled that here he made an ugly face.) "But there are better ways to go about this. Like all cleaning, there must be a system to it. So we will cleanse Europe, from West to East. In the course of this final solution, they will be allocated for labour in the East. This way, we will at least put them to some use. The able-bodied ones, separated by sex, will be put to work building roads for us. And a large portion of these will presumably die of natural causes, which will of course make our work easier. Now, unfortunately, natural selection and the survival of the fittest dictate that the remainder will be the most resilient and survivable strains. If they were released, it would be a disaster, for they would doubtless act as the seed of a new Jewish revival. So this most resistant portion will have to be…" Heydrich looked around the table, into every set of eyes. Heads bobbed, understanding. (These sources, and others who worked with Heydrich, made it clear that he would often neglect to finish his sentences, but still trail off in a way so as to make his intentions clear to the listener.) "At any rate, we won't leave this problem for our children and their children. How irresponsible it is, to pass large problems off on the next generation, rather than simply dealing with them! So we will bequeath to them, as our greatest gift, a Jew-free Europe. It will be a final solution to this problem. And one hundred years from now…" (Here, according to one participant, he gave a hopeful shrug.)

Then the meeting devolved into details and mundane minutiae. They discussed various criteria for special handling, including those deemed racial half-breeds, and those who had served in the Great War. Some of the participants reportedly fought off sleep.

After eighty-five minutes, though, it was over. The fourteen men stood and shook hands and left the room. Someone put on a phonograph of Mozart, and a domestic servant came around with a tray of cognac snifters.

Lest one think Heydrich was a mere paper-pusher or transmitter of orders, though, it is useful to look at the "cleansing" he had already facilitated by this stage of the war.

As Germany's armies advanced across Poland in 1939 and again across the Soviet Union in 1941, they were followed by SS Action Groups [Translator's Note: "Einsatzgruppen" in German] that were directly subordinate to Heydrich. Based on testimony from those few individuals who witnessed them in operation and lived to tell about it, their "Actions," repeated ad nauseum at various locations in Eastern Europe, usually unfolded as follows: First, a group gathered Jews at a designated assembly area. They then marched them in smaller groups to another site, often a large open pit in a silent pine forest. Here, the smaller group was lined up at the edge of the pit facing away from the men who brought them there. They had been brought in at intervals, and the pits were usually several kilometres from the assembly areas, so the most of the Jews were not able to clearly hear what had happened to their predecessors. But if they were in any group but the first, they could look into the pit and see the bodies of those who came before, often half-covered by a layer of sandy, bloody soil. If they were lucky, the last thing they heard was the crack of the rifles.

In all of Heydrich's various Action Groups, there were perhaps three thousand men. While the groups were in operation, it is estimated that they killed a million and a half people. At one location alone, a gorge known as Babi Yar in the Ukrainian S.S.R., the men of Police Battalion 45, Action Group C, killed 33,771 people over the course of only two days in late September of 1941.

Oddly enough, such killing proved too psychologically traumatic for the killers. All but the most hardened psychopaths eventually could not bear the sight of rifle bullets tearing apart silent victims. Sometimes such crimes destroyed the killers nearly as thoroughly as they destroyed the victims. Even Himmler had problems with it; according to witnesses, he "turned green" and nearly became physically ill the first and only time he witnessed a mass execution.

Heydrich, meanwhile, kept himself updated about the progress of the killing, sending and receiving reports via telex and radio, exhorting his men to greater and greater efforts. And since no records exist of many of his conversations with Hitler, there is some debate as to which man was more responsible. No one doubts that both men approved, but no one knows if it all happened because Hitler pushed or because Heydrich pulled.

And yet even in Heydrich there was maybe a longing to be something else. Despite the grey uniform, he kept trying to play the white knight: the dashing sportsman and fencer, the fearless aviator. While his men were getting their hands dirty on the ground, he spent as much time as possible flying Messerschmitts in combat alongside ordinary fighter pilots. He never shot down any Soviet fighters, and he destroyed one aircraft and damaged another through his own negligence. Presumably (given the time-consuming nature of his other duties and the difficulty of maintaining flying proficiency on such a limited schedule) he was of dubious usefulness in a front-line squadron. Yet none of the men who flew alongside him were about to tell the most dangerous man in Germany that he couldn't do something. Only two people in all Germany could do so—Hitler and Himmler. And Himmler only forbade his ablest subordinate after an incident that reportedly raised more than a few eyebrows.

While flying a combat mission, Heydrich was shot down. By purest chance he neither died a German hero nor lived unmolested to fly another day. Instead, what ended up happening was perhaps the worst possible outcome for him. He crash-landed some distance from the foremost German troops. As it happened, he was rescued by members of one of his Action Groups. When they reached the wreckage of his plane, they helped him unstrap himself from the cockpit. But after shepherding him back to their command post, they were bewildered. They sent a message to the rear reporting that they had saved a downed pilot who has apparently suffered a bump on his head and become disoriented, as evidenced by the fact that he kept loudly insisting he was Reinhard Heydrich.

```
DOCUMENT:    #47
DESCRIPTION: NARRATIVE OF J. KUBIŠ
PLACE:       ŽIŽKOV, PRAHA, OCCUPIED CZECHOSLOVAKIA
DATE:        19 JANUARY 1942
```

One expects great things from a mission such as ours. Excitement, energy. The thrill of doing battle at last. Instead we spent most of those early days cooped up. Nowhere to go and nothing to do.

A couple days after our arrival, a friend of HAJASKÝ's came over. He took Josef to a doctor who gave Josef a poultice and didn't ask too many questions. But we could not get much else done until his foot was fully healed and we had reliable identification cards. According to the doctor, the foot would take a few weeks. He also promised us medical waivers excusing us from factory work so we'd be able to roam the streets during business hours. But given JINDRA's attitude, there was no telling about the other identification cards. So we spent the next few weeks rotting and rusting in HAJASKÝ's flat.

Usually we woke up to the front door closing as he headed out to teach. I would then take some exercise. Usually I did sit-ups and push-ups in the cramped living room, taking care not to bump head and elbows on radiator and furniture. Josef's toe kept him from participating. It burned him up, being cooped up. He would have paced the room in frustration, if he could have.

For meals we did what we could with the meagre contents of the cupboards. Stockpiling food was illegal, but HAJASKÝ said most Czechs squirreled away what they could, especially flour and sugar. Heartier fare was harder to come by. One day we got bored and started experimenting, baking crude failures that vaguely resembled loaves of bread. Soldiers forced to play house. When our host came home he laughed at our ineptitude and choked down a few blackened chunks as a courtesy.

Fortunately HAJASKÝ's wife and son soon returned from the country. She was well used to rationed living and proved to be an ace at stretching limited ingredients into delicious meals. It seemed as if she could make a goulash and dumplings out of thin air. We later found out that she obtained many things using black-market ration coupons.

Occasionally they entertained guests. We were introduced in the vaguest possible terms. But thanks to this trickle of visitors, and occasional helpers like the one who had had helped us find the doctor, we gradually got a better sense of our countrymen. While it seemed most shied away from active resistance, nearly everyone lived in defiance of the law at some level. By German reckoning, most were criminals, even if their crimes were as small as storing up unused cigarette ration cards and trading them for food coupons. Or calling in sick for work frequently. Or sheltering people without reporting them to the police, like HAJASKÝ and his wife were doing with us.

The risks they took were never far from our minds. Simple hospitality put their lives in danger. But if it caused them any worry or trouble, they never let it show. HAJASKÝ never said a word.

Some time in January, there came a knock on the door.

It was a snowy day. I was eating and listening to the radio. Outside everything was fuzzy and hazy and cold. HAJASKÝ and his son were at school. Where was the school? I realized I didn't know that, even. The man knew how to keep his mouth shut. The woman had stepped out to run some errands. Leaving Josef and I alone.

So when the knock came, a thought popped into my head that we'd been set up. It was not a rational thought, but who else would be coming by? My automatic was by the radio, which was tuned in to the BBC Czech Service. I left the radio on. If I was arrested, listening to the BBC would be the least of my troubles. Also, it covered the sound of my footsteps.

I padded to the door and peered through the peephole. Saw a single man in civilian clothes. No one bad would have come alone. I uncocked the automatic and unlocked the door.

"Hullo?" I half-opened the door. Presented a smiling face but kept the gun hand hidden.

"JINDRA sent me to talk to you. May I come in?" the man asked. Another severe man, like JINDRA and HAJASKÝ. The occupation had driven the humour from everyone's face. Or maybe just the faces we were likely to meet.

"How do you know I'm the one you're supposed to talk to?"

He leaned close. Whispered. "Who else would be listening to the BBC Czech Service and answering the door with an automatic?"

I dropped my pistol hand from the door. He must have heard me uncock it. Now he looked at the gun as disinterestedly as if it were a loaf of bread. I shrugged. Opened the door further and let him follow me in.

Josef emerged from the water closet, by way of the kitchen. He looked down at my pistol and up at our guest.

"Greetings. JINDRA sent me," the new man said to him.

"I apologize for the reception. My friend lacks social graces."

"I don't mind," our guest said casually. "It shows he's on his toes. You should turn the radio down, though. I could hear in the hall. Lord knows what your neighbours are like. If they can hear it, they might do a lot more than rap on the walls."

"JINDRA really sent you?" I asked.

"You sound surprised."

"I got the sense he didn't want us here, didn't want to help us, and didn't trust us."

"Don't take it personally. No one trusts anyone these days." Our guest started to poke his nose around the flat like a prospective tenant doing a walk-through.

"So we've been told," Josef said. "What are you doing?"

"Having a look around," the guest said. "First thing you should do when you go somewhere new."

"Have a look around for what?"

"An escape route. Or people with guns."

"Oh. Sorry." Realizing I still had the pistol in my hand, I tucked it into my waistband.

"Don't worry about it." He nodded at my pistol. "That's about the only thing I trust these days. That, and the Bible."

"The Bible?" I asked. Maybe this man had a sense of humour after all.

"Why not? These are dangerous times, my friends. The abominable and destructive presence is standing on holy ground. Let the reader take note!" Our guest poked his head into the master bedroom, nodded, and turned back to us. "Let's have a smoke, shall we?" He walked past us into the living room, turned the radio down, and pulled off his gloves. On one of them, there were four cross-stitches, and on the other, three single stitches.

Josef gave him a strange look. "What are the stitches for?"

"Four Germans killed, three wounded," he said simply. "I have no illusions about my ultimate chances for survival, but if I can take a few more of them with me, I'll at least know I put my time on earth to good use." Now he pulled out a pack of Memfis and lit one. Finally I noticed that his left ring finger was missing.

I said nothing. But maybe my face did.

"This?" our visitor asked, holding up the maimed hand. "It's a strange social etiquette with things like this. Everyone wants to know what happened, no one wants to ask."

"What happened?" Josef asked.

"Well, I don't usually care for storytelling, but this one you need to hear. I lost it last year, when they tracked down the SPARTA II transmitter." He took a deep drag. Blew two smoke streams from his nose. "We were transmitting from a flat in Smíchov. Intelligence reports, updates, things of that sort for London. And suddenly our window man gave the signal that the Secret Police were on their way up. Now, we were mid-transmission, red-handed, stuck in a third-floor flat. So one of my companions stayed at the front door to trade shots with the Germans and buy us time to get out. The only problem was, we didn't know how to get out."

"But you got out."

"We slid down the drainpipe like it was a fireman's pole." He raised the hand with the ugly gap. "This happened on one of the brackets."

Josef and I winced.

"So my lesson for you is: find your escape route on the way in, so you won't have to look for it on the way out."

"That's a good lesson," Josef conceded.

"It was. Fortunately for me, I'd slid nearly all the way down the pipe when this happened. So I landed hard and limped away, bleeding. I wrapped a handkerchief around my hand. We could hear shots from upstairs but we didn't look back. I thought about ambushing them on the way out, but in this line of work, that's often the worst thing to do. So there's another lesson for you. Don't fight when you don't have to."

Josef nodded. Took a drag. "Do you wish you'd stayed and fought?"

"Every time I think about it. Even though I know I did the right thing. Still, there was another lesson that we almost missed. We saw a bread lorry parked out front with someone in the back. The kind a bakery might use to make deliveries to businesses. It hardly seemed important."

"But it was?" Josef asked.

"But it was. You see, it was about ten o'clock at night."

"And?"

"No bakery makes deliveries that late. As it happened, I didn't see the lorry again for some months. But I did see it again." He paused, puffed. "It was early October. I was on my way to a flat, to SPARTA I, and I heard that little whisper, the kind you hear when God wants to get your attention. The voice just said something was wrong. So I stopped. And I saw the van and remembered where I'd seen it before. And I just turned and walked away." He ashed, smoked. "Anyway, that was the night they took down SPARTA I. So pay attention to the little things."

"How did they find them?"

"They have radio direction finders. Very sophisticated. They can disguise them in commercial vehicles and prowl around the city, narrow you down to a block or so, and then they'll send out men with portable units on their backs to find the exact flat. They have a lot of ways of finding you."

"So this isn't a safe game," Josef said.

"No. Which is why I have to trust the pistol. I'm not going to Peček Palace. And I'll do whatever it takes to avoid it, but first I'm going to take as many of them with me as I can. The number of rounds I have, that, minus one, is the number of them I'm taking with me." The stranger finished smoking. Stubbed out his cigarette. "And now, I have two pieces of business here. One is to get photos of you two for your identification cards."

He dug into his knapsack and pulled out clothes. Which he unfolded to reveal a flashbulb and a camera. Deftly, he screwed everything together. Motioned for us to stand in front of a white wall. A few quick snaps and flashes and it was all done.

"What's the second piece of business?" Josef asked.

"A message. Memorize this. On Friday, one of you will go to the cinema off of Wenceslas Square for the 12:15 show of that propaganda movie."

"Which one?"

"The Jew Süss. There will be a man in the rightmost seat of the front row. Sit next to him, and he will take you somewhere important."

"Somewhere important?"

"This is of vital importance to the success of your mission. Trust me."

"Why should we?"

"Haha!" he said. "You're paying attention. For starters, I'm an officer. A captain. When we had functioning transmitters, my dispatches went directly to MUSIL. These other people…"

"You don't know what our mission is, do you?" Josef said.

"I know enough. A fair number of people know that you're here now. Far more than ideal, far more than you would like, I'm sure. And many of them are glad you're here. But still, there is talk, which is of course not good. Anyway, I know you're here to get one of them. Someone big. And that's all I need to know. And again, I'm a soldier. Not a civilian like these others. For me, it isn't even a question of helping or not helping."

"But…we don't even know your name!" Josef said. "What is it?"

"You can call me OTA," he said.

"That's my name!" I exclaimed.

"No it isn't. And it's not mine either, but somehow we both ended up with it. We need something else to call you. A code name instead of an alias. NAVRÁTIL, that would be a good code name." He smiled. "Anyway, my name, it is nothing. Does it matter what we're called? What matters is what we do."

A dim cinema.

Only three other people in the rows. Two lovebirds and a drunk. But no one in the right front seat. Anxious, I took my place and settled in.

As the room faded to darkness, an announcement flashed on the screen: "We kindly request the audience to refrain from loud comments during the newsreel. Thank you." The newsreel began with a shot of civilians lined up on a snowy street, carrying jackets, boots, sweaters and the like. "The Czech people turned out in great numbers over the past month to generously donate their warm winter clothing to the German Army's 'Winterhelp' program." Another shot showed the same civilians inside, handing bundles and baskets to a smiling clerk with a swastika armband. A woman was burdened down with furs, mittens and a pair of cross-country skis. In front of her, a well-dressed man literally gave the clerk the coat off his back. "These donations have greatly helped the Wehrmacht in its noble fight against the Bolshevist hordes." As if it was all part of the plan, to send the Wehrmacht into Russia with only summer uniforms. Now the screen showed German soldiers laughing and joking as they tried on their new clothes. A hodgepodge of smiling infantrymen with striped sweaters, and a particularly absurd chap with a fur-lined vest. I laughed aloud.

"Careful," a man said as he settled in next to me. "They'll kick us out without a refund." No sooner had he sat than he stood back up. Looked right at me. "On second thought, I need to use the water closet."

He left, and I followed a minute or so later.

The water closet had heavy marble partitions and a sink that looked like it weighed a hundred kilos. Glaze cracked and crazed. Rust stains trailing from the fixtures to the drain. My new friend was a tall, beefy fellow with blonde hair and pink baby cheeks. He looked under the partition of the toilet stall. Then he stood and washed his hands.

"I'm sorry I didn't arrive earlier." He dried his hands and looked at me in the mirror. "I have a hard time not laughing at their newsreels, too."

"So what's this all about?" I asked.

He shrugged. Chuckled. "I was hoping you'd tell me. I should have known better. It's best for all of us not to know too much. All I know is, the man I work with told me to give you these." He wiped his damp hands on his pants. Fiddled in his pockets and produced a set of car keys.

"OTA?" I asked.

He shrugged. "Maybe."

"And you are?"

"Call me REHAK," he said. "More importantly, the car. It's a black Tatra, parked about a block and a half down Water Street, whatever the hell they're calling it these days. Apparently there's something for you hidden behind the seatback. Take it to where you're staying, park it somewhere where you won't be observed, and take what's there for you. Then drive it back here and leave it parked with the keys in it."

"You don't even know what's in there?"

"Your guess is probably better than mine. I wasn't told, and I was told not to look." He dropped the keys on the heavy porcelain sink, patted me on the shoulder, and left.

I left the cinema after a couple minutes. Looked again at the ridiculous movie poster with its big red letters: Jew Süss. Under it, a green-faced Jew, with evil yellow eyes. Maybe the Jew Süss was jaundiced. Absurd. Next to it was a poster for the new Vlasta Burian comedy. Business as usual. Also absurd.

I stepped outside. Blinked hard against the cold noon sun. Found the car. Drove like a nervous old woman down the frozen streets back to HAJASKÝ's.

Behind the seat I found various items wrapped in waxed paper as if by the butcher. Familiar items, I could tell by the feel. Boxes of ammunition, grenades, and our two disassembled Sten guns.

"Why do you think OTA did it that way?" Josef asked.

Another wasted afternoon. A dead empty Saturday. After the cinema business the day before, we had unstapled the upholstery at the bottom of HAJASKÝ's couch and hidden the weaponry up among the slats and springs, but that had taken all of fifteen minutes. Not even enough excitement to last until supper. And now we were back to bored. Routine so monotonous it was difficult to imagine a different future or remember a different past.

"The same reason everybody does everything here," I said. "So no one knows everything, and a lot of people know almost nothing." (As a soldier I was not used to this logic. It was odd. Keeping secrets from friends as well as enemies.)

"This means we have to start planning," Josef said.

"How's your foot?"

"We have to start planning. MUSIL said we should get bicycles for when we scout out locations. If I'm on a bicycle it should be fine."

"But the weather…"

"The longer we wait, the riskier it gets for us. Even OTA had a sense of what we're up to, and we'd never talked to him before. Which means a lot of other people must be chattering."

"Like who?"

"These people who have visited and helped us, that doctor, the people back in Nehvizdy…who knows? We've rubbed shoulders with a lot of people."

"Shouldn't we wait for our identification cards?"

"I don't know if JINDRA's dragging his feet on them. He might want us to stay cooped up here doing nothing."

"We got our weapons back," I pointed out. Not that I agreed or disagreed about JINDRA. That was just how we worked. Taking turns as devil's advocate.

"We have them because of OTA. JINDRA said we'd get our identification cards, but we still don't have the cards."

I nodded. Now we'd both said our piece and it was time to think more. I retired to HAJASKÝ's room to read the Bible. Like the good simple Catholic Slovak he was, Josef loved his Rosary, but the Evangelical in me found the Bible more practical. A break from the day's monotony, rather than an enhancement. Besides, there wasn't much else to read, and after talking to OTA, I'd gotten curious. I'd long been a believer, but I wasn't very knowledgeable in my beliefs. God was sort of like a good-luck charm, a vague figure one would pray to for that extra bit of fortune. So I'd returned to the half-remembered book. I'd started by playing Bible roulette, but that wasn't satisfying. God was a bit of an ass in the Old Testament. Seemingly more human than most humans, always rewarding friends and punishing enemies. Almost insecure. So I'd gone to the Gospels. There was a God in whose image I'd like to have been created. And yet Jesus' teachings always alternated between comforting and jarring, ancient and relevant, indelible and impossible: The truth will set you free. My kingdom is not of this world. Offer no resistance to evil.

A key in the door. HAJASKÝ coming back unexpectedly from wherever he'd unexpectedly gone. You know neither the day nor the hour the master will return to the house.

"I saw the Realm-Protector today," he said in the kitchen. Snowflakes melting into the shoulders of his woollen coat.

"You saw the Realm-Protector?" Josef asked. Incredulous and interested. "Where was this?"

"Across the river. Beneath Hradčany."

"What, just walking around?" Josef asked with a chuckle.

"No, in his car. But it was just him and a driver, strangely enough. Why, does this interest you?" HAJASKÝ asked.

"You brought it up," Josef pointed out.

"I spoke to JINDRA as well," HAJASKÝ said.

"Does he have our identification cards?" Josef asked.

"He said OTA will have them for you in a few weeks. In the meantime he wants you to start switching residences. It will be safer for everyone," HAJASKÝ said. "Seeing people coming and going unexpectedly, neighbours start asking questions."

"Have the neighbours started asking questions?" Josef asked.

"I've gotten some looks," HAJASKÝ said. "Better safe than sorry these days."

DOCUMENT: #4232.17.07.1941
DESCRIPTION: U.K. FOREIGN OFFICE MEMORANDUM PRESENTED TO A. EDEN RECAPPING THE HISTORY OF FOREIGN OFFICE DEALINGS WITH THE CZECHOSLOVAKIAN EXILE GOVERNMENT AND ASSESSING THEIR CURRENT PRIORITIES
OBTAINED ON: 23.07.1941
BY: FRANTA

Sir:

In dealing with E. Beneš, the titular president of Czechoslovakia, the Foreign Office must first and foremost be cognizant of the fact that he was, until relatively recently, a private citizen. While his recent history is a matter of public knowledge, it is worth recapping here, in order that the Foreign Office might maintain an appropriate policy towards his quasi-legitimate government.

After Munich and his fall from power, he had faded into semi-retirement, having gone to America and accepted a post teaching sociology at the University of Chicago. When the Germans occupied the remainder of his country, though, a core of men from Czechoslovakia's intelligence service fled to London with the assistance of the British Government. Based on their previous track record of successful intelligence operations inside Hitler's Germany, we provided them with material and financial assistance. It is believed that, at around this time, the head of their intelligence service, one Colonel Frantisek Moravec, wrote to Beneš and placed the organization at his service.

At this point, the once and future president made his way here via steamer, arriving in July of 1939. He announced that Munich and everything after had been coerced by force and was therefore illegal. (Including, by implication, his resignation.) Still, given the understandable reluctance of other governments to recognize his exiled government, he was in a shaky legal position—arguably no different than, say, the head of a criminal syndicate.

In an effort to shore up his credibility, he undertook a variety of diplomatic initiatives. Upon the outbreak of hostilities in September, for instance, he travelled to France, where he established the Czechoslovakian National Liberation Committee and apparently met with some successes in his efforts to engage the Daladier government. Notably, they reached an agreement on 2 October 1939 allowing for the organization and re-establishment of the Czechoslovakian Army on French soil. He apparently had little confidence in the Daladier government, however, and returned to London within a fortnight.

Unfortunately for him, though, Mr. Chamberlain's Government did not accord him the same privileges as had the French. As far as our country's leaders were concerned, Beneš was still a private citizen, an ordinary man. (In fact, he was living in an ordinary house, his nephew's house at 26 Gwendolyn Avenue, Putney, London. It is a simple red brick house, scarcely different from its neighbours. In fact, to make it stand out, President Beneš hung a large bright red white and blue Czechoslovakian flag from the second floor window, obscuring the view from the living room.)

His situation, of course, changed dramatically as the war started in earnest with the fall of France. At this point, as the Foreign Office decided to establish relationships with the various exile governments that had arrived on our shores, it became apparent that President Beneš was the logical person for us to deal with. It was no longer to our advantage to treat him as an ordinary man. Our various ministers and officials started carving time out of their schedules for him.

Once the Blitz began, his situation received an added boost from a random—and for Beneš, fortuitous—act of war. In the course of the German raids, a bomb happened to land on Gwendolyn Avenue—a bomb that happened to be a dud.

Given London's increasing danger, and Beneš' increasing importance, the Foreign Office saw fit to arrange for him to move to a manor in the country not far from France's General de Gaulle and Poland's General Sikorski, a change of venue that has placed him on a more or less equal footing with those other exiled leaders, in terms of status and recognition.

We have undertaken these measures in the hopes that the respect and attention accorded to the members of the Czechoslovakian government-in-exile will translate into increased respect and authority among their fellow exiles. We do, however, expect greater efforts on their part towards our common war goals.

It is expected that President Beneš will press for a formal recognition of the legitimacy of his government-in-exile, a formal repudiation of the Munich Agreement, and the re-establishment of Czechoslovakia within its pre-Munich borders upon the eventual end of hostilities. We must not give him all of these things at once; it will perhaps be more useful to hold off, as a means of encouraging his country to greater efforts on behalf of the Allied cause.

Prepared for the Foreign Secretary by: E. Holmes

```
DOCUMENT:    #47
DESCRIPTION: NARRATIVE OF J. KUBIŠ
PLACE:       PRAHA, OCCUPIED CZECHOSLOVAKIA
DATE:        7 FEBRUARY 1942
```

During those boring days in February, I found myself thinking back to last fall, and the chain of events that sent us here.

When I found I was going on this mission, we were finishing the parachute course at RAF Wilmslow. (We lived in long draughty barracks. Metal frame beds lined the sides of the cavernous room. Black iron heating stoves stood in the centre, with chimney pipes like pillars. Every day during the course we swept and mopped the floor. Once a week we waxed. These barracks were not old but already the floors were so smooth that you could probably run your hand from one end of the room to the other without getting a splinter.)

It was a Saturday. It did not feel much like a Saturday. (There are no weekends in war.) Already the floors had been waxed and we had been fed. We'd filed through the squat cinderblock mess hall where they ladled lumpy mashed potatoes, slender meatloaf slices, and tepid green beans into the metal tray sections. (Hurry up and wait. Then mediocre food, but not enough. Armies are all the same.)

Now we were enjoying a sliver of personal time. Some were shining boots and rooting through foot lockers. Many of the Brits were gambling. Dice and cards. (Soldiers crave action and trouble more than most people, even if for most it is a silent secret desire. When these things aren't issued, many will manufacture them.)

Josef Gabčík, Honsa Klouda and I were playing mariáš when I glanced out the four-paned windows and saw a black Austin staff car pulling into the lot. Cinders crunching under the tyres. A Czechoslovakian captain got out. Walked to the front door and called out: "Gabčík! Kubiš!"

His tone of voice said the game was over. Josef raked the cards up. A ragged pile of crowns, bells, anchors and leaves. Made them neat and made them disappear. We exchanged glances. We had known each other for a while, and we had already become fast friends, but we were still unused to being mentioned in the same sentence.

The captain, a man named Sustr who would later accompany us on the Halifax that flew us here, walked us just out of earshot from the barracks.

"You've been picked for a special mission. Pack your bags."

"Begging your pardon, sir. I think we're on different teams. And doesn't the course end Tuesday, sir?" Gabčík asked.

"You're graduating early. And they're putting you together. Svoboda collapsed this afternoon. He had a concussion on the last jump, and he was trying to avoid sick call. Anyhow, whoever's behind all this has a bug up their ass about the timeframe. So you two are it."

"Yes, sir," Josef said.

And so, by the pure chance of someone else's bad parachute landing, I was thrown headfirst into our country's greatest undertaking of the war.

Within hours, we were on an evening train to London.

The city was a mess. Blacked-out and bomb-damaged. Once there, Captain Sustr walked us down a darkened blocks to what looked like an ordinary office building.

We were led into an upstairs office where sat a vaguely familiar man in an impeccable three-piece suit. He was tanned and healthy. Balding but vigorous. He reintroduced himself as MUSIL.

Sustr left. The door closed. Silent seconds passed, then: "We want you to assassinate the Butcher of Praha, Reinhard Heydrich. No doubt the radio and the newspapers have told you about the insane, murderous slaughter that's going on at home. Heydrich's responsible for it. He's one of Germany's most ruthless leaders. In our country alone, he's already been responsible for over four hundred executions. Our people are suffering under him, and we need to prove we can return blow for blow."

"Sounds like a worthwhile target, sir," Josef said.

"Yes. I don't mind telling you there was considerable discussion of the matter. A few other candidates were discussed, including Karl Frank and Emanuel Moravec..."

"Who, sir?"

"He's one of the leading collaborators back home, a former colonel in our army, and very active in creating their propaganda. But it was decided that such an assassination, though entirely well-deserved by its recipient, would not be noteworthy enough, given the effort and risk involved." It might be my imagination, but I thought I saw MUSIL make a displeased face. "It is the judgment of all concerned that Heydrich's death will best achieve our ends. Everyone's said you're great soldiers. But for this mission you must be something else. You'll be parachuting behind enemy lines in civilian clothes. By the laws of war, if such things exist anymore, that makes you not soldiers but spies. Any country would be within its rights in executing you. Any country. Germany, England, us."

We sat in silence.

"I know we told you other things in your interview. We had to tell you something big, to see if you could keep your mouths shut."

Josef spoke first. "Mine's probably open more than it needs to be, sir, but usually it just blows hot air. And Kubiš never opens his, so either way, you're covered, sir."

MUSIL gave something approaching a smile. "We'll give you a full briefing later. All I'll tell you now is that you'll be dropped in alone, and you will have to carry out your mission alone. When you go home you will be unable to contact any family or friends, and just as importantly, you are not to contact the resistance. We don't know how badly it's been compromised, and we don't want to find out the hard way. Again, I'm sorry for the discrepancy between what you're hearing today and what you were told. If you want to back out now, we'll understand. But as Masaryk used to say, there is no war without deception and lies."

We sat. Thought.

"I did tell you the truth about one thing. This may be the most important thing our country does in this war. It has been ordered by President Beneš himself."

Again Josef spoke. "I think we're both honoured to be chosen for such a mission, sir."

I nodded my assent. Flush with pride.

The next morning, they deposited us at one of the SOE's Special Training Schools. Land being scarce in England, they had commandeered a variety of manor houses with large grounds, and put said grounds to military use. So we found ourselves being driven towards a stately Georgian mansion situated behind a mirror-smooth pond. All very picturesque, except that the grounds were full of men in camo going to and fro. It called to mind a dollhouse overrun by toy soldiers.

The dirtiest, darkest secret about war, the one absolutely no one ever tells you before you enlist, is that it is often excruciatingly boring.

Much of that training had been tedious. And now in Praha, when one would have assumed that things would at last be interesting, it had inexplicably become even more boring than before.

It did pick up a bit when we first moved, though, in unexpected ways. As it turned out, our second residence was right across the street from HAJASKÝ's flat.

I went over there to check the place out before Josef and I moved. I found myself knocking on a door. Plain, wood-stained. Behind me another door opened. Nervously I spun around. Nobody. An elderly woman leaving her place, moving so slowly I wondered if she'd be able to make it anywhere before night fell. Anxiously, I waited for my door to open. Was I really so eager to get back inside? Even after so much time cooped up? Maybe JINDRA, HAJASKÝ and OTA were rubbing off on me.

Again I knocked. Abruptly the door opened beneath my hand. A red-cheeked man with a redder nose.

"HAJASKÝ told me to come over here," I said.

"Ahh, yes! Come on in!"

Behind him I saw a sliver of kitchen and what looked like three people. "I'm going to get a quick look around, if you don't mind," I said. I added the last as an afterthought but darted around him before he could even nod his assent. Yes, three at the table. Nobody. Middle-aged woman, young woman, teenage boy.

"Pleased to meet you," I think was what the man said once I turned around, but I wasn't really paying attention. I opened the door to my left. The teenage boy's room. Windows opening onto the street. A two-storey drop. Past that door and opposite the kitchen, a tidy living room. Small rug beneath the sofa, framed family photo on the end table.

"My name is…" he started. I darted past him again and found myself in the master bedroom. Windows facing the building courtyard. I looked out and saw a drainpipe. Doable in a pinch, although I wouldn't want to end up like OTA.

"It's good to have you here!" the man exclaimed. The others from the kitchen now stood behind him.

"I'm sorry?" I said, walking out of the bedroom.

"Oh, it's quite all right," he said.

I fidgeted. Opened a door next to me. Still distracted and edgy. "Well, that's good."

"That's a linen closet," he said. "You are?"

"Checking for escape routes."

"You only just got here! Your name, I meant."

"You can call me NAVRÁTIL."

"NAVRÁTIL?"

"You don't have code names?" I asked.

"No. We just have our regular names," the man—whom I will call S., for the sake of this narrative—said with a weary smile. "Well come in. Sit down. Let's relax a little, shall we?" He gestured to the other three, who were standing hesitantly, eyeing me curiously. "This is my wife. My son. And our neighbour." They all introduced themselves. [Translator's Note: Given the circumstances in which this manuscript was written, Kubiš was understandably concerned that those civilians who had assisted him would be identified by the Germans. He simply used the first letter of each individual's first name to identify all civilians who didn't have a code name. Based on subsequent events and testimonials, this conversation presumably refers to his first meeting with Stefan, Marie and Ata Moravec—no relation to Emanuel Moravec—and their neighbour, Anna Malinova.]

I nodded towards the neighbour—we'll call her A.—and she blushed. Maybe I did, too. She was too beautiful to ignore or to look at directly.

"She lives down the hall. She was just on her way out," S. explained.

"Well I could bring some food for dinner, perhaps," she said. "You're one of the parachutists, yes?"

One of the parachutists? I felt uneasy. She somehow knew this, and I didn't even know her. I said nothing.

"We've heard about you."

We? "You've…heard about us?"

"Yes," A. said. "We're very glad you're here."

"If there's anything you need, let us know," M. added. My welcoming committee looked at each other and smiled, like a small cadre of domestic staff pleased to be of service.

"Well, I don't want to cause you any trouble, ma'am," I said. "Just giving us a place to stay is a tremendous help."

"Nonsense," the elder woman—M., for our purposes—said. "You and your friend, you're going to need other places to stay, yes?"

I shrugged. Did not say no.

"I can help you out. I have a telephone. I can get in touch with others who can put you up when it's time to leave here."

"I appreciate the help, ma'am. But we do need to keep this quiet."

"We'll tell them no more than necessary," she said. "They'll know you're from out of town and you can't be registered with the police. That's it. You're submarines now."

"Submarines?"

"That's what we call people who have to stay out of sight."

"Very well," I said. "Once my friend joins me and we get the rest of our identification in order, we'll be coming and going more frequently. We are probably going to have to get some bicycles and keep them here, if that's all right."

"We have a few we can lend you," M. suggested. Important words, though of course I didn't know it at the time.

We ate. Pork and potatoes, set out in porcelain serving bowls. Small servings but delicious. The opposite of the army. Soon after dinner the son excused himself. Gave a look and fled, to his bed with a book. S. had dug out a bottle of slivovitz earlier, and we had been drinking with our meal. Now he and I smoked while the women cleared the table.

"I'm sorry," the missus said as she cleared away my empty plate. So clean it barely needed to be rinsed. "I know it wasn't a lot."

"If you want decent rations, you have to work in a munitions plant," S. chimed in.

"That's how it is these days, eh?" I asked. During dinner we'd discussed other things besides the war and the occupation. The scene around the table had become like a fuzzy picture of normalcy. But now the conversation circled back to our current abnormalities. It was what had brought us together, after all.

"That's how it is these days. The occupation, it is like bad weather. An inconvenience we're all subject to. On the plus side, less food and the same amount of booze means you do get drunk more readily." S. poured himself another slivovitz and then, almost as an afterthought, poured me one.

Behind me, the women loaded up the sink.

"You don't have to stay and help," M. said.

"No, I insist," A. replied.

Here there was some conspiratorial whispering. "Oh, very well," the missus said at last. She wiped her hands off with a dish towel. Turned to her husband. "Actually, you and I should go to bed. You've had a long day."

"I have?" S. asked.

M. bent over, whispered in his ear. He smiled and stood. "I should get to bed. I've had a long day."

They retreated behind the bedroom door, leaving A. and I alone. She poured me a new glass of slivovitz. Then she topped off hers and sat down.

"You're not concerned about the dishes?"

She smiled. "Why, you'd rather I did them?"

"Well, maybe not," I admitted. "So, you live down the hall?"

"Yes."

"With your parents?"

"Alone."

"Well, that's unconventional."

"It used to be their place. They passed on."

"Oh, I'm sorry."

"It's all right. It's been a few years now. What's your name?" she asked.

"My name?"

"I helped make you dinner. I've told you about me. I'd like to get to know you better. You can at least tell me your real name, yes?"

"Jan," I said. Instantly I regretted it. Sometimes guilt weakens your ability to hold things in. It is the most corrosive emotion. And then love, or lust, will push your words out through the rust.

"So where have you come from, Jan?"

"Where have I come from?"

"Yes," she said. "You must have come here from somewhere and for something." As she said this, she leaned forward. Smiling.

"I dropped in from the moon," I said at last.

"From the moon?" She smiled. "How lovely. How did you get there?"

"On a large silver dirigible, with tremendous propellers. It took us several days."

"What was it like there?"

"It was cold and lonely," I said. "There were people there, friendly moon men, but I didn't speak their language, and it took me some time to learn it. They had phonograph records to teach us, with different lessons. "At the Hotel," and "At the Seaside," and so forth, for the different situations we might find ourselves in while there."

"Still, it must have been exciting."

"When I first made it there it was, but I had so few people to talk to that it got lonely quickly. And by the time I spoke the language, it was boring being there. The most exciting thing then was gazing back towards home."

"So you came back out of loneliness." She smiled. Bit her lower lip and twirled her hair. And I was lost. And perhaps drunker than I would have liked. Too drunk for too many secrets.

"My partner and I were sent back here. On a special mission."

"A special mission?"

Abruptly the bedroom door opened. S. half-emerged, half-clothed. "I almost forgot, Jan. You'll be sleeping on the sofa, if that's all right. And you've seen the linen closet already. Good night!"

A. and I looked at each other. Giggled, blushed. Maybe she was tipsy too, at least.

"Well, then. You're on a special mission?"

"Yes. We're…counting the ducks on the Vltava."

She giggled. "That's a lot of ducks."

"Yes. The president is an ardent naturalist. Very concerned about the duck population and how it's holding up under the occupation."

"The president went to the moon with you?" She sounded sceptical but playful.

"He was there already when I got there."

"Do you think it will take a while to count the ducks, then?"

"Oh, certainly. Some months, at least. You cannot count them all in winter when most of them are gone. And along with the counting, there is the studying. Migration patterns, nesting habits. Perhaps…" Here I really reddened. Sipped slivovitz. "Perhaps mating rituals."

To my immense relief, she smiled. Blushed but did not move. "Ahh, yes. They say the ducks are mating more readily these days. What with the war and all." To my surprise and our mutual embarrassment, there now came from the bedroom a rhythmic low pounding. Again A. smiled sweetly. Downed the last of her slivovitz. "Blackout restrictions and curfews at night, there are only so many things for ducks to do."

For the sake of the young woman's reputation, I'll spare the details. Suffice it to say that by the time Josef made it over from HAJASKÝ's, I had moved down the hall, so he had the living room to himself.

On his first morning there, we lugged M.'s bicycles downstairs, desperate to do something, whether or not the weather allowed. Our tyres sliced through slush on the slick streets. At one spot, Josef's bicycle slid sideways and he landed hard on his foot. I saw him wince. Convinced him to lay up and rest a while longer while I scouted out the city on foot.

So he stayed inside and stewed while I walked wintry streets. Making notes of little things. Police patrols. Tram traffic.

I did not like doing such things without a valid ID. Josef was convinced JINDRA had been playing up the danger, to keep us inside and inactive. I wasn't sure.

In Old Town, the city felt claustrophobic. Or rather, more claustrophobic. Looming medieval towers, with steep roofs covered with small tiles that looked like fish scales. Streets and buildings laid down haphazardly over the centuries with no discernible plan. It felt like a different city around every bend. Here a platoon of soldiers marching by. Boots on cold cobblestones. And then a block or two away, children throwing snowballs. (Maybe this was the most shocking sight: I realized that I had not realized back in England that such things still existed here, even now.)

But always I was reminded of why we were here. By the sight of people I'd met, more than anything. Here and there I rounded a corner and saw a familiar face give a knowing nod. Like we had shared secrets. And I realized I had seen them in the rooms, behind closed doors. The doctor that helped Josef. The man that brought our equipment to the cinema. Random reminders. Somehow both comforting and unsettling.

After two weeks, we moved again. Southwest, past the big cemetery with its giant granite obelisks and towering trees and cracked crypts, to yet another family. They had a daughter, a lovely 19-year-old pear whom we'll call L. Josef took a shine to her, and she to Josef.

It was a Saturday afternoon when they reached what might delicately be called the penultimate stage in the getting-to-know-you phase of the relationship.

As he told it to me later, they were together on Josef's bed. (A day before, in what I suspect was an extraordinary bit of crafty foresight, he'd convinced her to move the radio into his room so he could listen for coded messages. Now, on this particular Saturday, he'd turned it on for noise camouflage. First the BBC, but President Beneš' voice came on, and as he told it later, it did not make for a potent aphrodisiac. So he'd tuned into a classical music station.) Presently she was stretched out on her back. He was crouched at the foot like a Mohammedan at prayer. Forehead down, focused. She writhed and gasped and bucked and shuddered.

"Oh, God," she said.

He crawled forward to lie beside her. Still she trembled to the touch. Exhaled, enjoying. Until she heard the front door open.

"Oh, God! My father!" she said under her breath.

"Zdeněk," her father called from the kitchen.

Undergarments, pants, shirts flew to and fro. (Getting dressed gets complicated and comical when it must be done quickly and quietly.)

The father burst through the door to find Josef alone in the middle of the room. According to Josef, L. was standing against the wall behind the door, visible to him but not her father.

"Uh…hullo," he said. Resisted so much as a glance in her direction.

"I just came back from meeting with HAJASKÝ. Somebody named OTA wants to meet you tomorrow. He'll give you the last of your identification papers."

"Good," Josef said distractedly.

"Oh, by the way...Zdeněk. Have you seen L.?"

"She was here just a minute ago."

"Here?"

"In the flat. Did you try her room?"

"I poked my head in."

"Well, she was in there earlier."

Behind the door, L. bit her lip to keep from laughing. (As Josef described it, she was not quite clothed enough to be decent.)

"Are you sure she didn't go out?" Josef asked, somehow staying straight-faced. (Or so he claimed.)

"Her coat's on the coat stand. Anyway, maybe you can answer my question…Zdeněk." He stepped through the threshold and was almost at the point where all would be lost when there came a loud knock on the door.

Josef and the father traded perplexed glances.

"Hullo?" The voice in the hallway spoke perfect Czech. But then again, so do many of the people they send knocking on doors. So the father walked to the front door but did not open it. "Yes?" he asked.

"Do you have a man staying here by the name of Zdeněk Vyskočil?"

Josef signalled to L. to make a break for it. She made a barefoot dash behind her father's back to the safety of the water closet. Confused by the sound and the situation, he turned around to see what was going on. Josef was signalling "No."

L.'s father turned back to the door and said, "No."

"Let me rephrase myself," the voice said. "We know you have a man by that name staying here. Is he here now?"

"No!" the father answered. Still Josef turned and opened the bedroom window, to escape from the devil he knew and the one he didn't.

"Tell him a man dropped by with a message from MUSIL," the voice said, suddenly eager, excited.

Hearing this, Josef stepped back from the cold window. Nodded at the father, who opened the door.

The stranger in the hallway was a blonde handsome man in his late twenties. He stepped in tentatively, smiled. Josef recognized him as Josef Valčik. We'd seen him at training schools in Scotland, and on the airplane that brought us here.

"Zdeněk Vyskočil?" Valčik asked, amused.

"You fucker!" Josef said he didn't know whether to hug or strangle Valčik. "Were you trying to give me a heart attack? Jesus, you're lucky I didn't have my pistol handy."

"Good to see you, too," Valčik said.

Finally Josef opted for the hug. "How did you find us? Where have you been?"

Valčik looked at the father and nodded Josef in the other direction. Josef's host noticed and obliged by going in the kitchen. Still Valčik lowered his voice so the other man wouldn't hear. "We've been in Pardubice. Myself, Potucek, and Captain Bartoš."

"Captain?"

"They promoted him once he got our radio set up and running. It was the first contact London had had with the homeland in some months. We got in touch with MUSIL, and he wanted us to get in touch with you, so they sent me. I don't know what you're up to, but I think London expected some sort of action by now."

"Yes. Well, unfortunately, I injured my foot when we were dropped in, so that's kept us from doing much." (I'm sure Josef put weight on his foot as he said this, just to confirm both his story and his memory.) "And we still don't have our full set of identification papers. We're supposed to get the last of them tomorrow. I think they've been dragging their feet."

"Dragging their feet?" Valčik said—looking down, I'm sure, at Josef's foot.

"I'll admit. We've been much less active than I'd like. Save the occasional distraction."

As if on cue, L. emerged from the water closet wearing a bathrobe. As if to prove to her father she'd been there all along.

"Well, we need new identification papers, ourselves," Valčik said. "That's been holding us up a bit. The Secret Police in Pardubice have been asking questions, so my boss wants us to get new names."

"Well, my partner and I are supposed to get ours soon," Josef said. "So maybe I can get you in touch. I don't know the man's name. He goes by OTA."

"OTA?" Valčik asked "You know him?"

"Yes. Why?"

"We're supposed to get in touch with him, too. Orders from MUSIL. They want a report from him, now that there's a transmitter up and running. They weren't sure where I could find him, though."

"Well, now you know. Lucky you," Gabčík said.

"Lucky you, you mean," Valčik said, with a glance back at L.

An outdoor hockey arena, down by the river.

Crowds of happy people, bundled against the late February chill, assembled to watch an afternoon game. Praha II vs. Podripsko. Stranovice stadium, with its tiers of seats for the proletariat and a building with indoor boxes for the powers-that-be. Germans, puppet government types, and industrialists, or so I imagined. Swastika flags and protectorate tricolours hung limply under the overcast sky. Bold advertising proclaimed the corporate sponsor. ULTRAPHON TELEFUNKEN. Near the top of the first tier, under the overhang for the press box and the upper level, Valčik and I sat in shadows. Pretended to pay attention.

"So you've been well?" I asked.

"Yes. Honestly we haven't been terribly busy. We've set up shop, kept an eye on things, and tried to stay out of trouble. I was working, actually."

The hockey game was OTA's idea. When he'd heard that someone new wanted to meet him, he'd gotten skittish. He only agreed on the condition that we'd meet him in a public place. Never mind the fact that I still didn't have my identification card. So REHAK had come over with two hockey tickets, and OTA had kept a third for himself.

"You were working?" I asked Valčik. Unsure I'd heard him correctly.

"Yes," Valčik grinned. "I had a legitimate job. I was a waiter at the Veselka hotel."

"Working as a waiter? You came…" It was so absurd, after everything, all the parachute training, that I forgot where we were. Finally I lowered my voice. "You came all this way and you were working as a waiter?"

"It was a great place to work!" Valčik said. The two Josefs always reminded me of each other. Genial Slovaks, good soldiers. Funny, friendly. Gabčík's perhaps more hot-tempered and headstrong. Whereas Valčik has a strange reserve about him. As if the friendliness was a way to keep people at arm's length.

"The hotel?"

"Sure. There were a lot of Germans dropping in. Army, Secret Police."

I looked ahead. The nearest other spectators were a few rows from us. "That seems like that would be the worst place for one of us to work."

"Well, like the saying goes, the darkest spot in the room is right beneath the lamp."

"So did you spit in their food, or poison their drinks?"

"Heavens, no!" Valčik said. "I poured their drinks, and lit their cigarettes. They never tipped, though, the bastards."

Below us on the rink, one of Praha's forwards raised his stick and slapped the puck. The goalie reached for it but missed. The crowd stood to cheer, and we tiredly hauled ourselves up for show. Down the side of the arena a little red-faced man manhandled a large metal number-plate into place on the scoreboard.

There came a tap on my shoulder from behind. I jumped with a start. Turned. OTA.

He had apparently come in through another section and walked through an empty row above us, presumably so he could see us before we saw him. Now he stood above us, sceptical. "Who is this man? This isn't your friend from before."

"He's one of us."

"How do you know?" OTA asked.

"I know him personally."

"This is someone you got in touch with here? That you knew from before?" OTA gave me a look as if I'd just strangled a newborn baby.

"No!" I almost shouted. "Sit down, I'll tell you all about it."

Warily, OTA sat.

"My partner and I both knew him…over there," I said. "And he's in touch with them."

"How do I know I can trust him?" OTA asked.

"We were all rigorously screened and selected," I explained. "Everybody who ended up…over there was dedicated enough to leave everything, to be there."

OTA shrugged. "Everyone here was dedicated enough to stay and face everything that's happened."

"I am who I say I am," Valčik responded. Curt, hurt.

Again OTA shrugged.

"Fine. How's this? I'll have…I'll have the BBC read something. A phrase of your choosing, at a time of your choosing, so you can listen in and know I'm telling you the truth. Would that put your mind at ease?"

"It would," OTA said. Now he relaxed visibly. "Enjoying the game?"

"They should pit us against a German team," I said. "I'd enjoy that."

"They don't allow it. Germans play Germans and Czechs play Czechs. Otherwise everyone would boo the Germans, and that would be embarrassing. Or the Germans might lose, and that would be racially unacceptable. I do like hockey, though. The perfect combination of grace and violence."

"He was just telling me about his work as a waiter," I said.

"That sounds like it would be good work for one of us," OTA allowed. I'm sure I gave him a look.

"It was!" Valčik exclaimed. "When you're a waiter, the only time anyone really pays attention to you is if you mess up. So when I worked well, I overheard a lot."

"They didn't stop talking when you were around?" I asked.

"No. They thought I didn't understand. I kept asking them to teach me things in German, and then I'd mangle it badly. So they didn't pay me much heed."

"Playing the dumb waiter," OTA nodded.

"Yes!" Valčik chuckled.

"You might be worth working with after all," OTA said.

"Thank you. Yes, it was a good job. I brown-nosed the brown shirts, waiting on them hand and foot. Sort of like the Good Soldier Švejk, but stupider, and more honest in my obedience. And they'd talk fast, thinking I couldn't understand it, and I'd get material to report back home."

OTA sipped his coffee. Made a face. Blew on it to cool it. "But you're not doing this anymore?" he asked.

"No. We'd gotten identification cards, so…" Here Valčik lowered his voice to the point it was almost inaudible. "Captain Bartoš decided we were going to come back up to the surface, start collecting food and tobacco rations, and declare ourselves with the police so we could live legitimately. And when we showed up on the police list, they randomly decided to turn my name over to the Secret Police. So they showed up at my work. Fortunately, I was off that day, and my employer, God bless him, told them he'd just fired me. Then he got word to me of what had happened. So I haven't gone back. And our leader wants us to get new identification cards now, but unfortunately our old source has dried up. So I need your help. That's one of the reasons I'm here."

"I can get those for you, if you do the BBC thing," OTA said. "I can't make it to Pardubice any time soon, and my camera's broken, so you should probably get new photographs yourselves and arrange to get them to me here."

"We can do that," Valčik said. "There's a photography studio near my old job. I don't think the owner will ask too many questions."

"Very well. I'll handle the rest. Which reminds me." He pulled a brown envelope from his coat pocket. Set it down next to me.

"Thank you," I said.

"You mentioned sending reports to London?" OTA asked.

"Yes. We also have a new transmitter. LIBUSE. So, like I said, we're in contact with them. That's the other reason I'm here. MUSIL wanted me to pass on a message to you."

"Which is?"

"He wants you to see if you can re-establish contact with RENE, whoever that is, and report back. I gather it's rather important."

OTA took a sip of his coffee. Nodded. "It is."

```
DOCUMENT:    #27
DESCRIPTION: PERSONAL DIARY OF K.H. FRANK
PLACE:       HRADČANY, PRAHA, OCCUPIED CZECHOSLOVAKIA
DATE:        22 FEBRUARY 1942
```

It was a rather dreary winter day at the Castle; I remember looking outside and seeing clouds darkening with the hour, but not heavy enough to bring snow.

Heydrich hates meetings, but he'd called one this afternoon; I showed up early and poked my head in. "My Lord?" I said, to see if he was busy.

"Come in. Sit down, please." Heydrich looked over his shoulder but did not turn to face me. Around the small wooden table in his office were typed copies of an agenda that, as it turned out, he had no desire to follow.

I stepped in and closed the door; I figured I'd win points by sitting down and perusing the agenda, but I soon saw it was full of items we'd already discussed. "My Lord..."

"What is it?"

"My Lord, these are matters we've discussed already. The transmitters, Geschke's arrest reports..."

"I know. Don't worry about it. It's not important."

"My Lord?" Now again he was not paying attention; he stared out at the twilight scene. (Ordinarily in those situations, it seemed like he was surveying the lands under his purview, the way the Leader had done at that same window; men of vision must surely spend a lot of time looking out the window, no? But today I had the sense he was just spending some time with his thoughts.)

At last, he asked: "What makes a man turn his back on his race, Frank?"

"His race, my Lord?" (Here again—I must admit!—I was nervous. There is often something accusatory and watchful in his tone. I don't think it was malicious today—perhaps just an indicator of his vigilance against all enemies of the Realm. Still, it sent a chill up my spine!)

"Yes." Finally Heydrich faced me. "Why would a man betray his own flesh and blood? His own race, his own folk…"

"I…I don't know, my Lord."

"One hears of people doing such things for love, so called. Lust, more likely. I suppose in some ways this is an understandable impulse. Lord knows there are other outlets for such urges, though. Perhaps…perhaps money is an issue for such men…"

"Perhaps, my Lord." Something in his voice had softened, but I resisted the urge to relax.

"Still, for a man of good racial stock, to shed his honour in such a manner…" Heydrich leaned back and lit a cigarette. (I'm sure I was surprised; it is a rare indulgence for him, a rare concession to human weakness.) "After all, when is a traitor ever held in high regard? Even to those he works for, he is odious. Look at how the Jews treated Judas. A race of money-grubbers. A race of back-stabbers. But when a man did so on behalf of them, how was he treated? Did they welcome him into their fold, the Pharisees? Did they thank him for what he had done?" Heydrich took a drag and waited.

"No, my Lord," I said. (I think I was glad to at last have an answer!)

"No," Heydrich echoed. "They threw a bag of money at him and said, 'Be on your way.' Barely a 'thank you,' and certainly no comfort in his time of trouble. What end can there be after that, except suicide? When you've betrayed your friends, and your former enemies, seeing your behaviour, do not welcome you with open arms…when you are that alone…"

He was interrupted by a knock on the door.

"Enough talk," Heydrich said. "The hour is upon us."

At the door, two men stood: Geschke and Thummel. [Translator's note: Paul Thummel was the head of Germany's military intelligence detachment in Praha.] Now there was no talk of substance, only cool pleasantries: greetings and questions about wives and children.

The others sat and began perusing the mimeographed papers in silence. Soon Geschke and Thummel looked as confused as I'm sure I'd been. Before they could say anything, though, the door opened. Two Secret State Police agents entered, followed by an inspector named Abendschon.

Neither of them reacted. Maybe by then we all knew what was really happening—the vague outline, if not the details.

Heydrich nodded towards Thummel.

Thummel turned towards his arresting agents; he somehow looked down on them from where he sat. Wordlessly they led him out; I breathed—I must admit!—a tremendous sigh of relief.

```
DOCUMENT:      #452
DESCRIPTION:   TRANSCRIPTION OF MAGNETOPHON RECORDINGS OF
               THE INITIAL POST-ARREST INTERROGATION OF
               PAUL THUMMEL.
PLACE:         PEČEK PALACE, PRAHA, OCCUPIED
               CZECHOSLOVAKIA
DATE:          22 FEBRUARY 1942
```

Notes from Lead Inspector Abendschon:

Due to the sensitive nature of this investigation, it has been decided that, quite contrary to standard procedure, we would do our utmost to generate a clear record of our interrogations of Paul Thummel. Given his own familiarity with the nuances of intelligence work, and his ability to come up with plausible alternate explanations for his activities, we would like to have incontrovertible proof of his statements to our investigators. Should any of his high-ranking patrons question our handling of the affair, we want to be able to prove to them that he has made statements at odds with our factual knowledge of his actions. Towards this end, we made loan of a magnetophon machine from the Propaganda Ministry.

Initial questioning took place in a basement room. Suspect's attitude was generally haughty and belligerent, with no admission of wrongdoing. Transcript follows.

[START OF RECORDING]

[ABENDSCHON] ...schon, and you of course are Paul Thummel, Captain and head of the Military Intelligence Services here. This is an initial questioning on charges of espionage and high treason. What do you have to say for yourself?

[THUMMEL]   Nothing. You're the one that's going to have to explain yourself, to Himmler, once he finds out about this.

[ABENDSCHON] Oh, I don't think so. [Here I held up a picture of a known fugitive, who is believed to be a captain in the Czechoslovakian military intelligence services working underground with their resistance.

Suspect showed no visible reaction.] Do you know who this man is?"

[THUMMEL] Enlighten me.

[ABENDSCHON] He's a captain in Czechoslovakia's military intelligence, which you would have known, if your men were doing an adequate job. But in fact I think you do already know who this man is. In fact, you have met this man. [Here I flipped over another photograph. This one showed Thummel meeting with this Czech outside in a park. They were clearly conversing. Suspect showed no visible reaction.] Do you deny it?

[THUMMEL] Well, it would be rather stupid to deny it now, wouldn't it?

[ABENDSCHON] What do you have to say for yourself?

[THUMMEL] Intelligence work requires one to meet with a lot of people for a lot of reasons. [Suspect shrugged.] I have my reasons.

[ABENDSCHON] And I have your contact logs from November, when we last questioned you, to the present. [Here I reached into my valise and produced several mimeographs.] And on the date this photograph was taken, as well as on several other dates for which we have evidence of you two meeting, your log sheets say, 'No Contacts.' I would love to hear your explanation of these discrepancies. 'Enlighten me,' as you say.

[THUMMEL] You asked me to admit I've been meeting with this man. I've admitted it. And as for reporting it, well, do you think the Czechs have no spies in our organizations?

[ABENDSCHON] Are you saying we have been compromised? That's preposterous.

[THUMMEL] If it was, I wouldn't be here.

[ABENDSCHON] Who are these supposed other spies, then?

[THUMMEL] Within days, I expect to have conclusive proof that a member of Geschke's staff, a closeted homosexual no less, has been funneling information to the Czech exiles in London.

[ABENDSCHON] You expect me to believe such…absurdities? Why would a man do such things?

[THUMMEL] Why do you think? Fear of blackmail.

[ABENDSCHON] And you think Geschke wouldn't know if such a man was on his staff?

[THUMMEL] I think he wouldn't report it, if he has such tendencies himself. And with them spying on us from within, do you think I want it known whom I'm meeting with? Not a chance.

[ABENDSCHON] What is it you're up to, then?

[THUMMEL] Here. I'll use simpler words. What looks to your thuggish mind like treason is in fact one of the most successful double-agent operations in the history of German Military Intelligence. We've had their intelligence service eating out of our hands for some time now. Since before the war, even.

[ABENDSCHON] I don't believe you. I would have heard of this.

[THUMMEL] Believe it or not, it's the truth. Do you think we share our triumphs with the Secret Police? Do you think good spies trumpet such things? [Audible scrape of chair obscured several words; suspect leaned forward somewhat belligerently.] ...the verge of totally shattering what little remains of their networks here. Taking everything down in one fell swoop. I'm talking about all of their most secretive and important agents. This is not the low-hanging fruit or even the higher fruit. We are cutting down the trees. This is the final culmination of years of effort. Years! Dating back to 1937. Tell me, inspector Abendschon. Are you willing to blow a massive and successful counter-intelligence operation, perhaps the most successful in the history of the Realm, based on your thuggish paranoia?

[ABENDSCHON] Tell us about this operation then, if you're so proud of it. Not all of us, just those of us you can trust. Provide us with details, dates. Names. Help us, and we can round up these people together.

[THUMMEL] I might. If you turn off that machine.

[ABENDSCHON] Machine?

[THUMMEL] The one that is recording this conversation. There is a microphone concealed atop the water pipes. If you cut the wires, we can talk freely.

[ABENDSCHON] Very well. Perhaps this can all end well, after all. I'd hate to see any harm come to anyone over a simple misunderstanding.

[THUMMEL] It would be a tragedy.

[SOUND OF CHAIR SCRAPING ON CEMENT]

[END OF RECORDING]

```
DOCUMENT:     #456
DESCRIPTION: OFFICIAL REPORT OF SHOOTING INCIDENT NEAR
              DEJVICE RELATED TO THE ATTEMPTED
              APPREHENSION OF PAUL THUMMEL'S PRESUMED
              CONTROL AGENT.
PLACE:        DEJVICE, PRAHA, OCCUPIED CZECHOSLOVAKIA
DATE:         22 MARCH 1942
```

Notes from Lead Inspector Abendschon:

The incident described herein occurred a month after the arrest of Captain Paul Thummel on charges of espionage and high treason. During this time, our agents held Thummel under house arrest and periodically questioned him on his contacts within Czechoslovakia's military intelligence apparatus. There was some suspicion that he was stalling for time, but he eventually arranged for a meeting with a man whom he said was his contact agent. [Translator's Note: We believe this was a captain in our military intelligence services who is referred to elsewhere in these documents by the code name OTA.]

On 22 March, we deployed eight agents in a park south of the Plaza of the Armed Forces so as to apprehend Thummel's contact on his way to meet Thummel. [Translator's Note: Plaza of the Armed Forces—"Platz Der Wehrmacht" in German—was their name for Benešovo Náměsti, formerly Vítězné Náměsti.] Everyone had been briefed on the physical description of the prime suspect, and all were given the most recent photographs of him with Thummel, and of Thummel with other unknown associates. I was partnered with Walter Buerger.

I stationed myself on a park bench along what was judged the suspect's most likely avenue of approach. Buerger and I had brought newspapers, and bread with which to feed the birds, so as to appear to be casual bystanders.

The appointed time of their meeting was 1900 hours, which would prove important as it was a little after sundown. Many of the casual bystanders and commuters transiting the park had cleared out by this time, and the lack of natural lighting, coupled with the absence of artificial lighting owing to the blackout restrictions, made identification of passersby difficult. It also made our ostensible reason for being in the park less plausible.

Shortly before 1900 hours, I became aware of three men conferring at a park bench not ten metres from me. Despite the fading light, I could see that one was an older gentleman with a moustache, one was a beefy, blonde, florid fellow, and one wore a green hunting cap and carried a valise. I suspected this third man was the man we had previously photographed meeting Thummel, but I could not get close enough to verify without arousing suspicion, and I did not want to draw my sidearm and make an arrest without being sure; I decided it would be best to follow him to his meeting spot to confirm.

We observed the first gentleman giving something to our suspect. They conferred, and the first gentleman left. The larger blonde fellow then got up and headed towards where Thummel had said he was meeting his contact. Our suspect remained on the bench. Buerger and I quickly decided that we would let the first man go, that Buerger would follow the blonde man, and that I would remain in sight of our prime suspect.

After a few minutes, this man, too, got up. He headed in a different direction, and I tailed him discreetly through the park. It was rapidly getting dark, so I had to remain close so as to stay in sight, but I felt reassured, as he had not looked back at me. But I soon realized he had looped around in the park so as to walk past the bench my partner and I had just vacated. When he saw the empty bench, he presumably knew we were following him, so I closed in, intending to apprehend him at last.

Suddenly there was a commotion closer to the Plaza of the Armed Forces, and I heard one of the agents give the apprehension signal. I heard loud shouting, and I was momentarily distracted. It was here that I lost sight of the prime suspect.

It was difficult to make out anyone by this point. Owing to the lighting conditions, one could only see dim shapes moving among the shadows. Occasionally I saw people silhouetted against the blackout slits on the automobile headlamps, but it was still nearly impossible to make any positive visual identifications. I left the park and headed down the street towards the Plaza of the Armed Forces to see what had happened; as it turned out, one of the other teams had apprehended the blonde suspect. They had handcuffed him and were leading him towards one of our staff cars for transport to headquarters.

Suddenly our prime suspect emerged from an alleyway between a restaurant and a tavern on the opposite site of the street. He levelled a pistol at the team that had apprehended the blonde suspect and shot three times.

None of the other team was hit. I drew my own sidearm and fired. The flashes from the suspect's pistol had impaired my night vision, but I saw him turn my way and fire at me. I took cover behind a parked automobile and fired several more shots. It was dark, and I don't think any of these initial shots hit their intended target.

The prime suspect then took off running towards the Plaza of the Armed Forces, where there are several tram stops. I followed him at a run, while yelling for assistance. I squeezed off another shot and thought I'd hit him in the leg, but at this point a tram passed between us, and I also realized I had emptied my pistol.

By the time I reloaded and caught my bearings, the suspect was almost at the tram stop, but from the dim light of the blackout automobile headlamps, I could see that the other teams were closing in. I yelled to remind them that we needed to take him alive.

As the suspect was nearing a tram, one of our other agents shot him in the leg from across the street. There was a considerable amount of tram and motor traffic on the street, though, and we were not able to apprehend him before he pulled himself aboard one of the trams and pulled the doors closed behind him.

Owing to the metal blackout covers on the tram windows, we could neither see nor shoot at the suspect once he was on the tram, but the tram did not start moving, and so we surrounded it. I had made my way around to the front of the tram and had nearly succeeded in forcing the doors open when I heard a single pistol shot from onboard the tram.

I boarded the tram and saw the suspect lying flat on the wood slats. There was a considerable amount of blood and brain matter, and it was apparent he had taken his own life. His pistol was empty; he had used the last round on himself.

Investigating and securing the scene proved difficult, owing to the lack of light. Presently we commandeered several civilian vehicles and removed the blackout slits from the headlamps so as to illuminate the area.

This proved fortunate, for we saw that the suspect had apparently thrown his valise under a nearby car before climbing on the tram. We searched it and found several thousand marks, and some small photographs of the type which might be used to make identification cards. The photos depict men of military age whose identities are as yet unknown. They bear a red ink stamp: Pavliček Studios, Pardubice.

```
DOCUMENT:    #47
DESCRIPTION: NARRATIVE OF J. KUBIŠ
PLACE:       ŻIŻKOV, PRAHA, OCCUPIED CZECHOSLOVAKIA
DATE:        22 MARCH 1942
```

In late March, Valčik was subjected to an interrogation of sorts.

"Twenty-seven." Valčik said simply and firmly. He looked directly at his questioner.

"Twenty-seven?" Gabčík repeated the number, incredulous.

"Too young, or too old?" Valčik asked.

"Too old! Far, far too old!"

We were at L.'s, playing mariáš. Josef, Josef and I. There were three of us, so it was a proper game. But it had degenerated into sex talk. Soldiers are soldiers.

"Are you kidding me?" Valčik exclaimed.

"How many good, unmarried twenty-seven year-olds do you meet?"

"Not many. But it is the best age for a woman. You want a woman who knows what she is doing. Or at least I do."

"It is nice," I allowed.

"The silent one speaks!" Valčik exclaimed. "Is this the voice of experience?"

"Recent experience." I blushed.

"See? Two against one. A little age is best. We want women who know what they're doing."

"Are you kidding?" Gabčík got a little loud, despite the fact that L. was sleeping in the next room. "I want one I can train. One that can't imagine being with anyone else."

"So what age, then?"

"Nineteen."

"Nineteen? Well, you should…" Valčik leaned forward. Got quiet. "That cute little one that lives here, you and her should…"

Gabčík grinned and raised his eyebrows.

"You didn't." Valčik said.

Gabčík blushed. Grinned even wider.

"You did!" Valčik exclaimed. "So both of you, since you got over here, have…I don't believe this. Bartoš and I have been fighting over women and you two…Jesus. Hail the conquering heroes, huh? Like you two are the…advance guard for the armies of Blaník, or something." He looked back at Josef. "Nineteen."

Abruptly the door burst open. L.'s father, trailed by HAJASKÝ. They both looked angry. Gabčík and Valčik burst out laughing.

"It's the authorities! You're under arrest!" Valčik exclaimed.

"Shush, you," Gabčík said. "I've done nothing wrong."

"Oh, there may be no legal basis, but that doesn't stop anyone these days."

HAJASKÝ and the father glared. Gabčík punched Valčik in the shoulder. "Your loose talk will get us in trouble!"

"Ha. Maybe they have an opinion on the matter. What is the perfect…" As Valčik spoke, Gabčík reached over to clamp his hand over the other man's mouth. Valčik leaned the other way, trying to stay free. "…age for a womphmam."

"OTA's dead," HAJASKÝ said.

The horseplay stopped. Both men froze in place.

"Dead?" Gabčík asked.

"How?" Valčik asked.

"I had just met him and was headed back here when the Germans ambushed him. He had to shoot himself to avoid capture," HAJASKÝ said. "I had just given him your identification photos. I'm assuming the Secret Police has them."

"Jesus," Valčik said.

"I spoke on the phone with JINDRA. He doesn't want you to go back to Pardubice. We're going to have to keep you here until this settles down. Maybe change your appearance." From his suitcase, HAJASKÝ pulled two bottles. "Black hair now. And I'd suggest losing the moustache."

Gabčík and Valčik walked into the water closet. Stood in front of the porcelain sink while Gabčík read the instructions on the dye. I observed from the hallway.

"I volunteered to be a soldier. I volunteered to be a parachutist," Gabčík said. "I did not volunteer to be a hairdresser."

"Don't complain," Valčik said. "I'm a wanted man now."

"We're all wanted," I pointed out.

"You may be first on their list, but I guarantee that we'll be ahead of you soon," Gabčík added. He put a hand on Valčik's shoulder. "Bend over."

"Bend over?"

"Yes, I have to wash your hair."

Valčik bent over. "It feels like I'm getting screwed."

"And you would know because…"

"Screw yourself," Valčik said. "No. By all of it. This whole situation. Living at the mercy of our friends and our enemies. Unable to come and go as we please."

"We'll be hitting back soon enough," Gabčík said. Turned on the spigots and scrubbed awkwardly in the shallow sink.

"Your mission?"

"We've got a lot of footwork to do, now that my foot's working. And now that this has happened, I'm wishing we'd gotten an earlier start. You don't believe in fate, do you?"

"No. Not at all."

"Nor do I. I can't think of a more absurd belief, to think that an individual's life is somehow not in their hands. Having said that, I do sometimes wonder if God has written the day for each of us in advance."

"The day?" I asked.

"The day it all ends. Not the contents of the book, just the number of pages. Anyway, this is a good reminder that we don't always know how much time we have. So. Well. Past is past."

"This may blow over yet, this OTA thing," Valčik said. He stood. Towelled his hair.

"Yes," Gabčík said solemnly. "I never thought I'd be glad to hear of another man's suicide. But HAJASKÝ was right. There is a certain…guilty feeling of relief."

"Don't feel guilty," Valčik said. "It was better for OTA this way, too. His end was in his hands."

"Still. I'm prepared to face death. I don't want it to happen, but I've made my peace with it. I pray every day that I may face it courageously. But the other way…they issued us pills. And I haven't made my peace with that."

"In our situation, I think most of our countrymen would see it as a moral act. Protection for those who have protected us."

"The priests always said that was the ultimate sin," Gabčík said. "The only one after which there could be no repentance." He read the label on one of the bottles. Realized he needed a bowl. I darted over to the kitchen and fetched him one. He mixed the components. An ammonia scent filled the water closet. "Careful. It'll discolour your skin if it gets on it." He bent Valčik over the sink to brush the black solution into his hair. For a few minutes, they worked in silence in the cold white porcelain room.

When they were done, Valčik stood to appraise the job.

"It'll take a few minutes for it to set in," Gabčík said. "Then you'll have to wash your hair again."

Valčik closed the toilet lid. Sat. "The Jews, when they were rebelling against the Romans in the first century A.D., they ended up holed up at Masada. They'd been looking to re-establish the kingdom of Israel, but it had failed. They were trapped. Making their last stand.

And eventually it became apparent that they'd have to kill themselves or be captured. But still there was this fear of suicide. So they drew straws. And every tenth person killed the other nine. Then the living drew straws again, and every tenth person killed the other nine."

"A better solution," Gabčík said. Now he took the towel from Valčik's neck and shoulders and looked at the mess he made of it. "The old man's gonna kill me when he finds out."

"Ha! Yeah, he is."

"Shut up, you!" Gabčík looked for a place to hide the blackened towel.

OTA's death breathed new life into our mission.

I have no reason to believe Josef had been stalling or malingering. But the fact of the matter was that we hadn't accomplished much. Mere survival since our arrival. What I had accused JINDRA of: no easy chore. And a bore. And we might have kept on like that. Days turn into weeks and weeks turn into months of their own accord. But OTA's death suggested that we shouldn't wait. Here was a man who had been on the run for months, who knew a lot more about the Secret Police than we did. And where had it gotten him? So while his death had not been good, it served a purpose nonetheless, as a necessary reminder. The end could come at any time. This wasn't news to us, but its urgency was new. Once you're an adult, life isn't so much about learning, but being reminded of old things.

And so, early that next week, we toured the vast stone courtyard outside the Mathiáš gate, atop Hradčany. Our guide was a nervous and shifty man. For purposes of this narrative, we'll say he was a maintenance man named Jiri. A friend of S.'s wife. [Translator's Note: Again, due to the nature of the story, Kubiš seems to have changed details of some characters so as to protect their identities. We have been unable to identify Jiri.]

As we spoke, his hands were in constant motion. Jumping in and out of his pockets, playing with the flaps on his clothing, turning his silver cigarette lighter over and over as if it were a talisman.

"How long will we be out here?" Jiri asked.

"As long as we need to," Josef replied.

I had to admit, I was a little nervous up here, too. In the big empty courtyard there were no shadows but ours. Everything more open than I had expected. (Actually, looking back, I don't know what I expected. When you finally see a place you have heard about for so long, you realize your mind has filled in the gaps in your knowledge. What you knew had been true, but it was also incomplete. And from those bare bones your mind had built a body both complete and completely different from reality. So it had been with Praha, and so it was with Hradčany.)

"Are there a lot of us on the staff?" Josef asked. Meaning Czechs.

"Yes."

"What do they do?"

"Simple domestic tasks. Cleaning and performing maintenance. Keeping the heat on, keeping the clocks set. Fixing things with our golden hands. Anything the Germans deem unworthy of a master race."

"So they treat you poorly."

"Actually, they tend to ignore us, unless we mess something up."

"Good," Josef pronounced.

Off in the distance, Praha spread out beneath us. Folds of land and countless rooftops, bridges over the Vltava, all hazy and distant in the damp spring air. With all that emptiness, I felt naked. Jiri fidgeted. But Josef didn't seem bothered at all.

"Let's make another pass," Josef said.

So we made a slow pass near the wrought-iron fence separating the public from the private. Spines stiff, staring straight, seeking sideways glances here and there. Like when you like a girl in school and you have to concentrate on looking elsewhere so she won't catch you looking at her.

"Who parks in there?"

"All the bigwigs. Heydrich, Frank…"

"Heydrich parks here?" Josef asked.

"Yes. That dark green Mercedes convertible. That's his."

Now Josef and I both looked over. This was of course too important to miss.

"Yes, I see it. Nice car," Josef said.

"He usually travels with just a single driver. Some of the other officials drive in local makes, Tatras and Skodas, but he's not about to be seen in a Czech car." Jiri pulled out his cigarettes and a lighter. Fumbled it and it clattered to the cobblestones and he scrambled for it. "This interests you?"

"Anything you can provide us about what goes on in there interests us," Josef said. "Get your golden hands on some schedules. That interests us."

"For Heydrich?"

"For everyone."

"You want me to pilfer documents?"

"If you can. Or typewriter ribbons, even, if they're getting thrown out. Whatever you can get without getting caught, give it to us. We'll decide if it's useful for our purposes."

We doubled back and went down Hradčany. Down a narrow street that sloped like a toboggan run towards the Saint Nicholas Cathedral and the Vltava. Two- and three-storey residential buildings lined our path.

"Who lives in these buildings?" Josef asked.

"Some of these used to be embassies. The ones up near the top of the hill mostly house German functionaries and Czech flunkies. Lower down there are some regular people. In fact, a woman who's a friend of ours lives near here." Jiri paused. Looked over to gauge Josef's reaction. "This interests you?"

"Maybe."

Had we brought our weapons with us, we could have killed Heydrich that next Monday.

It turned out that the woman Jiri mentioned lived in a painfully immaculate flat directly overlooking one of the streets Heydrich's car used when leaving the Hrad.

Of course, we didn't know that just yet. Jiri brought us to her house in the late afternoon and didn't tell her much. We drank tea and eyed her place like prospective tenants.

"Nice view," Josef said, looking up and down the sloping street. This time of day it was a shadowy canyon.

"Nice view?" she asked, mildly incredulous.

And just then, he showed up.

A single car, just like HAJASKÝ and Jiri had said. Right below us on the street. The dark green Mercedes we'd seen, with the passenger we hadn't, except in photographs. An eagle-beaked nose and a regal air. Self-absorbed authority.

"It is suitable." Josef turned to me. Whispered eagerly in my ear. "Jesus and Mary, I could have spat in his car. We should get our equipment out. Do it tomorrow."

Behind us, Jiri and the woman were looking at us suspiciously. They had to have some idea of what we were talking about. And who else had guessed our purpose by now? HAJASKÝ? JINDRA? I felt the knowledge spreading out from us like an ink stain. No way to clean or contain it. So maybe Josef was right.

"There are lots of Germans in this part of town," Jiri said. "Army patrols, police patrols, SS. It might be dangerous for what you're trying to do." He said this even though he wasn't supposed to have a clue about what we were trying to do.

Again I looked out. Now I saw a squad of troops. Grey greatcoats and pistol belts and helmets. Jackboots on the paving stones. They marched in two files down the sunny side of the street, slow and easy. Lazy, but lazy like a lion in the zoo. Stretching and yawning in the sun because no one is capable of challenging you. As they marched, four army motorcycles with sidecars roared past in the other direction. The noise was almost painful in the cramped street.

"They are everywhere in this part of town," Josef conceded.

Again we traded glances. Less enthusiasm now. Maybe we were thinking the same thing. There would be no chance of survival if we did it here. The first gunshots would summon every German within earshot. And that would be a lot. If they weren't coming through the front door by the time we got downstairs, they'd be close enough that it wouldn't matter. In London, close to MUSIL and far from the appointed time and place, it was easy to say yes to a suicide mission. Here, with that equation reversed, it wasn't. Still, what if this was our best chance?

As we watched, a gaggle of civilians headed down the hill. Heads bobbing like ducks. They were squeezed onto the low cobblestone sidewalks.

"Who are these people now?" Josef asked.

"Members of the domestic staff," Jiri said as he eased up to the window. "Many of us get off work about this time, and there's a tram stop down at the square. That man..." (Here Jiri pointed to someone somewhat distinctive in appearance. For purposes of this narrative, we'll say he had silvery hair.) "...I suspect he's one of us."

"Really?" Josef said.

"This interests you?"

"No." Josef smiled.

A child wandered in from the next room. A tow-headed tyke. He hugged the woman's legs and looked up strangely at the strangers who had invaded his house. She smiled, then turned to us. "Well, my husband will be coming home soon. But do you have need of the place?"

It occurred to me that they would be dead, too, if we did anything, regardless of whether or not they were home when it happened. The child stared up at me and I couldn't look him in the eyes. I looked up at Josef instead. Awaited his answer.

"I like the view," Josef said at last. "But it doesn't suit our purposes."

The next afternoon, Josef and I made our way to the tram stop at Malostranské Nam ěstí. Stared at cheap posters plastered on a wooden wall. Public service announcements reminding people in German and Czech that it was a crime to hide livestock.

"Do you think they have that problem here in the city?" Josef asked. "People hiding cows in their pantry?"

"Maybe they just want to remind us they don't have a sense of humour when it comes to crime."

"If that's a crime, even, we are going to be in a lot of trouble when this is all over," he smiled.

"And the people who've helped us," I added.

Alone we stood. It was a perfect early spring afternoon. Pleasantly cool. Sun so low it made the stones shine golden. We clutched our tickets and clucked at the propaganda.

"This tram stop's not a bad spot, actually," I pointed out. "We can wait here without anyone noticing."

Commuters started arriving. The people we'd seen the day before, trickling down the hill in dribs and drabs. And then the silver-haired man was there.

"Where the hell is the tram?" another man grumbled, not even a minute after he'd arrived.

"Light a cigarette. That always brings it," silver-hair said. "Once you light up, it'll show up just to spite you, just so you have to put it out."

The younger man gave him a look. But still he pulled out cigarettes and lit one. No sooner did he do so than the tram rumbled into view, as if it had been hiding and watching and waiting for this.

"See?" silver-hair said triumphantly.

Irritated, the other man pinched the ember from his barely-smoked cigarette and put it back in his cigarette case. (No one wastes tobacco these days!)

The tram trundled up, sweeping the stones with its long afternoon shadow. Humbly Josef and I climbed aboard and presented our tickets to the conductor. We found spots near the front. Facing each other but silent. Staring over each other's shoulders at nothing. Wondering where we were headed. Watching the white-haired man.

The tram ride lasted longer than I had expected. When the old man started gathering up his things, I nudged Josef. Jostled to the door ahead of him so it wouldn't be obvious that I was following him.

Outside I dawdled. Josef hung back. Still, the old man looked back at us.

We followed him into a sad quiet neighbourhood of tired houses. Missing shingles on roofs, cracked paint on shutters. Streets wide, but shadowy with the lateness of the day. So out of the way that if you didn't live here you had no reason to be here. Again the old man glanced over his shoulder, but now it didn't matter. I nodded over my shoulder at Josef and he walked faster. We accosted our quarry as he fumbled for his keys.

Finally he turned to face us. He spoke tiredly but with an edge of resentment. "Can I help you gentlemen?"

"That depends," Josef said. "Do you work for the Germans?"

The man relaxed visibly. Maybe he'd pegged us as Secret Police. "What of it? Is it a crime?"

"You work at the Hrad."

"A lot of people do," our man said warily.

"We're interested in you. You are..."

"Pavel," he said.

"Good," Josef said cheerily. Forgot to introduce himself. Or maybe he didn't forget. "What do you do, Pavel?"

Pavel told us what he did. (I will, of course, omit the details, but it sounded like he'd be a great asset.

Better than Jiri, perhaps.) [Translator's Note: We believe he is referring to a clock-setter named Novotney, whose duties required him to set clocks throughout the Castle, and thus allowed him unobtrusive access to virtually every room.]

"The Germans are demanding bosses, I'm sure," Josef said when our new friend finished.

"Why do you care?"

"I was thinking of seeking employment there, actually," Josef said, so smoothly even I almost believed him.

"And your silent friend?"

"Oh, him, too."

"You followed me all the way from Hradčany to ask about a job? I find that hard to believe," Pavel pursed his lips.

"Well, what of it? Is it a good place to work or not?"

"I don't believe you're looking for work," Pavel said.

"Suppose we were. Would it be a good place?" Josef said, smiling but mildly exasperated now.

"You really want to know!" The man was surprised and perplexed.

"Yes!"

"Frankly, I'd look elsewhere," the man said. Looked both directions as if to check and see if the Secret Police, too, had followed him. "I hate them. Condescending pricks. If you work on the domestic staff, you either won't be acknowledged, or you'll be treated as a slave."

"Excellent!" Josef grinned. "We'll be in touch."

We were starting to get information. But we had not settled on a site. There was some discussion of joining the domestic staff at the Hrad and accomplishing our mission that way, but the risks seemed too great. We could not guarantee we'd be able to smuggle our weaponry on to the grounds, and more importantly, there was some speculation that they did check backgrounds, which would have caused trouble. If we provided false ones, there was a chance the Germans would check them out, and if we gave true ones, we would be putting ourselves and our families at risk. It seemed a safer bet to attack Heydrich en route rather than trying to gain access to the Hrad.

So on the following Monday, a cool damp spring morning, Josef and I set out on M.'s bicycles.

We pedalled north. Found ourselves on a lonely country road, a high road, absolutely wide open. Trees on one side, but just a thin line. No shrubs or undergrowth. Heydrich lived near here, at an estate in Panenské Březany. And there were no places to hide. Still I felt freer than I'd felt since we'd landed. Under a grey sky and next to a grey road. But exercise and excitement made everything feel crisp and lively. The bicycle was freedom and vulnerability, and both were exhilarating.

"We might not be able to pull it off up here," I said when we stopped for a spell.

"We could pull it off. As for escaping…" He left the conclusions unsaid. This would be a suicide mission, after all. He shrugged. "The people who've helped us, maybe they will be safe."

The bicycles had been MUSIL's idea when we were still in England. He said they were innocuous and easy to get around on quickly. Staking out the road had been his suggestion, too.

"How's your toe?"

"It works. We'll find a spot out here that works. Here. Take the lead for a spell."

Happily I obliged. Pushed off and heard the wet squishy crunch of gravel and grit under my shoes.

Despite the talk, it was easy out here to forget why we were here. To forget there was a war or an occupation. Out here in the empty countryside there was nothing of consequence to prove that everything was wrong with the world. Open fields. Spring wheat pressing up from the dark earth. Clumps of country houses contentedly sleeping through the war in two small towns—Zdiby and Klecany. I couldn't imagine any of it looked any different than it had in 1937.

"Let's stop up there," Josef said.

"Up there" was the first place we'd seen that looked like a halfway tolerable hiding spot. A strand of trees that looked like it enveloped the road for some distance. We got off our bicycles and walked into the woods. Last fall's leaves, softened by this spring's rains, did not complain about being trampled underfoot.

After some minutes, we found our spot. A small rise in the earth not too far inside the wood. There was a slight bend in the road, and it was possible to see anyone driving south to Praha.

Still, when we first saw him from our new vantage point, it was so sudden we almost missed him. There had been traffic here and there all afternoon. Mostly sedans. A couple lorries. Never more than one car at a time, and often five or ten minutes between each. And then, without fanfare or escort, we saw the same dark green Mercedes heading away from Praha, probably going over eighty kilometres an hour. There were swastika flags on the fenders and two uniformed men inside. A driver. And a single passenger. Him.

"That was him. No escort, even out here," I said.

After all the preparation and difficulty, it almost seemed laughable. Josef and I actually looked at one another and grinned. For the first time in a while, I allowed myself to feel hope.

Soon it felt like a new routine.

Josef woke before the sun. Bumped and clattered around in the pitch-black of the living room. L. usually returned to her bed some hours before, which was fortunate, he said, because the noise awoke her father.

"Where the devil are you going?" the father asked once, groggy and blinking and confused.

"I have to count the ducks on the Vltava," Josef replied, and the father nodded and went back to bed.

Meanwhile I usually stepped softly so as not to wake my A. Retraced last night in reverse across the creaky floorboards, undoing the undressing. As I buttoned my shirt I would watch her pale naked back rise and fall in the sliver of light from the washroom door.

By the time I wrestled my bicycle down the narrow staircase and out into the dark city, Josef was waiting. Smoking the day's first cigarette by the white-painted blackout kerb. Buildings loomed black and nearly featureless in the pale dawn. Here and there one saw splinters of light beneath the blackout shades, as our countrymen grumbled and readied themselves for morning shifts at the factories. One by one they emerged from their homes. Congregated at the tram stops. Cigarette embers colouring their dark faces orange. Then the trams rumbled up. Narrow headlamp slits poked feebly at the dying darkness. The glowing cigarettes flew away. Bounced and died in the streets or disappeared down drains. And the men filed aboard. Faceless dark shadows once more.

As the sun came up we pedalled out into the silent fields. By the time we reached the small stretch of wood that encased the sleepy road, it was day, but just barely. Sun shone sideways against the trees. Tinting them orange and stretching their shadows forever along the forest floor. We dragged our bicycles far into the forest and laid them flat, then found our little hollow and nestled down for our lonely vigil. I felt the morning damp soaking through my shirt and suit pants as my elbows and knees and ribs pressed stones and twigs into the soft forest floor.

On Monday we hadn't made it out here until mid-day, but on every morning after that, we'd seen him. The earliest was at 8:39 and the latest at 9:12. Most evenings we saw him coming home. We hadn't seen him on Tuesday evening, but that could have meant he'd stayed late in the city and come home after dark. Today he whizzed by at 9:03.

"Still no escort," Josef said.

"Still no escort," I echoed. "If we take care of both of them…" If we take care of both of them, we might make it back to Praha by the time anybody realized what had happened.

Usually we spoke as little as possible. Which made for long and boring days, since we saw him in the morning and knew we wouldn't see him again for several hours. Today, though, dark clouds gathered. Rain came, cold rain. Soon the grey sky shone silver off the empty road and upon every dead leaf. Then it turned heavy and torrential, and we did not look around but just lay there and felt the ground turn to mud beneath us.

"Hooray. Liquid sun," Josef said with a grin, echoing one of the SOE instructors. Commando bravado. "Reminds me of Scotland."

Scotland. When you know someone well, a single proper noun can call forth a world of memories. Scotland meant trudging up and down dreary bald highland hills. Slate skies bringing the worst weather known to man. Torturous training exercises, land navigation and leadership used as a pretext for general character-building misery.

"I keep thinking of the pear technique, actually," I said.

"Ahh, yes." He chuckled. "The pear technique. It works, doesn't it?"

"Yes, it works," I acknowledged.

We had been in training when Josef had taught me the pear technique. It hadn't been in Scotland, but English weather was hardly better. All day rain, and we'd been soaked to the bone, but now we were waiting for Captain Sustr to pick us up for the ride back to the Nissen huts.

We'd been out on the grenade range at one of the SOE schools. It wasn't a terribly exciting place: three earthen berms and a row of foxholes. One of the commandos had rigged up a rusty car chassis to a motorized winch. Whoever was operating the range just had to flip a switch, and the contraption would pull the creaky hulk across the range. Then Josef or I would step from cover and throw one of the large antitank grenades. The car moved much slower than the one we'd be dealing with, and our surroundings would of course be far different. Still, most military training involves showing you things that are as similar as possible to what you will see later. If you shoot at silhouettes of people for long enough, it doesn't seem as strange when you have to shoot a real person.

"So you really plan on waiting?" I remember asking him.

"I'm trying to be a good Catholic. And there's some things you're not supposed to do. Suicide is one. And that—before marriage, at least—is another."

"Even now?"

"How is now any different?"

"Well, it's wartime," I said. "We won't be here more than another month or so. And when we get there…I mean, we can't really expect anything. And it's not like either of us is going to get married by the time this is all said and done. So why deprive yourself?"

"Who said I was depriving myself?" Josef grinned wickedly.

"Well, what about her, then? Are you just going to…get her to do things? That hardly seems better than just doing everything before marriage."

"Oh, no. Believe you me, I take care of them. Sex is anything that can get her in a family way, that's how I see it. Anything else is fair game. Actually, I think this makes marriage more likely."

"Talk, talk, talk," I said. "So much hot air from you."

"This isn't just talk. I can demonstrate. Practical training exercises."

"I don't want you to demonstrate!" I said. "I guess talk is fine."

"No, I can demonstrate. A pear actually comes in handy for this."

"A pear? You use a pear on them?"

"No, no, no!" He looked over at the grenade range. The sloppy jalopy on its bald tires. He pulled a pear from the pocket of his fatigues. Held it aloft like a conjuror. "But it is a useful training tool."

"What? You had that on you, just in case?" Here I chuckled. "Where did you get that, anyway?"

"Never you mind. This training is important. I had to make sure we had the proper equipment. You see, the mistake most men make is too much pressure, especially in the beginning. These are sensitive pieces of equipment they have." He produced a pocket knife. Cut the pear in half. "You see, you have to be very gentle. Flick your tongue so lightly the seed doesn't come out. This is important! You'd better practice." Josef handed me half the pair, and put the other half up to his mouth and started flicking.

Obliging, I tried to get to work, but now I was chuckling so hard my tongue wouldn't work right. "It's…hard to pay attention."

"Look. If ever there's a time in life when you need to focus, this is it." He went back to work.

Now I was laughing out loud. Abruptly, Josef put up a hand to silence me. I stopped and looked over. He now had his pear to his ear.

"My pear is having a massive orgasm," he said solemnly.

I exploded in laughter.

"She's begging to get married!"

By this point, I was convulsing. My stomach felt like I'd done a thousand sit-ups.

Suddenly behind us someone cleared his throat. Captain Sustr!

Josef and I jumped up. Spun around. Stood up. A cyclone of elbows and knees and pear halves.

"Humbly report, sir," Josef said. "We have finished our training and are ready for practical exercises."

"Practical exercises," Sustr said. Suppressed a smirk. "Actually, we have to get you changed. MUSIL is picking you up. He wouldn't tell me much, but he said to make sure you were looking your best." He hesitated. "I don't know what you two are being trained for, but evidently it's rather important," he added. Trolling for information?

"Evidently, sir," Josef said.

After collecting up our kit, we walked off to the lot behind the Nissen hut that served as range headquarters. When Captain Sustr opened the boot of the staff car, I noticed something on the corner of his mouth and gave him a look.

"What is it, Kubiš?" he asked.

"Beg pardon, sir. It looks like your mouth is bleeding."

"Sorry," he said. Studied his reflection in the passenger window and dabbed at his mouth with a handkerchief. "I had some dental work done a few days ago. Lousy British Army dentists."

Josef leaned over. Whispered. "Maybe his pear wasn't fresh."

Before long, we were standing outside the Nissen hut in our most immaculate uniforms. Scrubbed and fresh and pink-cheeked, aglow with anticipation.

MUSIL came alone to pick us up. Josef and I clambered into the back of the black Austin, while MUSIL took the right front seat. Chauffeur and chief.

We drove down sleepy side roads. Under the twilight sky, houses and trees and horizon melted into one another. Became inky blackness. Nothing to see. Nothing to do but converse.

"Do we know when we're going yet, sir?" Josef asked at last.

"Unfortunately not. We have to borrow a Halifax from RAF Bomber command. It's the only plane with the range to get home and back, but they don't want to give one up." MUSIL could be refreshingly informal compared to other officers. Such as Captain Sustr.

"Well, sir," Gabčík began. "If you want us to work alone when we get there, maybe we should get there on our own as well."

"Get there on your own?"

"Why not, sir?" In the darkness I could barely see Josef's face distort into a grin. "Swim the Channel, hike a bit."

MUSIL shook his head. "We do have a time frame for this mission. The president wants it done expeditiously. And, just so you know, I appreciate the humour. But don't expect the him to laugh at your jokes."

"Expect who, sir?" I asked.

"The president. That's where we're going. To meet the president."

MUSIL slowed the car. In the headlamps' soft glow we saw two Czech soldiers standing next to a wrought-iron gate. One of them opened it wide, and MUSIL nodded his acknowledgment and pulled through. Drove down a long dark drive. Finally he parked and we clambered out. We closed the car doors. The slam was deafening in the country quiet. The dark house loomed above us.

Inside, we walked through vast rooms filled with antiques and dimly lit by old lamps. Even the floors were ornate. Wooden parquet covered with thick rugs. There was an unnatural dark stillness about the place. Like a funeral parlour.

At last we came to the presidential secretary's desk.

"Good evening, Mr. Táborský."

"Good evening, sir," Táborský said, mildly surprised. Glanced down at his appointments calendar. "I didn't see you on the appointment schedule…"

"We didn't want this one written down," MUSIL said. "Just tell him these men are preparing for a long trip."

Táborský poked his head through the heavy oak doors. And Beneš came out. The man who had been helping Masaryk during those years of exile and diplomacy. Those four improbable years that had allowed Masaryk to leave Praha in 1914 as an unemployed professor and member of a rubber-stamp parliament and return four years later as the president of a country he had helped create.

"Come in, gentlemen! Come in!" Beneš beckoned.

Hesitantly we followed him into the study. A dim sleepy room. There were more books than I'd seen in some libraries. Overflowing the bookshelves and rising from the floor in ragged piles.

"Relax," he said. "It's an honour to have you two here. You're the most important people in the room. You are…"

"This is Jan Kubiš, sir," Josef said. "And I'm Josef Gabčík."

"Pleased to meet you," Beneš shook our hands enthusiastically. But quickly he turned solemn. "You know, I've had several proud moments in my political career. I worked with Masaryk for four long years and then stood next to him when our state was born. Then, years later, I was honoured to become president myself." He took a heavy breath. "I did not foresee this situation. It is always depressing, even for a stout-hearted man, to redo what has been done before, especially when that accomplishment seemed a miracle at the time. Masaryk raised an army of fifty thousand before our country was even a country. We have less than a tenth of that. But we must redo what he did, here in this second exile. Having this responsibility, I feel like a father must feel. Proud. Dutiful, but proud. Happy when times are good and sad when they're bad. But tonight I feel…humble." His voice broke. With a handkerchief he dabbed his eyes. "Our freedom will only be won back through your bravery. Through your…sacrifices. And it isn't fair, perhaps, that you young men should have to do such things while we old men stay safe in England. But I suppose war's always an inversion of the natural order…" Now he stopped speaking entirely. Eyes welled with tears. Like we were his sons and he was sending us off to die.

Gently, Josef patted him on the shoulder. "It's all right, sir. We volunteered for this."

I nodded. "We're…honoured to be chosen, sir. We won't let you down."

Good words. But now it was time to make them true. And I'd be lying if I said I was looking forward to it.

On Friday the weather was better. The sun dropped behind Hradčany. Greening hills, high castle walls, and the spires of St. Vitus. All had been solid shapes but became silhouettes. Black cutouts backlit by the orange sun.

We wanted to get back before dark. Not because of curfews, but because it is hard to ride bicycles in the dark. So we pedalled hard. Glided down sloping streets, reckless and fast. Past lazy homes. Crazy mothers chasing children. Hazy-eyed fathers tired from long days at the factory. (For some reason I imagined all of them at armaments plants. My sleepy countrymen, so unused to having a nation of their own that they had lapsed once more into servitude. Different German-tongued masters, but these ones were worse. Teutonic toughness replacing hapless Hapsburgs.)

I was eager to get back to A. But in a plaza near the Vltava, Josef suddenly slowed down. He looked to make sure I followed. Then he steered down a cement ramp that led to the riverfront.

By the river there were old men tossing bread to ducks. Some of the fowl had ventured onto land and were padding around. Josef pedalled hard towards them with a strange childish mix of antagonism and glee. He sent birds to flight in a flurry of feathers and honking. Then he finally coasted to a stop.

I squeezed my brakes and looped around in front of him. He stood astride his bicycle staring across the river. The birds and old men were departing, upset. No one was within earshot.

"We're going to have to do it on Monday," he said simply.

"Monday?"

"Can you think of a good reason to wait? The longer we hold off, the greater the chance they'll figure it out."

"I'm not worried about the Germans figuring it out," I said.

"I didn't say anything about the Germans. I'm worried about our countrymen," he replied.

"Do you think they want to stop us?"

"Do you think they want it to happen?" Still astride the bicycle, he fished in his pockets for a cigarette. "Some of them I don't trust." He lit the cigarette. Looked at me at last. "And the man's security precautions, for whatever reason, are a joke right now. We don't want to take a chance on that changing."

Suddenly the thought of actually doing what we came to do became large. Unreal. (Had I been deluding myself? Forgetting the end goal, and the likely consequences, of our time here? More likely I had just put everything off to a hazy tomorrow. Forgetting that tomorrow must eventually either become today or become meaningless.)

Still, what could I say? What good would all the training have been if I had balked then? I had no wife or children. So if my life had ended without doing this, it would have had no meaning. All the same, I wanted just a little more time with A.

"Don't you think?" he prompted.

"You're right," I said at last.

Instead of going our separate ways, we pedalled up the hill into Žižkov, to HAJASKÝ's. Up the same dim stairs to the third-floor flat. It's strange returning to a place you once lived. The familiar looks new when viewed from a distance.

"It'll be good to catch up with HAJASKÝ," I observed.

"I'm hoping he's not home," Josef said. "We can get everything and leave."

"HAJASKÝ won't mind us coming when he's out?" I said.

Gabčík lowered his voice to a whisper. "He'll mind a lot more if he finds out what we've hidden in his furniture."

"You haven't told him?"

Now he smiled, just a little. "Every good Catholic knows, it's easier to ask forgiveness than it is to ask permission."

I knocked on the door. No answer, but I heard movement. Knocked again. Finally Valčik answered, sleepy-eyed.

"Good evening, gentlemen. How goes it?"

"It goes," Gabčík said warily. "You were sleeping?"

"Yes." Valčik stretched lazily. Yawned. "It was the most wonderful nap. I dreamed I could fly, just by flapping my wings like this." He pedalled his arms like a demented albatross.

"Your arms," I corrected.

"Ha! Yes, my arms. It felt so real I tried to do it when I woke up. Alas, it didn't work."

"Too bad," Gabčík said.

"I don't have much to do, since I've been stuck here. Captain Bartoš wants me to stay put. It's been so incredibly boring, though!"

"Now you know what our life was like for two months," Gabčík said. "Is HAJASKÝ here?"

"No."

"Good." We walked in. The scene of so much unrelenting monotony. Now it was a prison without power.

"Good? Anything I can help you with?"

"Not really," Gabčík said. "Actually, I'd prefer it if you left the room for a few minutes."

"Might I ask why?"

"Because I don't want you in the room," Gabčík said.

"Good to see you, too," Valčik said. Plucked a copy of Jirasek's "Darkness" from next to the sofa and wandered off to the kitchen and the absurd water closet.

Hastily, Josef and I flipped over the sofa. Unstapled the liner from the bottom. The weapons weren't in there. The weapons weren't in there. The weapons weren't in there!

"Hey," Gabčík said to Valčik. "Did anything…happen to the sofa recently?"

"Oh, now you want to talk to me!" Valčik's muffled voice said from the water closet. "Don't worry. Your equipment's safe."

"Did you take it, or HAJASKÝ?"

"Jesus and Mary! Nobody took it. It fell out of the sofa the other day. The Sten became un-taped or something. It fell out right before HAJASKÝ came home."

"Did he find out?"

"No. I had the sense you didn't want him knowing. I hid it."

"Were you planning on telling me?"

"You didn't want to talk to me!" He emerged from the water closet. "And now you've interrupted my toilet reading."

"Sorry to inconvenience you," Gabčík said.

"Besides, I wanted to ask if you needed help…"

"The Secret Police has your photo. You're known to them. That would put the whole mission at risk."

"Suit yourself," Valčik said. Leisurely he walked into the other bedroom. Pulled the wardrobe away from the wall and leaned it back. Underneath, in the dead space between the floor and the bottom drawer of the wardrobe, he'd hidden everything.

"Not a bad hiding spot," Gabčík said.

"Thank you."

Josef had brought over two valises we'd borrowed from L.'s family. We were in the bedroom packing up the Sten guns when HAJASKÝ barged in, unaware we were there. He saw everything. Said nothing.

After that, we went back to where Josef was staying. Spent the next few hours disassembling, cleaning, and reassembling them in L.'s bedroom. Then we made plans, with her gramophone turned on for noise camouflage.

I didn't make it to A.'s until Saturday afternoon.

Josef still had to find a cable that we could string across the road to slow down the Mercedes. There wasn't much for me to do, so he let me go. I didn't know if it would be my last night with her.

She greeted me more coolly than I'd expected.

"I was just putting on some tea, if you want some," she said.

"Sure." I followed her into the kitchen.

She turned on the stove, lit a match to ignite the burner, and reached up into the cupboard for her blue teacups. I pressed against her as she leaned against the counter. I turned off the stove. Turned her around.

"I thought you wanted tea," she said.

"I changed my mind." I kissed her.

"Well, I still want tea," she said. She turned back around and turned the stove back on.

Again I kissed the back of her neck. Caressed her. She wore a simple housedress, a floral print thing that I rather liked. She smiled a little but kept spooning tea leaves into the metal strainer.

"The tea can wait," I said. Turned the stove off again and watched the blue flame disappear.

"You're going to do the same to me if you're not careful," she said, with something not quite like a smile.

"Is that a threat?"

"Jesus and Mary," she said. "You don't show up at all last night, you give no word about where you are or what's happened to you, and now you just show up and expect to just hop into bed at a moment's notice?"

"What's the matter with you?" I asked. "Is it that time still?"

"What's the matter with me? Jesus and Mary! You're lucky I have pity on you for what little you've learned about women when you were…up there on the moon. No, it's not that time still. In fact, I wish it was. I've been worrying about that. What happens, Jan, if I end up in a family way?"

"I'll be happy! I'll be excited!" I made a move to kiss her. Not long before, I hadn't dared to hope for a child.

She pulled away. "Yes, but will you be around? How long is this going to last, anyway?"

I shrugged.

"You don't know?"

"Maybe a few months. Maybe into next year. The president thinks..."

"We might last into next year?"

"Oh." Sheepishly, I smiled. "I thought you were talking about the war. Us? Forever, of course." I said hopefully.

"Forever," she spat. "There's nights where you act like it's the last night. And there's mornings where I wonder if it was. And…I mean, it was so wonderful when I met you. So great to meet a man who's willing to be a man, to do something about what's going on. But I expect some sense of what's going on with you, and what it means for us."

"You know I can't tell you that," I complained. "Look, all I can say is I was sent here for something very important. It needs to be done. When I volunteered for this, I was a soldier in exile...I had so little hope for the future. It wasn't that I wanted to die, but I didn't have a lot to live for, either. And now, with you…" I didn't know how to tell her about Monday. Didn't know if I should say anything. "But I did come here for this other thing. And I'll be honest, I'm not eager to do it. But I'm more afraid of not doing it. And it's hard, because there's so much else I want, too. I want a life with you. I want children, with you." I took a deep breath. "But the time is coming for this other thing."

She smiled strangely. "That's more words than you've said since I've known you." She did not turn the stove back on. She stepped into my arms and I held her. Felt her melt.

And Monday morning came.

Again Josef arose before dawn. Not knowing if he'd really slept. In the dark he disarmed the brass windup alarm clock and slipped into L.'s room to kiss her goodbye. Tender touches, whispered words. And then no more.

Back in the living room, he dressed quickly and quietly. Knew where everything was in the dark. Prepared for the routine now. From next to the door, he grabbed a valise. Heavy. We'd pared everything down to the bare essentials. Two pistols. Two grenades. One Sten.

Meanwhile at A.'s, I stopped fighting my excitement. Almost finished dressing before she woke. Maybe I hadn't wanted to wake her. To make it more difficult than it had to be. But she woke. And it was difficult. I could face death but couldn't face her. She said nothing but seemed to know. We shared a silent embrace. I kissed salty tears. On the way out I hoisted a knapsack freighted with the weight of a steel cable. I tripped heading out the front door and fell against the wall with a thud.

Passing M.'s flat, I could have sworn I saw their door cracked open. Imagined something or someone watching me.

I descended to the building basement. Flicked on my electric torch and found M.'s bicycle where I'd left it, leaning against the coal bin. Wrestled it upstairs.

Outside, Josef waited. We exchanged no words as we set out. Seriousness spawns silence.

Soon we were pedalling out of the city down the calm country road. We heard singing spring songbirds. Soft sounds, mild and metallic, chains catching sprockets. Saw silent sparrows. Sun slanting sideways on fields of wheat and barley, green shoots barely breaking through the earth. Then the trees. Long shadows blocking our path. So many times we had seen this. But today it all looked fresh and clear and sharp. I noticed things I had not noticed before.

I wondered if this would be the last morning of my life. I didn't know if I'd know if it was.

In the small woods, we selected our positions. This time we were not here for observation, but for ambush. So the plan was for me to stretch the cable across the road when we saw Heydrich approach. Meanwhile Josef would lie in wait with the Sten. They would slow when they saw the cable, or stop and do a U-turn, but Josef would be ready. And meanwhile I would back him up with the grenades.

But when I was affixing the end of the cable to a tree, I saw someone I hadn't expected to see. Another man on a bicycle, pedalling his merry way towards me. This was so strange I stood there dumbly as he coasted up and dismounted.

It was Josef Valčik.

"Good morning, gentlemen," he said cheerfully. "Fancy running into you two out here."

"What the hell are you doing here?" Gabčík asked.

"They sent me out here to stop you."

"What the hell are you talking about?" Gabčík said. Not terribly convincingly.

"Your mission, to kill the Realm-Protector. It isn't going to work anyway, not today, but still they sent me to stop you from trying."

"Who's they?" I inquired. I remember a frightening thought: the Secret Police already got to him, and he's turned.

"Why isn't it going to work?" Josef asked. Angry.

"He went out of town for the weekend. Off to see his Leader in Berlin. So he won't be here, he'll be flying in to Ruzyně and going to the Hrad from there. I ran into one of your friends that works up on Hradčany. He told me to pass on the message."

"He told you to pass on the message," Gabčík said. Practically bit the words as he spoke.

"I'm passing it on!" Valčik exclaimed defensively. "We can wait and see if you don't believe me. And, to answer your question, Bartoš sent me. He wanted to confirm what you were doing. And he wanted me to stop you."

Josef spat. "Bartoš has no say in this."

"He says otherwise. Some other missions dropped in recently, and they're in a bad spot. They need your help."

"We were told in London that our mission was the top priority."

"Priorities change," Valčik said simply.

"I'll have to have a talk with him," Gabčík said.

Valčik shrugged. "Anyway, I also think you could do this better with someone else on your team. I'd suggest myself, personally. But that's just me."

"Why do you want to be in on this?" Gabčík asked.

Valčik gave him a look as if his head had just fallen off. "You men are doing the deal! Getting the girls."

"You know the Germans have your photo," Gabčík said. "You know that puts us..."

And suddenly we heard an unwelcome noise. A German Army half-track appeared from the direction of Praha. Rumbled down the road towards us like a rhinoceros, squat and ugly. It was too late to move. They had spotted us. And Valčik started waving at them. Waving!

"Wave to them," he hissed.

Gabčík and I froze. Could not believe any of this.

"Wave to them!" Valčik practically shouted.

Reluctantly we raised our hands. And the driver, the German driver, gave a casual nod and lifted his hand off the steering wheel in tepid acknowledgement as he drove past.

"If you don't act like you're supposed to be here, people will think you're not supposed to be here," Valčik said simply. "And that's the other thing. I don't think you two ventured much farther down the road. But we're practically in Panenské Březany, and there's a substantial security detail at Heydrich's villa. If you tried anything here, they'd be on top of you in no time. You might pull it off, but you'd never get away."

"All right, enough," Gabčík said sharply.

"Well, we can stay here and wait for Heydrich if you'd like. But since he won't be here, personally I'd be happier heading back to Praha, changing my diapers and getting back to work."

Gabčík nodded. We pulled our bicycles upright and faced them back south.

"So am I on the mission now?" Valčik asked.

"I'll think about it," Gabčík said.

We pedalled slowly back to Praha. Saw the same things we'd seen that morning. But now all was flat and dull. Devoid of meaning. A strange morning. A reprieve. I had expected everything but I hadn't expected nothing. Now that the pressure was off I felt a dull ache deep behind my left eyeball.

Sooner than I'd expected, we were heading down a street the Germans had renamed Kirchmeyer. On the fringes of town, but far enough in that there were stores and tram lines and a power station and a hospital. And Gabčík took a hard right descending turn, and there was a screech of tyres as he almost ran over some poor chap on the sidewalk. The fellow froze and then jumped forward and Josef went up on his front wheel and then fell to the ground with a clatter.

"Jesus and Mary!" the stranger exclaimed.

"For fuck's sake! Of all the bad luck!" Gabčík ranted.

"I'm terribly sorry, sir," the stranger said.

Josef had scraped his hands. The wounds looked annoying but not overwhelming. "It's all right," he told the bystander. "I just didn't see you there." Then it struck him, what he said, and he stood, and looked around at this new spot.

```
DOCUMENT:      #6017
DESCRIPTION: STATUS REPORT ON OPERATION OUT DISTANCE
PLACE:         NEAR OŘECHOV, OCCUPIED CZECHOSLOVAKIA
DATE:          28 MARCH 1942
TRANSMITTED BY:    LIBUSE
FOR:           MUSIL
```

Operation OUT DISTANCE fell from the night sky in the wee small hours of March 28th, 1942. Outside having milder weather, their arrival in Bohemia was fairly similar to what we reported for ANTHROPOID.

That is to say, it was problematic.

Drifting down in the cloudy darkness, Lieutenant Opálka couldn't see any landmarks to gauge his landing. He fell forward and landed hard on his right knee. [Translator's Note: In this radio transmission, the sender originally used pseudonyms for the members of OUT DISTANCE. For clarity's sake, I have replaced the pseudonyms with their given names.]

Sergeant Čurda landed about two hundred yards away in the same field. He hit the ground properly and was uninjured.

The third member of the team, Corporal Kolařík, also landed successfully.

The two healthy men set about looking for their radio beacon. However, they soon realized that their valise with their papers and identification cards was also lost.

They searched fruitlessly for some minutes and found some of their equipment canisters. By this time, the eastern sky was turning grey. The two able-bodied men dragged the canisters to the edge of the field, where the land sloped off to a line of trees next to a creek.

Lieutenant Opálka determined that this would be the best place to hide their equipment and instructed the able-bodied men to do so. It was nearly light by the time they finished caching their canisters and coveralls. They then collected up Lieutenant Opálka and headed back to the road.

Owing to the manual labour, their hands were extremely dirty, with damp soil staining the knees and elbows of their suits. It was obvious to them that their appearance was not as it should have been, and they were desperate to avoid being seen in that state. They were torn between looking for the valise and getting a ride into town so as to put some distance between themselves and their equipment. Finally, they opted for the latter. They split up, travelled to Praha, and sought shelter with JINDRA's network, planning to return and retrieve their equipment as soon as was practical.

Unfortunately, when Sergeant Čurda returned several days later, he was unable to find the equipment, which included several Stens, several pistols, explosives, and a Rebecca radio beacon. Lieutenant Opálka says this latter item is essential to the success of their mission. He requests guidance as to how to proceed.

```
DOCUMENT:     #598
DESCRIPTION: OFFICIAL REPORT ON WEAPONS CACHE DISCOVERY
PLACE:       OŘECHOV, OCCUPIED CZECHOSLOVAKIA
DATE:        11 APRIL 1942
```

Notes from Inspector von Pannwitz:

We recently received a tip from a Czech policeman regarding a buried cache of weapons and radio equipment.

This policeman had been approached by a farmer who woke one morning to discover that large swaths of his newly-planted wheat crop had been mysteriously trampled, apparently in the middle of the night, by unknown intruders. The farmer followed the footprints and discovered several canisters of equipment buried near a creek on his property.

An itemised list of the equipment follows:
3 Sten guns
3 Colt pistols
1000 rounds of 9 millimetre ammunition
200 rounds of .45 calibre ammunition
3 parachutes
3 kilograms of cyclonite
2 radio transmitter and receiver
1 radio homing beacon
18 special demolition charges
40 incendiary devices
200 detonators

The Czech police removed this equipment from its location before reporting the find, which was unfortunate, in that we now have no leads as to who it belonged to. However, given the nature of the find, and other recent reports of large aircraft flying at low levels at night, it seems evident that the British are dropping in commandos to carry out a sabotage campaign within the Protectorate.

```
DOCUMENT:     #47
DESCRIPTION: NARRATIVE OF J. KUBIŠ
PLACE:       PRAHA, OCCUPIED CZECHOSLOVAKIA
DATE:        18 APRIL 1942
```

On a sunny mid-April day, Josef, Josef and I stood in line at a public fairground and purchased tickets to an exhibition of German propaganda.

"The Soviet Paradise" promised photographs and posters depicting the horrors of everyday life for the average Soviet citizen. Word-of-mouth said it was worthwhile. So we queued up outside the turnstiles. Above us loomed a large red banner. Bilingual, in the best tradition of the occupation, it read DAS SOWJET PARADIES, and below that, SOVĚTSKÝ RAJ.

We'd wanted a good public venue to meet Captain Bartoš. He had insisted on taking the train from Pardubice to Praha to personally talk to Gabčík and I about recent developments.

We almost missed him. People thronged past us, healthy men, old men, bald men, short men, full families, fine females, and everything in between. But no one resembled Bartoš. Until Valčik caught sight of a single infirm man hobbling nearby, wearing the vest and beret combination Bartoš said he'd wear, as well as the vaguely confused look of one who is meeting others in a crowded place.

"Is that him?" Gabčík asked, following his fellow Slovak's gaze.

"That's him," Valčik confirmed. "Jesus and Mary, he's gotten bad."

"Gotten bad?' Gabčík asked.

"I didn't tell you. He's been ill."

"Ill?" Gabčík asked.

Captain Bartoš walked up. Slowly. "Good day."

"Good to see you!" Gabčík got gregarious. Soon softened. "How are you?"

"Not as well as one might have hoped," Bartoš began. "It appears I've got rheumatoid arthritis."

"Rheumatoid arthritis?" I asked. Rheumatoid arthritis?

"My joints are swollen. In the morning I'm very stiff, and later it's not so bad. But it never goes away. Apparently it can strike at any age. So I've gone from young man to old man in a matter of months. I wanted a reason to have a medical card, and I got one." His features scrunched up with displeasure.

"Well, we can take you to the…back where we're staying, if you need a rest," Gabčík said. Almost slipped in a 'sir' despite the swirling crowds.

"I'd just as well stay out here," Bartoš said. "Truth be told, I've been laid up so long it's nice to get some fresh air."

"I know the feeling," Gabčík said.

For an hour we browsed the depressing dioramas. They featured photographs taken by the Germans in the wake of their initial advances last summer. One showed a collective farm whose dwellings resembled haphazard scrap heaps. Another presented peasants awaiting a doctor next to a bare table of wooden planks. A label alleged it was her operating table. Another collective farm looked positively medieval, with women cooking over wood fires and sleeping beneath piles of blankets. There was a decrepit orphanage with broken windows, battered mattresses, and children smoking cigarettes. Then, a church in the woods, rotting and decaying. Holes punched in ornate frescoes. Desecrated crypts. And yet the Soviets needed the building, so there was an electrical turbine where the altar had been, and technicians manning jury-rigged wiring and equipment that could charitably be described as unsafe. On the way out were posters calling for steadfastness in the fight against the "Bolshevist-Jewish conspiracy" that had caused such hardships for ordinary Russians.

"I'm not sure having them in charge of us would be much of a victory," Valčik observed as we headed through the turnstiles on the way out.

"They're not in charge of us, though," Gabčík said. "It's not the weak we need to fear, but the strong."

"The weak can still be dangerous," Bartoš said, walking slowly and stiffly. "The weak have nothing to lose but their suffering."

"Suffering can be useful," Gabčík replied.

"Spoken like a good Catholic," Valčik replied with a smile.

"Spoken like a man who's not suffering," Bartoš bitterly retorted.

Now we had ambled down the street and into a park. Walked along pleasant paths. Leaves were taking shape on the trees. We walked on our own. No ears near to hear us.

"Tell us, then, my good Catholic friend, how suffering is useful," Valčik said.

"It builds character, like they used to say…" Gabčík looked around. No one within earshot. "Like they used to say over there at the schools. Or, better yet. Taking exercise is a form of suffering, but it strengthens us in the end."

"But sometimes suffering just weakens us," Bartoš replied. "So it is not the suffering that makes exercise worthwhile, but the growth, the gain, the strength. Suffering is just an unfortunate by-product. On its own it is never useful."

"What does the quiet one say?" Valčik asked. Looked at me.

"It is one of the best ways to prove our love," I said.

"It is a selfish love which demands suffering as proof," Bartoš said gruffly.

"But it is an unselfish love which gives it, without it being demanded," I said.

"Love. Hah," Valčik said. "If ever there was a made-up word to describe something that people only thought existed—I mean, besides 'God' of course. What does love mean?"

"It means giving pleasure," Gabčík grinned and caught my eye. I laughed.

"But if giving pleasure gives you pleasure, is that love, or selfishness?" Valčik asked.

"I think love means acting in another's best interests, and not your own," I elaborated. "And the purest proof of our love is if we are willing to suffer so that others may have pleasure."

"Look at Our Lord," Gabčík said. "What purer form of love can there be, than to go through such suffering?"

"If he was God, he knew it wouldn't last," Valčik said.

"He had to at least wonder, though," Gabčík said. "When I read about the Garden of Gethsemane, I don't see the certainty, the perfection, of an all-knowing God. I see human frailty."

"He knew enough to know what was coming," I said. "He feared it."

"I fear what is coming," Bartoš said wearily. We had come to a park bench. Bartoš scanned all around as if to make sure again there was no chance we would be overheard. Then he sat.

"LIBUSE is foretelling the future," Valčik cracked.

"It isn't something to look forward to," Gabčík said. "I will agree with you about that. Your illness…"

"I'm talking about President Beneš!" Bartoš barked.

We all perked up. Where had this come from?

"How do you mean?" Valčik asked.

"He wants us to suffer," Bartoš said. "Have you thought, I mean, really thought, about the consequences of your mission?"

"No," Gabčík said. Glib.

"No?" Bartoš asked.

"It's not my job to think about such things," Gabčík responded defensively. "We're soldiers. Sir. Our job is to carry out our orders. Not to decide whether they're worth carrying out."

"Perhaps my orders were different than yours," Bartoš said calmly. "Mine explicitly said that, once we set up our transmitter and made contact with London, we were under the command of the home resistance."

"Mine explicitly said not to get in touch with them, sir," Gabčík said.

"You didn't have a problem second-guessing those orders," Bartoš pointed out.

"I did have a problem with it. Sir." Gabčík got a little angry. On his tongue the honorific sounded horrific. Worse than a curse. "But if I hadn't done it, we wouldn't have been able to accomplish our mission."

"The people who gave you that mission don't know what things are like here," Bartoš said.

"Whose side are you on, sir? You're worse than JINDRA," Gabčík said. "The Brits would say you've gone native."

"Native!" Bartoš barked. "These people are our countrymen! As soldiers, our job is to protect our countrymen! To suffer, yes, but for our countrymen! We have no other job! But we are making their lives more dangerous. Mark my words, if you're around to remember them! A lot of these people won't survive the war, because of the risks they're taking on our behalf!"

"They volunteered to help," Gabčík said. "They took those risks willingly, and they want us to succeed."

"Do they know what you are here for?" Bartoš asked.

"I've taken every possible precaution to make it safer for them," Josef said. "Still, they have proven willing to help in every way!"

"Do they know what you are here for?!?" Bartoš reiterated.

"No! We can't take a chance on that reaching German ears."

"Or unfriendly Czech ones," Bartoš said. "Your mission will cause untold troubles for our people. You know it. And London knows it."

"London said this mission is their top priority," Gabčík said. "MUSIL said so himself."

"MUSIL also ordered it to be delayed," Bartoš replied simply. His trump card. Played perfectly. "I can show you the transmission if you want. I can get them to re-send it, if you want. You can listen to it in code on the BBC."

For a few precious seconds, nobody said anything. Spring sun and green grass and ants crawling on the path in front of us. All was perfect and calm, except in our heads. Now Gabčík sputtered confusedly. "What the hell do they want?"

"What don't they want?" Bartoš asked. "They want more assassinations. They want a sabotage campaign, against railroads and bridges, to help the sainted Soviets. They want…and this is a mission you'll be involved with, mind you…they want us to help the British bomb the Skoda works."

"The Skoda works?" Valčik asked.

"Yes. The group that you men are going to have to help, they dropped in to set up a radio beacon that will help the British find and bomb the Skoda works. Unfortunately, they've lost their beacon. So you're going to have to help them carry out their mission."

"We are." It was not a question but an angry statement. Gabčík seemed almost belligerent.

"I can have MUSIL send you a confirmation if you'd like. This is ultimately for your benefit, even," Bartoš said.

"And why's that?" Gabčík said. Flat.

"Because they want to just drop more teams in instead."

"More parachutists?"

"Yes. Where they are planning on hiding them, I don't know. And that would make life more difficult for all of us."

"Did you tell London that?" Gabčík asked.

"Yes. And if you help the people who have dropped in already, I think we can get London to hold off on dropping more. But we might have to talk to MUSIL about your mission. ANTHROPOID. I think they also bumped it back because they know what will happen if it succeeds."

"What will happen?" Valčik asked.

"It will stir things up enough that nothing else will stand a chance."

After that, we found ourselves off in Plzen helping out OUT DISTANCE. It was a strange errand, lighting barns on fire to try and guide in bombers. It was a failure. The less said about it, the better.

But while we were there, Captain Bartoš allegedly held up his end of the bargain and sent a message to London asking that they stop dropping parachutists until the fall. (I say "allegedly" because what happened was far from what we'd expected.)

```
DOCUMENT:     #6038
DESCRIPTION:  MANIFEST FOR AIRDROPS OF 28/29 AND 29/30
              APRIL, 1942
PLACE:        RAF WILMSLOW
              WILMSLOW, CHESHIRE, UNITED KINGDOM
DATE:         1 MAY 1942
```

The following missions were dropped into Occupied Czechoslovakia on the night of 27/28 APRIL 1942:

BIOSCOPE
BIVOUAC
STEEL

The following missions were dropped into Occupied Czechoslovakia on the night of 29/30 APRIL 1942:

TIN
INTRANSITIVE

There was some discussion as to whether or not to proceed with these missions, given recent feedback from previous missions. However, a confluence of factors made it advisable to go ahead with the airdrops: the moon was nearly full, which hopefully made for safer landings for the various parachutists. Also, the sunrise and sunset times here and over continental Europe are such that it will not be possible to make further night flights until the fall. Lastly, political considerations continue to make it imperative that we make a substantial and visible contribution to the Allied war effort.

```
DOCUMENT:    #27
DESCRIPTION: PERSONAL DIARY OF K.H. FRANK
PLACE:       HRADČANY, PRAHA, OCCUPIED CZECHOSLOVAKIA
DATE:        20 APRIL 1942
```

Today was a perfectly pleasant spring morning, the kind of day where all but the chronically depressed or lovesick feel energetic as a matter of course. It was altogether too pleasant to ruin on the task at hand, though! I was forced to attend a ceremony of sorts that Heydrich and our lovely Minister of Public Enlightenment had cooked up to illustrate the supposed solidarity between us and the Czechs.

When I arrived at Heydrich's office, he had opened his windows to the fresh spring breeze and was perusing some documents from that treasure trove in his perpetually-locked desk.

"Yes?" he asked wearily—or was that my imagination?—when I stuck my head into his office.

"We'd better be going, my Lord," I said.

He sighed and slipped the documents back into a file folder, then slipped that into his desk, then locked the drawer and pocketed the keys before answering. "Are you looking forward to picking up the Leader's birthday present?" he asked at last.

I'm sure I rolled my eyes.

"I don't terribly want to go down there either," he said as he stood. "You know how I hate speeches. It is a sign of weakness, to have to explain things. It is...childish. True power means doing what you want, with no explanations—and if people don't like it, up against the wall! But we're not there yet. At least, not here. So for now..."

"The Czech people are already...somewhat docile, my Lord."

"Yes! Sheep, practically. And sheep respond most readily to the voice of a familiar shepherd. Which is why, for now, I'm deferring to Moravec's judgment on these matters."

"Do you think it sends the right signal, my Lord?"

"What signal do you think it sends?" Heydrich asked.

"That we view them as worthy of respect, my Lord."

Heydrich snorted. "The point is the story. Everyone knows that to rule, one needs rules. Most also know that one also needs people capable and willing to enforce rules, through force and unpleasantness if necessary. But when you are not at that point yet, you need most important thing of all: a good story…"

"What do you mean, my Lord?" (Here I was truly confused.)

"There has been no story here," Heydrich said. "Before going into Poland, we had a story ready for our people. We staged an attack on one of our transmitter stations. We left some corpses, people from the camps, in Polish Army uniforms to suggest who had done the attacking. So there was a story, and those who wanted to believe it could do so."

"What does it matter what they believe, my Lord?"

"If we really want to control these lands and these people, we have to first convince them it's what they want, too. These lands and their people are…well, many of them come from good Aryan stock, oddly enough. As much as I hate to admit it, many are brighter and more vigorous than many of the German-speakers living in their scattered little enclaves throughout Bohemia and Moravia. But they are confused by their weak Czech culture. They have always had to choose between the Teutons and the Slavs, but they're unsure where to find protection. So we have to perpetuate the story that we are the more benevolent masters and they would be lost without us. If we can do that…" Heydrich shrugged.

"So is that the end goal, my Lord? Just to keep them on our side? Germans and Czechs living hand in hand, sharing the land?"

"Of course not," he smirked.

"That was the status quo before, under Austria-Hungary. And what did it prove? That they are a nation of turncoats. They aligned with Teutons when it suited them, and when it became inconvenient, they were preaching Pan-Slavism and looking for salvation from Mother Russia."

"Rest assured, we don't want that. Why do you think there are no Czechs in our armies, even though they are part of the Realm? Hitler knows that if we put them on the Eastern Front they'd switch sides whenever it suited them, as they did in the last war. Culturally, if not racially, they are still Slavs. And again, the Slav is a slave. The Czech is perhaps more intelligent and duplicitous than the others, but perhaps that is only because of their Aryan bloodlines, and because they've had the opportunity. Under any masters besides the Hapsburgs, they would not even have been able to…" Heydrich left the thought hanging. "Still, even when they tricked the world into making them free, they were slaves. They wandered around confused without their yokes. Now we are here, and all we have to do is…" Heydrich trailed off again and smiled thinly.

"I still don't like them, my Lord." (I'm sure I scowled when I said this.) "And I still don't think we should pander to them."

"Come now. You know as well as I do that if I showed right now my end goals, we would have an uprising on our hands. And that would not serve our purposes. Now if, on the other hand, we can convince them that they are weak, that they are a tribe and not a nation, they will offer no resistance. And when the war's over, we will be able to deport the racially inferior, and send the children of the others off to summer camps and higher schools in Germany to be Aryanized…" Again he looked at me the mirror and smiled. "I mean, really, Frank. Do you think I give a damn about the Czechs?"

Here at last, I shook my head. He had a point.

Heydrich stood and nodded towards the courtyard. "Let's go."

Outside, his driver waited with the Mercedes; we climbed in and headed off, out the courtyard and down the hill towards the river. As usual, he was driving without an escort; I cannot understand such recklessness in someone otherwise so wise!

"These security arrangements always seem somewhat…minimal to me, my Lord," I said as we crossed the Charles Bridge, with its sad crosses of stone and statues of saints.

Heydrich remained as stoic as the statues. "There is a story of an emperor in the Far East who would walk, alone and unarmed, among his subjects while they toiled under the blazing sun," he said over the rush of air. "There was a machete in everyone's hand but his. And not one of them ever lifted an eye to look at him, much less put any effort into killing him. And here…I mean, we're talking about Czechs here…"

"Have you not even a healthy fear of them, my Lord?" I asked.

"Of what use is fear? Fear a thing enough and your very fears will call it into being. If you fear your wife cheating, for instance, your fear itself will be what drives her…"

"We've been getting strange reports from von Pannwitz, my Lord, about airdrops in the night. We've seized equipment. Radio beacons, guns, explosives. It might be wise to at least take some precautions, my Lord. Better security at these public appearances. Plus, of course, this car isn't armoured, and you travel without escort."

"It is a matter of national prestige for me to come and go as I please." Now we were in Old Town; the pedestrians on the narrow sidewalks gazed surprised as we whisked past, and Heydrich gestured dismissively towards them. "Why should I fear them? They are a weak people, a servile people. Capable of duplicity, but not resistance. And besides, if anything should happen…" He patted his pistol. (Here I at least had the good sense to turn away before I rolled my eyes. He can be so fucking grandiose!) "Besides," he continued. "They know if anyone were to try such a thing, it would be tantamount to national suicide."

Klein turned onto Richard Wagner Street, the broad boulevard that fronted the train station. Under the cast-iron awning in front of the large limestone edifice, a crowd of cowardly Czechs awaited: impotent potentates, servile scribes, mindless newsreel men.

The car pulled up to the kerb, and we got out. Inside to the lobby, a larger entourage awaited. At the centre stood Emil Hácha, with his face like a caricature of a sad forest gnome, and Emanuel Moravec, that fat animal; they awaited us under a large hanging swastika flag and a big bronze bust of the Leader.

"Hail Hitler," they raised their arms in eager salute.

Heydrich returned their salute as casually as if he'd been brushing off lint. All around was turmoil, the controlled chaos one always sees at these staged news events; someone had erected a microphone podium on a red carpet. And now everyone arranged themselves like iron filings around two poles of a magnet: Czech "government" types in black suits near Hácha, and grey-uniformed Germans around us.

Finally Hácha stepped up to the microphone. It had been set up for someone far taller, and he craned to come close, looking quite undignified in the process, like a schoolboy on tiptoes. (Here Heydrich gave me a knowing smile; I wondered if even this simple little indignity had been staged!) The supposed president of the Czechs tried to adjust it and failed; giving up, he gave his speech:

"Today, as the brave soldiers of the German Army find themselves locked in battle with the implaca-placa…implacable Bolshevist foe, we Czechs know that we must choose sides. It is a choice between civilization and barbarism, between progression and regression, between the backward-thinking Slavs and the forward-thinking Teutons. We must stand firmly on the side of our allies in their fight against the Red menace. And so on this special occasion, the birthday of Germany's great Leader, it is our pleasure to present this special gift which waits behind us. It is a hospital train for use by Germany's brave warriors on the Eastern Front."

Hácha eagerly shook hands with Heydrich, who was looking over his head at Moravec, who had presumably penned Hácha's remarks. "Good speech," Heydrich mouthed at the propaganda man, who nodded and smiled, self-satisfied.

And now Heydrich took the microphone—which was set up so as to be exactly right for his height—and spoke in his strangely high voice. "I thank you, Mr. President, for this gift from Bohemia and Moravia, which I accept on behalf of the Leader. This gift expresses the Czech peoples' sincere loyalty to the Realm in the tradition of St. Wenceslas whom you, Mr. President, personify. Wenceslas understood that the fates of the Czech and German peoples are intertwined, and he knew that, as a wise ruler, it was in his people's best interests to pursue better relations with the German people. He was a generous and charitable man, and by this act of charity, you, Mr. President, have established yourself as a worthy leader in that same image."

The flashbulbs flashed, and the scribblers scribbled, and Heydrich led the assemblage through the vast lobby and out to the train sidings, like the Pied Piper personified.

There a locomotive stood: strong and gleaming and clean and black and new. Behind it were six hospital cars painted glossy and green. Heydrich, Hácha and I filed up into the first one. The newsreel men and scribes scrambled off to the stairs at the far end to get shots of our inspection.

Inside, Heydrich looked things over, peering under the corner of a bunk here, and removing the metal lid of a mess pot there.

"What are you looking for, my Lord?" I asked quietly.

"Nothing," Heydrich said, glancing backwards; I followed his gaze to Hácha, who followed us expectantly, like a lapdog waiting for a pat on the head. Heydrich leaned closer, smiled. "I can't believe you are afraid of these people."

```
DOCUMENT:    #47
DESCRIPTION: NARRATIVE OF J. KUBIŠ
PLACE:       ŽIŽKOV, PRAHA, OCCUPIED CZECHOSLOVAKIA
DATE:        29 APRIL 1942
```

Thunderstorms came one night in late April. Several times I awoke. Saw flashes of lightning through blurry windowpanes. Spent much time in that fuzzy place between sleep and wakefulness. Dreamt dreams so vivid I was first convinced they were real. Then I was just convinced they were dreams. Then I wondered if they were just fragments of old memories jarred loose. The rain continued through the morning. Sheets of water covered the windows. Outside, I saw only slick stone and silver sky.

In the afternoon, when the storm became mere drizzle, I hefted M.'s bicycle on my shoulder and lugged it downstairs. Banged the pedals against walls and banisters and my ribs.

Outside among grey buildings and twisty streets, I picked my way east. Past staid crystal shops with signs proclaiming "This is a Jew-free store" and corner markets where placid civilians lined up for their daily bread.

Upstairs at my destination, A. greeted me with a pleasant smile. When I put my arms around her, though, she stood there. Body close, eyes gazing off into the indistinct distance, face half-buried in my chest.

"I dreamed about you last night," I said. "I dreamt we went to visit my parents."

"Where do they live?"

"In Třebíč. But it didn't look like Třebíč. It looked like the white cliffs of Dover."

"That is the strange thing about dreams," she said. "You know things that contradict your knowledge."

"It's also strange how empty they sound when you describe them to someone else," I said. "So what does it mean?"

"Dreams don't mean anything. It's just your mind's way of telling you what's on your mind."

"I haven't thought about my parents in months," I said.

"Why don't you visit them?"

"I can't. It is forbidden. Too dangerous, for us and them."

"Will I meet them ever?"

"Yes. When all of this is over."

"I would like that very much," she said, and squeezed me tighter.

Suddenly I became aware of noise coming from M.'s. Voices and music, indistinct, intermingled. Like when the radio dial is between two stations.

"You have new friends down the hall," she said.

"New friends?"

"From out of town."

She kissed me. But now it was my curiosity that was aroused. Now I was the one staring off into the distance.

"Well go down there, then," she said. "I'm sure they want to talk to you."

In the hallway one could hear loud phonograph music straining to conceal boisterous conversation. When I knocked, everyone went silent. M. opened the door, just wide enough for her face.

"Oh, it's just you," she said. Breath like a distillery. She flung the door wide open. Wobbled back to the assembled crowd in the living room.

Gabčík stumbled over. "Hullo. I popped in to HAJASKÝ's and he was on his way over here. London sent more people. At least, that's where this man says he's from. We've been…interrogating him, I guess you'd say. Čurda's idea."

I wondered whether I'd wandered into a war council or a party. Sure enough, Čurda was there. I'd been paired up with him in England, and we'd seen him a few weeks before, during the business at Plzen. Valčik and HAJASKÝ, were there too, and M. and S. and their son, and two others that looked vaguely familiar. With so many people standing around, the kitchen table looked like a flower with people for petals. The air was thick with smoke.

"If it gets any smokier in here, we'll only be able to see each other's legs," Gabčík babbled.

"They'll escape in the confusion!" Valčik exclaimed.

"Do you recognize this man?" Čurda asked me.

I peered closer. He'd been pointing at a wide-eared young man, clearly perplexed. But familiar. "Kouba?" I asked.

"Jan Kubiš!" he exclaimed. Relieved now. The civilians gave a look—they had not heard my real name.

"We were in the same platoon together back in training. In '34, I think," I explained. "What's this all about?"

"He claims they just dropped him in the other day," Čurda said. "But I never saw him back in London."

"I told you, I was a late substitution," Kouba said. "I was in a later parachute class, and I didn't spend much time in the training barracks. MUSIL and Captain Sustr were shuffling people around, putting new people in old missions, changing orders at the last minute. They wanted to get a few more missions off before the nights got too short."

"Bah," Čurda said dismissively.

"Well, I recognize him, and I saw him there," I said. "We can trust him. What's your issue with this one?" I gestured towards the other fellow.

"Miks was on my plane. I know he came here with us," Čurda said. "I just don't know why he took so long to contact us. For all we know, he's gone over to the Germans."

Here Miks hesitated. "I…I went to visit my parents."

All of drew a deep breath.

"Jesus and Mary!" Čurda asked. "We all want to see our family. You think you're special? You could get us all killed, doing things like that."

"That's enough, Sergeant," Gabčík said. Usually he wasn't one to pull rank, but Čurda was obviously drunk and looking to pick a fight. "What's done is done. We have to get things done now without reliving all that." He turned to Kouba. "Why are you here now? What do you need?"

"We buried a cache of weapons after we dropped in. But my mission was split up. I was put in touch with Captain Bartoš in Pardubice, and he said most of the parachutists were here in Praha. So I came to ask for help retrieving it."

"Perhaps these men can help you," Gabčík gestured at the others, who stood in drunken silence all around the small smoky room.

"Where is your materiel?" Valčik asked.

"In the Křivoklat Forest. Near Lany."

"Well, I'll help," Valčik said. "What the hell. It's better than doing nothing. How much equipment are we talking about here?"

"Forty kilograms," Kouba said. "I'll need a couple more people."

"I'll help, too," Miks said. "Better than sitting here and getting grilled for doing nothing." He looked over at Čurda.

"I'm not getting involved," Čurda said.

"We still need another," Kouba said, looking at Gabčík and I.

"I'm sorry, I can't help you. We already lost a couple weeks helping them out." Gabčík nodded at Čurda. "Our mission is too important to put on hold any longer."

"What is your mission, that it's too important for you to help your comrades?" Kouba asked.

"They are here to assassinate the Realm-Protector," HAJASKÝ said, heavy-lidded. Drunk, but hiding it well, until now.

Gabčík took a deep breath. "What are you talking about?"

The lie didn't faze HAJASKÝ. "I talked to Jiri. You've been asking him about Heydrich, just like you ashked me. You've been 'bserving his movements, getting his schedule. It doeshn't take a genius. 'f you want to know what people want, you just have to figure out what they're looking at. This is what you're looking at."

"Do you have a problem with this?"

"I don't," HAJASKÝ said. "I've sh-uspected it for some time, but I kept my mouth shut. For the most part."

"For the most part?" I saw the little quiver on Gabčík's neck I always noticed right before he blew his top. Blood rising like magma. "Who have you told about this?"

"Look, I support you. If anyone in thish war deserves to die, it's Heydrich. So I'm glad. I will offer a toast, to your health and your future success." Here he raised a lonely shot of slivovitz. Drained it.

Gabčík pounded the phonograph and it made an ugly noise. "WHO HAVE YOU TOLD ABOUT THIS?!?!"

"JINDRA." HAJASKÝ hesitated. "He wants to talk."

"JINDRA has no say in it!"

"If it wasn't for JINDRA, you two would be rotting in Pankrác."

"We might get there yet, if you keep talking." Gabčík pointed a furious finger.

"I sh-upport you," HAJASKÝ slurred. "I will back you up when you talk to JINDRA. But you do need to talk to him. He has helped you. Sho you owe him this."

A long silence followed. Gabčík cooled.

"We still need another," Kouba sighed.

"Perhaps I can help," the son said.

"This is men's work, son," said Kouba, who was (to my knowledge) only twenty-six.

"I want to be a part of it. I'm as big as any of you, I have as much at stake as any of you do."

"Do you know what you're asking for?" Valčik asked. "Everyone in this room knows enough that we can't let ourselves be taken in for questioning. Do you understand?"

"Yes."

As it turned out, he had no idea what was in store. Then again, none of us did.

```
DOCUMENT:     #612
DESCRIPTION:  OFFICIAL REPORT ON SHOOTING INCIDENT
              RELATED TO WEAPONS CACHE DISCOVERY
PLACE:        KŘIVOKLAT FOREST, NEAR LANY, OCCUPIED
              CZECHOSLOVAKIA
DATE:         1 MAY 1942
```

Notes from Inspector von Pannwitz:

One of our operatives, acting on a tip from a Czech policeman, recently discovered a substantial weapons cache in a forest near Lany. This find was reported to me on 18 April.

An itemised list of the equipment follows:
3 Sten guns
3 Colt pistols
1000 rounds of 9 millimetre ammunition
200 rounds of .45 calibre ammunition
3 parachutes
9 kilograms of cyclonite
1 radio transmitter and receiver
72 special demolition charges
40 incendiary devices
300 detonators

Owing to the size of this cache, and the failure to apprehend any suspects after a similar cache was discovered near Ořechov earlier in the month, I determined it prudent to leave it buried, and to keep the approaches to the site under covert observation in the hopes of apprehending whomever came to collect the materiel.

When I analysed the possible routes to the cache, it became apparent that we did not have enough resources to rely entirely on our own operatives, and so I was forced to station Czech police at a couple of the checkpoints. All operatives were in vehicles. Our intent was that they should be far enough from the cache that any parachutists or members of the resistance going to retrieve it would think they were normal officers on patrol, and would not think the cache itself was under observation. We instructed all operatives to watch for men of military age travelling alone on in pairs.

On the morning of 30 April, two Czech policemen monitoring one of the roads near the forest saw two such individuals entering the forest on foot.

When the policemen stopped them for questioning, one of the suspects produced a pistol and opened fire, killing one of the Czech officers and wounding the other. The wounded officer took cover and returned fire, bravely holding off the suspects until other officers arrived on the scene. These arriving officers in turn killed one of the suspects and seriously wounded the other.

Both of the suspects were carrying identification papers which appear to have been crudely forged. We still have not positively identified either man, but will be questioning the wounded survivor in the coming days so as to identify any additional accomplices.

```
DOCUMENT:    #47
DESCRIPTION: NARRATIVE OF J. KUBIŠ
PLACE:       ŽIŽKOV, PRAHA, OCCUPIED CZECHOSLOVAKIA
DATE:        2 MAY 1942
```

The errand Kouba had needed help with, to retrieve the materiel in the Křivoklat Forest, turned out as badly as it possibly could have.

There was a shootout. Kouba and Miks were gone. Valčik had somehow cheated both death and arrest yet again. But the incident made the papers, even. None of us were particularly happy about that. Čurda seemed particularly agitated.

After a couple days, we'd gathered around another smoky roundtable. A sober roundtable, except for Čurda. This time we were at HAJASKÝ's claustrophobic flat. Valčik, Gabčík, Čurda, myself. HAJASKÝ, of course. Still we were bumping elbows and egos in that dark little kitchen with its absurd adjoining water closet.

"We were stopped by a Czech policeman, the kid and I were," Valčik said. "We'd split up from the others and were approaching by a different route, and we were stopped, and he asked what was in our knapsacks, and I said, 'Nothing,' and he said, 'That's an awfully big knapsack to be carrying nothing.' He had to know what we were there for. He had to! They must have known something was up. And he let us go. He said, 'Turn around and go back, before someone sees us talking.' And when we were walking away, we heard gunshots, from further down, the direction the other two had gone."

"You heard gunshots. What does that prove?" Čurda asked.

"What does it prove?" Valčik exclaimed. "You saw the papers! There was a gun battle. One of them's dead!"

"And isn't it convenient that the two people we were suspicious of, the two we know least about, were the two who didn't return?"

"The two people you were suspicious of," Valčik corrected him.

Čurda shrugged. As if to say, yes, and events have proven me right.

"Why did they let us go then?" Valčik asked.

"So they could tail you discreetly. Follow you back to us," Čurda said simply. Slugged a stiff swig from a hip flask.

"That's absurd."

Čurda slammed his flask down on the table. "This whole fucking situation's absurd! We're not accomplishing anything! We've helped bombers drop bombs to kill our countrymen! And now we're just going to sit here and let the Germans round us up! Sounds great, sign me up!"

"What the fuck is wrong with you, you selfish fuck?" Gabčík exploded. "Let me get this straight. Let me see if I understand this. One of your comrades is dead, and another is held captive, probably wounded, and you're worried about you?"

"I'm worried we've all been hung out to dry. I'm worried this is an untenable situation. Even assuming you were correct and it was a shootout with the police, what's the point? To have our people come here for sabotage but end up in shootouts with our own countrymen?"

"Countrymen that are working for the Germans," Gabčík interrupted.

"Half this fucking country is working for the Germans!" Čurda exclaimed.

"And the other half is living in fear. Those that aren't already in Pankrác or Terezín. And as for the shootout, Miks and Kouba were ambushed by police officers with guns. If you were in their shoes, you'd have fought, too," Gabčík said. "If not, I don't want to wear the same uniform as you."

"Is it acceptable, to you, for us to kill our own countrymen? Just because it serves London's political ends?"

"You drunken fool!" Gabčík yelled.

"How many deaths are acceptable?"

"That's not why we're here, and you know it!"

"That's what your mission will lead to. That's what you will cause, if you kill the Realm-Protector. How many deaths are acceptable?" Čurda asked. "Fifty? Five hundred? Five thousand?"

"Look, you need to shut the hell up!" Gabčík's face was bright red. "You're going to get us killed, you know. This isn't a safe place to have this discussion."

"You don't want to have this discussion at all!" Čurda said.

Gabčík sat. Breathed deeply. Seethed. "You need to get the hell out of here," he said at last.

"Fine," Čurda said, and stood, and left.
"We know you don't want to have this discussion," JINDRA said half an hour later.

He'd arrived not long after Čurda left. It was the first time I'd seen him since January, but we'd often had the sense that he was the one pulling all of the strings above us. Moving us from house to house, arranging the identification papers for us, and for the others who had arrived afterwards.

"There's nothing to discuss," Gabčík said. Lit a cigarette with the ember from his previous cigarette and leaned back in his chair, defiant.

"There's a lot to discuss," JINDRA said. "The occupation has been relatively peaceful of late…"

"Whose fucking side are you on, anyway?" Gabčík asked.

"Our people's side! Our people have been safe. That won't be the case if you kill Heydrich. Our people will be slaughtered in the streets."

"What would you have us do? Learn to goose-step?" Gabčík asked coolly.

"Did you hear what I said?!?!" JINDRA's temple pulsed with blood. "I'm going to get in touch with Captain Bartoš. I know he has misgivings, too. We are going to get him to send a message back to London, asking them to call off the mission."

"There's nothing to discuss," Gabčík repeated. "We're soldiers, and we have our orders."

"You're spies! Assassins! Troublemakers!" JINDRA said.

"We're soldiers! Do you understand that? We're not civilians, helping out on a case-by-case basis whenever we feel like it! We have our orders, and we don't have the right to question those orders. This mission was ordered by President Beneš himself."

"He's out of touch with reality!" JINDRA said. "The people don't want this!"

"Plenty of people do," Gabčík said.

"I don't!" JINDRA said self-righteously.

"So you have the right to make the president's decisions?" Gabčík asked.

"At least I'm here with the people," JINDRA said.

"He can't be! He'd be rotting in gaol, or under house arrest, or dead. He's doing exactly what Masaryk did, in the last war."

"He's not even a legitimate president. He resigned after Munich."

"He has as much legitimacy as Masaryk had."

"Masaryk had the good sense not to do anything like this," JINDRA said. "Raising an exile army, that's fine. Sending them into battle, that's fine. But stirring up trouble at home in the face of overwhelming strength? That's the height of foolishness."

"He has his reasons."

"What reasons could he possibly have, besides the well-being of his citizens?"

"I don't know!" Gabčík said. "Foreign policy reasons! Big-picture issues! We know this is what he wants! He met with us personally before he sent us on this mission!"

"He spoke to you specifically about killing the Realm-Protector?" HAJASKÝ asked, breaking his silence at last.

"What do you mean?" Josef turned, surprised.

"Did he speak to you specifically about this mission?" HAJASKÝ asked. "Did you ever hear him say the word 'Heydrich'?"

"Well, no," Josef admitted.

"So there's a chance he doesn't know exactly what's been ordered," HAJASKÝ said.

Josef just sat there perplexed.

"I'm with JINDRA on this," HAJASKÝ said at last. "We need to at least send them a message asking for explicit confirmation. And stating, explicitly, that there will be reprisals. We'll send a messenger to Captain Bartoš. And he will send it. We know he's on our side on this. Soldier or not, we know he's on our side."

Again Gabčík just sat there. Flabbergasted at this turn of events. Finally he spoke: "And what are we supposed to do until then?"

"As far as I'm concerned, you're still on hold," JINDRA said. "When we hear back, we can have this discussion again."

"There's nothing to discuss," Gabčík said. Angry.

```
DOCUMENT:       #6039
DESCRIPTION:    REQUEST FOR CLARIFICATION REGARDING
                OPERATION ANTHROPOID
PLACE:          PARDUBICE, OCCUPIED CZECHOSLOVAKIA
DATE:           12 MAY 1942
TRANSMITTED BY: LIBUSE
FOR:            MUSIL AND PRESIDENT EDUARD BENEŠ
```

FOR YOUR EYES ONLY

SUBJECT: THE PROPOSED ASSASSINATION OF SS SUPREME GROUP LEADER REINHARD HEYDRICH

I am sending this message to alert the exiled political and military leadership of the conditions and circumstances relating to the proposed assassination of Reinhard Heydrich. This assassination would not help the Allies, and for the Czechoslovakian nation it would have unforeseeable consequences. The nation would be subject to heretofore unheard-of reprisals, and its citizenry would suffer terribly. Most likely, the reprisals and aftershocks of such an assassination would wipe out what remains of our resistance and intelligence networks here, networks that were built over a great length of time and in the face of tremendous difficulties. Therefore, we beg you to give the order through SILVER A to cancel the assassination at once. Do not delay, danger in delay. If for reasons of foreign policy an assassination is necessary, we would suggest the traitor, Emanuel Moravec.

```
DOCUMENT:    #27
DESCRIPTION: PERSONAL DIARY OF K.H. FRANK
PLACE:       WILSON STATION, PRAHA, OCCUPIED
             CZECHOSLOVAKIA
DATE:        2 MAY 1942
```

I found myself back at that blasted train station today.

We had an important visitor, so unfortunately it was even less pleasant than the last time we went there, on the Leader's birthday. We had to get there early and wait under the cavernous old iron train awning, as I imagine Moravec and Hácha had to wait for us that last time. An important lesson: if you are not the Leader, you will have to wait for someone, sooner or later. Oh, to be truly important!

Presently an armoured train arrived, a black behemoth, huffing and puffing after its journey from Berlin. We stood at attention as the train stopped, and at last the doors opened, and there appeared a bespectacled little man, with a familiar face nearly devoid of muscle tone and chin: Himmler.

There is a perception among those who have never been in uniform that everyone in the ranks stands still in mute uniformity, but those who have been there know this is not the case. There are always jokes and wisecracks and commentary, all delivered with head and eyes straight forward—and never more so than in the front ranks! And so, just as Himmler disembarked, Heydrich murmured, "Here comes the schoolmaster," just loudly enough for me—and only me!!—to hear.

Still, Heydrich greeted his superior as warmly as a brother, and they ambled together down the train platform, past their silent honour guard. A shapeless entourage followed them, with me at its head.

Heydrich's Mercedes awaited outside. In front and behind were two ugly half-tracks, with a squad of troops in each.

"This is the kind of security you should have at all times," I heard Himmler say as they settled in.

"Yes, Lord Realm-Leader," Heydrich said. (I was grateful that they couldn't see my face! It is, at any rate, somewhat harder to respect one's boss when one catches him kissing his own boss's ass.)

"I understand this isn't always the case," Himmler said.

Heydrich shot me an angry glance: so much hatred in those eyes! Then they motored off.

I was, unfortunately, not privy to the rest of that discussion; I had to return to the Castle in my own automobile, with Emanuel Moravec as a passenger. I did not speak to him the whole ride! But when I at last caught up with my boss and his boss, they were exiting Heydrich's car up in that great stone courtyard outside the Castle. I think I caught Himmler admiring the view.

"A beautiful city, is it not, Lord Realm-Leader?" Heydrich asked hopefully.

"It is."

"The Austrians should be proud of themselves. I had a most productive discussion and tour with Speer when he visited. We're going to build a new government centre near here, and a new German opera house. Once we're connected via highway to the rest of the Realm, this city will be as German as Frankfurt or Munich. In another twenty years…"

"I wasn't joking earlier when I spoke about your security measures, Reinhard," Himmler said, looking about edgily; he caught a glimpse of me hovering and lowered his voice, and I pretended not to listen. "Their resistance…"

"There is no resistance to speak of here, Lord Realm-Leader," Heydrich said. Patient but insistent. "Those who stayed behind tried to build a resistance, and we crushed that, and now the cowards in exile are trying to parachute in a new resistance, and we're crushing that, too."

"All it takes is one lucky man, Reinhard. Think of the damage our national prestige would suffer if something should happen to you."

"Think of the damage if we act like we're afraid of them, Lord Realm-Leader. For them to know they're defeated…"

"Your..." Himmler nearly shouted, then looked over at me and realized I was eavesdropping. I took a few steps away and pretended not to listen. "Your car isn't even armoured!" Himmler hissed.

Heydrich stayed silent.

"There's no excuse for you not to have had that done," Himmler continued quietly. "They would have no way of knowing."

"Let me show what we've done to their resistance, my Lord."

Within a half hour, we were back in Heydrich's office.

"…as a result of our efforts, we have seized the following equipment. Six Sten guns. Six Colt pistols. Hundreds of rounds of ammunition. Fourteen parachutes. Dozens of kilograms of cyclonite. Five radio transmitters and receivers. One radio homing beacon. 72 special demolition charges apparently designed for sabotage purposes. 6 charges for assassinations. 40 incendiary devices. Over 1000 detonators and fuses of various kinds." Von Pannwitz read the typed inventory in a matter-of-fact tone leavened with a pinch of self-satisfaction.

All of this equipment, lovingly cleaned of farm-field dirt, lay proudly before us on the heavy oak conference table in Heydrich's office. Himmler walked around the table and looked down at the weaponry. Nodded appreciatively. He and Heydrich were relaxed. The others in the office—myself, von Pannwitz, Geschke, Hácha, Moravec, and two Czech policemen—stood in frozen tableaux.

"It must also be recognized that these efforts would not have been successful were it not for the excellent co-operation between the Secret Police and various Czech police agencies," von Pannwitz added. "These policemen here are being decorated for their part apprehending two parachutists who were attempting to retrieve their equipment from the Křivoklat forest. The criminals were carrying pistols, and these men were wounded apprehending them. A third officer was killed. But in recognition of his sacrifice, we have provided his widow with a generous pension."

"The Realm is most grateful for your efforts on its behalf," Himmler said, and the policemen nodded their acknowledgement.

"Thank you. That will be all," Heydrich added.

Now there was some confusion. Finally I gestured for the others to leave, and they shuffled out.

"That will be all, Frank," Heydrich said, so I would leave, too.

I was quite displeased by this turn of events! Still, obviously I had no say in the matter, so I put on a calm face and left. I hovered outside the door, so as to catch snippets of the conversation; one of the staff officers noticed me eavesdropping, and I gave him a dirty look, then put my finger to my lips.

"I will say, this is a lot of equipment you've seized, Reinhard," I heard Himmler's muddled voice through the door.

"It says something about the passivity of their populace, my Lord, that the exiles are going to such lengths to stir them up…"

"You have fourteen parachutes. Have you captured fourteen parachutists?" Himmler asked.

Heydrich said nothing.

I leaned closer; I had the sense Heydrich was biding his time, angling for something big. But they apparently walked further away from the door; their voices faded, and I missed the rest of the conversation.

- 196 -

```
DOCUMENT:    #27
DESCRIPTION: PERSONAL DIARY OF K.H. FRANK
PLACE:       HRADČANY, PRAHA, OCCUPIED CZECHOSLOVAKIA
DATE:        14 MAY 1942
```

I was meeting with Heydrich today when the switchboard operator at the Castle patched a call through to his office.

Heydrich was perusing a report; behind his back, the open office windows overlooked placid perfection. There was no need to separate inside and outside; all was right with the world.

When the call came in, I expected to be ushered out, but Heydrich merely turned his back to me, so I sat and eavesdropped.

"Yes, Lord Realm-Leader," I heard him say to his caller—Himmler, presumably?

There was more talking on the other end; it sounded high and pleasant at first, but it flattened out—a note of concern, perhaps.

"Some issues, Lord Realm-Leader?" Heydrich furrowed his brow.

Again there was some haranguing. This time, Heydrich relaxed visibly, and turned towards me with a bemused look; he saw I was eavesdropping and didn't seem to mind! "Yes, Lord Realm-Leader."

More talking—I grew bored and envious. "Who questions it still?" Heydrich asked at last.

I heard a crackle as Himmler explained something.

"Bormann is a fool," Heydrich said dismissively. "If he wants a fight, I'll be only too happy to oblige. The bigger the fight, the bigger a fool he'll seem. Tell all interested parties that I will send a full report via teletype within the next two days. If anyone still wants to challenge me after that…" Heydrich swivelled in his chair and gazed out at the bright rolling city with its spires and orange rooftops spread out beneath him.

When at last the call was over, he turned back to me and smiled. "They want to pick a fight with me over Thummel. Over Thummel!" He gave a little incredulous head-shake, like a man amazed at his own good fortune.

```
DOCUMENT:            #458
DESCRIPTION:         TRANSCRIPTION OF MAGNETOPHON
                     RECORDINGS OF DISCUSSION BETWEEN R.
                     HEYDRICH AND P. THUMMEL.
PLACE:               KLADNO, PRAHA, OCCUPIED
                     CZECHOSLOVAKIA
DATE:                18 MAY 1942
```

Notes from Lead Inspector Abendschon:

At the request of the Realm-Leader, I travelled to Kladno in advance of his discussion with Paul Thummel, former head of the Military Intelligence in Prague, currently being held under a false name at the Secret Police headquarters in Kladno. I travelled with a Magnetophon machine on loan from the Propaganda Ministry; I was instructed to set up a room so as to record their conversation, and to monitor the recording. Again, Heydrich is determined that we obtain incontrovertible proof of his statements. In the event that our actions are questioned by our superiors, we want to be able to prove his duplicity, hopefully through a recorded confession.

As a safeguard, Heydrich requested that the suspect be chained to a chair in an interrogation room prior to his arrival and shackled, in order that he could be questioned with no one else present. He also requested that I turn over this transcript to him personally upon its completion, that I make no copies of it, and that I tell no one the details of our trip.

[START OF RECORDING]

[SOUND OF DOOR CLOSING.]

[THUMMEL] Good day, my Lord.

[HEYDRICH] It is night.

[THUMMEL] I'm surprised you are willing to tell me.

[HEYDRICH] You'll lose track soon enough.

[THUMMEL] Probably. I must admit, my Lord, it has been some while since I've had a visitor. I was beginning to think I'd been forgotten.

[HEYDRICH] Heaven knows I wouldn't want you to think that.

[THUMMEL] What brings you here, my Lord?

[HEYDRICH] You forget your role. You're the one in shackles, lest you forget.

[THUMMEL] I've forgotten nothing, my Lord. But at this point, with the way I've been treated, I have little to lose by being impertinent. I have friends in high places, you know.

[HEYDRICH] I am not concerned. Some of them did, in fact, try to intercede on your behalf, but obviously to no avail. And if anyone else tries to dig you up, I have more than enough dirt on hand to keep you buried for good.

[LONG PAUSE.]

[HEYDRICH] Ahh, yes. You forgot what we have known for so long, how inconvenient can be to have things written down. Both in your specific case, and in general. What is written can be stored away and used against you later. Cardinal Richelieu, who was perhaps more Machiavellian than Machiavelli, said it best: "Never send a letter, and never burn one."

[THUMMEL] He also said: "The pen is mightier than the sword."

[HEYDRICH] [Dismissively.] I don't believe it. That sounds like something a writer would say. Someone who has never held a sword, at least. I suppose there is some truth to it, though. The written word is dangerous. Unfortunately, of course, some things must be set down on paper for an organization to survive, but one must be very selective in what one allows to be recorded. The spoken word, unrecorded, is quicksilver. It travels from person to person, or from parents to children, but as it travels it changes. One man embellishes it to improve the story, and another leaves things out for the same reason. And this man lies to spare someone else, and that man lies to spare himself. And they are alive, these spoken truths. They can burn like a flame through the years and resist every effort to extinguish them. But they are deliciously unreliable. They can be changed as needed. Or affirmed or denied, to meet changing circumstances. Cardinal Richelieu understood that, even though the rest of the Church didn't.

[THUMMEL] What do you care of the Church, my Lord?

[HEYDRICH] You'd be surprised.

[THUMMEL] Ahh, yes. I forget. You, Himmler and Hitler. All lapsed Catholics, with the Catholic's love for ceremony and ritual and above all, rule and order, and the lapsed Catholic's belief that the rules apply to everyone but yourself.

[HEYDRICH] Masaryk, too, was a lapsed Catholic. Or had you forgotten?

[THUMMEL] What do I care for Masaryk?

[HEYDRICH] You were helping the country he founded.

[LONG PAUSE.]

[HEYDRICH] I will say this about the man. Show me a thinking Catholic and I'll show you a lapsed Catholic.

[THUMMEL] Still he remained haunted by it.

[HEYDRICH] And why not? Who can be interested in power and not care about the Church?

[THUMMEL] It is a kingdom of conscience. It rules no one without their consent.

[HEYDRICH] It only fell back on conscience and consent when the traditional methods failed it. The doctrine of papal infallibility, do you know when it was instituted? 1870. And why it was instituted? Because the Papal States were shrinking as Italy came together as a nation. It is a failing, elderly institution anyway. Unfortunately for itself, it has always had the written word to contend with. Rather inconvenient, Jesus' words, for anyone in a position of authority. For the church or the state...

[THUMMEL] For the church, my Lord?

[HEYDRICH] Of course! How can you read Jesus' words to the Pharisees and not think of the Church? 'You are like whitewashed tombs, clean on the outside, but the inside is filled with death and corruption.' And for an organization that purports to follow him to place such an emphasis on appearances…

[THUMMEL] [Laughing.] It never fails to amaze and amuse me how people who despise Christianity act as if they care more, not less, about Jesus' teachings. As if all they want is to bring the world back to his simple truths. What do you care about such things, except as a means to point out the inconsistencies of others?

[HEYDRICH] Oh, I suppose you're right. How could I care for Jesus' teachings? They are so impossible, so naïve. How can you love a neighbour who is of an inferior race? How can you call a man 'brother' when you don't even know if he is blessing or cursing you in his native tongue? When you don't know if he's content with your existence or planning to take everything you own? Such fuzzy thinking is…impossible in a world of men. But we have the luxury of trying something new. We can free the continent from these dusty and inconvenient Bibles. And what's more, we can do it by co-opting so many who profess to believe in them. Those people who give lip service to the ideals but really only care that their friends and family, their race and kin, get the best things in the world. For isn't that what most people care about, even most Christians? Despite their purported Saviour's insistence that we are all brothers and sisters with one father, don't most people just want to see their kind on top? To triumph in this world, not an imaginary afterlife, that's what people really want! And if it's not possible for an individual, it can at least come by being a member of a group, a superior race! That is what people really want! They want to be told that God loves their kind more than anyone else. They want a God created in their image, not the other way around! A God that loves those whom they love and hates those whom they hate! And unlike the Church, we can give it to them. For the first time since the Roman Empire, there will be a united Europe. And not just a unified Europe, but a Europe free from this culture of weakness and inferiority and suffering. A Europe where strength and might will be rewarded—which is as Nature intended!

[THUMMEL] It won't come to pass. And if it does, it will come and go. People always try such things and fail. Look at the French Revolution! They re-started the calendar and changed the week to ten days. They moved the months and changed their names, to Thermidor and Ventose and things of that sort. They tried to de-Christianize Europe and bend history itself to their will, to re-shade things to their viewpoint by telling everyone what was good and bad. The Dark Ages, the Enlightenment. What were these names but politicizations of history? And they thought they'd be able to spread their ideals to every land they considered to be enslaved. And eventually the ideals fell by the wayside. The so-called noble purposes were forgotten, and the wars continued on the basis of pride and vainglory and vengeance. So what came of all that so-called Enlightenment? Decades of bloodshed and a shattered continent.

[HEYDRICH] Your history is tailored to suit your needs. Still, were things any different when church and state were so closely bound as to be inseparable? Were those wars any less bloody?

[THUMMEL] [Laughing.] You speak to me of bloodshed!

[HEYDRICH] I'll admit, I don't despise it. But I don't pretend to, either. What great country got that way without bloodshed? The Romans are fondly remembered for their accomplishments. But how many people did they subjugate? How many did they crucify, besides that one famous carpenter? All history is written in blood. It only looks like ink from a distance.

[LONG PAUSE.]

[HEYDRICH] So despite all the cruelty the Romans are remembered fondly. And we will be remembered fondly. Because we will be the ones writing the history.

[THUMMEL] How grandiose.

[HEYDRICH] It is true! We have great things to accomplish. Lancing the Soviet boil, relieving the continent of this…Jewish pestilence that has infested it since the Diaspora..

[THUMMEL] [Unintelligible.]

[HEYDRICH] No, it is true! We have great things to accomplish.

[THUMMEL] Let me tell you about your accomplishments. Back in 1933, shortly after Hitler took power, my office was tasked with keeping tabs on a man named Fritz Haber. Do you know the name?

[HEYDRICH] No.

[THUMMEL] Fritz Haber was a senior scientist at the Max Planck institute, a Nobel laureate, one of the best minds our country has ever produced. Long ago, he developed, along with a man named Carl Bosch, a process to synthesize ammonia out of atmospheric nitrogen. This lead, for instance, to greatly increased fertilizer production, and consequently, greater crop yields. Literally, bread from air! And ammonia, too, is a precursor to manufacturing nitric acid in industrial quantities. Which, of course, is essential to making armaments. Do you know that without this man, we would have lost the Great War inside of a year? We would have simply run out of ammunition. Previously we had made explosives using nitrates mined in Chile, but with the naval blockade, only the British and French had access to those sources. But Haber's accomplishments kept us in the war. And yet when your ilk came to power he was suddenly in disfavour. We spied on him, we harassed him, we hounded out of the country. And do you know why?

[HEYDRICH] Enlighten me.

[THUMMEL] Because he was Jewish.

[HEYDRICH] So what?

[THUMMEL] Just think how absurd that is! All those theories about a stab in the back…and the reality was that a Jew kept us in the war.

[HEYDRICH] Who says he even supported the war?

[THUMMEL] He did! He lent all of his talents to our war effort! He helped bridge the gaps between science and industry and the military. He pioneered the use of poison gas for us. His wife was so despondent about his priorities that she committed suicide. But he kept on. So no honest person can say that this man, this Jew, didn't love Germany. That he didn't give his all for the Fatherland in its time of need. And to see such a man treated like a common criminal…

[HEYDRICH] What of it? So there was one useful Jew among so many. So what? Every country has its criteria for what is acceptable and what isn't. Every country decides whom to lock up and whom to set free. It just so happens that our criteria are based on blood, not behaviour. Which is just as well, since blood ultimately determines behaviour...

[Translator's Note: Here there were roughly four lines of dialogue blacked out in the original typed transcript, presumably by Heydrich himself. One can only guess at their contents.]

[THUMMEL] Since when do you care for the truth?

[HEYDRICH] [Angrily.] I care for it more than you think! You've seen my files, my index cards! All that information, what is it for, if not the truth?

[THUMMEL] It is for blackmail and backstabbing. Your truth is not a whole truth. No one keeps a file on you. No one spies on you. Your truth is sliced and dissected and used for your convenience.

[HEYDRICH] And given what we have in your file, it is most inconvenient. You speak of this Haber fellow. You speak of such noble things. As if that was what spurred to act, the plight of this poor Jew. Are you trying to tell me you never took money for your actions? We have the payment records, you know...

[LONG PAUSE.]

[HEYDRICH] Bank ledger books, in phony names, for amounts far greater than would be possible with your salary. We have photographs of you doing business at these banks, banks where there were no accounts listed in your name, and none associated with your organization. We have testimony from bank tellers concerning large cash transactions. We have forwarded this information on to Berlin...

[THUMMEL] [Unintelligible.]

[HEYDRICH] So you are a traitor, plain and simple. By all appearances a good German with a good German wife, and you decided to throw it all away for money. So perhaps there is some Jewish blood in you, after all. In which case we have more proof that we're on the right path. Again, you, too, have forgotten how dangerous it is for things to be written down. We have seen the ledger books. You can say what you want about your motivations, but your actions are what they are. You will spend the rest of your days as a prisoner...

[THUMMEL] You're as much a prisoner of these bars as I am. Without them, you're nothing.

[HEYDRICH] Oh, I think not. It is you who are nothing. It is you who has been forgotten...

[Translator's Note: Here again there were several lines of dialogue blacked out in the original German transcript. It is unclear whether this was the end of the conversation.]

```
DOCUMENT:    #47
DESCRIPTION: NARRATIVE OF J. KUBIŠ
PLACE:       PRAHA, OCCUPIED CZECHOSLOVAKIA
DATE:        23 MAY 1942
```

On a pleasant spring afternoon, A. and I went for a walk down by the river. The sun shone sharply. Sparrows sprung from place to place, pecking crumbs from between the cobblestones. (There are only two main kinds of paving stones in the city, I've noticed. Large grey bricks in the street and others on the sidewalk like dirty sugar cubes.)

Josef and I had been making new preparations. It would not be soon, but it would be real this time. I felt it like a stone on my chest. Usually when I was with her, that weight vanished, blown away like dandelion seeds. But today there was something new. A different unspoken tension. For once it wasn't from me.

"Such a wonderful day," I observed.

"It is." No argument from A., but little enthusiasm.

"What is missing?" I asked as we sat in the shade under a park bench.

"I can think of a few things," she said cryptically.

"Such as..." Next to us, a boy sat down on a patch of lawn. Not quite a teenager. He opened a valise and began grabbing fistfuls of grass and dropping them in the case. "...Now what on earth is he doing?"

A. looked over. "Gathering rabbit food, I imagine."

"A pet rabbit. How cute."

"I doubt it's a pet," she said with a little smile. "And if it is, it's edible."

I'm sure I shot her a strange glance.

She continued. "You've been too busy doing whatever you're doing to notice these things, but a lot of people have taken to raising rabbits. Since they don't have to be reported to the Germans like the pigs and the cows, people grow them and eat them."

"No!" I said in mock horror.

"You do what you do for a living, and that shocks you? People killing rabbits?" She gave me a look. "Yes, that's what they do. They keep them in rooftop hutches and keep feeding them, and the little things end up…" Here she blushed. "…multiplying like rabbits."

"Speaking of multiplying like rabbits…" I drew her closer to me and kissed her.

"If you wanted to do that, we should have stayed indoors." She smiled now.

"Maybe we should have."

"But you still have to count the ducks!"

"Ahh, yes. Counting the ducks." There were many ducks that day, in fact. Paddling on the sunny water and diving beneath it to peck food. Brown mallards and green-headed drakes shimmering in the sun. "So many ducks."

A. drew me towards her. Kissed me again and rested her head on my chest.

"You're going to make me lose count!" I exclaimed.

"Four hundred one, four hundred two, four hundred three…"

"Great! Now I've completely lost count," I said, feigning exasperation. "I have to start all over from zero."

"Great!"

"Great?"

"It's all part of my plan to keep you here as long as possible."

"Well, I do have to be thorough in my counting," I allowed.

"And all the while, the ducks are multiplying like rabbits."

"Yes, I suppose they are," I said, perplexed.

"There's a new one coming."

"A new duck?" Still I didn't get it.

"Yes. It will be here in seven months." Here she looked down and patted her belly.

And finally I understood. Felt an odd combination of fear and elation. Took a deep and heavy breath.

"Seven months," I said at last.

```
DOCUMENT:     #27
DESCRIPTION: PERSONAL DIARY OF K.H. FRANK
PLACE:        HRADČANY, PRAHA, OCCUPIED CZECHOSLOVAKIA
DATE:         23 MAY 1942
```

Today, there was a breath of real fresh air—an indication that perhaps all these months of patience will be paying off at last!

Geschke and I were summoned, quite unexpectedly, to Heydrich's office.

I don't think either of us had a clue as to why we'd been summoned, so we sat there, uneasy. Finally Heydrich cracked a crooked smile, and placed a teletype on his desk.

"I've received my orders. I'm flying to Berlin on the 27th in preparation for a private briefing with Hitler on the 28th. I'm going to brief him on our successes here and suggest ways to replicate them across the continent."

"Congratulations, Lord Realm-Protector," I said after a long pause. "We should celebrate."

"We should," Heydrich said. To the buzzer on his desk he spoke: "Please send in a tray of cognac."

"Very good, my Lord." (I was and I am, in fact, truly excited—perhaps more excited for him than I've ever been! If he's promoted, I don't see who else they'll be able to put in charge here, other than myself.)

"It is somewhat bittersweet," Heydrich continued. "Our work here is by no means completed. But we have much to be proud of. These lands are rapidly integrating into the Realm, and the workers now enjoy security and unemployment benefits comparable to those in Germany proper. Those who work for the Realm should share in its achievements, yes?"

Tentatively, we nodded.

"Of course, this will only be while the war in the east continues. We Germans are not all sunshine and smiles.

In order to fully integrate these lands, we will need to complete the weeding out of the various racial undesirables. Perhaps when the factories are no longer working around the clock…"

A silence ensued; Geschke eventually realized his boss was waiting for it to be filled. "We have been proceeding with the racial surveys, my Lord. The mobile x-ray devices have started to gather information on the racial characteristics of the Czech population. We've told Hácha it is part of a grand campaign to eradicate tuberculosis."

"They are not a terrible people, racially," Heydrich said. "As we've discussed before, there is a lot of Aryan blood here. Perhaps forty percent of them will be able to stay once this is all over. We will of course have to send their children off to be Germanized, and that will take some time. But we have a good start on things. The way things are going…" Heydrich stood and leaned his hand on the open windowsill; I thought again of that famous picture of Hitler on his first and only night here.

"The way things are going, you'll be Leader someday," I said.

"Perhaps," Heydrich said, and smiled.

An orderly arrived with the cognac; we drank and conversed awkwardly, then ambled off into the gilded halls. I must admit, I was too excited to work!

And now I'm too excited to sleep—again, this is a tremendous thing! I can't see how they can justify making anyone else Realm-Protector now; who, after all, knows and understands the Czech soul better than I do? Who is better qualified to rule them than I am? No one.

```
DOCUMENT:    #47
DESCRIPTION: NARRATIVE OF J. KUBIŠ
PLACE:       PRAHA, OCCUPIED CZECHOSLOVAKIA
DATE:        23 MAY 1942
```

By the time A. and I made it back to her place, I was ready to burst with desire.

"I guess it doesn't matter what time of month it is now," I said in her hallway.

"No, you idiot. It doesn't." She smiled. Kissed me. "But I am feeling…nauseous."

I'm sure I gave a disappointed look.

"Morning sickness," she explained.

I had not expected that. And it was all the more shocking to open her door and see someone sitting there. Waiting and smoking. Josef.

"How did you get in?" I asked. Sad and aching. Blue, as only a man can be.

"Through the door, like you did," he said.

"Did we…hear from London?"

"No."

"What's this all about, then?"

"Yes. What's this all about?" A. asked angrily.

"I'm sorry, could you step outside?" Josef asked.

"This is my flat, Josef!"

He shrugged apologetically but stayed. She left in a huff.

"What's this all about?" I asked.

"I just got word from our man. There was a teletype from Berlin that came in today. Heydrich's leaving on the 27th. Probably for good."

This. This was what I had hoped for, and feared. "I wish he could give us more time."

"We've been here five months."

"Yes, but…" I explained that A. was in a family way.

Josef darted to the door. Stuck his head out in the hallway. "You're pregnant?" I heard him say.

"Yes!"

"Congratulations!" Josef darted back inside and closed the door. Leaving her to wait in the hall still. "Good to know your gun works, huh?" he said to me.

"It's…" I didn't want to imagine how irate A. must be right now. Or how she would feel, with this. "It's a lot to think about."

"It is. Since we haven't heard from London, we have to make contingency plans. Move our equipment…"

"I meant this." I gestured towards A. and the hallway.

"All the more reason to act." Josef said. "We owe our children a better world than this mess we inherited."

"We do." I said solemnly. Still believed it. But also I felt, more strongly than I'd felt since we'd taken the mission, that I wanted to be there for it, too.

Again Josef flung the door open. "Come on in!"

A. came in, a half-smoked cigarette smouldering between her fingers. The other arm crossed over her slight but now-noticeable belly. A cross look on her face.

Josef flung his arms around her and kissed her on both cheeks. "We've got a lot to celebrate today!"

```
DOCUMENT:    #27
DESCRIPTION: PERSONAL DIARY OF K.H. FRANK
PLACE:       HRADČANY, PRAHA, OCCUPIED CZECHOSLOVAKIA
DATE:        26 MAY 1942
```

It has been a long day, and an eventful night.

There was a reception to celebrate Heydrich's last night here—although whether the primary purpose was to honour his time here, or to rejoice at his departure, I don't know!

I would have normally gotten properly inebriated, but I ended up leaving a little early, anxious and a little depressed despite all my good fortune of late. Still, I don't feel like I'll be sleeping soon, so I should perhaps jot down my recollections from the day.

I remember walking into Heydrich's office near the end of the workday; though his mood's been generally upbeat of late, today he seemed particularly jubilant. "Looking forward to the reception, I hope?" he asked.

"I am, my Lord," I said.

"We've got a lot to celebrate tonight!" he exclaimed, proud as a peacock.

"We do, my Lord." I glanced over the room. Apart from the furniture, everything had been placed in cardboard boxes, all neatly labelled and stamped. I believe many of his files are already back in Berlin under lock and key; those that remained here were in special boxes sealed in wax. "Well, it's all done then."

"Yes. Off to bigger and better things."

"I'm sure your new duties will keep you even busier than you were here, my Lord. Perhaps you will look back on this with nostalgia."

"I doubt it," Heydrich said. "Nostalgia is ultimately unsatisfying. New challenges, new goals: these are the only things that truly make men happy."

"I wonder if the Leader thinks so. At times I think it would be boring, with nowhere higher to go."

"There's always something more to be done," Heydrich said. "Still, I'll admit I've been looking forward to this night off. It's nice to have a break once in a while. What we've been doing is necessary, but it's coarse work. Rough. Sometimes one needs the finer things in life."

"They'll be playing your father's music tonight, my Lord?"

Heydrich stepped to the mirror to look over his uniform. "Yes. They'll be playing my father's music."

In the courtyard, we waited while Klein scuttled off to find the car. The sun was taking its time leaving the May sky; it did not feel like the end of the day. But others were leaving already; I heard car doors slam and starter motors crank on black Tatras and Mercedeses; I watched their brake lights as they headed out the courtyard and down the hill. Still we—the two most powerful men in the Protectorate, mind you!—waited; it was an unusual and unexpected state of affairs.

"Where the fuck is Klein?" Frustrated, I fumed—hoping to head off Heydrich, perhaps.

"Check on him, would you?"

"Yes, Lord Realm-Protector." This bothered me—was he determined to keep me playing the flunky until the very last minute? Still, Heydrich's questions were never questions, so I marched off smartly, as if I knew where I was going.

As soon as I was out of sight in the next courtyard, I practically ran over Klein, who was coming the other way. "Lord Frank, I was just coming to get you. Captain Boeckmann says he has work that needs to be finished up, and he's refusing to stop."

"I'll go talk to him."

Klein led me to the garage, where there were mechanics in white coveralls squatting next to the car. The doors were lying on the floor, and a captain strutted about, supervising.

"Captain Boeckmann!"

The captain turned; when he saw me, the confidence suddenly disappeared. "Hail Hitler," he saluted snappily.

"Hail Hitler. What the hell is going on here?"

"We were trying to install the armoured plating in the doors and seatbacks, my Lord."

"The armoured plating?"

"Yes. Himmler ordered it after his visit and shipped it with highest priority from Berlin."

"Jesus fucking Christ! Put the fucking car back together! (I pretended to be angry—in situations like that, it is a useful way to get things done quickly!) We've got an event to go to. Music, culture, a night on the town! And you're keeping the Realm-Protector waiting like some…Czech flunky?"

"Very well, my Lord," Boeckmann said. "I'll have the men complete the work tomorrow."

"You might as well not bother. The man's leaving for Berlin in the morning. He won't be back."

Here Boeckmann hesitated; he breathed heavily. "Does that mean you will be Realm-Protector, Lord Frank?"

Only then did I allow myself the thinnest of smiles. "Perhaps."

```
DOCUMENT:     #47
DESCRIPTION: NARRATIVE OF J. KUBIŠ
PLACE:        ŽIŽKOV, PRAHA, OCCUPIED CZECHOSLOVAKIA
DATE:         26 MAY 1942
```

For much of the week, the two Josefs and I had been shuttling to and fro on bicycles, moving various caches of weaponry. And now all was set. We were staying with new people, a family in Dejvice. Valčik was with M., and the other parachutists were out of the way. We had no cause to bump into anyone, and nothing to interrupt our plans.

Still, Gabčík wanted to pay one last visit. And so, on what I thought might be our last night in Praha, or anywhere, we ended up right back where we'd been on that first night. Back at HAJASKÝ's.

Again we knocked. Again he answered warily. But when he saw us, his face brightened.

"Gentlemen! What a surprise!" HAJASKÝ spoke more softly that I'd have expected. "What's the special occasion?"

"No occasion, no reason," Gabčík said. Sighed. "Well, I cannot lie."

"No?"

"But that also means I cannot say anything," Josef said.

"And you, silent one?" HAJASKÝ smiled thinly at me. "No final words, even?"

"Well…" Here I too had nothing. How does one say such things as need to be said on such occasions? Instead I pressed a small tin into HAJASKÝ's hand. Inside two pills rattled like beads. "In case they come for you some morning."

HAJASKÝ's face fell. But he nodded, serious now.

"And if you see JINDRA before we do, tell him…" Josef started. "Well, tell him something."

From behind HAJASKÝ, we heard a noise. I remember assuming it was his wife.

"I suppose you can talk to him yourself." HAJASKÝ opened the door wider. JINDRA was walking over from the kitchen. Curious, then furious.

"Fuck," Gabčík said under his breath. But he stood his ground. To leave now would be the height of cowardice. Then, to JINDRA he spoke: "Why are you here?"

"I'm told that your actions are imminent. I have received no confirmation of this mission from London, and so I came to tell him to tell you to hold off."

"You're in no position to stop us," Josef said.

"I'm head of this network!" JINDRA's voice was a sharp spike.

"You're head because you say you are. No one in London ever gave you authority over us," Josef says flatly.

"I built this network from fucking nothing! I sit on the council, on UVOD! This network, my network, has sheltered and fed you for five fucking months!"

"Are you finished?" Josef said simply. Acted as if about to leave.

"No, I'm not fucking finished! If you do this, innocent people will die. And good people, people that helped you and fed and clothed you, will be imprisoned and killed. Tortured, even! Are you comfortable knowing that? Can you sleep knowing that?"

"I don't like it, but they understand the risks they've taken!" Gabčík exploded at last. "They're patriots! We're patriots! We have our orders!"

"What monstrous egotistical maniacs! Your orders are more important than your countrymen?"

"We are the ones protecting our countrymen! Do you understand that? If we don't do this, if our nation fails to resist what's happening, we, as a people, will die! Our language, our culture, will die! It won't happen overnight, or in a fortnight, but eventually our people will be starved and subjugated and subjected to a darker darkness than we have ever experienced in our dark history! We'll be snuffed out! Extinguished! This is not a matter of glory or prestige! It is a matter of survival!"

"This war won't be won or lost here," JINDRA said. "You know it and MUSIL knows it and President Beneš knows it. It will be won or lost in the skies of England. On the steppes of Russia. In the deserts of Africa. Not in the streets of Praha."

"It is our duty to help those efforts in any way our President sees fit," Gabčík says. "And you can't stop us."

"We can. HAJASKÝ and I are going to go speak to your host household. We're going to ask them to place your weapons under our supervision until such time as this is all settled. You volunteered for this. The people who are sheltering you didn't."

"Yes, we did," HAJASKÝ said simply. Surprised, Josef and JINDRA both stared, speechless. So he continued, speaking softly but firmly. Almost mournfully. "At least, I did. I may not have known all the specifics. And I'll be honest, I fear the consequences. I truly and deeply weep at the thought of them. But we've been asked to choose sides, not outcomes. And I, for one, have chosen."

JINDRA turned and gave a surprised look to his fellow civilian. For a few moments he was speechless. "This will cause suffering beyond belief," he sputtered at last.

"Every nation and every people are suffering in this war," HAJASKÝ said. "We will either suffer for our allies or suffer for our occupiers. I'd rather suffer for our allies."

"This is completely unnecessary," JINDRA said.

"This is out of your hands," HAJASKÝ told him flatly. "These men are going to go back where they're staying.

I'm not going to tell you where they're staying. And they're going to do what they came here to do."

After that, we headed downstairs and out into the perfect spring night. As we grabbed our bicycles, Josef and I exchanged glances in the cool moonlight. Everything was calm but nothing felt calm. All was electric with excitement that evening. I didn't think I'd see another one.

```
DOCUMENT:          #7280.10.7.1947
DESCRIPTION:       EXCERPT FROM POSTWAR SUMMARY OF KNOWN
                   ACTIVITIES OF R. HEYDRICH
PREPARED FOR:      MUSIL
PREPARED ON:       10.7.1947
```

At the beginning of the century, Bruno Heydrich, father of Heydrich, ran a music conservatory in the Saxon city of Halle. He aspired to greater things and composed 43 works in various forms: piano pieces, choral presentations, string quartets, operas. But he was an undistinguished composer, frequently aping Wagner's overblown warrior epics instead of coming up with his own ideas. He died a third-rate imitator of a second-rate artist, with no following beyond his friends and family.

Which was fortunate for him, because his son became one of the most important men in Germany.

And so, on the evening of May 26th, 1942, the Rudolfinium, which had become Praha's German Concert Hall, inaugurated the city's music festival with an evening dedicated to Bruno Heydrich's chamber works, to be performed by four of his former students from the Halle conservatory. Heydrich himself had written the programs.

```
DOCUMENT:     #27
DESCRIPTION:  PERSONAL DIARY OF K.H. FRANK
PLACE:        HRADČANY, PRAHA, OCCUPIED CZECHOSLOVAKIA
DATE:         26 MAY 1942 (CONTINUED)
```

Following the delays with the car, we arrived in front of the Rudolfinium. Lina Heydrich had arrived separately; she's rather pregnant these days, but she also rather enjoys being a person of some importance, so she was not about to miss this outing. And so, side-by-side, but not hand-in-hand or even arm-in-arm, they walked together up the red carpet. A few of us followed at a moderate distance: myself, Geschke, von Pannwitz, and others I don't recall.

"Promise me you'll take it easy, Reinhard," I heard Lina say. "You've got a big day tomorrow."

"I've got a big night tonight!" he said brightly.

To my companions I muttered: "Our last night with the Blonde Beast."

"That's not a very nice thing to say about Frau Heydrich, my Lord," Geschke joked.

I laughed—I laughed all that much harder because I knew I shouldn't be laughing! And when the trembling subsided, I shook my head and spoke at last. "Ahh, there is truth in all humour."

"I suppose nothing makes a woman more bitter than being married to a philanderer," Geschke observed.

"She doesn't mind, as long as she gets to walk the red carpet," I replied. "Nothing makes a woman happier than importance by association."

"I heard she had quite the time renovating the chateau. She installed a swimming pool, even," Geschke noted.

"Well, who's going to turn down her budget requests? Or her labour requests, for that matter. She spared neither the gold nor the Jews."

"I must say, I am curious as to who the next Realm-Protector will be." Geschke said.

"I am amazed that the current one is actually leaving," I told him.

"And glad, my Lord?" he needled me.

"Indescribably glad." (It was true—it is true! For as much as I've fretted about my frustrations, though, all might yet be forgiven, for at last he will be gone. And again, who else can they choose to lead the Czechs now? Who knows them as well as I do? No one.)

"My Lords, shouldn't you show more respect to the man?" von Pannwitz asked.

"Believe you me, no one has more respect for the most powerful man in Germany than I do," Geschke replied.

"Fear is not respect," von Pannwitz said warily. "And the Leader would not be happy to hear you say that."

"Well, in a police state, the most important man isn't necessarily the head of state," Geschke said. "Sometimes it's the head of police."

Soon the ushers started shepherding us to our seats. The theatre darkened, and the curtain rose on a string quartet. They filled the darkened theatre with music—mediocre music, I must admit! Still, after two excruciating hours, when the last notes faded and the house lights came on, the applause was deafening—I'm not sure we wanted to clap; I think we just wanted to be seen clapping! And no one clapped harder or longer than I did.

```
DOCUMENT:     #47-J (CONTINUED)
DESCRIPTION: NARRATIVE OF J. KUBIŠ
PLACE:        DEJVICE, PRAHA, OCCUPIED CZECHOSLOVAKIA
DATE:         26 MAY 1942 (CONTINUED)
```

Back at the flat where we were staying, Josef wedged a towel into the crack under the bedroom door, and we went to work.

Scissors snipped stitches and slid under staples. We undid upholstery. Groped about for grenades. Found the Sten gun hidden among the slats and springs.

The SOE people had given us stick-type anti-tank grenades, the type the Germans referred to as potato-mashers. We placed two of them side-by-side in a battered leather valise we'd found in M.'s front closet. Then Josef assembled the Sten and dry-fired it. Then disassembled it swiftly into its 24 parts, lightly oiled and inspected everything, reassembled it, and dry-fired it again.

I loaded two magazines with bright brass cartridges. Empty, the clips felt familiar. Filled, they felt as heavy as my heart. Right and real, but strange still. Josef ventured out to the water closet. Retrieved the pistols, which were taped to the back of the bathtub and wrapped in waxed paper. And when he came back, we opened up the other valise, which was full of grass I'd plucked from a park on the other side of the river. We taped the weapons to the bottom of both valises and covered everything with grass. Precaution against what we figured was the worst possible outcome, a surprise stop on the way there.

All the while, our host family slept soundlessly. We listened but heard no creaking floors, no knocks on our door.

```
DOCUMENT:    #27
DESCRIPTION: PERSONAL DIARY OF K.H. FRANK
PLACE:       HRADČANY, PRAHA, OCCUPIED CZECHOSLOVAKIA
DATE:        26 MAY 1942 (CONTINUED)
```

When the applause finally died, we ambled up the aisles and wandered down plush stairs to the post-performance reception.

Nearly every hand cradled snifters of brandy and cognac, or glasses of wine. And as the drinks disappeared, the conversations crescendoed.

It ought to have been a delightful scene, and, for most, it was. I think there were only two people who were unhappy in the whole place: myself, and Lina Heydrich, who sipped water alone in the corner. (Her water is expected to break any day now!) I followed her scowl across the room, to where her husband was smiling at and flirting with two women, one blonde and moderately attractive, the other brunette and stunning.

Rather than talking to Lina, I ambled over to Heydrich and the women. (Misery loves company, true, and for a moment I had the most unmentionable thoughts...I had best not set them down!)

The two women talking to Heydrich gave no notice of my arrival; they were hanging off his every word, and looked so aroused that they'd have to change their undergarments shortly.

"...you're both from Vienna, then?" Heydrich asked.

Both women replied with dumb happy nods.

"Well, it's true what they say, then."

"What's true?" they asked. Almost in unison.

"That Viennese women are the most beautiful in all of Europe."

Again the women grinned stupidly and blushed. They whispered to one another, blushed again, and tittered. (Oh, how I look forward to the day he's gone and I'm in charge at last; all of your jokes are funny, and all of your come-ons are welcome, when you're in charge!)

"Who says that, Lord Realm-Protector?" the blonde asked, absent-mindedly toying with her hair.

"I've heard it said," Heydrich replied with a smile. "It's nothing to be embarrassed about, ladies! What is life about, except the never-ending quest for the important things, for beauty, for perfection?"

The women nodded dumbly.

"All my life I've been on that quest," Heydrich continued. "When I was a young naval lieutenant, I used to take my violin and climb to the crow's nest of the old cruiser I was assigned to. All alone, above anything, I'd climb up there by the light of the full moon, and gaze out on the beauty of the North Sea, soft and infinite in the moonlight. And I would play Mozart, and my heart would ache because it was more than I could bear, and I would be angry at God, for creating a world in which men could see such perfection but never posses it."

Now for a few moments all were silent. Sombre, not sober.

Finally Heydrich raised a glass. "Still, these are the things I've dedicated my life to. Perfect purity, perfect beauty, perfect truth, perfect knowledge. Man's never-ending aspirations, the search for strength and purity and truth, the elimination and eradication of weakness and backwardness. So let's drink a toast, then, to beauty and perfection."

The women drank; I raised a glass, too, but no one seemed to notice. The blonde blushed, and the brunette boldly brushed Heydrich's arm. "Your work must be exhausting, Lord Realm-Protector."

"Please. Call me Reinhard. It is hard work, yes. But well worth it for the better world we will leave for our children."

"I didn't know a man in your position would want to be called by his first name," the brunette replied; she touched his arm again and left her hand there long enough that no one could pretend it didn't happen.

"From my subordinates I expect fealty." (Finally he cast an acknowledging glance in my direction. The prick!) "But I myself am powerless before your charms." He grabbed her hand and kissed it; I wandered off at last, and plucked another brandy from a waiter's silver tray.

Geschke grabbed one, too, and sidled up behind me. "Perhaps that will be you in a few weeks," he said.

"God in heaven, don't think I haven't earned it," I replied—a touch bitterly, perhaps. I killed my brandy. "He is such a holy terror when he drags you out for a night on the town."

"An ordeal we've all suffered through," Geschke said.

"I think that's his secret," I said. "He makes sure to collect more dirt on you than you can possibly collect on him!"

"I accompanied him to Berlin a few months ago," Geschke replied. "And, of course, he scheduled the trip so that we'd have a free Friday evening, and an empty Saturday to recover. And…did you ever hear about the Salon Kitty operation?"

"Salon Kitty?" (I'm sure I grinned impishly.)

"Yes. He…" Geschke's eyes darted right and left; his voice volume descended several levels, from conversation to fear, and near to conspiracy. "I don't know that I had appreciated the depths of the man's cunning until that night. We had gone out drinking, private rooms at high-class clubs, and then we're somehow stumbling alone through late-night streets. Raising quite a ruckus. Think of it, the two of us, stumbling around like tramps, or…"

"Or law school students!" I smiled.

"Indeed! Haha. Drinking like we're back at university. So there we were, blind stinking drunk on the Alexanderplatz, and Heydrich started talking about an inspection tour. 'Now?' I asked. And he said, 'It's not what you think.' And he mentioned something called the Salon Kitty. Of course, I have no idea what is going on, but it is impossible to say no to the man when sober, even…"

I nodded knowingly.

"So we go to what, by all appearances, seemed to be an ordinary home. Elegant, stately, well-apportioned, to be sure, but apparently an ordinary house. But inside…Jesus, man! The most beautiful women I'd ever seen! And I know when I'm drunk, sometimes my vision gets…but these women were fucking flawless! And they behaved as if they'd been waiting to cater to our every whim. And…and I can't overemphasize how drunk I was by this point…so I have a single memory of myself naked with two of these women, but I'm not sure anything actually happened. But one of the last things I remember was seeing Heydrich headed upstairs with three of them. And of course, it turned out they were all…" Geschke practically whispered. "…prostitutes."

"Prostitutes?" I said, much louder than I should have.

"Yes. Heydrich had set the place up some time before. He had Nebe comb Germany for suitably attractive women. Most were already prostitutes, but some were ordinary girls. Or relatively ordinary girls, I should say. Sexual compulsives and nymphomaniacs all too willing to heed their country's call and perform a great service for the Realm."

"He never took me there…" (I was jealous! I am jealous! Yes, I am jealous of Geschke!) "How was this a great service for the Realm, though?"

"Well, the whole place was wired for sound. Double walls, double mirrors. Microphones in every room, leading to Magnetophons. They kept reels of magnetic tape rolling all the time. And when I found out about it, I appreciated the man's cunning so much more. I mean, I felt dirty, but I thought, 'Incredible! What better place to get secrets than a place where people do things they want to keep secret?' Because that was the whole scam. They brought important people there, dignitaries, diplomats, and the like, and they recorded everything they said and did. Men can keep secrets from their wives and their family, but they will spill their guts to a beautiful woman they slept with while drunk."

Someone wandered by, a drunk German; we moved away so as not to be overheard.

"So how did you find out all the rest?" I asked.

"Oh, yes! I was back at the RSHA main offices that Monday, and I started talking to Schellenberg about our weekend. And, so help me God, I mentioned the words 'Salon Kitty' and the man turned white as a sheet. And it turned out he was in charge of making sure the recording machines were turned off any time Heydrich went there. So thanks to that lapse, there was a tape recording chronicling the misdeeds of the country's prime chronicler of misdeeds. Something with which to blackmail the blackmailer. But fortunately for Schellenberg, he had issued standing instructions that, even if he personally wasn't able to call ahead, the machines were to be shut off if Heydrich showed up unannounced. And the fucking swine on duty had deliberately not done that. He'd played the tapes, and listened in, even! And now he's rotting in Dachau!"

"Hah!" (I laughed—yes, I appreciated the humour!)

"Anyway," Geschke said. "Here I thought we were a nation of laws, a nation willing to codify the popular will and enact it systematically, for the good of public safety and racial purity. And to see something like Salon Kitty…" (The whole time we'd been talking, Geschke's eyes hadn't left Heydrich's back. We all know how dangerous such conversations can be!) "And I wondered if this was some anomaly. But, no. Schellenberg said, 'Make no mistake. This is how it is with him. This man is the hidden pivot around which Germany revolves. In ways you don't know, with methods you might not want to know, he is the eminence gris, the one making everything happen. Even Himmler, even Hitler. Sooner or later he bends them to his will.'"

Here, unexpectedly, I was stricken with the most overwhelming malaise. I think it depressed me, to hear again how cunning the man can be. My best efforts seem insignificant when compared to such effortless guile!

I resolved to leave at once, to go back home to my wife, to set down my recollections of this unexpectedly miserable day. But first I looked back to the women who were moistening their panties in front of Heydrich. I felt helpless—impotent, even; I had not the energy for misbehaviour! But I understood something at last. Perhaps Heydrich has some touch of whatever it is that the Leader has, some ferocious instinct for making things happen by sheer willpower, something I don't have and may perhaps never have, after all.

```
DOCUMENT:    #47
DESCRIPTION: NARRATIVE OF J. KUBIŠ
PLACE:       DEJVICE, PRAHA, OCCUPIED CZECHOSLOVAKIA
DATE:        27 MAY 1942
```

Josef and I tried to sleep that night. I don't know why. You can never sleep on nights like that.

I don't know if I slept. I know I eventually dragged myself upright. Pressed the brass button on the torch. Saw that the hands of the round brass alarm clock had almost reached their appointed time. So I sat dumbly on the edge of the bed. Legs like logs. Staring stupidly. Finally I jumped up. Dropped to the floor and did fifty pushups, just to get the blood flowing.

From the living room I heard Josef stirring on the too-short couch. When I poked my head out, he greeted me with a thumbs-up. I trundled off to the water closet.

We dressed in groggy silence. Underwear, undershirt, pants, collared white shirt, vest, socks, shoes, cap. And a light raincoat for Josef. When I drew the front curtains, I saw sun on the trees. Good weather. Good.

Next I double-checked the valises. As if the Sten gun and the grenades might have disappeared in the middle of the night while I was lying awake next to them. They were there, of course. Hidden under the grass like evil Easter eggs.

"Good morning," the man of the house said. I snapped the case shut, alarmed. He was coming out of the bedroom and hadn't seen anything.

"Good morning!"

"I meant to tell you boys. I think the wife got a hold of some sausages yesterday. So we'll be eating well tonight."

"Um."

"We might not be here," Josef said.

"No?"

"Don't worry about us, though. We have plenty of friends around town now. So we'll be taken care of."

"Oh."

I looked at my watch and nudged Josef. We had to go meet Josef.

```
DOCUMENT:     #793
DESCRIPTION:  OFFICIAL REPORT ON R. HEYDRICH'S
              ACTIVITIES ON THE MORNING OF 27 MAY
PLACE:        PANENSKÉ BŘEZANY, OCCUPIED CZECHOSLOVAKIA
DATE:         27 MAY 1942
```

Notes from Inspector von Pannwitz:

I visited Klein at Bulovka and interviewed him at some length in order to get a fuller picture of Heydrich's activities on the morning of the 27th.

Klein had been up for some time the previous night; he'd shuttled Lina Heydrich back to Panenské Březany while the post-performance reception was going on at the Rudolphinium.

Heydrich had remained at the reception for some time, in the company of unknown individuals. Klein looked for him when he returned from Panenské Březany but did not find him for some time. When he did at last find Heydrich, he was descending from a staircase that led to a catwalk that led to the building's roof. According to Klein, he was somewhat inebriated, and was carrying a violin.

Klein drove him back to Panenské Březany at a very late hour; he says it was nearly dawn by the time they arrived.

[DOCUMENT CONTINUES]

```
DOCUMENT:    #47
DESCRIPTION: NARRATIVE OF J. KUBIŠ
PLACE:       DEJVICE, PRAHA, OCCUPIED CZECHOSLOVAKIA
DATE:        27 MAY 1942 (CONTINUED)
```

All the bicycles were back at M.'s, as was Valčik. So we waited for a tram over at the Dejvice roundabout, amidst a lumpy mass of grumpy people.

My excitement and tension had burned through the tiredness. So I fidgeted my way to the front of the crowd and peered down the street again and again to try and spot the tram cresting the hill to the west. It could not arrive quickly enough.

"Light a cigarette, that always brings it," Josef joked.

So I did. And sure enough, the tram appeared as soon as I'd taken a drag.

"See?" Josef said.

When it finally rumbled up, we mutely boarded. Grabbed seats next to one another, our heavy valises perched precariously on our jangling legs. The tram rumbled eastward, bucking and jolting along the steel rails inlaid in the cobblestone streets.

How slow the journey seemed!

Every stop took an eternity. One old man had to fish in his pockets for a wadded up ticket for what felt like five minutes, and I instantly hated him. I practically had to sit on my hands to keep from checking my watch every forty-five seconds. Meanwhile Josef jerked his head here and there like a caffeinated sparrow.

"I should have brought a book," he finally said. Gave a pained smile.

"I doubt I'd be able to concentrate on reading today," I replied.

The tram rumbled downhill, then crossed the river.

Then we had to catch another one that headed up the hill into Žižkov.

When at last we arrived at M.'s, Valčik was standing on the kerb. Three bicycles leaned against the street lamp next to him. Four fresh cigarette butts lay at his feet.

"We've got to get going," he said.

"I know," Gabčík replied testily.

They secured our valises to the handlebars with twine. Just before we set off, I allowed myself a peek at my watch. We were running seven minutes behind schedule.

```
DOCUMENT:    #793
DESCRIPTION: OFFICIAL REPORT ON R. HEYDRICH'S
             ACTIVITIES ON THE MORNING OF 27 MAY
PLACE:       PANENSKÉ BŘEZANY, OCCUPIED CZECHOSLOVAKIA
DATE:        27 MAY 1942 (CONTINUED)
```

[DOCUMENT PRECEDES]

Klein reported to me that, after depositing Heydrich with his wife, he found his way to the servant's quarters, where he had a room that he used on occasion when Heydrich's schedule made it impractical for him to return to his normal billet.

He was able to grab a few hours' sleep before it was time to rise. He got up, bathed, shaved, and went to Heydrich's room to wake him, only to be told by Lina Heydrich that he should come back in an hour.

[DOCUMENT CONTINUES]

```
DOCUMENT:    #47
DESCRIPTION: NARRATIVE OF J. KUBIŠ
PLACE:       DEJVICE-HOLEŠOVICE-LIBEŇ, PRAHA, OCCUPIED
             CZECHOSLOVAKIA
DATE:        27 MAY 1942
```

We rode north. After the edgy frustration of the tram commute, it felt good to be in control. To have an outlet for our nervous energy.

We rode hard and fast, screaming down the hill from Žižkov, then west across the river into Holešovice. One of the few parts of the city that was laid out well, in a smart, sensible grid. Past buildings and stores and clusters of commuters and trams we rode. Then north across the Vltava again. The river gleamed bright in the morning sun. Overhead the sky was its deepest possible blue. Across the bridge, the buildings stood out sharply. Bright brick and stark shadows. We rode uphill, standing on the pedals for the climb into Libeň. There was no sense in attracting attention, especially now, so Gabčík and I kept some distance between us, and Valčik stayed on the other side of the street. (His presence was problematic. On one hand, he'd been right, in that we did need him for the mission. On the other hand, as mentioned earlier, the Germans had his photograph, so for us to travel with him was especially problematic today. As a compromise, we'd agreed that we'd keep some distance between him and ourselves while on the final ride, and that he wouldn't carry any weapons.)

As we drew close, the buildings thinned out. People and trams and a smattering of cars bustled about in their placid routines. Soon everything would be different, and none of them had any inkling.

Finally we arrived.

There were several tram tracks running down the centre of the street, with small steel towers holding up the tram cables. Lining the street were silent two-storey houses, and a small electrical substation built against the front face of a hill. The street curved sharply and descended to the right in a hairpin turn. On the inside of the curve was a wrought-iron fence with a brick and cement base, beyond which the ground dropped away and there were several trees.

Gabčík and I took up positions on the inside of the turn, across the street from the power station and the tram stop. We leaned our bicycles against a street lamp. Valčik stationed himself further up the street.

"How are we on time?" I asked.

"Fine. Better than expected. We made up for it on the ride."

Josef's face was beaded in sweat. His raincoat wasn't needed for rain, but it was needed now. He shucked it off and perched himself on the cement part of the fence base and put his valise over his lap and threw his raincoat over the valise. Looking straight ahead all the while, he slipped his hands under the raincoat and into the valise. We had broken the Sten down into only three pieces, so it was a fairly simple job to reassemble it. His head and eyes looked about distractedly, as if they didn't know what his hands were doing.

Meanwhile I lit a cigarette. Surveyed the intersection. Thought: Everything is correct. Here is the place and now is the time. And the whole wide world doesn't mean so much to me, for this is where I belong. And whether I die today or live another fifty years, no day will be as momentous as today. And I have grown restless waiting for it, and also I wish I had more time. (How rarely do our thoughts and beliefs and priorities fit together neatly like puzzle pieces!)

Once Gabčík was done, he placed the Sten under the raincoat and under his arm and crossed the street to mingle with the commuters at the tram stop. There was a fair-sized crowd, and since Heydrich was set to come through around 9:00, Gabcik could use the commuters for camouflage and also see far up the road, to where Valčik kept watch. It was good that we had a third, after all. The placement of the hill meant that I would not be able to see when the car was coming, but the position of the morning sun meant that someone up the road could signal someone at the tram stop with a mirror. We'd told Valčik to do so once when he was in position, as a test, and he must have done it, because Gabčík put the raincoat-wrapped Sten down and stretched both arms in the air for a few seconds, which was the signal that he'd seen the signal. Everything was happening the way it was supposed to happen now, as smoothly and certainly as the trams on their rails.

I took another drag from the cigarette. My fingers grew hot from the ember and I stubbed the butt out on the brick of the fence. Then I cracked open my valise. Slipped my hand in and felt the reassuring shape of the grenade. Slipped my hand out, and into my pocket for another cigarette. Lit it.

Waited.

```
DOCUMENT:    #793
DESCRIPTION: OFFICIAL REPORT ON R. HEYDRICH'S
             ACTIVITIES ON THE MORNING OF 27 MAY
PLACE:       PANENSKÉ BŘEZANY, OCCUPIED CZECHOSLOVAKIA
DATE:        27 MAY 1942 (CONTINUED)
```

[DOCUMENT PRECEDES]

Klein estimates that Heydrich finally woke at 0900 hours.

After showering and shaving, he joined Lina Heydrich in the dining room for a breakfast of eggs and sausage. He invited Klein to accompany them.

They ate in silence, and only after the last forkful did Heydrich speak. He suggested that he and Lina take a stroll with the children, as it would be their last morning together as a family here. Lina expressed concern that he would be late, but Heydrich said he was flying himself to Berlin and would not be meeting the Leader until the following day, so time was not an issue.

The three children came downstairs, and Heydrich shepherded his family out the front door. They walked hand in hand around the grounds, and Klein trailed at a respectful distance.

Based on what he overheard, and what Heydrich mentioned to him during their ride, they discussed the fact that they would be leaving this home shortly. Heydrich didn't mention specifics about his upcoming assignment, but he told Klein he'd given his son Klaus some fatherly advice, telling him that he owed it to the world to live up to his capabilities.

[DOCUMENT CONTINUES]

```
DOCUMENT:    #47
DESCRIPTION: NARRATIVE OF J. KUBIŠ
PLACE:       LIBEŇ, PRAHA, OCCUPIED CZECHOSLOVAKIA
DATE:        27 MAY 1942 (CONTINUED)
```

Still we waited.

9:00 passed. As expected. And then 9:15. I worried a bit.

And then 9:30 came.

And 9:45.

And 10:00.

How long the wait seemed! Looking at my watch was heartbreaking, and not looking was excruciating. I would pick times, imaginary deadlines by which I was sure the car would be there, and the time would arrive, but the car wouldn't. And I'd check my watch again and the seconds would thud by, heavy and slow.

At the tram stop, people came and went, but more were going than coming now, so the crowd was thinning out. Then just after 10:00 another tram rumbled by, and everyone boarded. Still Josef stood. Alone now, without human camouflage. Cradling the raincoat under his arm. It seemed like he was clenching it tighter than he needed to. I was sure I could see the outline of the Sten. Or was that just because I knew it was there?

On the far side of the street, a policeman walked in the lee of the low hill, heading towards the electrical substation. He glanced over his shoulder at Josef, who was looking the other way, up towards Valčik.

I tried to signal Josef. He didn't see me. I looked both ways and stepped into the street. Now he saw me and waved me back.

The policeman looked back towards us again but kept walking. Now I realized that if I tried to get Josef's attention, the officer might notice both of us. So I leaned back against the fence. Wanted to light yet another cigarette, but I didn't. Maybe Valčik had given him the signal! I slipped my hand inside my valise.

Where was the car?

The policeman disappeared around the side of the hill. Finally I allowed myself another cigarette. Maybe that would summon Heydrich. It worked with the tram. It hadn't worked with Heydrich, but I hadn't specifically tried yet. So I lit one.

Sure enough, a tram appeared.

"Jesus and Mary!" I said in frustration.

The policeman came back from around the hill. Josef looked up and saw him this time. He saw Josef. Altered course ever so slightly. I thought I saw a glimmer in the policeman's eye.

A spot of sunlight flashed across Josef's face. The mirror!

Josef jolted and ran across the street, right in front of the tram, and took a spot on the kerb about ten metres up the road from me, and he dropped the raincoat and I could see the Sten and all I could think was: This is it. There is no going back.

The Mercedes rounded the corner, slow and fat and huge, and Josef's back was towards me and I could see his muscles tensing, but the Sten remained silent and the Mercedes swerved to avoid Josef. The car was right there! The car was right there! And Josef hadn't fired a shot! And Heydrich was looking right at Josef, and he was yelling! He was telling his driver to stop, and he was reaching for his pistol and standing up to better get at it, and the driver slammed on the brakes, and Josef slammed his Sten gun down in disgust. And the car was closer to me than Josef now, too close maybe, but my hand had already gone back inside the valise, and just as Heydrich was levelling his pistol at Josef, I released my grenade with a soft underhanded toss. Too soft! Too soft! It just missed landing inside the convertible and instead clattered off the door and fell to the street, and it exploded bright and deafening and I had never been this close to a grenade blast, even in France, and I felt it as a wall of hard hot air, and I felt something hard against my eyebrow, spinning my head.

When my senses caught up with everything and the hot blast had passed, I realized I was leaning against the fence, and I saw two uniform jackets draped over the tram wires, and there was a gaping ragged hole in the Mercedes right in front of the right rear tyre, and Heydrich and his driver were jumping out of the car, guns drawn. And the windows of the tram were broken and the tram was stopped, and people were screaming and pouring out of it, and the driver was coming towards me, staggering and waving his pistol. My bicycle was right there, apparently untouched. My eyes weren't working quite right and I touched my eyebrow and realized I was bleeding, and I grabbed the bicycle and wheeled it so it was facing downhill, and now the people from the tram were in my way, but in the way of the driver, too, and now I finally remembered my pistol and I drew it and started firing in the air, and a path cleared through the crowd, and I jumped on the bike and started pedalling hard down the hill.

And I knew we had failed.

Over the course of the past few weeks, Josef described the remainder of the scene well enough, and frequently enough, that I feel almost as if I've seen it myself.

Behind me, the driver was recovering his senses, but before he'd done so he'd accidentally thumbed his magazine release. So his magazine had clattered to the street and he'd fired once and missed and then dry-fired angrily for a precious few seconds while I made my escape down the hill.

Valčik, too, had already cleared out. He had no weapon and no way to influence events. How we regretted that decision now!

Meanwhile Gabčík was uphill from the car, taking cover behind a street lamp. And he had his pistol out now, and Heydrich was behind the corner of the tram, and they were trading shots. Josef fired twice, but from his spot it was hard to see if Heydrich had been hit, and so he made a move as if to charge around the corner of the tram, pistol blazing, but then there was the whang of a bullet ricocheting off the street lamp from a different direction, where the driver had found his magazine and put it back in his pistol. Seeing this, Josef fired two last desperate rounds, then turned and sprinted away, pistol in hand.

Down a side street he ran. There was a small open storefront, a butcher shop. Josef ducked inside, panting and out of breath, and the shopkeeper came around the counter as if to help, and the driver was yelling outside, and Josef said, "You've got to help me hide! I've just attacked the Realm-Protector!"

"Just…wait a second," the shopkeeper stammered, and rushed out the front door.

Only then did Josef notice a small swastika flag on the counter.

The name on the counter was an ethnically German name, Brauer. And through the front door, Josef could see Brauer shouting and pointing and frantically trying to get Heydrich's driver's attention. Alarmed, Josef started frantically searching for a back door.

During the chase, the driver had apparently lost track of Josef, but now he ran over to the front door of the shop, brandishing his pistol.

Josef hadn't found another way out, so he turned and bolted right while the driver was coming through the front door. They collided so hard that the driver fell back on his ass, and Josef had his pistol out, so he fired once, twice, and he hit the driver in the hip and leg, but he was out of ammunition and didn't know where Heydrich was, so he threw the pistol at the man's head and turned the other way and sprinted down the empty side streets until he was covered in sweat and his lungs ached and he could no longer hear the commotion back at the intersection.

```
DOCUMENT:    #803
DESCRIPTION: EXCERPT FROM OFFICIAL REPORT ON HEYDRICH'S
             ACTIVITIES ON THE MORNING OF 27 MAY
PLACE:       LIBEŇ, PRAHA, OCCUPIED CZECHOSLOVAKIA
DATE:        27 MAY 1942 (CONTINUED)
```

Notes from Inspector von Pannwitz (Excerpted):

[DOCUMENT PRECEDES]

After the assailants had fled the scene, the scene of the crime was in chaos for some minutes. The tram that had just arrived at the intersection was stopped, and several windows had been shattered by the grenade blast. Passengers had disembarked and were milling about and jabbering hysterically. Heydrich sat slumped against the side of the tram, alone.

The grenade blast had blown debris and metal splinters up through the car's side and seatback, wounding him. His uniform jacket had been off; it had been blown upwards by the explosion and had landed atop the tram wires. Heydrich was visibly injured, and there was a deep red bloodstain on his white uniform blouse, but no one was helping him.

Finally a blonde woman at the fringe of the crowd recognized him and alerted the other civilians to his presence.

There was a Czech policeman on the other side of the street during the attack. Upon hearing the blonde woman's cries, he ran over to the scene and flagged down a passing lorry. He instructed the driver that Bulovka Hospital was nearby and that they needed to take Heydrich there immediately.

The policeman and the blonde helped Heydrich into the passenger seat, although not without difficulty, as he was in some pain. The driver was in some confusion about the direction of the hospital and headed first down the hill, away from the hospital.

Although in considerable pain, Heydrich himself apparently alerted the driver to his error and ordered him to turn around. The driver made a three-point turn

and headed back through the intersection. At this
point, however, Heydrich instructed the driver to stop
and move him to the back of the lorry so he could lie
flat for the remainder of the trip.

[DOCUMENT CONTINUES]

```
DOCUMENT:     #47
DESCRIPTION:  NARRATIVE OF J. KUBIŠ
PLACE:        LIBEŇ, PRAHA, OCCUPIED CZECHOSLOVAKIA
DATE:         27 MAY 1942 (CONTINUED)
```

While Josef fought, I pedalled fast and hard, screaming downhill, here and there unclenching a hand from my handlebars to wipe at the blood that wouldn't stop welling from the wound over my eye.

Down I went, a different route than we'd taken. Feeling different emotions. Nearly opposite. Excitement and anxiety replaced by frustration. A strange relief at being alive, but that brought guilt. And anger at the failure. Morning's simple clarities replaced by something else. Then again, it was still morning, after all. (How much longer time feels after such an event! And how different things look when you simply reverse course!)

Near the foot of the hill, a pedestrian stepped out from the corner of a building and I swerved just enough to avoid killing him, but I struck a glancing blow and he fell backwards. My bicycle and I clattered to earth.

"Jesus and Mary!" the man shouted.

"I'm sorry, I'm sorry."

"Watch where you're going, would you?"

"I'm sorry." I realized I'd scraped my knee on the cobblestones. My pants were torn. I looked up and around. Imagined an extra alertness in every pedestrians. Waited for someone to stop me.

No one did.

The safe house closest to our position was a new place. We had visited but had not yet stayed there. I tossed the bike in an alley, walked calmly to the building, then unlocked the door and ran upstairs. The family was not home. Frantically I rooted through the bathroom vanity for the dye. Had I forgotten? I had.

I debated what to do.

I left.

Now I pedalled slowly and painfully up to Žižkov.

I left the bicycle a block or so from A.'s building. Walked the rest of the way. Calmly, or so I hoped. Cut through an alleyway and went in her back door. Just in case.

I didn't know if I'd be safe here. Back at the ambush point, I'd at least known that no one had known me. Whereas here there were neighbours who had seen me coming and going for months. And there was no disguising the fact that something had happened to me. I didn't think any of them was an informer, but in a circumstance like this, who could say? Should I have stayed at the first place? I didn't know.

I took the stairs in twos and threes. Jammed the key in the lock. Once inside her place, I slammed the door and leaned against it. Relaxed, a little bit. Breathed heavily.

"Jan?" Her voice startled me. I hadn't expected her to be home.

"Oh, hullo," I said. She hadn't seen me yet.

"I had to stay home today. Morning sickness." Finally she emerged from the bedroom. "Jesus! What happened to your head?"

"I had a little accident on the bicycle. I almost ran over someone."

"You look like you got hit by a car! Oh, Jesus, Jesus!" She darted into the water closet. "Where's my makeup mirror? It was just here the other day!"

Now I was curious as to what I looked like. And she wasn't going to find the mirror anytime soon. So I walked over to the water closet. Almost ran over her coming out with a towel and iodine. I saw my face for the first time. A massive ragged splotch of dried blood over one side.

I leaned forward. She cleaned. But I was so edgy and anxious her kindness felt intolerable.

"Could you turn on the radio?" I asked.

"Your face…" Again she dabbed me.

"I don't think it's as bad as it looks."

Still she stayed. Touched me tenderly. "What happened?"

"Could you just!" I almost lost it. Checked myself. "I'm sorry. It's been a rough day. Could you turn on the radio, please?"

Now she stopped at last. Gave me a look, but went and turned on the radio. Crackle and hiss gave way to an excited voice. "…nouncement from the Minister of Information, Emanuel Moravec." The first voice was replaced by a second. Serious. "The beloved Realm-Protector of Bohemia and Moravia, SS Supreme Group Leader Reinhard Heydrich, was wounded in a criminal attack that took place at 10:30 this morning in the outskirts of Praha. The would-be assassins threw a grenade which landed outside Heydrich's car. They escaped on bicycles and remain at large. Anyone with information on this cowardly attack is hereby advised to contact police immediately."

A. walked back to the water closet. Slower and wiser. "That was you." Not a question.

"Have you seen the hair dye?"

"The what?"

"Those tubes of hair dye. I thought I took them with me after we dyed Valčik, but I might have left them here."

"Let's clean you up first," she said. She sat me on the toilet and cleaned my wound. Gave me gauze.

Now she took a closer look at my clothes. "There's some other ones on your chest." She undid my shirt and, sure enough, there were a number of smaller cuts and scrapes.

I kissed her.

She kissed me back, reluctantly. Dressed my wounds. Then I led her to the bedroom.

"Jesus, Jan," she said. More frustrated than anything else.

We did not make love. She turned away and we just lay on the bed, holding one another in silence.

I could not just lie there for long. After a while, I opened the curtains and looked out. Were there more people than normal on the street? It was hard to tell. Hard to feel good, even after the attention. Especially after the attention. It felt undeserved. What had been within our grasp was now forever gone. Replaced by "if only," and maddening memories. (How quickly opportunity slips through our feeble fingers!)

Meanwhile A. got up. Rooted through the vanity. Finally she found the tubes, and I returned wearily to the water closet, and we dyed my hair. Brown to black.

```
DOCUMENT:     #803
DESCRIPTION: EXCERPT FROM OFFICIAL REPORT ON HEYDRICH'S
             ACTIVITIES ON THE MORNING OF 27 MAY
PLACE:       BULOVKA HOSPITAL, LIBEŇ, PRAHA, OCCUPIED
             CZECHOSLOVAKIA
DATE:        27 MAY 1942 (CONTINUED)
```

Notes from Inspector von Pannwitz (Excerpted):

[DOCUMENT PRECEDES]

The driver who had deposited Heydrich at the hospital did not stick around, but merely helped him into the waiting arms of several perplexed hospital attendants and then left. He remains unidentified.

The head nurse, a nun, found Heydrich sitting alone in an examination room after the attendants had deposited him. She looked him over, then, when she realized whom she was looking over, darted out to find one Doctor Snajdr. When Doctor Snajdr rushed in, Heydrich was still sitting upright, and the doctor helped disrobe him so he could inspect his wounds.

Heydrich asked his name. When he realized the doctor was Czech, Heydrich instructed him to find a German doctor. Snajdr departed and, after some minutes, found a German member of the hospital staff by the name of Doctor Dick, who completed the examination.

```
DOCUMENT:    #47
DESCRIPTION: NARRATIVE OF J. KUBIŠ
PLACE:       LIBEŇ, PRAHA, OCCUPIED CZECHOSLOVAKIA
DATE:        27 MAY 1942
```

According to what Josef later told me, he headed south on foot and crossed the Vltava. By this time it was apparent to him that things were not well. He said he felt vulnerable and naked in the open. On the roads lining the river he could see lorries and half-tracks, far more than normal. When he reached the south end of the bridge, he crossed the street and ducked between two buildings. Stripped off his vest and his hat and threw them in the trash.

He walked on, through Holešovice, then crossed the river again where it bent around to the west. Went another few blocks. Sat down and smoked a cigarette. Saw a knot of people talking at a tram stop. Walked up to eavesdrop on the conversations.

"…God helps us all," an agitated middle-aged man said.

"What's going on?" Josef feigned befuddlement.

"Haven't you heard? The Realm-Protector was wounded today."

"Wounded?" Gabčík asked. He remembered expressing genuine curiosity and evident excitement.

"Yes. Up in Libeň."

"Incredible! How about that!"

The man shot Josef a dirty look. "I'd be careful saying that in public."

"Yes," a shorter, older man said. "I'm not sure he was wounded that severely. And anyway, no good can come of this. All it can do is stir up trouble." His eyes darted back and forth. Then he and the first man looked each other up and down. As if each was wary that the other was an agent of the Secret Police.

"Of course," Josef said, disappointed.

He excused himself and stepped away from the tram.
Walked in lazy aimless circles through the fragmented
streets for almost two hours.

```
DOCUMENT:    #27
DESCRIPTION: PERSONAL DIARY OF K.H. FRANK
PLACE:       HRADČANY, PRAHA, OCCUPIED CZECHOSLOVAKIA
DATE:        28 MAY 1942
```

[Translator's Note: This entry apparently covers events from the 27 and 28 May.]

How much has changed in these past two days!

I am sitting down at last—exhausted, to be sure—to jot down some notes, to make sense of this cataclysm, this insanity, this unforeseen attack—which may yet prove a blessing! And when I sat down, I glanced over the hasty entry I penned the other night after the reception in the Rudolphinium, and it seems like it was written by someone else, in a different world.

The morning of the 27th, I should note, was ordinary, peaceful and beautiful—a perfect, perfectly ordinary day! And then came the news, like a bolt from the blue, and everything was topsy-turvy—hasty meetings and desperate phone calls and no understanding—none!—by any of us of how this could have happened. We have bent over backwards to treat the Czechs with grace and compassion and kindness, and now—this!

I remember, at some point, wandering in to Heydrich's old office—seeking solace from the chaos, perhaps.

All around were stacks of cardboard boxes, all stamped and taped and waiting for the dolly. After big unexpected things, the residue of yesterday's future feels so futile and useless! For a few moments, I just stood there, numb and dumb, and tried to breathe, to relax, to imagine none of it had happened.

The bakelite telephone on Heydrich's old desk rang.

"Hullo operator."

"State Secretary Frank?"

"Yes."

"I thought you might be in there, my Lord. I have a call from the Realm Chancellery."

There were pauses and crackles, and distant electric noises. Then, Hitler. "Frank?"

"Yes, my Leader?"

"Frank, I have been trying to get some answers about this mess that's happened."

"Yes my Leader." I breathed deeply—I was somewhat nervous, I must admit! "Apparently the Realm-Protector and his driver were rounding a corner when they were ambushed. A grenade exploded under the car. The Realm-Protector and his driver fought off the assailants, but they fled on bicycles."

"On bicycles?"

"Yes, my Leader. I'm expecting a report from our anti-sabotage chief soon. He…"

"This is absurd. How can two men on bicycles attack the most powerful man in the city? This is the height of foolishness!"

"Yes, my Leader. As I was saying, our anti-sabotage chief is at the hospital, and he will be…"

"The hospital?"

"Yes, my Leader. I don't have all of the facts yet, but he was wounded. I will speak to the investi…"

"This is the height of foolishness! You are not to travel anywhere without escort, Frank. I will be sending an armoured limousine from Berlin for your use."

"For my use, my Leader?"

"Yes. You are the acting Realm-Protector for now."

(Here I think I nodded, and perhaps smiled slightly. Still, I must admit, I'm concerned by the use of the word "acting," and the added "for now." Does he have that little confidence in my abilities?)

"We are going to have to discipline the Czechs," Hitler said. "Anyone found to have assisted in this evil plot is to be executed, along with their entire family. And on top of that, I want your men to round up ten thousand Czechs…"

"Ten thousand, my Leader?"

"Ten thousand! Round them up at random, to be executed later. No more of this coddling! It obviously didn't get us anywhere. We must have our vengeance."

```
DOCUMENT:    #803
DESCRIPTION: EXCERPT FROM OFFICIAL REPORT ON AFTERMATH
             OF HEYDRICH ATTACK
PLACE:       BULOVKA HOSPITAL, LIBEŇ, PRAHA, OCCUPIED
             CZECHOSLOVAKIA
DATE:        27 MAY 1942 (CONTINUED)
```

Notes from Inspector von Pannwitz (Excerpted):

[DOCUMENT PRECEDES]

At some point after they had made their initial examinations, I arrived at Bulovka Hospital.

Somewhat concerned by the prospect of further attacks, I had placed calls to the commander of our local garrison and had arranged for a company of soldiers to secure the hospital. They arrived with me, and fanned out to secure the building while I made enquiries and tracked down Doctor Dick.

The doctor was scanning x-ray slides when I found him. He held up the x-ray films to show me the extent of Heydrich's injuries. The blast had broken a rib and pierced his diaphragm. A grenade, or perhaps a piece of wire from the car seat, had been lodged in his spleen. (I placed some calls later and asked how this was possible; it seems the armoured plating from Berlin had somehow never been installed, but no one has yet been able to give me a satisfactory explanation as to why.)

Doctor Dick informed me that Heydrich would most likely need a splenectomy; he said the members of the hospital staff were preparing to perform the surgery.

This alarmed me; I issued firm instructions that no Czech was to be allowed in the same room as Heydrich, much less perform surgery on him.

Doctor Dick protested, but I was resolute. (Given the unexpected attack, and the unknown character of the Czechs on the staff at Bulovka, I could not and cannot risk something else happening through carelessness on our part.)

Here there was some contention and dispute between Doctor Dick and myself. He seemed concerned that Heydrich's condition might worsen if we waited for our own doctors to be flown in from Berlin.

Finally, we agreed to a compromise, to have the surgery performed by staff members from the local German Clinic, with Doctor Dick supervising. He was not entirely pleased with this arrangement, but I told him again in no uncertain terms that I could not risk having anything else happen to Heydrich.

Following this, I spoke to the detachment commander that had accompanied me to the hospital. We decided that our best course of action was to secure the second floor of the hospital and move Heydrich up there, to forbid any Czechs from going up to the second floor, and to paint the windows white so as to preclude the possibility of a sniper attack.

[DOCUMENT CONTINUES]

```
DOCUMENT:    #27
DESCRIPTION: PERSONAL DIARY OF K.H. FRANK
PLACE:       HRADČANY, PRAHA, OCCUPIED CZECHOSLOVAKIA
DATE:        28 MAY 1942 (CONTINUED)
```

Barely had my conversation with the Leader ended before the intercom buzzed again.

"Who is it?" I asked wearily.

"Emanuel Moravec, my Lord."

(I'm sure I swore under my breath.) "Send him in."

Moravec entered. Dressed in his full uniform with its ridiculous leather shoulder belt.

"What is it?" I snapped.

"My Lord, first off, I want to offer my condolences. This attack was a cowardly action by a few criminals and terrorists, and it in no way reflects the gratitude my countrymen have for all your nation has done for us."

I shrugged. "The Leader seems to think differently."

"May I suggest something, my Lord?" Moravec said tentatively. "I think it would be best for all involved if you don't overreact to this. There are many of us who have welcomed you with open arms…"

"The Leader wants harsh measures."

"May I suggest something else, my Lord?"

"What?" I asked, impatient and edgy.

"A reward."

```
DOCUMENT:     #803
DESCRIPTION:  EXCERPT FROM OFFICIAL REPORT ON AFTERMATH
              OF HEYDRICH ATTACK
PLACE:        BULOVKA HOSPITAL, LIBEŇ, PRAHA, OCCUPIED
              CZECHOSLOVAKIA
DATE:         27 MAY 1942 (CONTINUED)
```

Notes from Inspector von Pannwitz (Excerpted):

[DOCUMENT PRECEDES]

Upon leaving the hospital, I walked back to the intersection where the attack had taken place. We had driven past it on the way to the hospital. It was literally right around the corner; the road wrapped around a small hill and there I was.

The scene of the crime was now a strange tableaux where everything was frozen in place. The tram was still ascending and starting to turn the corner. The car was still just coming out of the hairpin turn. Everything looked nearly normal from my side of the street; it was as if time had simply stopped. The car was askew because of a flat right rear tyre, and the windows of the tram on the side opposite me had been blown out. And of course there were no people on the tram or in the car. But there were Czech police blocking traffic down the road, and uniformed and plainclothes Secret Police taking pictures and scribbling notes. (I couldn't help but notice an air of resignation and futility to their efforts, as is perhaps normal with police work, and perhaps with history as well. When one breaks something, a mug or a vase, there is often that simple urge to hold the pieces together. And this felt like that on a much larger scale—we were trying to look at something that would never be whole again.)

I walked over to the tram and found Lieutenant Weisskopf, one of the Criminal Police officers on liaison with the Czech police, whom I'd left in charge of the scene. He was standing near the open tram doors, giving instructions to a photographer. When he saw me, he patted the photographer on the back to send him on his way, then gave his report.

Based on Weisskopf's assessment, it seems all the damage was from one grenade. There was another grenade and a valise left on the kerb, and he pointed them out to me. The eyewitnesses he interviewed said that one man fled on a bicycle, but the officers had noticed a second bicycle leaning against a lamp post, and he pointed that out to me. Presumably it belongs to the other assailant. He said there are factory numbers on it, which we will distribute to our operatives so they can search sales records at local bicycle shops in order to find the owners.

After the initial report, Weisskopf walked me around to the other side of Heydrich's auto to show me the rest of the crime scene. (From the right side, the car looked like a toy attacked by dogs. The door was drooping off its hinges, and there was a ragged metal hole in the rear quarter-panel.)

Here he pointed out what may be the most important clue: one of the assailants had dropped what appeared to be an unfired British-made Sten gun.

Before I picked it up, I looked down at the weapon and looked out at the scene. In the next day or so, the car will be towed, and the tram will be taken back to the garage, where they will surely replace the glass and return it to anonymous ahistorical service. The crime scene cannot obviously remain undisturbed forever, but I didn't want to lose any important clues through carelessness, so I had Weisskopf make sure everything had been photographed before I picked up the weapon.

It was in fact a Sten—a type I believe is commonly used by British commandos, the same type we had captured at Ořechov and Lany.

I pulled back the bolt. When I did, several blades of grass that had been mashed inside fluttered to the ground.

[DOCUMENT CONTINUES]

```
DOCUMENT:    #27
DESCRIPTION: PERSONAL DIARY OF K.H. FRANK
PLACE:       HRADČANY, PRAHA, OCCUPIED CZECHOSLOVAKIA
DATE:        27 MAY 1942 (CONTINUED)
```

After some wrangling and discussion, I set down a statement for Moravec to read over the radio. Then I accompanied him to the studio, to ensure he recited it exactly as I'd written it. (It had occurred to me that he might decide to turn traitor again and say something else entirely on the air—a plea, perhaps, for a general uprising! As I've mentioned before, I do not trust the man. At any rate, I wanted to impress upon him that things will no longer be as they were under Heydrich. From now on, he can expect to have someone looking over his shoulder!)

So we found ourselves there, with Emanuel Moravec in front of the microphone, waiting for a signal from the sound technician.

The technician counted down, then pressed the buttons on the sound console with one hand and signalled Moravec with the other. The Minister of Public Enlightenment took a deep breath and began to speak:

"On 27 May 1942, an attempt on the life of the Realm-Protector, SS Supreme Group Leader Heydrich, was perpetrated in Praha. A reward of ten million crowns will be given for the arrest of the guilty men. Whoever shelters these criminals, provides them with help, or, knowing them, does not denounce them, will be shot with his family.

In the Praha region, a state of siege is proclaimed by the reading of this ordinance on the radio. The following measures are laid down:

- a. The civilian population, without exception, is forbidden to go into the streets from 2100 hours on 27 May until 0600 hours on 28 May.
- b. All inns and restaurants, cinemas, theatres and places of amusement are to be strictly shut, and all traffic on public highways is forbidden during that period.

    c. Any person who appears in the streets in spite of this prohibition shall be shot if he does not stop at the first summons.
    d. Other measures are foreseen, and if necessary they will be announced on the radio.

Signed in Praha on 27 May 1942 by the SS Supreme Leader and acting Realm-Protector in Bohemia and Moravia..." Here Moravec paused, and enunciated each name as he looked over at me. "Karl Hermann Frank."

Moravec stepped away from the radio, and the technician stopped the recording. "We are clear, sir."

"This is going to be rebroadcast several times, correct?" I asked the technician.

"Correct, my Lord. We are to replay it every half hour until 7:30, then every ten minutes until 8:30, and then every five minutes until 9:00."

"Very good."

"What happens at 9:00, sir?"

"We have been organizing the army, police, and SS units here, and bringing police in from the nearby German-speaking parts of the Realm. Tonight they are going to search the entire city, house by house, until they find these people."

```
DOCUMENT:    #47
DESCRIPTION: NARRATIVE OF J. KUBIŠ
PLACE:       ŽIŽKOV, PRAHA, OCCUPIED CZECHOSLOVAKIA
DATE:        27 MAY 1942
```

Josef said that when he finally got to M.'s, she was home alone with the radio on, huddled close so she could keep it low.

He joined her as President Beneš spoke: "The Czechoslovakian government-in-exile hails today's spontaneous attack on the monster, Reinhard Heydrich, by members of the home resistance. This act of just vengeance against the Butcher of Praha shows that the Czechoslovakian people wholeheartedly reject National Socialist rule. It is a shining example for all the oppressed people of Europe who are living in daily terror of the Secret Police."

"So that was you two," she said. "Mr. Vyskočil."

"Yes."

"Good job."

"No it wasn't," Josef responded bitterly. "If it was, he'd be in the morgue, not the hospital."

"Well, what's done is done."

Josef sat. Then, as he recalled it, he stood back up. Paced. Got a tumbler from the cupboard and downed several glasses of water. Tried to sit down again. Stood back up.

M. looked up from her work. "So you didn't want to spend the night with that girl?"

"You know about that?" Josef asked.

"I know all," she said. Smiled.

"I didn't want to get them in trouble," Josef said. Stopped. "Not that I wanted you to get in trouble. I mean…" Again Josef stopped. At a loss for words.

"It's all right," she said. "No one forced us to help you out. We accepted it. How did you get back here, anyway?"

"I walked."

"You walked?" M. asked. "What happened to the bicycle?"

"The bicycle?" Josef asked, incredulous. "Oh, Jesus and Mary, I think I left it up there! Oh, of all the fucking idiotic things I've done today! Oh! Jesus! I'm sorry. I'm so terribly sorry."

If M. was upset or worried, she hid it well, at least according to Josef. "Well, what's done is done," she said at last. Went back to her laundry.

Josef took a bath. Tried, perhaps, to rid himself of the grime and frustration of the day. When he finally got dressed and returned to the living room, M. silently handed him a set of her son's clothes. The radio was on, repeating State Secretary Frank's orders, as read by Emanuel Moravec. Outside they could hear rumbling. Lorries and tanks and half-tracks.

S. came home soon afterwards. M. cooked dinner and they ate in near silence, then sat in the living room smoking and listening to the radio as the sun set.

Near dark, other noises could be heard outside. Close by, there were belching lorries and clanking tanks. They heard the nervous chatter of a machine gun off in the distance.

"It's going to be a long night," S. said.

Josef and I waited it out without realizing we were down the hall from one another.

As darkness drew near, I helped my A. clear out the heavy oak chest which sat at the foot of her bed so I could curl up at the last minute if a lorry stopped on our block. Not a great hiding spot, but the best we could think of. Meanwhile Josef sat calmly on the M.'s sofa. Pistol within easy reach. Hoping, perhaps, for a chance to redeem himself after the business with the jammed Sten gun.

```
DOCUMENT:    #803
DESCRIPTION: EXCERPT FROM OFFICIAL REPORT ON AFTERMATH
             OF HEYDRICH ATTACK
PLACE:       WENCESLAS SQUARE, PRAHA, OCCUPIED
             CZECHOSLOVAKIA
DATE:        27/28 MAY 1942 (CONTINUED)
```

Notes from Inspector von Pannwitz (Excerpted):

[DOCUMENT PRECEDES]

Once I left the crime scene, much of the afternoon was spent in discussions with Geschke and Frank about the size and scope of the manhunt.

I had hoped to concentrate on doing some solid police work and developing leads based on the evidence we'd collected.

But they had no confidence in this approach. And they were not happy to find we had no informers who were able to identify any of the individuals who had apparently sheltered these people. Geschke is, indeed, rather upset that I do not have quality sources capable of providing such information. He made it clear that development of such resources would be my top priority going forward.

But in the meantime, we had to solve this crime. And more importantly, we had to look like we were solving it. So they decided to hope for a random success in a massive blind search. As it turned out, this manhunt ended up being perhaps the largest we've ever conducted in any of the occupied countries.

Throughout the afternoon and on into the night, Peček Palace and the various offices on Castle Hill were abuzz with criss-crossing calls and clattering teletypes, orders and counter-orders.

Out in the streets, a motley but massive force assembled. There were SS and Secret Police from Praha and Brno, and Criminal Police hastily brought in from Germany proper.

They assembled in parks and squares throughout the city. In the absence of knowledge, there was much speculation about whether this was an isolated incident or the signal flare for a general uprising. Consequently, as blackout darkness descended, there was some scattered gunfire here and there in various districts. It is believed this was all basically caused by trigger-happy troops who were unused to conducting what was still, theoretically, a criminal investigation.

And despite all of our efforts, there were still too many residences, and too few people to search through them. Hardly any of the troops conducting the manhunt had more than the most fragmentary knowledge of who they were looking for. They were ordered to arrest anyone who could not produce identification, and while this did lead to several hundred arrests, it is doubtful whether any of these will lead to any new breaks in the case.

In the meantime, I worked on collecting the evidence and finding the best place to display it.

By daybreak I had finished supervising the installation of a somewhat unusual display at a department store window the Baťa shoe store in downtown Praha. We had dressed up a mannequin with a raincoat and cap that were found at the scene. Arranged around it, we had put the bicycle, the Sten gun, and the valise we'd found nearby. We also had posted a sign in German and Czech advertising rewards for co-operation, and advising anyone who had seen these items to come forward.

[DOCUMENT CONTINUES]

```
DOCUMENT:    #47
DESCRIPTION: NARRATIVE OF J. KUBIŠ
PLACE:       ŽIŽKOV, PRAHA, OCCUPIED CZECHOSLOVAKIA
DATE:        28 MAY 1942
```

In the morning A. woke before me. Made tea and eggs. The noise and the smell got me out of bed. We ate at her small breakfast table and looked out at the silent stone courtyard. I was depressed and tired, but told myself I shouldn't be. It was another morning, at least.

"Anything exciting planned for today?" she asked me as we finished. Arched an eyebrow.

"No." I chuckled. Perhaps for the first time since the attack, I chuckled, if only just a little. "Jesus and Mary, no."

"I'm going to see if they've heard anything," she said.

I heard the front door open and close. Then open and close again less than a minute later.

"Your friend is over there."

Like a flash, I was out the door and down the hallway. Josef was sitting on their sofa, hand still on his pistol in his pocket. Eyes tired and bloodshot. Looking glummer than I'd ever seen him. Glummer than I'd ever seen me, even. And angry.

"It's good to see you in one piece, Josef."

He grunted.

I walked in. Sat down. "I was worried after I got away. Everything went to hell. I… And then I heard shots behind me and…"

Finally he spoke. "It's all right. I ran, too. I had to shoot the driver to get away, but I got away. I don't know if I even thought about the aftermath, I was so focused on the event. I think I'm still surprised I got away. But I got away. I ran, too."

"You're angry."

"Not at you. The…the fucking Sten!" He burst into motion and emotion. Hit the sofa with his arm, threw a pillow at the radio.

"It's all right."

"It's not all right! It's a fucking nightmare I can't wake up from!" He quieted down. Thinking, perhaps, of the neighbours. But the intensity stayed. "I failed, Jan! I failed! After all of that preparation, I failed at the simplest part of the task! You pull the trigger, the gun goes off. And I failed! And even after that, all might have still been well if we'd just given Valčik a weapon. But no."

I walked over. Patted him on the shoulder. His eyes glistened with tears of rage and frustration.

```
DOCUMENT:     #803
DESCRIPTION: EXCERPT FROM OFFICIAL REPORT ON AFTERMATH
              OF HEYDRICH ATTACK
PLACE:        PEČEK PALACE, PRAHA, OCCUPIED
              CZECHOSLOVAKIA
DATE:         28 MAY 1942 (CONTINUED)
```

Notes from Inspector von Pannwitz (Excerpted):

[DOCUMENT PRECEDES]

I came back to headquarters after supervising the shoe store display. By that point, I had been awake for thirty-eight hours. Still I was determined to keep the investigation on the right track.

Inside, all was chaotic. Everywhere one got the sense that events had gotten ahead of us. It was not just disorder, but the feeling that there would never be order again.

I stalked the hectic hallways until I found Geschke and a policeman standing over a table with a hastily patched-together paper map.

He needed an update before he left to brief Frank, so he dismissed the policeman, and I reported on the latest developments: Heydrich out of surgery and recovering, the evidence assembled and on display, the manhunt concluded and no leads.

I expressed concern at the quality of the information we were getting. Such harsh measures as were being practiced tend to generate a lot of worthless information and many arrested suspects, but no clear or useful information. And from what I had seen, this was the case here: the sweeps had netted so many people that it would take us days to interrogate them all, and in the meantime we would not have time or resources to investigate our legitimate evidence.

Geschke said that we needed to do such things, and that we cannot be seen to be soft. I repeated my points, but he said it didn't matter, because the Leader was out for blood. He said, furthermore, that if I expressed my opinions too loudly, I might end up being made responsible for the whole effort.

I told him that it would be an honour to be officially leading the investigation.

He informed me that I would be ultimately held responsible if the investigation failed, but I told him that I was not concerned about that.

He informed me that I would perhaps have to be more harsh than I was used to in my questioning. It looks bad if you're not harsh, he said.

After this discussion, I agreed to go with him up to the Castle to brief Frank. The trip took longer than expected. Geschke had to send a staff captain off to round up a squad of soldiers and a half-track. He was unwilling to take a chance on driving unescorted.

```
DOCUMENT:    #47
DESCRIPTION: NARRATIVE OF J. KUBIŠ
PLACE:       ŻIŻKOV, PRAHA, OCCUPIED CZECHOSLOVAKIA
DATE:        28 MAY 1942 (CONTINUED)
```

Later that afternoon, HAJASKÝ dropped by.

We met him in A.'s place. He sat hesitantly. Did not look us in the eyes.

"First off, I wanted to say congratulations. What you two did was the bravest thing anyone's done in this city since the Germans took over. On behalf of everyone involved in this second Resistance, I commend you for your heroism." HAJASKÝ fidgeted in his seat as he spoke.

"That isn't why you came by," Josef said.

"No, it isn't," HAJASKÝ said. "All of you are going to need to go into hiding."

"We are in hiding," I pointed out. I hadn't left the floor in thirty hours.

"I suppose I should explain a little…it's been decided that all of you need to be somewhere…out of the way," HAJASKÝ said. Looking as uncomfortable as I'd ever seen him.

"It's been decided?" Gabčík echoed. "Decided by whom?"

"All of us?" I asked.

"Every parachutist in hiding here in Praha must…"

"Decided by whom?" Gabčík said again. Emphasis on the whom.

"JINDRA."

Gabčík shook his head in disgust.

"He has reasons," HAJASKÝ pointed out. "You and the others are scattered in a half-dozen homes all over the city. They only have to find one of you, and they'll crack the whole thing open. It is safer this way."

"Safer for JINDRA," Gabčík snorted.

"We're proud of what you've accomplished. I'm honoured to have had a part in it! But…"

"But now you're going to throw us to the lions."

"…but there are consequences! And there will be more. Some who are hosting parachutists are worried."

"These are not new issues," Josef said.

"They are, though," HAJASKÝ said. From his valise he pulled a folded red poster with black lettering. On it was written a reasonably accurate account of the attack, and descriptions of Josef and myself. And it had Valčik's real name. The flyers had pictures of M.'s bicycle and Josef's raincoat. And my valise, which, come to think of it, I had borrowed from one of our host families. It was more than enough information to make one worry.

"Jesus and Mary," I said.

"I think it will alleviate those consequences and lessen those fears if you stayed out of mind and out of sight for a little while. And I don't always agree with JINDRA…"

"I don't always trust JINDRA," Josef interjected.

"But I still think this is…"

The door opened. Josef jerked, startled. It was A. She seemed surprised. Shell-shocked, even.

"It's a madhouse out there. I almost got stopped. What the hell have you gotten us into, Jan?"

"Jan?" HAJASKÝ asked. In all that time, I'd kept my real name secret from him.

"What's going on here? You are…" she asked HAJASKÝ.

"Just leaving." HAJASKÝ said.

"We were talking," Gabčík explained.

"I have to go into hiding," I said.

"For how long?" she asked.

I shrugged. Looked at HAJASKÝ.

He shrugged, too. As if as ignorant as me. "You'll know more when I do. Good day." With a wave, he left.

Josef stood. Pretended to stretch. Looked at his watch. "Look at the time! I really must get home before dark." He opened the door and headed back down the hall.

A. waited for the door to close before speaking again. "You knew this was going to be like this, didn't you?"

"Like what?"

"There's talk of executions. Reprisals."

I took a heavy breath. "I didn't know anything like that was going to happen."

"But you knew something was going to happen, yes? That it wasn't going to be just long walks by the river, counting ducks and holding hands…"

"I didn't know what was going to happen."

"You knew something was going to happen," she said.

"This can't last forever."

"It can last longer than us," she said at last.

```
DOCUMENT:    #27
DESCRIPTION: PERSONAL DIARY OF K.H. FRANK
PLACE:       HRADČANY, PRAHA, OCCUPIED CZECHOSLOVAKIA
             AND EN ROUTE TO BERLIN, GERMANY
DATE:        28 MAY 1942 (CONTINUED)
```

Today, too, was a most atrocious day. At the Castle two days ago, when we were preparing for the concert at the Rudolphinium, the halls had been as bright and warm and lethargic as an afternoon nap. And today all was manic frantic chaos.

Under the oil paintings of long-dead Hapsburgs, past the mirrors and the large windows overlooking the bright stone courtyards, I paced, had meetings, shouted orders, and paced some more. And the men to whom I'd given orders would depart, their heels clicking on the ornate wooden floors and padding across the lush carpets. And always there was someone else needing orders, instructions, guidance!

I must admit, it got to be somewhat overwhelming. Eventually, I had to go into my office again and close the door, to keep the chaos at bay and buy myself some time to think. (I had thought about moving into Heydrich's old office—he was, after all, vacating it anyway—but I felt that might seem unseemly.) Despite my efforts, the insanity made its way in anyway, via another telephone call from Berlin.

It was the Leader. He sounded rather upset.

"What's this I hear about a reward, Frank?" Hitler raged.

"Our Minister of Public Enlightenment suggested it, my Leader," I replied.

"We are not going to reward these people for attacking us!" Hitler exclaimed. "These are a duplicitous people! If backstabbing is rewarded, they will keep doing it! We need to have our vengeance!"

"Our investigators think that might not be the best way to catch…"

"I'm not sure you have what it takes to be Realm-Protector," Hitler said. (Oh, such a crushing statement that was! My heart froze as I heard the words.) "The Czechs obviously aren't going to appreciate a lenient master, so I'm going to send them someone who isn't afraid to wade through blood! I'll give them Daluge!"

"Daluge?" I asked, not sure if I'd heard him correctly.

"Do you have a problem with that, Frank?"

"He isn't the most intelligent man to…"

"I don't care! Look where intelligence got us! We need action now. Force! Daluge can give it to us. You're out."

After the line clicked dead, I just sat there for a few minutes, staring dumbly at the mute receiver, collecting my thoughts. And unfortunately that's how Geschke and von Pannwitz found me a minute or so later.

"We came to brief you on recent developments, my Lord," Geschke said.

"You're going to have to find Daluge, too," I said. (I said it with more than a touch of bitterness, I'm sure!)

"Daluge?" Geschke asked.

"I'm out as Realm-Protector. Acting Realm-Protector. Whatever. They're putting Daluge in."

"Daluge?" Geschke asked again, amazed. Von Pannwitz rolled his eyes.

"I know. Even Heydrich hates him. Dummy-dummy, he calls him. Brawn without brains is the worst combination of characteristics for a creature. That always gets you in trouble."

"He didn't give you much chance to accomplish anything. You had the job for…a day, my Lord?" Geschke asked.

(Here I'm sure I gave him a relentless look of pure hatred, to at least put him in his place.) "I'm still going to Berlin to brief the Leader."

"This is going to destroy our investigation," von Pannwitz said at last.

"I'll try and at least talk some sense into the Leader," I said. "But if I can't, God help us."

I am onboard an armoured train now as I set these recollections down. We are rolling towards Berlin through black countryside—through empty farmland as dark and as grim as my mood.

```
DOCUMENT:    #47
DESCRIPTION: NARRATIVE OF J. KUBIŠ
PLACE:       ŻIŻKOV, PRAHA, OCCUPIED CZECHOSLOVAKIA
DATE:        28 MAY 1942 (CONTINUED)
```

"I have spoken to the Czech people on the radio as a military retiree. I have spoken to the Czech people as a minister. I have written, exhorted." Emanuel Moravec's voice provided the soundtrack for a tense dinner. A. and I had popped by to eat. Gabčík had gone back to L.'s. But what we faced was so enormous that we had nothing to say. So S. had turned on the radio. Everything was propaganda now. But anything to silence the silence.

"But of late I lack words that might unlock the door to the Czech mind," Moravec continued. "The intelligence of a philosopher but the character of a bootlegger. The diligence of an ant but the horizon of a slug. These are the facets of our unhappy national peculiarity which culminate in the disgusting figure of a calculating sloth and a titular idiot Švejk. This so-called good soldier embodies everything that is wrong with the Czech character. It is a cowardly character. The criminals who did this did not have the courage to fight a fair…"

M. got up and turns the radio off.

"Speaking of good soldiers, what is to happen to you?" the son asked.

"We have to go away for a bit. It will turn out for the best," I said.

"I'm glad we've helped," the son said.

"I am glad to hear you say so," I said.

"It doesn't seem fair, to be rejected by our countrymen for what you've done," the son said.

"They are going to a safe place," M. said. "They will be out of sight for a while until we can get them out of the city. At least, that's what I've been told."

"Well there's no safe place for us. Mark my words, the Germans will be here before this is over," S. said. Eyed me angrily.

"Jan left me something in the medicine cabinet," M. said. "If the Germans come, I'll go where they can't follow."

I swallowed. Hard. Breathed hard. Looked away so I wouldn't make eye contact with any of them.

"Should I…" The son spoke. Stopped. Looked at his mother. Sanded the specifics off his words. "Should I go, too?"

"Jesus and Mary!" S. exclaimed. Stared at me. Stormed off.

"I've helped you," the son said to me. And to his mother: "I've done more than some of the parachutists."

M.'s eyes grew damp. She put her hand over her mouth. Shook her head no.

"What am I to do, then?"

M. walked closer to her son. Whispered instructions in his ear.

```
DOCUMENT:    #27
DESCRIPTION: PERSONAL DIARY OF K.H. FRANK
PLACE:       BERLIN, GERMANY
DATE:        29 MAY 1942
```

Another unpleasant day—when will it end?

When I finally reported to the Leader this morning, my stomach felt as if he'd clenched it in his fist.

"Have you found them yet?" he asked from across his heavy desk. (Those eyes—so intense, so pure! How disappointing it was to disappoint them!)

"We have several leads, my Leader. The clues from the scene, a bicycle and the gun. We think it was parachutists…"

"I know it was parachutists! Do you think they dropped in alone? Without anyone even noticing that they had arrived? No. There are people among the Czech population who knew about this beforehand! But has your reward brought any of these people forward?"

"We are still sorting through leads, my Leader. We…"

"It hasn't, has it?" Hitler paused. Pressed his fingers against throbbing temples. "I am…incensed. I give the Czechs the best man I have. A brave man, a strong man, but…a benevolent man. A man willing to listen to reason, a man committed to the best possible future for their people. And not only is he attacked in the street, but no one even comes forward out of sympathy or respect to tell us who did it! Well, if they won't come forward out of love, perhaps they will do so out of fear. So again, I want you and Daluge to round up and execute, at random, ten thousand…"

"My Leader!"

"…ten thousand Czechs! This is why…"

"My Leader!"

"…this is why you're not going to be Realm-Protector! Daluge understands these things! He may not be a smart man, but that can be good. People understand the simple things! You're too clever for your own good, Frank."

I paused and took several deep breaths. "My Leader, this will not help us in any way. Most of the Czechs have been helping us, or at least not interfering. If we execute people at random, everyone will know we are executing people who have helped us. People who have worked in our factories, people who have made our tanks and planes and guns. If we kill even the people who have helped us, we will give the others all the more reason to betray us."

Hitler glowered. "We must have our revenge."

"We will, my Leader!"

"This space, this land, must be German."

"It will be, my Leader!"

"Anyone who approves of this crime must be executed."

"They will be executed, my Leader."

"And we need to do something big. Something dramatic."

"Geschke is planning on a deportation of Jews. A thousand Jews, marked for death. In Heydrich's honour." (I did not necessarily like this, but I hoped it would placate him.)

"I don't know if it will make a difference. People sort of…expect such things from us. And the Czechs won't worry about it happening to them. You need to make a public example of someone. The Romans had the right idea. Nail people to crosses! Make them suffer for all to see! That's how you earn fealty in this world. The people who did this, and the people who helped them, must be punished. Publicly. The whole world must know."

"They will, my Leader."

"If you want to have a future where you're at, you must see to it."

"I will see to it, my Leader."

```
DOCUMENT:     #47
DESCRIPTION: NARRATIVE OF J. KUBIŠ
PLACE:        ŻIŻKOV, PRAHA, OCCUPIED CZECHOSLOVAKIA
DATE:         29 MAY 1942
```

Soon all the arrangements had been made, and all that remained was the departure.

I descended the stairs after my final goodbye with my A. HAJASKÝ was waiting at the base of the staircase.

"Did it go well?" he asked.

I did not want to talk about it, and I still don't. "It went. Let's go."

We walked down the bright afternoon street. Even on that first day here I had not felt so exposed. Even after the attack. Then I had at least felt edgy energy. Now I felt like I was already dead.

We took a tram across the silent fearful city. Not even in the dead of winter had I seen so many stone faces staring out at nothing. HAJASKÝ and I sat at opposite ends of the tram and acted like we never had met. Outside, people shuffled slowly. As if the sunshine on their shoulders was snow. I resented them all.

Finally HAJASKÝ made eye contact with me and stood up. I stood, too, and got off when he did. Then I pretended not to follow him as I followed him down the street.

A church loomed above us.

I stood in the doorway while HAJASKÝ went looking for his contact. It was Saturday morning and the place was empty. Solid stone floor, weighty wooden pews. Vaulted white ceilings. Placid, peaceful. The only sound was HAJASKÝ's disembodied voice somewhere beyond the altar.

After a while, HAJASKÝ emerged with a bearded holy man.

I stuck out my hand when they walked over. "Pleased to meet you, Father…"

He gave me his name with a warm handshake. He seemed genuinely glad to meet me. Which, in light of the circumstances, I found hard to believe. [Translator's Note: Again, Kubiš did not give names of civilians, so as to protect them, for he apparently intended for this manuscript to end up in German hands. The individual in question was most likely a layman named Petrek. To alleviate confusion, we have used his real name hereafter in lieu of the fake name Kubiš originally used. For the same reason, he avoided giving details of the church where they were sent, but obviously it was the Orthodox Church of Sts. Cyril and Methodius.]

"Father Petrek."

"No," he said. "Just Petrek. I'm a layman. Our Lord said, 'Let none among you call himself father. You are all brothers and sisters with one father.' It is good that you are here."

He led us to the front of the church and rolled up a rug to reveal a trapdoor in the stone floor. Grunting, he pried it up, then retrieved a long wooden ladder from the stairwell leading up to the choir loft.

One at a time, we descended into darkness.

Down below, in the slanted square of light coming through the hole in the church floor, the churchman retrieved a candle from the pocket of his coat. Quickly he searched his pockets and produced: nothing.

"For as many candles as I have to light every week, you'd think I'd always have matches on me," he said with an embarrassed smile.

"You're obviously not a smoker," I told him as I produced mine.

Candle-lit, we proceeded with the grand tour. I could not have imagined a more depressing place. The crypt was dank and musty, and aside from the shaft down which we'd descended, and a single rectangular slit cut in the wall, there was no source of light or air. And those sources were so narrow and insignificant they made the rest of the room all the more depressing by comparison. Further down, the flickering flame illuminated rectangular holes. Coffin-sized, filled with bones. Catacombs.

"I'll admit, it's a little…cosy," he said, as if he was a landlord, and I a prospective tenant. Which was the truth, come to think of it. "But it's quiet, and out of the way."

"What are we going to eat?" I asked.

"We will bring you food and water."

"And cigarettes?"

In the soft candle glow I saw him smile beneath his beard. "Yes, we'll bring cigarettes."

HAJASKÝ huffed. "It's not like you're paying them. And it's not like you have a lot of other options these days."

I gave him a look of some sort.

His voice softened. As if ashamed of his exasperation. "This will be the best. Only a few of us know your whereabouts now. And they'll take care of you until things die down and we can work out a permanent solution. With the sacrifices you men have made and are making, you do deserve better than this. And we will get you better than this." HAJASKÝ patted me on the back. Gave a comradely squeeze. "But for now, we'll make do with this."

I dropped my bag. And the notion that things were going to start getting better. I tried to absorb the fact that this was home for now.

"You're right," I said at last.

"We have business to attend to upstairs. But rest assured, the others will be arriving soon," HAJASKÝ added.

"And I will round up some food," Petrek said.

They ascended the ladder. Leaving me in the crypt. Alone with my thoughts.

My first hours alone in that cave were the worst.

In the dark, I had no companion save my dark thoughts. Was this the culmination of everything? All the training and sacrifice, all the planning and preparation? For this? I wondered what it all meant. Everything.

It had all been going as incomprehensibly smoothly as the plot of a trashy romantic novel. My A., all that had happened with her...I'd have not believed it if I'd not experienced it. Then the absurd, incomprehensible bad luck of the failed attack. Like a sudden change in fortune in a card game. Did it all mean something? Or was I reading too much into pure random chance? Events that just happened to happen near one another? What should we have done differently? (So many things!) And how would it all end? At least that needn't be left to chance, I found myself thinking. At least I still have my automatic if the Germans come. At least I still have my L-pills. (Perhaps that is the difference between Josef and myself: I fear the uncertainty of random unpredictable death, but I do not fear suicide, because that at least I can control.)

After some miserable hours, Petrek came down with Švarc, whom I hadn't seen since England, and Valčik. I don't know how much time had passed, but it was dark outside. Both arrivals made me practically ecstatic, and we hugged like long-lost brothers. Then I gave them the grand tour.

"Any reason we can't clean these catacombs out?" Valčik asked.

"They're filled with bones," I suggested tentatively.

"And?"

"Isn't that sort of...disrespectful?"

"Would you rather be disrespectful to someone who doesn't exist any more, or sleep on the cold damp floor?"

"We should clean them out," Švarc said. "They're the right size for sleeping, anyway."

"Yes!" Valčik said. "Two against one!" He reached head and arms into one of the horizontal holes and started raking with his fingers. Femurs and humerii and radia and ulnae and vertebrae clattered onto the floor. The skull rolled over and stared up at us, mouth agape.

"He's yelling at you," Švarc said.

"Shut up, you," Valčik said to the skull. He reached down and closed the jaw.

I shook my head. Smiled a little.

"I'll clean yours out too, if you're squeamish," he said to me, then repeated the process on the next catacomb over. "Get up, lazy bones!"

"Yes, you've been sleeping long enough. We're tired, too," Švarc said.

Against my will I found myself laughing as they scraped the bones of saints onto the floor of the crypt. The fact that I knew I shouldn't be laughing made me laugh all the harder. It uncorked my bottled emotions.

"He's gonna get us busted," Švarc said, about me.

"Yeah, some policeman's going to pass by on the street and say, 'Hey, that doesn't sound right. The skeletons weren't laughing yesterday.'"

Bublík and Opálka and Hrubý came on Sunday. Again my mood improved, a little. I hadn't known all of them well, but we'd had enough common experiences that the arrivals felt like a family reunion. Other brothers to lighten the load. What strange creatures we are! We may have food and drink and shelter, but without others to interact with, our minds work themselves into the most frightful fits. There can be no sense of perspective or scale regarding the immense things in our lives unless it is provided by another's presence. Like when you are on holiday and you take photographs of large buildings. You are the photographer and you can't see yourself, and only seeing others in the picture lets you know how large any of it actually is.

Quickly we grew used to the place. We held push-up competitions and smoked. Petrek had provided us with a battered tin can in which to relieve ourselves, and we sacrificed a blanket to cover it up, but the air rapidly grew foul with the scent of piss and shit and sweat and cigarettes. Corruption and death all around.

Finally on Monday, Petrek lowered the ladder again, and Gabčík descended into our midst.

We were sitting in two circles playing mariáš in the flickering candlelight, amidst piles of bones. And I can't imagine what the scene must have looked like to Josef. All of us playing cards and smoking cigarettes in the kingdom of the dead.

"Jesus and Mary," Gabčík said at last.

"Man! We had just the right amount of people to have two games going at once. And now, forget it," Valčik said.

Gabčík shook his head. Rubbed his face with his hand. His other hand held a crumpled piece of paper.

"Cleaning out the bones was Valčik's idea, by the way!" I protested, and the others laughed and hooted and someone threw a deck of cards at me.

"No, it's…" Again he shook his head.

I got up and walked over to him. Saw what he was clutching. A flyer. A list of names.

"What is that?" I asked.

"That's what we've caused. Reprisals. Executions. They're posting names in the streets, they're reading them on the radio. It's worse than anything that happened under Heydrich."

"It's all right," Valčik said. He'd materialized behind me.

"It's not all right! Nothing is all right! This is the worst possible outcome! Failure and reprisal. Either one alone might have been bearable, but this!" He gestured at the catacombs and the bare bones. "JINDRA was right. We are no good. We are troublemakers. Everyone who helped us has to fear for their life. And look where they've put us. Look who we're keeping company with." Again he gestured at the bones. "That tells you something right there."

"There's nothing we can do now," I said.

"Exactly! That's what's so…fucking frustrating."

"Cheer up, my friend," Valčik said.

"Yes, cheer up," I echoed.

Finally he looked up. "You're telling me to cheer up, silent one?"

"Yes." I patted him on the shoulder. Gave him something like a hug.

"Look on the bright side," Valčik chipped in. "You can sleep in tomorrow."

Gabčík shook his head. "It's depressing, having to sleep here."

"I might talk to Petrek," I said. "We'll see if there are other options. This isn't the end. It's all right. You're tired. Get some sleep." Again, I patted him on the shoulder. Put on a brave face. Tried not to think about what he had said.

Because he was right, after all. We had failed. Or so it seemed.

```
DOCUMENT:    #27
DESCRIPTION: PERSONAL DIARY OF K.H. FRANK
PLACE:       BULOVKA HOSPITAL AND HRADČANY, PRAHA,
             OCCUPIED CZECHOSLOVAKIA
DATE:        4 JUNE 1942
```

[Translator's Note: This entry appears to cover events from 2-4 June.]

It has actually happened.

The once-unimaginable, the thing I'd once perhaps darkly hoped for, has happened, and reduced me to a black despair deeper than I'd known, and a dark anger at this cursed land and its ungrateful people.

I had perhaps known it was coming for the past few days. There was something bleak in the air, some sense that nothing was going to turn out well, despite all our best efforts, despite the all the triumphs that seemed as good as won.

I felt it already the other day, when Himmler accompanied me back to Praha after our visit with the Leader. It was a quiet, tense trip aboard the train; green fields undulated past the window, and the morning sun was bright, but I had a hard time enjoying it. I had the feeling of an inept student who had repeatedly tried and failed to please the headmaster, and was now facing the harshest disciplinary measures despite his best efforts. And yet I knew that was not the end of it.

When the two of us—plus a retinue of guards—made it back to Bulovka, it was apparent that Heydrich's condition had worsened.

Alone in his now-windowless hospital room, he drifted in and out of consciousness. I had been in such a state after surgery once; I remembered it, how I'd gone back and forth between the black empty sea of oblivion, and a white morphine fog.

What was Heydrich's state of mind? One can only surmise. When I'd been in that situation, I'd had little sense of anything beyond the blurry metal bed frame, and few thoughts of the world beyond the bland walls. Hours meant nothing, and days themselves blurred together. Nurses and doctors and nurses came in and out; life broke into pieces like dreams. I assume it was such for him, but all I can describe for certain is our conversation.

I remember Himmler by the bedside, looking down his nose and over his wire-rimmed glasses. Again, he seemed like a schoolmaster; but here there was a new level of disappointment than what I'd seen, for he'd never expected much from me, whereas Heydrich was the star pupil who had suddenly and unexpectedly and utterly disappointed him. (And yet behind the steel frames and the stern gaze there was concern—beneath that tough facade, he is quite the compassionate man! He really does try to hide it, though.)

"How are you doing, Reinhard?"

"What day is it?"

"June the Second."

"June isn't a day. June isn't a day! June is a month." Heydrich giggled in his morphine euphoria.

"June the Second," Himmler repeated.

"Oh. That's a day."

Himmler pursed his lips. "You're delirious."

"I'm hilarious. But no one else is laughing! I'm having a great time in my head, but I cannot get anyone else in here with me! I think they have me on morphine!"

"Yes," Himmler said sternly. "They have you on morphine."

"They have me on morphine!" Again Heydrich giggled.

"How do you feel?"

"I have spent so much time running around! I never took the time to relax! And now I feel so relaxed!" His head lolled. Blissful but tired. "But today time has stopped. I don't know when it's going to start again. Do you know when it's going to start again?"

"Time hasn't stopped," Himmler scowled. "There is much to be done still. The Realm needs you. Your strength and virtue are an example for all of us."

"I feel weak. I never felt weak before. I never felt weak before."

"We need you to be strong," Himmler said.

"We are all the more determined to carry on because of what happened to you," I said, glad to talk at last.

"Frank! Friend! Are you in charge now?" Heydrich asked. "You always wanted to be in charge!"

I scowled, and spat out his next words as if they were poison. "Daluge is in charge."

"Dummy-dummy!" Heydrich smiled. "Such a shame! He is such a silly stupid man! Sillier and stupider than I am right now, even! At least I have an excuse! They are giving me drugs!"

"Yes," Himmler said.

"But he is that way without the drugs!"

"We are determined to find the people who did this to you," I told him, hoping, perhaps, to encourage him. "I assure you we will find them.

"We will find them, and everybody that helped them. And we will wipe them off the earth, along with their friends and their families," Himmler said. (His weak chin and jowly face were alive with emotion now!) "We will kill them publicly, for the whole world to see. History is not meant to be written by men like that. History cannot be dictated by the pathetic vermin that attacked you and fled into hiding. It must be written by men like us! Strong men, hard men that can do the difficult things we need to do. Like rescuing this continent from the treacherous vermin that are infesting it: the Slavic rabble, the decadent Franks, the detestable Jews. Weak, pathetic creatures, like the scum that attacked you. We were made strong, we were made fearless, we were made hard so we could rid the world of such inferior creatures. It is our destiny."

"Maybe this is my destiny," Heydrich said dreamily. "Do you remember my father's opera? Did you go see it ever?"

"Uhhh. Yes," Himmler said.

"I greatly enjoyed it, my Lord," I said, with perhaps too much feigned enthusiasm.

Then again, he seemed too drugged to notice. "Maybe this is my destiny. To get all these things started so that men like you can finish them. Maybe this is my destiny. You remember that line, right? The world is…"

"The world is…" Himmler parroted. (Such an actor he can be—he really looked as if he has heard the line in the opera and it was on the tip of his tongue!)

"The world is a pipe-organ which the good Lord turns himself. And everyone must dance to the tune on the drum."

"You're delirious. You're talking foolishness. You choose the tune," Himmler said. "You pick the drum and you put it in."

"Everyone must dance," Heydrich said. Closed his eyes. "I'm tired of dancing. I'm tired."

I followed Himmler outside into the hallway. Doctor Dick was getting ready to step outside for a cigarette. Anxious, Himmler walked over.

"What else can you do for him, doctor?"

"Honestly, I don't know what else to tell you, Lord Realm-Leader. There's shrapnel and debris in there. From the grenade, from the car. If the car had been armoured, maybe…"

"DON'T…" Himmler's voice spiked. He made a fist and punched the wall. "Don't tell me what could have been done differently. Just tell me what you're doing now."

"Well, as I mentioned earlier, we are giving him sulphonamide for the infections. And morphine for the pain. But the surgery…"

"What about the surgery." It was not a question or a statement. It was a challenge.

"I'm not sure how well…I'm afraid sepsis might be setting in. We'll do what we can, Lord Realm-Leader."

"You'd better." Himmler glared at the doctor for a few seconds before leaving.

Doctor Dick pulled out his cigarettes and walked towards the lounge; I don't know if I've ever seen a human more eager for a smoke.

Himmler took the train back to Berlin that afternoon. For the few remaining hours I saw him in Praha, he appeared nervous and agitated, as if there might be an ambush waiting around every corner. Meanwhile, I spent the remainder of the day, and all yesterday, being swallowed by dread. Everything felt wrong, and yet it also felt like there was no way to stop it.

And today the news came. I'd had a sense it was coming. Still, though it wasn't a surprise, it was still a shock; I found myself thinking simple repetitive mindless thoughts: this is happening, this has actually happened, there is no way to change it.

The news broke far too late for the morning papers, so I accompanied Emanuel Moravec back to the radio studio to oversee a broadcast.

As he pored over the typewritten text, I stood there numbly; I imagined the Czechs huddled together across the fearful anxious city, in living rooms, kitchens, offices at the back of factories, and out in front of department store windows; I imagined them huddled together around radios, straining to hear news which they had perhaps all hoped to hear, drawing comfort from Moravec's words, drawing strength, preparing to rise against us.

We had to stop that. We had to take away their hope, for their own sake. It would have been a great mess all around, far greater than was the case, even! We had to prevent that. And I had to make sure he said the right words, that he didn't change his mind and incite them.

He spoke slowly, clearly, with a gravity that matched the situation: "SS Supreme Group Leader Reinhard Heydrich, beloved protector of the Czech people, died at 4:30 this morning at Bulovka Hospital. His cowardly assassins remain at large. Anyone found sheltering or assisting them in any way are hereby warned that they will be shot, along with their entire family, for their role in this treachery. A generous reward of one million Realm-marks has been offered for information directly leading to the apprehension of these cowardly criminals." He leaned close to the stainless steel microphone, his eyes dead with apathy.

"And we're clear," the technician announced after he turned off the microphone channel.

I nodded my acknowledgment. It had been a decent performance, after all. Perhaps Heydrich had been right about the man. He was useful, at least.

"This is intolerable," Moravec said. Leaned back in his wooden chair, lit a cigarette, stared blankly ahead.

"What is, sir?" The technician deposited an ashtray on the console.

"This situation. This terrorist crime." Moravec ashed on the floor. "What good can come of it? Our people are suffering."

"Maybe someone will come forward for the reward," I said.

"They should have done so already." Moravec looked back at me and cocked a perplexed eyebrow. "What does it take to get people to do the right thing these days?"

I find myself wondering the same thing.

```
DOCUMENT:     #47
DESCRIPTION: NARRATIVE OF J. KUBIŠ
PLACE:        CHURCH OF STS. CYRIL AND METHODEJ, PRAHA,
              OCCUPIED CZECHOSLOVAKIA
DATE:         4 JUNE 1942
```

The day it finally happened, we awoke to the trapdoor opening in its little recess in the vaulted ceiling of the crypt. Down came the ladder. We saw the silhouette of a man descending from the bright daylight. HAJASKÝ.

We blinked hard. Eyes unused to the light. Probably we looked like cave people. At least, that's what I felt like.

HAJASKÝ tossed a newspaper on the stone floor in front of me. A late edition extra with a banner headline.

"Holy Jesus!" I said. Cracked a smile which kept growing until it turned into a cackle. "Holy Jesus!"

Finally HAJASKÝ smiled, too, and spoke. "You did it. You did it after all."

Without realizing I'd gotten up, I found myself clapping everyone on the back and hugging and grinning. Gabčík exhaled audibly and shuddered with emotion.

"See? I told you not to worry," I told him. Clapped him on the back.

"There is still a lot to worry about," HAJASKÝ said. "They were calling this the largest manhunt in the history of the Realm. And the price on your heads is now one million marks."

"A lot of people we've met might sell us out for that much," someone said.

"I might sell us out for that much!" Gabčík grinned. Back to his normal jokester self for the first time since the attack, or so it seemed. He cleared his throat, addressed an imaginary German. "My Lord, this Kubiš fellow here, he's the one that did it. I saw the whole thing!"

"Very funny, Josef." Again I clapped him on the back. Already my cheeks hurt from smiling.

"A million, huh?" Valčik said. "I'm gonna go outside…for a walk…I'll see you men later."

"Very funny, Josef," I said.

Now HAJASKÝ cleared his throat. "At any rate, this will keep the Germans mad for quite a while. So there's no telling when it'll be safe to try and move you."

"Can you bring the rest of our weapons?" Gabčík asked. A few of us had come to the church with automatics, but the remaining Stens and grenades were still hidden in various homes.

"I don't know that Petrek would be happy with that."

"Tell him it's better to have them here with us than out in some family's house." Gabčík said.

"I'll tell him."

"Is anyone else coming?" Valčik asked.

"That fellow that got drunk and started the big argument, when all those others arrived…"

"Čurda," Opálka said.

"…I'm not sure where he is. And that other one, the one who was hobbling. He might come, if he's in a condition to."

I read again the incredible headline.

It was an ending I'd given up hoping for. An ending I'd thought impossible. And yet I knew even then that it was not the end.

```
DOCUMENT:    #27
DESCRIPTION: PERSONAL DIARY OF K.H. FRANK
PLACE:       PRAHA, OCCUPIED CZECHOSLOVAKIA AND BERLIN,
             GERMANY
DATE:        9 JUNE 1942
```

For all else that has gone wrong in the past few weeks, all the troubles, the manhunt which still continues, all the unanswered questions, I can at least report that we have been able to give Heydrich a proper send-off.

I do miss him. I must admit it, as strange as the sentiment now seems, I miss him! It is an emotion I had not expected. I am, I suppose, somewhat jealous as well—he died like a warrior; he died triumphantly; everyone now speaks well of him.

And we gave him a warrior's send-off.

On the night after he had died, I accompanied the SS guard of honour that left Bulovka Hospital in a German Army half-track. They carried four torches; the flickering firelight illuminated their impassive faces and their polished helmets. Behind them was a gun carriage carrying the coffin holding the deceased Realm-Protector.

They wound their way through silent streets to Castle Hill—a single source of light in the blacked-out city.

The local Catholic Vicar-General had sought to send four Church representatives to the mourning services, and to have the bells of St. Vitus toll in his memory. We politely refused.

Instead, we put together something altogether more appropriate for a warrior. Under a large black SS flag, his body lay in state at the Castle for the next two days, flanked by six soldiers. They wore spotless uniforms; their boots and helmets were impeccably shiny. They held ceremonial swords rigidly against their shoulders. Evergreen branches lined the room—a Nordic touch I especially liked.

The mourning here was capped by a ceremony in which Daluge spoke warm lies about his bitter rival and predecessor, and the Czech contingent cried phoney tears for their protector.

Again the flag-draped coffin was loaded onto the gun carriage. The half-track drove slowly down Castle Hill and across the Charles Bridge. Soldiers stood at attention all along the route, beneath sad stone statues of saints and wrought-iron street lamps and Baroque buildings.

A few curious Czechs went out to quietly watch the strange spectacle. And it occurred to me why it all looked so familiar; I had seen a similar scene less than five years before, when Masaryk's coffin had travelled the same path from the Castle to the train station! (I had been a guest at that horrid event-the sort of perfunctory invitation that must be given, and must be accepted, whatever the feelings on either side. Such cruelties abound in politics!) And during the ceremony I realized this too—I realized, and I had to consult a reference service to realize it was the truth—they had the same birthday! Heydrich and Masaryk, they had the same birthday! March the 4th!

I don't know what it means, but amidst all of the grim remembrances, I found this strange parallel, at least, amusing.

Then, of course, I accompanied Heydrich's casket on the funeral train to Berlin—yet another trip on that blasted train! And there were still more ceremonies when we got there.

Hitler convened a massive assembly in the cavernous Mosaic Room at the Realm Chancellery. Everyone who was anyone was there in attendance. Before the ruler-straight rows of folding chairs stood an ornate setup, with still more evergreens. Massive pillars supporting large ceremonial torches, and gilt wreaths inscribed on red walls of polished marble. There were soldiers standing at attention, their swollen chests decked out with ribbons and buttons and patches, red and black and silver and gold on the grey woollen uniforms. And in front of the honour guard and the flag-draped coffin, there was a field of flowers: crocuses and immaculate white lilies.

Himmler spoke. "Here we mourn not just a friend and colleague, but a man who was so much more. A devoted family man, a father for his children and a leader of promise for his nation. In Heydrich we had a man with a heart of iron, always willing to do the hard things his country demanded."

We mourners in the front rank quivered with emotion. Göring and Goebbels dabbed red eyes with white handkerchiefs. Speer alone sat, stony.

"He had the difficult task of building and leading an organization which dealt almost exclusively with the seamy side of life; with the unreliable, with deviants. And he made many valuable contributions to police all over the world, based on his knowledge, and in the spirit of comradeship. His chief reward was that crime in Germany sank steadily to the disappearing point from 1936 onward, and despite the war now in its third year, it has now reached its lowest point ever. Everyone can go out on the street peacefully, without being bothered or getting robbed, even in the darkest hours of the night, in sharp contrast to the 'magnificently humane' democratic countries. I knew this man well, I know how this man—who was compelled to seem outwardly hard and strong—often suffered in his heart, often struggled. How painful it sometimes was for him! For our police, he will remain the creator and founder, perhaps never to be equalled." Himmler swallowed hard and left the stage.

Hitler wept.

Finally he composed himself and stood, then marched to a spot in front of the casket and saluted his fallen angel. At last, he ascended to the podium and spoke.

"I'm too…mournful to say much. So I only have a few words to dedicate to the deceased. He was one of the best National Socialists. One of the strongest defenders of the German Realm. One of the greatest opponents of all enemies of the Realm. And as Leader of the German Realm, I decorate thee, my dear comrade

Heydrich, with the highest order I can bestow. The highest stage of the German Order."

Everyone watched Hitler. To be honest, I expected more! His usual oratory is so incandescent, so spellbinding—I waited for a great speech worthy of the man—the great man, I can say now that he's gone!—that we were laying to rest. But Hitler turned and descended from the podium. After a prolonged and miserable silence, we mourners broke into applause. The military orchestra played "The Dead Soldier's Song" and Beethoven's "Eroica."

Outside, the day was all the brighter, and the sun all the more harsh, after the depressing dim funeral. The coffin was loaded onto yet another half-track. All along the route to the cemetery, soldiers stood at attention, sweltering in their field-grey uniforms and coal scuttle helmets as they saluted the slow procession. Behind their ranks, various ordinary Germans thrust their arms skyward in sloppy salute. And the sun hung high, casting short shadows.

```
DOCUMENT:      #7280.10.7.1947
DESCRIPTION: EXCERPT FROM POSTWAR SUMMARY OF KNOWN
             ACTIVITIES OF R. HEYDRICH
PLACE:         TEREZIN, OCCUPIED CZECHOSLOVAKIA
DATE:          9 JUNE 1942
PREPARED FOR:     MUSIL
PREPARED ON: 10.7.1947
```

In the small town of Terezín (which is, of course, surrounded by the brick walls of the old fortress named by the Hapsburgs in honour of Maria Theresa), the Germans had established the main ghetto for Jews from Bohemia and Moravia. Outside the brick fortress walls lay bucolic Bohemian countryside, pleasant and pastoral; inside was filth and misery and disease and overcrowding. Tens of thousands lived in squalor, chronically malnourished, sleeping in stuffy rooms and shuffling through the streets, wearing their yellow stars on their clothes.

On the day of Heydrich's funeral, a thousand of them were rounded up: men, women and children alike. Soldiers of the SS herded them from their temporary homes and down dilapidated stairs. Carrying their single suitcases, they trudged down brick-paved streets and out from the fortress gates, then out along the country road for three kilometres to the nearby town of Bušovice, where a train awaited.

The transport was anything but luxurious: boxcars behind a black locomotive. While the soldiers watched, the men and women stacked their suitcases next to the trains and climbed aboard, heading for disaster.

It is, of course, impossible to say whether any would have survived the war under other circumstances. Still, they were dying for a specific vengeance. All of their paperwork was in order, and everything was stamped with special stamps, with initials indicating: Assassination of Heydrich.

The world paid little heed.

```
DOCUMENT:    #27
DESCRIPTION: PERSONAL DIARY OF K.H. FRANK
PLACE:       PRAHA, OCCUPIED CZECHOSLOVAKIA AND BERLIN,
             GERMANY
DATE:        9 JUNE 1942 (CONTINUED)
```

A subdued luncheon followed the funeral orations at the Realm Chancellery. We munched crackers and cheese and sausage, and swirled snifters of brandy and cognac; I drifted from conversation to conversation, saying little, hearing much.

"You must be sad to see him gone," Göring said to Himmler. "You two worked so closely."

"It is quite a…transition." Himmler somehow looked neither displeased nor pleased.

"He was a force of nature," Göring added between mouthfuls of food.

"He was."

"If such a thing could happen to such a man…well, it could happen to any of us!"

"Yes." Here Himmler at last appeared somewhat emotional—again, he feels things more deeply than most people realize. "It is something to think about."

"What will become of his files, by the way?" Göring asked. "If those fell into the wrong hands…"

"They are secure," Himmler replied.

"It seems there are probably some that you won't see the need to maintain," Göring said—speculating or fishing, it was hard to tell.

"They are secure."

"It is quite a shock, though. Such a surprise. So many things have been going well…then this attack…"

"And the Cologne raids," Himmler said. "Many things are not as they should be. Perhaps the Leader will offer some guidance." They ambled over to where a cluster of flunkies was forming around Hitler; I followed along, curious myself.

"...they were…most eloquent," said some pissant—Eichmann, I think his name was—from some department I don't recall.

"Simple but eloquent," someone else said.

"Yes. He was and will remain an inspiration." Eichmann enthused. "We must continue his work and dedicate ourselves anew to finishing what he started. Now it is a matter of honour."

"Yes, we must remember his example," I added.

"Yes, by all means, continue his work. But if any of you follows his example, I will be bitterly disappointed," Hitler snapped crisply.

"My Leader?" Eichmann asked.

"He fancied himself a hero. Well, such heroism is not needed. Since it is opportunity that makes not only the thief but also the assassin, such 'heroic' gestures as driving in an open unarmoured convertible are just damned stupidity. We must not throw away our destiny by following that example."

We nodded and sipped our drinks. No one moved.

Himmler cleared his throat. "Yes. We cannot leave everything to the Good Lord and make him our personal security guard."

"Heydrich understood, more that anyone, that we have great goals," Hitler continued. "But he apparently did not understand that great goals bring about great opposition. And we cannot encourage such opposition by allowing it any successes, however temporary they may be."

Here I was about to voice my agreement, but an anxious orderly tapped me on the shoulder. "There is a telephone call from Praha, my Lord. They say it is urgent."

I excused myself, and followed the edgy captain down empty hallways to the orderly room.

"Frank?"

At first I did not recognize the voice. "Yes, what is it?"

"We have some extremely important information." It was Daluge.

"Yes, what is it?" I asked impatiently.

Daluge paused for effect, then spoke, slowly and proudly. "We think we may have found some of the people who were behind this monstrous crime."

"Excellent! How soon can we act?"

"The wheels are already in motion. We think we can make something happen tonight."

I listened intently as he laid out his plan.

```
DOCUMENT:    #7280.10.7.1947
DESCRIPTION: EXCERPT FROM POSTWAR SUMMARY OF KNOWN
             ACTIVITIES OF R. HEYDRICH
PLACE:       LIDICE, OCCUPIED CZECHOSLOVAKIA
DATE:        9 JUNE 1942
PREPARED FOR: MUSIL
PREPARED ON: 10.7.1947
```

Near Kladno, there once sat an unremarkable country village, one whose name we all now know too well. It was a tiny cluster of brick houses and barns hugging the bottom of a gentle valley in the Bohemian countryside, with oak trees scattered all about, and others lining the sides of the road that lead into town. On June 9th, 1942, the day of Heydrich's burial, its population stood just shy of 500 souls. 199 men, 195 women, 95 children.

Already by sundown of that day, the last normal day for that poor town, army lorries and black Secret Police staff cars were assembling two kilometres down the road in Kladno. According to the townspeople, there were so many that they filled the cobblestoned town square with the roar of diesel engines, and coughed smoky exhaust into the open windows.

Inside the canvas-covered lorries, the soldiers sat facing each other on wooden benches. According to one participant, the rank-and-file spent the early evening awaiting orders. Some grew sleepy in their warm wool uniforms, and others got restless and fidgety. Eventually word trickled down that they could get out and stretch their legs, and so they spilled out of the back of the lorries and stretched and joked and wandered off in search of water closets. At any rate, those we've talked to claim they knew little of what was going on.

As it grew dark, their leaders assembled indoors on long wooden benches in a plain white room normally used for detainees awaiting interrogation.

The battalion commander informed them that the Secret Police had assembled conclusive proof that the townspeople at their nearby target—this small town whose name is now, of course, large in our hearts—had not only approved of, but had materially assisted in, the attack on Heydrich.

By the time they filed back outside, it was dark, and many of their soldiers were standing around smoking. Electric torches came on and the leaders rounded up their men. The soldiers grumbled and clambered back on the lorries, and waited in darkness and silence. Then again came the cranking of engines and the grinding of gears as the lorries and cars started queuing up and driving out of town.

By midnight, they had surrounded their target.

The battalion commander went first with a squad of soldiers to the mayor's house. They did not knock but instead kicked open the flimsy front door and stormed inside, yelling and waving electric torches. Awoken by the noise, and afraid, the mayor met them at his bedroom door.

They forced him to produce a ledger containing the names of all the townspeople.

They then apparently brought the ledger back to a farm near the edge of town. There, other soldiers had set up a tent with tables and maps under a strand of trees, so the leader could study the ledger by the light of kerosene lamps.

Then squads of soldiers started going from house to house. They roused families from their beds and forced them to dress, then prodded them through the streets at bayonet point. Families were separated along the way, with the women and children siphoned off to the town schoolhouse and the men herded like sheep into the large barn owned by the Hořak family. When each family was rounded up, the squad leader wrote down the names, then went to the command post and had them crossed off the ledger.

Other squads searched the empty houses for valuables, and carried them back to the Hořak farm and deposited them on a tarp.

One squad didn't round up families or valuables but simply loaded a dozen mattresses into the back of one of the lorries, then leaned them up against the stone wall of the Hořaks' barn.

As dawn grew near, the men were taken in groups of ten. They were lined up in front of the mattresses.

Then they were shot.

They were reportedly shot by two squads of riflemen. Then the officer in charge of the detail used his pistol on anyone who still showed signs of life.

Inside the barn, the others waited in anxious silence. According to one of the guards, they could hear almost everything but acted like they did not.

Near the end of the shooting, the sun started coming up. Each new group of victims eventually got to the point where they could not feign ignorance. According to one eyewitness, when they lined up to meet their fate, they had to step over crumpled corpses whose blood had turned the ground to mud.

```
DOCUMENT:    #27
DESCRIPTION: PERSONAL DIARY OF K.H. FRANK
PLACE:       LIDICE, OCCUPIED CZECHOSLOVAKIA
DATE:        10 JUNE 1942
```

It has been a most ghastly day!

After the funeral, and various meetings and discussions, I took a night train back from Berlin. I could not sleep, and so I spent much of the ride again staring out the windows at the blackness; I could not see, but it was preferable to thinking.

In the morning, I headed out to the place Daluge had told me about, a small town out in the country near Kladno.

There had been shooting, but it was all done by the time I arrived. On the outskirts of town, cameramen stood behind tripods in a wheat field, filming the aftermath.

I found the leader of the operation at the command post under the stately trees. Behind him were—there is no easy way to say it—stacks of corpses.

I breathed heavily; even now, I cannot articulate the random emotions I was feeling; at any rate, I didn't and don't want to attempt to describe them. It seemed best to keep things professional. "How is the work proceeding?" I asked.

"It is all done, my Lord. It went very smoothly," the leader replied. "There are…or there were…173 men in town last night, out of 195. The remaining 22 are believed to be working in Praha or Kladno. We are sending their names to Praha so Geschke's men can round them up."

"What about the women?"

"The lorries are taking the women down the road to Kladno, my Lord. We'll process them there before sending them further. Ravensbrook or Terezín, probably."

"And the children?"

"They will be sent off as well, my Lord."

I will say that I did not necessarily like all of this; still, I did at least hope some good could come of it. So I said: "Some of them can possibly be Germanized, yes?"

"Germanized, my Lord?"

"Yes. Why not? Just the younger ones, the ones that will have little memory of this. They will have to be evaluated for the appropriate racial characteristics, of course. But if they are suitable, and they can be adopted by a German family elsewhere in the Realm, perhaps…"

The air still reeked of cordite; the leader looked over at the aftermath of what had happened there; how I wonder what he thought of me! Perhaps it all seemed foolish to him. "That's very…generous of you, my Lord," was all he said.

I shrugged. "It is the sensible thing to do, I think."

"It will be done according to your will, my Lord."

Now we both surveyed the scene, somewhat uneasily, perhaps.

I felt—I do not know why I felt it!—the sudden urge to explain myself. "I did not want things to turn out this way," I said. "This is mostly Daluge's doing."

"They will hate us forever, my Lord."

"Well they did not love us. They were never going to. So their hatred can be the only proof of our power. Our hands are tied. Again, I did not want things to turn out this way. But the Leader is right. It was necessary, I suppose."

"The Leader did not want to only punish those in the town who were proven to be guilty, my Lord?"

"Guilty?" I asked. (I was surprised; it hadn't occurred to me that he believed them to be guilty!)

"Yes. Those who were proven to have helped the parachutists, he didn't want to just punish them?"

"Proof. Guilt. Innocence. What does it matter in the grand scheme of things?" I said at last, wearily.

"What does it matter, my Lord?" The leader's face stayed somewhat impassive, but his heavy breath hinted at deeper emotions.

"Yes. What does it matter? As far as the Leader is concerned, the important thing is that we have taken action. We have made an example for everyone in the Protectorate to see. For everyone in Europe. We have told a story. Heydrich used to talk about the importance of having a story. The key to controlling the present is controlling the past, he would say. And the best way to control the past is to tell a story about it. Well, now we have a story. They sheltered the parachutists, they were shot. As to their actual guilt or innocence, well..none of them are alive to tell their stories."

The leader stared off into the distance, yet gave the impression he was not actually looking at anything; his eyes remained glassy and unfocused.

"I think we have more work to do here," I told him. "Once the buildings have burned, we have to set explosives. Blow up the ruins, then bulldoze the rubble, then bury the remains. And that will be that. The town will be wiped off the map. Literally. It will be broken into pieces too small to ever reconstruct. And people will whisper, but no one will raise their voice. There will be nothing left but our story. 'This is what happens to all who resist.'"

The leader of the operation looked towards, but not at, me.

"Our hands are tied." (Again I felt the need to explain everything, to justify it. Why did I feel such weakness? I am ashamed of myself now, as I write this.) "The Leader has decided that this must be done. And since it must be done, we should do it in the most dramatic fashion possible. I want corn to grow where the town once stood."

"It's very…Biblical, my Lord," the leader said, staring off again, eyes glazed. "Having our vengeance. Our justice."

"I would not say that," I said after some thought. "I would not try to justify our actions that way. True, I'm sure in the Old Testament such things happened, but even in the Old Testament there was talk of proportionality, whereas our whole point here is to have no proportionality whatsoever. No, it is not Biblical."

Now we both stared off into the silent distance. Soon the blasts would start, and the cameramen off in the wheat field would start filming again, but for now all was quiet.

"It is something the Romans might have done, perhaps. This is how the world works. This is how their empire was built. It was said of the Romans that they would impose a desolation and call it a peace. Well, this is that. Mark my words. There will be peace in the Protectorate after this. There will be peace."

(Strange words to say on such an occasion, perhaps, but it is my greatest hope now—that, at last, we will have some peace!)

```
DOCUMENT:    #47
DESCRIPTION: NARRATIVE OF J. KUBIŠ
PLACE:       CHURCH OF STS. CYRIL AND METHODEJ, PRAHA,
             OCCUPIED CZECHOSLOVAKIA
DATE:        10 JUNE 1942
```

When we heard the news, Josef and I were up in the church, collecting up our laundry.

We had to be careful not to go up there too often, and not to hang more clothes to dry than could plausibly be explained by Petrek. So we were off to the side next to the altar, amidst all the vestments and robes and crosses, taking our clothes off the wooden drying racks. And Josef had turned on the radio. And Emanuel Moravec was speaking.

We heard the news and froze.

"Did he say Lidice?" Josef said.

"I think so."

There was a wooden chair, and Josef pulled it over and sat. Placed his hand on his face and stared off. Furrowed his brow.

"We never went there, did we? I can't remember. What was the name of that town where we landed?"

"It was not Lidice."

"It was not Lidice," Josef said. Repeated the words as if that would give him reassurance. "Was it near Lidice?"

"No. It was east. Lidice is near Kladno."

"No. It was not Lidice. It was not Lidice. Did we know anyone from there? Were any of the men downstairs from there? Did any of them stay there?"

"I don't think so," I said. Felt a chill in my bones. "I don't know."

As it sank in, I felt empty and dead. I went downstairs and sought to stay busy, but there is not much to do here. So I went back upstairs and borrowed some paper from Petrek. Then I went back downstairs and began to set down this narrative.

DOCUMENT:	#5292.19.07.1942
DESCRIPTION:	U.K. FOREIGN OFFICE MEMORANDUM PRESENTED TO A. EDEN REGARDING THE CZECHOSLOVAKIAN EXILE GOVERNMENT AND THE RECENT ATROCITIES AT LIDICE
OBTAINED ON:	23.07.1942
BY:	FRANTA

Sir:

It is the suggestion of this desk that the Government should re-evaluate its relationship with E. Beneš, President of the exiled government of Czechoslovakia, in light of recent events on the continent, particularly the assassination of R. Heydrich and the German destruction of Lidice.

While for some time our relationship with the Czechs has been somewhat problematic, these events, particularly the destruction of Lidice, have been of immense propaganda value to the Allied cause. This latter event has made newspaper headlines around the world and seems a prime example of the stakes of this conflict.

On the Eastern Front, there have already been hundreds of Lidices; many have been ten times as bloody. But those atrocities have been largely unpublished and unremarked upon outside the Soviet Union, and many happened in conjunction with heavy fighting. Lidice, by contrast, was an act of terror against a random village in a peaceful countryside. It seems to have been a calculated atrocity for public show, designed to strike fear in the hearts of all peoples living under German rule.

Instead, it has galvanized the Allies.

In America, a member of President Roosevelt's Cabinet recently said that, "If future generations ask why we fought, we will tell them the story of Lidice."

Our own Prime Minister has threatened to bomb three random German villages into rubble for every Lidice.

Even the Soviets have made note of this event, and used it as a pretext to recast their relationship with the Czech exiles here. On the day of Heydrich's death, the Soviet diplomat assigned to the Czech exile government reportedly told President Beneš that Stalin supported the re-establishment of a strong and independent Czechoslovakia with its pre-1938 borders intact. And in the wake of Lidice, this policy has reportedly been confirmed by none other than Foreign Minister Molotov. "For the Soviet Union," he reportedly told President Beneš, "Munich does not exist."

It is this desk's recommendation that our Government should follow suit by formalizing our recognition of Beneš' exiled government and formally repudiating the Munich agreement. Given Beneš' newly increased stature among the Allied statesmen, and Stalin's evident attempts to curry favour with him, it would perhaps be wise for our own Government to stay in his good graces.

Prepared for the Foreign Secretary by: E. Holmes

```
DOCUMENT:      #47
DESCRIPTION:   NARRATIVE OF J. KUBIŠ
PLACE:         CHURCH OF STS. CYRIL AND METHODEJ, PRAHA,
               OCCUPIED CZECHOSLOVAKIA
DATE:          12 JUNE 1942
```

Two days after Lidice, Josef and I ascended the ladder to the church floor to talk to our host. We blinked hard against the sunlight streaming through the stained-glass windows. Our faces stubbly and dishevelled. Nostrils still filled with subterranean miasma. My hand cramped from writing.

Petrek had set out three chairs in a circle. He seemed glad to talk.

"We can't go on like this," Josef said, practically before we'd even sat down.

"What makes you say that?"

"What makes me say that?" Josef asked. "I can't sleep! I'm miserable! After he died, I thought we'd at least accomplished something, but after Lidice…"

"It is a serious situation," Petrek said. Nodded contemplatively.

"It is beyond serious!" Josef exclaimed. "Valčik heard a rumour from HAJASKÝ that the Germans are going to literally decimate the entire city of Praha, at random. They are going to kill everyone with an ID card that ends in zero, and everyone without an ID card, unless we are apprehended. Have you heard this rumour?"

Petrek closed his eyes. "I have heard this rumour."

"And?"

"Perhaps it is just a rumour."

"What if it is true?" Josef asked.

"What if it is?" Petrek asked. "Does your worry help matters? Can you stop the Germans from doing this?"

"We can if we turn ourselves in," Gabčík said. Heart heavy.

"Is that the right answer?" Petrek asked. He gazed into us. His face was strange, but serene. A bushy beard and piercing eyes. "If that is how they deal with some random village, how much more will they do when they have a focus for their rage? The Secret Police will break you. They will round up everyone you know and everyone you've come into contact with. Is that the right answer?"

Finally I spoke. "Perhaps there is another way."

Petrek and Gabčík both turned to me. "What other way?" Petrek asked.

"We could ask for an audience with Emanuel Moravec. Tell the Germans we have information on the assassins and ask for an audience with him. And then assassinate him."

"Assassinate him?" Josef asked.

"It is one of the missions. One of the things MUSIL seemed very enthusiastic about. We could take care of that, to prove we haven't been defeated."

"And then what?" Petrek asked.

"Then…well, the pills they gave us…"

"I don't like this talk of suicide," Josef said.

"I doubt that would even work," Petrek said.

"Or we could kill ourselves out in the park," I offered.

"Why? For what?" Petrek asked.

"To protect everyone else. I have been writing down our story. I've been telling it in a way so that the Germans will know I'm telling the truth but won't have enough information to go after anyone else. I'm nearly done with the manuscript. We could bring it with us, go out there and hang placards around our necks saying we were the perpetrators, and then take the pills, and the Germans could read what I've written and know that…"

"I don't like this talk of suicide!" Josef shouted. "I know it's been there all the while, hovering, this idea, but I don't like it."

"What would you have us do?" I asked.

For a while, he said nothing. Then: "Valčik talked about the Jews at Masada. They drew straws and had every tenth person kill the other nine, so at least most of them wouldn't die suicides. And…well, it's not an ideal solution, but compared to what you're suggesting…"

"This whole mission is suicide!" For the first time in a long time, I was losing my temper. "Oh, we put on a brave face and acted like it wasn't! We fed lies to our lovers so they'd think it wasn't! We tricked them into trying to build a future with us, but it was a suicide mission from the start! MUSIL never let us think otherwise!"

"I don't think that's the right answer," Petrek said. "Obviously you're troubled, but…"

"And for good reason! How are we supposed to feel?" I asked. "How can we not blame ourselves, and wonder if things would be better with all of us dead?"

"Keep in mind: you're not responsible. The Germans are the ones doing the killing."

"We all know it wouldn't have happened without us!" I replied. "We provoked it! We set it off! I never read the Bible much until we came here, but I know Jesus says to offer no resistance to evil. When someone strikes you, turn the other cheek. Violence begets violence. And we resisted evil! We begat violence! And that violence is being returned upon our people a thousand-fold! I shied away from those words, I had a hard time with those words, especially being a soldier, but I understand them now! And it is a horrible, awful understanding!"

For some seconds, we sat.

"It's all right," Petrek said at last. "They can be troubling and challenging, our Saviour's words. I don't always know how to live by them, but I know how empty and unsatisfying life can be when I run from them."

"Should we fight, if they come?" I asked.

"I don't know what to tell you," Petrek said.

"You know, we have our weapons now," Josef said.

"I'd like to think there's another answer." Petrek replied.

"Is there? This is the path we've chosen. We can't very leave it now."

"What if there was a…a path from the crypt?" the churchman asked. "A way to escape from the tomb? Would you take it?"

"I've thought about it already," Josef said. "It looks to me like we would be able to tunnel under the street. Through the vent I can see manhole covers. There has to be a sewer under the centre of the street."

"There is," Petrek said.

"So we could tunnel there."

"Why haven't you?"

"We'd still be in Praha. It would be easier to sit in on a service and walk out the front door with the crowd."

"What if we could get you all the way out of the city?" Petrek said.

"How?"

"We take coffins out of the church all the time. We could get some and use them to smuggle you out, one by one. Drill air holes in the bottoms. It would look like a series of ordinary funerals, and we could take you all the way out of the city without arousing suspicion."

"You'd be taking a lot of risks," Gabčík said.

"I'm already taking risks. I've accepted those risks. Jesus said to welcome the stranger, feed the hungry, give drink to the thirsty. When you came, you were all those things. Rejected by your friends and associates. So I don't mind helping you get out."

"And if the Germans come?" I asked.

"We will deal with that if it happens. But we don't need to seek that out or assume that's how it must be. And we don't need to act like we'd be doing the world a favour by destroying ourselves. So let's not get twisted up about that. These people live by retaliation. They would be exacting their vengeance even if you were dead. That's all they know how to do."

So we stayed put. We went back downstairs and told the others what we'd decided. I kept writing, for lack of anything better to do. We started taking turns sleeping in the choir loft, for a break from the dank depressing crypt. We waited for a knock on the door. And we waited for our coffins.

THE ATTACK ON HEYDRICH

(From top) Heydrich's Mercedes after the attack; a wider view of the scene.

A MANHUNT; A FUNERAL; AN ATROCITY

(Top) Clues and rewards on display in downtown Prague. (Bottom, L-R) Heydrich's funeral procession in Berlin; German troops at the destruction of Lidice.

CLIMAX

(Top) Saints Cyril & Methodious Cathedral during the battle on 18 June 1942.

(Left) The Prague Fire Brigade attempts to flood the crypt.

(Right) The crypt after the battle.

COLLABORATION

(Left) Karel Čurda (partly obscured by elbow of man in right foreground) helps the Gestapo identify parachutists during the battle at the church.

(Bottom) Emanuel Moravec, Minister of Propaganda and the public face of Czech collaboration.

CHAOS

(Clockwise from top left) A Prague street after the accidental American bombing on 14 February 1945; a smashed statue of Hitler during the Prague Uprising; ethnic Germans being deported from the Sudetenland; a cell door at Pankrác.

RETRIBUTION

(Clockwise from top left) K.H. Frank in court, flanked by guards; a view of the courtroom at Pankrác during his trial; the execution of K.H. Frank on 22 May 1946; K. Čurda awaits his fate.

The Prisoner's Journal

(Editor's Note: This collection of recollections was found handwritten, untranscribed, and in some disarray. We have made every effort to clean it up and place it in a legible format while still retaining the language, the tone, the spelling idiosyncracies, and most importantly, the spirit of the author's original writings.)

Never did I think my life—my life, which once seemed so full of drama and adventure that I could barely believe it!—would end this way—treated like a common criminal, awaiting execution in a lonely gaol cell.

When I entered the army, I had imagined much greater things—medals, awards, commendations for bravery, promotions. I'd ascend through the ranks with grace and good humour, all the while acquiring tales of—what did the English used to say?—derring-doo. Yes, tales of derring-doo with which to woo the ladies back home. I even fantasized about keeping a journal of my experiences, something I could perhaps one day turn into a book or a play—but I didn't have time or opportunity to start in those first frantic weeks, and by the time I did, I felt like I'd missed too much. And I didn't know how I could write the beginning without knowing the end!!! How wrong I was! What a story it might have been!!! And now I do at least have what I once longed for, the time to write, and the knowledge of the ending!!! Oh, how one must be careful! Fantasies have a way of coming true far later than expected, and in the most frightful ways. But I do have time and opportunity at last—I know how it's all going to end, and I have time to write it down, to hopefully make sense of all the madness.

It has been an eventful life, at times! But most of the drama's over now—the business with Heydrich, the battle at the church that ended the great manhunt, the insanity that came afterward—and I'm left living in the boring remainder.

What remains? Not much. A bag of troubles, my own historia calamatia, the collected memories of a series of misfortunes so complete that it seems God Himself has arranged my life so as to deny me any happiness. (Even chronicling these calamities depresses me! Still, I'm setting pen to paper—if for no purpose than to avoid talking to my cell mate!)

I'm writing in a quiet gaol cell; the cold sun casts a bent rectangle on the concrete floor, an un-shadow sun shape subdivided by the iron bars. I barely talk to my cell mate. (I suppose I don't like people very much, after all!) So it's a lonely life, a dreary life, as depressing as death—even more so, perhaps, because that at least would be a new adventure!

I suppose I should be glad for the peace and quiet, though. And things have at least improved slightly in these past few months.

I arrived here in the back of a windowless lorry, still sore from multiple beatings; I remember wincing from the fresh bruises and cuts, and the various sore and stiff and tender spots on my body—these uncountable injuries that hurt every time I shifted positions, every time the lorry took a hard bounce. I had no sense of surroundings or destination, save that provided by my imagination.

When the doors finally opened, we were at Pankratz. (I am spelling it in the German fashion!! I should—no, I will not cross it out.) Behind us, a large metal gate rumbled closed—the only gap in the featureless walls. Ahead of us stood guards with clubs and truncheons.

My next memories are a shoddily-spliced film featuring varied scenes of casual violence. The jailers—glorified thugs, really—had formed a gauntlet through which we had to pass. A few of us disembarked hesitantly—how very hesitantly!!—until a guard came from behind and smacked the first fellow full on the leg with all his might, taking him down; I'm sure I heard the man's bones break.

Whatever discipline had been holding the guards in line evaporated; we were yanked from the lorry and thrown into what had rapidly become a surging angry mass of uniforms, truncheons, feet, fists. There was no time for thought, no time for anything but blind animal fear; we were thrown down on the stones, kicked and punched and picked up and shoved and hit again; I saw pavement and sky and faces and limbs.

Then we were lined up against a courtyard wall. Hands on the wall and head straight forward, they yelled, and the one time I didn't obey, someone slammed my skull into the cement. I remember tasting blood in my mouth, staring intently at the stucco, and thinking—absurdly—of being forced to sit in the corner of the schoolroom when I was a child.

I heard a pistol shot.

It echoed off the stone walls, and I flinched in spite of myself.

Then I heard another, and another, and they were coming closer, and I died with every shot.

At last I felt a hot barrel nuzzling my ear, and I cringed, and I felt the barrel move as the invisible hand pulled the trigger, and then—it would be hard to write this otherwise, ha ha!!—I heard the click of the safety catch.

Then came another trigger pull, and a blast like a cannon very near my ear, and I flinched, my face pressed hard against the prickly stucco of the courtyard wall. And this was repeated again and again and again until their intent at last became clear; they didn't want to finish us off, but to send a message, to establish a simple social order: we are everything, and you are nothing.

My days and nights soon settled into an endless cycle of alternating aggravations, far worse than anything I'd experienced—and complained about!!!—as a commando. I was crammed in a two-man cell with as many as eight others. We would fight like animals when it came time to apportion the pig slop they served us at mealtime (mouldy cabbage and near-rancid meat, rotting potatoes and watery soup) then sleep closer than lovers, waking to stumble over squirming bodies on our frequent trips to the toilet. (Illness and gastric disease ran rampant, and there often seemed little difference, quality-wise, between the mushy mess we'd been shovelling into our mouths and the chunky gruel our spasming bowels deposited in the ever-clogging porcelain bowls.) One had to fumble about in the darkness to find one's own sliver of the lice-infested bedding, often waking others who would then realize they, too, needed to make the trip. (These have been—especially in the beginning—the worst beds I've ever slept in. But I always return eagerly—in here, there's no better place to be!! Blessed, blessed sleep—the one escape route they can't quite seal off, ha ha!! On second thought, though, there's another one, one I haven't had the courage to try. Perhaps I should have done so, before it all ended at the church! Perhaps I should have spared myself all this. I...I digress.)

God's cruelty—or monumental indifference—seemed particularly obvious in those early months. The summer sun hung forever in the cloudless sky, and I would stand for hours by the windows, straining at the bars for the slightest breath of fresh air, the weakest breeze—any respite from the foul odour inside, a co-mingling of sweat and shit and piss and come that smelled worse the higher the temperature. The buildings were ovens—and we were ducks, roasting in our own foul (fowl?) juices!!!

But now—I must reluctantly admit—it isn't quite so bad. The temperature and the overcrowding have gone down. Although the food is not great, even I must admit it is better. And while there isn't a good time of year to be imprisoned, winter's probably the best: you don't want to go outside! You're stuck in this walled-in clump of cement buildings, this diamond of suffering squeezed in on this hilltop, this ugly cracked lustreless gem set far too prominently in this quiet stone city. You're stuck here, and the outside world's more drab and depressing than normal, but at least you miss it less.

Still, one never expects such endings! It has been such a long time since the world felt normal that the word's lost its meaning. But in all that abnormality—Munich, war, exile, return—there were at least a multitude of possibilities, more questions than answers. That uncertainty had been uncomfortable; how I miss it now!!

I was a soldier, then a spy. And now I'm a prisoner, waiting to die.

I could have avoided this outcome, had I but had the courage to take my own life. Courage—that's what's expected of a soldier! Courage and superhuman selflessness. Well, the honest truth—as much as I hate to admit it, even (especially?) to myself—is that I never had those virtues, and eventually got tired of acting as if I did. I can admit to it now, at least! I have that much courage, at least.

It does me little good, though, with my options dwindling and the end drawing near. I'm facing justice—or what passes for justice these days!! A kangaroo trial, I believe that's the English phrase, and a trip to the gallows within two hours of sentencing. That's what passes for justice these days!! Still, when it comes, I suppose I'll need some measure of courage to walk those final steps to the gallows with some measure of dignity.

And I will be executed. I'm writing it again so it will feel more real, more definite. After all, how else can this end? Escape? To where? Acquittal? Impossible, now that they know who I am. I can hope against hope for another rebirth, a new new life, but that won't happen. Not without a miracle.

Two hours. Barely enough time for a last supper and a last confession—if I even decide to go, ha ha!! (Will they even allow it? Who knows? I dare not hope for more.) Until then, I'm stuck here in my cell—far emptier than it used to be, but still miserable!!—with nothing but my stories, and nothing to do but tell them as I wait around to die.

When I stare out at the snowy courtyards reminiscing, I don't usually think about what got me here—the attack on Heydrich, the horrific wave of revenge killings that followed, the tragic battle at the church that seemed to be the end of it all.

No, I spend most of the time thinking—with some guilt, mind you—about my unexpected new life—my improbable resurrection!!

I remember seeking shelter at a quiet country inn. (It was December of 1942, or thereabouts.) When I came in from the cold, every head looked me over, but slowly, casually, each in turn; the place was dark and smoky, full of old men who looked like they'd been hunched over their beers at those wooden tables since before the war started and would be there after it ended, provided they didn't topple over dead first. By the time I'd plopped down at a table near the hearth and started peeling off my damp socks, they'd all turned back away. No worries, I remember thinking—they'll all be talking about me soon enough.

The hostess came over to see if she could get me anything. "A good strong Czech beer," I told her. Hearing my accent, she frowned a little, and asked if I was a Slovak.

"What is it to you?" I asked, and she said she was curious. (I knew this was necessary, but I didn't like her attitude. Or her face, for that matter.) "Just…could you bring the beer please?" I asked at last.

She bowed, left, returned with the beer. I ordered a goulash and wolfed it down in silence.

We didn't speak again until she brought the bill; only then did she apologize and say she hadn't meant to be nosy.

"It's all right," I allowed; my spirits were improving now that my belly was full of food and my head was filling with beer. "I was rude. I'm sorry. I'm just…under a lot of stress, with our situation these days."

"These are difficult times," she agreed.

I sensed this was my chance. I leaned forward conspiratorially, darting my eyes back and forth, the way one might do while on the run. "Can I…speak freely with you, ma'am?" I at last asked. "These are dangerous times. One cannot always speak freely, lest the wrong ears hear."

She smiled, just a little. "If you're worried about German ears, you needn't worry here."

Only at that point did I lean back, relax, and give what I hoped was a weary but contented smile.

(My hand grows tired. I will finish the story tomorrow.)

Where was I? Ahh yes. The inn.

Night had fallen and snow was falling. I don't remember what else we said, but at closing time I was motioned into a back room, where the hostess tied a blindfold over my eyes and led me outside.

My heart beat louder than my footsteps on the snowy ground; my guide told me nothing, so I tried to concentrate on the latter. We walked across cobblestones, then stumbled across the furrows of a frozen field. Then I remember shuffling through snowy leaves and twigs — a forest floor. And then, more cobblestones. I was a little confused — truth be told, the beers had gone to my head, a little — but I wondered if we'd really gone that far.

I heard knocks on a wooden door. We were let in, and I was pointed towards a staircase. It may have been my imagination, but I thought I heard my guide chuckling as I tripped and stumbled awkwardly upwards. At the top, I nearly toppled back down, but at last she offered a helping hand.

"Thank you," I said, though I wasn't sure I meant it. "Who is it I'm meeting, anyway?"

"It is not for you to know," she said, quite annoyed.

"What am I to call him, though?" I asked, to which she told me — in quite a cold manner, I might add — that he would tell me what he was to be called, but only if he trusted me.

"I'm trustworthy!" I exclaimed. "I'm an honest man! You could be bringing the Gestapo here, for all I know."

She said I was being absurd. Then she led me though what felt like a doorway and sat me on what felt like a bed. And then — she had the nerve to ask my name!

"I'll tell your friend my name. If I trust him." I smiled, and she made an exasperated noise. Truth be told, this was already getting boring for me, too — this depressing theatre, these tired roles. Also — unfortunately — by this time the beer was having its usual effects; I had the simultaneous desire to empty myself of piss, and to get started on making more.

"Is there a water closet up here?" I asked my guide; she replied—in a tone I really didn't care for—that I should have asked when we were out in the woods.

"I didn't," I pointed out, and she sighed and led me to another door. "There, go in there."

The blindfold complicated things somewhat. With my shins I found the toilet bowl, then undid my trousers and aimed. I heard a spattering sound, all wrong. I stopped, re-aimed, and tried again. No luck—I was making water but not hitting it. The third time I tried, I felt piss soaking through the front of my pants legs—"Fuck," I swore, and tore off the blindfold. And they'd left the toilet lid down! Not just the seat, but the whole lid!!

"Jesus and Mary, who leaves the lid down?" I yelled.

Through the door I heard the bitch chuckle. Then, at last, an apology; she told me there was a dog here, a drinker.

"I am too, but I don't leave the lid down," I said, and she laughed with me at last. Good, I remember thinking—after all, you do need to win these people over!

Inebriated and somewhat forgetful, I cleaned up my mess, then opened the door and saw my hostess.

"Jesus and Mary, put your blindfold back on," she said, and I obliged sloppily. She tied it again, harder—so tight I saw stars—and sat me back on the bed.

"You'll soon see that in my case, your precautions are unwarranted. And in fact, once you find out who I am, you'll see that I have far more need for caution than..." I pontificated, before realizing I was speaking to an empty room.

Now that half of my needs had been taken care of, I'd like to think I was half happy, but my thoughts wandered back to the flask in my back pocket. I thought about pulling it out and belting down a few swift swigs. No, the voice in my head said. Wait a few minutes. Control yourself that long, you disgusting pig.

Were they watching me? I really didn't think so. So I wrinkled my brow and tried to get a little give in the blindfold—enough, perhaps, to see out the bottom. There was a glimmer of light; I saw carpet, and tilted my head back to try and get a peek at the rest of the room.

"Stop!" A man's voice called out, startlingly close to my head; I might have pissed my pants, if I hadn't already done so.

I froze.

In a warm but firm voice, he asked what I was looking for.

"I want to make sure I'm not being set up. For all I know, you've sent for the Gestapo. I usually trust people, but these days…"

"No," the voice said. "What are you looking for in Moravia?"

"Can I trust you?" I asked again.

"I am nothing if not trustworthy."

"Very well." I smiled. "I'm looking for soldiers. Soldiers for the armies of Blanik."

"We're far from Blanik," he said cautiously. "What makes you think you can find them here?"

"I think I can find them anywhere. The question is, can I wake them?"

"Perhaps. It has been a long winter."

"It's been here since spring," I replied—a poor joke, but it was, after all, the truth. "No matter. The storms are ending. Given the right leadership, we can rouse people from their caves to fight."

"The storms were hard," he said.

"They were. But I've heard the exiled government has taken to dropping in more parachutists."

My host said sternly that he'd heard the same thing. He seemed anxious not to reveal too much, but he did ask: "What of it?"

"I would be interested in contacting these people," I told him hopefully. "I'm sure they're having a hard time of it."

My host said he was sure of it as well, and asked again: "What of it?"

"I would like to help them out. I know what they're going through." It was hard to gauge the impact of my words with the blindfold on, but I tried to deliver this next sentence so as to make an impression. "You see, I'm…I'm a parachutist myself."

"I don't believe you. There aren't any others still out there."

"Ask me anything!" I said. (I'll admit it now—I was nervous!) "I trained at RAF Woldingham, my commanding officer was Captain Sustr…"

Still he didn't believe me; he asked if I had a code name.

"I have a real name!" I exclaimed. "Can I trust you with it, though? I know I'm an honest man. Are you?"

"If we wanted to do anything other than get to know you, we could have done so already," he reminded me. "What is your name?"

"Josef Gabchik," I told him. "I'm the man who killed Heydrich."

He spat. "It's not even a credible lie, seeing as how everyone who was involved with that died at that church in Prag. The Germans love to make examples of people," he said, sounding strange...and...was it my imagination, or did I hear him fumbling for something? He admitted that such tactics did serve a purpose...and then...did I hear him cock a revolver?

My heart thundered; I tried to stay calm, and redoubled my efforts. "Who says I'm dead? The Germans?"

"Everyone," he said.

"The Germans were the only ones in a position to tell the story. Of course you heard that. The truth was too embarrassing!"

"And what is the truth?" he asked, but humbler now, quieter, with a touch of hope that gave me hope.

"Oh, they were right about the attack. They couldn't conceal that. And they were right that I was at the church. There were three of us in the choir loft, keeping watch, and four of us in the crypt. And…well, here I am!"

Scepticism crept back in to his voice; he didn't believe anyone could have escaped, with hundreds of troops around.

"Oh, I thought the same thing!" I exclaimed. "But the crypt, you see, was half below street level. And the south wall was but ten metres from the sewer line running down the centre of Resslova. So we started digging a tunnel. And when the Germans came, we started digging harder, while the three in the choir loft held them off."

"All the parachutists died," the voice said.

"Those three did, yes. Kubish, Opalka, Bublik. But oh, how they fought!" Finally I could stand it no more—I pulled out my flask and took a swig, to loosen my tongue and keep the story flowing. "They fought like lions, to buy us time. How I wished we could have fought with them!! But we'd talked about it before they went up there. 'Save yourselves if anything happens,' Jan said. I told him I didn't want to hear it, but he said it again. 'We'll buy you time,' he said. 'Save yourselves to fight another day.' And so we dug. We wanted to fight—oh, how we wanted to fight!!! But we knew it wouldn't make a difference, so we dug. They held the Germans off for hours, from up in that choir loft!! And I know they fought to their last bullets. There was gunfire, followed by explosions, and it all started dying down, and then…there were three final shots."

He was eager for the rest of the story. I held out the flask and he took it; I heard him take a swig.

"Unfortunately we hadn't finished digging. The fighting had covered up the sound, but when it stopped, we still hadn't hit the sewer. Oh, I cannot describe the anxiety!!"

He asked—eagerly—what we'd done.

"We kept digging. We tried to dig quietly. But somehow they became aware of our presence."

"I heard a rumour that there was a traitor."

I swallowed hard before I spoke: "I heard that, too. He almost cost us our lives. They started throwing in tear gas through the vents, then grenades, and then they started trying to flood us out with fire hoses. One of my men, Svarc, was wounded. Oh, I thought we were done for. But the most wonderful thing happened—a miracle!"

"What?" (I almost felt bad for my host; he wanted so desperately to believe!)

"The water they were pumping in, it loosened the rock and soil in our tunnel. It did our work for us!! Everything loosened, and we had our path to the sewer. We practically fell in, and we were nearly overcome by the smell, but I wanted to jump for joy! We figured the

Germans would have people waiting where the sewers emptied into the river, so we headed uphill, into the city, and we waited out the day. Since Svarc was wounded, he volunteered to stay behind to hold them off, so it was hours before they even got down there to look for us. And we heard dogs and angry voices; we saw electric torches far off, but the smell threw them off. They never made it down to where we were. And when night fell, we snuck out a manhole cover, under cover of the blackout."

My host seemed perplexed as to why he hadn't heard any of this.

"Who would you have heard it from? The Germans? After the supreme embarrassment of having one of their most important leaders killed in the very heart of the continent, do you think they wanted it known that the perpetrators had escaped their grasp? No! They wanted at all costs to hush it up!!" I was on fire now, telling this tale; I was in my element at last. I was even starting to believe myself! "So they did what all governments do in such situations. They concocted a version of the story which fit the publicly available facts, and made sure no other information saw the light of day! It is easiest to lie when you build from the truth, yes?"

My host mentioned the fact that they'd found bodies after the battle, that they'd taken bodies from the crypt—still, I could feel his resistance crumbling!

"You think the Germans would have a hard time coming up with three more corpses?" I asked, incredulous. "When they were killing hundreds a day?"

Here he asked why my family didn't let it be known that it wasn't me. Again he sounded sceptical—but I could tell he was searching for a reason to believe, for a reason—any excuse—why faith and hope should triumph over logic and evidence!

"Ahh, but that was the horrible beauty of it," I said, calm and appreciative now. "Since everyone knew they were killing friends and family of anyone even remotely involved, they knew no one was going to come forward and say, 'That wasn't Josef Gabchik.'" Here I paused, and let myself sound somewhat emotional. "Of course, they went after those people anyway…"

"Your friends and family?" he asked.

"Yes. I lost my fiancée, even, Libena, the love of my life. All the more reason to keep fighting, though! We have been hiding in the forest, using our training and keeping out of sight. And now the spring has come early. It is time to resurrect our resistance!"

And here: victory! He untied my blindfold.

I blinked hard and looked around. A stale musty bed, two plain wooden chairs, a wooden table, a threadbare rug, clumps of dust congregating in the corners, an ancient lamp casting an anaemic circle on the ceiling and another, larger but distended, on the floor and bed and wall. My host—my captor—was an older man, in his 40s, with grey hair and a moustache. He introduced himself as Tomas; he shook my hand and said it was an honour to meet me.

"The honour is mine," I told him. "It is a relief to know there are still men in this country willing to fight."

Here—at last—he mentioned that there might be other parachutists, and asked if I might be willing to meet them.

"That would be a tremendous help." I wandered over to the window and cupped my hand to peer through the lamp's reflection and into the darkness. Down below I could just make out a set of footprints leading towards the dark woods, and another set coming back from the woods. That stupid ugly bitch had led me in a circle!! We were upstairs at the inn!!

Tomas tried to contain his enthusiasm, but did a miserable job. He shook my hand eagerly; he said it would be an honour to help.

I am not Josef Gabchik, of course. Karl Jerhot is what I go by these days. Not my birth name, but it works.

(Should you get to choose your own name, as an adult? I tend to think so. It doesn't seem fair otherwise. Why should your most personal attribute be something you didn't choose, something you're saddled with from birth, something that tells others your ethnicity, something that follows you wherever you go? Can you ever be a different person if you're stuck with the same name? No. And what's the point of living, if you are cast in a role from birth and never get a chance to play another? Granted, people you've known don't always accept a new name. My mother, for one, resolutely refused to acknowledge mine in all of our correspondence; she resolutely kept addressing her letters using my full birth name, no matter the inconvenience it caused me. Which makes me wonder—does your name belong to you, or everyone else? Is it there for your convenience, or theirs?)

Ahh, I digress. It's more fun to do so than to finish this particular story!! But there's so little to do in here. Writing and masturbating, one by day and one by night—and how the latter becomes an art form in here! You have to perfect your technique, and stroke very quietly, so as not to rouse—or arouse!!—your cell mates. (I do not fear rape—I fear consensual sex! It is far more common here. Some people quickly lose their sense of shame in such matters, but— strange as it may seem—there are still some standards I have for myself. Despite the many other ways in which I've debased myself, I still have some standards!!) So that is a challenge. And coming up with new fantasies—another challenge!! One gets bored with the same old memories—and their details fade. Surrounded by such swine as one meets in gaol, one forgets what a woman looks like, what a woman feels like, what a woman smells like. One of the guards—the tall fellow—has been giving me pen and paper for writing; perhaps I can talk him into bringing in some old magazines, so I can stroke off to the advertisements. Otherwise I'll have to start masturbating to memories of other times I masturbated!!

I suppose I should get on with my tale, rather than pleasuring myself with these digressions. This story doesn't have a happy ending, but I suppose I should tell it anyway, if only to make some sense of it.

But not tonight. My hand's getting tired. Mental masturbation has the same effect as the other kind, ha ha!!

Where was I?

Yes. I'm not Josef Gabchik.

Maybe I want to be, beneath it all!! Yes, maybe that's the point of this whole story—no need to go further. Despite the bloody mess he caused, the disgusting abortion-that-lived that was Operation Anthropoid, people spoke highly of him. Even the people who thought it was more trouble than it was worth to kill the Reichsprotektor—and most people felt that way, believe me!—even those people spoke well of him! They knew they could not do what he did. And that is the surest way to be held in high regard—not by getting people to agree with you, but by doing what they can't do! That's all I've ever wanted, for people to speak well of me. Is that such an outlandish, unreasonable goal?

Yes, they all spoke well of Gabchik, and praised his courage. And though I still say it was all just foolhardiness, the fact still remains that I stole his name when it suited me. So perhaps I wanted to be him. Or perhaps I just want what he had—the posthumous praise, the hero worship, the perfection in death that none of us have in life.

Or maybe I just want to be anyone but me. That could be it, too.

I need a drink. A good stiff drink, or two, or twenty, to wash away these memories, if only for a night.

Granted, there are some good things about not having that option here—no headaches, no shakes, no (or rather, fewer) voices in your head, less questioning of your own sanity, none of the terror of trying to remember yesterday, then realizing you didn't want to, after all.

But I do want to forget it all!! So I do want a drink. No, make that a thousand. Enough to obliterate my memories, enough to flood through the walls so I can escape the most insidious prison of all, the one whose walls follow me wherever I go—the prison of my waking mind!! Me!! My face, my body, my skin—this is the prison from which I cannot escape. The same ugly face staring back at me every time I'm unfortunate enough to catch a glimpse of myself in the mirror in the morning…

Perhaps I should stop shaving. Yes, that's what I've been missing—a beard. A new look for a new life—and why not? How can I possibly feel different if I don't look different?

18 December, 1945

I've decided to start putting a date to these entries. I don't particularly want anyone to read through them! Still, dating them will perhaps give my ramblings some focus.

Back to the story.

Tomas made arrangements for me to stay with a couple in the next town over, a fellow tavern-owner and his wife; they put me up in the cold dusty attic of their small country home.

The wife was a flabby dumpling of a woman, as wide as she was tall; she greeted me at the door with a candle the night I arrived and told me I'd have to stay out of sight.

I nodded appreciatively. It seemed like the thing to do.

"I don't mean to be rude—this is for your protection," she said. "It's a small town, and if people saw you downstairs while my husband's at work, they might think I've taken a lover!" (As she said this, she pinched me on the cheek. Such absurd fantasies, I remember thinking!)

It only took one person to talk, she said: a neighbour with his eye on the property, a business competitor of her husband—or perhaps one of her jealous lady friends.

She winked as she said this; I nodded dutifully, and gave a little smile, mildly flirty. (Again, it seemed like the thing to do.)

"Anyhow, everyone saw how many heads ended up on the chopping block during the Heydrichaida," she said. "So no one wants to stick their neck out these days."

"Don't I know it," I said.

It was hard work keeping her away from me, as it turned out!! Her husband was usually off running the tavern—this was a small town a few kilometres from Welehrad—so she would pop up to the attic more frequently than mere hospitality required; she provided me with a mountain of blankets, ample servings of bread and cheese and rabbit, and a woefully insufficient flow of wine—which I hoarded by saving the first quarter-full bottle she'd given me and pouring every subsequent bit in after it, mixing red with white because I only wanted enough for one really good drunk. And—though in not so many words—she offered herself, too!! So I kept our conversations friendly but terse, so she'd leave the cold attic warmed with fantasies I hoped would never materialize.

During those long boring days I pleasured myself by pleasuring myself, jerking off into an undershirt that soon grew filthy and crusty—you could have probably soaked it in hot water and used it to repopulate the country!! Strange as it may seem, though, I started to think of her while doing it—my little dumpling!! (It wasn't that I wanted her, per se—I remember thinking that we'd fall through the ceiling if we tried—but fresh memories make for easy fantasies; there was very little effort required to cast the production, or write the dialogue, or to design the sets, or envision how the scenes would play out. And—this is how strangely my Catholic mind works!!—masturbation seems like less of a sin when it involves someone who would enthusiastically give consent if asked!!!) So there, too, I had to keep quiet, lest someone get aroused—how little some things have changed!!

Still, something had to give. Eventually I got word about the meeting with the other parachutists, and everything was set, and I was celebrating the coming end by drinking all the wine I'd hoarded, and sure enough, as if she knew I was at my weakest, my little dumpling came upstairs and threw herself upon me!

And finally I yielded.

Yes, I made that trip between my little dumpling's fat thighs to that soft infinity that waited—how is it that the most unappetizing women make for the best sexual experiences?—and when I was spent—we hadn't fallen through the ceiling, probably because it hadn't lasted very long!—when I was spent, I turned away, disgusted with myself. And she tried to cuddle up to me! She actually tried to hold on to me!

But right at that moment—oh, how fortunate!!—we heard her husband coming through the front door. As she scrambled for her clothes, I kissed my hand and placed it upon her lips and said, "It only takes one person to talk." She went back downstairs, hasty and dishevelled.

Her husband knew something had happened. Through the rafters I heard them shouting.

I don't know why he didn't come up after me right then, but I didn't want to wait for him to change his mind. So early the next morning, while they still slept, I stole down from the attic. Though still somewhat inebriated, I remember making sure to take my crusty t-shirt with me—and leaving a note on the kitchen table with some excuse explaining my sudden absence.

(Do I miss those days in the attic now? Do I actually miss my little dumpling, and wish we'd spent more time in adulterous ecstasy? It all seemed like such agony at the time that I'd fantasized about my old life, but now I would go back to that attic in a heartbeat!! My little dumpling—what I wouldn't give for her to visit me in these cramped confines! Certainly she'd be a better companion than my current cell-mate.)

At any rate, I remember creeping through the back door and out into the snowy moonlit pines; I smoked a cigarette with heart and lungs and head aching, thinking of those endless summer days in the forests near Wittingau. Then I walked downhill into town, sent an urgent telegram as soon as the operator's office opened, and drank the last of the wine while I waited shivering at the station for the morning train. One's thoughts become very basic in such situations; I wondered why so many parts of my life echoed so many other parts, and I remembered to throw the undershirt in the trash, and I wondered why I'd made such an effort to take it. Was it because I didn't want the husband to think less of me? I'd already given him plenty of reasons to hate me; I knew I'd be giving him far more, soon enough.

<u>19 December, 1945</u>

The train ride was an unfamiliar one, west and north out of Moravia, the snowy terrain flattening out as we went. Or rather, the route was unfamiliar, but I felt exactly how I'd felt in June. (Had that been only six months before? It felt longer. Truly 1942 was the longest year of my life! Time is supposed to be the same always, steady and invisible like gravity; it's only the transitions that make these forces seem greater — the smack of one's body hitting the ground after a fall, the pain of a broken relationship, any change so complete and dramatic that whatever came before feels irretrievable. And there were many transitions that year — no wonder it felt so much longer than most!! I went from London to Prag, soldier to spy, Czech to German.)

I digress. As in June, I wanted the train ride to last longer than it did. I dozed fitfully, I fretted — I wished I was somewhere else, but I don't know where! Somewhere different, somewhere I'd never been. Brazil or Australia, perhaps — warm and far from this madness.

I'm not sure I specifically remember getting to Prag, but I know what I must have seen: the intricate awnings at the station, the smoky brown vaulted lobby, the passengers clenching themselves in anticipation of the cold as they walked out the station doors. I cannot remember if it was sunny or cloudy. I do recall looking north at the frozen swath of city spread out before me, grim greys and whites, skies growing dim as the winter sun made its anxious early exit.

Had anyone followed me? I remember remembering that I'd forgotten to check, and wondering what was wrong with me for forgetting—this was a simple precaution in intelligence work, well beneath my intelligence, but still I had not done it! I tried to make up for my obliviousness by taking a few random detours, cutting back and forth down side streets and then looping back around, then walking north across the Moldau on that open bleak bridge—I have never been colder!!—nakedly alone in the icy December wind.

North of the bridge I forced myself to stop in a park and light a cigarette. And I remember—for some reason I remember, after three years!!—how excruciatingly long it took to light that one cigarette. Was it the cold that made my hands tremble so?

Finally, content that I'd atoned for my earlier ineptitude, I headed again towards my destination, past sleepy flats and the snoring electrical plant and into the heart of Holesoviche. There were no pedestrians in this part of town, and I rather liked the silent solitude. Nothing but factories and warehouses, and streets as empty as my soul.

The place I was looking for was a small tool-and-die shop; I walked down a narrow alleyway to the back and forced myself to stand out in the cold for another cigarette. No one had followed me.

At last I allowed myself up the battered brick stairs and onto the loading dock, then through the rusty door that led to the warehouse floor.

Pannwitz was in a small windowless office behind the glass office that overlooked the desolate factory floor—idle machines, crates of metal parts, cold cobwebs in the corners.

He had turned on the radio, a large cabinet-style one. He was listening to a news broadcast and leaning back in a leather chair, taking a pull from a bottle of brown liquor.

"Have you been here long?" I asked.

"Long enough to start a fire," he said; he took another swig before handing it over. "Here. Warm up for a bit."

I took the bottle but — strangely — hesitated. I'd been good all day in anticipation of this, but I didn't want to seem too eager. Best to wait just a little, I remember thinking. And I remember being absurdly proud of that brief wait — ahh, the meaningless victories which cause us to gloat in the midst of a losing campaign!!

Pannwitz cracked a bemused smile. "What are you waiting for?"

The radio crackled: "Merry Christmas from the forces of the Reich." Over its hiss the various troops introduced themselves — Merry Christmas from Oslo, from Tunis, from Paris, from Stalingrad.

Pannwitz added: "There you have it, if you're looking for a reason. Merry Christmas, and Happy New Year."

"I wouldn't call it that, exactly," I said as I finally took a drink — a nice long pull, but I remember watching his eyes watching the level of the bottle. The judgmental prick!

He wanted to know if I'd been followed. "I don't think so," I said.

"You don't think so?" He echoed my words crossly, turning them into a question — a question of my honesty and devotion, after all I'd done for him!!

"No one followed me," I said, more firmly.

He said I'd sounded unsure; I just shrugged. (In all honesty, I wasn't sure of much back then.) Then he asked — quite insultingly — if there was anything I did know for sure.

"The rumours are true. They've dropped more people. And there are a couple others left over from the spring and summer that somehow held out."

Of course, he claimed to have already known these things; furthermore, he said he wasn't sure this warranted an emergency telegram, or a meeting back here in Prag. (He took the bottle back, drank, and set it on the desk, but kept his hand on it.) He did want a number, though.

"Four or five parachutists, at the most," I told him.

(He scowled.) "Four? Or five?"

"Four, then."

"Have you seen these people, or talked to them, or just heard about them?" he asked, quite condescendingly.

"I've talked to people who have talked to them. At an inn in Welehrad. The man I talked to was a pot-bellied man in his mid 40s, with longish hair and a moustache."

"Ohh, a moustache." Pannwitz repeated the end of my sentence, but coated it in a distasteful mixture of disbelief and disgust. "Now at last we are getting somewhere," he said, in a tone sarcastic enough to invert the meaning of his words.

"He called himself Tomas," I said, to which Pannwitz reminded me that I, of all people, should know how little names mattered in this business.

"He arranged a meeting with three of the parachutists!" I exclaimed. (Surely this merited some reward; I eased the bottle from his fingers and drank.) Still he wasn't impressed. He wanted to know where I'd met the man—the name of the inn.

"You know how little names mean in this business."

He gave me a dirty look.

"The Ugly Duckling," I said at last.

He asked if I'd learned any other—what is the phrase? Ahh, yes...proper nouns.

I kept my mouth shut.

"Wonderful," he said. "It's an astonishing piece of detective work you've done—clearly enough to wrap this investigation up. Your dedication to the Reich is to be commended." He sneered as he took the bottle back.

I sighed; this was too much. "Did you hear me? They arranged a meeting with the parachutists."

He took a swig. "I'll withhold judgment until it actually happens."

"Look, this is hard work!! These people are suspicious!! No one gives you names!! No one tells you where anyone else is staying!!"

"The people you're staying with. You know their names," he said; his drunk eyes looked dead.

I said nothing.

"These people are criminals. Enemies of the Reich." (He said this after another swig—the pig!!)

"They know nothing."

"They knew not to shelter you," he observed.

"These people are skittish. It is hard!" I exclaimed.

"No one said it would be easy," he replied. "You do know their names, right? If not, you're not of much use to us after all."

"Cherny," I said at last. "Peter and Anna Cherny." (I gave him the names—my little dumpling! What was I supposed to do, though?

One doesn't really have a choice in such matters. He was going to find them anyway.)

Finally, he sounded pleased; he said he'd talk to them later. Then, he asked what name I'd used — if I'd used Gabchik's name.

I said nothing.

"You're going to get yourself killed, you know."

I shrugged.

"Maybe that's what you want," he observed. "Still, we must get through this. They must be wondering where you went. We need a plausible explanation." He figured he had to arrange something before I went back there — a shootout, an escape, an act of sabotage, something to make the character complete, something to make it seem that I was, indeed, who I said I was.

I remember nodding, just a bit, and not grabbing for the bottle — not just yet!! He made it clear that I needed to press for a meeting with the other parachutists. And it would be far more difficult now that I'd come back here.

"You agreed to meet me," I pointed out.

"You sent the telegram, so either way, I needed to meet with you. Either because this truly was urgent, or because we needed to talk about your performance — and the latter seems to be the case. This arrangement, it is...comfortable for you, yes?"

I shrugged. "Financially, it is comfortable." I took a drink at last; he gave me a dirty look.

"Well, let's keep things the way they are, then," he said. "I'd hate to see you go through any kind of...difficulties, because of some…misunderstanding." (He spoke slowly, drawing out the words; he apparently didn't trust me to catch the meaning otherwise.) "These things are a headache for all involved. All the paperwork. You understand, yes?"

"Of course," I said angrily.

I don't remember what else I did that night, but there was one more incident related to that trip that I feel compelled to recount.

When I was on the train back to Welehrad the next day, there was a bit of a delay—someone had torn up the train tracks! What should have been a routine trip turned excruciating; we had to walk several hundred metres through the cold dark woods, past the wrecked section of track, then wait in the little station in the next town for hours while another train was brought up. I was furious at the delay!! Irate!! In that station I paced and fretted and fumed and smoked and steamed; I complained so much that even my fellow inconvenienced passengers grew weary of me. Sabotage, the stationmaster said.

And it only occurred to me later that night—it was me!! In a manner of speaking, at least; it was the diversion Pannwitz had spoken of, the sabotage. He'd sent some agents off into the forest on my behalf, tearing things up so Anna and Peter Cherny wouldn't be suspicious of my sudden and unexplained absence.

20 December, 1945

After I'd been here in Pankratz a few months, I was the victim of an unexpected denunciation—cruel, vindictive, and without cause. They learned my true identity because of this denunciation. So suddenly, rather than being an anonymous nobody, I was important. Mine was now a prestige case; not only did my charges carry a potential death sentence, but I was notorious enough that the powers-that-be didn't want to risk the chance of someone beating them to the punch by doing me do death whilst among the general population, the petty denouncers and minor traitors and common criminals.

I was upset at the situation, at first—certainly my odds of surviving the justice system had dropped dramatically. Because the Czechs had not correctly identified me until then, I might have made it out with a relatively light punishment.

But the more I thought about my predicament, and the fact that my outside life was shattered—no, pulverized, with no recognizable pieces to pick up and reassemble—the more I realized my situation at least had some things to recommend it. They transferred out of the regular population and into a section on the first floor near the front of the complex, along with the other notorious prisoners. Certainly it was nice to feel important again, at last!! And the living conditions, I had to admit, were much nicer—two to a cell, with bedding actually fit for human use. The view was much poorer, but that was both bad and good; I could no longer see the adjacent streets, the peaceful neighbourhoods, the ordinary people going on about their business or, in the distance, Vysehrad, all those buildings golden and perfect in the low sun. Now I can only see the tops of a few buildings—but it is easy enough to forget what they are; it's easy to imagine them as other divisions of the prison. Does that make me happy? Imagining the whole world to be sharing my misery? Yes, I suppose it does!! For that's one of the peculiar and unexpected tortures about prison— not just the fact that one is confined, but the fact that so many others aren't!! How troubling that can be—just knowing they're going on about their business, that life goes on with no apparent disruptions when you're not around—that, surely, is at least half of the punishment!

I digress. I suppose I'm avoiding the parts of this story I dislike, the nasty end, with its ugly echoes of the summer. Anything to avoid looking in the mirror—more mental masturbation, self-love trying unsuccessfully to stave off self hatred! My hand is cramped again. I'll tell more tomorrow, perhaps.

Oh, yes. I should mention that while all this was going on—the mopping up of the remaining parachutists, my espionage on behalf of Pannwitz, and so on—Paulus' once-mighty Sixth Army was being encircled and slowly strangled, so many kilometres to the east in Stalingrad. (We knew nothing of it at the time, of course! We heard the barest report directly after it was over, when the Germans could no longer cover it up, then much more at the end of the war.) They were cut off from resupply and forbidden from withdrawing, a quarter of a million men subsisting on horsemeat and half-rations, living like dogs amid the snowy piles of rubble, fighting desperately while their ammunition slowly dwindled, then dying. Anyway, I only mention it because it struck me as odd, later on—and emblematic of my luck!! When I fought for the Allies, the Allies kept losing, and virtually as soon as I switched sides, the Germans started losing!! It just figures, somehow.

<u>28 December, 1945</u>

All right, the meeting.

I don't remember exactly when it finally happened. I'd been staying above Tomas's inn, back in that old dusty room—and before it happened, I bumped into Peter and Anna Cherny again.

That happened quite by accident. The place was nearly empty, and I was coming out of the water closet, and there they were. My little dumpling gave a shameless look of admiration and lust! Meanwhile, her husband greeted me with the same look of warm regard one gives to animal manure that's stuck on one's shoe.

There were a few other patrons in the bar. Still, she carelessly walked right up to me.

"I heard something about an act of sabotage on the train line!" she said—with a heavy wink and a nod, so obvious that it was more noticeable than if she'd come right out and asked if I'd been responsible!!

So I looked around and said, somewhat sheepishly: "Oh, I hardly did anything."

Peter glared at me for a while before speaking: "You needn't be so…modest. My wife seems…quite pleased with all the destruction you've caused."

I just smiled. "Well, hopefully there will be more to come!" And then—shameful me!—I patted him on the shoulder. At last I went back upstairs, determined to stay out of sight until my meeting with the other parachutists.

I remember one or two delays. Each time I was careful to go through the normal procedures, sneaking out of the inn and sending coded postcards with no return address to an anonymous post box in Prag.

The meeting was finally arranged to take place at a small country cottage. (I don't think the parachutists had been staying there—that sort of thing didn't happen. You met people at third-party locations, so if the first party was rounded up, the second party could go home safe—unless, of course, the first party was me! No one knew your real name, and you didn't know anyone else's. And no one knew how big the resistance was, or how small, but everyone knew no one wanted to do anything earth-shattering until the end was near. That had been the chief consequence—quite unforeseen in London, I'm sure!!—of Heydrich's assassination.)

At any rate, Pannwitz had insisted I accompany his agents, so I found myself wedged into the back of a small black sedan, poorly heated, that rocked to and fro down a narrow wooded country road as it followed another sedan that straddled several sets of snowy footprints. We knew where we were going, but we followed the tracks anyway; they wound back and forth amidst the snowy silent pines and papery birch. Then they veered off down a drive, and we stopped.

Pannwitz stepped from the lead car, taking care not to slam the door. He walked back, and the agent next to me rolled down the window to the bitter cold.

"We want you to go talk to them," Pannwitz said with icy breath.

"Why?" I asked, and he said we wanted to take them alive.

"I don't think that's realistic," I told him, but he didn't care.

"They might shoot me if they recognize me," I said. "We all knew each other back there," and then...was it my imagination, or did he actually shrug?

And he mentioned that they'd had a denunciation — of me! A report from the local police, which had filtered up to him, of a British-trained parachutist taking shelter locally — me! And the person filing the report — none other than Peter Cherny!!

"That backstabbing prick!" I said.

"Well, it gives me an excuse to go easy on the man, at least," Pannwitz said. "But it also gives us further reason to question your judgment..."

"Jesus fucking Christ," I huffed — what the hell did I have to do to prove my worth to these people?!?! I climbed out and slammed the door. Pannwitz gave me a dirty look, but I didn't much care.

Fuming, I trudged down the long snowy drive towards the cabin, which was perched on a knob above a frozen lake. Behind me, the other agents got out of their cars and started fanning out through the woods, pistols drawn, stumbling over roots and branches and swallowing their swearing as they wiped the snow from hands and knees. The devil with them, I remember thinking.

Angry and alone, I stopped at the end of the drive. I thought—I doubt anyone will believe me, but it's true!!—I thought about running up and joining them, switching sides again for one last stand. But I didn't. Pannwitz had not given me a gun, and I knew even then that he never would. So I stopped at the end of the drive, hopefully in range for shouting but not shooting.

"Men!!" I yelled, and raised my hands. "They got me!! They ran me down."

There was no answer—were they even there? I wondered. I waited. I nearly froze my fingers off searching under the snow for a stone, cursing myself all the while for leaving my gloves in the car. I found a rock, threw it at a window. Nothing.

"They tracked me down, after the railroad sabotage!" I yelled again. "I'm sorry! They made me lead them here. They beat it out of me!! You might as well come out—you're surrounded!!"

I hadn't expected it, but I felt exactly as I'd had in June, back at the church. The same old role—I'd been typecast!! What a bitter realization that was!!

There was nothing for maybe half a minute—I was shivering and bending over so my frozen fingers could find another stone when I happened to look up and see a pistol butt smashing a windowpane. (It was the first I'd seen of the men inside.) I turned and tripped, and landed just shy of a woodpile; I scampered to safety with banged-up knees and torn pants.

I don't remember who fired first, but there were many shots back and forth, all muffled by the snow; I remember Gestapo agents clutching pistols with their gloved hands as they peered out from behind trees; I recall clumps of snow falling from the pristine pines with every shot from the cottage. And I remember Pannwitz, that fool, red-nosed in the bitter air, waving everyone forward and motioning for them to encircle the house, striding confidently with no apparent regard for his own safety, puffing steam like an angry locomotive. His agents moved like pros, taking turns covering for one another and advancing. But somewhere it became apparent there was no more gunfire coming from the cottage.

And then came the final shots. One, two—I froze in place waiting for the third, but there was no third.

The front door opened. Pistols were levelled and fingers tensed, but no one shot. A man emerged, hands held high, and beneath them, a familiar face.

Pannwitz barked to the two nearest men to put him down.

The first agent holstered his pistol and circled around behind our new captive, while the second kept his weapon trained on the man's head. Coming up from behind, the first agent kicked the parachutist's feet from under him and pushed him down and straddled him and frisked him while the others searched the house.

Meanwhile, the parachutist—Srazil or Janisek, I don't remember who it was—lifted his head to get a glimpse of me; clumps of snow clung to his eyebrows and ears.

"Josef Gabchik, huh?" he said with a venomous look, practically spitting out the words. Clearly he was mad I had outwitted him!!! Finally the agent straddling him barked at him to shut up and shoved the man's red face down in the snow.

I felt somewhat bad for him; he was clearly mad at himself for falling for such an outrageous ruse, a lie so outlandish I'm still somewhat amazed it worked. Is it my fault the man was an idiot? No, of course not. But so often the idiotic lies are the ones people most want to believe. And I'd given him that! For a few short weeks, I'd given him something he wouldn't have otherwise had, a brief chance to believe the impossible.

Still, I figured I should help him out of his predicament—it was the least I could do! "They're reasonable people," I told him. "If we talk to them together, we can work something out. They can give you a new life!"

30 December, 1945

His mission, we later learned, was called Antimony.

We learned it because he did decide to co-operate, in a way—we learned it from him. For whatever reason, London had gone through a phase of naming missions after metals—Tin, Antimony, Silver A, Silver B, Steel. (Not that they'd always done that; mine was Out Distance, if I remember correctly, and Gabchik and Kubish were Anthropoid, and there was also one called Intransitive. But the names made no difference, as far as I was concerned—they were all pointless. So it was right to try and stop them!! I still believe that, even now. They were trying to stir things up, just as we'd been trying to do back in May and June, and that had caused problems for everyone—so it was right to prevent it from happening again!! I still believe that, even now. No one else will admit it, of course, but it was right to keep things peaceful!!! I don't regret what I did, not a bit.)

I think Antimony had been sent to set up a transmitter—yet another transmitter!!—and get in touch with the missions from the spring—like mine!!—to determine their fate. So I suppose they accomplished their mission, ha ha!! Just like—God's honest truth—I accomplished mine, before everything else happened.

From what I gathered—Pannwitz did not let me in on the questioning, mind you, but I'm sure he wished he had, afterwards!!— Srazil or Janisek, whoever it was, mentioned to his interrogators that there were at least two other parachutists on the loose, and he somehow convinced Pannwitz that he'd do a better job than me at sniffing them out. So Pannwitz reluctantly gave him a little leash to go hunt the others down.

He promptly disappeared.

He wasn't gone long, mind you! All his old contacts had been burned—by me! All the doors he might have hidden behind had already been kicked open—thanks to me! So Pannwitz rounded the wayward parachutist up within the week, before his own superiors even found out about his blunder. And he shipped the man off to Terezinstadt, to a dank cold cell in the dreaded small fortress, as punishment and as a matter of general principle, to dissuade anyone from attempting anything of a similar nature.

Still, after that, there was something new in Pannwitz's voice when he spoke of the man, something I hadn't heard in a while—something almost like respect.

It didn't matter in the end, though—for when we rounded up Srazil or Janisek, whoever it was, we got a line on still another parachutist—possibly the last one, at that point, that hadn't been killed, captured, or come over to our side. (I wasn't the only one, you see!!!)

That one went down differently. But that—alas—is a story for another day.

2 January, 1946

The New Year is here. Nothing has changed. The guards are giving me plenty of paper, but beyond that they don't pay me much heed. I have seen them escorting Karl Hermann Frank out in the courtyard. Oh, to be truly important!

Back to the story. On a surprisingly specific tip, we'd driven out to the country, to a dark little farmhouse badly in need of new shingles and a fresh coat of paint. It reminded me of home.

Pannwitz had brought me along mainly for linguistic purposes — I don't think his men had a good grasp on Czech, or cared to get one. (Not that I blame them — it is an absurd language! There are so many strange letters, Rs with hats that sound like "dz", Cs with squiggly marks that make them sound like "ts," and so on, and so forth.)

Anyway, we knocked on the door of this place, and the husband answered so nonchalantly that I wondered if we'd made a mistake. He was a baby-faced man with sad watery eyes and arms devoid of muscle tone. (I can remember the face well, because I saw it years later at a most unfortunate time. Did I have an inkling, even then, that he'd be important? Did I have some knowledge, some out-of-time understanding, a voice whispering back in the black blank part of my mind?) At any rate, I was struck by his girlishness. There were two young daughters and a wife in the house, and it seemed whatever masculinity he'd had had either vanished entirely or rubbed off on his wife. She had a perplexing hard-edged hatefulness about her. I couldn't tell whether it was aimed at us or her husband.

At any rate, the agents fanned out through the house and found nothing, and they were on the way up the staircase when I saw something from the husband, a signal to Pannwitz, a short little nod in the direction of the kitchen.

Pannwitz signalled; his men came over and placed hands on pistol butts. In the kitchen there was a freestanding wooden cupboard, and one of the agents pointed a silent finger at it and gave a look at the husband, who closed his eyes and gave another quick little nod.

Now everyone had drawn pistols, and one agent reached up and tipped the cabinet over, and it fell with a crash. And behind it, there he was! In a little nook hollowed in the wall, there on his back with the pistol; he squeezed a shot or two off — I can still see the flame!! — and the agents emptied their revolvers, pulling triggers until hammers clicked on empty cylinders and the parachutist was lying with his head lolling to one side and bullet holes like furrows angled up and into his chest.

As soon as the shooting stopped, Pannwitz barked orders to secure the house and photograph the scene.

The wife buried her face in her hands. The husband offered no consolation. Instead he turned his back and walked over to Pannwitz, who was saying something along the lines of: Do you recognize this man? What is his name?

It took me a second to realize he was talking to me — my hands had started to shake, and my eyes were fixed on the doorframe next to me, where a bullet had lodged a hand's breadth from my head.

4 January, 1946

Not long after those near-death experiences — perhaps in early February of '43 — I remember being back in Prag, on the drunk to end all drunks.

What do I remember from those weeks? (Were they weeks, even? Who knows?)

I remember scenes. Drinking like that — drinking with no thought for the morrow — is like going to the cinema and leaving too many times to use the water closet — there are breaks in chronology, and unexpected plot developments which no one around you is entirely willing to explain.

I remember drinking alone at some barrel-vaulted pub in Old Town that looked like it had been in business since Jan Hus roamed the streets; I remember solid wooden tables and chairs, dark red tile floors, and lighting as dim as my conscience.

How hard it was to slow my head down, though!! My thoughts raced; all the machinery threatened to overheat and fly apart if I failed to keep it well-lubricated. And yet my estimations of how much lubrication always seemed off! My life dissolved into a slippery mess; many nights, I had a hard time standing it, or standing at all.

I do remember stumbling across some agents from Pannwitz's team one night; we were not really supposed to be interacting in public, but I wanted something from them, some break in the infinite loneliness, some acknowledgement, some willingness for them to bend their rules because of all I'd done for them. They were seated at a table in the back, so as to talk freely, and I stood above them expectantly. They must have seen me — my familiar face and my anonymous civilian clothes — but they did not make space for me.

"Come on now! A drink makes all men brothers!" I think I exclaimed — something Pannwitz was fond of saying. One of them answered with a dirty look.

I think they'd been talking about our recent work. Apparently the parachutist was boffing the wife while the husband was at work, and the daughters had told father about mother, and father had in turn told the Gestapo. (I remember being jealous of that parachutist; he'd at least had a decent-looking partner for his adultery!) Someone said it figured, that the Czechs were a nation of denouncers and turncoats, and it was as much a part of their genetic makeup as their bone structure or eye colour. (I swear he stared at me as he said it!)

Still I tried to stay with them, to be a part of the group. I think I overheard speculations about Jewish blood and racial characteristics, and references to Judas and Shylock.

At some point, I was asked to leave.

But — was that how it happened? I might have confused that with a later incident. My chronologies are skewed. And looking back, I do remember drinking a toast with one of them, then having an extended and meaningful conversation whose contents I cannot remember. Was that around the same time? That same week, that same night? Who knows?

7 January, 1946

Where was I? Ahh, yes. That miserable winter stretch, three years ago now: quick liquid days, and nights of dark solitude.

Somewhere in there, it all came to a head.

Was it a morning? It might have been night. I remember waking up, still drunk—the brass alarm clock read a little past six, and it was dark, but Prag's winter nights are long enough that such times are often subject to multiple interpretations—in fact, I remember peering out from the blackout shades trying to determine which six it was, and being unable to tell, because of the blackout, whether people were coming or going from work, then falling back into a blackout of my own without ever determining the answer.

And I remember—was it the same day?—waking up again to definite daytime, sunlight stabbing me in the face when I lifted the window shade—I recoiled like a vampire!! I lay back down—cold, tangled in the bedding, and inexplicably naked.

Then came the same voices, voices of terror and anger and skull-splitting frustration and disgust: You've got to stop doing this to yourself. You're living like an animal, a disgusting, filthy pig. How did you let this happen again? What did you do last night? Who saw you do it? Do you want to remember? Do you even want to remember?

And then: why the devil is it so cold?

I tottered to the kitchen and pulled up the blackout shade to cast sunlight on all its filthy glory. There was a forest of bottles on the little kitchen table, some toppled over, all empty. Nothing to take the edge off. And the sink was clotted with dishes caked with rot and stewing in greasy water. (The last time I'd eaten at home, I'd left them in there to loosen up the baked-on food crust, but now the whole mess smelled so badly I didn't want to be in the same room as it, much less clean it. Squalor Victoria.) I turned my back on the catastrophe; the floorboards creaked beneath my cold bare feet, protesting my cowardly retreat.

I felt the draught behind me—the bathroom!! Ahh, that was it—I'd left the bathroom window open. In the breeze, the door pulsed as if mechanized, never quite closing, but acting as a valve for the winter wind. I pushed it open, only to be assaulted by odours that would likely have been unbearable were it not for the cold. Such a scene: vomit and excrement, with most of the latter in the toilet, and much of the former in the bathtub, but enough of both misplaced that I had quite a bit of cleaning to do.

How had this happened? Why did I not remember it happening? And why was I naked?

Seeing the mess, I had a glimmer of a memory. I think I'd been unable to place both ends of my digestive tract over a receptacle at the same time—or, perhaps everything hadn't happened at once, and I'd tried to use the toilet for all of it. And I'd tried to clean it all up, apparently without success. Oh, how absurd such mornings are!! How incomprehensible—like a pulp detective novel in which the only mysteries are your own motives and actions!!

It was too much to handle in my current state. I scrambled over to close the window, but it was, in fact, closed—closed and broken, a starburst of jagged shards. (I felt shattered, too, in the terrible light.) Curious, I stuck my head out and saw my filth-encrusted clothes lying crumpled in the snowy courtyard—as if they'd leapt to their death rather than be associated with me!! I became aware of cuts and scrapes on my arms— all more annoying than serious, I determined after a brief inspection, but bad enough to add considerable fuel to my burning self-hatred. It was a wonder I hadn't killed myself—perhaps I wanted to, after all.

Yes, perhaps I wanted to! Yes, perhaps that was it. After all the business at the church, perhaps I did really want it all to be over.

But of course I would have to open the window all the way to get around the broken glass—no sense hurting yourself while you're trying to kill yourself, ha ha!! I strained my fingers against the painted-shut window frame and moved to get more leverage, grunting in frustration. Such a terrible headache I had—but I knew it would be cured soon enough, ha ha!! I grew angry, though; the window wouldn't budge. And as I adjusted my body to get a better grip, my bare feet slipped on the tile, which was slick with my own filth. I fell and hit my head on the windowsill. Not hard, mind you! Just enough to knock me out.

When I woke up—I don't think it was long—I remember staring up at the broken window in disgusted defeat, thinking: Jesus and Mary, you can't even kill yourself properly!! Then somehow—miraculously—I laughed at my ridiculous absurdity.

I beat a hasty retreat from the cold—like the Germans before Moscow the year before, ha ha!!—pausing only to open the baseboard vents leading to the basement coal furnace. I stopped, too, at the linen closet—and the dirty clothes hamper, which was far more full—and grabbed armfuls of laundry. Finally I collapsed on the bed, burying myself under an impromptu mountain of clothing and towels.

I closed my eyes—it hurt to close them, but it hurt to have them open, too; even with the blackout shades, there was too much light. And I could not quite fall asleep. Instead I fell into an in-between state that was still far preferable to outright consciousness. I remember thinking about my dark moment in the bathroom, telling myself: That is not the answer. In spite of the filthy mess your life has become, that is still not the answer.

Wandering about the city later that day, I spotted a church, and figured I might as well go inside, to at least talk things over with a priest. I lingered on the stone steps, then finally mustered the courage to pull open the heavy wooden doors—echoes of that fateful June! For a few minutes, I lurked in the shadows of the massive stone pillars, stepping out here and there to stare at the flickering candles. But when the priest spotted me and started walking over, I abruptly came to my senses and left. The thought of repentance nauseated me. (And I wonder now—why did I think I needed to repent? I have done nothing wrong—nothing any reasonable man wouldn't have done in my place!!!)

It was only back at home, while finally at last half-heartedly cleaning my disgusting messes, that the real answer became clear: I needed a woman in my life!

9 January, 1946

I haven't had a drink in a long time now—almost as long as I haven't had a woman, although I couldn't tell you which I miss more, or less.

It's been more than half a year now for both—not an abnormal length of time without a woman, but certainly the longest I've been without a drink since sixteen or so. (I have gone without for months here and there—on account of training, say, or giving it up for Lent. And I could do it! When I wanted to, I could do it. So I am not a drunkard. I have that, at least!!! As for my periodic sexual abstinence—well, I was just doing what the Church asks. Not voluntarily, I'll admit, ha ha!! Still, I have abstained. I have suffered. That must count for something!!)

I'm despairing of ever seeing a woman up close again—God Himself seems particularly determined that I never again enjoy that pleasure—but I am holding out hope for a drink.

It's not as far-fetched as it sounds. Some of the guards have been somewhat friendly; they've been downright generous in giving me paper and pen with which to write. If I can stay in their good graces, who knows?

10 January, 1946

My thinking about the guards has evolved quite a bit, mind you.

They have remained a constant presence, but in the earliest months they made it a special point to make their presence felt. Stupid lazy thugs, grotesque in their sloppy uniforms, fat and unshaven, their breath reeking of alcohol, erupting at unpredictable times into fits of casual fury. And when they'd get tired of beating you, they'd make you pummel each other, for sport—they'd put two of you amidst a circle of guards and shove you at one another until you took out your frustrations on your hapless fellow prisoner. The violence hasn't quite gone away—even now, some of them think nothing of pulling you aside for a beating if you look at them wrong. But nowadays it usually lacks something, some level of fear and fury.

Still, one remembers the exceptions.

One evening some months ago, for no apparent reason other than sport, the guards manhandled a shrieking prisoner to the fourth floor railing and pitched him headlong over the side. My cell was near enough to see the scene but not its grisly aftermath, except in my mind; I remember his eyes wide with terror, his fingers clutching at the rail as they pounded his knuckles, first with fists, then a club; I remember the strange distant sound that followed, heavy like a sack of potatoes toppling over, wet like a melon breaking. I heard the death was reported as a suicide; I was furious about that—such a cruel lie to tell a man's family!

And yet there have been times when being transported on the gallery where I've thought of launching myself over that railing and into eternity.

What stops me? Catholic guilt? Shame? Fear I would feel, even for a split second, the heavy hard smack as I hit the cement below? Or—stranger still—fear that I would fail again somehow, even at that? Perhaps it has been sheer spite, an anger at the guards that translates into a refusal to do their dirty work for them.

At various times, the thought of ending it all on my own terms—of controlling my life's end, since I can't control its contents—has nearly overwhelmed these reservations. Still, I haven't done it. I don't know why. Who could ever know why? Decisions seldom come from a rational and calculated thought process—otherwise I might have done it! Sometimes I think it is the rational choice. Sometimes I think I'm a coward for not doing it.

(These have not been pleasant thoughts, mind you—I've often felt a dark depression, a blackness shooting out from my heart and coursing through my veins, an evil feeling so ugly I can't endure it for long—nor can I escape it! At times I've been certain this would overcome me and I'd take matters into my own hands; at times I've felt more certain of this than of anything else in my life.)

Of course, it's going to end here anyway, with or without my consent or participation. An appearance before the People's Court—exactly what the Germans used to call their courts!!—a verdict, and, assuming the sentence is death, execution. No appeals, no retrials, no delays—that's what passes for justice these days.

11 January, 1946

I meant to keep talking about the guards, but I got sidetracked.

During summer's hot insanity, I hated them all; now I suspect they're not all thugs. (Most of them, yes—but not all!!) The personalities behind the uniforms have emerged; some of them have shown themselves to be at least somewhat human. As was the case in the army, their individuality became visible at first only in the small details: the level of shine on the shoes, the barely discernible differences in cleanliness between one uniform and the next, the angle of leather belts and the lustre of buttons, the freshness of haircuts and shaves. (Generally standards in these areas are far lower than in the army, but a few of them do at least take some pride in their appearance!) Only later could I see that mannerisms, too, set them apart—there are still jokesters and silent ones and perfectionists and slobs; the percentages may be different than in society-at-large, sometimes wildly so, but they still do all the things normal people do. They grow uncomfortable and restless when they have been working too long; they scratch at their necks when they're chafed from the wool uniforms; they tug at the leather belts that loop diagonally about their torsos; they pick their noses and scratch their asses when they think no one's looking. The ones on the night shift sometimes get drunk.

Among them is a moon-faced man named Stefan; he's probably my safest bet. I spoke to him a little tonight; he was wandering the tier outside my cell supervising a group of inmates who were scrubbing the floors.

"Guard," I called him over. Softly, he asked what I wanted; he was somewhat drunk.

"I wanted to see if there were any job openings here at the prison." He responded with incredulity, but he didn't seem upset, so I kept going: "I've been out of work for a while, you see."

Stefan had the decency to chuckle a little. "You can come out and scrub floors if you'd like."

"I'm a lazy man. I'd rather be supervising the people scrubbing the floors. Much more pay for much less work!"

From down the gallery, I heard keys jangling—another guard walking up. I'd been avoiding this one; he was a thug and a slob. Stefan told him I wanted work, and he laughed explosively; his derision made my blood boil!!! He told Stefan to put me on the work detail, then waddled off.

"Bah." Stefan said to his co-worker's back.

"Well, I won't be asking him for a recommendation," I observed.

Stefan's drunkenness was more evident now. "If you are to be considered for employment, we of course need to see your party membership card."

"Party membership card?" I asked, quite cluelessly. "Are you all communists?"

"The government is divided," he said. "The KSC runs the Interior Ministry. The Interior Ministry runs the prisons."

"So you're a communist?" I asked.

"That's what my membership card says," he responded, with some shame.

"So you don't believe in it," I observed.

He hushed me, then looked both ways down the gallery, presumably to make sure no one was within earshot. Only then did he speak again: "I believe in feeding my family. I sought work, I didn't find it; I joined the party, I found it."

"Was this something you wanted for yourself, growing up?" I asked.

He smirked. "Was this what you pictured for yourself?"

So I said: "Yes, of course," with as much sarcasm as I could muster. "As I said, I'm a lazy man. So I figured, rather than spending time and energy working to keep a roof over my head and food on my plate, I should have society do it all for me. When the army was no good any more, this became my best option."

"And such good food it is, too," he observed. (He smirked, but sounded somewhat sympathetic.)

"I suppose I have your communists to thank for that," I said.

"You talk a lot for a prisoner."

"I've got nothing to lose but my yoke!" I exclaimed. "And my boredom."

He chuckled a bit, and shook his head. "I assure you, it is every bit as boring on this side of the bars."

"You meet important people, at least," I pointed out. He gave me a quizzical look and asked who I might be talking about, and I told him: "My old friend Karl Hermann Frank, for one."

"Your old friend?" he asked, suspicious now.

"I knew him during the war, you know. I was with him for some very historic moments." I said, sounding prouder than I'd meant to.

He shook his head, disappointed. "That isn't something I'd advertise."

"What does this fool say now?" Another voice—the thug—and surprisingly close! He'd come back around, holding his keys to his hip so they wouldn't jangle and warn me.

To the thug, Stefan spoke: "He says he's friends with Frank."

"We should put them together," he called out. "Scum with scum."

"We can put you together," Stefan echoed. Much of the warmth had left his eyes—showing a front for the thug, perhaps. "You can rekindle your friendship."

Something in his tone made me reticent. "I don't know about that."

Stefan mentioned that I might get better food. "Fattened up before the slaughter," the thug said, then stumbled off again.

"I suppose I'd feel a little more important, to be in such company," I admitted.

At this he snorted, and said Frank was just another man, after all.

"It must be interesting to be guarding him, at least," I observed, but he responded that eventually it was all another routine, and he didn't take any particular pleasure from it.

"So you became a party member to do a job you don't enjoy?" I asked.

(Here he grew mildly annoyed.) "There is a revolution on the way," he said at last. "It has already begun, and with the elections it will be complete. At times like this, it is good to be on the right side of the bars."

I must admit—he makes a good point.

13 January, 1946

I've had only the smallest glimpses of the world outside the walls, but I feel everything it's going through, the dying convulsions of the recent war.

Like any large thing, wars such as the one we've lived through do not stop abruptly—the machinery still whirls about, all the flywheels and gears and pistons; although the combustion that propels it has stopped, it takes a while for the rest of the machine to do the same. There are still populations to be displaced and resettled, revolutions to be completed, justice to be meted out.

To do so, the government has set up the People's Courts, whose judgment I now await. These are not normal criminal courts, mind you; they have ordinary judges, but the judge presides over a panel with representatives from each of the four political parties that are still legal—Communists, Democratic Socialists, National Socialists (Benesh's party, unrelated except in name to Hitler's party, ha ha!!) and Catholics. So the justice system itself has been politicized; in these revolutionary courts, there is more emphasis on the revolution than the court, or so it seems.

And I have unfortunately already seen the fruits of their labour.

When was that? It seems it must have been mid-August, hot August, impossibly miserable, in spite of the so-called peace here in Europe, and the rumours of peace from across the globe. (There had been news so great it had momentarily erased all human distinctions of ethnicity and class, all distinction between prisoner and guard. A bomb, an impossibly large bomb of a type never before seen, brighter than the sun and large enough for just one to destroy a city, had been dropped on the Japanese—a bomb large enough to startle a world that was too jaded from all the bloodshed to pay attention to anything less outlandish.)

And yet the bloodshed was not quite over.

On one of those disgusting and sticky August days, I witnessed a ghastly scene just outside the walls. This was before I'd been denounced; I was still on the top floor, and I could see an immense crowd, tens of thousands of people gathering in a hot angry mass as the sun dropped torturously slowly from the hot summer sky.

They were centred on a large wooden gallows with three crossbeams and three nooses. One would have thought every European would have been sick of bloodshed by that point, and disgusted at the thought of more killing, but—no!! They filled the square and peered out of every window in the neighbouring buildings; some bloodthirsty souls even climbed onto the rooftops for an unobstructed view!! And those in the crowd below kept jostling ever forward, as if everyone was afraid someone else might have a better view of the proceedings.

Finally the victim was led out of the courthouse by a phalanx of justices and guards. The crowd surged as the foreign bodies passed through its midst. Some spectators craned for a better view; others yelled and even spat at the condemned man, who had been pronounced guilty just an hour before.

I did not want to watch. But I couldn't turn away.

My stomach clenched as if my thoughts were a fist reaching down to squeeze it. And the thoughts were as repetitive and simple and implacable as a heartbeat: if they find out who you are, you'll be up there, too.

And then it came. The drop—so sudden, so startling! Even though I'd been waiting for it, it took my breath away!! Three more deaths in one instant—had I heard the sickening cartilage crack, like the popping of a giant knuckle? It seems impossible, but I imagine that I did; I heard it in my mind, where it still echoes today. And the sights, too, I cannot purge. Bodies instantly lifeless, swaying slightly, heavy hooded pendulums.

Some in the crowd left as soon as the matter was done, but others pressed forward to get a glimpse of the grisly aftermath. And the authorities left the corpses hanging for an hour, so everyone could get a look, although people only cared about the middle one.

The man had been mayor of Prag.

18 January, 1946

Stefan, the guard I've been talking to, was walking by last night after I stopped writing.

He was drunker than the last time; he held it well, but I can smell!

"Can you spare a nip for a thirsty friend?" I asked.

"My boss wouldn't be happy if I did such a thing."

"I won't tell anyone."

"I'm sorry, friend." (He moved backwards, just slightly.) "There are roles to be maintained." (As he said this, he looked over his shoulder, down the gallery; the thug, the other guard I'd talked to before, was sneaking up.)

The thug was drunker, and somewhat unkempt. (It is strange how strange people look when they're drinking, and you're not—the bloodshot eyes, the grandiose motions.) He wanted to know what I wanted.

Stefan chuckled. "He wants to get drunk, too."

"Who does he think he is?"

"Someone important, evidently, Stefan said about me. And to me: "You're not allowed to get drunk. There is no fun allowed for the prisoners!"

The thug added: "You must abide by the rules, at all times! You are entitled to food, shelter, and doctor's visits, and nothing else. These are the rules."

"What do the rules say about drinking on the job?" I asked, vaguely aware that this was not a wise thing to say.

"Oh ho ho ho," Stefan said, backing off.

The thug's mood grew dark; he asked if I was threatening them.

"No, of course not," I said, feigning courtesy to this man I—I hope they are not reading this when I am out!!!—this man I despise.

"If you do not give me respect, I will take it from you." He drew closer, grew more malevolent. "Is that what you want?"

"No, of course not."

Here he tilted his head back, as if reappraising me. (It was a look I particularly despised; the asshole seemed to regard me as if I was some sort of specimen.) He asked if I was an informer.

I did not know how to answer, but he did not wait for a reply: "Once an informer, always an informer," he sneered. Then at last he spat on the ground and stalked off, his angry eyes now dull again.

Stefan waited until his co-worker was nearly out of earshot to speak. "We shouldn't get too familiar," he said. "Lest you forget who is in charge." He produced a flat bottle of schnapps from his back pocket, and took a deliriously long swig. Ohh, it was so close!

"I promise, I won't forget around him," I said, to which Stefan replied that he and the other guard were not all that different.

"You are not the same," I told him.

"You're right. He's more honest than I am. My words may be nicer, but if I do the same work, what does it matter?"

"You take no pleasure in it, though," I pointed out.

Hesitantly, he admitted that the work did not sit well with him.

"Well, of course not," I said. "You seem like a decent man. You check in on us, even when you don't have to..."

"What of it?" he asked, surprised and suspicious. "Are you going to inform on me now, too?"

"No, of course not. I just noticed."

Here he reminded me of Jesus' biblical words — I was in prison, and you visited me. But it seemed strange — he was trying to curry my favour! "I thought you said you were a communist," I said at last.

He asked why he couldn't be both a Christian and a Communist.

"You can't!" I exclaimed, exasperated. "It doesn't work! Marx said religion's the opium of the masses!"

And how did he respond? With a shrug, a typically ambiguous Czech shrug that could have meant many things.

All I could do was shake my head.

Finally he smiled, a happy big drunk smile, and said he was just preparing for every eventuality.

22 January, 1946

I no longer feel like writing about Pankratz, about the unpleasant present. But I must write something. And so: more mental masturbation.

The first time I pleasured myself was, not coincidentally, not long after I met Elena, the girl I always pined after, the unattainable one who was to haunt me until the day I met my wife, and longer.

Elena was not my first fantasy, though, strange at that may seem!! I ran into her here and there in Wittingau — I made extra trips in the hopes of seeing her!! — but when the sleepless hours grew too long, when the temporary torture of unrequited lust finally grew greater than the eternal torment that awaited — indeed, that still awaits!! — and I went out into the woods to commit the sin of Onan for the first of many, many, many times, it didn't seem right to despoil her!! Her, of all people!! Even in my fevered fantasies, it felt wrong. If only I'd known what cruelty and corruption lurked beneath those blonde locks!!

So out in the dark forest, I focused my considerable powers of imagination on another girl I knew, a fat sow whom I'd known as long as I could remember, a slut I could have had at any time if I were willing to endure the brief wait in line, the not-so-brief period of ridicule from those in town who had not yet sampled her so-called charms (and those who had, and refused to admit it publicly!), and the possible trip to the town doctor with my tail tucked between my legs, so to speak. There in the dark, I imagined scenes and conversations with this girl, things I'd say and she'd say and I'd do and she'd do, and I stroked off furiously. I remember wondering if I was going to yank my peter loose.

Then it was over. I remember feeling good, but not as good as I had expected. What had I expected? I don't even know. Something overwhelming. And what I got was far less — a slight release, more of an absence of desire than a presence of pleasure. (Any good feelings I had were subtle enough to be easily overwhelmed by my anxiety over what I had done!) I trembled to think I might have been observed. Inside under the candle light, I looked myself over for any stray stains — I'd seen enough pigs and cows copulate that I at least had an idea what it would look like. And again in the morning, I looked myself over and found the most unimaginable thing — my member was swollen, angry at being abused, apparently — it was going to fall off! I was sure of it. And it would be my just punishment for my sinfulness.

And despite the lack of outward evidence, I was convinced that everyone knew. They knew!! They knew!! How could they not? These thoughts were so loud I was sure everyone else could hear them. I imagined they were not speaking to me out of embarrassment and shame, and I came very near to telling everyone, even mother, just so it would be out in the open and we could all get back to our business.

I swore I would never touch myself that way again. I went to confession promptly. And yet I found myself back out in the woods again, far sooner than I'd expected!!

All the while, though, I made my impromptu pilgrimages to Wittingau, trying to convince Elena of my devotion. She would talk to me somewhat pleasantly, but she also had an artful knack for evading anything beyond the barest hints of the possibility of future courtship. So I would walk home in a strange mix of longing and frustration, thinking angrily: This is the thanks I get for keeping your image chaste!!

So eventually — I was still alternating between going to the woods and going to confession, and given my obstinacy in this sin, I was amazed that I hadn't been struck dead or blind or member-less — but I eventually allowed Elena into my fantasies, figuring that if I couldn't have her one way, at least I would have her the other.

And strange as it may seem — and granted, I may be mis-remembering this — that broke the logjam with her!! For I was so embarrassed afterwards, so quick to avert my gaze when I'd accidentally run into her, that eventually she started to actually *try* to talk to me!!

And yet, not much ever happened with her. Enough to keep me hoping for more, but not enough to keep me from going back to the woods many, many more times.

We did make an excursion together to watch a theatrical performance in the town square in Wittingau. A Shakespeare production—Macbeth. I was mesmerized; I thought about pursuing a career in the theatre, which seemed the only logical place for a young man who always wanted to be someone else. (It also seemed an appropriate occupation for my Czech blood: we are, in many ways, a nation of actors.) Mother, of course, did not approve: actors were vagabonds and rogues, she said, and she'd had enough of that in her life already with father.

23 January, 1946

Lest I forget to mention it while reminiscing on my life before the army, I should point out that somewhere in there, I got drunk for the first time.

Mother had always warned me that father had died of the drink; she'd admonished me to drink nothing but communion wine. But one day I was at church with another altar server, and he suggested that we avail ourselves of the many bottles there. It occurred to me that I could thereby honour the letter of mother's decree while ignoring its spirit; I proceeded to get blind stinking drunk.

And it felt miraculous!

Here, at last, was the release, the calm, the peace I'd been looking for with the other, with my frequent trips to the woods! This was as pleasant as I'd imagined that would be! Granted, it didn't last long; when I made it home, my mother gave me a good thrashing, in spite of my protests: "You never said how much Communion wine!" I'd drunkenly wailed, to no avail.

And so when I at last joined the army, it was with mixed motives. I wanted to impress my mother—while also escaping her constant watchfulness, her endless harping about my vices! And I wanted to impress Elena, and to escape from her as well.

It wasn't long into the training that I started wondering if I'd made a tremendous mistake. (I can say it now—I can admit to it now, at least!!) The endless days in dirt pits at the rifle range, the wearying bayonet drills against unyielding straw dummies, the long marches under heavy packs with shoulders and feet aching and weary—it all somehow seemed flatter and less dramatic than I'd imagined, as boring in its own way as life on the farm had been.

And yet I couldn't go back. Not without some sort of triumph under my belt, a trophy to shield me from their incessant harping. Surely that was why I stayed a soldier, why I went to France rather than demobilizing, why I made my way to England—and even why I volunteered to go back home as a commando! The training, more rigorous than what I'd yet had, would prove that I was someone, that I had accomplished something on my own, quite apart from their hectoring.

And so—I cannot help but think—without my mother, and without Elena, none of this would have happened! I'd have become an actor rather than a soldier; I'd have made myself happy rather than endlessly trying to impress them.

Without them, I'd be free.

27 January, 1946

It occurred to me that these memories somehow seem pleasant now. How is that? Looking back at my youth, and at those early years in the army, I know I wasn't happy, yet I still feel a certain something that is known in English as nostalgia—a word, curiously enough, that comes from the Greek, and actually means homecoming.

I remember going back home in early 1943—my first visit after all the Heydrich business had finally played out.

I remember being on that winter train—echoes of that recent trip to Moravia, but now I was headed south—and thinking of that first incident with the wine bottle, and of my relationship with mother in general. She never understood how deeply unhappy and lonely I have always been! And when I drank, those feelings went away! If only she'd tried it, she might have at least understood! I don't remember much about father, other than that he'd been a drinker, but I felt connected to him after I found myself on the course that had supposedly brought about his demise. Father understood what mother did not. Life is misery most of the time, and we must escape however we can.

South we rolled, past valleys where clumps of evergreens clung to the earth's damp creases, past lakes dotted with ice-fishing huts, past snowy fields as pristine as paper.

In Wesseli an der Lainsitz I changed trains; I could have spent twenty minutes there and gotten on the next one, but I dropped in to a nearby tavern instead—hoping, perhaps, to run into Elena; I'd heard she'd moved there. (Though it might have been awkward to run into her, I looked for her all the same! No luck.) I did get a couple glasses of beer in me so I could relax before that final trip to Wittingau, and home.

There, too, I dilly-dallied, dropping in on the likely haunts for some more scouting. I wondered what would happen if I saw her. I wondered if I wanted to see her, given the rumours I'd heard. I suppose it didn't matter; I saw her anyway when I forgot to forget. (Though the fantasies had long ago grown hollow and dry, still I tried to suck some final flavour from them!) She had moved on; she was perhaps off in uniformed arms already even as I searched, or in bed waiting for the deed to be done and the money to be placed on the nightstand. (Perhaps this was an uncharitable assessment, given my own employment situation—perhaps we were both actors after all, playing similarly grotesque roles for similarly outlandish sums!) At any rate I made my rounds, and made myself sit still long enough to choke down a bitter beer in each of the likely spots, and finally stumbled again down the dead cold road to Nova Hlina, the town that never woke up.

The less said about that homecoming, the better. I barged on in, and they all looked up from the kitchen table. Scarcely could I bear the stony stares from those of my brothers who still lived at home. The devil with them, I remember thinking finally, and sat down and served up a plate as if it were a normal evening.

My brothers simply excused themselves without saying a word. At last, my mother spoke, coldly; she asked how I was.

"I'm well," I said, but she immediately contradicted me. (In my mind, I berated her—why did she even ask, then, if she already had an answer of her own? Instead, I took a deep breath.) "No, I suppose I'm not," I acknowledged at last. "I will be once this is all said and done."

"Perhaps," she said dismissively. Then: "You've been drinking again," in a tone which immediately set my heart beating faster. Who did she think she was? To think she could still run my life, who did she think she was?

"I'm nearly 32, mother," I pointed out, trying to contain my temper. "I had a few in town. I don't see how it matters to you."

"No," she said. "In Prag, too. You need a woman in your life."

While this was, again, a conclusion I'd already reached, I wasn't about to tell her that. "I need a different woman, that's for sure." I retorted.

This, she said, was a cruel cut. Yet her own voice was a cold knife blade!

"Fine. I need a woman. I agree. Probably for different reasons than you want me to have one, but I agree." To this she asked what I thought her reasons were; she asked—quite insultingly!—if I had acquired powers of telepathy in the army.

"You want grandchildren! I get it already!" I breathed deeply, to cool my boiling blood. "I want to be happy, and you just want grandchildren."

"I want you to be happy, too." (How could such a sentence sound like a weapon? Somehow she made it so.) "That was all I wanted for any of you," she claimed.

"I am happy," I told her.

She said it was a lie.

"All right, I'm not," I acknowledged. "Not now, anyway. Who could be, with such a homecoming?"

"Grow up. Find a woman and settle down." She said these words with such hostility that I wanted to be alone for the rest of my life, just to disobey her!

"I don't have many opportunities to meet a good Czech girl in my line of work," I told her. "The ones I meet don't end up thinking very highly of me." To this, she said I could meet a German girl for all she cared—it wasn't like they were going anywhere.

(I must at this point mention how correct I thought she was. How inevitable it seemed, the German triumph!! True, there had been rumours of reverses on the Eastern Front, but we knew nothing of substance, and it still strained belief to think any of it would affect our status here in the centre of what seemed destined to be a German continent. I defy those who would judge me to look back at their yellowing wartime newspapers and remind themselves how inevitable it seemed when one simply looked at a map! How insignificant we looked!! With Slovakia lopped off, and Bohemia and Moravia like a shrunken morsel about to be masticated by a tremendous Teutonic skull—Prussian brain, Bavarian cheeks, Austrian jaw and Sudeten teeth—what was our fertile farmland but a tasty treat on the verge of being devoured?!?! In retrospect, I can say that there's nothing more absurd than a political map, especially in wartime. It makes these temporary realities seem etched in stone, as if when you crossed those borders, the ground itself would change colour. Whereas at most such boundaries nothing changes—least of all you.)

At any rate, that visit started on a low point and headed downward.

The very next morning, my mother barged in on me in the back room and finally—for the first time ever!!!—caught me doing what I'd fled to the woods for all those years ago. After I was living on my own and presumably free from such concerns, my mother had to catch me in the act then, of all times!!!

I was mortified. I had to drop into town for a few hours after that, just to clear my head.

Then, back at home—truth be told, there were some unpleasant scenes. I don't remember all the details. I either left or was asked to leave. Either way, it didn't matter; I was bound and determined to never return.

28 January, 1946

Was that the trip when I found the mistake in our family Bible? Until recently I thought it had been during the Heydrichaida, but now that I'm looking back in more detail, I'm not sure it was. Memories of my actions are somehow not always solid.

(Solid—there's a thought! Sometimes it seems like memories come in three phases, like matter itself. You have your gaseous memories, which are so insubstantial that they dissipate almost instantly—what you ate for lunch on such-and-such a day, or what time you went to bed three Wednesdays ago, or whether you shaved four days ago. But many are liquid—somehow not entirely substantial, more often turbulent and changing—the first time you saw someone, the first time you knew something, or heard something worthwhile, or realized something needed to be done. And solid memories are perhaps the rarest of the three, but they are the only way to subdivide and hold the others. The church shootout, the mission against the Skoda works, the trial, Ash Wednesday of the last year of the war: these are solid memories. Many other memories I can only place approximately, and only because they logically must have come before one such event and after another.)

I only mention the family Bible because it marked a turning point in my estimation of myself. The book was a heavy gilt-edged thing, rarely opened except to inscribe important dates; it had an ornate leather cover whose cracks and creases were encrusted with dust. I remember cracking it open to look for words of guidance, but was that during the Heydrichaida, or on that winter trip in early '43 when I was feuding with my family, or both? Sometimes you have a sense you have done something before, but there is no proof as to whether it is déjà vu, or a forgotten memory, or an echo of a dream.

I know I was looking for guidance and I found a riddle, a mystery, a clumsy ink chicken-scratch over my parents' wedding date. And I'm not sure whether I had ever realized or noticed—or thought much about—how I, an October Libra, had somehow been born exactly nine months after what I'd always been told was my parents' wedding date! (The approved Catholic story being, of course, that they both saved themselves for their wedding night and yet also had waited so long and so patiently and loved each other so completely that God had blessed them with a child after their first congress.)

Does it not seem more likely — I remember realizing in a thunderous flash — that they lied about their wedding date? Who gets married in January, after all?

That must have been it! Such an epiphany — it turned everything upside-down, and shattered whatever remaining delusions I'd had that my parents' union had been a wholesome holy one. And yet — to preserve the fiction of happy obedient Catholicism, my mother had gone back and erased the documentary historical proof of her misbehaviour! And if she lied about that, what else was she lying about?

A lot, I realized. These thoughts refused to die when I got back to Prag. Indeed, my speculations intensified. Perhaps my father was not my father after all — I didn't look like any of my brothers. Perhaps I was not entirely Bohemian but some mix — half-German, perhaps! Certainly it was not beyond the realm of possibility in our part of the country — is not Eastern Europe dotted with enclaves of ethnic Germans? And did we not, in fact, live rather close to Austria? Could it be, I remember thinking, that my last name should not be what it is after all?

It was a while after that before I discussed this with mother. When I mentioned something along these lines, she responded strangely — but strangely enough to tell me something! I did not and do not know the complete truth. But I know that most of what my mother had told me about my parentage was, in fact, a lie.

29 January, 1946

Oddly enough—as if mother's wishes were coming true, and she was still somehow controlling my life despite my efforts to be rid of her—it was not much later that I met my wife.

It was in Old Town, in a tavern dark enough that even I looked good. She was blonde like Elena, with darker eyes but a warmer face. (Was she prettier than Elena, or was I just drunk enough to think so? At any rate, she reminded me of Elena, which was good, and she was not Elena, which was also good—but as it turned out, they had far more in common than I realized straight away!!!)

When I came in, she'd already been there, sitting alone at one of those bare wooden tables. Fortunately I'd had just a few nips at home before heading out, so I didn't look away when she looked at me, but I wasn't quite numb and dumb enough to sit right down at her table, either.

Instead I found a place for myself, not directly across from her but within sight, at least, and ordered a beer, and looked at her. (I'm sure I was nervous, but I remember thinking: this is why you go out to the taverns, is it not? If there were women at your house, this wouldn't be necessary, but there aren't.)

The waiter went over to her and I heard her order: German. (Such an awesome language! In all honesty, I've always preferred it to Czech! Everyone sounds more respectable when speaking German.)

For the next few minutes, I pretended I was capable of ignoring her; I sipped my beer and put on what I imagined to be a peaceful, carefree, normal air. Then at last I dared a glance in her direction, and she caught me, but she smiled, looked down, and blushed. I looked down, too, at my golden glass, and when I looked back up, she was looking at me. I sensed—as I so rarely do, ha ha!!—that the timing was right and auspicious. A few fewer beers and I'd have not had the courage to go over there; a few more, and I might have slobbered on her.

"Ist hier noch frei?" I said, pointing at the available seat diagonally across her table.

"The seat is available. Nothing in life is free." (Her air was not quite I-like-you; it was more keep-talking-and-let's-see.) So I sat, silently. At last, she asked if I was going to say something.

"I'm working on it," I told her. "I suppose I'm surprised to see such a beautiful woman in here by herself."

"Work harder," she said dismissively. (Had I had fewer drinks in me, the cut to my pride might have done me in!) "And who said I was here alone?"

"I said it," I told her, undaunted. "I'm a spiritual medium, trained by gypsies. I'm possessed of great psychic fortune-telling abilities, and capable of incredible feats of telepathy."

(A sceptical smile crossed her face when I said this, but a smile nonetheless!) "What else can you tell me about myself?"

"You're German," I said. ("You're good," she snickered.) "From Schwabia!" I continued. "You're practical and stylish, but frugal. Independent but conservative. Your astrological sign—you are familiar with the astrological signs, yes?" (She nodded.) "Your astrological sign is Pisces."

"A Pisces?" she chuckled. "Very well. And what do I do for a living?"

"You're an undertaker," I said, with a straight face.

She laughed at last—a small but real victory! "You were doing so well!"

"No, I know you're not an undertaker," I said. "You're a nurse."

She smiled and said that, for argument's sake, we could just say that she was a student. (In retrospect, this was a statement full of evasions and omissions and ill portents, but I just went along with it—how blindly did I submit to her machinations!)

"Studying nursing?" I asked.

"No," she chuckled.

"Undertaking?" I asked, hopeful, but again she said no, we could say she was a student of humanity, and studying to be a teacher. She wore a bigger smile; I could not believe my luck. Finally she asked my occupation.

"I can't tell you," I told her. "It's a state secret."

"German, though?"

"Half-German, actually. And half Czech."

"You must really like beer, then."

This was quite a funny comment in retrospect, but I was feigning a general attitude of indifference, so I just shrugged.

"There is nothing wrong with that!" she exclaimed. "I'm of a like mind."

"The devil knows his own," I told her.

She gave an impish smile. "Who told you I was a devil?"

"Is it a secret?" I asked. (She said of course it was!) "Well, then, I suppose it makes sense that you're going into teaching. You can hide your devilish nature amidst rows of rosy-cheeked schoolchildren." (She feigned shock, but I could tell she was delighted by the attention, so I kept going.) "And I must say, it is a good plan. For what better place for the devil to hide than in the classroom? It presents a veneer of respectability and kind-heartedness to the world. While in the meantime you get to corrupt an entire generation."

"You think like the devil!"

"I'm familiar with his ways," I said, world-weary and wise. "I've seen him around."

"And what have you learned?"

"He's a trickster. And the smarter and prouder you are, and the more you want, the easier it is for him to trick you. And he does give you what you want! He fulfils the letter but not the spirit of his obligations. He gives you what you want, but never what you need."

"Everyone knows the devil's a trickster," she said. "But they say people vomit in the presence of the devil, and I don't see you running off to the water closet."

"I hadn't heard that," I said. I hadn't heard it, but I didn't like it; my stomach clenched anxiously, like a fist before a fight. I put my hand on it and sighed.

"Are you feeling all right?"

"Now that you mention it, my stomach is a little..."

She gasped, offended and amused, and gave me a playful pat on the shoulder. "I'm not really the devil! He probably wouldn't have the patience for teaching, at any rate." (She wrinkled her eyebrows and crinkled her mouth in a most delightful way.) "Haven't you ever read Faust?"

"Not yet," I admitted.

"You should read it; it will get you to understand your German blood."

"Did it teach you to bedevil men?" I asked.

Feigning outrage, she tapped my shoulder playfully and exclaimed that her name was, in fact, Gretchen. (I think I responded with a dumb look.) "Gretchen saves Faust," she explained.

"So I am to play Faust, then?" I asked; she said I would have to give it a read and tell her myself. And she said there was something of young Werther about me as well.

"How did that one go again?" I asked.

She said it was something else by the same man — Goethe, I think — a story about a passionate man, full of sorrow and self-hatred, who was destroyed by his love for a woman he could never have.

"You read a lot," I commented, to change the subject.

She said she adored reading; she batted her eyelashes and asked if I felt the same.

I lied. "I love it."

She asked what I'd read recently. "The Good Soldier Schweik," I said.

"Czech literature," she said in an ugly tone, with an expression to match. She asked if I could relate to it.

"Not really," I said. "The main character was a drunken buffoon, a soldier who didn't much care for soldiering, and who subverted his superiors at every turn. No, I couldn't relate."

"Did it tell you anything about your Czech blood?"

"Nothing likable," I replied. "Czechs are sly. They get their way through crafty subversion, not outright opposition. Pretending to do what people want, but doing it in a way that obeys the letter of their instructions, and not the spirit."

"Like the devil," she said, and smiled.

"But with Czechs it is benign, absurd. Pathetic, perhaps, but not malicious. One's overseers end up quitting in simple frustration."

"You sound…divided in your loyalties." (She made the most delightful eye contact as she spoke!) She asked if half of me was going to quit the other half in frustration.

"I hope not!" I exclaimed.

"No?" (She prodded.)

"I think Czechs and Germans can coexist peacefully. Even amiably. We must start with our shared love of beer and let everything build from there." I raised my glass and we clinked in celebration.

Her eyes sparkled. She said it was the wisest plan she'd heard yet.

"Why not?" I added. "It is a lubricant, is it not? Do not all machines need lubricant? And surely it will work on the large scale as it does on the small—usually one can only bring together a roomful of people with alcohol. Why not the centre of the continent?"

She smiled impishly; she liked the idea. "Think of all the money that would be saved on administration!" (She looked delightfully philosophical as she spoke.) But she added that, in her experience, alcohol was more like mineral spirits than lubricant; it stripped away the paint and varnish and let us see things for what they really were.

"A good thing, too, is it not?" I asked, to which she replied that sometimes we needed our stage masks. After all, she asked, we don't want people to know everything about us at first glance, do we?

"You tell them more than you know, in spite of the masks," I said.

"Do I?" she smiled.

"Your watch gives away a lot. More you're your clothing does, usually. It tells me at a glance if you're rich or poor, stylish or functional—and if you take care of personal possessions. But your clothes say a lot, too. I have to pay attention to such things in my line of work. Accents, too…my supervisors tell me I'm exceptionally good at languages and accents…"

Here, she interrupted, and pointed out that I'd said Pisces was her zodiological sign.

"Pisces are free spirits," I explained. "You are here alone…"

A man appeared, a uniformed German who negotiated his way through the tables, said Guten Abend, apologized for being late, and kissed Gretchen on the cheek. To me, Gretchen simply said she'd never actually said she was here alone—and her zodiological sign was actually Taurus.

"Of course it is," was all I could manage.

I don't remember exactly what happened next. I think I went to use the water closet, and when I returned they had gone.

3 February, 1946

More winter bleariness today. It actually feels good to be vacationing in my memories!

That first time I met Gretchen might have just as easily been the last. (How different my life might have been! Would I be here? Possibly not—probably not!)

I must stop speculating on alternate possibilities. Such fantasies are ultimately depressing—though they do provide at least a few moments of pleasure. Gretchen might have remained a pleasant fantasy rather than a horrible reality!! Another pleasant illusion with which to pleasure myself. And I might be free!! Granted, a free German is not always in a great spot these days. But it would have been some kind of change.

As it happened, I was back in that part of town the very next night. I somehow ended up by the same tavern —I don't think I went there deliberately, but who can say? And I was trying to stay away from the drink for a few days, so I didn't have a good reason to go inside, but I convinced myself that I needed to use the water closet. So I walked into the establishment and walked around and—I am embarrassed to admit—walked around a second time, just to make sure I hadn't missed her. And then—I walked all the way out the door before I even remembered the purported purpose of the visit! So I ducked back in to go to the water closet. And when I left, she was still not there. No luck, I remember thinking—as if it was unlucky that I hadn't run into that she-devil! Such lengths I went to, to find the agent of my demise!

(Are all women evil spirits? Sometimes I wonder. Their actions often seem calculated to cause confusion and discord; they cannot be counted on for anything, least of all rationality! And if God is male, and came to earth as a male, and selected only male apostles, might that not signify that women come from somewhere else?)

I digress.

So I walked off through Old Town, telling myself—if I remember correctly—that I hadn't actually wanted to run into her after all. In truth, I was lost in my thoughts, and lost in the general sense. (I never got the hang of that part of the city! It was two months before I could walk consistently from Old Town Square to the Charles Bridge without getting lost—and that was while sober!! When inebriated, forget it!! It was a night-mare labyrinth, seemingly designed to trap hapless drunks. In my longer flights of fancy I always imagined people trying to stumble out, getting lost, stopping at another tavern to gather their wits and have another drink, and repeating the process until finally passing out on a kerb; I imagined them finding lodging the next morning so as to not suffer through that again, and settling in, and growing old without ever leaving that part of town. Again, I digress.)

At any rate, the labyrinth worked in my favour that day—or so I figured!

I rounded a corner and there she was—I almost trampled her. I'm not sure I'd have spoken to her if I'd seen her from afar, but as it happened, I didn't have time to avoid her.

(She smiled; I remember being pleasantly surprised at her pleasant surprise.) Then she said something like: Well, well. If it isn't Doctor Faust!!

"Guten Tag, Frau Gretchen," I said, as nobly as I could. She still looked good, better even than she'd looked in my semi-drunken memory, strangely enough. "I wasn't…"

"Fraulein!" she exclaimed. She apologized profusely for running out on me the other night. "My brother had tickets to the opera, you see, and we were running late…"

"Your…brother?" At the time—at the time, mind you!—it was the most wonderful word I'd ever heard.

"Yes. My brother…" (She stopped her hurried explanation and dissolved in bright giggles that filled the silent street; she touched my arm, then apologized again and explained that she wasn't laughing at me.) Truth be told, she said, she wished she'd stayed; it was a rather frightful Wagner production. Again she touched my arm, spoke: "I am really sorry, Doctor Faust, I…"

"That's all right." (I chuckled at last and shook my head with friendly disbelief.) "So I'm still Faust?"

"Oh, no," she said. "It's just that…I never caught your name!"

"Karel," I said.

"Karl?" She misheard me, rendered my name in its Germanized form—which suited me fine. Pannwitz had wanted me to come up with another name for my work—I still had to use the Czech form for that, and I unfortunately still needed a Czech last name—but I'd wanted a new one anyway, for the new me. And so Karl Jerhot was born.

9 February, 1946

More bad weather outside. Some conversations with Stefan, but nothing substantial. So—back to the fungible past, to the last spot at which things might have been made right.

All might still have been well even then, even after everything else that had happened, had I but left Gretchen to her own devices. Unfortunately, I lacked the courage to do anything but pursue her wholeheartedly. For it seemed like this relationship was—well, I shouldn't say the missing piece of the puzzle, for that is an overused turn of speech. No, this was a new puzzle entire, with a complete set of new pieces, and a new pasteboard box, and (most important of all!!!) a new picture on it, a complete new scene that I'd never seen.

And was I not entitled to this new life? Isn't that the ultimate point of the faith I was born into? Not the death and the suffering—no, those are but waypoints that most people confuse for the whole point. Isn't it ultimately about the resurrection? The possibility of a new life?

And yet, how badly it is ending.

I almost forgot—they executed the man whose wife was sleeping with the parachutist, the man who was there in that kitchen with us when I almost got shot, all those years ago. They say denunciation is a womanish crime, a quick and easy divorce for wives with no other recourse. I suppose that's not always the case.

10 February, 1946

The thug came over last night, drunk and angry, yelling that I was a denouncer.

"You knew this already," I pointed out.

"You are not just any informer. You are the one who…" (Here he described what I'd been accused of.)

I shrugged. (Inwardly I raged—Stefan must have told him!)

The thug asked why I'd done it. (He seemed like he'd somehow lost respect for me—where he'd found any, I'll never know!)

We stood there for a few moments. "I don't have anything to say," I said at last, in case he hadn't understood my silence.

He said people were killed, because of me. I told him: "They would have been killed anyway."

He said I was scum. He also said he'd lost family back then—I suspect he's lying, but what could I say?

"You would have lost more, had it not been for me!" I pointed out. (It is the truth—why does it sit so poorly with them?)

It certainly didn't sit well with him; he shouted: "You betrayed our blood. You should shed yours!"

Knowing I was being entirely unwise, I still felt unable to stop the words coming from my own mouth, the bile bubbling forth like froth. "Our blood betrayed itself! I prefer being German! The Czech culture is ridiculous; the language is womanish!"

I heard the angry jangle of keys; he started stabbed one at the lock. I braced myself for the beating that was sure to follow. (In truth, I almost welcomed it, so great was my boredom!) My blood was flowing, my adrenalin surging; I felt alive for the first time in months! Electric, excited, almost aflame!

And something happened to stop it.

"Jan!" Stefan was stumbling down the gallery, calling the thug's name. (In truth, it had not occurred to me that the thug even had a name!) "I need..." And here there was a crash, a clatter I could not see: Stefan falling over drunk, presumably.

Jan withdrew his key and turned, distracted.

"Jan!!!" Stefan yelled. "Jan!!! Oh, shit, I think I cracked a rib. But I didn't break the bottle!"

I craned my neck to see. Jan stumbled off to help Stefan; for the next few minutes, I heard them fumbling and falling and cursing and eventually even laughing. Meanwhile, I stood there perplexed—alone and unscathed.

11 February, 1946

Stefan appeared last night to continue our discussion—sober this time.

"How is our language womanish?" he asked quietly.

At first I didn't understand. Nor did I particularly want to talk to him, once I remembered the ugly scene with Jan. But I was angry and wanted answers. "You told your friend—the thug—about me," I said at last.

He shrugged.

"Why?" I asked.

He asked if I'd ever gotten drunk and done something I'd regretted.

I thought about it, but only for a moment. "Nothing like that!" I exclaimed at last. "I know how to hold my liquor."

"Really?" he smirked.

"Yes. Years of practice. I am an expert."

"You were begging me for a drink the other night."

"An expert always needs more practice. I've gotten somewhat rusty of late."

"I'm sure you could pick it up again without too much trouble. It is like riding a bicycle," he said dryly. He looked about; he seemed bored, and desirous of conversation. Again he asked how the Czech language was womanish.

"You remember me saying that?" I asked. "You seemed...too drunk to remember anything."

"I seem like a lot of things," Stefan said cryptically. (What did this mean? Who is he, really? I've been wondering ever since we talked; I'm sure there's more to him than meets the eye.) Again he spoke: "How is our language womanish?"

"How is it not? Rules that change all the time, depending on little more than mood! What's more womanish than that?"

"That is funny," he said, but he did not laugh.

"It is a womanish form of self-defence," I continued. "As if those who wrote it down were thinking, 'If we can't keep foreigners out, let us speak and write a language so complicated they can't understand what we're saying about them behind their backs!' Sure, it worked against the Austrians, but how did the Germans respond? By putting their language first! And I can respect that! What I can't respect is Czechoslovakia. A lion on the coat of arms? How absurd."

"It is a mighty animal." (Stefan pointed this out as if I might not have considered it.)

"It is wishful thinking! Nothing more! If they put an accurate animal on it, everyone would laugh."

He asked what I would suggest—a lamb, perhaps?

"No, not lambs. Lambs die, and there's something noble in death, at least. Whereas Czechs refuse the dignity of martyrdom. No, the Czech nation is a nation of pack animals. Donkeys, all working with heads down, and no protest besides feigned sloth and stupidity."

"You insult yourself as well, friend."

"I think not. I'm half-German. I became a German."

"So you figure you've done nothing wrong?"

"Oh, I've done plenty wrong! Just not that."

"What does it matter if people know about it, then?" he smiled.

"It matters," I said. "Who else have you told?"

He said, somewhat coldly, that this was not of my concern. And then he asked if I truly thought I'd done nothing wrong, and I said again that I hadn't.

"No? Under four eyes, as the Germans say, you would still say you'd done nothing wrong? You still wouldn't talk about what got you here?"

This I couldn't believe. "You're asking me this, after I almost got thrashed for it already, on account of you?"

"Oh, I don't expect you to talk to me," he said. "As I said the other week, there are roles to be maintained. And we have already perhaps become too familiar with each other for our own good." But, he added, I was disturbed, and I clearly needed to talk to someone.

"Like who?" I asked

He shrugged. "There are a couple priests who used to come in and make the rounds every so often. I was always curious as to what they got to hear...I'm sure some of them knew more of the truth than some judges..."

"You could get a priest in here?"

"Possibly."

"Send me a nun instead," I said, which surprised him; he asked if I'd talk to a nun and not a priest, and I laughed: "I'd talk to a woman and not a man."

He seemed incredulous. He asked if I really didn't regret any of it.

"I'm a German!" I shouted, unexpectedly angry. "I completed all the citizenship requirements!! I had all the paperwork done!! My father was German, I married a German!! I am a German!"

He walked off, disappointed. I didn't mind, though; he's been acting strangely, and the more I think about it, the more it's apparent that he and Jan, despite their apparently different personas, are really colluding against me, playing good and bad to see if I'd talk to one of them about everything.

I did tell him the truth—legally speaking, I was a German! Gretchen and I wanted to start a new life together, and by the time we were married in that summer of '43, it was a done deal. Not long after that—three months after the wedding date, and I'm not ashamed to admit it, ha ha!!—we welcomed a lovely set of fraternal twins, a boy and a girl.

It was all downhill from there. I don't suppose I'll describe much of that trip, though. Suffice it to say that was ugly enough that even my current situation sometimes feels pleasant by comparison.

12 February, 1946

Another empty day.

I was given a new cell mate two days ago, but we haven't spoken. The man literally has said nothing, even in situations that have clearly called for a simple "Excuse me" or "Thank You." Another strange character, like the fellow from the sticky summer months who would pick dead skin from his feet and then get into shouting matches about religion, or the fellow in fall who incessantly cleared his throat and made disgusting phlegmy noises and never even pretended to be quiet while masturbating. My cell is like a stage in a bizarre play—there are no changes in costumes or scenery, but the characters enter and exit with no explanation. They say lines which don't match their actual history, and try to play roles for which they've badly miscast themselves. (Even the guards—I have no idea what they're actually doing, once they're outside my field of vision! I only know what they choose to tell me. They're obviously colluding against me, but it could be worse than that. They could be spying for the prosecutors, for all I know!)

It is tiring. There has been far too much theatre in my life; I can't tell if anything's been real.

13 February, 1946

I've been avoiding my cell mate. I've been avoiding the guards. I do not wish to speak to anyone. Again, the only refuge is the pen.

This new life I'd stumbled into dragged on for some time after I met Gretchen, but in truth, before long, it felt much like the old one. And by early 1945, it was all over but the shouting, and the shooting.

Prag at last was suffering from the war. For some time, the strains had been minor and nearly invisible; now they were tangible and growing. There were more restrictions on food and clothing—I had money but little to buy with it, so at last I was saving, at least! Petrol was extremely scarce, and by that point there were few enough automobiles on the road that people often forgot to look for them while crossing the street. (Prag was obviously not built with motor vehicles in mind, and there are many spots where it is hard to tell whether one is on a road or in a plaza. So even during normal times—or busier times, I should say, because I haven't seen many normal times there—one often forgot to watch for them. In early 1945, though, it was as if the city had somehow reverted to a time when the internal combustion engine was still a rarity. One went long periods without hearing one, and then there would be a single baffled German Army half-track, or a car which had been retrofitted with coal gas tanks on top, or a nervous ambulance carefully tip-toeing through the oblivious pedestrians, as if unsure whether it could make it to the hospital without taking more lives than it saved.) Meanwhile the streetcars were growing swollen with extra passengers, and tired from carrying them; there had been several catastrophic accidents, and I'd grown wary of public transport, except in the most dire emergencies.

But I still had to travel to and fro, to keep up appearances for Pannwitz. By that point, he'd been made head of the entire Prag Gestapo, but he still insisted on running me personally. And he still wanted intelligence — unfortunately, our sources of information were drying up as it became more and more clear who was going to win the war. (For much of the past year, I'd taken to brushing up on my English, listening to illegal broadcasts of the BBC and transcribing them, and reading black-market novels, both to find out what was really going on, and in the hopes they'd give me a chance to go elsewhere to spy. I would have even settled for some radio work — something, anything different!! But Pannwitz wouldn't recommend me.)

So somewhere in there, I'd started making up reports. In lieu of previous activities, I frittered the days away drinking in vaulted taverns, concocting tales of plots and conspiracies — against Emanuel Moravetz, against Frank, against Himmler and Hitler, even — the more outlandish, the better!! (This was, it must be remembered, not long after the Wolf's Lair plot against Hitler, and after the Slovak National Uprising, so the larger plans were actually very plausible; nearly everything was plausible now.)

We would then meet in a variety of places — after hours in empty offices, or in darkened corners of dim taverns — and I would brief him on my so-called efforts, and on the outlandish plots I was bringing to light. I don't think I gave any specifics; I'd just say that the people I'd met with were too crafty to pin down. I'd divulge rumours and hints and half-clues, all based on sketchy recollections of anonymous meetings in public places with people who resolutely refused to plan things far enough in advance for me to alert the Gestapo.

Meanwhile Pannwitz would take pulls from a silver flask, from which he seldom shared. (Over those few months he'd started asking fewer questions and taking fewer notes.) I was still trying to put it together, I remember telling him more than once; he'd take his long swigs and stare at me with dead eyes.

After a while I knew he knew I was lying! And yet we still had our meetings. Eventually I took a chance on bringing a flask of my own, and he said nothing.

So I would tell stories we both knew to be untrue. And he'd tell stories of his own, about his earliest days as a policeman, chasing pimps and thugs, cleansing the Berlin streets of their human filth. (How people cling to their favourite stories! They clutch them like trophies as their world falls apart, as the triumphs themselves grow tarnished with their fingerprints.)

And there was another story I remember well, because he only told it once.

It was about the end of the Heydrichaida, when the outcome of everything hinged upon a single interrogation; I think he told it to put me in my place.

They had rounded up a family that had been sheltering parachutists—a family I'd met before, Stefan and Marie something-or-other, and their son Ata. His men had knocked on their door in the wee morning hours, and he'd been questioning the father in the kitchen while the mother and son were in the hallway. And one of the guards—quite against instructions and protocol, Pannwitz pointed out!!—had let the mother use the water closet. And she had cyanide in there, and she took it before Pannwitz realized what was going on. They kicked in the door, but it was too late; she gave a little smile and collapsed, and that seemed to be that. They'd realized, too late, that they'd been questioning the wrong person, and any knowledge she'd had about the whereabouts of Heydrich's assassins was now permanently out of reach.

But Pannwitz was convinced that the other two at least knew something. And his superiors wanted him to use harsh measures, but he had a slightly different idea. He did let the thugs have their way with the son for a bit, down in the basement cellars there at Petschek, but then he went down there and pretended to get mad at his own interrogators, and he brought Ata up into his office and cleaned his wounds and gave him something to drink.

And he talked to young Ata, talked to him like a human being. We Germans, we're just like you, he said — we, too, need something to take away the pain. So let's have a drink and forget our pains, he said. Let's forget our divisions. A drink makes all men brothers.

The youth had initially been somewhat un-sociable — sullen and silent, in no mood for chit-chat — but Pannwitz dealt with that simply by suggesting that if Ata didn't share a drink with him, he'd just have to go on about his business and leave the youth back downstairs.

And so the youth took a drink. And Pannwitz even drank with him — just as he'd done with me! Coffee with brandy, trying to make it seem like a friendly chat. And he gave Ata some more claptrap about the brotherhood of man, and how, whatever one personally thought about Heydrich, the attack on him had been a crime, after all, and such crimes made a mockery of that brotherhood. He went on like this for some while, and then — just when the youth was at his weakest and drunkest — Pannwitz arranged it so the guards brought in the mother's severed head.

They'd placed it in an empty aquarium so as not to make a mess. She'd already been dead, of course, but the youth hadn't known that yet, so naturally the sight was quite disturbing. (Pannwitz said this reluctantly, almost apologetically.) In his drunken stupor, Ata moaned and wailed and wept; finally Pannwitz walked over and patted him on the back, as if out of sympathy. And, Pannwitz claimed, he had felt badly for the boy! He said he felt badly, and he wanted to protect the youth from these bloodthirsty thugs, but he could not do so unless the boy gave him some information.

And Ata talked.

Ata didn't say much, mind you — he didn't know much, after all. But he knew the name of an Orthodox church in downtown Prag that his mother had mentioned as a place of refuge.

And that, of course, was enough to wrap things up.

I wondered at these storytelling sessions — me with my frightful fantasies about our bleak future, and him with his glorious visions of a golden past; it seemed so unproductive that we might as well have been whiling away the hours at the tavern! But of course I was beholden to him, and I had to keep going through the motions. It only occurred to me later that he had to keep up appearances, too, to keep his own bosses happy.

14 February, 1946

I wanted to write more. What else is there to say about those days, though?

After meeting with Pannwitz, I would walk home if things were well with Gretchen, or stay out on my own if they weren't.

Still, taking refuge in the taverns did not mean I was free from care. Far from it! The Red Army was raping its way across Eastern Europe, and while most Czechs were fine with that, I was drinking with other Germans at last, and they discussed the Soviets with the same tone of fear and helplessness a farmer might use when awaiting a swarm of locusts. (The Americans and British were coming, too. They had already shown their own bloodlust by incinerating much of Germany, but most of us figured they would at least be nicer once one got to talk to them face-to-face.) As the two fronts drew ever closer, our already-prodigious levels of alcohol intake rose in inverse proportion to the distance between them; the level of inebriation necessary to make reality palatable steadily ascended until the only real solution was oblivion.

As I've mentioned, we all knew the two fronts were not equal, and we all had the same preference. Still, our first experience with the Americans was not auspicious—they came in aeroplanes dropping bombs, and on St. Valentine's Day, no less!! High explosives and white phosphorous falling on the Mozart Brucke (near where I am now, come to think of it) and the nearby buildings and hospitals on what some overly logical German bureaucrat had renamed Krankenhaus Strasse. (After the war, I heard there were apologies for the tragedy, for the 413 innocent dead Czechs. It seemed the hapless pilots had been trying to bomb Dresden. All was forgiven, of course—apparently there's nothing wrong with wanting to bomb Dresden.)

21 February, 1946

I haven't written for a while now. A heavy depression has settled over me, like low dark winter clouds.

I should write. It is something to do, at least.

Where was I? I have written about the times near the end, but not about the end itself.

Again, I regret to say that I was in the taverns a lot by that point. Sometimes Gretchen would meet up with me, although more often not, thanks to the twins and the nanny situation. (I suppose it depended, too, on what I despised more on a given day—the sight of her face, or my own soul-crushing loneliness.)

Truth be told, she was not a great mother to our children. She was not capable of spending money wisely, or consistently minding them when they were in her charge, or effectively disciplining them when they cried in the night. She wanted a full-time nanny so she could get out of the house more often, but I always asked why, and she never had a satisfying or logical answer. So our marriage was devolving into an escalating series of unreasonable demands on her part, coupled with greater and greater efforts on my part to at least maintain some independence and freedom of action. Indeed, there came a time when the Gestapo became less oppressive than she was!!! All I really had to do for them was keep turning up; they were getting remarkably forgiving about the details of what I actually said.

Still, it was all incredibly stressful. My life had become a whirlwind; nearly all of my actions revolved around deceptions—of my employers, of my wife, of myself. Yet in all that time I gave no serious thought to leaving Gretchen. Where could I go? I could not leave my children. And besides, the life we'd built together was comfortable. Not pleasant, but familiar. The performances we gave might have been emotionally taxing, but they were not otherwise difficult. We were familiar with the set; we knew where to stand, and when to enter and exit; we had long ago memorized our lines. There were threats and accusations and more threats, and some unpleasant scenes, but I figured nothing would come of any of it. I, of all people, thought that this, of all things, was stable enough!

So we made plans for our escape together, our flight west, away from the rampaging Russians and towards the amiable Americans. And by March it was all in place. I'd even finagled Mother into coming up to take the children—we did not know what to expect during our flight, but I was pretty sure it would not be good for toddlers. Gretchen and I wanted to get a good running start; I hoped by the time it all settled down we'd be in American hands in Germany, and no one would bother to figure out who I really was, or what I was running from.

But then I awoke on Ash Wednesday to find—catastrophe!

It was a slow realization, a creeping sense of unfathomable betrayal that dawned on me as I stumbled about in my stupor that morning. At first, I'd thought Gretchen had taken the twins for a walk. But then I came to realize that not only was everyone gone, but a substantial portion of their clothing and possessions, too — and, of course, the money!

I found a note on the kitchen table. I have neither the desire nor the ability to remember its exact contents. Still, it was the grossest collection of one-sided stories, half-truths, myths, fantasies, and outright lies I had ever laid eyes upon.

And yet, on the plus side (I remember thinking after I calmed down), being alone had its advantages.

After a few hours, I sauntered down to the tavern (not the one where she and I had met — even I'm not quite that pathetic!! — but another favourite haunt in Old Town) and realized I didn't have to come up with a cover story, or submit to a lecture beforehand!!

On the way, I noticed sad-faced commuters with ash crosses on their foreheads, and I reminded myself that I should get to Mass before mother's train arrived that afternoon. What would I tell her about Gretchen? My head felt thick and sticky. I hoped the drinking would loosen it enough to let me think up a story.

I found myself alternating between the blackest depression and a strange light freedom. An edginess hung in the air; there were noises too, low propellers droning again, high and far off, just like on Valentine's Day, just like during the business at the Skoda works. And then — explosions in the distance, a low menacing rumble. My heart raced. Had everyone miscalculated? Could the Soviets be here already?

In the tavern, I drank, thought, smoked, thought, drank. Meanwhile the tavern-keeper hunched over the console of a radio, steering the dial from one static-choked channel to the next. Out front I saw pedestrians with ash-cross foreheads talking excitedly, and others heading down into the underground stations, fearful. Above the slanted rooftops and spires across the square, I could see plumes of black smoke rising into the clear blue sky. Taking no chances, I moved farther from the window.

At last the tavern-keeper's radio needle pulled a slender strand of news from the crackling static. "…Americans apparently deliberately targeting the Bohmen und Mahren Works with a combined air armada of fighters and fighter-bombers. Dozens, if not hundreds of dead…"

"Turn it off," I roared. The tavern-keeper gave a strange look over his shoulder. "My brother works there," I explained.

I drank—a river of beer deep and wide enough to erode the rocky edges of my recent life. It took a while, given the magnitude of the mountain of rubble that had been steadily accumulating over the previous few months, but eventually time started accelerating nicely, then skipping about, and I was almost content in my oblivion when I realized I was late for mother's train.

Catastrophe!! I darted out into the square, bumped into a passer-by; I wobbled in the bright cold sun and got my bearings. And I realized again that I'd failed to make it to church before mother's arrival.

After the great catastrophes, those little lapses can feel particularly onerous; I felt miserable, low—worse than I'd felt that morning even. (How little did I realize how much further I had left to fall!) Then I had a thought—an absurd, ingenious thought!! I darted back into the tavern, grabbed my ashtray from the hands of the perplexed tavern-owner, stuck my thumb amidst the forest of fag ends that had sprung up over the course of the day, and laughed at myself as I drunkenly inscribed a cross of ash on my forehead.

4 March, 1946

They tell me I'm going to get a solicitor soon.

Revolutionary justice is chaotic. People are quick to use trite metaphor when describing justice, to speak in terms of machinery, wheels and gears and cogs—but revolutionary justice is like being in a poorly-maintained machine that is simultaneously falling apart and being operated faster than it was designed for; the parts are grinding, and the gears don't always mesh; pistons slip and misfire; the whole assemblage threatens to shake itself apart. Many who were in custody with me during the first months were essentially here for no crime other than being German; they'd been rounded up by angry mobs with clubs and pipes during the wild lawless days after Prag fell, then detained in schoolrooms and cinemas before being passed off into the marginally more capable hands of the newly-arrived so-called authorities. Establishing a justice system in a city that has been recently recaptured, using people who had recently returned from exile or who had, in some cases, been imprisoned themselves by the people they were now imprisoning—it did not make for orderly or efficient administration!! For many months, I had the distinct sense they didn't always know who they had in custody, or why. I know they did not know who I was.

But now at least I am finding out what I've been charged with, and I'm getting to meet with my solicitor.

I wonder what I'll tell the solicitor; I don't remember everything, not by any stretch of the imagination. Strange how easy it is to forget faces, events, details, exact chronologies! So much passes through our heads, and so little hardens into tangible memories—and even those can acquire shapes and textures different than what they represent!!

(Memory—is it something God devised to torture us?? Certainly the pleasant portions of my memories have nearly evaporated. I can remember some wonderful moments—getting married, seeing my children in my wife's arms — but not without remembering other things that produced them and followed upon them. Has it always been this way? Was the present ever pleasant? Or have I always been sorting through bitter memories and awaiting an unendurable future? Those regrets and fears — jagged and misshapen and ugly — often feel more real than my surroundings, which can change if I am moved from one cell to the next; they are more real than my cell mates, who can be rotated in and out. They never go away; they are the true stones from which my prison is built!)

7 March, 1946

The final days of my old new life — all the weeks after Ash Wednesday — are a blur; I am still not sure what happened, or why. I know I did not have the patience to submit to mother's hectoring for very long, and so I sent her packing. I was resolved to enjoy my new-found freedom! I took advantage of the situation to drink as much as possible for as long as possible.

But then, far in my fog, came the day Prag at last erupted into total chaos. It wasn't long before the Soviets' arrival and the end of the war when it finally happened, the uprising we Germans had so long feared. From the perfect calm of an average May morning — May, again!! — there suddenly came the most unexpected and frightful violence unimaginable.

Waking, still in my fog, I heard beneath my windows an unexplained roar, as implacable and continuous as the ocean, yet human. And outside in the harsh sunlight — Czech flags! People waving Czech flags! Where had they come from, those flags?

Then I turned on the radio and heard the most frightful words I have ever heard, repeated over and over: Death to all Germans!

It was odd, and yet more horrifying and real than everything else had been; I felt like I was getting up at last to face the cruel morning after a night where I had not quite slept but had instead lingered in that hazy place between dreams and consciousness. I did not take time to pack. What good would it do? If I took a suitcase, they would know I was leaving. So I grabbed a flask and the cash I'd scraped together since Gretchen's departure. Then I dressed hurriedly and took my bicycle downstairs and out onto the bright chaotic May streets.

Such a beautiful day! Sunlight streaming through tender leaves, and the air bright and full of hate—not a hint of bad weather to dampen the city's inexplicably implacable fury! Rifle shots cracked—where had the docile Czechs found rifles? My heart raced as I mounted the bicycle. Rumbling over the cobblestones, I swerved around clumps of Czechs hastily erecting barricades, and others yelling and waving flags; I saw hordes in an animal fury, kicking and punching a hapless civilian—a German?—lying on the sidewalk amidst them; I rounded a corner and saw a German soldier lying dead, a dark stain spreading across his grey uniform. I froze.

And looking down, I saw: a Czech flag! A Czech flag, a good-sized cloth Czech tricolour which someone had apparently hastily sewn together from three pieces of plain cloth. (One never stops to think that even a sewing machine can be a weapon of war!) I clenched it in my fist as I placed my shaky hands back on the bicycle's rubber handgrips. The flag would be my salvation!

"Death to all Germans! Death to all Germans!" I yelled lustily in Czech as I pedalled north, clutching the makeshift flag like the security blanket it literally was. Across the river twice, north into Liben on the relentless climb, and then past the spot—the very spot, I had not planned it that way, but I passed the same place where Gabchik and Kubish had lain in wait those years ago! Daluge had erected a memorial the year after the attack, and now angry passers-by were taking out their frustrations on the bronze bust of Heydrich, beating it with sticks—sticks!!—as if six years of frustration could be relieved by attacking an inanimate object. On a whim, I stopped, grabbed a loose paving stone, and hurtled it at Heydrich's big bronze nose. And I was mad! — had it not been for him, none of this would have happened. I would not be fleeing.

But did I have to flee?

I thought about sticking around and taking part in the festivities. "Death to all Germans!" I shouted myself hoarse. It was strangely invigorating to yell; it was exciting to be part of something so great and energetic! Was there a way to stay? A place to hide out? No, not in Prag; there was always the chance I'd be recognized. Best to flee. The statue would be toppled soon enough; the perpetual SS Honour Guard was, of course, nowhere to be found — forever was over.

I got back on the bike. Soon I'd been pedalling for an hour, and my armpits were soaked with sweat, but the buildings were finally giving way to glorious yellow fields of rapeseed, and I knew I'd make it after all.

I remember patting the flask in my inside jacket pocket and telling myself: not yet.

9 March, 1946

All still might well have turned out well.

Unfortunately, it turned out so badly that I later became furious at God for teasing me with that delirious taste of freedom! The flag, that flag that had appeared as if by magic, that I'd somehow noticed right when I needed it — that had been such a fortuitous gift that I could not help but chalk it up to divine Providence! And yet, my miraculous escape came to naught; my freedom was taken away, just as easily as it had been given.

After an exhausting and wearisome journey northwards, my bicycle at last gave up the ghost in a small frontier town not far from Tereisenstadt. The front tyre had been slowly losing air for a few kilometres. I pretended it was of no great consequence — even as I felt the rumble that told me I was rolling on my rim, I kept pedalling! But eventually I flung the machine into a roadside ditch and cursed myself for not bringing a spare inner tube.

The countryside was chaotic in those wild lawless May days. According to rumour, the partisans — who had been practically nonexistent just months before — now roamed at will; one could see their handiwork in the burnt-out hulks of lorries and half-tracks, or the eyes of the fleeing German soldiers. (These men travelled in haphazard convoys; when they ran out of petrol or were shot up by the partisans, they abandoned their vehicles and headed north or west on foot in ragged groups, wearing uniforms that had lost all traces of uniformity — tunics were optional; blouses were tucked or un-tucked or torn or bloodied; trousers were rolled up, or torn to make shorts.)

And there were civilians, too, fellow ethnic Germans from Prag and other enclaves fleeing the madness; here and there I fell in among them and traded stories, or bartered for food; mostly I walked alone.

I remember giving in and draining the flask at last, and feeling no better, only slightly different — an abatement of my nervous tension, rather than pleasure.

I remember fantasizing about where I would have been right then had it not been for Gretchen's perfidy. And yet I still wanted to talk to her again! Even if only to demand a proper accounting of our life together, an acknowledgement of all the time and money I'd spent on her. (Even if I never admitted it to myself at the time, my actions indicate what my thoughts would have denied — what I haven't admitted until now!! I was headed to her family's home in Schwabia. How pathological is that? How depressing, how diseased, is my soul?)

I remember—was that that same day?—wandering down an eerily deserted country road in the twilight. I came across a stranger sitting in the shade of a tree, drinking from a bottle of schnapps, with another bottle or two by his side. And I thought: a man after my own heart! (Or liver, perhaps.) This stranger I never knew, whose name I never learned—this demon. Who was he?

I remember waking, still drunk, in the woods on the outskirts of a small town that seemed nearly deserted; I remember seeing German signs and thinking perhaps I had at least made it to the Sudetenland. I don't think it was where I had lain down the night before—but I can't say, because I don't know where the previous evening had ended.

Go into the town! Find your people! something said in my head—not audible, but just as real.

There were a few people out and about, a few baffled souls wandering the empty streets, but no one gave me a second look. Something had happened here; there were many broken windows, and the brick sidewalks were covered in shattered glass and trash and piles of ash. In my stupor I saw what looked like a tavern; the proprietor's name was German.

Go in there! something said in my head.

I stuck my head in, and there she was! At the end of the bar— Gretchen!

Her face was turned away, but from behind I saw (in my drunken stupor) the same glorious blonde locks, the same build, the same posture.

It couldn't be her, I remember telling myself. (Drunken thoughts are simple and repetitive, though they don't seem that way at the time!) It couldn't be her.

It couldn't not be.

I caught a glimpse of her face and couldn't look away. (There are times when you end up staring at someone simply because you cannot believe—your mind cannot comprehend!—that it isn't the same face, or at least related to the same face, that you had known before.) Had I somehow magically directed myself here? And how? Some fierce desire, some intense telepathy or psychic force guiding me like radio waves?

Whatever the reason, it clearly was meant to be. For it was her.

Go and talk to her! (Something in my head said.)

I walked in and put my hand on her shoulder. "Guten Tag, Fraulein," I said.

"Nemec!!!" (She spun and screamed, and darted from her chair as if it was on fire.) "Nemec!!! Nemec!!!" (Nemec means German—in Czech!!!)

I realized at last I'd made a terrible mistake; I mumbled some vague apology in Czech and backed out. I shook my fuzzy head and looked around—the place was a mess, it was not a working tavern. Something was not right!

"Nemec!!!" The strange woman—whose face now somehow looked nothing like Gretchen!—backed away in fear, then bolted past me for the door. She screamed in the street, and the dead souls took note. And all I could think was: This is going to be bad. This is going to be bad!!

Before I realized what was going on, a couple coarse country-town boors were grabbing me and pulling me out into the bright dusty street. And as if by magic a crowd had appeared—a strange belligerent crowd, shouting at me in Czech, spitting, swearing, throwing shoes, shouting again. Where had they come from? Where had this fury come from? My own anger overpowered my lingering drunkenness; I yelled back but was knocked to the ground; I covered up in a foetal position as they kicked me. I remember thinking this, at last, was the end — and I felt a strange sense of relief at the thought! (Provided, of course, that they knocked me out soon.)

Unfortunately I did not die.

Salvation, if I can call it that, came in the form of the local police. (There were many cases in those weeks where the police stood by — or actively helped — while Germans were being killed by angry Czech mobs. I don't know why they intervened in my case!!) I felt the blows stop, and I heard shouting. When I opened my eyes, the cocoon of people had abruptly split; there was daylight, painful daylight, and sun and clouds, and then, eclipsing the sun, a policeman, balding with sad eyes, and another, fat and florid and angry.

The sad-eyed one asked my name.

The endless issue: who am I? I was torn between two unacceptable alternatives: an anonymous German-Czech name, and a Czech one I was sure was notorious.

I suppose I could have made up something new, but Pannwitz always said such things get hard to keep track of in such situations.

"Karl Jerhot," I said at last. Once more for good luck.

They asked why I was here. I told them: "I'm trying to rejoin my wife and children in Germany." (At the time I thought it was a lie.)

They asked what I did. Was there an acceptable answer? "I'm a farmer," I said.

They searched my pockets and found a wallet, keys to my flat (now somewhat useless), and roughly ten thousand Reichsmarks.

They asked why a farmer had so much money. I could not answer.

They did not know who I was, but they knew I was not nobody.

And so I found myself in a narrow iron-barred holding cell in the local police post—the first of many cells!—shaking from nerves and lack of alcohol, aching and wanting to die, undone again by that unholy trinity: money, and pussy, and drink.

11 March, 1946

It was a bad time to be German, for a change.

There had been many revenge killings, and there would be many more before the summer was out. Czech civilians, who had been unwilling to lift a finger when it had been dangerous to do so, now made up for their docility with an abrupt and perplexing rage. There was some fighting in Prag between the beleaguered German garrison troops and the riotous populace—aided by the Vlasov Army, soldiers that had twice turned traitor—but within a matter of days the real Soviets had finally arrived, and the war was officially over.

When President Benesh returned to Prag in their wake, the populace hung German corpses from the lamp-posts to greet him.

I made my own somewhat-less-triumphant return not long afterwards. There was the windowless van, followed the aforementioned beatings by the Revolutionary Guards.

I also remember—I'd almost forgotten!—how, after all that, we had to be registered. We were lead, beaten and weary, into a hot stone building. The air was heavy with sweat and fear. We were told to present ourselves to two angry guards who sat with a ledger book at a heavy wooden table.

It turned out I was suspected of being a werewolf. These were the dead-enders, the Germans reportedly plotting and organizing themselves into an underground army, waiting for the right moment to emerge and wreak havoc on the Red Army. A lie, of course, but I didn't want them to know the truth.

I hoped I'd serve a few months, or a year, and be let out — to do what, I don't know. Still, that beginning time was the roughest, for reasons I've already mentioned — the overcrowding, the abysmal food. Fortunately or unfortunately, though, my life as a normal prisoner soon came to an end.

It was late in the summer, and we were out in the courtyard; I got a look of recognition from the womanish man whose wife had been sleeping with the parachutist — the parachutist who'd been hiding in the wall, who had almost shot me — here was the cuckolded husband who'd turned him in, the one I'd seen in the kitchen of the country house all those years ago!

I didn't have any particular desire to talk to him, and I tried to ignore him, but then he called out to me by my real name: Karel Churda.

Either one of the guards overheard, or one of the prisoners mentioned it to them, or perhaps the womanish man made it a point to tell them himself. Whatever the cause, I was pulled out of my crowded cell later that night, severely beaten once more for good luck, then thrown into a deliciously spacious cell.

And despite my fresh bruises and cuts and innumerable aches — and the knowledge that they would now be much more likely to put me on trial for my life now that they knew who I was — I felt a deep and strange and sudden sense of self-satisfaction. My desire to kill myself was even — briefly — lifted. Obviously I was important!!

12 March, 1946

I finally sat down for my first visit with my solicitor — or rather, the man I'm told is my solicitor.

We were seated across from one another at a large table wedged into a small room near the front of the Pankratz complex; it was such a tight squeeze that we couldn't lean back in our chairs at the same time.

For the first minute or so, he said nothing, and just rifled through his papers. I grew anxious; I could understand the guards not talking to me, but this was absurd!

"Are you my solicitor?" I asked at last.

"Are you Karel Churda?" he asked, without raising his head or his voice. "If so, then yes."

"Not a very friendly one," I observed; here at last he looked up and pointed out that he was not being paid to like me, but to defend me.

"How are you going to do that, if you don't like me?" I asked.

"I dislike the People's Courts a lot more than I dislike you," he said. "And I like arguing more than anything. And this case promises plenty of opportunities to argue."

"Do you like being the devil's advocate?" I inquired.

He raised an eyebrow. "Do you like thinking of yourself as the devil?"

I shrugged. "This is the role they've cast me in. I did nothing wrong, nothing anyone else in this cursed country wouldn't have done in my shoes. But I'm being villainized, I'm being demonized..." I was eager to continue, but he cut me off.

"I hate to disappoint you," he said, "but you're really not that important. A nuisance, an inconvenience, but certainly no devil, or at least not one they want to publicly demonize."

"I'm not?" I was confused. "How do you figure?"

"Everything is in flux," he said. "Here in this prison, history is being written. Its events are being hammered to fit various ideological moulds. The past is often more malleable than the future, you see, for if one writes a future, the real future always eventually arrives to contradict it, but if one writes a different past..." He looked deep into me. "You can tell whatever story suits you, and sooner or later, your stories become more real than your memories."

I frowned. "Are you saying I'm making things up?"

But he claimed he wasn't talking about me, specifically. All he'd meant was that my case—the mere fact of its existence!—threatened the Communist Party's narrative, for in their version of history, they were responsible for everything good and noteworthy—including all heroism, and all resistance. (It seems the past is malleable, but only if one ignores whatever facts contradict the desired narrative. Like me—and all the parachutists that were with me.) Because we trained in Britain and not the Soviet Union, he said, we were standing in the way of their story; we had made their history unwieldy. And history could not be memorized and used as a basis for action if it was too complicated. It had to be simplified to be remembered and made useful, and they already had a simple story: the Soviet Union had offered to stand behind us at Munich, the Soviet Union had liberated us, the Soviet Union was now the beacon our Communists would follow to lead our country into the future...

"What does all this matter to me?" I asked, to put a stop to his blathering.

"It is a tremendously good thing!" he claimed. "There is now some reluctance to bring you to trial and publicize all this. Especially with so many more useful defendants around, like Karl Hermann Frank."

Was he being serious? I found myself quite unexpectedly agitated. "How long are they going to keep me here? Are they going to forget about me?"

He said he didn't know—but given that fact, we needed to take advantage of the situation. He claimed he needed to hear my side of the story, everything I knew, so we could at least devise a defence strategy while there was still time. He said that our—he said "our," as if we were both in this together for equal amounts—our only advantage was that their attention was fixed, for the time being, on the higher-profile cases, Frank's trial and the like.

I said nothing. Something seemed strange. He was far too eager!!!

He gave an unpleasant look and said: "I do not have much time here. The government is giving me far more cases than I can manage effectively. I may not be able to come back for some time. I need you to tell me everything, today!"

"How do I know you are who you say you are?" I asked at last.

He feigned puzzlement. "Who else would I be?"

I shrugged. "One of them. Someone sent in to set my mind at ease and trick me into divulging evidence that they don't have, so they can convict me on the basis of my own words, spoken in confidence."

To this he just smirked. He claimed they had more than enough evidence to convict me, with or without anything I said. And even if they didn't, that wasn't going to stop them these days, for the People's Courts were all about politics, not justice...still, after all that, he asked if I was ready to start talking!

"I don't have anything else to say right now." I crossed my arms. "Tell the thugs they'll have to beat it out of me."

He shifted uncomfortably. "No one's going to beat you to get you to talk."

So he was admitting it was going on! And that he knew about it! "Why not? They've beaten me already, for nothing."

For a second, he looked as if he might burst with frustration. Then he stopped, breathed, and leaned back, as if preparing a different course of argument. When he spoke again, he sounded sympathetic; he knew that, at the time I'd done what I'd done, a lot was going on; I'd probably had every reason to believe I was ultimately saving lives.

So he knew more than he'd admitted! I smiled. He'd revealed too much. "If you know all that, why do you need me to talk? It sounds like you know enough to defend me."

He glared. "Still, the fact remains that you were arrested with a German-provided identity and a very large sum of German money after three more years of war with the Germans. So obviously..." (And this he said quite judgmentally—far too harshly for someone who was supposedly defending me!) "...obviously you didn't mind working for them."

"A lot of people worked for them," I pointed out.

But I'd made the mistake of making enough money for the others to hate me, he pointed out. And if there was a reason for that, I should tell him now, otherwise they would hang me for it, eventually.

"What do they know of me?" I asked, agitated. "I put an end to an unpleasant and bloody situation! I saved lives! Is it my fault I was well paid for that? What do they know of my situation, besides biased eyewitness testimony from people who are only trying to save their own necks? What do they know?"

And he said—and this was the first I'd heard of it—that there were also captured payment records, proving that I'd continued to work for them long after that situation was over.

I was speechless. And furious!!! Pannwitz—that alcoholic prick!!! He'd either forgotten to burn them, or deliberately not done so, so as to burn me.

Into this void he said—in a tone I found almost too much to bear—that it was one thing to make a mistake, and it was another thing entirely to profit handsomely from it.

"So they're faking evidence," I said at last. "They don't have enough real evidence to convict me, so they're making things up."

"They're doing no such thing!" He sounded frustrated—tired, perhaps, from putting up the front. And here he said more than he meant to say: "Is it too much to admit they paid you?"

Aha! He was asking me to admit to things! "I had other reasons for doing what I did," I said, exasperated. Almost immediately, I regretted it. Was this too much to admit?

"Fine," he replied. "Tell me your other reasons, at least." (He looked as if he really expected me to start talking!)

"I've said more than enough already."

"I am your solicitor!" His face was growing red; I could tell he was having trouble keeping up the charade! "I need to hear your side of the story, if I am to defend you!!"

"So you say," I replied, enjoying this game.

"Fine," he said, and started to gather up his papers. "When their attention comes back around, they will convict you, with or without your other reasons. I would make my peace with God, if I were you."

"Well that's terrific legal advice!" I shouted, just to get a rise out of him. "Some solicitor you are! You don't even know what to say!"

"I have to work with what I'm given," he said, somewhat snippy. And with that, he stood to leave. He did not shake my hand.

On the way back to my cell, I was escorted by the Jan, the thuggish guard who is friends with Stefan. He taunted me, asking — quite mockingly — how everything was going.

"They are going to let me go," I said brightly.

He didn't believe me. I was an exploiter of the people, unreliable. Why, he asked, would they let scum like me go?

"Simple," I said. "So I can get back to pleasuring your wife."

(I knew he was steamed. I didn't care. Sometimes there is a perverse pleasure in making people angry. Especially now, these days, here. It's the only control I have, really!)

The thug slammed me hard against the wall, then caught me with a thunderous right to the jaw. I went down and he kicked me a few times, and then it was done.

14 March, 1946

Stefan came to my cell today and told me I was being moved.

When I asked why, he said it had been determined that my friend needed companionship. "My friend?" I asked.

I gathered my toiletries and uniforms and undergarments and bedding and followed him clumsily, dragging the bedding behind me, struggling to keep hold of everything. He led me down the gallery, cold and aloof, and offered no assistance until he reached our destination, where he produced his large brass keys and unlocked the cell door.

I walked in hesitantly, pulling my meagre personal possessions, and when I got them all through the doorway, I could see my new cell mate appeared to be none other than Karl Hermann Frank.

Was it really him? I wondered if they'd hired a double, to set me at ease and get me talking. But no—he had a glass eye. They wouldn't be able to find a man who looked like Frank who also had a glass eye. I straightened up, took a deep breath, and smoothed my uniform. "It is good to see you again, Mein Herr," I told him at last.

"Again?" He asked, but didn't turn to look at me; he was lying on his back on the bed, an arm over his eyes, but I could tell he wasn't sleepy, or even tired.

"Don't you remember me?" I asked.

With a frustrated huff, he turned and looked over at me at last, a quick once-over with his one good eye, and said: "Not particularly."

"No?"

Again he looked over at me, just a little more intently, and said that yes, perhaps I did look a little familiar.

"I was at the battle at the church back in 1942," I explained. "After Heydrich."

At last he nodded. He mentioned the trial; he'd seen me there, too, when I'd testified.

"I forgot about the trial," I said. I had forgotten it. It was not a pleasant memory—out of all of them, that was the one I wanted least. All those faces, the rows of defendants, the Orthodox clerics and their thick beards, the civilians who had fed and sheltered me—no, enough about that. "Your trial started today, yes?"

He huffed angrily and said it was tomorrow. He asked if I knew the significance of the date.

"Friday?" I guessed.

"Seven years ago tomorrow," he said, "We rolled into Bohmen und Mahren." Hitler's visit, the start of the occupation—it was the anniversary. He was convinced they'd scheduled it deliberately.

"Beware the Ides of March," I said; he just snorted and said something vague, which I took as permission to continue: "Here we are, Germans, but I suppose in their mind we're just Czechs who wanted to be German."

Here cocked a curious eyebrow and looked over at me again, as if I was suddenly worth looking over, by virtue of my ethnicity; he asked if I was, in fact, German.

"Well, half," I said.

"Half?" he asked.

"The good half," I smiled, and he chuckled a little, at last.

15 March, 1946

Frank and I spoke again today. Having him in here—a man who was once so remote and mysterious, but who now wears the same clothes as me and faces the same fate—has overcome my normal reluctance to speak at length with my cell mates. But I may yet go back to my old ways!!

They came and got him early in the morning; he washed his face and shaved and did his best to look presentable. He was gone most of the day.

When he returned, I was lying on my bunk relaxing; I didn't want to get up, but it seemed the situation called for some basic pleasantries, at least. "How did it go, Mein Herr?" I asked at last.

He said — quite mournfully — that they were going to crucify him.

"They're angry, Mein Herr," I pointed out, staring up at the solid cement ceiling. "They want a villain." I think I said this not as judgment, but as a statement of fact. But he took it as an insult. He claimed he was not as bad as they were saying, that he'd done what anyone would have done in his shoes.

This I found hard to swallow. "Are you saying you had no choice in the matter, Mein Herr?"

"No! I did what I had to — I tolerated the Czechs!" He claimed he'd been extraordinarily gracious and magnanimous. And he said Heydrich — Heydrich, of all people!!! — had taught him to do so!!!

I'd been lying down, but now I sat up and swung my feet to the cold cement floor, interested at last. "You have a strange definition of tolerance! And why would Heydrich want to put up with the Czechs, Mein Herr?"

It was obvious, Frank said — they worked well for whoever co-opted them. Technically speaking, they'd always been the most proficient of the Slavs, because of — as he put it — the intermingling of German bloodlines. (He gave a gracious nod, as if this was a courteous statement.) And because of this, Frank and Heydrich had decided that some Czechs were quite suitable for Aryanization. But their behaviour... (He asked if I'd known Emanuel Moravetz; he did not wait for an answer.) Heydrich had chosen Moravetz to be the propaganda minister. And obviously, Frank said, the Reich had worked with foreigners all across Europe, with Quisling and people of that sort. But Moravetz had been one of the Czech Army's most decorated soldiers! Not some failure waiting out the years to retirement in a desk job, but a very stellar soldier! He'd led the Honour Guard at Masaryk's funeral, Frank pointed out; he'd written newspaper columns during Munich urging the Czechs to fight us. (I remember noting that I was part of his "us" now—apparently as a result of my intermingled German bloodlines. I think I smiled thinly, although his blather was starting to annoy me. Though I agreed with him, he was starting to truly annoy me!) If a leopard such as that can change his spots so easily, Frank asked, what did that say about the country on the whole? He and I were of German stock, he pointed out, and we'd been loyal to that, first and foremost. But, Frank asked—full of arrogance and annoyance—what had Moravetz been loyal to? There had been ultimately no loyalty in the man, he said, no sense of duty or consistency.

"I don't know how you can say that," I interjected, glad to at least interrupt the tirade for a few seconds. "Perhaps he thought he was doing what was best. And he did help us out..."

"Moravetz shot himself, you know," Frank reminded me. "To avoid arrest as the city fell..."

"Sometimes I think that's the braver path," I said, just for argument's sake. "I don't know that I could do it."

Frank just scowled. "It is the coward's way out. That's all Moravetz was. If he'd had the courage to face the consequences of his actions, he'd be in here with us."

Here—rather politely, if I do say so myself—I bit my tongue so as not to remind Frank that he'd been captured while fleeing. Instead I just said: "Hitler shot himself."

Again he glared angrily, then spoke almost reverentially. "Hitler was the symbol and embodiment of a national spirit. When his nation was gone…" Frank's voice trailed off. He looked towards me, but not at me; he smiled, as if remembering a joke he hadn't bothered to share. And finally: "But perhaps Emanuel Moravetz was, too, come to think of it."

"Was what?" I asked angrily.

"The embodiment of the Czech national spirit—all of their moral cowardice, their servility, their sophistry and self-hatred, encapsulated in one man!"

"That's a rather offensive way of putting it," I said.

"Oh, but it's true! If only the man had thrown himself out of a window, it would have been truer, still." (Again he almost smiled; he looked at me, eyes slightly askance—one real, one glass.) "This city was saved by treason, after all," Frank said. "The Vlasov Army. Those Russians that had been fighting for us under that traitorous Soviet general. When the Czechs had their morning uprising in early May..."

"I was there for that!" I interjected, but he didn't seem to care.

"...they were still almost put down!" His voice dripped with condescension. "Imagine it! The waning days of the war, the Reich collapsing under the terrible assaults, and still the Czechs were almost put down when they tried to revolt! But the Vlasov Army saved them from having their city pulverized at last. So the great cities of the Reich are now piles of ash and rubble—Berlin, Frankfurt, Hamburg, Dresden—and still here Prag sits, unscathed—a great shining monument to human cowardice and treachery!!" (He'd been pacing excitedly, but with this he finally sat, strangely self-satisfied.)

16 March, 1946

A boring empty Saturday. Frank's trial is, of course, due to resume Monday, but in the meantime we have more time together than normal.

We'd just turned over our breakfast trays this morning when he asked how I'd ended up working for the Gestapo in the first place. So we whiled away the morning talking about that time I've been reluctant to even think about, that fateful spring of 1942.

Because Frank's such an ass, I didn't get to tell the entire story. But because I couldn't, I actually want to, now!

My original mission, for which I'd trained in England and parachuted home, had nothing to do with Heydrich or any of those other crazy plots, although—as I explained to Frank—I suspected we had all been sent by the same people. No, my mission was simple, easy, and somewhat absurd—I was dropped in with two other men to set up a radio beacon near the Skoda Works. (This factory complex, run by my erstwhile countrymen, was a major source of both German war materiel and Czech embarrassment.) Our radio beacon was to guide in a flight of RAF bombers to blow the whole place to—what was it the English always said?—smithereens. Presumably, the mission was meant to send a message not just to our enemies, but to our friends in London—that at least some Czechoslovakians were committed to smashing the German war machine, rather than building replacement parts for it.

Strange as it seemed later, this logic had sounded logical to me, and so I'd kept my spirits up and given it my best, even after the Gestapo dug up our radio beacon while we were finding shelter in Prag. One would have thought this would have necessitated a change of plans—but no, London insisted we proceed, even with no beacon!

As I told this story to Frank, he interrupted to ask what my fellow commandos had thought.

"They saw that things weren't quite right. We all saw that, once we got here," I told him—and it was the truth! Even though I didn't always like Opalka, my team leader, I must admit he wasn't a bad fellow, and I could tell he'd had his doubts about all of it. As I told Frank: "There was this discrepancy between what we'd been told in London about the home resistance, and what we were seeing for ourselves. And the most logical conclusion was that they'd lied—after all, if the resistance was as strong and active as they'd said, then why bother sending us at all??"

Frank nodded appreciatively. I think I was glad—and surprised!!—that he was actually allowing me to talk for a spell.

And so, I explained, in late April or early May of 1942, Opalka and I found ourselves on a train to Plzen—along with Josef Gabchik, Jan Kubish, and Josef Valchik. (A star-crossed five-some, to be sure—I was the only one fated to survive the summer.)

Once there, we spent several days holed up with a resistance member, whose name (fortunately for him!) I did not and do not recall. Opalka went off a few times to do reconnaissance, while the rest of us spent much of our time indoors, smoking and drinking and listening to the BBC Czech Service. It was tense—Gabchik and Kubish kept insisting this was distracting them from their mission, but I wasn't so sure. They hadn't accomplished much in Prag besides finding themselves girlfriends. (Much less production than seduction, ha ha!!)

But then at last in that smoky stressful room, we heard the prearranged signal: President Benes' voice, straining to be strong as he said the magic words: "Have patience. The day of revenge is approaching."

We set out by bicycle, pedalling strongly on the country roads—our spirits (as I explained to Frank) much improved after the deathly claustrophobia of that upstairs room. Opalka headed off with

Valchik in one direction, and Gabchik and Kubish followed me in another.

I remember — something I did not describe to Frank today!! — coming to a fork in the road and not knowing which way to go. Opalka had written his directions on a single sheet of foolscap, and when I pulled it out of my pants pocket, it was surprisingly damp and smudged.

"What's wrong?" Gabchik asked.

I tried to decipher the mess — Opalka's poor penmanship certainly didn't help matters any! But after a while, I was able to figure it out. "Nothing," I said at last. "We're fine." (This is one of the difficult things about being a soldier, and being a man. Whatever is going on, one must always give assurances that all is well — and if it isn't in fact the case, one must make it so before anyone figures it out!)

We pedalled along the road, and sooner than I expected, we came to a country barn. "This is it," I said. Gabchik said it didn't look abandoned, and I remember being upset — he wouldn't trust my judgment! "This is it," I repeated.

I did tell Frank what came next. The sun was a little ways from the horizon, but I didn't see anyone around, so we'd put ourselves to work. Opalka had provided us with small jerry-cans of black-market kerosene, which were wrapped in blankets and strapped over the rear bike tyres; we loosened the straps and carried the cans into the barn; there we stacked hay bales against the walls and soaked everything in kerosene.

Here and there, I'd cast a glance out of the dark barn at the bright countryside, checking if anyone had been alerted to our presence. And no one seemed to have noticed — the barn was far enough from any farmhouses that it felt like an orphan, and the few cars and lorries that drove by showed no sign of being aware of, much less alarmed by, our presence. Our only witnesses were two donkeys that stood there in their stalls, placid and idiotic.

When we'd set everything up, we withdrew from the barn to have a smoke under a stately oak. Gabcik took our lanterns from our knapsacks and inspected them while Kubish and I puffed merrily away. Here I pulled out a flask; I took a pull and offered some to the others, but they refused—Kubish politely, Gabchik disdainfully. (At this point in my retelling, Frank interjected with a snide comment of some sort, which I did my best to ignore.)

Gabchik asked me what time we were supposed to light it, and I pulled the instructions from my pocket and held them up to catch the light of the falling sun. (Unfortunately—I can tell the truth about this now, at least, though I didn't mention it to Frank—that section of the instructions was a series of unintelligible smudges.) "Another hour," I think I said.

Whatever it was, Kubish seemed sceptical; he wondered if the fire was going to last that long if we lit it now.

"These things take a while to really get going," I told him. "There was one near home when I was a child. It burned for hours." I tossed my smouldering fag end off into the grass.

"Be careful!" Gabchik said anxiously.

I'm sure I gave him a look.

"We don't want to start a fire," he explained with a grin.

"Very funny," I replied. Gabchik had finally relaxed a bit; we chatted under that oak like friends on a picnic, and he at last allowed himself a cigarette before the sky darkened.

(Here Frank interjected, to ask what Gabchik was like. "He was a decent enough fellow, all in all," I admitted. "As much as I hate to admit it, he was not a bad guy. People seemed to look up to him. And he was of a type one often came across in our Army, especially in England—so perfect that you wanted to hate him, but just funny enough that it was hard. He was wrong about many things, though.

And he had a temper. Oh, what a temper! And he could be incredibly stubborn." Frank said that must have been why they'd picked him in the first place. He seemed interested in knowing more, but I got back to the story at hand.)

Time passed. Slowly but uneventfully. Gabchik left to relieve himself, and Kubish and I lit new cigarettes. The moon shone plump and lopsided, barely visible through the tree leaves; out there everything was cool and washed-out blue, but under our tree, all was black, except our slowly pulsing cigarette embers and the warm orange masks they made of our faces.

And I remember another tidbit I didn't relay to Frank—when Gabchik came back from relieving himself, he insisted we extinguish our cigarettes. It was, in retrospect, a small correction, but it made me unaccountably upset. "Why?" I'd asked. "For all anyone knows, we're just friends out in the countryside."

"We not just friends out in the countryside," he said coldly—to me, not Kubish, even though he'd been smoking as well!

"Let's light it then," I said. "It's time, anyway."

I kissed my butt for one last drag, then stepped out from under the tree and flung it sidearm into the cool blue grass. Then I pulled out my Ronson, unscrewed the globes of the oil lanterns, and set each wick alight.

Kubish and I both took a lantern and walked up to the barn. The door opening was now a black rectangle; the rest of the barn was painted in pale moonlight colours. Kubish made a move as if to guide the donkeys out.

I flung my lantern against the opposite wall, and the barn's interior was suddenly bright, alive with fire. "They'll figure it out," I said about the animals. Kubish followed suit, and we scampered halfway back to the oak, then turned to survey our handiwork.

Gabchik walked up to us. "We should leave the scene of the crime, at least," he said—though he, too, seemed transfixed by the fire.

(Again Frank interrupted my telling, to ask why we were lighting the barn on fire. "To guide in the bombers!" I explained. "They thought that would work! As if they were going to be able to navigate all the way from England and successfully bomb a factory complex that was only illuminated by two burning barns miles apart on either side!" But rather than agreeing with me, Frank asked why we hadn't used a radio beacon. I nearly exploded! He hadn't been listening at all! This is why I'm writing it down now—at least I can tell it without interruption!!!)

In flickering orange light we untangled our bicycles, anxiously pulling pedals from between spokes and putting chains back on sprockets.

We pedalled in silence back to the rendezvous point. It was another abandoned barn; I didn't know why we didn't burn it, too, for good measure; it looked like it had been fighting a delaying action against gravity for some years and was preparing now for the final surrender.

Here we walked around back; there was a spot of ground behind the barn where we couldn't be seen from the main road. We could just barely see the factory spread out, soft and peaceful in the moonlit distance, smokestacks trailing silvery plumes into the crisp night sky.

Ducking around the corner, away from Gabchik, I snuck a cigarette. Off in the distance I could see one of the barns burning, and my pulse quickened. I wondered what we'd see after the bombers; I imagined great fireballs, vast columns of smoke rising into the sky and blotting out the moon; I wondered if the smokestacks would topple or stand alone in the morning amidst mountains of ash and rubble and twisted scorched metal.

Then came a low sharp voice in the darkness, from an unexpected quarter—Opalka telling me to put out my smoke. (He was walking his bicycle towards us with Valchik trailing behind.) Jesus and Mary! Grudgingly I extinguished it.

"I could see you from the road," he said sternly. Then: "Are you sure this is the rendezvous?"

"It matches your description," I said as we went back around the corner to rejoin Gabchik and Kubish.

We waited in darkness.

After a while, we heard the angry hum of propellers, high and distant. Then came searchlights, stabbing up into infinity and then slashing at the sky like swords. We heard distant hollow thumps from flak guns and saw tracers ascending to heaven, so lazy and peaceful it was hard to remember what they were. Then explosions in the sky, disembodied bursts with no immediate sound like a faulty talkie at the cinema, distant like summer lightning, impressive but ineffectual.

And then—a series of explosions! On the ground, very close! I almost jumped out of my skin. They were far closer to us than to the factory, and it took some time before my heartbeat slowed enough to realize all the other sounds were dying out. The propellers faded; the tracers sputtered and stopped; for a time the searchlights still searched, but I felt what they couldn't know, that there'd be no more.

Gabchik said—grinning in the darkness, I'm sure—something like: "That was fun! I'm awake now, at least."

I was furious—our mission had come to naught, and that was all he could say? "That was pointless," I said. I had expected many things, but I had not expected this. My mind throbbed, angry and hot. Was this really it? Really and truly? Was this why I'd trained, parachuted in, put my entire life at risk? They'd come nearer to killing us than to damaging the factory.

Valchik said: "We did our part, at least."

"We did nothing," I replied, bitter.

"Enough talk," Opalka said. "What's done is done."

Silently we picked up our bicycles and pedalled towards Plzen. Our tyres crunched softly on the white gravel of the empty country road; in the cool moonlight, it looked frozen.

17 March, 1946

I suppose the Skoda mission unlocked something in me, some sense of the futility of it all, an entire shift in my attitudes. Back in England we had been training merrily, listening to rousing speeches and believing we were the heirs of the first generation, the soldiers of the Czech Legion who had thrilled the world with their brave Siberian exploits while winning their nation its freedom. And I was starting to see that things weren't quite so glorious — but it took a little while for it all to play out.

The early morning hours after the bombing found us waiting listlessly on an empty train platform. Two hours' sleep makes any day feel wrong, makes sunlight itself feel like blasphemy — and it had been fitful anguished sleep, the kind you get when your brain's machinery has been whirling so rapidly that it simply will not come to a halt. It was hell, that sense of negative accomplishment — the recent past had made our lives more dangerous without actually accomplishing anything. Such feelings — such torture! One has, in such times, that most futile desire — to simply turn back the clock. Did they even feel it, the others? Did they understand?

"That was useless," I said, to find out. "We accomplished nothing."

Valchik said we'd done what we'd set out to do, and everything else was out of our hands.

"For all we know we killed some poor farmer," I said; Gabchik motioned me to be quiet, but that only made me mad—there were things I needed to get off my chest that morning! Besides, there was no one in earshot. "This is ridiculous, helping the Brits bomb our own people so President Benesh can…"

"Enough!" Opalka said.

Valchik even had the nerve to say it was our fault, that if we hadn't lost our radio beacon it all would have been fine. This really steamed me, because it was patently unfair to blame us. "The Gestapo dug it up!" I exclaimed, louder than intended.

"Enough!" (Opalka almost shouted. He pulled rank to shut us up, then pulled me aside, and we had words with one another.)

After that, I went off to by myself and plopped down on my knapsack, alone in the tired blank morning.

On the train back to Prag, I slept the sleep of the dead. I do remember one fragmented moment of consciousness, waking with my head slumped against the window and a thin strand of saliva draped across my arm like a spiderweb, my neck stiff and sore from holding up my deadweight head.

When Gabchik shook me awake back at the station, I jerked, startled. For a few seconds I forgot where or who I was. It was like my mind had been erased and I was a blank person, a nobody, a newborn in an adult body.

<u>18 March, 1946</u>

Frank's trial is serious business—for him, for the prison, for the city, for the country.

You can tell without even seeing a newspaper—you can see it in the eyes of every prisoner and guard. When Frank's escorted out to the yard or down the galleries, chatter dies down. It is not reverence—it is anything but reverence! But there is something more than disdain in the silence—perhaps the guilt the living must always feel in the presence of those about to die.

For the public-at-large, I'm sure this is all still just theatre. (All trials are theatre, perhaps, but this seems to be the highlight of the season—a show trial, in fact, for I doubt there will be any real justice, any truly blind attempt to add up and weigh the evidence on the law's measuring scales. It's more like a popular film or play that's interesting because the stakes are so high, not because the outcome is ever in doubt.) But for Frank, it is anything but entertaining.

Still, any brief moments of empathy are far overwhelmed by his endless justifications and petty complaints.

Last night, for instance, I had just drifted off to sleep, and he woke me. It was just after the night count, not long before lights-out, but he was grumbling about getting up in the morning for his trial.

"You can sleep all you want, soon enough," I pointed out, then rolled over and tried to do the same.

This, he said, was not funny at all; he sounded displeased—or rather, more displeased than normal.

"I'm facing the same fate," I pointed out, to which he said that his would be arriving much sooner.

"I'll trade places, if you like," I suggested; I meant it, too.

Again he glared with that glass eye. He said they kept harping about Liditz; they refused to believe it wasn't his fault.

I think I made a dismissive noise, and said: "Even I don't believe that."

Here he shot me the dirtiest dirty look he'd ever given me—an ugly face made uglier by stress and confinement and old age and bad food. "It was all Daluge's idea," he claimed. "This is the problem with political matters—eventually the loudest and stupidest win out, because they also care the most, because they have nothing else."

I nodded, or said something noncommittal—which he apparently took as an indication to keep talking. Truth be told, I did not pay attention because, again, I am sick of his self-importance. After having played second fiddle for so long; after finally becoming the most powerful man in the city, then ending up the most despised; after sharing a cell with me when he used to spend his nights boffing starlets from the Barrandov studios, he seems at least determined to run this little prison cell. (No fun being second-in-command here, ha ha!!) But I have a hard time thinking highly of him—it is hard to respect a man once you've watched him take a shit, and given the layout of our cell, that's something I've probably seen more than either of the two Frau Franks ever did.

I suppose I should at least write down some of what he said, to keep record of his idiocy.

Somewhere in there, he talked about Liditz being counterproductive, because they'd wanted to be civil to the Czechs until the war was won and they could ship them off to Siberia. He said he was informed about Liditz after the decision had been made, and he'd arrived on the scene after the shooting was over. (The Siberia matter he said almost offhandedly—as if there was nothing wrong with it!)

Here I should say that, as far as my own behaviour is concerned, I wouldn't have done what I did, if it wasn't for Liditz. But I did not want to tell Frank—I didn't want to prolong the monologue! For a long time I stayed silent. Then—because he wasn't getting the hint—I buried my nose in a book I wasn't even reading; eventually, he stopped talking.

1 April, 1946

Frank told another excruciatingly boring story the other day. Something about sneaking into St. Vitus with Heydrich after some reception. Emanuel Moravetz had told some story about how anyone putting on the crown of Wenceslas would die unjustly within the year, and all his male heirs would die, too. But Heydrich got drunk and decided it was a good idea, to try on the crown. So they went over there and banged on the door drunkenly until the priest let them in, and Heydrich put on the crown and pretended to have a heart attack, just to be an ass and scare Frank. But eventually it happened, Frank said—it all happened as they'd been told; Heydrich had died, and his sons had died, one taken ill, the other run over accidentally by a German Army lorry.

On the plus side, we've started another side project—brewing homemade alcohol!! He has been hoarding apple juice for some time, storing it in a washed-out milk can that was pilfered from the kitchen service. To this we added bread crusts and sugar, also pilfered from the kitchen and delivered via our friend with the laundry cart. We'll see what happens!

26 April, 1946

I haven't set anything down for almost two weeks.

I don't want to write more, but I don't want to talk to Frank—or rather, to be talked at by Frank—either. So I suppose I'd better get writing!

When Liditz happened, I'd been living in a forest not far from home.

Hiding in Prag with the others, hopping from safe house to safe house, had become pointless after Plzen and the fiasco at the Skoda

Works. What use did I have sticking around? My mission was done, after all. Did London expect me to stay? What was the sense in that? Did they expect us to keep bouncing from place to place until we slipped up? Until some nosy neighbour called the Gestapo?? (That's the problem with the military. Because so much of soldiering involves difficulty and hardship — the training, the marching, all the physical exercise — there is this tendency to automatically equate the hard thing with the right thing.) Anyhow, I'd done all they'd asked me to do. My war was over.

I don't remember exactly how or when I went back home.

I remember mulling the matter over after meeting other parachutists who had dropped in after us. They were entirely too hard-headed, too unwilling to look at realities on the ground — there was talk of sabotage, of more assassinations, of all kinds of insanity that would have lead — that did in fact lead!! — to disaster for all involved.

There was an incident, for instance, when a few of them took the train out to Lany to retrieve some equipment they'd stashed in the forest. That was a mess, a disgusting abortion of a mission — even Gabchik and Kubish hadn't wanted any part of it!! At least one of the other parachutists was captured. I knew it was only a matter of time before he talked to the Gestapo and the rest of us were rounded up.

It was stressful. I had to have a few drinks now and then to blow off steam. Lord knows I had reason to!! And there were only so many ways to relax. Gabchik and Kubish had — somewhat foolishly, I must say — taken lovers, women they'd met at one safe house or another. It seemed a distraction and a diversion on their part — I don't think they particularly wanted to do what they were sent there for — but I can't say I wouldn't have done the same in their shoes. That might have kept me in Prag!! That might have kept all this from happening!! They got their warmth and comfort from their women, but mine came from the bottle, and I could take that anywhere.

I do remember finding myself at a tavern in Wittingau, looking for Elena. No — I ran into her!! Was she with a German, that night?

Maybe. I know I ran into her, and I remember remembering that I'd forgotten to forget about her.

And I remember coming home to mother. It had been—what? Two and a half years, by that point? Three? Still, I vividly remember the look on her face through the front door of the house—pleasantly surprised, for a change. She embraced me and wept.

My brothers trickled in—the older ones from the fields, and the younger ones still cavorting through the forest. The older ones seemed sceptical—they looked at me in the weary wary way that workers look at shirkers. But there was joking, too, laughter and joy and hugs and kisses. Mother mentioned that I'd been drinking—an observation and a tone I didn't much care for—but all in all, it was a pleasant homecoming, and I'm sure mother would have killed the fatted calf, but for the fact that the Germans sent the Czech police around every month to count everyone's livestock. So she cooked up several rabbits to celebrate the return of her prodigal son.

I did not know what to tell them when they asked where I'd been. Here I was, still single, apparently unemployed, a loner and a loser with nothing to show for the past few years.

I didn't know what else to do, so that next morning, I went back to work in the fields. I think I wondered what life would bring, now that my time as a soldier had come to a close; I figured I'd settle down and raise a family of my own, at last. The work was so monotonous, and the scenery so familiar that, within days, it felt like the past few years had been a strange dream—Munich and exile, and the fall of France, and that roundabout trip to Algiers and then to England on the sunny decks of those rusty tramp ships, and the training, and the night flight back—all of it! Only the present was real, and strangely pleasant—sweat and toil and soil.

Then, crackling over the radio in town, came news of the attack on Heydrich—a bolt from the clear blue sky, an electric reminder that all was still not right with the world.

27 April, 1946

I suppose I should continue where I left off.

To be perfectly honest, I can look back on it now and say that I wasn't actually that happy in the fields. There was the certain knowledge that the past few years had been no dream after all, and that I wasn't much safer at home than I had been in Prag. After all, I'd come back suddenly after an absence of almost three years, and such things do not go unnoticed in the country! In the city, the sudden presence or absence of one face in the crowd makes little difference. But the country is different—it is like throwing a stone into a small still pond. Whereas the same stone might have disappeared into the ocean without a trace of its passage, in the pond the ripples go back and forth forever, and there's nothing to do but watch them.

I suppose it did occur to me to go elsewhere, even before the attack. But the news about Heydrich sealed it. The Germans were clearly ready to turn the entire Protectorate upside-down to find anyone who knew about this beforehand. Emanuel Moravetz was on the radio every day, all anger and menace. The message was obvious: they were going to shoot the innocent until the guilty started talking.

Somewhere in there, I packed a knapsack and stole away in the night. I had some food and a little money, and all I wanted was to hide out in the forest until they found Gabchik and Kubish and everything settled down.

I remember the long dark walk down the empty country road, and into the great silent pine forest—I'm sure nothing looked different from when I was a child, and yet everything felt different! I eventually decided one spot was as good as the next, so I walked away from the road and lay down on the soft needle bed of the forest floor. It took a while to fall asleep—I was anxious, and more alone than I'd ever been.

29 April, 1946

Frank and I have not been talking much lately. I would not have expected it, but things now are much the same as they were with any of the anonymous cellmates that preceded him.

It is a lonely life. I do not feel a part of life, though I suppose I never have. But perhaps I prefer it that way! Have I ever had a relationship that didn't end in pain and suffering?

And still I wish things could be different, although I don't know how they could be. I find myself staring out again at the courtyard—silver and shiny, with puddles of spring rain reflecting the cold grey clouds above—and thinking of days gone by. Here and there they have been giving us time out there—rarely, because they cannot let us mingle with the unimportant prisoners, lest some anonymous inmate try to go from criminal to hero in one fell swoop by doing illegally what the state is waiting to do under the cover of the law. Still they give us an hour a week to ourselves out there, just to keep us from going even more mad. Oh, how I live for those hours! But this week, our allotted hour fell in the midst of a rainstorm. I would have gone anyway, but the guards of course didn't take us.

I would like other things to think about. I think Frank has been asking the fellow who delivers the laundry about smuggling in some magazines, so we'll at least have pictures of women to look at.

I find myself wondering where Gretchen is. I hate myself for wondering, but I wonder all the same.

1 May, 1946

On my first morning in the forest, I awoke to the sound of the train.

It tore through the woods not ten metres from where I slept, and I jerked awake, heart pounding, sweating, breathing hard until I remembered where I was.

The distant rumble of steel wheels gradually gave way to morning forest solitude. I ate some bread and cheese I'd taken from home, and took a few swigs of wine, and that calmed me down somewhat.

It wasn't bad, actually, once you remembered how to live without plumbing or furniture. Certainly I'd gone through worse in the Scottish Highlands—less than a year before, that had been!! And here there were no forced marches, no hills to ascend and descend. No one yelled at you to stay awake for your watch rotation at night; between trains, there were no sounds at all, save from the oblivious songbirds. You could take naps. You could drink. There was no undergrowth, nothing except the soft carpet of pine needles, the high green boughs; you could wander off and find yourself in one of those magical spots where all you could see between the tall straight pine trunks were the trunks of more distant trees. You could almost forget about Heydrich and the war. You could almost forget, except for the nagging knowledge of why you were here, and what you were hiding from.

2 May, 1946

Still few words between myself and Frank. I do not think the trial is going well for him. The fellow with the laundry cart gave him some pictures of some sort, but he's been hoarding them. I am waiting for the right moment to bring the matter up.

Our little project has been fermenting beneath the bunk bed for some time now. It's covered, but still the smell is seeping out. I'm looking forward to trying it out—maybe we'll be able to have a good honest pleasant conversation then!!

5 May, 1946

Where was I in my recollection? When I've taken a few days' rest, I often have to turn back and find where I'd left off. And when I read it, it's always different than I remembered—sometimes better, often worse, but always different. What a slap across the face the written word can be! What an unwelcome link to our past!

I digress. I was writing about my time in the woods, after Heydrich.

That pine forest soon grew boring. I tried to stay active by moving from here to there and back again, or keeping on the lookout for whomever might come looking for me. (The Gestapo weren't likely that far out in the countryside, but there were always local police, some of whom were surely willing to assist such an investigation.) Still, there was really nothing to do. I found myself restless and discontent, and though I had enough food for a couple days, I knew I'd eventually have to sneak into town.

My other bodily functions drove me from the woods first, though. It's hard to wipe your ass in a pine forest!!

Presently, then, I found myself walking into Wittingau, so I could shit in a proper water closet. And I needed a newspaper, both for informational purposes and to make future forest shits more pleasant. And I figured it wouldn't hurt to have a decent meal and a drink or two while I was there. So I went to one of the taverns and sat down for a proper meal—a goulash, preferable at least to that roast beef with creamed shit that so many Czechs love. (Oh, of such trifling stones are catastrophes built! How different it would have been, but for my desire to empty and re-fill my bowels that day!)

So I was in there, minding my own business, polishing off my meal and washing it down with a beer when one of my old school classmates, Peter something-or-other, stumbled in. And he was about the last person I wanted to see: an obnoxious ass, a braggart, and — based on the latest gossip — a notorious drunkard about town.

Of course, he headed right for me, even though I was ignoring him. He called out my name — my old name, of course, because at the time that was the only one I'd had — quite loudly. And he asked why I was here, given that I'd joined the army. "I thought you went off to England!" he said, far too loudly.

I wanted to choke the prick. I wish I had! It would have shut him up, and none of this would have happened. Instead, I just shot him a dirty look. "You must have been imagining things."

And here — the ass! The drunken obnoxious ass! — he said: "No, you did go off. I remember now! And yet here you are, back at home, the conquering hero — so why be so modest?"

"Shut your mouth," I told him in no uncertain terms.

"Why?" The drunken ass asked. "Are you on some kind of secret mission? Don't tell me you helped kill the Reichsprotektor!!" (He actually laughed when he said it — the prick!)

Come to think of it, that was the first I'd heard they'd actually succeeded, but I just wanted him to stop talking. "You better shut your goddamn drunk mouth before I rip out that idiotic tongue of yours," I said, then slammed my beer down hard on the wooden table.

And he laughed. He laughed at the very idea that I'd been involved! The fucker.

For a few moments there was silence. I wanted to smash my glass against his fat fucking face. But even slightly inebriated, I sensed that wasn't wise.

The middle-aged man at the next table grumbled that whoever had been responsible for it had caused quite a bit of trouble.

"How do you mean?" I asked.

Now the other patron glared at me. "Where have you been hiding, that you haven't heard this! They're killing people in retaliation! They're reading the names on the radio every day! How have you not heard?"

Peter leaned back and guffawed heartily. "He knows all about it. He organized the whole thing!" (I don't know what offended me more, the fact that he was being such a loudmouthed ass, or the fact that he thought it so absurd that I might actually be involved!)

Oh, I was furious! How I wanted to shut him up—to smash him! I could imagine the blood; I nearly broke my glass with my clenched hand just thinking about it. But it would have caused more harm than good, and brought far more attention than peace of mind. So I stormed out of the tavern, still steaming.

Across the town square I went, my dark mood impervious to the bright sun on the white buildings. It hardly seemed fair that such a pleasant day should be ruined by all this stupidity. And to be blamed for it, and endangered by it—this was most unfair!! After I'd argued against it, to be blamed for it!! It wasn't right.

Across the square, I dipped in to another tavern and persuaded the reluctant proprietor to turn on the radio, and I had a few more beers and sat alone staring into my glass, and on the radio there were bulletins and advisories and a relentless list of the dead.

Someone had to put a stop to it! (What spirit was this that told me that? Was it me or not me?) I realized that this was why I was here, and that this was how things were supposed to be.

I think that's when I sent the letter to the police.

On the way out of town I picked up a newspaper, a couple bottles of wine, some bread and cheese, a few apples, and some tobacco and rolling papers. I walked south down the bright empty road, past the glorious yellow rapeseed fields and back towards the dark looming pines.

<u>5 May, 1946 (Later)</u>

I looked over what I wrote earlier and felt compelled to add something.

Knowing who I was and what I'd just done made for the most unbearable torture imaginable. It was—at the time, it was!!—the loneliest feeling I'd ever felt, being alone in the woods with an ache in my chest that food and wine and cigarettes could not sate.

I woke up that night to thunder and lightning, followed shortly by rain so heavy I thought it would strip the needles from the pines. And amidst the chaos and confusion, I realized: God is mad at me.

I wondered if I was going to die, and if I deserved to.

6 May, 1946

Another harsh May day.

The sun has been coming out, which makes for misery in here: the world is blossoming again, and we can only enjoy it during our short hours on the yard. Otherwise, it's torture to see! Going outside — how rarely do we appreciate such things! What wouldn't I give to be back in that forest now!!

I've been tossing and turning at night, staring at the ceiling, bored and frustrated, tired of body but with a mind so energetic it seems it might leap out of my weary skull. My mind is an out-of-control motor, and I've no way to cut the electrical power!

It occurred to me last night how I used to deal with this problem. And…well, I did what I could about it. (Best not to write it down!)

7 May, 1946

After the thunderstorm, I tried staying in the forest for a few days, but it just didn't work. I'd either forgotten, or gotten too lazy to apply, everything the SOE instructors had taught us about surviving in the field. My bread was soggy; the cheese I'd opened, slimy; the rolling papers and newspaper toilet paper, a pulpy mass; the tobacco, a series of damp clumps that stained the bottom of my knapsack. Only the apples and the wine were impervious to the rain.

It made for a strange drunk, sitting under the dripping pines, their dead needles like a sponge on the forest floor, re-soaking my trousers every time I sat. It was a hungry, angry drunk, and the two bottles of wine were only partially successful at allowing me to forget that I was hiding from a world that had been made inhospitable to me through no fault of my own. Misery, misery, misery!!! I did not think there could be a day worse than that one—how little I knew what waited!!!

I was so depressed that I thought about ambushing a train. (So to speak!) I would jump from behind a pine and onto the tracks in a sudden surprise attack—oh, I imagined it all! The shock on the engineer's face and the smile on mine; the metal-on-metal braking screech, too late; the brief but unimaginable shock and pain I would have to endure. How long would it last—a second, two seconds? Too long. (Yes—I thought about it then, too!!)

Truth be told, I was afraid. My heart raced at these thoughts; I prayed to the Almighty Lord that I would not do it, that I would just stay there passively the next time I heard a train whistle in the distance.

Also, I knew mother would find out, and I couldn't bear the thought of that.

Had I known what was to come, I might have done it, all the same.

Instead, I toughed it out for another night, a hot damp sticky night of tortured half-sleep. (Hell has to be humid!! They always talk about the flames, but it wouldn't be hell if it wasn't somehow humid, too.)

I knew I had to get out of there. I did not know where I had to go, but I knew I had to get out of there.

When I finally gave up on sleep, I walked home and drew a bath and explained to mother that I was going to go back to Prag for a bit. She asked if that was going to be dangerous for me. I told her no, and that at any rate I wasn't afraid. After my bath, I put on a change of clothes—blessedly dry, pleasant clothes! We chatted, and I wolfed down some food, and we talked more, and it started getting late, so I spent the night.

The next morning I almost changed my mind—but on the radio they were talking about Liditz, and that sealed it—I had to put a stop to all of this! So I walked down the long flat road to Wittingau, heading out of the empty pine forests and past the bright silent fields.

In Wittingau I didn't linger long. This time I didn't run into anyone I knew, but still I couldn't escape the nagging feeling that even the strangers knew what I was going to do, that their eyes could see inside me and didn't like the view. So I stayed just long enough to have a couple drinks and read the newspapers. And nothing had changed, except that the things that seemed like they couldn't get worse had, in fact, gotten worse. There was talk of Liditz, and rumours that the Germans were literally going to decimate Prag, killing every tenth citizen until the perpetrators came forth.

It was clear that someone had to put a stop to it. And I was the only one who could.

11 May, 1946

A nun came by to see us late last night — or someone dressed as a nun, at least.

Given past conversations with Stefan, I am doubtful — I haven't seen anyone in religious garb in months, and I don't think I've ever seen this woman! And I did not notice her last night until she was at the cell door wishing us a good evening. (She said it in German; she said it as if there was a chance that the evening might be good!)

"Good evening?" I asked. "Why would it be, here?"

She said it could happen; she claimed she'd met people in here who were happier than many out in the real world.

"We are not those people," I told her.

She asked what the problem was, and I gave a short nod toward Frank: "Him."

Of course, Frank the busybody overheard me; he exclaimed loudly that everything was my fault, that I'd taken something of his.

"It was my idea to make it!" I told him, because it was.

"What was it?" she asked, sounding concerned. (Granted, it was hard to be sure, because it was the first time I'd heard that emotion in some time.) "The guards said you were fighting terribly."

It was only here that I remembered telling Stefan I'd be willing to talk to a nun. I realized I shouldn't tell her too much, for she was most likely an impostor—like the man they'd claimed was my solicitor, the last one that tried to get me to tell my story. "The…guards sent you?"

"Yes! You were fighting, yes? What was so important that you had to fight about it?"

"Does it matter what it was?" I asked at last.

Here she furrowed her brow and admitted that no, perhaps it didn't.

"Is there a priest around?" I asked. She asked if I'd prefer to speak to one, and I shrugged.

"They have been in, here and there, but the guards sometimes turn them back, if they can think of a good excuse. So when they do get permission, they tend to visit those about to be executed, those in most need of the sacraments. The harvest is plenty, but labourers are few." She added that she'd be happy to speak to me.

I shrugged. I did not want to say no. And, truth be told, even if she was another fake, an actress trying to gain my confidence and get me to talk about what I'd done, they had at least selected a relatively attractive woman for the role. (How long has it been since I've seen one?) She looked to be in her early forties, perhaps; there were wrinkles at the edges of her eyes, but enough light and warmth in them that I tended not to notice.

Frank withdrew—surprisingly respectfully, I thought—to the window and pretended not to listen. Still I knew it was an act on his part, so I whispered, and stuck to Czech so he couldn't listen in. "My cell mate is...intolerable," I told her.

"I'm sure you're both under quite a bit of pressure." (I could not tell whether she was more comfortable in Czech or German—she spoke both well, though. Clearly the guards who'd sent her wanted to set us both at ease!)

"It's easy for you to be sympathetic," I reminded her. "You don't have to live with him."

She simply responded that we all had our own crosses to bear. "I've had more than most people," I told her. "Anyway, I don't need this one right now."

She switched back to German—for Frank's benefit, presumably. "Another prisoner told me something recently that I rather liked. He said our crosses were attached to us—tied to our feet, perhaps. So when we don't pick them up, we end up dragging them, or simply being unable to move, which causes more pain and frustration than if we'd simply shouldered our burden." (I have to admit, this was a good lie; it made her sound credible.) She then asked if I had a Bible.

"No," I told her. She asked if I would like one. "I suppose it would give me something to read," I said. (I've never liked reading, but I like dealing with my cellmates even less, so it's becoming more palatable lately.)

As if by magic, she produced a Bible from beneath her habit. There was a slot in the door through which they slid our meal trays; she unlatched it and passed the book through.

Karl Frank stood and walked over at last. "I am to be executed soon. Can you send a priest? One who speaks German?"

She promised to see what she could do. Then she looked down the gallery, as if someone out of our sight was signalling her. She nodded in the direction of this unseen stranger. Then she turned back to us, said a simple good night, and left.

14 May, 1946

Frank and I had a somewhat decent conversation today, at last.

"Do you think she's real?" I said this aloud, out of the blue; I suppose I said it to Frank.

He gave an odd look and asked if I was talking about the nun; I replied, "Of course."

"Why do you ask?"

"It did seem like a strange visit," I said. "Altogether too convenient. I can't help but wonder if she is who she says she is."

"Who else would she be?"

"An impostor."

"Does it matter?" he shrugged. "Anyhow, we'll find out eventually."

"Or we won't. We're stuck here in our cells; we only see what they want us to see," I said.

Frank merely grunted, then added that he did, in fact, need to speak to a priest; he looked troubled, shrunken, hollow.

"I have to admit, I was surprised to hear you say that," I told him.

"Believe me, I was just as surprised to say it," he said. "I used to believe, but it's been some time."

"But you want absolution, just in case?"

"I don't know." He gave a crooked look. "Perhaps I just want to talk to someone that has to just sit there and listen."

And here I laughed—the first time I'd laughed in a while, it seemed.

Frank went on to say that all of this reminded him of a funny story that had circulated about Canaris.

"Canaris?" I asked, unsure if I'd ever heard the name.

"Well, about Canaris and a priest," he said, as if this explained everything. "Well, I shouldn't say funny. It was an interesting story. They said Canaris was a young lieutenant on an intelligence assignment abroad, and he'd been captured and was rotting in some dusty jail awaiting execution. And he'd requested a priest to come and hear his confession. And the priest came by, late at night, and Canaris killed him..."

"Killed him?" I repeated involuntarily; for all my depravity, this shocked me.

Frank hadn't listened, hadn't even paused in his story. Canaris had strangled the priest, he said, and put the priest's body in his prison clothes in his bed, and dressed up in the priest's robes, and simply walked out of the prison. And the guards just had not paid attention to the priest. Maybe they'd been lazy, maybe they'd been new and did not know him, maybe the priest was new. But they just hadn't paid attention—they saw a priest go in, and they saw a priest come out—and how many times, Frank asked, do you remember what someone looks like the first time you see them? Usually you don't, he said, and you usually only recognize them a second time because they are where you saw them the first time, doing the same thing, or wearing the same clothes. (Finally here he paused for breath. Good Lord, the man can talk!)

"Who's Canaris?" I asked at last.

"Who's Canaris?" (He sputtered.) "The head of the Abwehr."

I smiled and nodded.

"Germany's military intelligence service," Frank explained, mildly exasperated. "You might be interested to know that Canaris and Heydrich served together in Kiel, in the navy, in the 20s." (I wasn't particularly interested, which of course didn't stop him—but I did at least try to pay attention.) "Heydrich used to dine in Canaris's house as a young lieutenant, and listen to the old man's stories, and then after dinner he would play violin while Canaris's wife played cello. But later on, Canaris and Heydrich had a falling out. Canaris was no saint, but he pretended to be high-minded. He claimed the SS would lead Germany to ruin. And but for Canaris..." (Frank gave a gesture that somehow indicated everything, the city and the war and the last four years of our lives) "...but for Canaris, all of this would have been different."

"How do you mean?"

"The Abwehr was feeding information to the Czechoslovakian military intelligence service for almost the entire war—very valuable information!! And they in turn passed it all on to the British, who used it to defeat us."

"Why?"

Frank shrugged; he said Canaris was a mysterious man who did not leave fingerprints on many things. "We arrested an Abwehr man here in Prag, and he seemed like the usual spy, a drunk, a womanizer, betraying everything for money. That is the disheartening thing about such work, you see—at the end of the day it often boils down to money! A despicable thing to do, to betray one's people for money."

"Disgusting," I said.

"Still, there was speculation that it was more than that, that Canaris might have somehow been involved. It did not all make sense, though. There was never a clear picture of these things. All we ever knew for sure was that this Abwehr man had passed on a lot of information."

"What kind of information?"

"Given his position, we could only assume the worst, once we found out. But without that, who knows? We might have subdued London. We might have taken Moscow." (He gazed out the window, wistful.)

"I wanted to resettle in the East," I told him. "There was talk of resettlement programs, to colonize the East and make it ours. An army of farmers in the new breadbasket of the Reich. It seemed like a good place to start a new life."

"As a farmer?" Frank snorted.

"Why not?" I was a little indignant—angry again at his eternally condescending manner, at his willingness to disagree for the sake of disagreement, and his unwillingness to even let me be right on such a trifling matter. "It would be a nice change now, I'll tell you!"

I expected an argument. Instead he chuckled a little, at last, and allowed that it might be preferable to our present situation.

19 May, 1946

Outside in the courtyard we can hear workmen, carpenters clattering away with hammers and saws, a tremendous racket that seems all the louder because of what it represents.

They are building a special gallows for Frank.

It is a bare wooden plank structure, Austrian-style, with a central pole upon which to hoist the victim, and a staircase for the executioner to verify death—far different than the scaffolding they'd used on the mayor, which had looked like something out of an American cowboy film. They are building it in the corner of the courtyard, in the crook of two buildings. They are building it with a raised platform, shoulder-height. Evidently they are expecting another guilty verdict, and another crowd.

21 May, 1946

As promised, a priest came tonight.

I did not get to speak to him or look at him. He spoke at the cell door with Frank for a long time. I did not hear much of what they said, and—unlike Frank with me!—I tried not to listen. So I don't know if he confessed any sins, or if he asked for absolution, or if he got it. I only know that when they were done, Frank's eyes were moist with tears, and when he lay down, his bunk shook with sobs.

22 May, 1946

They executed Frank today.

It was the last day of his trial, the sentencing day. The guards passed our breakfasts through the slot in the door, and we ate silently—not quite the stony quiet we'd had before, but something simpler, a silence that was almost peaceful. I think we both knew the time for arguments had passed. And even if we had other things to talk about—what can one say in such situations? The emptiness can be more eloquent than you ever could—it alone is as big as death.

For his trial, Frank had been wearing the German Army private's uniform he'd been wearing when he was taken into custody. (I don't know—we never discussed it—whether it was his choice to wear it, or whether it had been given to him, for the sake of the show. For are not costumes an essential part of theatre? Anyhow, it was a sight—the once mighty man, whose SS uniform had been immaculate, gilded and ornate, draped with braids and dripping with medals, now an old man clad in plain humble garb. Maybe Frank wanted to send the message that he was a simple German following orders; maybe the Czechs wanted to send the message that he used to be somebody but was now a nobody, being sent to the gallows like a common criminal.)

At any rate, last night he scrubbed his uniform out on the floor, away from the smeared ruin of our old chessboard, using water from the sink and the meagre suds from our shrunken and cracked grey soap. On his hands and knees he scrubbed everything, then laboriously rinsed it all out, trousers and then blouse, before wringing it all out and hanging it to dry on a crude clothesline he'd made by sacrificing the hem on his bed sheet. ("I don't trust the prison laundry service," he said. "I want to at least meet my judge in clean clothes.")

And from then until he put it on and left this morning, it seemed Frank was doing his best to face the situation. I cannot say, "To face it well," for that implies nobility, and I did not see that. No, I just saw a tired old man who shuffled off, weary and resigned to his fate. It was hard to recognize in him the insufferable pride I'd seen so many years before, or the anger I'd faced during our time together; he did not just look older and in worse health; he looked greyed, defeated, haunted, shrivelled.

There was no need for a dress rehearsal; we had seen others do this too many times, out across the gallery. So when Frank shuffled off amidst his quartet of guards, it felt like the most natural thing in the world, as if I was not seeing something new but instead observing something that had always been—and yet there was the terrifying knowledge that it was, in fact, real; whatever the man's considerable faults, he'd be gone, unable to tell a story or make an argument or do anything else but stand in judgment before his Maker.

Outside I could see the scaffolding, and a reviewing stand of some sort for dignitaries. For some hours, there was little activity out there. But then spectators started filing in, gathering in clumps in the courtyard and trickling into the reviewing stand. I'd heard something from Stefan about survivors of Liditz being in attendance, but I think some of the observers were judges and prosecutors from the court. (Apparently justice is not blind!)

Before long, there must have been a couple thousand people in the courtyard, and I could barely see the platform and the gallows pole—a sad island in a sea of heads. There were photographers, too, snapping away—photographers and newsreel men!! And spotlights, though I don't know why. It seemed the only thing missing were vendors selling peanuts and candy, or perhaps a brass band.

It disgusts me, how they made such a spectacle of it. Still, I strained to see!! I stood on tiptoes and pressed my face against the barred window, unable and unwilling to look away.

Finally they marched him out. The low chatter of the vast crowd died down somewhat. There was at least some seriousness now, a hushed reverence. And ritual: the reading of the sentence, and jeers from the crowd, and then a statement, and I couldn't hear much, but I caught mention of Liditz. And then a priest said a prayer and gave a blessing—although whether he was blessing Frank or the proceedings, I couldn't tell.

The executioners manoeuvred Frank over to the pole, then tied his feet, then looped a thick belt of cloth under his arms. With that, they hoisted him to the top of the pole. (It was a strange way of hanging people, the Austrian style—ascension and death, with no resurrection.) The lead hangman then ascended the short staircase next to the pole, then placed the slender noose around Frank's head.

And then abruptly—even though I had seen it before, it took my breath away—he dropped, and his body lolled to the side.

I gasped and covered my mouth and turned away.

The hangman looked into Frank's eyes, and a doctor came up with a stethoscope to verify his death. And then—horror!! Frank's left arm rose halfway. It seemed he was trying to point at the executioner. There were gasps in the crowd, and then—at last—his arm went back down.

The hangman took the band of cloth from around Frank's chest. He hung there lifelessly, his head slumped forward as if terribly ashamed.

There was some scattered cheering and applause in the crowd.

Meanwhile I sat down, turned away from the spectacle at last, and stared at the opposite wall of my cell, empty. And it started, the same repetitive thought that's keeping me awake tonight, alone in my empty cell: This is how I am going to die.

25 May, 1946

I am depressed.

Picking up the pen, brushing my teeth, shaving: these seem like Herculean tasks. During the past few days I have been laying back down after the morning count and sleeping as long as possible. One would think a man facing death would try to stay awake. But no.

28 May, 1946

I am still slack.

After morning count I return to bed. Every morning. When I do get up, it isn't long before my body feels heavy and weary, like the force of gravity has been increased. I feel like I'm going to fall apart, like my skeleton will surrender at last and I'll collapse into a pile, a bag of bones and loose ligaments and toneless muscles.

29 May, 1946

The guards—especially Jan, the thug—have been prattling on and on about the elections the other day.

It occurs to me that Frank's trial was scheduled to culminate before the elections, to bolster the Communists by sending a message: the people are having their vengeance. If so, it worked: the Communists won 40 percent of the vote, more than any other party. Benesh is still president, but Gottwald—the biggest thug of them all—will be premier now. More importantly, the outsized win might give them the momentum to win an outright majority the next time around. They claim to have a million party members—a staggering number in a country the size of Czechoslovakia, and the largest membership any political party's ever had in this country's brief history, as the thug never tires of telling all who will listen, and all who won't.

Even Stefan now says their final victory is historically inevitable. (Historical laws, to them, are as relentless and implacable as physical laws; there are certain logical progressions, and certain foreseeable results, which are rapidly becoming unstoppable, like a boulder gathering speed as it rolls downhill.)

I read something from the New Testament yesterday, from the Bible the nun left, something I'd never seen. In Romans, Chapter 9, it talked about how God makes some vessels for noble purposes and some for ignoble ones. Surely they're talking about me.

What I did was historically inevitable—if I hadn't been me, someone else would have, sooner or later. They talk of history, but none of them remembers it properly!! No one remembers how it felt after Liditz—the pressure, not just of what had happened, but of what was to come. Such a hellish thing the future can be!! Terrifying in its immensity, its horrible possibilities, its relentless advance. Someone had to at least set it on a different course, before there was another Liditz, or two, or ten. And no one else stepped forward, so I had to! How many more would have died, had I waited?

So I came forward—which was how it had to be!! Jesus needed Judas, and Gabchik needed me, so the story could end and everyone could move on to other things.

31 May, 1946

The nun—if that is what she is—came back today.

My cell has a door, not bars, so when we talk I have to stand very close to it; I see her through the narrow rectangular window a section at a time—eyes but not mouth, then an ear and a slice of habit but not eyes, and so on.

"Is it a nice day outside?" I asked, and she nodded and said it was, and added: "God is good."

"Not to me. When I had my time in the courtyard yesterday, it was cold and raining. Today I'm stuck inside and it's sunny."

She suggested that perhaps I needed the rain. She didn't seem particularly mean-spirited, so I let the remark slide, although I did ask: "Why?" And she just shrugged and said that God knew what I needed better than I did.

"Well, I have a wife and children I need to take care of," I said—somewhat spitefully, I'll admit. "If God was good, if God knew or cared what I needed, I wouldn't be here. I'd be with them."

Here she changed course and tried to offer me some sympathy, at last. She said this was one of the biggest hardships about being in here, knowing that family and friends were still out there, still living life, and that one was powerless to be there with them

"Have you been in here?" I asked, to which she admitted that she hadn't. So I spoke again: "So you don't know how hard it is for us."

She said she had a sense of our hardships from talking to us—but she finally admitted that she didn't know herself.

"It's beyond hard," I said. "It's intolerable."

Here she mentioned something about some old Greek philosophers. They'd said—or so she claimed—that it wasn't situations themselves that were intolerable, it was our opinion of those situations.

"Well, they weren't in here either," I pointed out. "My situation is intolerable."

She claimed—on what grounds, I don't know—that she'd felt the same way about her own life, at times. But, she said—and this I found hard to believe—that it was truly her choice as to what opinion to take of things. For instance, she lived with several other nuns, and was often stuck inside with them, eating a lot of bad food. And there were times, she claimed, where she longed for the company of men...and it seemed like she was flirting with me!

This was absurd, and proof she couldn't be a nun; it had to be a trick concocted by the guards—all of it, even the supposed priest I'd seen talking to Frank! Still, I was willing to play along, so I said: "We should trade places, Sister!! We can both be happy!"

And here she blushed, harder than I've ever seen a human being blush. "You've gone red, Sister!" I said excitedly.

"Like the country," she said—hoping, perhaps, to change the subject.

"I am serious, though, Sister," I told her, enjoying this playacting. "We can trade places! Life would be better for us both!"

For a moment she seemed at a loss for words. Then, unexpectedly, she gave a small smile. "Most of my fellow nuns are some years older than I am."

"I am not picky at this point, Sister!" I said, which was, in all honesty, nearer to the truth than I'd like to admit.

"I simply meant we have to choose how to perceive things. We are all capable of making life unbearable, if we choose to. We all choose our own prisons."

This made me incredibly upset. "I did not choose this," I reminded her. "I did something that needed to be done, and I was the only one in a position to do it, and there were consequences I neither intended nor expected. So that's the only conclusion I can come to. God chose me for this, then turned his back on me! God wants me to be miserable!"

"How can you say that?" she asked, feigning shock.

"Does it not say in the Bible that there are some vessels made for noble purposes and some for ignoble purposes?" I asked.

She furrowed her brow and asked where it said that. She had no clue! About the Bible, she had no clue! It makes no sense—unless, of course, she's a fraud, in which case it makes perfect sense. "In Romans, Chapter 9," I told her. "There's also something similar in the Second Letter to Timothy."

She pondered this as if searching for a suitable answer, and even looked away from me and down the gallery—which was, I supposed, the general direction from which her puppet master was pulling her strings. "I should know by now not to question prisoners on matters of Scripture," she said at last.

"Why not?" I asked, perplexed.

She gave a slight smile. "No religious person, whether nun or priest or cardinal, has as much time to study the Bible as the average prisoner."

A clever answer. "Or the same need to look for loopholes," I said with a smile. "So what do you say, then? God is all-powerful, yes?" And she said yes, that she supposed so. "So does that not mean," I continued, "that God wants me to be miserable? I mean, if God knows everything, and God is all-powerful, and I am miserable, then what other conclusion could one come to?"

And here, she claimed it was not always our choice what happened to us, but—and this I find I really have a hard time believing, given current circumstances—we choose how much to suffer. She claimed that if we embraced our suffering and picked up our cross every day, we actually suffered less than if we ran from it.

"How is that a choice at all, then?" I asked, more upset now—clearly she was being sent here just to antagonize me! "If we cannot even choose our crosses, then we are actors reading lines that are already written, heading towards an end that's already been decided. Then it is true what the Communists say, that it is all historically inevitable."

She did not have an answer, and I was not sure I wanted to talk more anyhow, so I lay back down, and she went on her way.

At first I was glad that I'd won the argument, but now—strangely enough—I'm worrying that I've driven her off.

2 June, 1946

Still I have no cell mate.

They have also taken to closing the slit in the door for much of the day.

On the plus side, I can masturbate without consequence.

On the minus side, I am depressed most of the day. Pleasuring myself can only take up so much time. And my fantasies are more disturbing now—I dare not even write them down! I thought my past cellmates were excruciating, but at least I had people I could respond to, people I could react to, if only by avoiding. Now there are stretches where I find myself wondering if the world has ended, or if everyone has gone away and left me stranded—perhaps the

Rapture came, and I've been left behind! I know these thoughts are absurd, but I think them anyway.

This is hell. Being so alone.

I am starting to question my own sanity. No, I have always questioned it. Perhaps I am starting to know the answer.

There are things happening that cannot be true, but my rational mind is not functioning any more, and I perceive them as true. Am I remembering it all correctly? Did I share a cell with Frank, really? Did we say everything I think we said? Looking back on those pages, my recollections seem detailed and real, but my memories are starting to blur together with my dreams and my imagination. And some things — I can admit it now — I wrote days and weeks after the date I put on the page. And other things I've written and thrown away. I suppose it's been a project, something to pass the time in here. Perhaps I am writing what I wished I'd written. Perhaps I am writing about the conversations I wished we'd had. Or about what I wish had happened. Obviously he's no longer here to correct the record.

There are times when it feels like the walls themselves are moving, pulsing in and out. I know this cannot be true, but I perceive it as true.

There are times I hear people whispering out on the gallery, just out of sight. There are times I hear people talking on the other side of the walls — often at night, when it seems no one should be awake. I did not notice this before, and I did not think it was possible to hear through the thick walls, the heavy doors, but it might be true.

There are times it sounds as if the walls themselves are talking. I know this cannot be true, but I perceive it as true.

I have been conducting mental exercises, to try and retain a little sanity. Trying to figure out events from my childhood and their exact sequence, based on what came before and what came after. Trying to recall jazz songs, and the plots of cowboy novels from America that I read in England.

I caught myself talking to the walls, the other day.

I was bored and I caught myself talking to the walls. So I took a nub of charcoal and drew a stick man next to the door, where the guards cannot see it unless they come in the cell. I have not yet given him a name. Or is it a her? No, it must be a him! No woman could stay silent so long!!

The stick figure's useful. I need someone else to tell my stories to, besides my meagre and incomplete journal, and telling them to him somehow feels more normal than talking to a blank wall.

Some of my stories I have never told and will never write down. Others I have told so many times that at some point the story became more real to me than the truth.

Does this retelling distort the stories? Is there a truth beyond them? If no one else remembers as well as I do, are my stories the truest truth? Do I need to retell them and change them—to strip away the unnecessary parts—to keep them alive? The past does not exist any more, though we bear its scars—is there any other way to preserve it besides stories? The scars are meaningless wrinkles of flesh on their own; they change shape and fade.

Or perhaps the past is like dead wood—retaining the shape, but not the function, of something that was alive. And stories are the fire that brings it back to life—a fleeting life, a transformed life, altogether different than what came before, but still not dead. But is the past better off dead? Certainly it burns us as completely as any fire. For what are prisoners, if not men constantly being burned by their past?

7 June, 1946

There's still no sign of the nun.

I have been reading in the Gospels about the blind man who was healed by Jesus. When the Pharisees asked him if Jesus was a sinner, he simply said that he did not know, that he only knew that once he was blind, but now he could see.

Is that what faith means? To know things as certainly as if one had seen them? Certainly there would be no need to discuss theology with someone whose eyesight had been restored—what argument could be stronger than a miracle? For what use are logic and reason if they contradict one's experience, and the emotions and feelings that flow from it? And yet, Christ does not always make faith so easy; later, he tells Thomas: Blessed are they who do not see but still believe!

I believe the guards are reading this.

They are reading it while I am outside for the slender hour I get every week. Surely that is just a ruse, to allow them to read what I've written. Why else would they give me time outside? Me, whom they so clearly despise?

I must be careful what I set down here.

11 June, 1946

The supposed nun—Sister Ignatia, she says her name is—finally came back today.

"You've been avoiding me," I told her.

When she asked why she would do that, I just shrugged. "Why wouldn't you? I'm full of doubts, I question your way of life. I am a wicked and sinful man, Sister!"

She responded far more blandly than I'd have imagined; she simply said that we all doubt, from time to time.

"And you still believe?" I asked.

"I've seen God work in my life." (She said this simply, as if she did, in fact, have complete faith.) "It is like the blind man who was healed, and went to the Pharisees..."

Here I got chills on the back of my arms. "What made you bring that up?" I asked, wondering how she'd known what I'd been reading.

She seemed perplexed, and said she'd only mentioned it because that particular passage was one of her favourites. After all, she said, this work—presumably meaning the prison, the prisoners, everything—kept opening her eyes to what happens when we turn away from God. And she claimed it was something she'd seen in her life, too; she said she could relate to everyone she met here.

"How can you relate to them? You're a nun. These men are murderers."

She said she'd met a murderer when she was new to this. She claimed—and this I found tremendously hard to believe!!!—that she did not ask people what they had done, or what they were accused of. But he'd told her. And he'd been miserable; he'd said he had not bathed or groomed himself in six months. There were dark patches on his face, blotches of mould or mildew. And part of her brain had screamed—literally screamed at her!—saying: You are talking to a murderer! You are talking to a murderer! And she didn't know what to say.

"But you did say something," I pressed her, somewhat curious now.

"Yes. In Christ we are made new."

"Hmm." For once I did not have a response. She went on to say it made her realize that such a crime often takes two lives—for this murderer had felt so cut off from God that he did not feel alive, and could not even take care of himself on the most basic levels.

"I've felt that way," I admitted. "I don't know if I'm cut off from God, or just depressed."

"Perhaps they are the same thing."

"Perhaps," I mused.

She told me she'd done some thinking after our talk, for she had not known what to say. But she'd had a dream in which an ant was crawling up her arm. And the next day that image would not leave her head. And she claimed that something in her head—but not her—said: The ant is moving, but you are still.

"So?" I asked, quite clueless as to where she was going with all this.

She said it was about our relationship with God—how we are moving, but God is still, and we are walking through time, but God is eternal, so it isn't 1946 for God—it is somehow 1946 and 2046 and 2046 B.C. all at once, and a thousand years are as a single day, and whatever direction the ant went, God could place a finger in front of him...

"...or crush him," I interjected.

"God is not looking to crush you, Mr. Churda!" she exclaimed. "This is all for your benefit!"

I breathed.

"I have felt far from God lately," I said again, and—quite surprisingly!—tears welled up in my eyes. I could not even describe the feeling as good or bad; it was simply overwhelming emotion. "I've been...afraid."

She grew excited and passionate—full of some great charisma! "It does not matter what you fear. For God can put whatever we need in front of us. God is like a person with an ant, but a benevolent person, moving fingers and limbs to keep the ant from falling, or to remove obstacles the ant cannot see. Or better yet, God is like the author flipping through the pages of a manuscript, always revising, always editing. God knows what we need and when we need it, and God is not bound by time, so if we make a wrong turn, God can still flip back to the earlier chapters and change things to put what we need in front of us, and we won't even know it's happening. God can keep whispering to us to go one way or another. And we may not listen, we may not always do our part, but God continually gives us other chances, for God can go back and whisper in other peoples' ears, too—God still finds the hearing ear and the seeing eye!!!"

"What happened to the murderer?" I asked at last.

She admitted humbly that she didn't know. They'd moved him; she'd never seen him again. "Perhaps he started bathing again and reading his Bible. Perhaps I was the one being taught the lesson. I have to choose how to interpret these things."

"How," I asked, "can one interpret things as anything other than what they are?"

I think her main argument was about the difference between facts and the meaning we give them. One of her fellow nuns, for instance, had gone on a mission to India. And rather than having Father, Son, and Holy Ghost, in their three main Gods they have a creator, an embodier, and a destroyer. And she said her order, the Jesuits, had been unexpectedly successful in China, partly because they wore black, and there, black and white mean the opposite of what they mean here. (Here, of course, we associate white with life and purity, while black is the colour of corruption and filth and death. But to them, black is the colour of the fertile soil, and white is the colour of bones.)

"So we cannot know right from wrong?" I asked, confused now.

"No," she said. "Our Lord said 'Offer no resistance to evil,' not 'There is no such thing as evil.'"

"So what are you saying?"

After thinking it over, she said that perhaps the whole point was to be suspicious of dualities. "After all, how can one tell light from darkness when the darkness calls itself light?" she asked. "On my own, I can convince myself that bad is good, that wrong is right, that top is bottom. One needs a third point of reference, an understanding of what black and white mean in any given situation…"

"An understanding of the spirit," I suggested.

"Yes! An understanding of the spirit!" she exclaimed excitedly; I'd not thought it was possible for me to bring joy to another person and to myself, but here it was!

Or so it seemed.

Then she said: "Thank you, Mr. Churda! I learned something new today!"

The guards came by, and she had to leave, but I felt well. And it only occurred to me later that I'd never actually told her my name.

So obviously — despite her protestations to the contrary — she's paying attention to who I am and why I'm here.

So why is she here? What spirit animates her? It seems my initial suspicions were correct — they sent her to get me talking. I'd started to believe that she might actually be who she said she was — and I suppose I'll keep treating her that way, for the sake of convenience — but I must keep my defences up.

<u>14 June, 1946</u>

They moved Gerik in here the other day.

I don't know why he's here. Or rather, I know exactly why, but I don't understand. He was a parachutist, like me; he worked for the Germans, like me; we're charged with the same basic offences, various violations against President Benesh's Great Decree, offences against the national honour and things of that sort. But he doesn't have any particular affinity for the German race or people. He was probably just afraid, plain and simple. He says he had other reasons, but I suspect he's just not willing to admit to his fear. Which makes sense, I suppose. I don't think I'd admit to that, either.

Why does anyone do what they do? People give reasons that are publicly acceptable, but there's usually a darker motive, hiding — still, it's easy to find if you look!!! Gretchen claimed to love my wit and sense of humour, but she loved my money, and she left when it was gone. (She claimed differently, in her note, but nothing else was grounds for leaving! She put up with my misbehaviour until the money was almost gone — and then she took the last of it!!) Sister Ignatia claims she's visiting because of the Gospels, but she is obviously angling for information, trying to get me to reveal things — and she knew my name before I told her, after all! Stefan, too, claims good motives, but he's keeping his distance of late; I'm sure he's afraid of what the other guards think. And the prosecutors claim to be prosecuting me because my actions were treasonous, but they just want the attention!!! I did what any of my countrymen would have done in my shoes. Try getting them to admit to it, though!!

(I still do not understand how they sit in judgment — and on behalf of the people! Absurd! I at least had the courage to switch sides, while most others helped the Germans and later claimed to have offered resistance. Ha! What little resistance they offered was more in the mould of the Good Soldier Schweik, a passive, almost feminine behaviour; a feigned compliance that lacked either the courage of true resistance or the courage of a change of heart. The behaviour of the average Czech under the average occupation is far more cowardly than either; it does not so much drive off foreign masters as annoy them to the point of distraction and frustration. It is nothing more than a steady slow drip of feigned idiocy; it sort of works, but it does not look good in the history books!)

Now that I think about it, the fact that I went one fateful step ahead of the crowd makes me useful to the prosecutors—I am a good person for the people to look down upon! I talked to the Germans, whereas most people just silently went along. I worked for the Gestapo, while they merely worked for the German—and Czech!!—industrialists who were busy turning our country into one of the Reich's biggest armaments factories. I stepped forward, alone, while they stood amidst large crowds, trembling in fear, but safe in public anonymity.

I am remembering the rally they staged, not two weeks after the assassination and the gun battle in the church. It was planned as a way for the people of Prag to come out and show their support for German rule, thereby atoning for the troublemakers they'd evidently sheltered. And the people of Prag showed up in droves!! (Those same people will no doubt now claim that they'd supported the resistance in private, that they'd hidden weapons for some man whom they only knew by a code name, or that they'd passed information between two other men—also conveniently anonymous—or perhaps even that they'd sheltered one of the parachutists! "Perhaps it was this Gabchik fellow himself, although we never knew his name, of course!"—that's what they'll say!!) They surely will not tell you how they filled Wenceslas Square in droves, a slanting mass of people hundreds of thousands strong, spilling from the National Museum and spreading off down the side streets like a stain. And while they watched, Emanuel Moravetz spoke from the podium about the true and eternal bonds of friendship and amity between the Czech people and the German people. And did the crowd grow irate? Did they surge to the stage to tear him limb from limb? Did they even boo or hiss or jeer from the safety of the crowd? No!! They applauded the German mouthpiece; they cheered him as he announced their continued enslavement!! He denounced the cowardice of the exiled government, Benesh and his illegitimate cronies stirring up trouble from abroad while the people suffered the consequences; he denounced their democratically elected leaders, and they cheered!! I cheered too, but at least I'd made a commitment to my choice—whereas they cheered from the crowd, knowing no one would ever call them to task for their fickle nature! I saved them from more Liditzes, and under their breath, they thanked me—but now they're calling for my blood!

It reminds me of the people of Jerusalem laying their palm fronds in front of Jesus as he rode into town on a donkey, then screaming for Pontius Pilate to free Barabbas a week later!! How many people were in both crowds?

I saved them. Why are they not grateful?

18 June, 1946

An anniversary I don't care to remember. Four years now in this new life—or, perhaps, four years since I knew there was no going back.

Gerik tried to bring it up, but I didn't want to talk about it. Is he working for them now, too? Did they offer him a deal—get the rest of my story, and testify against me, in exchange for clemency? Probably.

I did talk to him about the Czechs and their servility, and their shame about being occupied, and how they were trying to use me as a scapegoat for all of that. He simply asked if it was hard for me to admit I was wrong. Wrong about what, I don't even know—he obviously didn't understand my point, and I eventually grew tired of explaining. He always was a little slow in the head.

On the plus side, the other day he showed me something most useful—a small broken section of mirror which he'd ground into an oval and crudely mounted on a ruler. The mirror was affixed at such an angle that one could stick the device through the slot in the door and use it as a sideways periscope to see if anyone was coming. (I'd seen such devices in the hands of other prisoners, but hadn't had the materials or the patience to construct one myself; besides, the guards would never let me alone with such contraband!)

29 June, 1946

Again I am not sleeping well.

I was in court for a preliminary hearing of some sort. I found myself looking up to the giant coat-of-arms behind the dais. Lions and eagles—absurd!! Again, has there ever been a worse case of wishful thinking? As if anyone in this country has the soul of a lion!!

And then I remembered I'd been there before.

It was back in 1942. When was it? September, perhaps? The Germans had a trial (People forget—the Germans had trials!!) for everyone involved in the plot against Heydrich. The Orthodox bishop and priests and lay people were up front, and behind them, various civilians. That young girl that Kubish had knocked up was there, visibly pregnant by then. And young Ata Moravetz, once a brash hothead, now bitter and broken and distant. Everyone was there—everyone who had not reached for their cyanide quickly enough when the Gestapo came around.

I will admit, it was not a pleasant experience, seeing all of them; I remember them staring at me, while I did my best to look away. And it is not a pleasant experience remembering it—but I suppose I should write about it anyhow. Either way it will be on my mind.

But I refuse to feel too badly for them! They knew what they were getting in to, after all!! And they could have changed their minds even then. I know because I was not the only one who did so!!

A fellow named Ladislav Vanek—known to us as Jindra—was there, too, as a witness for the prosecution. He had been in charge of virtually the whole network of people we'd come into contact with. I don't know when he'd come over. I heard he gave up a lot of people, far more than I had—everyone he knew who had sheltered a parachutist or carried a message.

I wanted to find out why—or even just talk to him and reminisce—but I didn't get a chance. When we bumped into each other outside the giant red-and-white court building back on that September day in 1942, he shot me a dirty look and walked away. As if he was fit to pass judgment on me!

Oh, yes—I now know the date of my trial, which is to say, the date of my death. April 29th, 1947. Ten months off, still—so for now I can let myself go with the venial sins, the masturbation, the petty quarrels with my cell mate, and then confess it all the night before the trial. They are still executing people within two hours of sentencing, which is good, in a way—if I go to confession the night before, then hold my tongue (and not my cock!) for a few hours, all should be well.

<u>2 July, 1946</u>

Sister Ignatia—if that is her real name—came back.

"I am going to be executed," I told her. She asked when, and I said: "Soon."

She looked at me sceptically. Had they already told her the truth? Probably, assuming she's one of them. "Early next year," I admitted.

"Are you afraid?" she asked.

"I'm actually looking forward to it," I told her—which is more or less true, though I suspect my feelings may change as the day approaches. "After all, what do I have to live for? And besides, the others already faced it, so whatever else they did, whatever their wrongs, people can say they're heroes and no one can question it. But I didn't face it, so whatever else I did, people can call me a coward—and I can't question it! But after that..." And here she tried to interrupt me—whether to denigrate my logic or try and dissuade me, I don't know.

But I stopped her in her tracks with a question: "Tell me, what is braver? To walk up the gallows, or to fight, to struggle, kicking and screaming until the bitter end?"

She reminded me of Jesus' admonition to offer no resistance to evil.

"They are evil, aren't they?" I replied. (Gerik was on his bunk, asleep, but I'd been holding his mirror device; I stuck it out the gap in the window of the cell door and swept it both ways, to see if any of the guards were watching us.)

She asked what I was doing. "Don't worry about it," I said as I snapped the mirror back inside. She then asked why I'd call the Czechs evil, and I grew excitable. "You basically just said they were, yourself! When you said not to resist them!" But she said she'd simply mentioned the verse as a reminder to be peaceful, and not as a judgment against the Czechs.

"They are evil, though," I said. "They pretend not to be, but they pretend well. I was arrested right after an anti-German riot—Czechs beating and killing German-speaking civilians, simply for their ethnicity. There was that massacre at Usti. And the ongoing expulsions—Germans being forced to wear white armbands, being beaten, deported, losing their homes…"

"It is strange," she observed. "Everyone who fought the Germans became like them in some way. The British, who were bombed, ended up bombing; the Soviets, who were pillaged, ended up pillaging. Here in Czechoslovakia, President Benesh is talking about a Final Solution to the German problem, and they're putting armbands on them and shipping them off on railroad cars. And meanwhile the country is being taken over by thugs who have won 40 percent of the vote…"

"How can you not resist that, Sister?" I exclaimed. "If you were in here, being beaten by their thugs, would you turn the other cheek?"

"I don't know if I could. But Our Lord could. That's the example we have to live up to. And resistance allows evil to pretend it's good. When you're locked in struggle, it becomes easier for your opponents to claim they are justly responding to provocations—and harder for observers to judge the truth."

"Still, surely there are cases where the evil is so great, and truth so apparent, that one must fight," I said.

But she pointed out that the Germans thought they were resisting evil. For they were angry, she said; they blamed their troubles on the Jews, on Bolshevism…

"The Germans had every right to be angry!" I felt the words tumbling forth unbidden; I felt I could not stop them even if I wanted to. "It is incredible, how unjust it all has been! The Poles were a military dictatorship. They killed fifty thousand ethnic Germans at the outset of the war. Does anyone remember that? No! Does anyone even look at how much blood is on Allied hands? No! I remember listening to Goebbels, on the radio. He spoke eloquently about Allied hypocrisy and self-righteousness and selective memory. He said, 'How little they speak of Stalin's victims, now that Stalin's on their side.'"

To this, she unexpectedly mentioned that there were German Jews here in Prag, before the war. (Here she was quiet but forceful. Was she angry? Was this her ploy all along—to hide her true feelings until after I revealed mine?) And now, she said, there were none, except those who hid so they wouldn't be shipped off to Terezinstadt. She asked me if Goebbels ever spoke of them, other than to say they deserved whatever came to them.

"What of it?" I asked.

But to her it was a major concern; she claimed there were millions of Jews killed, not just here but all across occupied Europe. She said some were calling it a Holocaust, as if such a level of human sacrifice was somehow necessary, as if God was the hungry angry God of the Old Testament, a God who always required sacrifices. But, she claimed, the Jews themselves had a different word, a word that simply meant disaster.

"I did not know anything about that," I said.

She said I must have noticed something. She talked about the people one used to see in Prag wearing yellow stars, and how they'd gradually disappeared. Had I not noticed that they were disappearing, she asked? (Was she being sarcastic? I couldn't tell.) I think she said we shouldn't get hung up on the suffering of people who looked like us and spoke like us, for there were many who died in great numbers. She talked about Poles and Gypsies, about whole families perishing after Heydrich…

"I wanted to put a stop to that! I didn't want that to happen to anyone!" I wanted to stop talking—I knew she was goading me into talking, so she could tell the guards—and yet I could not contain my own words! "I went to the Germans to get them to stop it, and they beat me! And I fell back into Czech hands and they beat me! And now, for saving people's lives, I'm being executed!"

She pointed out that I was not the only one who suffered injustice in the war.

I couldn't think of a good response.

"You know, I was starting to think you were German," I told her at last. "You speak the language so well, you've shown such sympathy for them."

"Are they not God's children, too?" (She asked this simply; it sent chills down my spine.) "If what Jesus said was true, and we are all brothers and sisters with one Father, then how could any death be weighted higher or lower in God's eyes? If you are a parent, you love all of your children, even the ones who have disappointed you. And if you love all of your children, then every death is a tragedy."

"Even the guilty?"

"Especially the guilty. For how many of them die without knowing God's love?"

Here I felt something welling in my heart, like a bubble. I had so much I wanted to blurt out! But there would be no going back. So I changed the subject. "Does it bother you that God's called Father?"

She asked why it should, and I said: "You are a woman."

"Thank you for reminding me. I'd forgotten."

I sensed something here—some sarcasm, perhaps—but I pressed on: "Doesn't that make you feel like less of a child of God? Like He can't relate to you, if He is male and you have to call Him Father?"

"It is our language that's limited, not God."

"Jesus was a man," I pointed out.

"Jesus had to be one or the other. We'd have a hard time relating to a Saviour that was neither male nor female..."

"Why not a woman, then?"

"I asked my Mother Superior the same thing once. It was the only time I ever saw her smile. She said that if a woman had come down and told us all to be nice to one another, no one would have noticed. Women usually figure these things out on our own. It's the men that need to be led in the right direction."

I chuckled a little; she pressed on. "And it was necessary for God to come down in human form. If not, it would be too easy for us to believe in God and yet be mad at God—to say God doesn't understand suffering, to say God doesn't know what it's like down here, doesn't know what it's like to be hungry or hurt or upset or aroused..."

"Aroused?"

"Why not?" she asked. "It is part of being human, is it not?"

"The Church doesn't seem to think so."

"The Church spends the bulk of its time talking about other things."

"The Church spends the bulk of its time on things it shouldn't care about! Look at all the wars, the politics! The Crusades, the Holy Roman Empire, burning Jan Hus at the stake..."

She smiled thinly and asked if I was a Czech patriot now. I couldn't think of a good rejoinder, so she kept on; she claimed that these things were tremendously regrettable, but rare; she said she focused on the good, and others focused on other things...

"Burnings at the stake? Holy wars? Can you blame anyone for focusing on these things?"

"Not particularly," she said, and added that the bad was always louder than the good.

"How do you mean?" I asked, and she simply said it again: the bad was louder than the good. And I must have seemed curious, for she elaborated—when things went the way they were supposed to, nobody cared. People being born, getting married, having children, growing old, dying a natural death—these things were not news. The Church visiting prisoners, feeding the needy, giving comfort to the sick—this was not news. But wars, famines, murders, betrayals—these were the loud things, the things people wanted to know about.

I could tell she wanted to know about me, about what I'd done; she could hardly contain herself! But I just said: "The bad certainly seems more powerful."

To this, she claimed that it was not more powerful, which was why it needed to be loud—to call attention to itself. And—I did not quite follow her logic here—she said it was our attention to it, and our resistance, that made it stronger. But I didn't say anything. My bladder was filling up, my mind was elsewhere, and I didn't want to give her an excuse to keep talking. Still, she kept going—she was worse than Frank!! She claimed she didn't want to talk about bad news, but good news—repentance and forgiveness and new life.

Again the bubble grew in my chest; despite the pain in my bladder, I found myself speaking without thinking: "I do have much to confess. I fear I cannot even face it all."

And she suggested, simply, that I write it all down.

This stopped me short—here it was again! After all the religious talk, this—this is what she's wanted all along! She wants me to tell my story! Otherwise, why would she have known about me, why would she have known my name? Surely they recruited to betray me, to listen to my story and testify against me!!! Still, I didn't confront her. I simply said, "I have been writing."

And she nodded towards my half-hidden stack of papers and admitted that she'd noticed. She already knew I was writing! So my initial suspicions were correct! (After all, what is more likely — that her favourite story just happened to be one I'd just written about, or that they were spying on me? Which leaves me wondering, of course, whether I should leave these musings in here for them to read — but it is better for them to know that I know. Guards, whoever is reading this — I know you are reading!!! I will not write down anything I don't want you to know!!!)

Of course I didn't tell her I'm on to them. I didn't say anything — and again she looked down the hallway, as if looking for guidance! Again I produced Gerik's mirror device and held it out — and I saw Stefan, just out of range down the gallery, motioning to her! She asked what was the matter, and I just said: "I am afraid to write it all down."

"It might give you peace of mind," she suggested.

"What am I supposed to do? Tell them everything, so they can use it to execute me?" My chest grew heavy and tight again. "If I walk to the gallows without so much as a word of resistance, will I have peace of mind? If I face what I avoided during the war? Is that what it will take?"

"Dying isn't the only thing that takes courage. Living well, living differently, takes courage — sometimes more than dying." (Here she touched my hand, gently. I am ashamed by the physical response it produced! It has been so long since a woman has touched me tenderly.)

"I am troubled. I need to speak to a priest." I hung my hands on the hole in the door and looked off, downcast, feeling guilty (about physical reactions I dare not describe) and confused — why was she so tender, all of the sudden? I wanted to grab the mirror device and see if Stefan was still nearby — but I did not want to disrupt things.

She withdrew her hand and said she'd see about a priest.

7 July, 1946

I'm reviewing what I wrote the other day.

I wonder if I want to confess. I told her I did; still, somewhere in the dark recesses of my mind is another thought that will not leave.

Some time ago I gave up hope of escape—there are cells on either side of me, and although I am on the first floor, the guards keep a close enough watch that tunnelling through the floor or escaping through the window would be impossible. The window is barred by a wrought-iron grille whose bolts are anchored in the outside wall, quite out of reach, and even if I somehow made it into the courtyard, I would still have to scale the outer wall. The cell floor is solid cement of indeterminate thickness, and I don't even know what lies beneath—it could be solid rock, which would be frustrating; it could even be basement offices for the guards. (I do not think this is likely, mind you, but it's the scenario I always imagine—scraping through the cement floor with a succession of spoons, feeling a momentary sense of triumph after months of concealed effort as the last bit of cement crumbles away, then—despair! Staring through the hole in the floor at some senior guard, or the warden, even, then falling through the floor in a rain of crumbled cement and landing on their desk.)

But if I could do what that Canaris fellow did…kill a priest, and escape in his clothing…

It is a dark and evil thought. Even I know as much, and I don't always recognize such things. (My thinking is so confused! For it occurs to me that if this plot were to succeed, its very success would prove that he was, in fact, a priest, and that the nun was actually a nun; if they were just actors posing to gain my confidence, surely they would have guards waiting to rescue them!) I burn with shame and embarrassment just having these thoughts, and I must be insane to be writing them down. Of course I can tell no one—especially not a priest, ha ha!! What would they think of me? And yet, I am still writing, even though I know the guards are reading—so do I want them to know what I'm plotting, so they'll stop me? (Guards, stop me!! If you are reading this, stop me!!!) Or is it too late? If I already have this desire in my heart, is the damage already done? Is the sin as good as committed? The Bible suggests it is so!!!

I am rambling. I am not quite sane. Or it is late, and I am tired, and I am having a hard time sorting through my thoughts and desires and determining what is real.

I only know this dark fantasy will not die. It has taken up residence in the dungeons of my mind. And I have tried to keep it chained there, but I have been feeding it, too, scraps of angry leftover memories, all the rubbish I should have thrown out long ago; I have been feeding this ugly thought, and keeping it alive.

21 July, 1946

I've done little writing lately. I have been in a foul mood.

When I got here, I would look at the buildings and find myself perplexed by their wear and tear—strange stains on ceilings, metal surfaces painted and repainted, chipped and pitted, smooth troughs in certain spots on stone staircases, worn away by hundreds of feet striking the same narrow path day after day.

And now I understand why prisons are not the neat and pristine and perfect structures one imagines!! In here we take our frustrations out on the building itself, in ways big and small. Several men above us recently blocked up the toilets and flushed them repeatedly, flooding the floors, sending water spilling out from under the doors, dripping from the tiers and cascading down the stairs.

As for me, I have been so upset at our treatment here that I ignited my bedsheet in protest—which of course earned me a beating and a spell in a cell by myself. It was a change of pace, at least!

Yet I still have my journal. I hid it in my pillow before they moved me. Perhaps they allowed me to keep it so they can keep reading it—I fear this, for they will know how truly disturbed I am!

And yet I am writing again.

The guards have been getting drunk and taunting me about being on the wrong side of history.

The Communist Party now holds the key government ministries—defence, interior, agriculture. (Agriculture does not seem important until one considers that all of the ethnic Germans are being expelled from the country, and their land is being appropriated and redistributed—to party members first, naturally.) So the guards are excited, full of hope, and themselves.

Even Stefan sounds like a party hack now. He says Jesus was the first revolutionary, and that God killed people—in the New Testament, no less—for not being Communists. (He cited Acts Chapter 5, and I'll be damned if it wasn't there! I had never noticed it before! Are they rewriting the Bible now? I wouldn't put it past them!) He says this is the world Jesus wanted—a world in which none are rich and none are poor. The exploiters of the people are gone, he says, and the party is redistributing their wealth to the people—the Kingdom of Heaven is at hand.

1 August, 1946

The woman who claims to be a nun came by the other day.

I hadn't seen her in a while. She asked if I'd been writing, and I said, "Some," and she said yet again that I needed to make a thorough examination of conscience so that I might confess when it came time. "The truth will set you free," she said.

I just laughed out loud: "The truth will get me hung."

She said it would give me peace of mind; she said it simply, as if it was not debatable—which it most clearly was! "Ha!" I laughed. "The truth has given me many things, but never peace of mind."

She asked if that was because of the truth, or my reaction to it.

"Tell me, Sister. Did Jesus love the truth?"

She exclaimed: "Of course! I am the Way, the Truth and the Life!"

"Were Jesus' stories true then? Was there a prodigal son, or a man who hired workers in the afternoon and paid them the same as workers he'd hired in the morning?"

Here I'd caught her! She did her best to explain her way out, though: "Stories…have their own truth…an artistic truth," she sputtered. "They have life and spirit depending on whether they're true to the ideals of beauty and the rules of human behaviour." ("Human behaviour can be ugly," I pointed out, but she kept going.) "Besides, one cannot put the fullness of truth in a story. One cannot describe a walk in the woods, say, and make note of the position of every leaf. One can only describe what they've seen of the truth, what they remember of it, which is what Jesus did."

"But those are pleasant stories! They are memorable because they are so different from what really happens! In real life, in my truth, there is no make-believe! How can I accept a truth that is unacceptable? When I am in here facing death, unable to see my wife and children and family?"

"You should love the truth for its own sake, not because it's favourable or unfavourable to you."

"I do love the truth! The courts don't care for it, but I love it!"

"Does that mean you'll tell it at your trial?"

"I'll tell it to my confessor," I said. "As for the courts, I'll try telling it in a way that won't get me killed, so I'll probably leave some things out. Does that make me a liar? Are you judging me, then?"

She shrugged. "I am not sure what's reasonable in these situations. I don't know what I would do. You've been writing, though, I see."

"Yes! I've been writing, I've been writing, I've been writing!" I exclaimed. "And the question I have is: Why do you care so much?"

She shrugged.

"Do you talk to them?"

"Them?" She pretended to be confused.

"The guards. Do you talk to them?"

And she admitted it!!! But she claimed—quite cleverly—that she had to talk to them, for they granted or denied her entry depending on their whims. She also claimed that she didn't talk to them about us.

"They signal you while you're out there," I pointed out. "They don't let you come in the cells."

She claimed—cleverly, again—that they kept an eye on her for her safety; they did not want her out of sight. She asked why it mattered.

"I might feel more comfortable if could speak face-to-face, Sister. With no doors between us, and no guards watching."

She promised to see what she could do. She said I should keep writing in the meantime.

"There are some things I can never write down," I told her again — but although I know what's really going on, that she is not a nun (for why would Communist guards allow a nun, after all?) my resistance is waning.

They'll probably torture me if I don't get it all down on paper.

I should at least give them something new.

7 August, 1946

The truth has caused far more trouble for me than lying.

After Heydrich, I sent a letter to the police. I told them they were looking for Jan Kubish and Josef Gabchik. I told the truth!

It seemed like the right thing to do, to give the Germans two names they were sure to get sooner or later — to save lives, by giving them an excuse to stop the killings! But when I dropped the letter in the post box, I felt the awful irrevocable finality of what I'd done. I heard the dull paper-on-metal thud as it hit the bottom: proof that my written words still existed outside of my sight. Proof they were beyond my reach. Proof there was no going back.

It was hell, waiting for something to happen after sending that letter! I think I spent the next several days in the forest, depressed and tired, my head so heavy it was hard to keep it upright. I knew I needed a drink. I remember going back to town and getting drunk, and still it didn't shut off the voices in my head.

I'm not sure if I remember getting on the train.

I do remember being on the train, drunk, knowing I had to do what I was doing, and still wanting to be anywhere else, doing anything else. Wanting to be anyone else.

I remember the countryside rolling by, sunny tall pines and flat land and silver lakes, all the same as I'd seen as a boy. And yet—how my sad heart now polluted these pleasant views!

How tortured I felt! Ill, odd, old: my stomach churned and my bowels twisted. My contents were trying to come out of both ends; I envisioned a tube of poorly-made toothpaste being squeezed by a fist. At one point, I stumbled off to the train's cramped water closet, where I spent some time suffocating in the fetid air, pants around my ankles, knees knocking against the metal sink cabinet, wracked by waves of nausea. And when I finally tried to clean myself up, the roll of toilet paper was empty. How can I not think life's been one great conspiracy—even that bathroom's previous occupant screwed me over!

I stumbled out, sick and miserable and eager for fresh air. I remember pounding on the window to open it, then sticking my head halfway out—half-hoping some un-pruned tree branch would reach out and smack me into oblivion. But no such luck! Instead, the wind shifted. Smoke came into the train, and the other passengers started yelling at me. And no sooner had I closed the window than a huge tree branch struck the train with a smack! Right where I'd been standing! It felt like a giant slap in the face from the Almighty.

I'd taken that train route many times before, but it never felt faster than on that day! I found myself hoping for a train derailment! For death! Anything to end this trip early and remove this burden from me. I had a pill in my pocket, still, rattling around in a tin. It had stayed dry, despite the rain. Was that a sign? Why did I not take it?

Unfortunately I arrived alive in Prag.

Out in the captive city, I stopped a passer-by and mentioned my destination. He looked at me nervously before disappearing, darting off to Lord knows where. No one wanted to go where I was about to go!

As it happened, it was not far away. But how I dreaded the journey's end!! I'd wondered if I'd be able to spot the building, but when I got nearby I saw it seemed unmistakable: a dark grey building surrounded by lighter ones, a massive proud corner building, stately and sinister. (Was that in my head? I don't think so. If the police had presented the row of buildings as a line-up, I'm sure I would have correctly picked the guilty one.)

Still I delayed!! A drink might help, I reasoned. So I procured a bottle of spirits and parked myself in a park across the street, a pleasant grassy spot equidistant between the National Opera and my dark destination.

I drank away the hours as if on holiday; I lay down and stared at the sky and tried to imagine everything was normal. But no amount of alcohol could let me forget what had to happen next. And there were no other options — I had no place to stay, and after buying the bottle I didn't even have enough for a return ticket.

Turn back. (Something said this within me — my thoughts, or my fears, or something more than me, or something less.) Turn back — it isn't too late. (Then there came another voice.) If it isn't too late now, you can make it so.

And so, limbs heavy with liquor, heart heavy with hatred for what I was about to do — for what I had to do!! — I hauled myself up from my crushed patch of grass, then stumbled across the street and knocked heavily on the cast-iron door.

8 August, 1946

I must keep telling my story. Although the guards are reading this, I must at least tell this part. (And I know you are reading it, guards! Over the past few weeks, before each trip to the yard, I've plucked a few hairs and placed them between select pages—where they would have remained undisturbed, except that you disturbed them! A bit of tradecraft I learned from the Gestapo—and I am writing it down because I want you to know that I know! No matter. I will only set down the things I want to set down.)

Where was I? I had just arrived at the headquarters of the Gestapo in Prag.

I do not know what I expected when I got inside.

I do know I did not expect what I got.

Inside was a spotless lobby of gleaming white marble, cool and pleasant and peaceful. I stood there confused—the effect was as disorienting as if I'd entered a dungeon door and found myself magically transported to heaven's pearly gates.

"Enshuldigen Sie, mein Herr?" (I became aware of an orderly at a wooden duty desk. His tone was somehow both condescending and perplexed; he wore something like a smile on his face and something like a Luger on his hip.)

"I have important information about the attack on Heydrich," I told him.

He shifted in place; I suspect he pressed a buzzer under the desk. At any rate, I heard boots clicking on marble, and an officer appeared.

"I'd like to speak to the officer in charge of the investigation," I told him.

"The officer...in charge of the investigation?" he asked, sounding quite dubious. "You think you can just wander in off the street and speak to whomever you choose? You could be one of the parachutists, for all we know!!!"

I took a sharp deep heavy breath. Should I tell them? Would they find out anyway, if I didn't? Then I spoke at last, with confidence: "With the information I have, I guarantee I will be speaking to him within the hour."

They ushered me in to a small bare holding room. Others searched me and found the cyanide. It was a small white pill, big enough in my mind to crowd out all else. Why hadn't I been man enough to take it? Fear of mother? Or of people in general? Either way—fear. I could handle being a suicide, but not having people know it. I was afraid of what people would think; God already knew I was a failure.

Before long, a man named Fleischer was sitting across the table from me.

He said I was a parachutist, and I admitted it.

He asked why I was here, and I told him: "I was homesick. I volunteered so I could return home. Perhaps I wanted to do my mission, too, but when I got here, I realized it was stupid and counter-productive for the exiles to stir things up. I could not in good conscience allow it to continue."

(Was that what I said, or what I remembered, or what I wished I'd said? Maybe it was the truth. I do not know any more. My so-called solicitor was right. When you repeat your stories often enough, when your explanations run through your head for long enough, they become your memory. Or at least they're fresher than your memory. I don't think that is lying, though! You are just remembering something different, a story rather than an event.)

Fleischer asked about my mission, and I told him of our fool's errand against the Skoda Works...and when I mentioned the radio beacon, he nodded, almost involuntarily—I do remember that! And it felt good! I felt proud! Better than I'd felt in weeks! So they do have it, I remember thinking—I'd was right after all!

He and his assistant left me locked in the small room. They'd taken my shoes and socks and belt, presumably to inspect them for hidden weapons or spy tools or things of that sort, and they'd taken my shirt, presumably to humiliate me. Sitting there half-naked, I felt like a child waiting on the examination table for the town doctor— slumped and numb, lonely and empty.

But I was talking to Pannwitz before the hour was out!

22 August, 1946

It's been a week or so since I've written anything, but I feel compelled to write more.

Where was I in my recollection? Yes—meeting Pannwitz.

I must admit—when I first met him, there was some discussion of the reward money the Germans had offered. I'm sure that's going to come up at my trial—even though it wasn't why I went to Prag and talked to the Gestapo, it was a considerable sum they'd offered. So I'm sure they'll bring that up. But what was I supposed to do? Was it so wrong, to change sides? Is it always wrong? I should think not— otherwise St. Paul would be regarded the same way as Judas. Perhaps it's only wrong if you pick the wrong side.

At any rate, I didn't do it for the money. But I wasn't going to turn it down, either. Is it wrong, that I didn't turn it down? Is the right thing suddenly wrong once you get paid for it?

Talking to the Germans, and accepting their money—it doesn't feel like the worst thing I've ever done.

23 August, 1946

A new development—the so-called Sister Ignatia showed up last night with a key to my cell.

I'm still trying to piece our conversation together. I was tremendously distracted; such proximity to a woman might have been somewhat normal in my past life, but I felt unaccountably uncomfortable. And I'm not sure I believe her.

We'd chatted in a disturbingly personal manner about her life before the convent—what she called her old life of sin. She said she'd been the mistress of an older man. A wealthy, charming man. A famous industrialist whose name I'd know, she said, though she would not give it. A married man. She said he'd spoken of all manner of things, and had even mentioned leaving his wife; he'd spoken of burning, undying love.

But she'd gotten pregnant—or so she claimed. She'd been vomiting. And he'd supposedly given her a choice: either she could go to a doctor who would take care of it, or he would have to pretend they'd never met. It was all on account of his family—he said the scandal would ruin too many lives. And when he said it, his eyes had burned with the force of his conviction, with his belief that he was doing the right thing, the unselfish thing. (That was the thing about the devil, she said—he was a wily, capricious, destructive spirit, a trickster that could make you think the wrong thing was the compassionate thing and the right thing was the cruel thing. And I thought back to my first conversation with Gretchen when she said this; so help me, I thought about Gretchen!)

At any rate, she said it had all ended badly. She did not say what choice she'd made—she resolutely refused to say what she'd done! She only said they'd gotten the scandal they'd been trying to avoid. But she remarked on how strange it was, how obstinately we'll refuse to change course when it also means admitting we were wrong about something so great.

"It is strange," I allowed. "Do you miss it? Being with him?"

She said she sometimes did. Even though it led to misery and heartache, the life of sin she'd lived, even though her current work was far more rewarding and gratifying, she said she sometimes missed her old life!!!

How am I supposed to believe her? Why did she tell me these things? Perhaps—oh, I can see it now!—perhaps so I'd confess my own sins! My crimes! She must be a spy for the guards—with this, and having gotten a key. A clever actress! She wanted me distracted! She wanted me off-balance, uncomfortable! She must be a spy!

It occurs to me there is a way to find out for sure.

But I cannot write it down.

3 September, 1946

Again, I've been delaying my recollections!

Sister Ignatia has spoken of God whispering in our ear, of the Holy Spirit suggesting other paths. In the first book of Kings, Chapter 19, verses 11 and 12, Elijah stands on a mountain before the Lord, and faces wind, an earthquake, and a fire, but the Lord was in none of these; the Lord was in the gentle breeze, and the Lord whispered in Elijah's ear.

I don't always know what to make of this. Many times when I thought I heard God's whisper, it led me to disaster—the day I was captured after escaping Prag, for instance. What spirit was that? God, or the devil, or my own fevered mind? Is religion a form of collective insanity? Am I insane?

I heard a whisper at the church.

First I had to endure a whirlwind of questioning and re-questioning, a sustained and troubling evening in which the Germans' moods and tones seemed to change by the minute. Were they interrogators, captors, or friends? Was I a valuable source of information or a prisoner? That was never quite clear. I did feel more like a clue than a human being—an important but inanimate piece of information, a valued possession that had been found after a long and frantic search and needed to be held on to tightly lest it be lost again—but not a person! No, not a person. So I spent my night locked up under a rotating watch of overseers, begging for all the basics—a hurried trip to the water closet with a Gestapo agent practically looking over my shoulder as I tried to coax piss from my full-but-fearful bladder; a meagre meal of bread and water; a few shattered minutes of fitful sleep on Pannwitz's office couch with that same baby-faced agent standing guard again—clearly they were afraid the prize might somehow slip from their grasp!! As this dragged on in that nearly-sleepless night, I found myself in a foggy hung-over dreamlike haze, my thoughts reduced to numb ramblings interspersed by periods of emptiness.

I knew they were making arrests, based on what I'd told them—that family, Marie and Stefan and Ata, the ones I later saw in court, the ones he talked about in that damnable story he told me just once all those years later. I tried not to think about it.

Finally, after many long hours, I found myself being hustled outside and wedged into the back of Pannwitz's car, which took its place at the rear of a column of canvas-covered lorries. Pannwitz occupied the front passenger seat but never quite sat, for he was constantly yelling at the driver, conversing with the agents on either side of me, and throwing up his arms in frustration at every unexpected stop. All the while we tasted the diesel fumes that belched forth from the troop transports ahead of us, dim shapes outlined by the dark blue sky and barely highlighted by our blackout headlamps.

When we stopped at the church, all was purposeful chaos, a lot of muffled grumbling and shouting and milling about: soldiers erecting roadblocks, directing lorries to park, emplacing machine guns.

Around us, the noises died down. We were still some blocks from the church, which was now ringed by wooden barricades. Inside the cordon, all was dark and quiet, the buildings featureless black shapes against a morning sky that grew lighter by the minute. And I remember thinking the war wasn't entirely terrible, if it brought such peace and quiet and darkness to the city, the inky stillness of the blackout calm.

Numbly I stepped out of the car and lit a cigarette. Someone practically yanked it from my hands and ground it underfoot.

Meanwhile Pannwitz assembled a squad to accompany him into the silent church.

I sensed that this was it. (Or did I? When I'd been hiding out in Prag, I'd never heard anything about a church. So I'm not sure if I expected Pannwitz to find anything, or if I wanted him to. I think I might have still hoped this was all a wild goose chase.)

Pannwitz and his men went to the front of the church. For a few minutes, nothing happened.

And then—gunshots!! Noises muffled by walls, not quite escaping intact, but still unmistakable. Then explosions—grenades. Still we could barely see anything—stained glass breaking, and dim flashes inside like distant summer lightning.

And then, silence.

Pannwitz and the others hustled back in twos and threes; at least one of them limped. It looked like he'd been shot high on the outside thigh—a serious wound but not life-threatening.

They took time and took stock of what had happened, and Pannwitz and the commander of the SS troops squabbled. It sounded like Pannwitz wanted prisoners, or defendants—live captives, at any rate. Whereas the SS man was more concerned about the lives of his soldiers than with jeopardizing an ongoing investigation. But Pannwitz said he was in charge of the manhunt. It was a criminal investigation, and this was its conclusion, and if the commander had any problems, he should take them up with Karl Hermann Frank.

By the time they went back in, the early summer sun was nearly up; the sky softly painted the stained glass in light pastel colours.

From a rooftop across Resslova, a machine gun opened up; an angry woodpecker destroying the morning calm, sending real birds to flight, chewing through the stained glass.

Apparently they'd holed up in the choir loft, and there was but one small staircase leading up there—a great place to defend, except that it lacked a fallback position. (Maybe that's what they wanted! Maybe I gave them that, at least—a final fight with their backs to the wall, a public battle after all those weeks in hiding, an opportunity to play the lion, or at least the obstinate donkey, after weeks of feeling like sacrificial lambs!)

The sun came up and the fight dragged on; the early edgy excitement gave way to grim monotony. Some more SS troopers limped back. Several others were carried off, lying motionless on stretchers with gaping head wounds or uniforms growing dark with blood.

Eventually the shooting died out.

By then, the sun was blasting straight down Resslova, glinting off the cobblestones when you looked east, turning everything golden. And the people of the city were milling about beyond the barricades, perplexed by this battle which had suddenly sprung up in the midst of their peaceful city. None of them had expected this! I suppose a few might have been intrigued and hoping for heroism, but I think the general feeling was that the poor fools were done for.

They started bringing the bodies out from the choir loft.

There were three of them, and the first was brought out on a stretcher. Someone started yelling, and the soldiers cleared a path through the barricades for an ambulance van, but I caught a glimpse of the head on the stretcher—a bloody mess—and I knew he wouldn't last long even if they got him to a hospital. And he didn't. That was Kubish.

The other two were more obviously done for; the soldiers carried them by twos, grabbing hands and feet like the dead men were but sacks of flour. Pannwitz pointed and shouted, and the corpses were unceremoniously dropped on the cobblestones in the shadow of the building across the street from the church.

All around was a chaotic, unforgettable scene: I remember the SS commander shouting orders, and his men counting their ammunition and their dead while the church tapestries burned behind them; I recall Pannwitz pacing as he awaited the fire brigade, whose sirens were already sounding in the distance. Still, I was distracted by the stillness and the silence of those two dead men on the cobblestones.

I found myself walking over there to look, and hating myself for walking over, and feeling unable not to. There was a ghastly unnatural blue tone to their lips and mouths. Cyanide.

That's when I heard the whisper.

Was it the same whisper I heard before, before I went to the Germans? Have I heard it since?

The whisper said: That's enough. Just nod and act like you're thinking, and if anyone asks, say you're glad that's all over.

But I did not listen to the whisper.

Pannwitz saw me and walked over.

"Is this it?" He asked with authority, as if he already knew but wanted confirmation.

"That's Opalka," I pointed. "I think that's Bublik. And the one on the stretcher was Kubish." And I looked up, breathed hard, and spoke—a short heavy sentence I knew I could never undo: "I don't see Josef Gabchik."

4 September, 1946

I really don't know what I was supposed to do that morning; I have a hard time believing my actions had any real impact on the final outcome by that point.

There were, I was later told, upwards of 700 Waffen SS troops surrounding the Karel Boromesky church, in which seven parachutists had holed up—three in the choir loft and four in the crypt. The soldiers had formed a double cordon around the church; they'd even stationed troops down where the sewer emptied into the river. I tend to think that, by the time I identified those bodies, Gabchik and the three others in the crypt weren't in a much better spot—in a box, in a state we couldn't determine, but sure to be dead if we made any effort to open it up.

Still, I've often wondered: What would have happened had I not said anything? Or if, for instance, I'd told them that Bublik was really Gabchik? Maybe Pannwitz would have declared the whole episode over and done, and the troops would have cleaned up and gone home. Had they not known there were more parachutists, they might not have discovered the crypt.

But they did discover it.

Pannwitz swore up and down when he realized they hadn't gotten everyone. Fleischer, the first interrogator I'd spoken to, was on the scene as well; he grabbed the churchman and threw him to the ground. He kicked the man and yelled at him. And at last the man admitted there was a crypt under the church floor where the others were holed up.

So they found it, and I helped them, even though I could have kept my mouth shut. Why?

Maybe I felt trapped already in this new life, this role. Or maybe I felt important at last. To use a chess analogy—which I hate to do, for I still despise the game after playing it with Frank!!—I was no longer a pawn but a queen—or better yet, the only one on the scene who'd ever seen of the other side of the chessboard!!

But all this is speculation, an attempt to give shape to formless memories. Almost five years on, some scenes remain sharp, but others have faded, for this is a story I don't like to tell. Maybe I simply had not thought at all on that numb tired morning. I don't know why I did what I did; I only know that I did it.

10 September, 1946

18 June of 1942 would have been an absolutely perfect day under different circumstances.

The sun was high and bright behind scattered clouds—just enough to make the sky interesting.

Nearly all of Prag was at peace. Perfect, placid and docile as ever, except for those few strange blocks around the church. It was bizarre — you looked one way and everything seemed normal, and then you stuck your head around the corner and there was the war. Yesterday it had been burning far away, at the distant edges of the continent; today it had somehow arrived in the centre, like a single spark borne on the wind.

With all the barricades, and the way they tried so hard to contain it to those few bizarre blocks, it did seem more like a fire than a battle — something the Germans had to extinguish lest it spread. And the firemen were there too, now that half the battle was over and the men in the choir loft had taken their own lives — Czech firemen, with engines and hoses, trying to extinguish tapestries and other decorations that had caught fire during the battle for the loft.

Off behind the fire engines, Pannwitz huddled with the SS commander to plan their assault on the crypt. And when they finished, he came over to talk. He seemed calm on the surface, but angry underneath; he wanted me to talk to them — the other parachutists.

"How?" I asked.

He pointed to a spot in the church wall along Resslova, and said it was the vent for the crypt.

"What am I supposed to tell them?" I asked.

"Tell them to surrender. Tell them they'll be treated well. Tell them this doesn't have to end today." He stared me down — those eyes were so implacable! "I don't care. Tell them…whatever. I want to take them alive."

I remembered them beating the priest. I wondered if they were telling the truth. I did not ask.

Our side of the church stretched along Resslova; the bottom portion of the wall was the top of the crypt, an impenetrable wall of thick cement. On the cobblestoned sidewalk and in the street, Czech firemen spooled their hoses, and Germans huddled with their men, but very close to the vent was a dead space that everyone avoided. The parachutists in the crypt hadn't made their presence known, but no one knew what they might do if presented with a target of opportunity. (The overall outcome of all this wasn't in doubt, so none of the Germans wanted to run the risk of not being around to see it!)

With some trepidation, I stepped past the barricades and into that dead empty section of cobblestones. I found myself directly in front of, and staring up into, a black rectangle of empty space.

(What were my thoughts? If I remember correctly, there had been no shooting from the crypt yet, no communication, nothing. I think I hoped even then that it was somehow all a mistake, that maybe the others had been hiding elsewhere all along, or that they'd escaped. Oh, how I wished with all my might for the situation to be different than it was!!)

I looked back. Pannwitz nodded towards the vent. I cleared my throat and spoke: "Come on out, boys! The priest told them you're in there."

There was no answer, nothing. I became aware of young Ata standing next to me, sullen and silent. How long had he been there? (Is it not strange, how you can suddenly notice things and people that must have been there all along?) He looked battered and broken.

"Come on, Josef!" I yelled. "These are reasonable people, if you reason with them. You don't have to die today!!"

Finally a voice—Josef—yelled out, loud and blustery: "Save your breath, you...traitor. We're not going to surrender."

"Don't be a fool! It's over upstairs!" I shouted. "The others are dead!"

"We are soldiers, too! We're prepared to die, too!" (Was it my imagination, or did he say this as if trying to convince himself?)

"This doesn't have to end here, Josef. You can have a new life!!"

Again, the disembodied voice called me a traitor. (The vent was high enough in the wall that one could only see a dim image of the ceiling—and Josef didn't show his face, for obvious reasons. I never actually saw him alive that day, come to think of it! But I could not understand—I still cannot understand—why he would not leave his cave!)

I remember looking back and wondering how many machine guns, how many rifles, were trained on that little vent. I saw riflemen and machine-gunners in their coal-scuttle helmets in position on the rooftops, their barrels barely visible; I felt their eyes on me and their gunsights on my back; I imagined the tension in their trigger fingers and wondered if they'd really care if I got clipped by mistake.

"What was that, Josef?" I asked, turning back to the task at hand.

"You're a traitor, you motherfucker! A traitor and a coward!" (He was yelling; he'd lost his temper. Big surprise!)

"Why don't you come out and say that?" I asked, and chuckled, and turned towards the Czech firemen to gauge their reaction. Nobody laughed. I thought it was funny.

Josef apparently wasn't amused, either—I saw the barrel of a Sten (the only thing I saw of them during the standoff) and stood transfixed for what seemed like forever. The gun spouted fire and I—I must admit—scampered off, tripped on the kerb, tumbled and got up and ran again. (Here of course there was actually some laughter from among the Germans—those fuckers!!! I was not amused.)

On the rooftop across the street, the machine gun opened up; the bullets chewed chunks from the cement and ricocheted to the ground, flattened and smeared like coins left on train tracks.

When the shooting stopped, someone in the crypt placed a mattress over the vent hole. Dusting myself off after the fall, I saw this and chuckled: a simple solution. Now they could move about freely, and no one could see inside.

Pannwitz started rounding up the firemen. They listened, slack and unenthusiastic, but when he stopped talking, they started unspooling the hoses. They were going to try to flood the crypt.

The firemen brought up ladders and hoses; although the vent was covered, they hugged the wall anyway, so Josef and the others wouldn't have the angle to shoot even if they'd been watching. But they worked slowly, and you could practically see their typical Czech thoughts written across their typical Czech faces: a little effort toward meeting the Germans' demands, and a lot of effort toward not getting shot, and everyone will be happy.

Finally they had placed ladders on either side of the vent; two men climbed, and other men passed hoses up to them. The men on the ladders pushed away the mattress and fed the hoses in, and others turned them on, and they pulsed and tensed and twitched as if alive.

Someone inside cut the nozzles off and pushed the hoses back out.

Across the street the machine gun opened up, firing in short angry bursts followed closely by the high bright sound of cartridge brass falling like a rain of coins.

Pannwitz signalled the machine gun to stop and motioned for the reluctant firemen to replace the hoses. The SS commander delegated a few soldiers to stand at the ready with hand grenades. The hoses went in first, and then the grenades, and then came explosions, and then silence.

It seemed everyone held their breath. Was it really over? But the end of a ladder appeared from within the crypt, moving and poking. They were trying to push the hoses out.

Again the machine gun opened up. Stray rounds nicked the hoses, and bright arcing fans of water sprayed onto the cobblestones. (Somehow I remember this sight better than any from that day—how strangely beautiful, the sunlight in the water!)

When the gun stopped, the ladder was still pushing at the hoses, and the hoses came back out. And right then an intrepid—or perhaps bored—soldier ran up, jumped and grabbed one of the rungs, and seesawed down like a circus acrobat; when his feet touched ground he started running, pulling the ladder from the crypt, and for a second it seemed like it wasn't going, like the men inside were playing tug-of-war, but the machine gun opened up and the troopers threw in more grenades, and the ladder came loose. Again the reluctant firemen climbed their own sad ladders and half-heartedly pushed the hoses back in.

The SS commander frowned; he said to throw more grenades if they pushed them back out.

He walked around the corner and sure enough, the hoses came back out, and now the troopers threw in both regular grenades and tear gas. Again came explosions, then silence. Tear gas billowed from the vent. And I wondered again—was it over? And the tear gas canisters came sailing out.

I was tired—deliriously tired—and for some reason here I imagined the crypt as a living thing, a squat fat monster with a ladder for a tongue, an animate object that regurgitated everything put inside it. I started laughing uncontrollably, which drew a lot of dirty looks from the haggard soldiers. Then the Gestapo agent at my elbow elbowed me. I realized Frank was on the scene, and had been for some time.

"What the hell is going on here?" Frank raged. (I'd never seen him in person, but I wasn't impressed even then. He wore an intimidating uniform, but he was a small man, and his busybody nature, his nervousness shone through—weakness and fear masquerading as strength and decision. He knew everything was slipping from his hands!) And Pannwitz told him they were trying to flood the crypt.

Frank asked: "Why, in God's name?"

Pannwitz seemed confused by Frank's confusion. "We want to capture these men. Bring them to justice. We need to make an example of them."

Frank looked at him as if he'd started drooling on himself. Then he exploded: "This is ridiculous!! This is absurd!! They're fighting to die, and we're fighting to keep them alive!!"

The SS commander tried not to gloat; Frank directed him inside to see what was happening.

(Inside the church, I found out later, there was a hole in the church floor through which the parachutists had entered and exited the crypt via ladder; it had been covered hastily by the priest, but the Germans had now uncovered it.)

At any rate, when the SS commander came back, he said his men had been shining electric torches down into the crypt, but the water wasn't rising. And he wasn't sure how to get an assault force down there without getting them all shot.

Frank practically burst: "Just get them in there! Get them in there any way you can and put a stop to all this insanity!"

(From the crypt came the muffled rattle of a Sten, presumably shooting at the troopers on the church floor.)

Frank continued, quieter. "If the water isn't rising, it must be flowing out somewhere. There might be a passage to the sewer, or some other underground pathway. This city, the low parts were filled in centuries ago; there is a lot underground..."

Still the SS commander looked perplexed.

Frank was frank: "Look, the longer people hear shooting here, the weaker we appear. We need to put a stop to this before it inspires a general uprising. I don't care if they all die."

11 September, 1946

I did a very bad thing today.

Sister Ignatia came by, and...and I can't even bring myself to write about what I did! And I couldn't confess it, either, if the priest ever came by. I am not human, not human at all, but a dirty sinful monster overcome by the flesh. Surely everyone knows it now.

I am going to hell, without a doubt. There is no salvation for me.

17 September, 1946

I should finish talking about the church. They'll probably beat me if I don't, and it is more pleasant to ponder than the present.

After the business with the vent and the ladder, there was a lot of milling about that, upon closer inspection, turned out to be pointless.

The firemen looked as if they were tending to their hoses and engines, but if one really paid attention, one could see they were moving slowly, and repeating their tasks, and undoing one another's tasks. (It seemed they were too patriotic to speed the demise of the four in the crypt, and too afraid to prevent it.) But the Germans were delaying, too; they were garrison troops, and their comrades-in-arms were fighting and dying on the steppes of Russia and the sands of Egypt, but Prag was so peaceful that their heaviest duties probably involved lifting the larger glasses of Pilsner. I wonder how many of them wished they had gone to sick call, so as to miss this mess of a day and return swiftly to the lazy rhythms of the occupation! They surely had not psychologically adjusted to the idea that they might die on such a fine sunny day.

As for me, I kept to myself, sucked down a succession of cigarettes (all begged from my increasingly resentful Gestapo babysitter), stewed in my thoughts, and waited to be needed again. I watched the Czech civilians on the other side of the barricades; they'd cluster in curious clumps until one of Pannwitz's men walked over as if to question them, and then they'd disperse, heads down, trying to be invisible. I realized I would never be one of them again, would never again be anonymous — there was some strange satisfaction in that!!

As the commanders planned the final assault, someone realized no one had touched the hoses in some time, and there was hopeful speculation that the parachutists were dead. But finally the Germans dispersed for the final assault.

Now came a hand signal from inside, and the troopers outside threw more grenades, and the machine guns on the rooftops opened up again. And there was firing inside the church, too; they were shooting down through the hole in the church floor; the muzzle flashes flickered on the inside walls of the crypt.

Then: a signal. The machine guns outside stopped. From inside, I heard shouted orders in German — they were trying to lower men by rope through the hole in the crypt ceiling.

For a second all was silent: was it really over?

Then: more firing from inside the crypt. Through the broken church windows I heard Germans shouting and swearing. The parachutists had been playing dead, it seemed.

Morning dragged into afternoon. The Germans regrouped, tallied the dead, pointed fingers, and plotted their next moves.

Still, it was getting somewhat boring! More of the same, more of the same! How quickly the extraordinary becomes ordinary, and even annoying, when one is tired and isolated, with nothing to do but wait for the end! I wanted to eat, I wanted to sleep, I wanted a drink—Lord, how I wanted a drink!! I wanted to slip off and be ordinary again, a face in the crowd! I wanted to be anywhere but there! How could a life-and-death struggle be so tedious?

They found out about another entrance to the crypt, a staircase covered by a stone slab behind the altar. There was talk of blowing it open and attacking from two directions at once. More preparations ensued. And finally the troops took up positions again.

An explosion shook the church. The last of the stained glass now blew out from the massive windows, a delicate colourful crystal rain that ricocheted off the masonry and fell amidst the cobblestones.

From the crypt, I heard four muffled shots.

Were they bunched together or evenly spaced? I don't know. I cannot remember. Does it matter? I don't know. I only know that I must have heard four.

Inside the church, they had cleared away the broken stone slab covering the staircase, and the first man stopped halfway down, either when he heard the shots or when he heard the silence afterwards. And I think—I did not see it directly—he took a few more steps, then saw what he saw, then turned back and shouted two words, two magical words that were repeated from man to man, from leader to subordinate, from inside to out and German to Czech—two words that snuffed out all other conversations: Ist fertig.

It is finished.

12 January, 1947

I haven't written in months.

I am depressed again, as bad as I've ever been.

Is there any purpose to any of it? I have told my story—or most of it—and nothing has changed! Have they even read it? Are they going to read it? Do they care? Perhaps not—perhaps not!!! Is no one even interested in this chronicle of my depravity? Perhaps I shall burn it.

29 March, 1947

My trial draws near.

We've had months and months of boring winter nothing, days blurring together and becoming indistinguishable, and the weather outside turning ever-so-slightly warmer. I have little to discuss. I have a month to live.

There's certainly no chance for another visit from Sister Ignatia; I did, however, sit down yesterday for a visit with my solicitor—who may, in fact, be a solicitor. (Perhaps everyone has been real, after all! What a horrid thought!)

"How are we looking?" I asked.

"Now you want to work with me?"

I shrugged.

"Well, the good news is, the general climate is better. The Communists are still hungry for vengeance, but the general population's been sated. And ironically, one of the methods the Communists were using to bring about their version of justice — stacking the People's Courts with people who survived the German prisons — is backfiring." I raised an eyebrow, and he continued: "Those people are actually more inclined to be fair-minded, because they know what it's like to be on the receiving end of injustice. And as it turns out, the general punishments, particularly the mass deportations, have also backfired, by getting in the way of specific punishments for individuals."

"What does that mean?"

"It means they've inadvertently deported many of their German-speaking witnesses along with the other ethnic Germans. Some defendants have no one to testify against them."

"And the bad news?" I asked.

"The particulars of your case are still not great," he said. "They are probably going to try you with as little fanfare as possible, and hang you."

"What's our courtroom strategy, then?"

"Pray, my friend," he said. "Pray like a priest on fire."

This was not, of course, what I wanted to hear. I actually want to get on good terms with God — now more than ever! And yet it seems less possible than ever.

17 April, 1947

The priest finally came the other night.

I had been alone in my cell, reading Job until lights-out, then lying there in the dark thinking on the various calamities that have befallen me. On such nights, I often think I hear noises, so I waited a few seconds to respond—I am not always sure what is real in these situations! But the knocking returned, slightly louder, and I went over, and there he was, the priest, alone in the dark late-night corridor. I could barely make out his dim outline.

"I'm told you're in need of a priest."

"I am, Father! I have much to confess," I said.

He asked if I could turn on a light.

"Not this late, Father. The power is cut off," I explained. So he reluctantly passed matches and a candle through the grating covering the door hole.

Once I got it lit, I studied his face. He stood crookedly, leaning on a cane or a walking stick or some such thing, but he was a handsome, tanned, rugged man, who seemed too healthy to need such an implement. And I could not help thinking that he looked vaguely familiar.

"Bless you, my son," he said, but something seemed strange—and it occurred to me that it might be better to get him in my cell. Did I want to arrange it so we could speak more easily? Or did I want to do what they said Canaris had done? Did he even have a means to get in? I didn't know, but—oh, how pleased I was—he brought the matter up himself! He asked if he could come inside!

"That would be best, Father," I said. "But how?"

Like magic, he produced a set of keys.

Oh, how delighted I was as he unlocked the door! In the candle's orange glow I saw he wore a beautiful black woollen cassock that stretched from neck to ankles—and it even had a hood! My evil thoughts, my dark fantasies—how easy it would be to escape in such clothes!

And yet he really did seem astonishingly familiar, and I could not shake the sense that I'd known him before. And my curiosity got the better of me. "Are you sure we haven't met, Father?" I asked.

He said he couldn't imagine where we might have met—but he spoke as if trying to preclude the possibility.

"Where are you from, at least, Father?" I asked, and he named some town in the country—Caslav, I think.

"Have you ever seen someone who reminded you of someone else, but you knew it could not logically be that person?" I asked, and he said yes, it was a most peculiar phenomenon—but he seemed reluctant to discuss it.

"Do you have relatives in the army, Father?" I prodded.

Here he gave a look of surprise and mild excitement. "Ahh, yes. I believe my brother was in England with the exile army."

"You believe, Father?" I asked, surprised at his uncertainty.

"We have not spoken in years. He left abruptly when the Germans came," he said sternly. "Look, I don't mean to be curt, but...time is of the essence. The guards might throw me out if I stay too late."

"I don't like them," I said. "They are thugs."

"They are. Everyone in the Interior Ministry. The Communists won forty percent in the elections, and now they think they can push everyone around."

"Many people support them," I pointed out, perhaps just to argue.

"They are radishes! Only red on the outside." He practically spat the words, disgusted. "I doubt the Communists could win a majority even with their help, but they will try through any means available. And are we to end up like the Germans under Hitler? With thugs unable to win a clear majority but determined to muscle their way to power anyway?"

"Ahh, yes. Sister Ignatia said something similar," I noted.

"Sister who?" he asked, then added: "Oh, yes. It is true, though."

"You seem…very concerned about such worldly matters, Father," I commented.

"They are a godless bunch," he said sourly — but then smiled and said: "You are right, though. I should pay attention to the next world, not this one. And now, about confession…"

"Yes, there's a lot we need to discuss," I said distractedly. The dark thought formed: if I want to kill him and take his clothes, I should do it now. "But…I can hardly form the words, Father."

And then — he pulled out a silver flask! He took a swig, and handed it to me: "Perhaps this will loosen your tongue."

"Your boss won't mind you drinking on the job?" I asked.

He grinned. "My boss turned water into wine."

I took a swig: unholy spirits!! Shocking, and yet so wonderful — the vodka blazed down my throat like lava and burst in my stomach like a meteor, with fireballs shooting down my arms and legs and up into my head. I was a new man!!

He smiled again, but there was something crooked in it. "Well now. Where were we?"

"Bless me Father, for I have sinned. It has been…" I glanced at his wristwatch, as if it held my answer. "…over five years since my last confession."

"Five years," he echoed, amazed.

"I…" And here I broke down, crying with regret and shame. Was it the liquor already? I hadn't had much, although I reached up, tearful, for another swig, and another. "…I have been such a bad man, Father! I was a cruel man when I drank, a violent man sometimes, with women."

"Yes, yes, of course," he said—but he said it as if it didn't matter!!! As if my depravity was boring!!!

"I consorted with prostitutes, Father! I visited houses of ill repute!!! I married a whore, and continued to sleep with other whores!!! I believe I have contracted a venereal disease, Father, and my mind has been not quite right. And in spite of this, I…I attempted to have sexual relations with a nun, a sister of the church!! Oh, Father, I am a wicked man, with no hope of salvation!!!"

And was it my imagination, or did he shrug? He said: "Very well."

"Very well?" I asked, incredulous, and he said: "What of the war?"

I took a deep breath and—I'm sure—gave a quizzical look. "What of it, Father?"

"Did you do things you regretted?"

"Some things, perhaps, Father…but…."

"And you have nothing to confess from the war—now, in this time of reckoning, you have nothing to confess?"

Now I was upset. There had been something about the nun that set me at ease, but this priest set me off. He had an unexpected proud air about him, something of the lion in his demeanour. I took another swig; I felt rejuvenated, courageous. "This feels more like an interrogation than a confession, Father. I did nothing wrong but back the losing side. That's the only real war crime."

He scowled. "The Germans perpetrated evil. Injustice!"

"People claim to hate injustice because it sounds good," I said. "They really hate losing. They only look for injustice afterwards."

My visitor huffed and shook his head. "You're being preposterous. The Germans started this war. They committed horrible crimes! Look at Liditz!"

"Yes, look at Liditz! The Allies loved it! You can stop counting the dead when the other side has done something like Liditz! President Benesh got to return and purge the country of Germans, because of Liditz!"

"The Germans did far worse than that. The way they treated the Jews..."

"No one cared about the Jews before the war! And no one knew it was happening during the war!" I exclaimed.

But he claimed—and how he would know this, I don't know—that it was known during the war. The Polish Underground had pictures of what was being done to the Jews, he said, and they'd smuggled them out to England—horrible pictures, nearly too hellish to believe, piles of corpses, stacks of people being burned...

"And what of the people burned in Hamburg, in Dresden?" I fumed. "Anything the Germans have done, their enemies have done too, in the course of fighting them! So this is not justice, what's happening here, now. And yet when all is said and done — all these executions will be forgotten, all the German civilians incinerated by the Allies will be forgotten, while what the Germans did will be remembered!" I took another drink; I had nearly drained the flask on my own, but he did not seem eager to take it back. "I regret nothing. Prag survived the war intact, unlike so many other cities. A few bullet-marks on a church wall — a small price to pay for a city!"

"You forget the fighting at the end of the war. The citizens rose heroically..."

"They rose foolishly!! And even then it was suicidal!! They almost provoked the city's destruction!! If it wasn't for General Vlasov..." I killed the flask, and felt the spirits doing their work. So long without a drink — one grows unaccustomed to the once-familiar sensations!! But still the feeling was easy to recognize — old but familiar, ally and adversary in one, far more powerful than appearances would suggest. My face flushed; my mind blazed; my tongue was on fire. "But then, where would our country be without traitors?"

"What do you mean?" He threw in a "my son," almost as an afterthought.

"The soldiers who left the Austro-Hungarian Army, who walked East in the Great War — I did what they did! I was following in their footsteps! I just followed them in the opposite direction. A new Good Soldier Schweik, for a new war..."

And was it my imagination, or did his jaw clench angrily? He said nothing but pulled out a flask—another flask, Hallelujah!!—and took a swig, and offered it to me.

Obligingly, I drank. "After all, I did nothing others didn't do. How many people listened to Emanuel Moravetz's…"

"Do not speak that name!" The priest practically exploded! I could not understand the sudden rage—his face turned red!

"You're a radish, Father!" I drunkenly laughed at his new colouration.

"I am not a radish! I am anything but a radish!" For a few moments, I thought he was going to burst a blood vessel. And I dared hope—if he died on his own, or rather, by God's hand, what a happy accident that would be! But he calmed down: "I'm sorry, my son. I…do not like hearing that name. He represented everything that was wrong about the Czech national spirit."

For a few moments we sat in silence. Somehow my dark thoughts faded. This blessed man had brought me alcohol, after all.

"Frank said the same thing," I observed. "I shared a cell with him, you know." And he shook his head and said that he and Frank agreed on that, at least.

And I don't remember exactly what I said after that; the alcohol was having its usual blessed effect, at last—far more quickly than it used to, for I've lost my tolerance!—and I was deep in a rosy-minded fuzz. But I think I shared some stories about Frank, and about why I'd done what I'd done during the war—I told him the Germans had beaten me during my initial interrogation, to get me to talk, and I'd wanted to hate them, but once I saw what the Allies did to win the war, I wasn't sure they were any better.

And I'm pretty sure he said that this was sophistry, the type of argument Emanuel Moravetz would have made. And he grew excited, and somewhere in there he started on a long speech about Plato, about Plato and fire and a cave and a lot of other things that my drunken mind couldn't quite follow, and all the while his eyes gleamed like embers, as if possessed by the memory of some long-ago triumph. And I think I smiled and nodded, just to go along.

Did he give me absolution? I seem to remember him fumbling over the words, and me helping him out—he must have been drunk himself. But I do not completely recall.

Did I black out? I do not know. Did the guards come? I seem to remember them in here. Did they drag the priest out? Did he leave on his own? So much is hazy. I only know that this conversation happened, not how it ended.

18 April, 1947

Of course, there has been more.

Every good drunk has its hangover, and for me, so long without one, the next day was an extended misery—I was crabby and irritable.

And today, without the hangover, I am still miserable. One day closer to trial, one day less to live. Have I had absolution? Am I forgiven? Can I be, if I still dwell on it? If I still want parts of it back? For I do! Another chance with Gretchen, for instance—that might be nice. Or one last rip-roaring drunk—salvation though oblivion.

But all this is foolish talk. All I can hope is that they'll let me speak in my defence. And if they do—and even if they don't, because, really, what would it matter?—I'll give them a piece of my mind. Those faces in the courtroom—I'll ask them, "How many of you were there for Heydrich's funeral? Or for Emanuel Moravetz's rallies? Maybe you told yourself you were 'curious' or that you worked in the armaments factories because you were 'hungry' — but you did it nonetheless! And you dare sit in judgment? You look down on me, mock me, ridicule me, say evil things about me — and why? Because we are different? Or because we are the same? I was offered more money than you, but I had the misfortune to be stuck with my choice!"

I do regret that. I did not mention all my regrets, talking to the priest. And some of them I may never admit, but I do regret that.

19 April, 1947

Where was I? Ahh, yes. Regrets.

I remember sitting down with Pannwitz after the battle at the church.

During those whirlwind hours when I'd first come to them, we'd briefly discussed the matter of the reward money they'd posted. He'd said it would take time to make the arrangements, but they were men of their word, honourable men, good Germans, and they were going to pay me my million.

And I remember that first real discussion a week or so after the battle — we were back in his office at the Gestapo headquarters.

Of course they would pay me, he said. It was in their best interests to do good to those who had done good to them. After all, who would come forward in the future if they didn't reward the man who helped close the case on the greatest crime in the history of the Reich? Rest assured, he told me — I would get my money.

"I do not want this to be widely known," I told him.

He looked perplexed.

"My role," I said. "I don't want it publicized that I claimed the reward money, or that I was at the church."

They were not planning on that, necessarily, he said. And anyway it would be easy to come up with some other story for how they'd figured it all out.

"That would be ideal," I said.

Perhaps, Pannwitz suggested, they could say they'd happened to interrogate the right family, and then at the church, they'd found additional weapons, or articles of clothing, or some such thing that told them there were others down in the crypt.

"That sounds plausible," I said.

Gerik was there, too, if I recall—he had come in at around the same time I did, but I hadn't seen him at the church. Pannwitz spoke to both of us, but his eyes kept wandering over to something on his dresser—an empty aquarium. I vaguely remembered seeing it before, full of goldfish, but I didn't know what had happened to them. It was a beautiful day outside, a perfect summer day, and the windows were open to catch the wind. There were just enough clouds to give the sky depth and form, and a glorious sun behind them turning their edges a heavenly white, but still Pannwitz stared at that aquarium.

They tried to tunnel their way to freedom, he said; finally he looked at me; I had no idea what he was talking about.

"The four in the crypt. They tried to tunnel out," he said. "Given a few more hours, they might have made it to the sewer. And we had people watching where it let out down by the Moldau, but of course you never know. They might have snuck out after dark, or gone the other way, further into the city, and disappeared before anyone knew they were gone. So it is good that you were there."

I remember squirming and looking out the window at the park where I'd gotten drunk just over a week before—it now seemed like a previous life. I wanted to be back there. I wanted to be elsewhere, anywhere!

Pannwitz said they'd found eleven weapons in the church. Eleven weapons, and not a single round of live ammunition remaining; he sounded impressed.

Finally Gerik spoke. He said that when the Jews were surrounded at Masada, they had drawn lots, and every tenth person killed the other nine. And they had repeated the process again and again, so that as few people as possible would die as suicides.

Pannwitz sneered. "What do I care for the Jews?" he asked.

Gerik grew quiet; he said it was just a story he'd heard somewhere, one that seemed relevant.

"It is not healthy to show such interest in the Jews these days, you know," Pannwitz said distractedly. He rooted around in his desk drawer, consulted something, transcribed it on two pieces of paper, and handed one to each of us: a bank name, and an account number.

Again, Pannwitz said, they were men of their word, honourable men. Everything we'd discussed had been taken care of, but in the future, we'd be meeting elsewhere. It would be best for everyone going forward, he said, to meet somewhere more…discreet. And I'm sure I looked confused, but he promised I'd know what he was talking about, soon enough.

I do not remember if we talked about anything else. I do know I did not want a future with him, going forward. My only plan, going forward, was to take my money as far as it would take me. I wanted to be elsewhere. I felt sick.

On the way out, I burst into the water closet and retched until my stomach was empty. Then I cleaned myself in the porcelain sink; I made the mistake of looking myself in the eyes, and I shook my head in disgust.

Within fifteen minutes of leaving that nasty grey place that used to be a bank, I was at a bank that was still a bank, shifting impatiently between the velvet ropes in a line of anonymous customers. My head filled with fantasies as I stared at the tellers sitting behind their shiny metal gates, moving vast sums about in their ledger books! Oh, the paradise that awaited! I wanted to travel—to Sweden or Portugal, or perhaps Switzerland, to exchange all of my money and go overseas, to Brazil or Australia, to start a new life beyond this hellish continent.

When the teller finally called me, I explained my business, then drummed my fingers on the marble counter while he made his way back to the safe.

He came back, far sooner than expected, and placed a brown envelope in front of me, far smaller than expected.

"What the hell is this?" I exploded.

"Five thousand Reichsmarks, sir," the teller said flatly.

"Five thousand? Impossible."

He nodded at the envelope and told me to count it.

I didn't, for I knew it was true, but that wasn't what I'd meant. "My balance should be somewhat…larger than that," I explained.

It was indeed far larger, he said, but I should not worry—I'd be able to withdraw five thousand every month. So another five thousand next month, and five thousand the month after that, and so on until it was depleted, which would take some time, as it was a considerable balance. "And meanwhile… (Was it my imagination, or did the little prick smirk at me?) …meanwhile your money will be working for you—earning interest all the while, even while you sleep!"

"Great," I told him.

He said five thousand Reichsmarks a month was quite a sum.

"What if it isn't?" I asked. "What if I need a little more in a given month?"

He shrugged, the helpless shrug of the lowly peon taking comfort in simple obedience and clear instructions. "I'm sorry, sir," he said. "The gentleman who set up the account was very specific."

"Of course he was," I said. Of course he was.

The teller raised his head as if being helpful. "The gentleman left an envelope with some other information. Would you like it now?"

"Maybe next month," I told him, and turned and walked out. Oh, how I wanted to punch that smirking over-obedient little prick! In a perfect world, perhaps.

29 April, 1947

My trial is today.

It is strange to see the date written down as a real date, as today's date; it has loomed so large in my mind for so long. And now it is just past daybreak, and almost time for the morning count, but in my restlessness I have already been awake for some time. Perhaps I shouldn't care—there will be sleep enough, soon enough!

Outside, the guards are making the rounds—I dart to the door; I see them on the other side of the gallery, rapping on the cells to wake people for the count—I do not have much time!

And now morning count is over, and they're distributing our meal trays. Mine sits untouched as I write, growing ever colder. There are a few more things to set down, and so little time now!

I spent those lonely predawn hours looking back, thinking, pacing, unable to stop my fevered mind. Maybe I shouldn't be so upset, but it's hard. I want a new life and a fresh start, but there are so many accounts left unsettled in this one!!

But would I really want another life? How could I, when this one's been so unpleasant? Maybe I just want it to be over—created, embodied, destroyed, a proper ending. Still, what happens next? After the sure exit, the ultimate escape, the trip no one ever returns to describe? Whatever awaits, it won't be long coming. Outside in the courtyard, I can see the hangman's pole, and the slender loop of rope swaying gently in the breeze.

I know they are coming for me. I am scribbling furiously now, eager to get a few more things down! Despite what I've just written—even now, so close to that end—I keep saying: "If only a few little things could have been different!!" So do I fear a new life, or do I still somehow yearn for it? I don't even know any more. For I can see the list of things I want stretching ever longer, off into unreasonableness, and how can one ever be happy if one wants so much? So perhaps I am not Schweik, after all. For Schweik wanted nothing but to be left alone, whereas I want too much: everything.

But amidst this despair, another spirit tugs at my heart. What is this whisper in my ear? It could have been different? It can be different now! How I want that to be true!! I do hope for something else!! I am sorry for so much!! (I'm crying like a woman as I write—sobbing and dripping unsummoned tears!)

Noises in the gallery—I dart to the door. Gerik's mirror—I stick it out to see how much time is left. And they are collecting the trays, but down the gallery, four guards, led by Stefan—not long now. "I'm writing it all down, Stefan! You'll be able to read it! I'm writing it all down!" I yell, and try to watch his reaction in the mirror. He seems...perplexed?

And as I write these last lines, I am weeping, overwhelmed with emotion! (Are you reading this, Stefan, now that I'm gone? A few more lines before you take me away!!! Know that I am sorry, my brother; know that I wish, at last, that I had done it all differently. Do you believe me? I'm leaving this out so you can read it. I know that you are a radish — pure at heart!!! Do you believe me? Will I be set free, because of this? Will it matter at all? Either way, I do regret it all! Do you believe me? My tears are curling the paper — is that proof enough?)

And now you are outside, banging on my door, telling me I have two minutes to get ready.

I relax and breathe. It is all down. And I know at last — this is how it ends.

But now — a breeze brushes my cheek. A breeze, a feeling — where did it come from? I cannot tell. But I breathe again, and — what is this feeling?

And now — you are fumbling with the keys. I must finish.

I breathe. What is this feeling?

I feel new.

DEDICATION

This book is humbly dedicated to the United States Military Academy's Department of History, and to the wonderful instructors I met during my four years there.

ACKNOWLEDGMENTS

This book release would not have been possible without the generous financial support of the following people:

My parents, Gerald D. Brennan Jr. and Veronica Kay Brennan

My lovely fiancée, Octavia M. Bragg

My fellow members of the Long Gray Line—both the non-Spartans (Bob Underwood, Charlie Fagerquist, Mark Amato, Jennifer Pampuch, Kearson Farishon and Charles Taumopeau) and the Spartans (Nick Hallam, Susan Galich, Jubert Chavez, Gregory Stopyra, Erica Hemmy, Cullen Jones, Jack Jones, and Jim Cook—a pretty hefty percentage of the A2 '99 Drill Roll!)

Liz Tieri, founder of *Back to Print* and The Deadline. (Her do-it-yourself attitude and can-do spirit was a particular motivator for me to get this project out there!)

Columbia J-Schoolers: Phil Klein, Laura Angela Bagnetto, Aaron Rennie, and Nathan Woods

Co-workers at Nitel: Pat Raynor, Nat Topping, Jim McCabe, Milan Saric, Clay Hulen, Bill Hager, and Maria Arteaga

Random other friends and family from Chicago, Toronto, Orlando, and various other locales: Laura Faye, Andrew Rae, Brent Maclean, Mark Maclean, Jeff Cadieux, Matt Baron (my Kickstarter Sherpa), Jeff Frumess, Karen Porter, Rachel Walters, Sam Bleakly, Nick Bianco, Chris Vena (my brother from another *alma mater*), Tony Kelly (Ride it like you stole it!), Deanna Trejo, Aunt Kathy Eagan, Charlotte Ferris, Mike Miller, Scott Jarrette, Anita Applebomb Mechler, Julian Gonzalez, Victor Gonzalez, Patricia Herrmann, Sean Rohwedder, Mercedes Gomez, Scott Tribble, Chrissy Burbach, Terra Dankowski, Jim Page, Tim Gurnig, Gary Bradford, Heather, Rachel Kimura, Rachele O'Hare (who designed the awesome Tortoise Books logo), Doug Busack,

Darren Brown, Ted Winiarski, Diana Hawkins, Clint Work, Dr. Mike Tax, Aunt Pat Kovacs, Aunt Mary Jo Martyn, Eric William Green, Dave Ip, Tom Hanke, and Paul Backhouse

And last, but not least, Jim Graziano, of the J.P. Graziano Grocery Company. This is a great family-owned place, and their Mr. G. might just be the best sub in Chicago. Go get one if you're in the West Loop—they're at 901 W. Randolph St.

WORKS CITED

PART I

Much of the first part is based on events in *Master of Spies* by General František Moravec. Rather than merely retracing the outlines of his story, though, I tried to rewrite it for my purposes, as a singer might cover another musician's song, or as a DJ might sample from or remix another's music. Frequently, Moravec mentioned that an event or a conversation took place, and I imagined what the scene might have looked like and how the conversation might have unfolded. Also, I omitted many important events that did not fit into the narrative and thematic arc I wanted, and played up other events for the same reason. As in the rest of the book, my goal was historical plausibility, as opposed to historical accuracy; only in select instances (such as the meeting between František Moravec and Emanuel Moravec, which never happened) did I deliberately sacrifice historical accuracy for the sake of the story.

Many of Tomas Masaryk's utterances were taken from his writings, particularly *Modern Man and Religion,* and *The Making of a State* (Original Czech title: *The World Revolution*), and from Karel Capek's accounts of conversations he'd had with Masaryk, published as *Talks with T.G. Masaryk* and *On Thought and Life*.

Accounts and descriptions of fighting on the Eastern Front in the First World War were taken from *Memoirs of a Spy: Adventures along the Eastern Front,* by Nicholas Snowden, from Moravec's memoirs, from the novel *The Good Soldier Svejk* by Jaroslav Haśek, from the 1968 film version of the same, and from the 1981 movie *Austeria*. Corporal Baloun and Captain Sagner are characters in *The Good Soldier Svejk* by Jaroslav Haśek.

Descriptions of Russian prison camps were heavily based on the experimental color photography of Prokudin-Gorskii.

Descriptions of Odessa were taken from Wikipedia, from various online photo albums, and from the movie *Battleship Potemkin*

Major Gletkin is a character in Arthur Koestler's *Darkness at Noon*.

The account of Tomas Masaryk's funeral was based on the description in Peter Demetz's *Prague in Black and Gold*.

Hitler's speech during the Nuremburg rallies at the height of the Munich Crisis was generally transcribed from the text of the speech in English as reprinted in *Foreign Policy*. However, I made some edits to clean up the quotes and make it a better read.

PART II

Much of the second part follows the historical evidence and conclusions presented in *The Killing of SS Obergruppenfuhrer Reinhard Heydrich* by Callum MacDonald and in *Target: Heydrich* by Miroslav Ivanov.

Descriptions of the interior of a Halifax bomber outfitted for parachuting were taken based on photographs published online.

The feelings and sensations of a parachute jump were based on my experiences earning my jump wings at US Army Airborne School, Fort Benning Georgia, 1997. I did not do a night jump, though.

Historical background on occupied Prague came from *Prague in the Shadow of the Swastika* by Callum MacDonald, *The Failure of National Resistance* by Vojtech Mastny, and *Prague in Danger* by Peter Demetz. *The Hitler Kiss* by Radomir Luza was particularly helpful for reading about the moods and attitudes of members of the Czech Resistance; I stole the title of the book and used it as the foundation of an anecdote, and I also read about the pear technique here. Another important source of information on moods and attitudes was a brief interview I conducted with Josef Novotney, a tour guide at the National Czech and Slovak Museum in Cedar Rapids, Iowa, who lived in Prague during the occupation.

Some scene descriptions, background information, and text from Heydrich's speech at the train appeared in historical and newsreel footage shown in the documentary *SS-3*.

I backed up the historical research for this section by renting a bicycle while in Prague and travelling to many of the surviving locations, including the safe houses that belonged to the Moravec, Fafek, and Orgoun families, the road from Prague to Panenske Brezany, and the eventual ambush site. I also visited the church of St. Cyril and Methodius on multiple occasions.

Text from the speeches given at Heydrich's funeral, and some descriptions of the funeral, were based on descriptions and text published in *Reinhard Heydrich, The Biography, Volume 2: Enigma* by Max Williams.

PART III

Very little is known for certain about Karel Čurda's life: he was from Nová Hlína, he was a sergeant in the Czech army and drank heavily, he married a German woman and became Karl Jerhot, and he was executed in Pankrác Prison on April 29, 1947; this section relied heavily on imagination, conjecture, and the author's projections of his own personal experiences onto the life of a total stranger.

Information about the justice system in postwar Czechoslovakia primarily came from *National Cleansing* by Ben Frommer, which was a tremendously useful piece of scholarship. I also read *Documents on the Expulsion of the Sudeten Germans*.

Struggle for the Soul of the Nation by Bradley Abrams was an invaluable source on the general social and political conditions, and on the various strains of ideological thought, that coexisted in Czechoslovakia during the brief period of postwar democracy.

I watched the documentary series *The World at War* several times in its entirety while writing this manuscript, mostly for general historical background. However, some scenes—including Curda's descriptions of German-speaking refugees fleeing Czechoslovakia—were heavily based on imagery from that series.

The radish quote came from the memoirs of President Benes' secretary, Dr. Taborsky.

I supplemented all of the research in this part by visiting Pankrác Prison; I did not take a tour, but was able to survey the grounds extensively and supplement that information with aerial photographs published online, interior photographs published online, historical photographs obtained from ČTK (The Czech Press Agency), and a film of the execution of Karl Hermann Frank posted in the archives of the Stephen Spielberg Institute for Holocaust Studies.

I also visited Třeboň and the surrounding countryside, where Karel Čurda was born and raised.

ABOUT THE BOOK

In late December of 1941, two parachutists dropped into occupied Europe on a mission to assassinate Reinhard Heydrich, an SS leader whom one contemporary called "the hidden pivot" of Nazi Germany.

Six months later, they succeeded.

Resistance tells this oft-forgotten story in epic and memorable fashion. Part Dostoevsky and part *Dirty Dozen*, *Resistance* is thrilling, tragic, and darkly comedic. It is also a powerful meditation on the nature of history, and on the ways we distort the past in order to preserve it as memory.

ABOUT THE AUTHOR

Gerald Brennan earned a B.S. in European History from the United States Military Academy at West Point and an M.S. in Journalism from Columbia University in New York. He's currently a co-editor at *Back to Print* and was a co-editor and frequent contributor to The Deadline. He usually divides his time between the South Loop and the West Loop.

Follow him on Twitter @jerry_brennan

Made in the USA
Lexington, KY
08 September 2012